The King's Craft

The King's Craft

The Petralist Book 6

Frank Morin

The King's Craft
Book 6 of The Petralist

This is a work of fiction. All characters and events portrayed in this book are fictional, and any resemblance to real people or events is purely coincidental.

ISBN: 978-1-946910-17-2

A Whipsaw Press Original

Edited by Joshua Essoe
(http://www.joshuaessoe.com/)

Cover art by Brad Fraunfelter
(http://www.bfillustration.com/)

Illustrations by Jared Blando
(http://www.theredepic.com/)

Book design by Kate Staker
(https://katestaker.com/)

First Whipsaw printing April 2021

Other Works by Frank Morin

The Petralist Series

Set in Stone, Book One

A Stone's Throw, Book Two

No Stone Unturned, Book Three

Affinity for War, Book Four

The Queen's Quarry, Book Five

The King's Craft, Book Six

Blood of the Tallan, Book Seven

When Torcs Fly, A Petralist Origins novella, Tomas and Cameron

Game of Garlands, A Petralist Origins novella, Anika

Builder of Intrigue, A Petralist novella: Ailsa

The Facetakers Series

Saving Face, Book One

Memory Hunter, Book Two

Rune Warrior, Book Three

Aeon Champion, Book Four

Short Stories

"Odin's Eye," included in *A Game of Horns: A Red Unicorn Anthology*

"The Essence," included in *Dragon Writers: An Anthology*

"Only Logical," a purple unicorn story

"The Seventh Strike," included in *Cursed Collectibles: An Anthology*

Find all these books on

frankmorin.org

Amazon

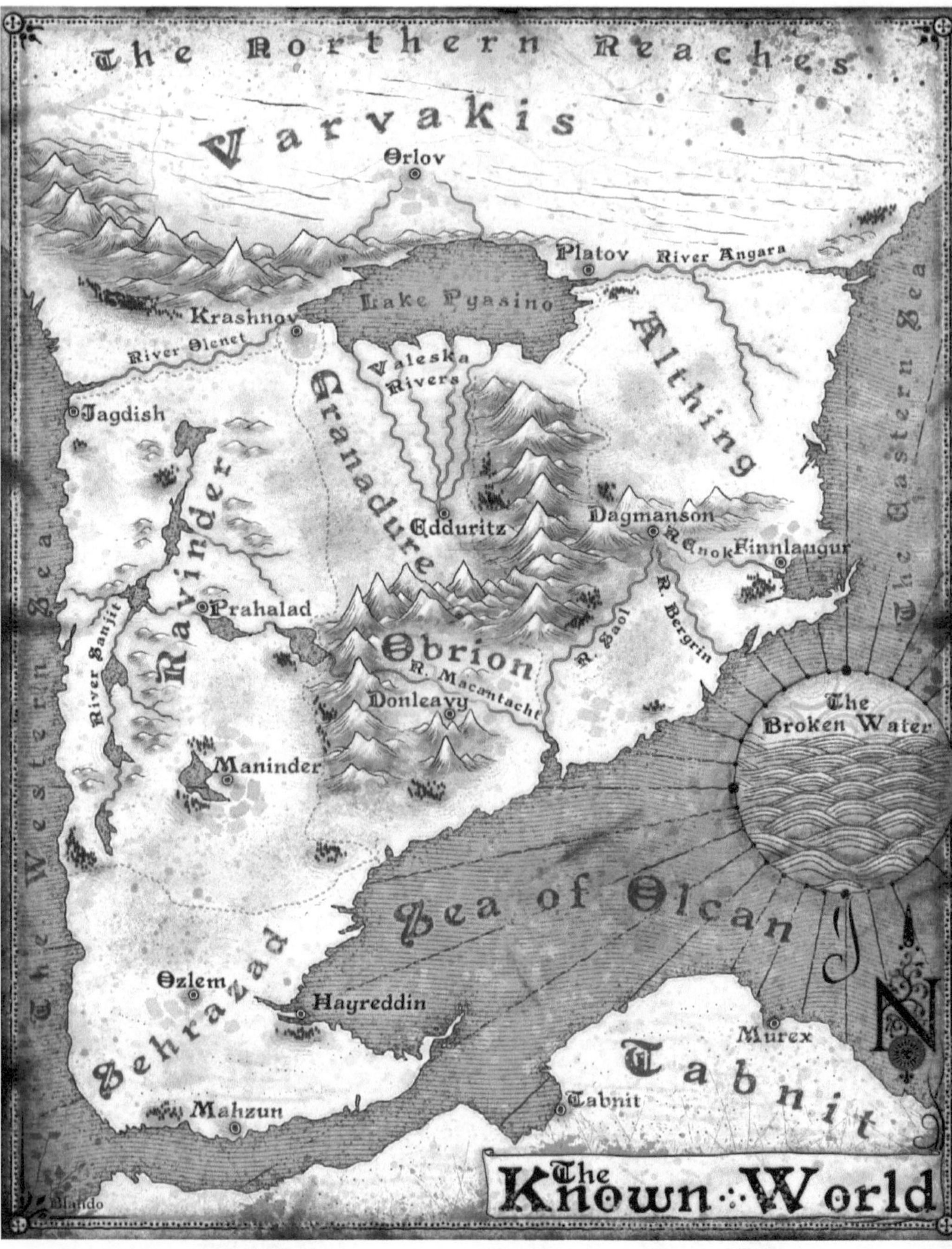
The Northern Reaches
Varvakis
Orlov
Platov
River Angara
Lake Pyasino
Krashnov
River Olenet
Valeska Rivers
Granadure
Althing
The Eastern Sea
Jagdish
Ravinder
Edduritz
Dagmanson
R. Enok
Finnlaugur
Prahalad
R. Saol
R. Bergrin
Obrion
R. Macantacht
Donleavy
The Broken Water
River Sanjit
Maninder
The Western Sea
Sea of Olcan
Sehrazad
Ozlem
Hayreddin
Murex
Tabnit
Tabnit
Mahzun
N
The Known World

Southern Granadere

100 miles

The Northern Reaches
Farmlands
Nister River
Edderitz
Faulenrost
Builder Compound
Altkalen
Wetter River
Harz
Emmerich Quarry
Schmitten Quarry
Althing Nation
Taunus Mts
Abwehr Mountains
Badurach Pass
B Lando

THE LANDS OF
OBRION
N
W
E
S
GRANADURE
GRANITE MINE
ALASDAIR
QUARTZ-ZINC GOLD MINE
THE WICK
PUMICE MINE
BASALT MINE
MARBLE MINE
MERKLAND
SLATE MINE
OBRION
SAOL RIVER
CRANN
TRODAIRE
DONLEAVY
MACANTACHT RIVER
GRANITE MINE
BASALT MINE
FREASTAL
GRANITE MINE
CASUR
MULRENNAN
CARRAIG
DEIFUR
LAIGE
LIMESTONE MINE
RAINEACH
SANDSTONE MINES
CHOSTALAN
SPEIRMOR
RADHARC
THE DESERT
BLANDO

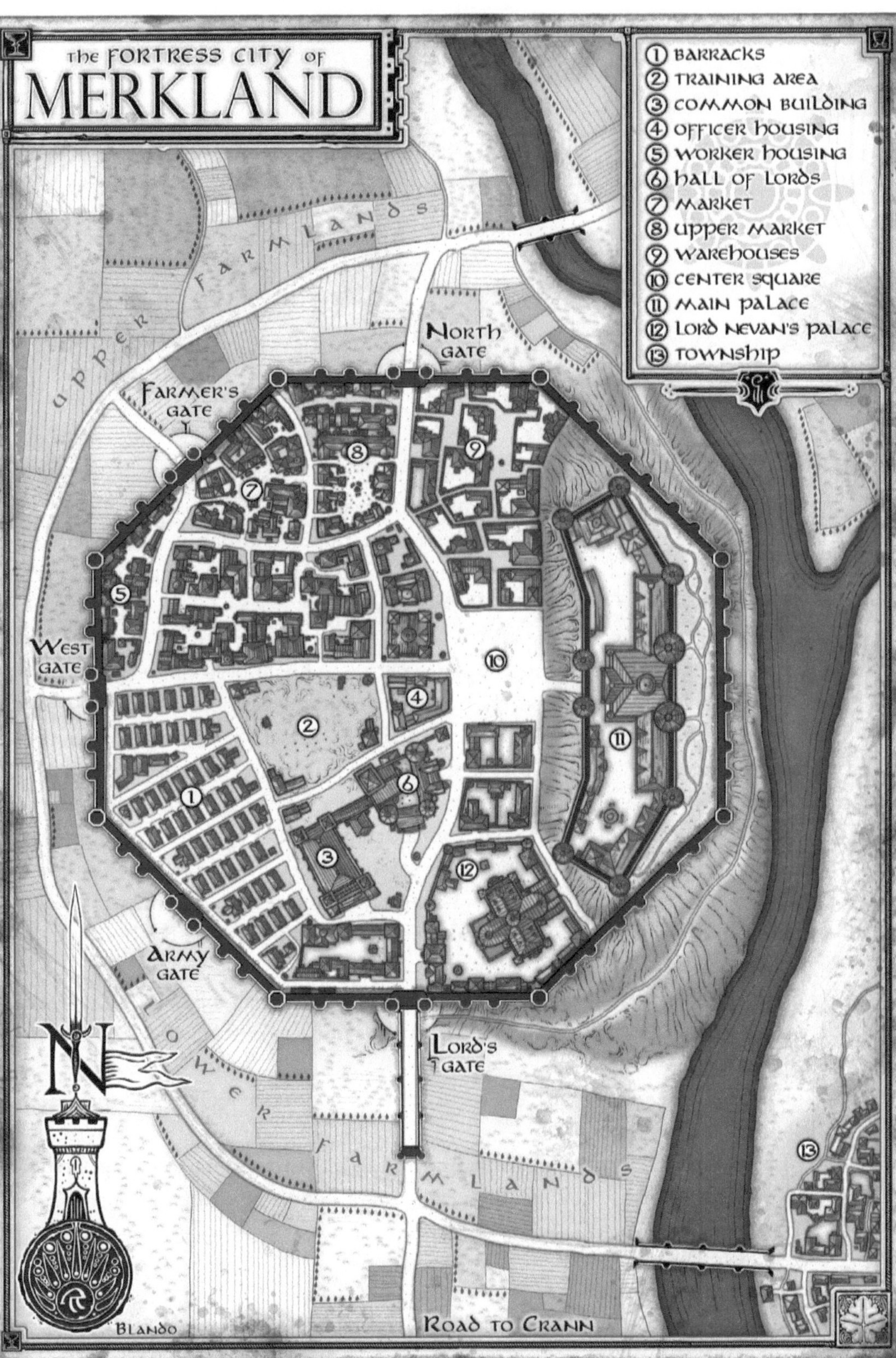
the FORTRESS CITY of
MERKLAND
1 barracks
2 training area
3 common building
4 officer housing
5 worker housing
6 hall of lords
7 market
8 upper market
9 warehouses
10 center square
11 main palace
12 lord nevan's palace
13 township
upper farmlands
North gate
Farmer's gate
West gate
Army gate
Lord's gate
lower farmlands
Road to Crann
Blando

Acknowledgements

This awesome, epic book is a testament to the constant support I receive from my family and from you, my enthusiastic fans. THANK YOU!

There's no way I could create such an intricate, in-depth story, packed with such incredible characters, without your support and encouragement.

So here we are! *The King's Craft* is awesome.

And it almost never existed.

I had intended to complete the series with one final book—*Blood of the Tallan*—which will now be book seven. But as I worked on this book, the story kept expanding until it was clear I had more than one novel's worth of story here. I knew you would love more story instead of less story, so I changed focus and recrafted the adventure into two huge, epic novels. You're going to love them.

As always, thanks to my family for undying support and invaluable input. Kyle, the idea guy, helped me push the magic far deeper and far grander than I could have done alone. The girls—Jenny, Kate, and Emily—offered great opinions and insightful feedback, and Jacob helped me explore the best jokes and best recipes!

Joshua Essoe again provided an excellent edit, asking all the questions I was secretly hoping he wouldn't, and pushing me to never take shortcuts. The story shines far brighter as a result.

Brad Fraunfelter is an artistic wizard. Every cover gets better, and this one is the best one by far. Well done.

Thanks to my beta reader team, and for all of you who have been politely but insistently asking, "When is the next book going to be ready?"

It's done! Enjoy.

Frank

Chapter One

Start the Day with Terrible News, and Nothing Worse Will Happen. Probably.

Verena knocked on the door to Kilian's suite in the recently completed New Schwinkendorf grand palace, suppressing her frustration at the unexpected summons. The hallway smelled of fresh paint, and the woodwork gleamed with recent polish. Rebuilding was progressing fast, but time was so short and she had so much research to finish.

Kilian opened the door, dressed casually in linen trousers, white shirt, and a black leather vest, but his expression was serious and tiny crimson sparks danced in his eyes. His black hair, tinted to blue at the edges from his centuries-long association with water, looked wilder than usual.

Verena followed him toward his spacious sitting room and asked, "This isn't about the appointment of the new lord, is it?"

Kilian chuckled. "No. The rumor mill is giving that topic too much attention already."

"Then is this about your mother?"

He didn't answer immediately, so her concern escalated sharply. Was the much-dreaded invasion from his mother, the mad Queen Dreokt, finally beginning?

They weren't ready.

It was a miracle the queen hadn't launched war upon Granadure already. Winter snows might slow regular armies, but not her. She alone could threaten the full might of Granadure and all of their allies combined.

They'd dealt with several of her saboteurs in recent weeks, and Student Eighteen had identified three other spies embedded in some of the research teams. Strangely, Kilian had chosen only to monitor them.

Those spies had to be reporting on how fast rebuilding of New Schwinkendorf was progressing and at least a little about the remarkable progress they had made through the winter on research and development of new mechanicals. Yet the queen still hesitated. Why? Had they overlooked something critical?

Surprisingly, Aifric was already there, sitting on the couch facing the fireplace. She wore baggy Longrunner pants and her thick, brown hair was braided for running, but she also wore a very cute cotton top. Interesting. Usually the more military personalities in her head insisted on leathers or tougher fabrics. Maybe they'd been undercover in town dealing with spies.

A glowing bed of coals in the hearth emitted an even, warm heat across the room. Plush carpeting covered the floor, and several tapestries on the walls lent the room a cozy feel. Aifric waved, and Kilian gestured Verena to sit on the couch with her, while he took a comfortable chair nearby. "I've sensed no new disturbances from my mother."

Aifric's face shivered for a second and Student Eighteen took the control position in their shared head. "This is something else entirely, although it is related to the queen, and it posed a direct threat to all of our plans."

Verena felt a chill. They both looked grave. It had to be something bad. "Is she launching that army of summoned creatures against us instead of Merkland?"

They'd suffered sporadic incursions by deadly summoned creatures, but all of them had been discovered early and destroyed quickly. With so many mighty Petralists and such a concentration of the most advanced Builder battle mechanicals assembled around New Schwinkendorf, the occasional attacks had proven little more than good training exercises.

Another question, another inconsistent action from the dread queen. Their contacts in Obrion assured them the queen had built many more nightmare elemental creatures than she'd sent against them or Merkland, so she had to be planning a major assault soon. Verena started chewing on the question, considering all the defensive measures they'd already put into place, and how they could augment them.

Student Eighteen said, "No. This is worse."

Verena paled. The meeting was shaping up to totally ruin her day. "Worse?"

"The threat is already among us. It's Connor and Ivor," Kilian declared.

"What are you talking about?" Verena demanded, suddenly wishing for that horde of summoned monsters.

Student Eighteen said, "They don't even know they pose a threat. It dates back to when you were still in your coma, that time I took them to Donleavy to try to rescue Ivor's fiancé, Alyth."

Verena remembered the story. The doomed attempt had been remarkably bold and romantic, and stupid.

Student Eighteen's features shivered again and her posture changed. Her smile widened, her shoulders adjusted, and she sat forward a little. Her voice changed to the warmer, enthusiastic tones of Aifric the Healer. She tapped the side of her head. "The queen killed me, and that trauma was severe even for my mind sisters."

"Mind sisters? I like that," Verena said.

"Kilian's idea," Aifric said with another bright smile.

"It seemed appropriate," Kilian said.

Aifric continued. "After Connor helped resurrect me, we've been able to rebuild a vital memory from that encounter. Queen Dreokt implanted directives in both of their minds, ordering both Connor and Ivor to wait until the spring thaw and then murder every Builder before returning to her."

Verena scowled. Vile beast of a woman! That was worse than she had dreaded, and exactly the kind of horrific evil she'd come to fear from the dread queen. They'd heard grim tales from Ailsa of the carnage the queen had wreaked among her own ruling classes. The cold-hearted, brutal efficiency of the queen's efforts to secure an iron grip on Obrion terrified Verena, but also strengthened her resolve. Such a monster could not be allowed to rule Granadure and the rest of the continent.

Kilian spoke up. "My mother rarely chooses the route of subtle deception. Usually she goes with overwhelming force and simply destroys the minds of any who oppose her. In this case, it appears she thinks she can get some usefulness out of Connor and Ivor. In her twisted sense of black humor, she probably thinks killing the Builders through them is a form of poetic justice."

"That's why she's been waiting to strike," Verena realized. "She's not just building up her army, but she's waiting for us to tear ourselves apart. If they succeed in obeying those commands, it would throw our entire revolution into chaos and make it a simple matter for her to step in and mop up the pieces."

Kilian nodded, and Aifric said, "That's what we suspect."

"How long have you known about this?" Verena asked.

"Since before the battle of Merkland," Kilian stated.

"So long?" Verena exclaimed. They'd let Verena and the others interact with Connor and Ivor for months, when murder rages were hovering in the blackest part of their minds, waiting for a chance to spring. She whispered, "Why?"

Aifric shifted back to Student Eighteen and shrugged. "If we lost the battle of Merkland, none of us would've survived until springtime anyway. We've been monitoring them and working on a plan to try to save them."

Kilian added, "The challenge is that we can't just step in and remove the order. They're like mind bombs. Even if Student Eighteen figured out how to diffuse them, there's a risk my mother might have included alternate commands in case the original one was foiled. There's no way to know, and it was not worth taking that chance unless we had no choice."

Verena rubbed at her arms, suddenly feeling chilled. She was wearing a skirt and blouse instead of flying leathers, but now wished she'd worn a jacket. She sat back on the couch and considered how she would've reacted had she learned about the danger sooner. "That's why you didn't tell us. You thought one of us might somehow give away that we knew and accidentally trigger one of those secondary directives."

Student Eighteen nodded. "Now that the spring thaw is drawing close, we need to act."

"That's why you're here," Kilian added.

As she considered the horrific position the queen had placed Connor and Ivor into, Verena wanted to scream with frustration. If the queen really could implant an order to blind Connor to his love for her, if he actually killed her and Hamish, she doubted he would be able to live with himself once he realized what he had done. That was probably part of the queen's plan. If she couldn't use him, the revolution would lose him too. Her hands began to tremble with horror and a growing rage, so she clenched them in her lap.

Kilian was watching her and seemed to read her emotions. "You need to understand the danger. We will need your help if we hope to save them."

"Please tell me you have a plan," Verena said as she tried to settle her mind and focus on the solution rather than the cold, stark terror of the danger. The queen couldn't snatch Connor away from her, not now that she'd dared hope for victory, for peace if they survived the looming war.

More than once in their crazy relationship, driven by the demands of duty and the unique challenges posed by his special affinities, she had been prepared to destroy Connor. She had thought those days long past, and in recent weeks had begun dreaming very seriously about the day they could be wed.

Now all of those plans felt fragile. She wasn't sure she could fight or destroy him. She might not have a choice. Too many lives depended on her. Even worse, if he was rational at the moment he fell to the mind bomb, he would beg her to destroy him before he could hurt anyone, despite how that would destroy her too.

Kilian said, "We do have a plan. It's risky, of course, but doing nothing is riskier."

Student Eighteen added, "Linking to Connor's mind in advance and trying to remove the mind bomb is beyond my abilities, and perhaps beyond the abilities of anyone but Connor himself once he ascends the third threshold."

"Are you suggesting he ascend?" Verena asked, surprised.

Kilian shook his head. "Not yet. The risk still outweighs the potential reward."

"That's why you keep pushing off the idea of ascension. All that talk of needing to train and prepare was a diversion," she guessed.

"The training was necessary, but yes, I delayed on purpose. If he were to fall to my mother's command and we couldn't intervene in time, I doubt we would be able to stop him if he'd already ascended."

"So what do we do?"

Student Eighteen said, "We orchestrate a controlled triggering of the kill order. We need him to think the spring thaw has come. If the mind bomb is triggered, any concealed secondary orders should be erased by that fact."

Verena grimaced and drew in a long, shuddering breath as she considered the proposal. "We just need to stop Connor in a blind murder rage."

Kilian flashed his roguish smile, easing the cold knot of fear gripping her heart. "Connor's been training hard all winter, but I haven't taught him everything. Even without another ascension, stopping him won't be easy, but I believe we can do it."

Student Eighteen added, "We don't need to beat him. The plan is to trigger the rage, then for me to link to his mind with chert. I will try to help him realize the directive is external. At that point, working together we should be able to overcome the order and set his mind free."

Kilian added, "Then when Connor is free, he can help us free Ivor before he can do any serious damage."

Verena didn't miss how many *shoulds* and *coulds* and *probablys* they used. It seemed all too often of late their plans were like that, but she didn't see a better way to do it.

She forced calm into her voice. "What do you need from me?"

Kilian rubbed his jaw. "This is the tricky part. We need to schedule a city-wide high alert drill without revealing the nature of the threat. If things go badly, we need everyone ready to defend themselves."

Student Eighteen added, "In that eventuality, you would need to spread the word that Connor has fallen to a mind attack and that he's not himself. That might give us a chance to stop him, or at least slow him down long enough for some people to escape."

Verena shivered again. Connor and Ivor together in a fit of murderous rage could probably level New Schwinkendorf all over again and possibly kill everyone there. It sounded like they would target the Builders first, so she considered ways to move them to better defensive positions and distribute some of the more powerful defensive mechanicals among them.

Frustration at the awful situation interrupted her thoughts. She rose and paced to the fireplace, fists clenched. "I hate that we have to prepare to kill him! He's sacrificed so much so many times already. It's so wrong."

Kilian gave her a reassuring smile. "I know it's hard, but refusing to face reality only puts more people at risk."

She sighed and sank back onto the couch. Student Eighteen shifted back to Aifric, who gave her a sisterly hug and pushed a gentle current of warm healing to her. It helped calm Verena and she smiled her thanks.

"Consider this the first step toward freedom," Kilian said. "If we succeed, we'll prove that my mother's mind control is not insurmountable, and use that as a rallying cry for the revolution."

"Although maybe not right away," Student Eighteen said with a wicked grin. "We'll still want to ensure the queen's spies send word that her command was successful."

That was brilliant, and it explained why they'd kept a few spies around. Verena had suspected they were sending misinformation, but Aifric was suggesting an unprecedented coup. If the queen thought Connor and Ivor had succeeded in killing the Builders and been either captured or killed themselves, she would think the road to victory was open and might make a foolish mistake. Unfortunately, that meant that either way, win or lose, their actions would trigger the next major battle of the war.

Verena drew in a deep breath and nodded, accepting the duty and tackling the challenge with the same determination that had carried her through to that point. "Does all of this have anything to do with the challenge course you had Wolfram design for Connor to run today?"

"Absolutely. We do need to demonstrate to our Arishat allies the extent of his powers and present a united front to help dispel the rumors of a weak lord being appointed by the crown to rule New Schwinkendorf. Most importantly, today's run will help identify any weaknesses in his training we might have to exploit when we trigger the mind bomb."

Verena shivered again at the term. It was so accurate, but it carried with it the full weight of danger that hung over her beloved Connor's head. She wanted to protect him from danger, but she was agreeing to push him off the cliff right into the fires of Queen Dreokt's mental assault.

They would defeat the murder rage. There simply was no other alternative.

Chapter Two

Dig Deep, Go Fracked, and Hurl

Connor sprinted across Schwinkendorf valley, basalt-enhanced legs flashing over the brown grasses, matted down by the fading winter snows. He moved faster than a diving pedra, the whistling wind the sound of freedom. He reveled in the open air and wide space, letting the stresses of intense training and the constant fear of an all-out attack from the queen fade from his mind for a moment.

He lacked a Wingrunner's protective face mask, but he didn't need one. He maintained an invisible wedge of air just in front of himself to split the cold, dry wind, forming a pocket of moving calm through which he ran.

Running fracked was great. Fighting a running battle against Kilian with elemental powers was simply awesome.

A fresh wave of intertwined water and fire lanced out from Kilian as he raced past in the opposite direction. Connor was already tapping marble and soapstone, with flames coiled around his left hand and rippling water flowing around his right.

He didn't dare try to wrest the elements from Kilian, but threw his will into deflecting the blast aside long enough to zip past. Then he banked after him in a turn so tight he nearly went horizontal and his legs started to slip on the dew-covered grass.

Good thing he could also tap slate for a second to secure his footing. How Kilian avoided slipping was a mystery, but he banked just as tight in the opposite direction. Connor needed every advantage, because any mistake would guarantee Kilian got the win.

"Not today," he vowed as he poured on more speed.

In his mind, Fire and Water took human form as they'd started doing since his second ascension. Fire was a wild youth who loved to laugh, and who courted Water with desperate longing. Water always looked like a beautiful, mature woman whose long tresses flowed around her like crashing waves. She flirted with Fire, but still kept a cautious distance. Connor enjoyed the glimpses of their personalities, even if they were just his own projections.

He couldn't resist laughing as his legs blurred with superhuman speed, blood pumping with the thrill of the important match. The wide, northern end of the valley had been designated as the location for the ultimate challenge course to test Connor's mastery over his second-ascension powers. He'd practiced intensely all winter to master them, and when he won today, he'd prove he was ready for the final ascension.

Hundreds of spectators were watching the event, including senior delegates from the Arishat League. The crowd stood on a high ridge of earth to the north that Evander had raised for that purpose. They were watching the proceedings from behind a tall screen of white canvas. The Builders had created a number of sightstone viewing posts scattered across the field, as well as nearly a dozen more hovering above the challenge course on little remotely-guided hover platforms that Verena had dubbed Bumblebees.

With the Bumblebees managed by one of the other Builders, the observers could watch every angle of the competition as if they were standing right next to Connor instead of two miles away. It was important to perform well for them, but more important to finally face the daunting challenge of ascension. Connor had no idea why the queen had granted them such a long reprieve, but time weighed heavily on him. He needed that ascension to master the full range of Petralist powers so he could take the fight to her and keep everyone he loved safe.

Only then could he let himself enjoy the dreams of a life with Verena. But for the moment, if he didn't focus, Kilian would wreck him, and Kilian was only the first challenger Connor needed to defeat. Nothing like taking on the toughest challenge first.

And he didn't get all day to do it, either.

As Connor banked after Kilian, he glanced toward the first of four earthen pyramid pylons placed in the wide, flat valley in a rough box shape, about a mile to each side. Connor's challenge was to reach each pylon and touch it in turn, defeating everyone who tried to stop him.

He wasn't off to a great start. He hadn't even reached the box yet. He'd foolishly expected to not face much opposition before that first pylon, but Kilian had intercepted him on the wide open grasses, closing like a living meteor.

Connor tapped a little more porphyry to help solidify his connection to the elements. He was already sucking on a small piece of quartzite, tucked into his cheek, and another wafer of marble pressed under his tongue. He wore a necklace with additional stones, including serpentinite, tucked under his battle jacket, wafers of slate were wedged into special pockets inside of his boots, and he'd downed a gritty draught of soapstone in water twenty minutes ago.

He was going to need every one of them.

Connor didn't need to waste time dipping a finger into a bag of powder at his belt to access porphyry. He wore removable leather battle plates strapped to his thighs, with precious grains of porphyry sprinkled onto the sticky inside edge of the right one. He could absorb what he needed the moment he needed it, without wasting effort or needing to purge.

With porphyry ignited in his heart, the rampager stirred there, pacing in the cage he'd fashioned out of willpower. He and the beast had reached an accord and usually it submitted, but he would never let down his guard. He couldn't risk the beast raging through him, forcing him to transform into a deadly rampager again.

Instead of engaging in a time-wasting running battle, Kilian abruptly reversed course by fashioning a sloping ramp of ice that acted like a slingshot to hurl him back at Connor. That was a fantastic move, one Connor had practiced many times recently, but somehow Kilian pulled it off with a level of flair that Connor couldn't match.

Connor was maintaining a light connection with chert, but Kilian was adept at shielding his thoughts. All Connor managed to pull from him was a vague sense of confidence and a thorough sense of enjoyment.

Again the two of them flashed past, too far apart to strike with powder-coated weapons, but within easy reach of their elemental powers. Connor struck with every bit of skill, slinging fire and water at Kilian, who responded in kind. Elements erupted all around them, exploding into brilliant bursts of multi-colored lights and glittering shards of ice, quickly saturating the late morning air with warm humidity. Kilian yanked that water back out and formed a horizontal waterfall right in front of Connor.

Connor whooped as he burst through it, but it felt like he breathed in more water than he threw back at Kilian. The two of them had practiced this type of running elemental battle many times, and they could keep it up for hours if they wanted to, but today Connor lacked the time. He only had ten minutes to complete the entire course.

Time to take the duel to the next level.

Connor tapped slate as he banked around again. Earth appeared in his mind, and as always reminded Connor of Evander. He used earth to spin the ground beneath him, allowing him to make a perfect about-face in an eyeblink and run back in the opposite direction.

The hardest part about that maneuver was handling the gut-wrenching twist as everything spun around him. He lacked time to enjoy the excellent stomach-lurch, so tried to ignore the intriguing flopping of his guts. Then he twisted the ground beneath Kilian, altering his direction too so that instead of running past Connor at thirty yards, he suddenly ended up on an intercept course.

Kilian could have blasted himself into the air to avoid a collision, but instead he grinned, and a huge sphere of water appeared between them. It had to be at least twenty feet across.

They both struck it from opposite sides at the same time, moving so fast that anyone without a soapstone affinity would have simply splattered. Connor used the waters to slow his momentum to a standstill in a matter of yards, bleeding the excess energy out into the waters. Kilian did the same, and they ended up within spitting distance.

Usually that would be the moment Connor would crack a joke and Kilian would groan and try to say something ancient-arcane-masterishly-awesome.

Not this time. As the waters bled away, Connor drew his powder-coated wooden long-knives and lunged for Kilian's torso.

Kilian deflected both of Connor's blades with his own long-knife, while whipping a wooden meteor hammer around his head to deliver a brutal strike at Connor's sternum. Even though it was supposed to be a non-deadly practice weapon, he struck so fast that he might still crack Connor's chest since he wasn't tapping granite. Connor appreciated friends who trusted his reflexes so much.

He was still tapping quartzite, and Air flitted over the other elements in his mind like a mischievous young woman, dressed in exquisite robes as if clothed in sunset-streaked clouds, black hair whipping about her lovely face. She no longer fled his touch, but granted stable access to air.

With her help, he deflected the meteor hammer with an invisible barrier, barely an inch from his chest. He'd learned the shielding technique from the Builders and had recently perfected his Petralist version of it.

Good thing, because Kilian hit his shield seven more times in the next three seconds. He fracked his arms, forming new joints halfway down his biceps, allowing his arms to spin ten times faster. They blurred, and that meteor hammer hummed through the air.

Connor fracked his arms too, groaning against the sharp stabs of pain, and redoubled his attack. His blades whipped around him so fast they looked like shadows. Connor poured on every ounce of speed and skill to reach Kilian.

It wasn't nearly enough.

He could have switched to obsidian, which would improve his fighting skill, but not his pure speed, and against Kilian the speed was more important. So he trusted his shielding and threw himself at Kilian, slashing dozens of times every second.

Kilian dodged or deflected every single stroke. Connor didn't even come close to hitting him. Sure, his blades sometimes missed by mere fractions of an inch, but against Kilian they might as well have missed by yards.

He grinned as he fought, riding a wave of battle thrill as he pushed the limits to the uttermost edges of control. Somehow basalt helped him understand where his blows would strike, or almost strike, and helped him aim.

Kilian struck Connor eight more times across his shielding, despite Connor's best efforts to defend himself. Meteor hammers were graceful weapons, and in Kilian's hands, his looked like a cloud of wooden spikes whizzing around him. Even though Connor was replenishing his air shield, the blurring meteor hammer was peeling it away just as fast.

The practice weapon wasn't designed for such a brutal onslaught and began to crack, and several spikes ripped free. It would disintegrate in a few more seconds, but that might be long enough.

Connor urged all the elements to join hands, then drew a little earth into the mix of his shielding air. He added a bit of fire, then water, creating an impenetrable mixture of combined elements that not even Kilian could penetrate. The enhanced shielding shimmered around him, a constantly shifting blur of colors. Quicksilver water mixed with crimson fire, laced with black earth and wisps of transparent air.

Then he added a touch of serpentinite. Of all the elemental powers, serpentinite did not yet manifest in his mind like a living person. He envisioned it as the sound of Verena's laughter, circling the other elements. Connor wove it into the mix and unleashed it all into Kilian's face.

The elemental barrage struck Kilian and catapulted him backward. Not even *he* could stop that.

Of course, not even getting clobbered hard enough to send Boulders crying for a Healer slowed Kilian much. Somehow he managed to still strike back. The insidious weight of stilling settled over Connor as Kilian shifted to inner-focused basalt and tapped the weird power.

Connor slowed, his fracked arms snapping back to normal, but even that flash of pain felt subdued. With stilling, Kilian could drag Connor to a halt, steal away his life, stop the beating of his heart, the pumping of his blood, and even the movement of his thoughts.

It would take about eight seconds.

Way too long. Connor also tapped inner-focused basalt, embracing the strange feeling of stilling. He immediately sensed Kilian's power wrapping him like an invisible hand. He threw his own senses against Kilian's, grappling to throw off the ancient Dawnus, but he was fighting from a compromised position.

Holding stilling in place was apparently a lot easier than breaking free. Made sense. Connor had never managed to pry Hamish's fingers from a sweetbread once he grabbed it.

He did manage to slow the effect, but a trickle of energy still siphoned away, weakening him and strengthening Kilian at the same time. Kilian jumped back to his feet and approached, that confident smile on his face. Connor knew that as hard as they'd been fighting, Kilian had not been pushing his uttermost limits. Their elements drained away as their entire focus turned to the invisible battle of wills fighting for control over Connor's life force.

"I doubt my mother would try using stilling, but it's possible. You can't let yourself get tripped up by it," Kilian said in a conversational tone even as he intensified his attack.

The flow of energy siphoning away from Connor increased, triggering a memory of the abject terror of standing helpless before Queen Dreokt in Donleavy. When he'd gone to help Ivor save his fiancé, they'd arrived too late, found Alyth's mind wiped. The queen had somehow realized what they were doing and intercepted them. She'd beaten them down with terrifying ease, denying them even the ability to defend themselves. That sense of helplessness returned, sparking a rising sense of panic.

He needed to think, to fight, to escape, but exhaustion settled over him, whispering with ever-increasing intensity to give up. It would be so easy, but he'd lose before the game had really begun.

He refused to allow that, refused to accept that he was helpless again. Thinking of the queen and that doomed attempt to stand against her triggered an unexpected flood of rage, so intense it burned away his panic and left him gasping, despite Kilian's stilling.

Connor had no idea where that came from, but couldn't waste time wondering about it. That blast of rage gave him the tiny sliver of hope he needed. He couldn't beat Kilian with stilling alone, and his access to the elements felt weak and flighty. He needed a new approach, and fast.

The beast of porphyry stirred, aroused by Connor's fury and angered by their position of weakness. It had grown content to allow him to lead most of the time, but now it flexed itself against its bounds.

"Release me and together we can burst free of these shackles. Let us transform and hunt in our perfect form, and not even this pack master could withstand us."

It was tempting. Porphyry tapped into the more powerful frequency of green-tinted energy. Embracing it and transforming might just allow him to break out of Kilian's tightening stilling. But if he released the beast, would he be able to control it? The last time he transformed, the day he started the revolution in Merkland, he'd managed to rein it in, but the effort had taxed his will to the uttermost.

If he failed to control it, he'd attack Kilian with deadly intent. Kilian might be able to restrain him, but he might not. If pushed to defend himself or die, what would Kilian do? Could he still destroy Connor, even in rampager form?

The thought disturbed Connor, but also gave him the idea he needed.

We'll hunt soon, but not today, he promised.

Then he purged the little porphyry that remained in his bloodstream. The beast growled as it faded away. Without porphyry, the effects of stilling seemed to magnify, and Connor stumbled to one knee under a flood of weakness.

He was almost out of time.

Kilian took another step closer, frowning. "Concentrate, Connor. You can't just give up."

Connor muttered, making the words unintelligible while he focused on the removable plate of armor over his left thigh. He felt the powdered stone stuck to the inside edge and willed it in.

Kilian took another step closer, barely three strides away, and leaned forward. "What?"

Perfect.

As the lightning-like power of diorite ripped through Connor's limbs, he also tapped blind coal. That sedimentary stone was the secret to not blowing himself up when he tapped diorite, but it required him to apply that external-focused power of blind coal internally.

It was a strange concept, one that he'd struggled to understand at first. The slippery feeling of blind coal instantly wrapped him, but to apply it internally, Connor envisioned it like an invisible serpent. Grimacing, he swallowed the snake. Blind coal was weird, and the feel of its protection slithering down his throat and coating his bones nearly made him gag.

Just the set-up he needed.

Kilian frowned. Maybe he sensed the activation of blind coal. It did seem to deflect the stilling momentarily. In fact, blind coal by itself might be enough for Connor to break free of the trap. That wouldn't be nearly as much fun.

Connor looked up, tapped diorite, and vomited an explosion into Kilian's face.

The force of the blast knocked Kilian tumbling, although no flames could hurt him when he walked with fire.

In that moment of distraction, stilling evaporated and Kilian's mental shielding flickered. Connor was still connected to chert, so he distinctly heard, "*I can't believe I fell for that. Hamish will never let me live this down.*"

Connor chuckled as he climbed back to his feet. Hamish had been trying to figure out how to explosive vomit using quickened stones ever since Connor used the trick on Harley during the desperate battle for Merkland. He hadn't succeeded yet, but had managed to give himself explosive stomach aches seven times.

As Kilian flipped over in the air, already seizing Connor's vomited flames to catch himself, Connor got another idea. He tapped limestone and as the bright sunlight streaming past became visible to him as streaming waves of light particles. He seized them and gave them a mighty twist.

Kilian righted himself and with a concentrated blast of fire, shot up into the air.

Except Connor had dropped a mirage over him, making him think up was down.

Before Kilian realized his mistake, he shot right down into the twenty-foot hole that Connor opened beneath him with slate, and plunged right into the deep, soft earth at the bottom.

Feeling deeply satisfied, Connor dropped the mirage and sealed the pit over Kilian just as his tutor spat out a mouthful of earth and started to laugh.

Connor grinned and saluted the sealed pit, feeling relieved he'd figured out a way to get past Kilian. Even when he wanted to lose, he pushed Connor to the limits.

That fight had wasted too much time, so he fracked and raced north toward the first pylon. He'd reach it in seconds.

Well, he might have if the front of the pylon hadn't split open to release Evander onto the field, half-reclined on his signature sliding earthen chair.

Chapter Three

The Best Teachers Inspire

Evander accelerated toward Connor on that earthen seat, feet propped on stirrups and hands grasping long handles. It might look awkward, but Connor had tried it once in Althing to annoy Harley. He'd found it surprisingly comfortable.

Giant Evander was over seven feet tall, with huge shoulders and hands. His mahogany-skinned face radiated strength, his shaggy black hair whipped in the wind, and although he wore his usual black leather jacket, for once the front was buckled. Harley had fought Evander to a standstill and destroyed the entire Carraig in the process.

All Connor had to do was beat him in a few seconds, but without all the collateral destruction.

No problem.

As the two of closed at terminal velocity, wind ripping at Connor's face, he tapped chert and focused on Evander in time to catch a fragment of thought. "*. . . stumbles without injury while learning to walk.*"

Sounded like part of a great line of Sentry speak. Evander's convoluted speech challenged everyone's ability to understand. It built upon simple truths, but combined them in vague ways that left open many interpretations. Had Evander figured Connor would try to read his thoughts and prepared that in advance, or did he really think that way all the time?

Connor had no idea, and suddenly it didn't matter because Evander flung open his coat, revealing a brilliant band of intense golden light hovering right in front of him.

"No fair!" Connor shouted.

Evander had used the trick of concentrating a beam of light to help defeat Harley. Connor tapped limestone and instantly felt that light-turned-weapon glowing in his affinity sight, so intense it was like Evander had squashed the sun into a slender blade.

Verena had dubbed it the Death Beam.

Connor had practiced the technique with Evander in recent weeks enough to know he'd never stop it. At best, he could deflect it if he grabbed it quickly enough. Today he had a better idea.

Evander released the death beam and it flashed across the distance in a blink. It was aimed at Connor's shoulder, but he managed to deflect it down to strike him in the stomach.

Instead of blasting through him and possibly tearing him in half, the light ricocheted away from the thin piece of extra armor he wore there. As it shot away, the beam of light punched a hole through the air, creating a booming thunderclap. It crossed the valley in an eyeblink, angling up and away, and struck a large maple tree on a high hill to the north of Faulenrost. The tree disintegrated in a fantastic explosion of fire and splinters.

As Connor and Evander passed each other, almost close enough for Evander to snatch him off the ground with one of his huge hands, Connor easily read Evander's surprise.

"How did you deflect that?" Evander shouted as he slung himself around impossibly fast using earth. Through slate, Connor could feel Evander's presence in the earth like a beacon, his influence underground as overwhelming as the golden brilliance of the death beam had been in the air.

"Mirrored Sehrazad steel glass," Connor explained, not slowing. He tapped serpentinite and sounds became visible, like brightly colored hummingbirds that easily outpaced him. Before they could flit away on the wind, Connor caught them. Sounds were so much fun with serpentinite. He tossed the words over his shoulder to Evander, then concentrated on running.

He didn't bother fighting Evander for control of the earth, but focused all his will on shielding. Even that wouldn't help much against Evander, especially when running so fast. The blurring movement of his legs weakened his connection with earth.

As he feared, the ground erupted in front of him, and a twenty-foot wall rose to block his path. He veered sharply, leaning so far over that the limp, brown winter grasses caught at his armored shoulder. He couldn't quite make the turn to get past the wall, but ran up onto it, going horizontal and racing down the wall's length. He planned to jump off the end and try to circle it, but the wall extended, and the end began to turn in toward him.

"Tallan take it and boil it in Hamish's socks," Connor muttered.

He accelerated, but the earthen barrier lengthened faster, the ends sliding across the ground, bending inward until they touched, forming an unbroken circle three hundred yards in diameter. Connor was tempted to see how fast he could make a circuit, but that wouldn't get him closer to his target, and would just make him dizzy. He'd already explosive-vomited, and the diorite had left him feeling drained, so he lacked the enthusiasm to try again.

So he tapped quartzite. Air returned to his mind, fickle and flighty and beautiful, but she did not pull away when Connor grasped her hand. His connection solidified and he sensed the air currents all around. Many were young and eager, created by the elemental battle with Kilian. They raced around the valley with little purpose but lots of energy.

Just what he needed. Ignoring more mature currents higher up, Connor seized a couple of the eager young ones, and they immediately swept in, whipping around him and lifting him into the air.

As he soared up over the wall, Evander rose on the opposite side, lifted by a miniature whirlwind that somehow didn't even stir his hair. Evander didn't usually tap air nearly as much as earth, but apparently that didn't mean he wasn't good at it.

Was he as good as Connor?

Connor grinned as he accelerated into the air. One way to find out. "Duel in the skies? You're on."

Except that's when he sensed Verena swooping down out of the thin, obscuring clouds high overhead. She moved like a ripple through his air senses, and he glanced up, looking right at her. Verena's new Swift was colored in mottled blues and grays that blended into the sky extremely well. The speedslings along the front of the nimble attack craft were already spinning. Connor and Evander might be two of the most powerful Petralists alive, but in some ways, Verena owned the sky even more.

Connor loved Verena fiercely, but that didn't mean he'd let her win. Usually he loved dueling with his friends, but this epic challenge course had been designed by General Wolfram as a way to reassure their Althing allies that they really did stand a chance when they faced the queen in the coming weeks, and time was running out.

He hoped a victory would ease his own worry too. The longer the queen waited to attack, the more he felt convinced they were overlooking something vital. He'd started worrying he saw distant enemies lurking in shadows, preparing to strike. Just the day before he'd been convinced he saw the silhouette of a big man lurking outside the command building where Shona and Ivor were holding a remote conference with Rory and Anika in Merkland.

He had to shake off his worries, though. He couldn't defeat both Verena and Evander together, not if he got distracted, and definitely not in the air. He'd risen to about a hundred feet above the valley floor. Verena would get within range to release her deadly mechanicals in seconds. Evander was swooping in from the right, frying-pan sized hands already open, as if he planned to pluck Connor out of the air and spank him.

So Connor tapped the flowing power of soapstone. The Nister River, running to the north of the Arishat encampment, glowed in his water senses, as did the snow on the nearby hills. The air was pretty dry, but Connor squeezed it and managed to suck out a couple of small globes of water.

He slapped them both across Evander's eyes.

Then he tugged again on the current holding him aloft, urging it to swoop sideways. He hoped to position Evander between him and Verena. That might give him a few more seconds to figure out how to defeat her without hurting her.

Evander kept coming, altering course to continue closing on Connor even as he pawed at his eyes. Connor kept the water in place, flowing it around and through his massive hands. He tried yanking Evander's air current away from him, but although Evander might not usually like flying, his control was impressive. Even blind, he swept in, huge arms reaching toward him.

Connor gestured Air to keep going. She winked, seeming to like the ploy, and the air current he'd been riding continued on its course. Connor didn't continue with it, but released his connection and slipped free. For a couple seconds he fell, completely untethered to anything. Cold air whistled around him and he relished the absolute freedom.

Verena wrecked the moment by firing a missile at him. She hadn't fallen for his ruse, but in her nimble Swift had slid sideways even as she continued her dive. With a clear field of fire, she didn't hesitate. He loved that about her.

Evander plowed right through the air current Connor just released, scattering it. If Connor had remained in it, he'd have gotten clobbered.

Connor tapped quartzite again, and Air returned instantly. The piece of quartzite in his cheek was nearly spent, but it should last long enough. Her windblown hair gave her a wild look, and she was grinning as she slipped her hand into his mental fingers to reestablish the connection. Another air current swept in to catch him about thirty feet above the hard ground, and he sent another one gusting against the missile, pulling it off course.

He aimed it at Evander's back.

No doubt Evander would feel it coming. Deflecting it might keep him busy a few more seconds. But Verena had learned painful lessons fighting Harley. The queen's deadly general had turned Verena's missiles against her and deflected her hornets against Dierk's windrider. The latest model of the missiles contained more aggressive stabilizer fins as well as tiny quartzite blocks set near the front that Verena could activate remotely to help steer.

Not enough. As soon as she realized she couldn't compensate for Connor's wind attack, she triggered the remote detonation. The missile exploded in a spectacular pink cloud.

It was nice to know she hadn't actually been trying to kill him. If the missile had struck, the blow would have rattled him and covered him in powder, marking the kill. A regular diorite-tipped missile would have really hurt, and would have suggested that maybe he needed a little motivation in his courting efforts. He'd planned to give her flowers during the big feast. Maybe he should think bigger, like a new sharpening stone for her throwing daggers.

Evander, still blinded by those annoying water plugs, settled into a hover fifty feet away and turned toward Connor. "Starlight is prized by romantic hearts seeking quiet solitude, but even the pedra sleeps during the darkest nights."

That sounded like a threat. Verena had slowed and begun circling about a hundred feet up and maybe eighty feet out. She kept the speedslings pointed in his direction the entire time, but did not release them. She seemed content to see what Evander had in mind.

Had they coordinated this beforehand? Definitely not good. Time to wreck whatever they were planning.

Except that's when Evander snuffed out the sun.

Well, that's what it felt like. One second Connor was flying through bright sunlight. The next second, everything turned pitch black. It wasn't the darkness of a moonless night where the stars were covered by heavy clouds. It was the absolute darkness of a sealed tomb.

It was inspirational.

Connor nearly settled into a hover, but realized that would probably just get him clobbered, so he kept moving even as he tried to figure out what Evander had done. It had to be limestone, but Connor had never realized he might be able to use the stone to remove light too. The effect wasn't as completely debilitating as sensory deprivation, which stole away all senses. That much about the situation was positive.

He tapped limestone, but sensed no light at all. He was flying in a void far more complete than the little pockets he'd created sometimes by splitting light around himself to create temporary invisibility. Evander had blocked all light from entering a huge area.

Connor couldn't wait to try it, but he didn't have time to play right now. He could reach out through limestone and try finding the light, try wrestling with Evander for control over it. He might manage to pierce the bubble of blackness.

That wasn't epic enough for today. Connor grinned as he gripped Air's hand in his mind and urged her to accelerate. The wind seemed subdued somehow as they shot higher. Evander had stolen his sight, but he could still hear. The problem was that the rushing wind made it extremely difficult to hear anything else. He could tap quartzite to enhance his hearing, but Evander could do the same thing. Connor needed an edge.

So he tapped serpentinite.

He might only have access to sounds, but with serpentinite Connor owned sound. He'd practiced with serpentinite a lot over the past few months and had noticed a peculiar property of it that had never seemed very useful until now. He shouted, emitting a burst of high frequency sound, too high for humans to hear. He doubted even Evander would hear it unless he was max-tapping quartzite to his ears. The sound erupted away in every direction, visible to him as a bright red expanding wave.

Part of the wave bounced back from a huge figure swooping toward him on an intercept path from the left. Another part bounced off a Swift-sized shape moving into position almost directly above him. The echoes formed a clear map of the area, reinforcing what he saw.

The idea was working even better than he's hoped. Connor laughed, but caught that before Evander heard.

The giant was doing an admirable job of shielding his approach, and Connor wasn't sure how Verena was targeting him, but it looked like she planned to drop a bomb on his head. So Connor took that laughter he'd just captured and tossed it in her direction, wrapping it around her Swift. That might make her hesitate.

For Evander, Connor tapped slate.

Earth appeared in his mind looking grumpy that he'd called upon him while flying with Air. She winked, making Earth scowl. Connor could sense that Earth secretly envied Air sometimes and he liked her flirtations more than he'd ever admit, but he didn't like getting summoned into her domain.

Connor explained what he wanted with a thought and extended his mental hand. Earth approved of the plan, and the connection solidified.

The frozen ground beneath Evander erupted. So high above the ground, Connor couldn't draw deep from the earth, but he only needed a couple of inches across the top. A mushroom cloud of fine earth particles blasted into the air directly into Evander's path.

For perhaps the first time in Connor's experience, Evander must not have been tapping earth because he reacted a critical second too slow. As he swept through that cloud of earth, it dissipated his wind current enough to make him falter. Air didn't like flying through dirt.

In that second, Connor struck. He yanked Evander's current, and fickle Air abandoned Evander. He dropped like a stone.

He'd recover before crashing into the earth. Probably. Not that it mattered. Evander enjoyed a close relationship with Earth so wouldn't get damaged, no matter how hard he struck. But that still put him several seconds behind.

"The greatest warrior proves his skill in the moment of battle, but a cake removed too soon from the oven saddens an entire household." He tossed the cryptic Sentry speak at Evander and set it spinning around the giant's head, whispering the message over and over. Let him decipher that one while he tried to catch up.

Grinning, Connor gripped Air's hand and accelerated into the sky. The impenetrable darkness didn't leave, so every four seconds he emitted another burst of sound to map his position and close on Verena. Whatever she was planning hadn't included Evander getting stumped. Maybe he'd promised to punch Connor out of the darkness cloud so she could strafe him with pink hornets.

Instead, Connor swept in close to the Swift. She was hovering and had dropped her window shielding while she peered vainly out into the darkness. With serpentinite he could see her profile in exquisite detail, like a softly glowing tracing of her on black paper. Her head was tilted slightly to one side as she tried to listen, but the sound of her own thrusters would drown out the sound of his wind current.

Even hovering close enough to touch the Swift, Connor couldn't see anything with his natural eyes. The blackness was complete. He was enjoying it, but by the hunching of Verena's shoulders, he sensed it was getting to her. Flying blind was a great way to crash again, and she had way too much first-hand experience with that.

Connor had planned to knock on her window shielding, but got a better idea. With another serpentinite mapping burst, he silently slipped through the window and as wind gusted through the cockpit, he kissed Verena on the cheek.

Dummy. Surprising Verena was never a good idea.

Verena yelped and instinctively punched him in the face. The blow knocked him right out of the Swift.

That could have gone better.

Air caught him and drew him back to Verena. Connor rubbed his cheek where she'd struck. He hadn't been tapping granite, and she had an amazing right jab. Before she could restore the window shielding or trigger her hornets, Connor called, "Ow. I thought you liked it when I came to visit."

"Connor, what were you thinking?" she demanded, clearly annoyed. He'd hoped to help her relax, but she seemed even more anxious than before. That was unusual. Usually she loved combat and flying above almost anything else.

He dared draw closer again. This time he leaned on the window. She couldn't see him, but his weight pushed down the front of the Swift. She quickly adjusted, and the pressure would help her know where he was. "I figured a kiss would be a nicer way to tell you that you're out than forcing you to crash another Swift."

"Don't you dare," she warned.

In each of her crashes, she'd risked her life trying to save him or others. Connor loved her fierce spirit and sometimes-idiotic bravery, but she had nearly died. This latest model not only included many new weapons, but lots of improved defensive mechanicals. She would not go down easily again.

"I'm coming in. Don't punch me again."

This time when he slipped inside the tiny canopy, she reached toward his voice. He caught her warm hand, then touched her cheek.

"How can you see what you're doing?" she asked.

"Magic," he said with a grin.

She chuckled, pulled him closer, and planted a quick kiss. He made sure she found his lips. As always, he loved the smell of high mountain air that clung to her and the subtle, minty taste of her lips.

"How are you feeling today?" she asked casually, but there was something odd in her voice.

"Winning so far, but low on time."

For some reason that seemed to help her relax. He felt her smile as she said, "If I'm out, you've got work to do."

"Can I borrow one of your missiles?"

Her tone turned mischievous. "Take what you want, Connor. I know you'll make it up to me over dinner."

"Done." That one was easy. Everyone would get a feast tomorrow.

He rolled back out of the Swift and caught the missile that she released from its rack under one of the stubby wings. Then he accelerated again. Within seconds he burst from the strange blackness bubble into bright sunlight that seemed blinding after that pit of darkness. Glancing back at it, he whistled softly. Evander had dropped darkness over a globe of space several hundred yards in diameter, stretching all the way down to the ground. Connor really needed to learn how to do that.

First, he had to win. He dove for the first pylon, slightly northwest of his position.

Evander broke out of the darkness, sliding across the ground and heading toward the pylon to intercept.

Connor didn't have time to fight Evander again, and couldn't hope to beat the giant with earth. So he tapped limestone. As beams of light became visible as streaming bands, he gave them a twist, creating a mirage of himself dropping straight toward the ground. He remained in the air current this time, deflecting light around himself to make himself temporarily invisible as he swooped away at an angle to come at the first pylon from the east.

As Connor hoped, Evander took the bait, focusing on the mirage of Connor falling. When mirage-Connor was still thirty feet above the ground, earth erupted in a giant, grasping hand. It snatched the fake Connor out of the air, and only then did Evander realize his mistake.

He spun back around toward the air current, but Connor had already created a second mirage and let it take his place inside the current. He was dropping down toward the pylon, untethered to anything, still wrapped in a bubble of invisibility. Wind whistled past as he picked up speed, and he used serpentinite to squash the noise he made. Unless Evander had noticed him create the disguise, he'd never figure out the trick in time.

With instincts honed by centuries, Evander struck the second mirage with an air current that corkscrewed the fake Connor out of control back toward the ground. He again sent grasping fingers of earth to capture him, and a rare smile began forming on his huge face.

In that second, Connor landed atop the earthen pylon, tapping granite to not break his legs. Even though Connor tried to shield his landing, Evander immediately spun to face him. Just in time to catch Verena's missile in the face.

It erupted in a very satisfying cloud of pink powder.

"Tag, you're out."

Connor didn't wait for Evander to reply, but leaped off the pylon and tapped slate. Earth was grinning with approval as Connor accelerated in a slide across the ground toward the second pylon, situated a mile to the east.

"One down. Three to go," he said to himself. He caught the sounds and set them running around his head, the words repeating like a mantra. He reminded himself to grab some music from one of the minstrels and preserve it in one of Aifric's diamond sound recorders. Using it during a duel like this, filling the air with stirring music, would make his victory even sweeter.

Even though Connor was still tapping a little granite, he could have also tapped basalt and made a run for it. Since his second ascension he could tap two primary affinity stones simultaneously, and doing so offered unique benefits that he'd been practicing with. Even Kilian barely kept up with him in a fully fracked sprint any more. The amazing freedom of basalt speed always thrilled him, but he wasn't sure who was going to attack him next, and a solid connection to slate gave him a better chance of sensing danger before it struck.

Without warning, Aifric erupted out of the ground about a hundred yards away and sprinted in his direction, a braided-steel meteor hammer in her hand. She moved so fast that Mariora or Rith were probably the personalities in control.

He should've gone with basalt.

CHAPTER FOUR

The Unexpected Fruits of Chemical Weapons

Connor would love nothing more than to engage in a super-fracked running battle with Aifric and all of her personalities. She could shift control between the nineteen women living inside of that head in the blink of an eye, and each of them possessed a different set of affinities. That made her almost as versatile as him.

The only thing she lacked was the ability to combine multiple affinities at the same time. He had trained hard with her in the past couple of months, working to fine-tune his tap rate and absorption rate. She could keep up with him unless he really pushed the limits or started combining multiple affinities.

Getting into a fight like that with Aifric could take all day, and he'd already spent too much time. Besides, he'd consumed too much of his allocated power stones. A long battle could exhaust an important affinity he might need to defeat the next challenger. So Connor tapped basalt, but not to frack.

Instead, he hit Aifric with stilling.

He didn't like using stilling on living things, not since he had stilled the entire city of Merkland. Forty thousand lives provided lots of motivation.

He'd felt every single death caused by his attempt to save the people of Merkland. They still haunted his dreams. If he hadn't stilled them, thousands more would have died, driven to berserker rage by the quickened porphyry bomb that Harley had detonated over the city. Knowing that didn't help as much as he wished it did. He had held those lives captive in his power, siphoned away their life forces, and sacrifice them for the greater good.

He'd hesitated to use stilling much since then, but today's test was designed to prove his mastery over all of the weapons in his affinity arsenal. If he was fighting the queen, he couldn't hesitate. So he grimaced with lingering unease, but unleashed it anyway.

Aifric was always pushing him to fight harder, seek for every possible advantage. She would understand why he had to do this, would congratulate him on using it even as she fought to defeat him. She was an assassin and a healer, so she was used to weird personal conflicts.

Stilling settled over Aifric like an invisible blanket. Her blurring strides slowed and she stumbled. Her life force glowed in his mind like a Solas, so much more vibrant than any he'd seen. He had never realized that having so many people sharing that head of hers resulted in such a noticeable effect. The rush of energy that he siphoned away from her and absorbed was delicious in a way that he hated to acknowledge.

Aifric shifted rapidly between multiple personalities, trying to find a way to beat the stilling. One of them, he wasn't sure which, struck at him with earth, but the blow lacked power and he easily blocked it. He recognized the tilt of her head when she switched to Isabell, who tried to call forth fire, but the flames flickered, and he snatched them away.

As she stumbled to her knees, Connor slid across the remaining distance to her, snatched the powder-coated meteor hammer from her grasp, and touched it lightly to her temple.

"You touched steel to every kill location on my body and spared my life. Today I'm returning the favor."

Then he released stilling. When he had stilled the city of Merkland, their energy had poured into him like a raging flood as forty thousand souls reinforced his own life force. Releasing stilling had been far more difficult than he'd ever admitted to anyone.

Although Aifric's life force was as strong as any twenty other people, he found he could release stilling without that same hesitation. She was one of his dearest friends. Besides, if he actually did injure her, Student Eighteen would cut out his heart.

He loved having friends that helped him know proper boundaries.

As soon as he released her, Aifric drew in a sharp breath, gave him a disgusted look and said, "You are such a pebble brain, Connor. That little show means nothing compared to what I did for you that day."

Connor grinned and extended a hand to haul her back to her feet. "I don't mind still being indebted to you."

She rolled her eyes, and Tresta took control. Her stance became wider, her shoulders somehow blockier. The rather grumpy Boulder scowled at him. "We had such a great plan for that duel. I hate missing out on a good bash fight."

That was a sentiment shared by every Boulder Connor had ever known.

"I promise that as soon as we can find a little time, I'll bash fight with you for twelve hours straight."

She grinned, and Aifric's face shivered as multiple other personalities took control long enough to add their smile. Connor would need twelve hours to bash fight all of Aifric's Boulder or Rumbler personalities. He doubted any of them would feel fully satisfied, but he would do the best he could.

Then she shifted to Student Eighteen. "That stilling worries me. We even tried pumice, but couldn't break out."

"Do any of you have affinity with blind coal?"

"Not yet. We haven't ever gotten our hands on enough to try."

"I'll get you some."

She flashed a grateful smile.

"You've shared enough secrets with me, least I can do," he added, then turned to leave.

Student Eighteen grabbed his arm. "My meteor hammer?"

Connor handed it over with a sigh. He'd wanted to get his hands on one of those for months, but seemed to always get distracted before he could get one and schedule some time with Dietmar, Ilse's lead Wingrunner, to learn how to use it.

Aifric hefted it and said, "On loan from Ivor."

He should have recognized it. "I'm surprised he loaned that to you. He loves that weapon." Ivor had won it from a Grandurian noble in a card game while stuck in Altkalen as a prisoner of war.

She sighed. "He only loaned it because I promised I'd hit you with it."

"What did you have to promise in return if you missed?"

Her only response was a scowl. Connor laughed, tapped basalt, and sprinted east toward the second pylon. Ivor was a champion negotiator. Aifric didn't really need the weapon, so he doubted Ivor had leveraged much out of the deal, but he would have gotten something. With all of her personalities, there was almost no limit to what Aifric could do.

His musings were cut short by a diorite missile exploding just in front of him. He was moving so fast that he didn't have time to swerve before running into the cloud of blinding dirt and fire.

Connor dove straight through, tapping both marble and soapstone. He grabbed the fires from the explosion, wrapped himself in them like a full-body shield, and rolled back to his feet.

Hamish roared overhead in his flying suit, barely ten feet off the ground. Behind the protection of his face mask, he was chewing on a bit of breadstick. He gave Connor a jaunty salute and dropped a tiny vial. It fell toward Connor's feet.

Oh, no.

Connor was not about to let that vial hit the ground and break. Hamish absolutely loved the Althing chemical weapons. He had assigned himself the chief liaison from the Builder group to the Althing scientists. He regularly showed up after sampling the latest inventions with his skin tinged some weird color, or looking like he had just puked everything he'd eaten in the last month.

The Althing researchers considered Hamish something of a legend. Not only did no one else want to sample any of those chemicals, but they were convinced no one else would have survived so long.

So Connor wrapped that little vial in flames and shattered it, planning to incinerate whatever devilry Hamish had prepared. He was not expecting the flash of phosphorescent brilliance that erupted from the vial.

Shouting in surprise and clapping his hand over his blinded eyes, Connor tapped slate and dropped straight into the earth and sealed the hole over his head. Half a heartbeat later a stream of hornets chewed into the ground.

What was Hamish thinking? Those hornets could have torn Connor apart if he was not tapping granite. He liked having friends with unshakable faith in his instincts, but maybe he needed to have a talk with Hamish. Sure, they liked testing diorite-puking on each other, Hamish regularly asked Connor to hit him with sensory deprivation, and they'd nearly killed themselves several times trying to figure out how many times they could make a death beam bounce between pieces of Sehrazad steel glass, but . . . Well, maybe discussing limits wouldn't work so well.

So Connor erupted out of the ground and threw himself back into the air, again releasing a pulse of sound. His eyes still saw nothing but dancing light from that flare, but he didn't need to see to find Hamish. This time he filled that burst of sound with a hundred times as much energy. It erupted away from him like a thunderclap. It caught Hamish, who was swooping toward his back, right in the face.

The blast knocked Hamish over backward several times. He fired thrusters all over his suit to stabilize his flight. It was an impressive display, but it took him too long. Connor tapped quartzite to pull the air away from Hamish and form an exhaustion pocket. Verena had mentioned they ran into weird holes like that sometimes when flying.

Hamish maxed his thrusters, but with so little air there was nothing for them to push against and he began to descend. Connor's eyes finally cleared as Hamish twisted and threw a tiny dart in Connor's direction. It flicked through the exhaustion pocket and the tiny thruster at the back then caught the air and accelerated the deadly little dart straight at Connor.

It was an impressive move. Connor would not waste that kind of creative battlefield thinking by simply deflecting the dart with a blast of air.

So he tapped basalt and fracked his arm.

The dart was coming fast, but in a fracked state everything seemed to slow as Connor's speed and reflexes accelerated a hundredfold.

He caught the dart, turned it, and released it back at Hamish.

Builders were starting to include remote self-destruct triggers on all of their big explosive weapons, but that dart was too tiny. Hamish couldn't stop it, although he contorted mightily in a vain attempt to escape. The dart exploded against his armored chest in a spray of blue powder.

He landed a second later and Connor released the exhaustion pocket. Hamish looked at his blue-coated chest in disgust. "That should have worked."

"It almost did, but why blue?"

Hamish chuckled. "As if I'd let Verena choose the colors. She already names everything, and between how brilliant both she and Jean are, I can hardly get a creative idea to call my own anymore."

No one but Hamish could have kept up with those girls. He could maintain a sugar-saturated state of pure inspiration longer than anyone Connor knew. Most of the people who tried his technique either fell into a sugar stupor, or got violently sick.

Connor raised a fist for Hamish to bump and said, "We need to finish those vomit rockets. You might have gotten me with one of those."

Hamish grinned. "You're on. Just don't mention it around Jean."

"Of course." Connor tapped basalt and sprinted the last quarter mile to the second pylon. As he ran he thought of Jean and the terrible injuries he's suffered at the battle of Merkland. Talk of missiles and explosions sometimes still made her uneasy. He and Hamish would perfect the vomit rocket, but not anywhere around Jean.

Luckily no one else intercepted him before he reached the pylon. He touched the rough stone with a grin. "Two down."

Connor spared a glance to the north and tapped quartzite to scan the crowd of observers. He spotted all of the principal Althing leadership, plus General Wolfram, Gisela, and scores of people he didn't know, but didn't see anyone who stood out like Grandurian nobility who might be the much talked about new lord of the city. That was a problem he'd deal with later.

Time to win.

Chapter Five

Never Underestimate Motivated Friends

Connor sprinted north toward the third pylon, almost a mile away. He kept a low tap rate with slate, questing in every direction for additional danger. He also pulsed out invisible bursts of echoing sound to make sure he didn't miss anyone using the new Blind Curtains. Those were mechanicals rendered nearly invisible using reflective materials and carefully applied sightstones. The amazing development was being adapted for some of their flying machines to help conceal them from Obrioner scouts.

He found no threats as he quickly crossed the distance, but the closer he approached that pylon, the tenser he felt. There was no way they would give him a free leg of the challenge. Still no danger appeared as he slid to a stop a dozen feet short of the pylon and approached it cautiously, every sense alert.

He pulsed out a final blast of invisible light and sound. Only then, standing directly in front of the pylon, barely three strides away, did he realize that the sound was bouncing back from a space right in front of the pylon just large enough to conceal a person standing perfectly still and splitting the air around themselves with limestone. He hadn't noticed it before because the rest of the sound bounced back from the pylon right behind the person, so the difference in bounce-back time was minimal. From a distance everything looked normal.

Shona erupted out of that invisible bubble with a shout of triumph, her powder-coated wooden sword already sweeping down toward his head.

Connor instinctively tapped granite and leaped to meet her. His close-in bash fighting instincts were honed from months of intense practice with Tomas, Cameron, and Erich. Shona was an excellent fighter, and if he hadn't already been focusing on that spot, the ruse most likely would've worked. Instead, he caught her hand and stopped her sword half an inch above his head.

"Connor, you can be so annoying," She grunted as she increased her tap rate, her muscles growing.

He'd perfected the art of annoying Shona during the hectic months when he'd served as her Guardian. Her devious plotting hadn't worked out the way either of them had expected.

Shona max-tapped, her body shifted into perfectly sculpted lines. Connor could draw far more strength from granite than Shona, but he did not want to simply overpower her. His relationship with Shona was very complicated, but he still felt reluctant to damage her honor by making her look weak.

So as they struggled, her scent of roses wafting over him, her expression one of intense concentration, Connor winked and tapped external quartzite. He hit her with sensory deprivation.

Her skin returned to normal, her body shifting out of the perfect lines of living stone back to her excellent native figure, and complete calm settled over her exquisite features. Connor knew from experience how unnerving sensory deprivation could be. It robbed one of all their senses. It left them in a state of limbo even worse than that creative darkness that Evander had dropped over him earlier.

Hamish seemed to love it, particularly when Jean was nearby so she was the first thing he saw when he recovered. He claimed that everything seemed more vibrant right after being released from sensory deprivation. Most people just freaked out. Connor was not sure if Shona had ever experienced it.

So he gently took her sword from her grasp and scraped the flat of the blade down the center of her face, leaving a coating of pink powder behind. He also tapped chert and focused on Shona. Her thoughts seem to scream into his mind.

"*Let me out! Connor, I know you can hear me. If you don't release me this instant, I'll rescind . . .*"

She hesitated. One of her favorite threats when he was her Guardian was to rescind patronage, but now they both knew that was a lie. Still, for most of her life she had believed the lie, and old habits died hard.

Connor turned her slightly to face the pylon, touched it himself, then released her from sensory deprivation.

Shona gasped and lunged forward. Instead of grappling with Connor, she collided with the pylon, tripped, and plopped down on her backside.

Connor was already sprinting away to the west, his legs fracked. Tapping serpentinite, he captured the colorful curses that she shouted after him. Hamish would have loved to hear them, so he was tempted to save a few of the choicest ones to share later, but resisted the urge.

There must be some kind of final defenses ready to block him from the fourth pylon, but he'd already faced most of his closest friends, and he was starting to feel a little impatient. So he decided to give the watchers a show. He was running low on powder to fuel his primary affinities, but he still had plenty of stone left to fuel his mighty tertiary affinities. He decided to demonstrate what he could do with the elements. That meant tapping porphyry again to help solidify his connection. He could tap two igneous stones simultaneously but was already using granite and basalt.

Which to purge? He could absorb more powder quickly if the need arose, particularly if he absorbed only enough porphyry to keep the connection going. He could move fast with the elements, so decided to purge basalt. Hopefully he was making the right choice.

Connor purged, absorbed a little porphyry and tapped it. At the same time he called upon the elements. The rampager arose in his heart, pacing in its restraints, growling low. Connor got the sense that for some reason it didn't like him calling it and the elements at the same time. That was strange. He'd never felt anything like that before, but didn't have time to wonder about it.

As always, the clothing worn by the mental projections of the elements was striped with bands of both red and green, representing the different frequencies of power that fueled the affinities. Life had been simpler when he could only access the lower frequency red energy, but his mightiest new abilities were tied to the difficult higher frequency green. He'd accessed it after his second ascension, but the two sources of Petralist power tended to crash into each other and cancel each other out. Tapping porphyry helped solidify his connection to the green frequency without red interfering.

Connor also tapped chert. Like porphyry, the sedimentary stone was somehow linked more strongly to green, and when he tapped both stones his elemental control increased dramatically. The elements seemed more content to work together than ever, even though his tape rate with porphyry and chert was still pretty low. That was a good sign. Kilian had promised that eventually he wouldn't need to keep tapping porphyry to stabilize them.

Good, because his supply was getting low, and no one but High Lord Dougal had known the location to quarry more. There had to be someone living who knew, maybe one of the cutters who had worked at that secret quarry, but no one knew how to identify them. He had access to a better supply of chert, but it tended to get consumed fast, so managing that supply was challenging too.

With his connection stabilized, Connor tapped Water. She stood closest to him and seemed to approve the fact that he called upon her first. He pulled water out of the ground and wrapped himself in a sphere of glittering silver liquid. Then he called upon Fire, who laughed silently as the wild insanity of his element swept through Connor, filling his mouth with the taste of ash and creating the scent of charred wood in the air. Connor was so glad that walking with fire no longer hurt like it had before his second ascension. Crimson flames appeared out of thin air and wove among the water. Fire grinned at Water and she winked back. That was the closest they ever came to touching.

Earth and Air came next, adding snaking lines of brown and ropes of translucent air to the bright mix wrapping Connor. Finally he drew upon serpentinite, wrapping some of his favorite sounds into the sphere, including Verena's laughter, Jean's beautiful singing voice, and Hamish's joyful cry when he witnessed a tray of fresh cookies drawn from an oven.

Surrounded by the impenetrable sphere of mixed elements, Connor set it spinning to accelerate west. He kept his arms and legs spread eagled, maintaining contact with the inner edge of the spinning sphere as it sped up. He'd used a similar technique, although only with water, to knock Gregor from his tower the day he'd freed Nicklaus and Verena from captivity in that little cave south of Alasdair.

With that act he'd broken with General Carbrey. He hadn't comprehended what insane adventures would result from that decision, but he never regretted the choice.

Sure enough, as he closed on the last pylon, still nearly half a mile to the west, the Arishat League unleashed their weapons. Explosions of fire and waves of not-quite-lethal acid washed across his path, fired by Althing trebuchets and Tabnit death tubes that Hamish had dubbed Sparky Sparky Boom Drums. Connor really liked that name, but the Tabnit officers had seemed oddly insulted by it. Verena had settled on Death Tubes as a compromise since no one could pronounce the Tabnit native name for them.

The boom drums fired impressively explosive ordnance, but he rolled right through them and everything else the Arishat League rained across his path. He grinned as he accelerated more and closed on the last pylon. Nothing would block him from this easy victory.

He barely noticed four steel pillars rising out of the ground on either side of his path. He wasn't sure if it was Evander or Ilse or Aifric pushing them up, but they were moving far too slow to interrupt him. Filled with confidence, he did not alter course but zipped right between the posts.

Sparks exploded from each post, and blue lightning rippled between them. Somehow it punched right through his elemental barrier and sizzled against his armor. It plunged through him, making every muscle spasm with pain. The shock of it felt like that time he'd unleashed his father's diorite hammer to blow the mountain above Alasdair.

That blast of energy severed all of his affinity connections, and his elemental shield shredded. Connor tried to scream as his body tumbled forward, but his throat was seized shut and he couldn't breathe. His vision blurred as the world spun out of control and all he heard was crackling.

As he tumbled to the ground, he heard a voice shout in his mind, "*Keep rolling, Connor! Get out of the field.*"

He couldn't see, could barely think, but instinctively followed the voice, rolling over the grass the best he could, despite the wild convulsing of his muscles. Somehow he managed to keep tumbling until he rolled beyond the far side of the box formed by those posts. As soon as he did, the deadly current cut off, releasing him from its brutal grip. He collapsed to the grasses, his muscles still twitching uncontrollably, just happy he could breathe and think again. A few more seconds of that might have killed him.

Where had that voice come from? He looked around, but saw no one. Had he imagined it? The voice sounded familiar, but he couldn't place it.

"Ow," he groaned. He really should have paid more attention to the Arishat research teams. They'd developed something truly painful. It had rattled him, body and mind.

For a moment he let himself recover and decided he hadn't actually heard anyone. As control returned to his limbs, he smelled lightning wafting in the air like sharp-scented smoke, and the taste in his mouth was like charred steel. He tapped sandstone, and healing warmth flowed into him from the sandstone pendant affixed to his necklace of stones. It was a rather plain stone, smoothed to a cylindrical shape. It lacked the sheer, concentrated power of the sculpted pendant that his Aunt Ailsa had gifted to him months ago.

That one had crumbled to dust after the battle of Merkland, its powers exhausted. The one he wore now was a gift from Gisela. It held far more power than an unsculpted piece, but she had lacked time to work the stone to the concentrated magnitude of Ailsa's master works. Still, he appreciated having it.

As sandstone washed away the worst of his aches, he managed to sit up, tap quartzite, and glance over at the distant observation post. Most of the observers were still hidden behind the huge screen, but several of the Varvakins, dressed in gleaming plate armor, had stepped around it and were jumping up and down in glee, hands raised in victory.

The test was supposed to prove he could defeat whatever they threw at him, so it rankled that they seemed so pleased to have disabled him. Maybe they hoped their invention could hurt the queen too. If it could, then Connor would celebrate with them because that meant he wouldn't be the only possible hope for the revolution.

All he knew about the Varvakin inventions was that they worked with stones that snatched steel from a distance, and also somehow harnessed a power they had referred to as the Merry Dancers. That ignorance had just cost him a very painful crash. He couldn't wait to learn more.

Captain Ilse rose out of the ground nearby, carrying Ivor out of concealment with her. Ivor's hands were already encased with water and fire, and he looked eager to jump into the fight with Connor. The two of them hesitated, looking surprised to see him so disabled. His connection to his elemental affinities still felt shaky. He doubted he could defeat the wily captain with earth, let alone best Ivor with water and fire at the same time.

"Most of today's run was impressive, but you still failed to reach the final pylon," Ilse pointed out.

She looked willing to wait for him to make a move before crushing him. Ivor was grinning, with flames curling around his teeth. He looked confident they'd easily stop him.

"What pylon?" Connor asked with a grin.

"Oh, no you don't," Ivor snapped and together they spun to glance at the final pylon.

He should have attacked because Connor was already tapping sandstone again, but this time externally. The boiling, destructive power of sandstorm ignited from the stone, and he cast it at the pylon.

He'd practiced with sandstorm through the winter, although he hadn't yet learned to enjoy the process of tearing things apart at a fundamental level. All the stones with both internal and external focused powers resulted in opposite effects, but none seemed as dramatic as sandstone.

A brown storm of sand materialized around the pylon and within seconds consumed it, melting it away to nothing.

Ivor whirled back to face Connor, his expression offended. "Hey, no fair."

"I thought you were supposed to stop me," Connor said, projecting calm confidence, although internally he was still groaning.

Ilse chuckled. "I'm not sure that exactly fits the parameters, but some part of you definitely reached that pylon."

Ivor released his elements and sighed. "You owe me a duel, Connor."

"Gladly. But you might owe me a lot more."

"How so?" Ivor asked, drawing closer, instantly intrigued by the discussion of debts.

"Well, the way I see it, I won you a debt from Aifric and saved you public humiliation in front of all the Arishat League officials. Your account is adding up fast."

Ivor laughed. "Aifric's debt is on her, and humiliation is a strong word."

"I guess we'll never know. Another duel is a good idea. Later," Connor said.

Ilse extended a hand and hauled him to his feet. "Clever use of your affinities, Connor. I approve."

He grinned at her. "It helps that I have such interesting friends."

She slid them north on a platform of earth toward the crowd of onlookers, and Connor gratefully let her manage it. He wondered again if the new lord of Schwinkendorf was concealed among the watchers. Had he seen Connor fall? Connor didn't like that idea, especially if it encouraged the new lord, whoever they were, to think him weak and easy to push around. He'd be severely disappointed if he tried. Connor wasn't Grandurian so did not owe official allegiance to any Grandurian lord.

He hoped the new appointee recognized that the best thing they could do would be to stay out of everyone's way, but he'd known enough nobility to be prepared for the worst. He hoped the king had made a wise choice, but Connor would be ready. All of their lives, all of the lives of everyone they loved depended on their success.

They were preparing to fight the dread queen herself. If the new ruler of New Schwinkendorf endangered the vital work they were doing to prepare for the looming war, Connor would remove them and deal with the consequences.

Chapter Six

Going from Bad to Worse

Ailsa stood atop one of the nine high towers that reared above the throne room, perched above the central palace of Donleavy. Mealt Falls thundered past, almost close enough for Ailsa to touch.

Heights did not usually bother her, but standing on that tiny catwalk at the top of that slender tower made her just a bit nervous. Worse, with the falls roaring past so close, the billowing spray clouding everything in mist and coating the stonework, slipping and plunging to her death became a very real danger. That would be such a stupid way to die after all the risks she'd survived.

Nearby, Rosslyn was gleefully rushing around the narrow catwalk, hand outstretched to the falls. Of course, if Ailsa was a powerful Spitter, she wouldn't have any reason to fear either. Surrounded by all that water, that narrow, slick catwalk was probably one of the safest places Rosslyn could witness the events unfolding just below them.

The expanse of the multi-leveled capital city stretched to the north in a breathtaking vista, but Ailsa's eyes were drawn to the intense blue flames crackling in the air above the semicircular throne room directly beneath her.

General Aonghus was ascending.

Ailsa watched the proceedings with great interest. Buried deep beneath her facade as the queen's trusted advisor, Ailsa allowed a rare, well-shielded personal thought. "*I've only got Connor's ascension at the Carraig for comparison, but Aonghus doesn't seem to be having such a good time of it.*"

He stood in the center of a column of intensely hot flames, little more than a shadowy figure etched in fire. The flames were growing so hot Ailsa could feel the heat even standing a hundred feet higher and surrounded by the cool, billowing spray.

Only Queen Dreokt could venture close during a fiery marble ascension. She seemed impervious to the flames and ignored the fact that she was walking on thin air high above the palace. The dread queen was pacing in the air around Aonghus, who stood in the flames several dozen feet above the roof of the throne room. He was beginning to writhe, as if struggling to escape the conflagration.

Queen Dreokt wielded such mastery over the elements that sometimes she seemed to forget that they were not actual extensions of her hands. She stepped to the very fringes of the flames and began calling out encouragement. It was perhaps the first time Ailsa had ever seen her openly support anyone but Harley.

"He doesn't look so good," Rosslyn commented as she paused at the railing beside Ailsa.

"I've heard that marble ascension is the most difficult. Flames purify, but also destroy, and from what I've heard this ascension could easily accomplish either result. Or possibly both."

"How could it do both?" Rosslyn asked with a frown.

"Stepping through that threshold strips away all the dross from a person. Even if they survive, if the parts that were stripped away were the parts that most defined them, what would be left?"

Rosslyn frowned. "I hadn't considered that."

Ailsa kept her expression neutral and verified her surface thoughts were focused on Aonghus, but again allowed her inner self to think. "*Rosslyn fascinates me. She's a new addition to court, and she has much to worry about. More than the ever-present fear of death or mind-wiping, she must agonize over the fate of her dear children.*"

From all accounts, Rosslyn seemed a very capable young woman. In her thirties, daughter of High Lord Feichin, sister of Redmund, the hero of Drumwhindle Pass, and mother of two adorable toddlers who had arrived in the capital with her a few weeks earlier.

She and her children still lived. High Lord Feichin had stepped into Dougal's vacant seat as one of the queen's high counselors, along with Ailsa. She might not be a Petralist, but as one of the senior sculptresses in the realm, she merited sufficient respect that her position serving the queen was not entirely unprecedented. Since Ailsa was not a high noble, she often provided insights that the queen found refreshing. So far she had thrived in the dangerous environment. High Lord Feichin and Rosslyn both seemed to be performing satisfactorily. That didn't mean all was well, though.

The queen had insisted on interviewing Rosslyn's children. They appeared undamaged by the encounter, but Ailsa doubted they were unaffected.

Queen Dreokt had brutally responded to rumors of insurrections stirring in other cities across the realm. Anyone even suspected of revolutionary thoughts was killed or mind-wiped. And she'd started interviewing the children of all the high houses.

No one was completely sure what she did in those private interviews. Most of the children survived, and like Rosslyn's kids, seemed fine. But Ailsa had picked up enough hints from the queen's occasional angry ramblings against wicked servants that she felt more worried than ever. "*If she's not implanting into those children's minds orders to rise up at the first sign of revolution by their families and murder their own relations, I'll eat my last sculpture.*"

She wasn't the only one who suspected that. Rumors abounded, and the entire kingdom huddled in fear. "*Only Merkland stands free, but even with all the contacts I've helped them establish, no one else dares openly join the revolution.*"

With the country cowering under her heel, Queen Dreokt had used the winter to build up her decimated army. Like she had done with Lady Shona, she somehow could sense Petralist potential in people and spark it to greater intensity. She had helped scores of Petralists gain a secondary or tertiary affinity, and had gifted hundreds more a primary.

Her army was growing every day, bursting with new Petralists. They were training hard in new military encampments near Crann and Belmullet. When the queen finally unleashed them, they'd field overwhelming force.

That was not her only weapon.

Ailsa's musings were cut short by a wave of heat from below, so hot it warmed the steel catwalk underfoot and consumed some of the billowing mist, flashing it to steam in a hissing cloud. Ailsa cringed back from the steam, then risked another look over the side.

The flames surrounding the writhing form of General Aonghus blazed from blue to white hot. The heat intensified as he slowly rose higher. It looked like the ascension was reaching its conclusion. Queen Dreokt was rapidly circling him, shouting encouragement, clapping and laughing as Aonghus suffered.

Then abruptly the fires winked out. For a second, Aonghus stood in the air, white-hot fires burning in his eyes as he tipped his head back, threw his hands out, and shouted in ecstasy. Then he collapsed.

The queen caught him and drew him to her like a mother might an injured child. She hugged him, stroking his head, whispering words too soft for Ailsa to hear. She floated higher with Aonghus still in her arms until she stepped onto the walkway beside Ailsa. There she gently released Aonghus, placing him carefully on his feet. He staggered, nearly falling.

Ailsa steadied him and he leaned against her. His eyes popped open, and in that first glimpse, Ailsa read pain but also clarity.

Like most Firetongues, Aonghus had always seemed rather unhinged. He possessed an exceptionally powerful affinity with marble and had seemed to love the wild insanity of walking with fire more than most.

Now, for the first time ever, he looked completely in control. That was unnerving.

The queen had done something to Aonghus, touched his mind and perhaps a little more than that, before sending him off to Merkland with Harley and Dougal. Although their mission had ultimately failed, Aonghus had accomplished his secret orders.

"*Poor Jean. So many suffer along with that pure soul.*" From the accounts Ailsa had read, Jean's exceptional grace in managing her terrible injuries had lessened the horror of what he had done, but could never erase it.

While Ailsa kept her surface thoughts focused on joy that Aonghus had survived, sprinkled with reverent appreciation for her mighty liege, inwardly she shuddered to think what Aonghus could accomplish now, ascended in marble, stabilized and more in control than perhaps ever in his life.

Queen Dreokt laughed again, clapping her hands together in glee. "Well done, General. You handle the burn exceptionally well. I expect great things from you."

Aonghus found his balance, turned to the queen, and executed a deep bow. "I appreciate your confidence, your Majesty. I owe everything I am, and everything I hope to be, to your good will and your most excellent gifts. I am your humble servant."

"Not too humble, I trust," the queen corrected.

Aonghus laughed, his normal, wild laughter with flames dancing in his eyes. "Never that humble, your Majesty."

"Good. Rosslyn, you're next." The queen turned to her with one raised eyebrow, as if challenging her to object.

Rosslyn had survived several weeks in the capital, so she would never make such an obvious blunder. She curtsied, her expression eager. "At your command, my queen. I look forward to ascending. We'll see if Aonghus can keep up with me then."

It was rather daring to joke in the queen's presence, but somehow Rosslyn had managed to do it before, and the queen seemed to enjoy the levity. Few others could pull it off, but Ailsa silently applauded the younger woman for managing it.

The queen chortled. "Oh yes. You two must train together daily and test your new limits. I need you at full strength before you lead my great host forth to battle."

Aonghus looked eager for a chance to spar with Rosslyn. The two had a running bet about who would prove most deadly. Aonghus usually pointed out that he alone of the senior leadership of Harley's army had escaped alive, and touted the fact that it was well known that fire was the best battle element after slate.

Rosslyn usually countered that if he hadn't turned tail and run as fast as he had, he would not have survived either. She pointed to reports that suggested enormous casualties were attributed to Ivor, who had commanded the river during the battle.

The queen seemed content to let them argue about it. She challenged them to try harder and dig deeper during their practice sessions. She seemed desperate to prove to the kingdom that she had powerful leaders under her command, even after losing both Harley and High Lord Dougal.

Rosslyn said, "Once I'm ascended too, we'll be able to spank Ivor, and maybe even challenge Kilian."

Aonghus laughed, but Ailsa could read him well enough to tell he was wise enough to still fear Kilian. Again, he seemed far more in control than she would like. A wild Aonghus was dangerous, but a calculating, controlled Aonghus was far deadlier.

Queen Dreokt frowned. "You leave my naughty son to me. Kilian would destroy you both. As for Ivor, my plans for him work better if he lives."

That was about what Ailsa expected her to say. "*Why have you been waiting to strike Merkland and destroy Kilian and dear Connor? They pose a threat I don't yet understand or you would not have hesitated. This secret I must know.*"

Perhaps now she had a chance to find out more. "Dealing with Kilian and the other revolutionaries will indeed be a challenge. May I ask if you plan to lure them out by attacking Merkland again?"

She had not dared such a direct question before. Luckily, the queen did not seem angered by the query, but waved a dismissive hand. "We'll move against

Merkland soon enough. The spring thaws will arrive in Granadure soon, and my wicked boy will have plenty to keep him occupied until I arrive to take his head."

Aonghus rubbed his hands together. "So we move against the Mhortair first?"

She shook her head. "I have plans for them and the pitiful forces assembled from the so-called Arishat League. We will discuss the specifics in time, but today is a day of ascension. Rosslyn, as soon as you succeed we'll feast to celebrate your successes." She extracted an exquisite sculpted soapstone figurine from one pocket of her crimson and gold gown.

Ailsa had completed the sculpture just a week prior, and although she knew it would be used to further the queen's plans, she could not hide a little smile of pride as she looked at the exquisite figurine. The queen had provided an exceptional piece of soapstone, with excellent vortexes of power that Ailsa had worked and magnified until the final piece, shaped like a leaping dolphin, magnified the innate power of the stone nearly twenty times.

It was one of the most powerful pieces that she had ever produced, and it helped a bit to know that Rosslyn would be ascending with it. As Ailsa got to know the young noblewoman, she liked her more and more. Rosslyn was a true patriot, eager to do her duty for the throne and her family honor, and innately possessing a sense of right and wrong.

"*Your integrity is the leverage I will use to gently turn you into a future ally.*" One more step in the deadliest game she had ever played.

Rosslyn took the stone and gasped at the first touch. The billowing spray all around them shook, as if from an invisible thunderclap. Her expression turned to a look of ecstasy. Slender arms of silvery water formed out of the spray and clasped Rosslyn. She laughed with pure joy as they lifted her off the catwalk and into the center of the thundering falls.

While Ailsa peered vainly through the mist, her thoughts turned to the queen's words. "*Why mention the spring thaw? What do you have planned for Kilian and Connor and the others? Oh, I hope they're ready.*"

When she glanced back, Aonghus was pacing away with bits of blue fire flickering along his hands. Queen Dreokt had turned away from where Rosslyn disappeared, and her impenetrable gaze was resting instead on Ailsa.

Chapter Seven

Kids Do the Darndest Things

Connor opened the reinforced steel door into Mechanical Testing Bunker Number Three and stepped through, with Hamish right behind. Hamish had flown across town to meet him at the testing site, but now carried his helmet tucked under his left arm. It looked like he'd swapped the leather outer shell of his amazing Builder battle suit. Connor wondered what new enhancements he'd built into the incredible construct.

"Sure you should be pushing open big doors in your invalid condition?" Hamish teased.

"Eat rocks," Connor retorted with a smile. Hamish had checked on him several times over the previous day since the painful end of the challenge course run. Connor had felt weak, and his muscles had occasionally twitched at random times, but he hadn't suffered any lingering issues from the Varvakin lightning attack other than his hair still standing out wildly from his head.

Hamish had seemed a bit disappointed that he hadn't exhibited more side-effects. He'd hoped for explosive flatulence at minimum. As interesting as that might have been, Verena, who had stayed by Connor's side most of the day, had been extremely grateful it never materialized.

The testing bunker was situated just outside the western boundary of New Schwinkendorf, behind a heavily reinforced wall, inside a bunker fifty feet beneath the ground. At first Connor had thought the location was a little extreme, but through the winter they had experienced a number of truly fantastic failures.

No one had been permanently injured, but the thick, reinforced steel walls bore a number of scorch marks and cracks.

Jean was already there, standing in the observation balcony, a platform about twenty feet up one high wall, completely encased in reinforced Sehrazad steel glass. The wonderful invention looked like normal glass, but once fashioned, somehow became virtually indestructible. It offered excellent protection with unrestricted views. A crowd of assistants, researchers, and military officers clustered around Jean.

She might be an Obrioner commoner, but everyone treated her like Lord Eberhard's adopted daughter. She was clearly the leader and looked poised and confident, despite her terrible injuries.

Seeing the sleeve of her blue, cotton dress pinned over the stump of her right arm reminded Connor that he'd failed to save her, failed to heal her completely. Her golden hair was regrowing well, but a patch covered her right eye, and some faint scarring remained across the right side of her face, despite everything Connor and other Healers had done to erase them.

Jean waved with her good hand and Connor forced himself to ignore her injuries and see her the way she portrayed herself. She did not hide her injuries, did not apologize for them, but moved forward despite them. Her inner fortitude inspired him.

The crowd parted for them and they exchanged greetings. Connor smiled at Gisela, who worked as Jean's personal secretary. The pale-haired Althin sculptress was another skilled administrator, who helped Jean manage her extremely busy schedule. Hamish seemed to know everyone, but didn't stop to chat with them until after he gave Jean a quick kiss.

Connor asked, "What's being tested today?"

She grinned. "Personal defensive shielding. We've enhanced them significantly since the last iteration."

Gisela added, "We have adding secondary components to extend the livings of the shielding, and the makings of easier to deploying."

That sounded good. Several heavily armored soldiers were already assembling in the main testing room below. Connor recognized some of the mechanicals they wore, including blind coal gauntlets and personal shielding packs.

Hamish frowned. "You moved the shields to the back?"

Jean nodded. "It reduces interference and we can include larger stones."

"The last time we tried positioning them there, we suffered too much risk of failure. The activation mechanism could be broken too easily," Hamish pointed out.

"We're discovering new things almost every day, and this change was one. Danhildur, why don't you explain?"

She gestured to the middle-aged Althin researcher standing nearby. Gray streaked her straight blond hair, but her eyes sparkled with vigor and she smiled warmly. She led the rapidly growing Althing contingent of researchers and scientists, and acted as one of Jean's chief administrators of the Schwinkendorf Academy. She was an enthusiastic leader and no doubt equally thrilled by the amount of data she was funneling back to Althing.

"Indeed, leveraging the experience we've gained in combining chemical agents with remote Builder activation of mechanicals, we isolated a way to automatically trigger the shielding by measuring impacts to the wearer. For example, if they are struck hard in a critical location, the shielding will activate to defend them from additional harm or secondary impacts. Also, the wearer only needs to bang on one of several activation points on their armor to manually activate the shielding."

That was impressive. The previous design had seemed incredible too, but the activation process required turning a keystone. This way sounded so much better, and could trigger even if the soldier was incapacitated or struck from behind. Connor loved it.

Hamish looked fascinated. "How do you ensure the remote trigger activates?"

She started to respond but Jean held a hand up to quiet them. "We'll discuss more details in a minute. Look, they're about to start."

The soldiers had indeed assembled into battle formation, all facing a diminutive figure who was trotting out of another doorway across the testing room. Connor recognized him and laughed. "Nicklaus?"

Jean smiled. "He's one of our most enthusiastic testers."

Nicklaus' governess stepped to the front of the group. Christin looked less harried than the last time he had seen her in Altkalen and actually wore a smile. She was a slender woman in her sixties, with calm, brown eyes and shoulder-length brown hair pulled into a braid. "Plus this gives him something to do to focus his energies and curiosity. Captain Ilse has been assigning him duties. Helps him feel like he's part of her elite company, and it's much more constructive than chasing him around the city putting out fires and repairing accidental damage."

Jean nodded. "Nicklaus is already an immensely powerful Petralist, but he's still just a seven-year-old. He has far more enthusiasm than good sense."

Plus, he could use both Builder and Petralist powers. No doubt that was the reason he'd been permitted to come to New Schwinkendorf. His rare talent offered unique insights into how both sets of powers functioned, with the potential of one day unlocking how to help other Petralists and Builders cross that gap.

One important area Connor's friends had been testing was trying to figure out how Harley had managed to loan quartzite to Shona. Not even Kilian had known that was possible, and it was a critical breakthrough they needed to understand before meeting the queen's forces in battle. Once Connor actually managed to loan Petralist powers, he hoped that process would also help him learn how to help others establish new affinities.

The queen had done it with Shona, and reports suggested she was using that unique ability to build an unstoppable army, full of new Petralists. If they didn't figure out how to do it too, all the mechanicals in the world might not be enough to save them. If they did figure it out, the possibilities could save the revolution, and very well transform their entire society.

Down in the testing chamber, Nicklaus saluted the soldiers then leaped into a fracked sprint around them. He moved incredibly fast, as if young legs could somehow frack more efficiently. As he zipped around the soldiers, who shifted back to back so at least one of them was always watching the deadly little boy, he tapped his Dawnus affinities and began flinging fire and water at the soldiers.

Connor was impressed. He'd struggled to wield both water and fire together at first. Ivor had taught him some tricks, but it wasn't until he ascended the first threshold that combining his elemental affinities had come easier. Nicklaus was just a kid, but already he wielded his Petralist powers like an experienced warrior.

And he was also a Builder. While attacking with the elements, he also activated small diorite missiles from holsters in his arms, and even pulled a speedsling over his shoulder and unleashed a deadly volley.

Connor watched, enthralled as the soldiers activated the various defensive mechanicals. Luckily the equipment worked extremely well, allowing them to slip through explosions or step through grasping tendrils of elements. A couple of the soldiers were struck by missiles or hornets, knocked backward by the impacts, but shimmering shields of quartzite instantly wrapped them, protecting them from additional damage. A couple of them looked battered by the initial impacts, their armor scored or even cracked, but in any other situation the entire company would've quickly fallen to such a barrage.

No doubt Hamish and Jean were cataloging everything happening to the defenders, while Gisela and the other secretaries furiously scratched notes of their own. Connor just enjoyed the show.

The boy was having a blast, and Connor didn't blame him. He loved running with basalt and throwing around elements, but not even he with all of his affinities could trigger speedslings and diorite missiles. He usually didn't need them, but watching Nicklaus shift between Petralist and Builder powers so seamlessly made him grin.

He could only imagine how much fun he might've had as a seven-year-old wielding such incredible weapons. Nicklaus didn't even have to sneak out back to play. The biggest challenge was probably getting Nicklaus to put away the speedsling and the missiles when they were done testing. Connor had no doubt that if he checked in Nicklaus' room he would find at least one contraband weapon concealed under his bed.

He had always liked Nicklaus, and now he decided the boy was destined for great things.

The test ended all too soon, and Nicklaus immediately rushed to check on the wounded soldiers. Connor and the other observers descended from the observation room. Smoke and dust and the scent of melted metal hung in the room, despite the advanced air exchangers that had been set up to extract fumes after one of the Althing chemical weapons had melted through its protective container a few weeks ago.

Healers appeared to tend the wounded, so Nicklaus jogged over and saluted Jean. "That was fun. When can I shoot some more soldiers?"

His governess said in a long-suffering tone, "Nicklaus . . ."

He sighed and added, "I mean, when can I help test new ways to protect people?"

Jean ruffled his hair. "As soon as we analyze the test, I'll let you know. Thank you so much. You've definitely earned dessert today."

He grinned up at his governess to make sure she had heard that. Then he turned and exclaimed, "Hamish! Can we fly together today?"

"Today's pretty busy, but how about tomorrow?"

Nicklaus jumped up and down with excitement. "When do I get my own battle suit?"

Hamish chuckled. "We're still waiting on authorization for that."

By the terrified look in the governess' eyes, Connor doubted that authorization would come for at least ten or fifteen years. Nicklaus on the ground was a force to be reckoned with. Nicklaus flying around in a battle suit like Hamish could terrorize entire nations.

The boy turned to Connor and added, "When I learn to use the Varvakin lightning strike, will you let me zap you with it?"

"I'd like to understand how it works too," Connor said carefully. He loved Nicklaus' enthusiasm, but did not plan to volunteer for another lightning strike if he could help it.

Jean said, "We don't understand the lightning effect enough to build mechanical weapons using it yet."

The boy looked crestfallen until Hamish added, "But I'm sure we will."

He grinned and grabbed Hamish's hand. "You work with them, don't you?"

"I do. In fact, we're heading over there right now for one of the Juggernaut tests."

"Can I come?" Nicklaus begged, somehow making his eyes wider, his expression pleading.

It was a great show, and by Hamish's expression it had worked on him more than once already. Luckily, Christin was hovering nearby. She said, "Enough Builder work for today. You must prepare for tonight's feast."

Nicklaus sagged with disappointment and Hamish said, "Maybe some other time."

"Yay!" Nicklaus beamed, and Christin cast a reproachful look over the boy's head at Hamish. He shrugged in apology, but didn't actually look apologetic.

Jean said, "Hamish, I don't think I can join you. My teams will analyze the results of this test, but I've got a meeting with Ilse." She nodded toward her stump.

Gisela added, "All testings are being strenuously documenting this week."

"You don't think the new governor would block any of your work, do you?" Hamish asked, sounding offended.

Connor also felt a rush of annoyance. No one knew who would be appointed to govern New Schwinkendorf, but rumors suggested that many high nobility were negotiating to get one of their relatives appointed to the desirable post. The city might be new, but it already played a vital role in the war effort, and promised to become a strategic asset. All the nobles wanted the prize, but Connor doubted most of them would understand how to govern such a unique place.

He knew enough nobility in both Obrion and Granadure not to worry about how badly a purely political appointment could mess with all of their work. The thought of the king making such a stupid choice left him tense with worry.

He wasn't alone. Hamish scowled as he thought about it, and Connor noticed a lot of other angry looks, most of which were quickly suppressed.

With her usual impenetrable optimism, Jean said, "We want to make sure whoever is appointed receives all the information they'll need to become effective as quickly as possible."

"They'd better be," Connor muttered.

Hamish sighed, kissed Jean on the cheek and said, "We'll find you later."

Chapter Eight

The True Power of the Forgotten Sense

Hamish landed in a whoosh of thrusters just outside the long, low hangar that concealed the enormous underground Builder Cavern One. Connor skidded to a stop nearby, his fracked legs snapping back into position. Hamish was so glad he didn't have to break his legs every time he wanted to move fast.

They headed inside and stopped at Verena's workroom, located on the ground floor. As expected, she was working on another test of her marvelous new engine. It was running, secured behind a protective wall of reinforced Sehrazad steel glass. The workroom was large, despite that walled-off testing area. Verena was the senior Builder, after all. Hamish approved of the clutter of tables, shelves, and crates of supplies, although Verena kept them far neater than he would have. Still, the room smelled of stone and fire and the pungent scent of various fuel mixtures she was testing.

Verena waved them over and Connor led the way. She greeted him with a kiss and slipped under his arm. Hamish preferred holding hands with Jean, but didn't begrudge them their preference. Their relationship started with Verena hitting Connor a lot, so maybe standing like that brought back good memories.

During that midwinter trip to Verena's family estate, Connor had won approval from her father to formally begin courting her. That had helped them overcome the lingering issues that had threatened to drive them apart. Like the memory of Mattias. Hamish loved seeing them so happy together.

Hopefully nothing new would drive new wedges between them. Verena was Grandurian and closely related to the king, so she'd probably feel obligated to support whoever the new lord was being appointed to run the city. Hamish trusted her to warn them if she expected problems from whoever won the post.

"What are you doing here? Isn't Fyodor testing the coupler today?" Verena asked Hamish.

"Heading there next." He tucked his helmet under one arm and gestured toward the huge windows on the far wall that overlooked the rest of the cavern. Most of that space was dedicated to the construction and testing of the Juggernauts, and Hamish spent much of his time down there, immersed in the enormous project.

The teams included Varvakin engineers, Althin scientists, a huge team from Jean's Academy, and hundreds of assistants and workers. All of their international allies were working together to pool resources and brilliance in an unprecedented level of cooperation. Everyone was motivated to come up with strategies and weapons to defeat the dread queen. Wagonloads of the best foods from six nations fueled the effort and Hamish firmly believed that their better meals would ultimately turn the tide against the queen's army, whose culinary range was just so limited.

"Hear anything about this new mystery lord getting appointed tonight at the feast?" Hamish asked.

"Nothing's been announced publicly," Verena said with a shrug.

"The timing is so weird," Connor said with a frustrated scowl. "They should have waited until after springtime, at least."

"Why wait so long?" Verena asked, and Hamish noted a new tension in her voice. Did she know something about the appointment they didn't?

Connor shrugged. "We have a lot of work to do. A lot's going to happen once the snows melt."

"Probably more than most of us suspect," Verena agreed, her voice somehow fragile. She glanced at Hamish, and he read a deep worry in her eyes, but she was trying to hide it.

"You're positioned better than any of us. If you're nervous, we should be worried," he said.

"Have you been listening to all the ridiculous rumors?" she asked, glancing between them both.

"We've got enemies everywhere, probably some lurking right among us. It's not ridiculous to think a new player in the mix might cause a lot of problems," Connor retorted. They'd argued the point many times, but something about the conversation felt off in a way Hamish couldn't quite identify.

"Let's just not overreact to anything, okay?" Verena asked.

"Fine, but I won't pretend there's no danger," Connor said.

"There had better be a lot of food, or we could see riots," Hamish added. Leaders had been talking up the feast for weeks and people were ready for something memorable.

Verena chuckled. "I've seen Jean's plans for the meal. It'll be exceptional, don't worry. And Connor's feeling better." She nudged his shoulder. "And yesterday you proved you're tough but maybe not invincible after all." Strangely, she seemed more comforted than worried by that.

Hamish would never understand Verena. So he asked, "How's your engine?"

Several feeder tubes were connected to the engine heart, pouring various components of the fuel mixture into the main combustion chamber. This model was made of Sehrazad glass so they could watch the fuel exploding with fantastic colors, driving pistons connected to gauges that monitored force output. The readings looked good. The strange Sehrazad raiders had brought little else beyond their enthusiasm for battle to the alliance, but that little had been Sehrazad steel glass, and it was quickly becoming a critical component to many projects.

Verena beamed. "It's ready. The fuel mix is the best we've seen so far. Maximizing force while minimizing the need for diorite consumption."

"Good. Diorite is becoming the limiting factor on several of the explosive mechanicals," Hamish said. Their supply had never been huge, and it seemed every day they found a new application for explosions in both military and civilian mechanicals. Sometimes he worried they were becoming too dependent on diorite. Verena's research with the engine offered the first real alternative.

He added, "I've almost finished my tests distilling the tongue-burn component out of spice roots. I think we should add it to your fuel mix. Might make it better."

"No one but you would worry about how fuel tastes," Connor laughed.

"I'm the only one who understands the true power of the forgotten sense," Hamish said, assuming the slightly nasal tone and posture of one of the Althin scientists he worked with to test their chemical weapons. "Nothing can achieve its full potential unless taste is taken into account."

They both laughed and Verena said, "Hamish, don't you dare sip my fuel mixtures. They would be deadly."

He made a noncommittal sound in response. It constantly amazed him how little most other people understood about taste. Connor had talked about his remarkable experience in that spice-eating contest against Verena's father, but didn't seem to have taken the right long-term lessons from it. Hamish would find a way to help them ascend the taste threshold eventually. He would find the right recipe.

Verena said, "Hamish, if you'd piloted the new Juggernauts instead of that prototype against Harley, you might not have needed Connor's help to take her down."

"If only," Connor said.

Yeah, that would have been amazing. Harley had wielded incredible Petralist powers and many people had died or suffered terrible injuries, including Ilse, and of course Jean. To take his mind off of Jean's plight he said, "So now that the engine is working, you need a new project to keep dodging Wolfram's treaty meetings."

Verena grimaced. In addition to the vast resources pouring into New Schwinkendorf from across Granadure, the nations of the Arishat League had committed many of their finest minds and newest weapons to help.

They'd created an entire encampment for the Arishat League, a small but rapidly growing city of its own on the northern boundary of Schwinkendorf valley, near the Nister River. Complete with earthen buildings to garrison several military companies, huge workrooms for their pieces of joint research, and a palatial hall to house the international delegates and high officers.

Not surprisingly, the Althin diplomats had insisted on formalizing the arrangement through a new treaty. Granadure temporarily ceded the land of their encampment to the Arishat League so they didn't have to live and train on Grandurian soil. In that small space, everyone met as equals. Lady Briet of Althing and General Wolfram served as the two joint commanders and led the international military planning.

Lady Briet had been trying to get Verena to participate more in the never-ending political meetings. She was good at it, and as a close relation to the king, the Althins were eager to get her signature on more documents. Luckily for Verena, there was so much work to do she'd never run out of excuses, and now that there would be a new lord of the city, they'd receive the brunt of new treaty attention.

"When is that test with the Varvakins?" Connor asked.

"Soon." Hamish wouldn't miss it.

He led them to the big windows overlooking the vast workroom and the literal army of workers, scientists, and Builders who swarmed over the shells of a full dozen Juggernaut mechanicals. The work continued at a feverish pace. The energy was contagious, and since they had no idea how much time remained before the queen launched her war, everyone expected it to come any day.

Hamish couldn't imagine why the queen hadn't struck yet, but she wouldn't wait forever. The spring thaw was already beginning. He doubted she worried about dry roads and clear passes for her armies. Hamish worked as hard as possible in the calm they were enjoying before that storm, fueling his creative drive with buckets of sweetbreads. He hoped it was enough.

According to the reports they received from Connor's Aunt Ailsa, who somehow still survived in Donleavy as one of the queen's chief counselors, the queen was consolidating her hold over Obrion. The political situation was crazy. It sounded like the queen had beaten her own nobility into submission. She would soon turn her attention to the rest of them.

Connor whistled softly. "I've been so busy training, I haven't been here in weeks. Last time, they were little more than frameworks. Now they look almost done."

Verena snuggled closer to him. Seeing it made Hamish wish Jean was with him. "We've actually had the outer shells done for a while, but they get in the way when we're testing the inner components. We've made some exciting breakthroughs with magnis and strum."

Connor grunted and ran his hand through his unruly hair. "Those are what they used to knock me down yesterday, right?"

"Yeah. They're new even to the Varvakins. They know enough to channel some of those forces, but we're all still figuring out what they can do."

"What do you know? How did they rip right through my elemental defenses?" Connor asked, looking disturbed and fascinated in equal measure.

Hamish was happy that strike had worked so well. If those forces could surprise Connor so much, they might be a key element in defeating Queen Dreokt. He'd started working on miniature versions of those spark posts. Might be able to drop them down the breeches of the new lord if they started making trouble and help them feel better connected to the research teams.

Verena said, "Magnis is the force that fuels a lodestone. It pulls steel."

"It's more than that, though. We're finding ways to activate and deactivate the magnis grip force by coupling it with strum currents," Hamish added.

Verena had dubbed the power of magnis "grip force" initially. He still preferred to think of it as "Invisible Breakfast". He couldn't imagine anything exerting a greater pull on someone in the morning than breakfast.

She had originally dubbed strum "Dancers' Fury" since it seemed to be the same power that fueled the Merry Dancers that lit the northern skies of Varvakis on winter nights. Hamish still preferred that name over strum, but when Verena chose a name, no one overrode her opinion, and she'd decided strum was easier for folks to remember.

Verena said, "Strum is an energy current that reminds me of diorite, but it's power the Varvakins have learned to harness in really remarkable ways.

That crackling energy was like bottled lightning. Hamish loved it. He hadn't told Nicklaus that he was already developing a personal lightning mechanical. It was still early in the development phase, but he liked testing the miniature spark posts against his tongue. "The two energies are interrelated and we're studying how to apply them. With Verena's engine fueling it all, the Juggernauts will pack a lot of punch."

"Well, let's go see them up close," Connor urged.

CHAPTER NINE

The Bigger the Challenge, the Bigger the Toys

Hamish was eager to share the amazing developments with his friends. The three of them exited Verena's workroom and took the nearest stairs down toward the lowest level.

While they walked, Connor said, "I'm glad you came up with names we can pronounce. I can't say the Varvakin words."

"I thought you were working with Aifric to figure out how to use chert and serpentinite to learn new languages faster," Verena said.

Hamish hoped it worked. Everyone needed to learn the languages of their allies, but most people struggled to pick up new words. It surprised him that most of his friends did not seem able to pick up languages as quickly as he did.

He loved how foreign words rolled off the tongue. He'd been practicing Varvakin and Althing. To him, new words were like new dishes, something to seek out and to relish whenever he could get one. He memorized new words as quickly as he memorized new tastes. It worked for him, just like tasting rocks.

Every language had its own flavor. The staccato rhythm of the Althing tongue was like hot-roasted almonds. Althing was a large country to the east of both Granadure and Obrion, along the Sea of Olcan. It served as the political seat of the Arishat League with no standing army of its own. Hamish didn't think they had almonds there, but that's what the language tasted like.

Varvakis was an enormous country even farther north than Granadure, and apparently the northern reaches of their lands never thawed in summer. They were burly warriors who made the best steel on the continent. They boasted few Petralists but were renowned as mighty warriors anyway. Their more guttural tongue felt more like pot roast and potatoes.

He hadn't learned much about the Tabnit language yet. The strange people from the continent across the Sea of Olcan to the south kept to themselves. They were amazing sailors, and their sparky sparky boom drums, fueled by an explosively fast burning black powder rivaled diorite for destructive power. If only they'd brought more of it with them.

He loved the little he'd learned of the flowing, singsong tongue of Sehrazad. It was like a sweetbread flavored with foreign spices, perfect for a people who dressed in robes, rode camels, and wielded long, curved scimitars.

He'd heard snatches of Havaen, the native language of the Mhortair, and agreed with reports that it was considered the most beautiful language on the continent. Those sounds felt like a dessert smorgasbord. So many things to learn, and only one lifetime to learn it in. Sometimes that seemed unfair.

Connor said, "The last language test we did showed a lot of promise, but we haven't had time to follow up on it."

She nudged him with her elbow as they trotted down the long stair that zigzagged down into the bowels of the earth. "Find time."

"My schedule is pretty busy. You want me to sacrifice the little time I get with you to do even more research?" he teased.

She squeezed his hand and said, "Of course not. We're all doing our best. Did you discover any new secrets to linking minds with Aifric?"

Her tone was light, but Hamish noticed the same tension in her eyes he'd seen up in her workroom. She couldn't be worrying about him mind-reading the new lord, could she?

Hamish was sure neither he nor Connor had mentioned the fact that they'd considered the idea. They'd quickly discarded it. Messing with other people's minds was one of the queen's most evil powers, and no matter how just their cause, they couldn't start using those same horrific tactics. Connor couldn't control other people's minds like she could, but he was testing the limits of what he could do with Aifric. Understanding how chert worked could help him better defend himself.

Connor seemed oblivious to Verena's tension. "We've practiced a lot, but it's hard to get a strong connection. Both of us have to want it, and it's draining. We managed it when we resurrected Aifric, but usually we can't link that closely."

"Do you think Aifric could initiate something like that without your help?" Verena pressed.

Good question. Hamish hadn't considered that.

Connor thought about it as they descended the stairs. Walking down was so slow. Hamish preferred flying. Connor finally said, "I'm not sure. Maybe if she was ascended, but right now usually we have to work together. Why?"

"Oh, nothing important," Verena said quickly. "Just trying to understand all that you can do."

"Some days it's tough to keep it all straight," Connor said with a grin.

Hamish just listened. Verena was hiding something. Those questions hadn't been for nothing.

Verena added, "Keep working at it. I know language learning isn't high on the priority list, but like Jean always says, it's good to spend some of our time doing research not directly tied with killing people."

Hamish agreed completely, but they reached the bottom and he pushed open the door to lead them into the workroom. He paused to take a deep breath, savoring the smell of the giant workspace. In addition to the scents of steel, dust, and grease, the air vibrated with a low humming and carried a faint scent, like a whiff of charred toast.

Verena grinned, her eyes shining. Research rooms energized her. Connor glanced around, looking impressed.

He should. The room was packed with the dozen Juggernaut shells, rising like twelve-foot, spherical skeletons. Clusters of thick-coated wires crisscrossed the huge workroom like a swarm of really busy snakes, linking the shells and pumping life-giving energy into them.

Some of the wires crackled with strum, and the humming of that energy emanated from the Varvakin power supply in the far corner of the room. The big, blocky thing had been charged up by cables connected to some kind of power-collecting turbine in the Nister River overnight, then transported inside. Nine Varvakin scientists were scattered around the room, monitoring a series of gauges that measured the current.

It looked like they were ready for the coupling test. Strum energy was being fed by the generator, along the snarled mass of wires, and into the shells of a pair of the Juggernauts. None of the other interior components or weapons were installed. The test was only for the outer shell.

"We got here just in time," Hamish exclaimed. With a thought, he activated thrusters and lifted off the ground to get a better view.

Fyodor, the lead Varvakin, gestured to an assistant standing by the power source, and the woman flicked a switch. The humming intensified and a couple of the wires with frayed coatings began to spark and crackle. Apparently it wasn't serious enough to stop the test, but Hamish reminded himself to look twice before licking anything in there.

A couple of the other researchers pulled additional levers, causing hydraulic arms to roll the two Juggernaut shells together. Connor and Verena cautiously approached across the obstacle-covered floor. Hamish was too eager to wait. He pulled on his helmet and remotely activated sightstones connected to stones inside each of the shells that allowed him to see what was going on.

Hexagonal plates in each outer shell slid aside, powered by magnis instead of by quickened stones. The frames had been altered with openings so that as the hydraulic supports twisted the two Juggernaut shells, they interlocked. A series of clamps along both frames snapped closed, reinforcing the bond.

Hamish whooped and did a backward somersault as the Varvakins chattered excitedly in their guttural, native tongue. Hamish crossed the room to Fyodor, a burly man who always looked more comfortable in his plate armor than in his research clothes.

Fyodor listened to reports from several of his assistants before turning to Hamish with a wide grin. "Welcome, Builder. You arrive just in time. Test is good. Locking is tight and secure."

Hamish pushed up his faceplate. "It looks good to me too. Those shells are as tight as teeth stuck in a smashpacked caramel cake."

At Fyodor's questioning look he said, "I'll get you one later."

Verena and Connor caught up and Fyodor bowed over Verena's hand then gave Connor a happy smile. "Yesterday's test was very good."

He chuckled. "Better for you than for me. I can't wait to learn more about how you did it."

Hamish added, "It looks like you've stabilized the strum flow."

Fyodor nodded. "We began harvesting this strum as you say only a year ago, but great progress has been made. Our capital city of Orlov is already being strung with wires for permanent lights. No longer will the long dark of winter hold us prisoner. This energy will change the world."

The man had the heart of a poet, and Hamish knew by experience that he could also out-drink any three other people combined. They still hadn't found a chance for a borsht eating contest. Fyodor insisted it was food fit for kings.

Hamish would believe that when he saw it. He'd eaten food fit for kings. What he didn't doubt was that strum would indeed change the world. Builders were pushing the limits of science and magic with their inventions, but their work was always limited by the availability of power stone.

The Varvakins weren't. They generated their power somehow from the moving waters of rivers and the movement of special lodestones that produced magnis. They'd only just started understanding the basics of the relationship between magnis and strum. To Hamish it still seemed as much like magic as any of the affinity powers.

Connor said, "It looked like you succeeded in locking those shells, but I don't understand how you're doing it."

Hamish and Fyodor took turns explaining the recent test, how they used strum to power the hydraulics that moved the spheres, and how they used magnis to manipulate those outer plates in the shells. The techniques were so new, it felt like those early days of flying when they had been leaping into the sky without understanding anything about what they were doing.

It was really exciting.

Verena paced along the cables and over to the Juggernaut shells, her expression thoughtful, absently chewing on her lower lip. That was a sure sign that she was having a moment of brilliance, even though he had not seen her eat a single cookie or piece of cake. Hamish regularly tried to encourage her to eat more sugar.

Think of what she could accomplish on a sugar high.

Then again, Verena liked punching people in the face. If she got too hyper, she might not be able to restrain herself.

She returned and reported on her most recent engine test. Fyodor looked thrilled to hear she'd stabilized the mix.

"Is very good. With so much power, we should be able to drive the rukoyatka."

"He means magnis," Hamish explained at Connor's confused look.

Verena was nodding. "When we connect my engine to the gears linking to your magnis lodestones, we should be able to generate more than five times as much power as we did in the original Juggernaut."

Fyodor gestured at his power source. "That is similar to how we harness this energy through the rivers. The waters move the lodestones, which create the rukoyatka. That in turn generates strum. We have always loved watching the Merry Dancers in the night sky in winter, but now they dance for us."

Hamish loved how the pieces were coming together. "We should be able to use that stable flow of strum to drive more mechanicals." He gestured at the two Juggernauts. "And it will help us lock the shells together to make Ilse's Revenge."

Connor laughed, but Verena gave Hamish that annoyed look she always did when he tried to name something. "I still don't think that's the right term."

That was a nice way to put it. Usually she told him his names were stupid. He shrugged. "When you come up with a better idea, let me know. Until then, the super mechanical when we link all of these Juggernauts together into one greater whole will be known as Ilse's Revenge."

Connor smiled. "I like it."

"And you like explosive vomiting on each other," Verena pointed out with a laugh.

Hamish exchanged a look with Connor and together they shrugged. Best friends threw up on each other sometimes. Didn't she understand that?

"We'll still need power stones for thrusters, and as backups in case some of the wires get cut, but by having two separate power sources in the shells, our chances of being able to do some real damage should improve significantly," Verena said.

"And if we need to self-destruct like I did against Harley, the explosion will be even more amazing," Hamish added.

Fighting Harley had been a remarkable and terrifying experience, one he was not looking forward to repeating. On the other hand, he had proven conclusively that Builder mechanicals could in fact stand against even some of the mightiest Petralists.

With Ilse's Revenge, hopefully they could take on an elfonnel, or even help give the queen something to think about until Connor and the other Petralists spanked her down and ended her reign of terror.

Thinking about it all made Hamish suddenly very hungry. He decided he was actually looking forward to the big feast. Maybe the new lord wouldn't be too bad. Even if he was, they'd be best able to deal with him on a full stomach.

Chapter Ten

True Friends Never Give Up

Are you ready?" Jean asked Ilse.

They sat on wooden chairs facing Jean's desk, which was piled high with paperwork she hadn't found time to organize and file. A couple of comfortable chairs, both flanked by little tables covered with notebooks and pencils, faced a small, cold fireplace nearby. The rest of her small personal office was covered by floor-to-ceiling bookshelves, making the space feel cozy.

Jean loved it, but did not spend nearly enough time there. She was too busy in the larger workrooms, conference rooms, and testing sites where her teams were so busy developing mechanicals and working on the school curriculum.

Ilse was lightly touching the earthen flesh that she had summoned to sheath the stump that ended a few inches below Jean's right shoulder. As Jean focused on that scarred stump, memories flashed unbidden into her mind as they still so often did.

She stood outside of the Army gate of Merkland, her newly won army charging the rear of the attacking army. Her euphoria at commanding the mighty force evaporated as she watched Aonghus rise and viciously savage the big, burly caller who had already demonstrated such loyalty to her, despite only serving her for a few minutes.

She quailed in fear as Aonghus focused on her, his red hair aflame, his face twisted with marble-fueled madness. He snarled, "There you are, you wicked little imposter!"

Aonghus launched himself over her troops, driven by crackling flames. He swooped toward her, fire billowing from his mouth, his expression completely insane. He laughed maniacally and shouted, "Now you pay the price for everyone's follies, Lady Jean!"

Hamish's voice rose from her speakstone. "Run! Jean, I'm coming!"

She glanced up and saw him shooting over the wall, thrusters roaring, aiming for Aonghus' back. The sight of him filled her with joy, but he'd never make it in time. Jean stepped away from her Healers and the fallen wounded, moving to a clear bit of ground, and turned to face Aonghus. She couldn't outrun him, and she refused to endanger her patients.

She hoped to try speaking with him, but Aonghus formed an enormous spear of white-hot fire and threw it from fifty feet away.

Terrified, Jean screamed and tried to dodge. The spear split into many fiery shards. Those smaller spears plunged into her body, and flames boiled over her. Intense pain exploded through her as superheated air singed her lungs.

Jean snapped back to herself with a start, breathing fast, fear burning through her like remembered flames. Sweat coated her face and she couldn't fully suppress a shudder.

Ilse gripped her good left hand, her expression compassionate. "The nightmares will fade. Until then, you must be strong."

"Have yours faded?" Jean asked softly. Ilse's husband Lukas had been brutally killed right in front of her by Harley's mini-elfonnel, and Harley had shattered Ilse's hips and the bottom of her spine, leaving her crippled.

"Not yet, but they will," Ilse replied softly, but with determination.

Jean squeezed her hand back. She didn't need to say more. They had spoken many times of their mutual tragedies. Ilse's legendary determination inspired everyone. Despite her grievous injuries, she'd summoned earthen legs to regain mobility and continue fighting Harley. She hadn't retired, but forged on, committed to honoring Lukas by celebrating all the good things they'd enjoyed together. Her bravery had helped Jean cope with her own tragedy. She in turn tried to share strength and comfort with all of her patients.

Any of their burdens could easily destroy any one of them, but by lending each other of their strength, somehow they coped and crept forward along the path toward recovery. None of them might ever recover physically, but Jean was determined to reach a day when she was no longer haunted by that black and burning day. And she would see her patients freed of their burdens too, if possible.

Ilse tapped the earthen arm she'd summoned for Jean and said, "Try it now."

With a mixture of nervous anticipation, Jean started humming softly as she lifted her stump. The earthen arm attached to it rose weightlessly along with the movement.

It was working!

She flashed a delighted grin at Ilse, whose expression had turned to one of mixed elation and concentration. Jean shifted her pitch and the arm stopped rising, but the forearm section extended instead.

Ilse was beginning to nod, looking pleased, and Jean shifted pitch again. In rapid succession, she hummed several different notes, and each one triggered a different movement. With growing excitement, she worked through the sequence that the two of them had developed through more than a hundred painstaking tests.

This time they worked. The forearm moved forward and back at the elbow, the wrist turned and twisted, the hand articulated, and each of the fingers closed or opened on command. Jean barely believed it.

The idea for using sound to control the summoned appendage had taken weeks of other failed tests to figure out. So many people had worked so hard to help Jean find a way to mimic Ilse's remarkable summoned legs. That singular summoning had eclipsed anything anyone had ever dreamed of doing with summonings and it allowed Ilse to move despite her crushed spine.

Jean was no Builder or Petralist, but that hadn't stopped her friends from the ambitious goal of succeeding. At first, Hamish had suggested combining quickened stones, embedded within the summoned limb. Not a bad idea, but activating those stones proved cumbersome. The failures had mounted, and despair had threatened to crush her fragile hope.

After one particularly frustrating day when Jean felt like giving up, she had moved apart from the others and started humming to herself. She always enjoyed singing, and it seemed to calm the boys too. In that moment they all needed a little calm. As the gentle melody filled the small room where they worked, Connor's head had snapped up.

He had looked at her with fresh excitement. "That's it!"

So they switched their experiments to quickened serpentinite embedded in the limb to move it. It had worked better, but still had not given her the degree of precision she needed.

She had nearly resigned herself to the fact that it was the best they could come up with, which was still remarkable, but the others would not accept defeat. Ilse and Connor had spent a great deal of time discussing the process of summoning, and exactly what they could do with a summoned creature.

Those discussions were necessary, even if they had proven fruitless in helping Jean. She'd filled entire notebooks with that research and hoped to apply it to her plans to build autonomous summoned creatures with the mission to help or heal or rescue instead of killing and destroying.

To give an autonomous creature those more humanitarian missions required a greater level of sophistication in the commands used to give the automatons life. While Connor and Ilse worked on fine-tuning greater control, Ilse had discovered that she could create a summoning with the ability to move in certain ways depending on specific voice commands.

The next logical step would be to combine that breakthrough with Jean's extensive vocal range and to define an autonomous limb to perform very specific actions based on very specific notes. The only problem was, Ilse was not a great singer.

Jean had worked over the last few weeks to teach Ilse the different notes clearly enough for the automaton to accept the commands. They'd failed so many times that Jean had started thinking it was never going to work. With all of her other duties pressing down relentlessly on her time and attention, she started questioning the value of wasting more time on the failed project.

But now as she hummed, her voice rising and falling in pitch, the amazing summoned limb reacted smoothly. It was more than she'd allowed herself to dream. She laughed and gave Ilse a hug. Her new arm even managed to grip the incredible Petralist in a pretty good approximation of a normal hug with Jean humming softly to command it.

"I think this might be our most incredible breakthrough so far." How many others could they help with such an invention?

As she released her, Ilse grinned. "I'm glad you're a good singer."

"Mm . . ." Jean started to respond, creating a sort-of hummed note. Without hesitation, the arm swung around and clipped Ilse in the side of the head.

Jean grasped it and pulled it down, barely remembering to hum the notes that would help it relax. Ilse chuckled as she rubbed the side of her head. "I guess the next step is to include a command to tell it when to stop or start listening."

"Can we do that?"

"We'd better figure it out or you're never going to be able to talk with anyone again."

The door to Jean's office opened and Hamish stepped through, followed by Connor and Verena. Jean leaped up to embrace Hamish, careful to use the correct notes this time and make the arm wrap around him.

He whooped with joy and lifted her off her feet, swinging her in a circle, nearly knocking Verena into a bookshelf. "It's working! I can't believe it."

He didn't even seem to notice her eye patch or the scars still marring her face, even though she wasn't wearing the amazing helmet he and Verena had designed for her. Similar but more streamlined than the helmet he wore for his flying battle suit, it was enhanced with eight sightstones that she could activate with her keystone. They were linked to stones set in various workrooms that allowed her unprecedented ability to monitor the work of Builder teams, Althing scientists, and school researchers. It also helped cover the terrible scars Aonghus left on that side of her face.

At least her hair was starting to grow back. She didn't let her disabilities define her, and forced herself not to let self-consciousness of her injuries make her hesitate to interact. Hamish and her other friends had impressed her by not seeming bothered by them. They saw her injuries only as another challenge to overcome together. Their support helped more than she could ever express.

Jean hummed a couple more notes to get the arm to relax, then grinned. "We just barely finished the first test."

"I've always loved it when you hum. Now we'll get to enjoy it all the time. Have you tried practicing while eating lunch?"

Jean laughed. Leave it to Hamish to try combining all the things he loved best.

Ilse said, "We have a little more fine-tuning to do, but we're nearly there. By tonight, she should have a working arm."

"Perfect timing," Connor said, grinning as widely as Jean had ever seen. She knew he somehow felt guilty that he had not managed to save her arm, but it was a miracle he saved her life.

Verena gave Jean an enthusiastic hug, looking close to tears. "You can show it off at the feast."

"Give the new lord another example of how amazing you are," Hamish added.

"I'm sure we'll all get along fine with the new lord," she assured him.

Connor and Hamish scowled in exactly the same way. Hamish said, "He'd better appreciate you. You've been doing most of his job."

"If he's smart he'll keep you on as his assistant and not get in the way," Connor agreed.

Verena rolled her eyes. "Relax. Someone has to be appointed. Do you really think the king would make a bad choice?"

"Depends on how much he has to listen to advice from counselors with agendas who don't understand what we're doing," Connor said.

Jean had heard the rumors, but couldn't bring herself to believe the king would botch such a critical appointment. She felt a certain pride for how well rebuilding had progressed, and a sense of ownership for the city. She felt the same unease about transitioning the reins to someone new, but that had always been the plan. She just hoped she could continue serving the wonderful people she'd grown to love, although she'd welcome a lightening of her load. Maybe she'd get enough time to focus more on her personal projects.

Hamish tugged her toward the door. "Let's go. You girls need hours to get your teeth ready to eat."

Ilse laughed and said, "You do realize girls do a lot to prepare for a formal event, but very little of that preparation has to do with their teeth, right?"

"We need to teach better priorities," Hamish said, tugging at Jean again.

"Careful," Verena cautioned, extending one hand to make sure Jean remained stable.

"It's okay. Bruno fine-tuned the leg brace today." Jean extended her right leg so they could see the framework of slender steel rods, springs, and the clever joint that wrapped around her knee. It was Bruno's twenty-third prototype. The clever blacksmith hadn't given up, and the brace felt wonderful.

She hadn't lost her right leg in Captain Aonghus' firestorm, but it had not healed properly either. Connor, Aifric, and other Healers had tried repeatedly to fix it, but there was something fundamentally broken. Not even Aifric could explain why they couldn't heal it. Jean could walk, but the leg gave out occasionally, and it was very weak.

Verena had offered to make her a flying chair, but as tempting as that was, Jean had refused. She worried people might think she was growing too self-important, floating around everywhere like the dread queen herself. Now with Bruno's brace supporting her leg, she finally felt strong and stable on her feet again.

While her friends examined the brace, Jean felt herself flushing. She didn't like being the subject of so much attention and effort when there were so many other people suffering. She had made herself accept the unprecedented level of assistance because it was clear her friends would feel more hurt if she refused them. Besides, the research they were doing for her could easily be applied to other people suffering similar ailments.

Jean slipped an arm around Hamish's waist and allowed him to help support her. It helped him feel useful, and she loved the close contact. She grinned at Hamish and assured him, "Ilse and I will finish soon. I'll be ready in time."

She dearly hoped the feast proved as amazing as everyone expected. Her many teams deserved the celebration. They had performed remarkable work through the winter.

"Do you have an official title as General Jean? Wearing a new insignia along with your new arm would be perfect," Hamish said.

Jean gave him that look that used to cow him but now just made him grin. "You know I'm not a general."

"You should be," Connor said. "You do have a private army, after all."

"Please don't bring that up tonight," she urged. The transition to new leadership would be fraught with enough challenge without the new lord having to worry about her army.

"Lady Jean's Legion is something everyone knows about, and you are the commander," Ilse said gently, but firmly, a little smile tugging at her lips.

Hamish happily ignored her displeased stare and added, "You've finalized the rest of the command structure. You have to accept your position at the head."

Connor grinned. "She's just worried she's piled up so many titles she can't fit them all in one notebook."

"Very funny," Jean said sarcastically. It wasn't her fault that she was good at what she did, and that she'd been asked to help out in so many areas. Her army was definitely one area she hadn't planned on. It just sort of happened.

Of course, now that she had her own army, she wasn't about to give it away. The small force she had won during the battle of Merkland had swelled in numbers as more and more volunteers came forward to sign up. It was humbling and embarrassing for so many people to put their trust in her leadership when she was but a common linn from Obrion.

Her legion was growing into something wonderful. Not only were they working in tandem with Ilse and the Builders to create autonomous response summonings, but with Jean's mastery over the keystone that allowed non-builders to activate mechanicals, her core of trusted officers were quickly becoming well-known as an elite flyer corps. Few other non-Builders were trained in advanced flight tactics, but Jean had convinced Verena and Hamish that her people should act as the first test cases.

She already had four main squadrons. Mender Flight focused on healing and reaching wounded on a battlefield. Render Flight was focused primarily on the autonomous summonings and delivering other mechanicals. Sender Flight were primarily transport flyers, supporting her other flights and the broader army as needed. And Defender Flight were her main fighting soldiers who would deploy to ensure the other flights weren't interfered with.

Their mission was constantly evolving, though. They were becoming a unique, specially trained expeditionary force and it was one aspect of her many-faceted responsibilities that she was coming to thoroughly love. Tonight all of her teams, all of the people of the fast-growing New Schwinkendorf, all of the residents of Faulenrost, and all of their international allies would celebrate the innumerable accomplishments they'd managed through the difficult winter. Together they had raised a city from the empty valley and pushed the boundaries of science and magic faster than any other time since the Age of Discovery. Jean had helped coordinate the effort, tried to inspire people with the vision of what they could achieve, and celebrated every victory with them.

Tonight she hoped everyone felt the same stirring of pride she did. They deserved so much more than a feast, but hopefully they would sense the depth of appreciation she felt for their hard work. She felt convinced the other leadership of the city shared her feelings, and that the new lord, whoever he ended up being, would quickly understand and support them.

If he didn't, she would have to take steps.

Chapter Eleven

Work Hard. You'll Earn a Bigger Dinner.

Connor walked with his friends toward the enormous central hall down one of the wide boulevards, paved with stone, and smiled to think how much they had accomplished. As much as the Arishat League compound had grown and developed through the winter, it paled in comparison to New Schwinkendorf.

From the air, New Schwinkendorf looked orderly and impressive, the haphazard warren of buildings of the old Builder compound replaced with a grid-like pattern of streets. Every block was bursting with magnificent new buildings. Up close, it was even more amazing.

Despite the speed of construction, the workers clearly understood that they were building something remarkable. They had expended the extra effort to ensure joints were snug, doors and windows fitted perfectly, and even added engravings or flutings in places that might not be easily noticed. Connor spotted so many examples of work elevated from mere construction to craftsmanship.

The community was rapidly growing into a city, with more people pouring in all the time. Already Jean had assigned a team to start working on additional housing neighborhoods and the supporting infrastructure those would require. Managing New Schwinkendorf was quickly becoming a full-time job for a large staff.

He glanced at Jean and felt a surge of pride for her. She'd always been the smartest person in Alasdair, but in recent months she'd proven herself exceptional among the brightest minds gathered from across the continent. She was a skilled administrator, a tender healer, and a ruthless pursuer of truth. The grace she'd exhibited dealing with her terrible injuries inspired everyone.

Seeing her walking unassisted beside Hamish, smiling without concern for her scars, and with that miraculous new summoned arm helped ease some of his lingering guilt for not doing more to heal her. He liked to think that his personal training schedule made him tough, but in her own way, Jean was tougher.

With no affinities, Jean not only oversaw most of the rebuilding effort, but she was also heavily involved in the Builder research and development programs. Then there was the Schwinkendorf Academy, which had grown to several thousand researchers, scientists, and other academics. Plus Jean still continued her personal projects researching medicine and infectious diseases with a small team of healers and Althin researchers. And she commanded an army.

It was a wonder she found any time to spend with Hamish.

If the new lord disrespected her in any way, he'd get lynched by an angry mob.

The central hall was an enormous structure that rose six stories above the street, and four more belowground. The outer walls were sheathed in polished stones of all of the major affinities, although none of the stone was power grade, as far as Connor knew. Although, come to think of it, he wouldn't put it past Jean to find a way to include some power-grade stone in the mix, just in case they needed it. He'd have to ask Hamish to lick a few pieces later.

He doubted he could get Hamish to lick anything at the moment, though. Hamish eagerly led their small group, hand in hand with Jean, tugging her to walk faster. If not for her brace, her right leg would have buckled.

"It looks like everyone is trying to get in," Verena said, pointing at a crowd of at least three thousand people gathered outside the doors into the main hall. The dining halls inside were probably already full. People looked willing to wait as long as needed for their turn to join the feast and learn who their new lord would be.

Verena was dressed in one of her fine gowns that reminded him that she was a Grandurian high noblewoman. He no longer felt intimidated by that, and loved how beautiful the emerald satin made her look. Despite being dressed formally, she still wore her battered leather satchel over her shoulder. Connor had offered to carry it for her, but she refused to be parted from it. He didn't mind. Verena was even more a Builder than she was a noblewoman.

The central hall included many different rooms and functions, including a huge assembly hall in the first basement level. It also included four large dining halls that could each accommodate three hundred people. There were other dining halls scattered around the city, but for the night's inaugural feast, everyone who wanted to was invited to dine in the main halls.

"How is everyone going to eat?" Connor asked as they neared the crowds.

Their group also included Ilse, Gisela, and several of Jean's central team, including Artur the carpenter and Bruno the huge blacksmith. The two men dressed in fine doublets and cotton trousers, although Connor doubted many people would notice them.

Most people would be staring at Verena, Jean, or Lady Carolin who walked beside the huge Bruno. Jean wore a beautiful blue cotton dress, and she was perhaps the most popular person in New Schwinkendorf beside Verena. The elegant Lady Carolin was matron of the girls' school in nearby Faulenrost. She walked with grace and poise, dressed in a tasteful crimson gown.

Jean said, "We planned for up to five thousand people, and the cooking and serving staffs are ready to rotate people through every thirty minutes."

Verena looked impressed. "Coordinating that many meals that fast is as logistically challenging as planning a large-scale battle."

Carolin chuckled. "Probably harder."

Bruno, who's Obrioner was improving added, "The kitchens are packed with all the latest cooking mechanicals."

Arthur grinned. "And every other kitchen in the city is funneling their food into the back doors as well. Don't worry, we'll get everyone fed."

Connor wasn't surprised. The team had demonstrated in so many ways they were rising to the enormous challenges with exceptional skill. Jean was brilliant at picking talented people and motivating them to accomplish far more than they ever could alone. This night was as much a celebration of her team and their successes as it was anything else.

As he glanced around at the rest of the group, he realized they all had so much to celebrate. He felt incredibly lucky to associate with such amazing people. Quite often the military officers focused on Connor's unique abilities as Blood of the Tallan. His powers would certainly play an important role in the upcoming confrontation with the queen, but he couldn't do it alone. Together he and his friends were so much more, and that was their greatest strength.

Somehow he doubted the queen understood that concept. Good. It was one of their few advantages.

Instead of taking a side entrance reserved for special guests, Jean led the company to the main entrance where the crowds gathered. As soon as people recognized her, they took up the cry of "Lady Jean."

They recognized Verena too and other voices shouted her name. The entire crowd surged forward, eager to greet them. Between the two of them, Verena and Jean made up the glowing heart of the new community.

They spent several minutes greeting friends in the crowd, excitedly exchanging news about their most recent breakthroughs in their many projects. Connor hung back a little, enjoying watching the girls work the crowd.

He'd been so focused on battle training and ferreting out all the deepest secrets of the arcane mysteries of the higher thresholds that he knew only a fraction of the people that his friends did. He knew even less about the specifics of the work everyone was involved in. The girls and Hamish seemed to know everyone, and they chatted excitedly with them, switching back and forth between Obrioner and Grandurian without seeming to realize they were switching languages. This was their home even more than it was Connor's, and they loved the people and the work.

Connor decided it would be a great place to spend his life with Verena. All they had to do was survive a barking mad, super-crazy-powerful dread queen intent on enslaving the world.

Many voices called out questions about the new lord, but Verena only shrugged and said, "We'll all find out soon."

Jean added, "I'm sure they'll be wonderful."

Most of the crowd didn't look convinced, but none of them challenged her.

They were finally ushered through the crowd, still waving and calling to friends that they would save a special dessert for them. They were directed to the first of the four dining halls.

The kitchens took up a huge portion of the ground floor, while storerooms took up much of the rest, so the dining halls were all situated on the second floor. In the first dining hall, which was packed to overflowing with eager citizens, they found most of the leadership already assembled.

The huge room felt spacious, its vaulted hardwood ceiling supported by only twelve slender stone pillars, polished so smooth they shone. The floor was clad in dark tile with a slightly gritty finish that offered excellent footing, even when wet. The opposite wall, behind the high table, was made up of huge windows with an excellent view of the nearby city during the day. Now the views were muted by early evening.

The stone walls were draped with bright tapestries. Some displayed the flags and national seals for Granadure and all of their Arishat allies. Others depicted the best Builder mechanicals in epic detail. The one of the windrider made the ponderous transport wagons seem exciting. Connor had expected to see the crest of the new lord, but it hadn't been raised yet. The air of mystery shrouding the appointment was getting really annoying.

The room was crowded with long tables, packed with people on benches, dressed in their finest, filling the room with a riot of color and a heady mix of perfumes. Overlaying it all was a thick scent of cooking food, wafting in through swinging doors from the serving prep rooms on two sides. Mouthwatering meats, delicious bread, and a hundred other scents tugged at Connor's attention. He tapped quartzite to his nose and simply breathed in for a moment to savor them.

At the high table sat many of the leadership of both New Schwinkendorf and Faulenrost. Kilian and Evander sat on opposite ends. Kilian lounged in his chair, that roguish smile on his lips, already holding a glass of wine. Evander had shed his enormous leather jacket and wore an equally enormous blue doublet that seemed about to burst trying to contain his huge frame.

Aifric sat beside Kilian, looking resplendent in a gown of gold and silver, her thick hair piled in a complex pattern atop her head, leaving her graceful neck bare. Ivor was already there too, sitting next to Evander. In that position, he managed to look tiny, but he didn't seem to mind. He was chatting with Shona, who sat on his other side, gorgeous in her house colors of blue and green. She wore her golden hair with only a single diamond-studded pin to pull it back from her face, and her hair literally glowed.

Connor suppressed a chuckle. She'd been playing with limestone again. Not that he blamed her. He spent most of his days practicing with all of his affinities. If he only had limestone, he'd play with it constantly too. Nicklaus sat near General Wolfram, dressed like a miniature nobleman, but his hair was wild, and he was bouncing eagerly on the edge of his seat. He waved mightily when he spotted them.

Other leaders at the high table included Lord Eberhard, ruler of Faulenrost, along with his wife. Lady Briet and several other Arishat officials and officers packed most of the rest of the table. They made an impressive sight.

Connor frowned as he crossed the room. He didn't spot anyone he didn't recognize. He'd assumed the new governor would be seated there for all to see. Apparently Lord Eberhard planned to hold the suspense until the last possible second.

Connor and his friends slipped into the remaining chairs, reserved for them. Lord Eberhard rose, and an expectant hush settled over the crowd. He smiled warmly and spoke in Grandurian, his voice magnified by a Pathfinder.

Since Connor's Grandurian was still rough, Verena leaned close and translated. "My dear friends, this is a wonderful evening. We've worked so hard all these months and you have accomplished amazing things. Who would have imagined such a magnificent city could rise so quickly from the ashes of your old home? And yet here we are, better than ever, joined by so many new friends."

That triggered a round of enthusiastic applause. He let it run for a while before continuing. "Just as importantly, we're involved in the greatest work of our day. We are the tip of the spear. Or, more accurately, we're building the tip of the spear."

That generated a round of laughter. "Our research, development, schools, and Builder workshops are producing the tools that will turn the tide in these dangerous times and preserve our freedom."

Again thunderous applause drowned him out, forcing him to wait while everyone cheered, clapping hands, banging knives on the tables, or stomping feet. Connor cheered right along with them. They had every reason to celebrate. He really liked Lord Eberhard. The man had provided incredible leadership, taking in the refugees from the old Builder compound and coordinating efforts to get production running again even while rebuilding commenced. He'd championed Jean's efforts and supported her like his own daughter instead of a foreign commoner.

When the cheering subsided, Lord Eberhard continued. "There is much work still to be done, but I'm confident that together the people of New Schwinkendorf and the people of Faulenrost will continue to succeed. Tonight's feast marks the official birth of this city. Such a momentous event deserves a momentous feast."

As cheering resumed, Hamish cheered loudest of all and triggered a burst of multicolored lights from his battle suit, eliciting laughter from people all across the room. Everyone knew that he loved good food as much as he loved their precious Jean. The fact that he loved Grandurian food as much as he did his native Obrioner food pleased them that much more.

Lord Eberhard gestured for Jean to stand and said, "To explain the epic nature of the food we'll be feasting upon, I will let our own Lady Jean share some incredible news with all of you."

Chapter Twelve

Well-deserved Desserts

Connor was happy Lord Eberhard was giving Jean a chance to shine before the new lord was announced. He did not even seem bemused that everyone cheered Jean even louder than they had him.

She flushed under the attention, which only made her look even more beautiful. No one seemed to care that she wore a patch over one eye, or that her face was scarred. Her golden hair was starting to regrow, but still barely reached the nape of her neck.

She raised both hands, and only then did people realize she was wearing that marvelous summoned limb. Cheers redoubled and increased yet again when she quietly hummed the hand open and made it wave. Connor doubted anyone outside of his small group understood how it was possible, but seemingly miraculous discoveries were becoming an almost daily occurrence.

Jean spoke, and Connor applied quartzite to her voice to magnify it. Hamish also pushed a small piece of quartzite onto the table. No doubt, it was paired with the stone that he had left with the crowd outside so they could hear the proceedings. Speakstones were becoming ever-present in this new city of Builders.

"New Schwinkendorf rose from the ashes of old Schwinkendorf."

A voice from the crowd interrupted. "Only because you destroyed the elfonnel trying to kill us!"

A new cheer erupted. "Lady Jean, elfonnel's bane!"

Jean flushed again and waved futilely for them to stop, but they kept chanting, and Connor happily joined in. He had fought elfonnel, had defeated them, and nearly been destroyed in the process. The terrifying monsters were elements come to life, raised by the mightiest Petralists, who were often consumed in the process.

Spitnail Camonica had raised a water-bound elfonnel to attack the Builder compound during the battle of Harz valley. She could've wiped out both the compound and Faulenrost, laid waste to the entire region, and killed everyone.

Jean had risked her life and demonstrated remarkable bravery and her normal incredible brilliance by using a keystone, which was still so new at that time they barely grasped its potential. She not only managed to fly a windrider for the first time and save hundreds of trapped villagers, but also activated an enormous Last Word bomb and dropped it on the elfonnel's head. That had stunned it long enough for Connor, Hamish, and Verena to arrive and finish it off.

When the cheering finally subsided Jean said, "Thank you, my friends. We all risk our lives every day. I'm so grateful that you took me in, and I'm proud to call myself one of you."

The cheering resumed, and Connor felt moved by her simple yet heartfelt statement. The people all loved Lady Jean, the Hero of Schwinkendorf. He hoped the new lord was concealed among the crowd, paying attention.

They eventually quieted and she said, "If you don't let me get more than five words in, we'll never get to eat."

That generated a round of laughter and a very brief bout of cheering. Hamish seemed torn between enjoying Jean's moment in the spotlight and calling for the feasting to begin.

"As some of you know, the original town of Schwinkendorf was named in honor of the great, royal chef. He served the royal house over a hundred years ago, and some of his dishes are still enjoyed to this day. However, his greatest recipes, saved in his personal cookbook, were lost to the ages."

Jean smiled, seeming to light up the entire room. Connor wondered if someone had tapped limestone to her face. "We have enjoyed many incredible miracles in this journey together over the last few months, but one of the latest, and one that I think you'll agree will easily be the tastiest, was when I discovered Schwinkendorf's famous cookbook!"

She produced from under the table a huge leather tome and turned, extending it toward Hamish. The tome was a popular local legend, but no one ever thought it would be found again.

Hamish rose, eyes glued to the tome, and walked with stunned reverence to her side. He extended a shaking hand to touch the huge book and his soft voice carried easily across the silent room. "How?"

Jean laughed and kissed his cheek. "Oh, Hamish. You are adorable." She pressed the tome into his hands and he hugged it, looking close to tears.

Connor laughed, as did many people across the room. Anyone else would have looked a fool responding with such awe to a cookbook, but Hamish and his well-known love of food somehow lent the moment great importance. Connor glanced back at Verena and caught her dabbing at her eyes.

She shrugged helplessly. "He's so happy."

Hamish laughed with delight, launching into the air, thrusters firing and sending him up toward the high ceiling. He somersaulted several times, triggering bursts of multicolored light.

The crowd packing the tables cheered with him, and Connor spotted more than a few other women dabbing at moist eyes. Grandurians were more emotional about food than he'd realized.

Hamish returned to land next to Jean, grinning like a mad fool. Over the noise of the crowd, Connor barely heard her explain, "We were looking in the wrong place. I found it down in Lord Eberhard's records vault. I was searching for information on some of the original histories of Schwinkendorf. I discovered this with them."

Then she added loudly, "Tonight's feast is made up entirely of dishes from this cookbook. We couldn't think of a better way to celebrate the birth of New Schwinkendorf."

Cheering resumed, and Hamish could not contain himself. He swept Jean and the book both into a bear hug and lifted them into the air, laughing.

When they landed again, Jean left the book in Hamish's hands and said softly, "I think you should be the guardian of Schwinkendorf's secrets. I know no one else who appreciates food like you do."

Hamish looked like he was about to faint with joy. She added, "Of course, we've made copies for all of the chefs in New Schwinkendorf, and are preparing copies to gift to the royal family in Edderitz, but this tome needs a special home."

Hamish turned toward the crowd and raised the tome in victory. "What are we waiting for? Let's feast!"

As everyone cheered, and many banged their tables with utensils, Lord Eberhard rose once more and gestured for quiet. Jean started to return to her seat, but he pulled her back to stand beside him.

"Indeed the feasting will begin soon, but there is one other item of business we must attend to in order for the birth of New Schwinkendorf to be complete."

An expectant hush settled across the room and much of the good cheer was snuffed out. Clearly the moment had arrived for the announcement of the new governor. An eager energy seemed to emanate from many of the people gathered, and Connor noted Evander and Kilian both grinning.

They were keeping secrets again.

Why did that not surprise him? Knowing that they seemed to know something about the appointment helped ease some of his worry. At least this time, the secret was being revealed in a fittingly epic manner. That pair might be two of the most powerful, ancient Petralists on the continent, but they had a terrible habit of dropping mind-boggling secrets without any flair whatsoever. Maybe they were finally taking his feedback to heart.

"I have done what I can to assist in rebuilding New Schwinkendorf, and I and my people remain committed to assisting in every way possible. We consider this community to be one with us in every respect," Lord Eberhard said.

This time people remained quiet, and most leaned forward, expectant and eager to learn the identity of their new leader. It was not terribly common for a lord to be appointed a new city, but it was not unheard of either. Connor glanced around the room, wondering which door the new lord would enter from.

Then he glanced back at Lord Eberhard who was smiling widely, with Jean standing beside him, and understanding struck like one of Evander's death beams.

"Therefore, it is with enormous pleasure that I announce Lady Jean as the governor of New Schwinkendorf!"

Jean gasped, looking thunderstruck. For a second a stunned silence hung over the room, then it shattered under a torrent of cheering so loud it shook the hall. Connor felt like a fool.

Of course he should have realized what Lord Eberhard planned. Jean was the only choice that made any sense. Lord Eberhard had already taken to calling her Lady Jean along with everyone else, but no one had expected the king to appoint an Obrioner commoner leader of such a vital community.

Connor leaped to his feet, along with everyone else seated at the high table, all clapping and cheering. The rest of the hall followed a second later. People cheered Jean enthusiastically, and an undercurrent of tension that Connor had felt all evening bled away.

Well, almost everyone looked pleased. Shona's expression as she too rose to clap with the others looked like she'd eaten a handful of sour grapes. Although she was smiling, he knew her too well not to note the signs of displeasure.

He couldn't help tapping chert. Instantly emotions boiled into his mind from all around. Enthusiasm, joy, gratitude, and hope made up most of them. Thoughts from the multitude clamored for his attention, forcing him to carefully focus to avoid getting overwhelmed.

After a couple seconds, he managed to limit it to the high table alone. Many of those gathered were skilled at shielding their thoughts, but most weren't bothering at the moment.

Wolfram was thinking, "*She's come so far from that scared but determined healer in Alasdair.*"

Ivor was thinking, "*Good for you, Jean! Obrioner lords were fools to let you escape. Smartest thing I ever saw Lord Eberhard do.*"

When Connor focused on Shona he picked up, ". . . *was he thinking? Yes, Jean has proven herself, but are they so short of nobility that they needed to raise a commoner, and a foreigner at that, to lead this vital community?*"

Then she glanced at him. When their eyes met, her thoughts went quiet. She might not know he was listening, but she was smart enough to know to shield against the possibility.

So Connor winked at her. Let Shona stew on political ramifications. She'd been brought up tangled in political intrigue all her life so she wouldn't be able to help herself. Connor didn't have that limitation. He could simply cheer a dear friend for a well-earned promotion.

It took almost a full minute for Lord Eberhard to speak over the din. "For months now, my dear Lady Jean, you've demonstrated every quality that best defines nobility. Today we can finally grant you Grandurian citizenship and the formal title that you have already been living. Congratulations, Lady Jean."

He bowed over her hand, grinning. She curtsied, then wrapped her arms around him in an exuberant hug. Tears glistened in her eyes, and Connor didn't think she had ever looked lovelier.

Then Hamish swept her off her feet and soared with her around the hall so friends could reach up and touch her hand. Friends who were now her adoring and enthusiastic subjects.

Connor clapped loudly. Often nobility made little sense, although Lord Eberhard was a refreshing exception, but today they had done something right. Jean deserved the title more than anyone he had ever known. She was already acting as administrator, governor, and the beating heart of the community. No one else the king could've appointed could ever hope to do half of what she was already doing.

He gripped Verena's hand and laughed. "This is amazing."

She was grinning as wide as he had ever seen, and her eyes glittered as if on the verge of tears. "A lot of nobles wanted this post. New Schwinkendorf is already becoming a vital national asset, but Kilian's opinion still carries a lot of weight."

Connor laughed again, glancing over at Kilian. Aifric was speaking into his ear. The two sat just beyond Verena, but the cheering was so loud he didn't bother trying to thank Kilian yet.

"I didn't think he interfered with politics," he commented.

"I made sure he did this time. He is the king's uncle, after all. And my father helped convince the rest of the ruling council to ratify the decision."

"Your father?" Connor could scarce believe it. Verena's father had at first been very opposed to their courtship, and had only come around during their recent visit to the family estate.

"You won a lot more than my father's blessing," Verena said with a grin.

"I'm glad, although courting you is all I ever want to do."

That earned him a quick kiss.

A new thought struck him and he asked, "Once the king approved Jean as the new governor, why let all the rumors build like they did? People were worked into a frenzy over it."

"Lord Eberhard could have quelled those rumors, but they were necessary."

That didn't make sense to Connor, but she read his confused look and added, "Look around, Connor. By letting everyone stew over the threat of some unknown lord arriving and messing up everything, Lord Eberhard helped everyone realize just how important Jean's work is."

"But everyone loves Jean already," Connor protested.

Verena nodded. "They do, but she's an Obrioner commoner, and she's getting appointed to rule a very important city. The people love Jean, but there is opposition among the Grandurian nobility. By playing his cards this way, Lord Eberhard has sealed this community to Jean with an unbreakable loyalty. Word will spread and no one will be able to oppose her. There are no weaknesses to exploit here."

She was right. Everyone was so thrilled, so relieved with the way things turned out, they would never allow Jean to be removed. Lord Eberhard had proven himself an adept political strategist more than once already, but this was a much more sophisticated display of his skills. Jean deserved to have such powerful friends.

Kilian laughed at whatever Aifric had said. She turned toward Connor and Verena, leaned close and spoke in her Student Eighteen voice. "You think they'll grant you and Hamish titles too?"

"I doubt it," Connor said.

"Why? You two have done as much as Jean in your own ways, and you're both risking your lives every day to help save this country. That should earn you something."

Connor gestured to where Hamish was just dropping back into his seat after returning Jean to her spot. He was again hugging the cookbook. "We're already getting rewarded. Hamish has his cookbook and Jean, and I've got Verena. What more could I want?"

"Oh, that's good, Connor," Verena said with a dazzling smile. Then she added, "We actually considered the idea, but decided against it."

Aifric laughed, her face shivering for a second as she shifted to another personality. Connor recognized Cacilia's flirtatious tones. "Oh, Connor. You're going to have to work a little harder to help Verena overcome that politically savvy mind of hers. I can suggest a few ideas." She added with a wicked laugh.

Verena rolled her eyes. "Connor is managing just fine. The work they're doing is vital to the war effort. They're both serving in critical capacities with our allies."

Connor said, "Makes sense. We do have the rank of commander in the Althing military, and we're both working a lot with the Arishat League. Right now our statuses are pretty independent."

Student Eighteen nodded approvingly. "I agree. If you and Hamish were given Grandurian titles, it might complicate some of your work."

Verena nodded and took Connor's hand again in her warm one. "Let's just focus on surviving this next year. At that point we can worry about titles and whatever else comes next."

Connor hoped they got to that point. He was looking forward to a time when he didn't have to focus most of his energy on trying to learn deep, arcane secrets to try to stay alive for just a few more weeks. He'd love to simply spend time with Verena, maybe travel the continent and visit some of their friends from other countries, and enjoy life a little bit.

With encouragement from Lord Eberhard, Jean lifted her hands high and declared, "Let the feasting begin!"

The side doors flew open and servers rushed in carrying what was already proving to be a singularly epic meal.

Chapter Thirteen

Old Man Schwinkendorf's Mad Chef Skills

Dishes fit for a king flowed like a flood tide across the dining hall. There were so many, each cooked to perfection, each seemingly better than the last. Connor forced himself to sample only a little bit of each one, even though any individual dish would've made a fine meal on its own.

Unfortunately he was sitting too close to Hamish, who clamored to try every single dish. The servers all knew his love of food and his long quest to find the missing cookbook, so they eagerly obliged. He consumed the first three dishes all by himself.

Jean thought that was hilarious, but Connor saw it as a challenge. Verena took a meat pie with a crust of woven bread, dripping with warm honey. It looked amazing, but Connor diverted one server heading for Hamish and snagged their pot of stew before Hamish got it.

The tall ceramic bowl was filled with thick, spicy stew, bursting with chunks of savory sausage, crunchy greens, and maple flavoring that momentarily made him forget he wanted to try other plates.

As more servers swarmed the room and pushed dozens of dishes at the diners of the high table, it was hard to decide what to try next. Connor suddenly felt ravenous as he dug into a savory pork roast with a delicate balance of subtle spices that rippled across his tongue, each flavor building upon the last until he almost forgot to swallow.

It was not flavored like anything his mother had ever made, but somehow the first delicious bite seemed to melt into his tongue and remind him of long autumn evenings lounging with Hamish near the Wick. He sighed and tapped quartzite to his tongue. Instantly the flavor intensified like an erupting volcano. A really delicious volcano. If only tapping marble tasted like that every time, he wouldn't be able to stop.

A warm sweetbread came next, rolled into a twist and coated with sugar. Inside it was filled with cream that was somehow still chilled, and the unexpected mixture of warm and cool made him grin. Next he dove into a dish of beef slices layered over a bed of Sehrazad white rice. The beef had been marinated until it was so tender it fell to pieces off his fork. He closed his eyes and for a moment forgot to breathe as he slowly chewed, drinking in the savory taste with quartzite-enhanced taste.

Across the room, everyone was eating with unrestrained gusto. It seemed like every person had at least one server assigned to them, providing a never-ending stream of delicacies. Conversation faded to exclamations of delight. No one could waste breath in needless chatter. There was too much eating to be done.

Connor was happy no one interrupted as he next consumed a dish of chewy pasta chunks in a rich, tomato sauce that left him feeling warm and content. He lost track of all the dishes he sampled and could not have chosen his favorite.

Schwinkendorf was a culinary wizard, and the city's chefs had lived up to their namesake. If King Henrik ate that well every night, it was a wonder the man fit through the door. Maybe that's why so many palace doors were so huge.

At one point, Connor caught Hamish's eye and in unison they raised their forks in salute.

Verena paced herself better than Connor did. She was more accustomed to big feasts. He continued to tap just a little quartzite to his tongue to increase the magnitude of the flavor, although the food was so good he did not really need to. Still, using quartzite while he ate was quickly becoming one of his favorite habits. If only he could share the wonder of it with Hamish.

If he ever could, Hamish might eat himself to death. He was already eating with such enthusiasm that it was inspiring the entire high table. Everyone else had plenty of reason to smile, with the birth of New Schwinkendorf and appointment of Jean as the governor, but Hamish's enthusiasm helped take the feast to a higher level.

The table was filled with more laughter and cheer than they'd usually enjoyed through the long winter of frantic work and fear of attack. During that feast, Connor felt like perhaps the spring thaw had finally come.

A sudden headache stabbed him behind his eyes. He winced, dropping his fork and rubbing hard at his temples. The pain seared into his thoughts, snuffing out his joy and for a second he forgot where he was. He stared down at his meal, and it disgusted him.

"Are you all right?" Verena asked.

When Connor glanced at her, he growled with sudden fury, and he felt an overwhelming urge to scream a vile curse at her. Shocked by the intense feeling, he only barely remembered that he loved Verena.

How could he love a horrid Builder? More angry words tried boiling out of his mouth and he frowned, trying to make sense of his wild emotions. He loved her. . . . But he hated her too. He wanted to kiss her, but he also really wanted to grab his dagger and ram it—

Connor recoiled from the thought, rocking back in his chair, horrified by what he'd been thinking.

Except she was a Builder, a vile—

Connor seized chunks of his own hair and pulled, the pain helping center his thoughts for a second. What was happening to him? He hadn't tapped porphyry, but it felt like the uncontrollable rage that had swept him away the first time he tempted the dangerous stone.

He fought against it, but felt his mind slipping under the boiling torrent. He was going to lose control. Somehow he was going to unleash rampager rage when not even tapping it. He felt chilled with horror and slapped himself hard, trying to wake up from the nightmare slipping over his mind, but it didn't help.

Then Student Eighteen arrived, one hand gripping his shoulder painfully hard. Instead of offering healing warmth, she connected with him using chert. He was not tapping chert, but recognized its effects. She was pushing calm and peace into him. He wasn't sure how she knew he needed it, but that rush of peace helped reinforce his mind against the fury that was already setting his hands shaking with the need to smash . . . Verena?

Desperately Connor opened himself to Student Eighteen. How could he feel angry toward Verena? Close to panic, he embraced the peace she offered him like an invisible lifeline. He closed his eyes and simply absorbed the calming piece and let the whispers she pushed into his mind urge him to relax.

"*It is still winter, Connor. Spring has not yet arrived,*" she whispered.

What? That was so weird, but it seemed to help. His headache eased and the terrible anger faded like oil seeping through his fingers. He felt tainted by it and shivered at how close he'd come to totally losing control.

After a moment he opened his eyes. She winked and said, "Pace yourself, Connor. Some of these dishes have more kick than you realize."

Verena, who had been watching him with concern bordering on fear, leaned farther away, suddenly looking worried. "Don't you dare explosive vomit, Connor. Not tonight."

It was a good way to divert the conversation away from what had just happened. He sensed that neither of them wanted him to talk about it yet. He couldn't imagine why, but he refused to ruin the feast.

So he took a deep breath and forced a smile. "Don't worry. Whatever that was, it's past. I'm not about to waste any of this food throwing up tonight. I can throw up any meal."

He forced himself to return to the feast, but his appetite was gone. He felt a little unsteady, his thoughts still fuzzy, even though he tapped sandstone and drew in a warm current of healing power. For some reason it didn't seem to help as much as it should.

After a few minutes, the weird effects of his unexpected rage wore off. He couldn't explain it, but definitely didn't want to experience that again. He triple-checked to make sure he hadn't accidentally absorbed any porphyry, but he hadn't. He avoided chert too, just in case he'd unwittingly tapped into someone's concealed anger. External anger shouldn't affect him so much, but he didn't want to take any chances.

The rest of his friends continued feasting with undiminished gusto. Hamish was consuming enormous quantities of food, but seemed ready to go all night. Maybe that was why he'd worn his battle suit. He rarely took it off, although meals were common exceptions. Had he worn it with the hopes it could help hold in his stomach if he ate himself to exhaustion?

That was cheating. No way Connor would ever agree to an eating duel with Hamish again while he was wearing the suit.

More dishes continued to flow around the room as many of the diners were shepherded out groaning, patting full bellies, and exclaiming the wonders of the feast. Eager newcomers rushed in and took their spots. One of the benefits of the high table was that they did not need to rotate out. Connor wondered if Hamish would insist that Jean include that as a bylaw. He wouldn't complain.

Despite Hamish's inexhaustible appetite, most of the table began to slow. The servers noted the change and shifted to desserts.

The main courses had been epic, although Connor didn't know their names. The desserts looked even better, and the sight of cakes and cookies and puddings presented on silver trays helped Connor regain his enthusiasm. He shouldn't have eaten so much. He needed more room for dessert.

Some of them were variations on desserts he already knew. His Grandurian was pretty basic still, but he'd memorized the names of most of the desserts.

The light, fluffy krapfen rolls, still warm from the oven, surprised him when he bit into one and found it filled with Althing chocolate. He chewed slowly, letting the sweetness curl around his tongue.

Eating windbeutel cream puffs, drizzled with honey glaze, was like licking a sweet cloud, and he wished he could eat a hundred of them. He only managed to grab four before the tray emptied, though.

He didn't have time to feel sad because the frankfurter kranz cake showed up next. The four-layer confection was shaped like a crown, complete with seven tall points, topped with bright, jewel-like cherries. He served one tower to Verena and got a piece with another for himself. The cake was light and fluffy and sweet, and eating it was like consuming one of Verena's laughs.

The crispy-crunchy springerle biscuits with their uniquely chewy centers delighted him. Somehow they were cooked with patterns on the top, like the Grandurian royal crest or Lord Eberhard's crest. Others were shaped like the healer symbol or tiny Builder mechanicals. The artisanship was fantastic, and the crunchiness reminded him of the feel of striking stone with his father's hammer.

Verena's iron will finally crumbled under the onslaught of sweets, and she consumed more than he had ever seen. Hamish had been trying to get her to embrace a higher sugar diet for a long time, promising that sugar-induced state of creative brilliance that he referred to as Mind Fracking would double her best creative day.

She usually insisted she didn't need it, but that night she experienced what he was talking about. Connor watched her with growing concern. She half-closed her eyes while slowly chewing one sugary dessert, made up of a flaky pastry filled with cream. She looked like she had reached the sugar saturation state. If she kept going, she might push herself to the stomach revolt point, or simply pass out like well-bred ladies were trained to do.

He'd never seen her pass out. He'd also never seen her throw up, although he bet that if she put her mind to it, she could challenge any of them for the record.

Aifric was chatting happily with Kilian, who didn't seem to have any trouble keeping up with the many personalities that kept switching in for momentary control. Connor caught occasional snatches of their conversation, enough to realize he would've been hopelessly lost.

They were talking in several different languages, and by the bits he understood, it sounded like they were discussing customs and peoples across the continent. Connor doubted anyone but Kilian could keep up with Aifric. Or maybe Aifric was finally the one person who could keep up with Kilian. They both seemed to immensely enjoy the conversation.

He did notice them glancing in his direction more than once, and in those moments their lighthearted chatter faded to more serious expressions and softer words. He was tempted to tap serpentinite and listen in, but the moments passed quickly and he decided that sugar was addling his mind and making him see things that weren't there, like the shadowy figure lurking around town the past couple of days.

Verena eventually pushed her plate back abruptly and stood. She glared at the last sweet on it. "No. That's enough. I will not be controlled by sweets."

Connor glanced from her to the innocent pastry. Her outburst had caught the attention of other people at the high table, and Hamish wandered over to join them, stretching and looking supremely satisfied. When he reached Connor's side, he leaned past, snatched up the offending pastry, and popped it into his mouth.

He gave Verena a reassuring smile. "Don't worry, I'll stand as your champion and defend your honor against any other desserts thrust upon your unwilling gullet."

"Unwilling gullet?" Verena laughed.

Connor added, "Hey, I'm her champion, remember?"

Hamish shrugged. "It was worth a try, right? I did get one more desert out of it." He patted Verena on the shoulder. "It's okay. Not everyone can handle full-contact desert combat. You'll get used to it."

She rolled her eyes and shooed him back to his seat. Smiling after him, she leaned closer to Connor. "If he doesn't pop before the night's through, I'll be amazed."

Connor grinned. "If he pops, he'll die a happy man."

"He'd better not die. Lady Jean has definite plans for him." She winked at Connor and added, "I feel like I'm about to pop. I can't believe you ate so much. I need to stretch."

He moved to stand, but she gestured him back. "Finish your meal, but don't overdo it. I want to go chat with some of the newcomers."

Connor wasn't sure any of the newcomers wanted to chat with anyone. They were all trying to catch up. Verena moved off into the crowd anyway.

Connor returned to his food, but did eat more slowly. He felt it his duty to remain at the high table until every rotation of other diners passed through. That meant he had to continue eating for perhaps several more hours.

Duty could be hard, but sometimes it was sweet. And savory.

Chapter Fourteen

With Shona, Surprises Are Rarely Unexpected

Connor looked up in surprise when Shona settled gracefully into Verena's vacant seat. Luckily Verena did not notice, or she might have flown across the room to issue a death battle challenge. Verena and Shona had managed to coexist together through the winter in sort of an uneasy truce. They had promised not to kill each other, or even maim each other, but that did not mean they would not happily get into a fight at the drop of a hat.

"I'm not sure it's a good idea for you to sit there," Connor advised.

"Don't worry, Connor. I'm not interested in hurting Verena today. I need to speak with you."

"Okay. Speak away."

Good thing he was already stuffed to bursting. He could not have enjoyed feasting while sitting so close to the beautiful, deadly high lady of Merkland. Sure, she had switched sides during the battle of Merkland and thrown in with the revolutionaries, but that didn't mean as much as it might if anyone else had made the bold move. Connor's relationship with Shona was far too complex to trust she had made that choice out of simple patriotism.

Shona glanced to either side, even though no one was paying them any attention. "It's a private matter, Connor."

It was not the first time that winter that Shona had tried to get Connor alone. She and Ivor had spent much of the winter in Merkland, but every time she saw Connor, she had tried to pull him aside. He had managed to deflect all of those invitations, usually by ensuring he was with Verena or Hamish.

He did not believe Shona would try again to twist his heartstrings and pull him away from Verena like she had so many times in the past. She seemed to have accepted his choice, but what if she was going to try to get him to fulfill that promise to kiss her one more time? Breaking his word had been necessary to prove to both her and to Verena where his heart was.

So he gestured at his plate. "I'm not really finished."

She didn't buy it. He only had only one pastry left. She had timed her approach well. The servers were busy with the flood of new diners and had left the high table unattended for a few minutes.

"This will only take a moment, I promise. It's important, Connor. It's something I've been wanting to tell you for a long time. Please trust me that I have no ill intent."

She looked at him with those big, hazel eyes, her expression open and honest. Despite all the time and experience he had with her, he still felt moved by that look.

When he hesitated again she added, "I promise. No more than one minute. And if you feel uncomfortable at all, you can leave and fetch Verena."

They had to start trusting each other eventually if they were going to work together to overthrow the queen and free their country, but did that moment have to be now?

She took his hand and tugged him to his feet. He did not pull away. That would've drawn too much attention, but he did slip his hand out of hers. He would never allow Verena to see him walking hand-in-hand with Shona. Not only would Verena probably attempt to murder Shona right there, but she'd probably maim him too.

Both Aifric and Kilian glanced up as they passed, and Connor said, "We'll be right back."

Neither of them looked convinced, but they did not interfere. Connor glanced across the room, hoping Verena might spot him with Shona. She would move to intercept them, which would be perfect. Unfortunately, she was sitting at a table on the far side of the room with a couple of Builders and a few of the Althing researchers, engaged in a lively discussion. Even though she regularly received brilliant insights to help other projects, if she had one now, Hamish would insist that he'd proven mind fracking worked and redouble his efforts to addict her to sweets.

Connor followed Shona cautiously across the room. Nicklaus trotted up to them as they wove through the crowds. "Hey, Connor, are you getting a special dessert?"

"No, just a boring meeting."

"You're not supposed to have boring meetings during a feast, you know," Nicklaus pointed out.

Shona gave him a reassuring smile. "We won't be long."

"I'll come get you when the next round of desserts are served," he promised and sped away.

Connor suppressed a grin. With any luck, Nicklaus would mention to Verena that Connor had left with Shona. She could still catch up. Unfortunately, no one else stopped them as they exited the room.

He expected her to stop in the hallway, but she continued down the stairs and outside into the chill air of early evening. The crowds seemed bigger than ever. Connor wondered if word of the singular feast had drawn people who had previously not planned to tempt the long hours in line.

Shona led Connor a block to the south, stopping in a pool of lantern light at the corner of a side street. The new Schwinkendorf Academy administration building rose four stories on the next block, but it was unusually dim and quiet. At that moment they were very much alone, even though thousands of people stood barely a block away.

Shona paused there, looking somber, but not angry or intense the way she did when she was planning to attack.

She almost looked nervous.

It was hard to tell because that was such a rare expression for Shona, but as she opened her mouth, then hesitated, that's what she looked like. Seeing Shona nervous made him very nervous. He was tempted to tap chert to figure out the mystery, but something in her mood made him hesitate.

Shona had thrown herself into battle without reservation. She had survived a lengthy stint in the dread queen's company. She was clever, ambitious, and very deadly. Anything that made her nervous, Connor did not want anything to do with.

He wondered if she was about to ask for more aid for Merkland. It was a wonder that the queen had not swept north from Donleavy to crush the budding revolution. The attack had to come soon and she would raze Merkland to the ground, despite their preparations to defend the city.

He was completely unprepared when she grabbed his hands and burst into tears. "Oh, Connor. I'm so sorry!"

Connor recoiled from her anguish and glanced around in both directions, preparing to tap his affinities. Had she betrayed him to the queen? Would the queen dare strike all the way into Granadure to come fetch him?

They were still alone.

Shona continued, not seeming to notice his reaction. "Queen Dreokt personifies everything that I used to think was great about being a noblewoman. She's powerful, experienced, and has a clear vision of what she expects the country to become under her reign."

Connor wasn't sure where she was going but asked cautiously, "What you used to think?"

Shona nodded, actually sniffling as she rubbed her nose and then her eyes with the back of her hands. "Connor, she enforces absolute obedience. She takes the lives of everyone around her without consideration of their will or their intent. She owns them and considers that her absolute right."

She paused, stepping a little closer, her teary eyes wide and vulnerable. Her voice fell to a whisper. "Just like I used to treat you."

Connor blinked. He couldn't think how to respond. Was she actually apologizing? Shona, the high lady with all the answers? She was usually so confident. She'd even negotiated a place as one of the three commanders of the revolution right there on the battlefield.

She embraced him, sobbing. Connor was forced to awkwardly hold her, more shocked in that moment than he'd ever felt about her.

That was saying something.

Shona had done a lot, but always she had felt convinced that she was not only doing what was right for her, but right for Obrion, her realm, and for Connor. He wondered if the queen had messed with Shona's mind after all.

"I realized that's why you had to leave. It's not that you didn't love me or want to serve me, but you had to break free of the shackles around your freedom." She pushed away from him, her face a mess, her hair disheveled, looking more alluring in that moment than she probably ever had.

That was weird.

"I don't blame you, Connor. I blame myself. If only I'd understood, we could have avoided some of that heartache and accomplished so much together."

She seemed to be coming back around to dangerous territory. That helped Connor feel that she would be okay after all. "Lady Shona, I appreciate it. I really do. I think you know that I only ever wanted to be your Guardian. I think we should leave all that in the past and try starting fresh."

She sniffled again and nodded. "I would like that. I know we can never be what I'd hoped we could be, but being your friend and regaining your trust, and knowing you'll no longer recoil from me when I approach would be more of a victory than I ever hoped I could get."

She seemed to be acting in earnest, although with Shona one could never entirely tell. Well, most of the time one couldn't.

Connor tapped chert.

It was probably considered bad form to listen in on a high lady's thoughts right after she had bared her soul and apologized for evil behavior, but he couldn't help it. As he met her gaze the connection snapped into place.

"*I can't believe I actually said that. I've never been so terrified in my life, but it feels so good to get that off my chest. Is he believing me? Does he think I'm lying?*"

Connor opened his mouth to respond, but caught himself. He managed to say, "Ah, good."

Her eyes narrowed and she added, "Connor, if you're listening to my thoughts, know that I'm telling the truth."

He started to relax. She wasn't angry.

Then she thought, "*But don't you dare ever do it again.*"

She spoke aloud, "I'd love to know your thoughts, Connor." Her poise had returned, and she lifted one fine eyebrow as if to challenge him to respond with as much honesty.

"I appreciate your apology, Shona. I really do, and I think now maybe we can start over."

He hadn't actually released chert, so easily picked up the next thought, which she wasn't even trying to shield. "*I'll prove myself to you Connor. Somehow. And this doesn't mean I won't kill that vixen wench Builder if I ever get the chance to do it in a way that you won't know it was me.*"

Yup. Shona was still Shona.

A strange, scratchy sort of voice spoke out of the shadows to their right, interrupting his response. Connor and Shona both turned as a huge figure of a man approached from up the street. He was a burly fellow, wearing a heavy overcoat, but no hat. He looked Obrioner, and he spoke in their native tongue with a slight accent that Connor recognized as from Lord Feichin's realm.

"Lady Shona, I bring word from her Majesty, Queen Dreokt."

He stopped about a dozen feet away, but Connor recognized him. He was the big, shadowy figure Connor had noticed lurking around. He instantly tapped granite and porphyry together. He'd adopted the idea of sticky armor plating and had added similar sticky surfaces to the inside edges of his front pockets. It made for instant, easy access to his affinities.

The porphyry beast awoke in his heart and flexed its muscles, and his lifelong curse of granite rolled through him with the itchy crawly feeling he knew so well. He also popped a tiny piece of marble into his mouth and reached for the wildness of fire. Whoever the stranger was, they would regret interrupting.

Beside him, Shona settled into a battle stance, her skin fading to gray and her body shifting into the perfect lines of sculpted stone.

The messenger said nothing, but flung open his huge overcoat. A creature of nightmare that had been wrapped around his torso flung itself across the distance toward Shona, spitting a huge gout of fire.

CHAPTER FIFTEEN

Bad Hair Days Never Get Old

Connor lunged to intercept the strange creature, but it reached Shona with the speed of a fracked Strider. Its body was strangely square, with only two long arms extending out the front, capped with grasping, clawed hands. As it flew toward Shona, its thin torso inflated like a Sogail bladder balloon.

Flames were already pouring out its enormous mouth, which looked far too big for its face. Strangely, it didn't seem to have teeth, but was covered with weird suckers, like the ones that lined that octopus Connor had seen in Althing.

Shona shrieked and lifted her left hand to shield her face from the flames. The creature slammed into her so hard she stumbled and almost fell.

Its fiery breath washed over Shona. Even though she was tapping granite, the flames still melted her hair away. If she hadn't closed her eyes, no doubt that intense heat would have boiled them in their sockets. Connor winced to see the damage. He'd burned off her hair more than once and knew from painful experience to leave a girl's hair alone.

He tapped marble and snatched the flames away, intending to wrap them around the creature and incinerate it. The creature's strange mouth suddenly made sense as it tried to suction around Shona's face, its clawed arms dragging at her hand to complete the seal. Then it could fire-vomit its burning breath right down her throat when she opened her mouth to scream.

That was both disgusting and inspiring.

The huge messenger erupted into the blinding light of a Solas and he charged at Connor. His body shifted into ponderous lines as he tapped granite too. Worse, water erupted out of his pockets, snaked out, and yanked Shona's feet out from under her.

She struck the ground hard, vainly trying to pry the disgusting creature off her face. The creature had to be summoned, but it was unlike anything Connor had seen. Flames were spraying out the gaps where Shona's hand broke its seal, so it was still spitting flames against her face. If Connor hadn't been draining away the heat, it would have boiled her insides when she tried to breathe.

Connor whipped the fires that he stole from the summoned creature back against the messenger's face. That fiery whip cracked against his cheek, sending him stumbling. Normal fires couldn't project that kind of physical force. The fact that it could when Connor wielded it was one of those amazing effects he still couldn't explain, but he was grateful for. Connor also tapped soapstone, yanked the water away from Shona's feet, and shoved it up into the creature's mouth to drown it.

All he managed to do was nearly drown Shona. Since the monster's fire lacked heat, it didn't boil the water to steam, but the water didn't seem to slow it down. Annoying.

Connor also tapped serpentinite and cast a warning thundering across New Schwinkendorf. "Alarm! Alarm! We're under attack from the queen."

Help would come fast, but Connor had to deal with this threat before Shona was seriously hurt.

The messenger recovered remarkably fast and again charged Connor, arms thrown out wide as if he planned to carry him off his feet. More water erupted in front of him like a dozen grasping tendrils.

That kind of fight was exactly what Connor excelled at. If only he had a little diorite. He'd eaten enough that explosive vomiting into the man's face would've been exceptionally powerful.

He didn't have any, so he tapped limestone and yanked all that light that the man was emitting and gave it a savage twist, forming a mirage. Queen Dreokt appeared beside Connor, her fiery gaze scowling at the messenger.

She snarled, "You fool. That's the wrong Shona."

The voice was the crowning part of the mirage, accomplished with serpentinite. It made the mirage seem so real that Connor almost believed it himself. The messenger never hesitated, though.

Tallan take it. Had the queen warned him against mirage? That seemed terribly unsportsmanlike.

The man crashed into Connor, leading with a flood of water. Connor slid back a foot under the onslaught until he split the waters with his own soapstone affinity. Slipping through the gap, Connor curse-punched the man on the tip of the chin. Hard.

Connor could draw far more power from granite than anyone who hadn't ascended through two thresholds. The man had an unusually powerful affinity to granite, but that was not enough. His jaw shattered, and the blow catapulted him off his feet. He crashed to the ground, arms thrown wide, eyes crossed, unmoving.

Connor hoped he hadn't killed the man. They needed to interrogate him, but he didn't have time to check. He seized the summoned creature that was rolling around on the ground with Shona. It was still single-mindedly vomiting fire into her face.

Shona did not seem to realize that Connor was sucking away the heat. She was beating at the creature with a stone hardened fist, but lacked the leverage to do much damage. Its weird, square body absorbed blows like it had no bones, but was simply a leather bag filled with fire.

Connor tapped soapstone, wrapped the thing with water, and yanked it with a mighty heave.

He forgot it was connected to Shona's face with about a hundred suckers.

It came free, but also launched Shona into the air so hard she soared up and into the darkness. If she hadn't been max-tapping granite, that brutal wrenching of her head and neck would have snapped her spine.

She got great distance and looked like she was on track to clear the top of the school administration building. Connor interrupted the impressive flight, throwing out tendrils of water to catch her. She had suffered enough with losing her hair, he didn't want her crashing through a building and destroying it in a fit of rage.

The monster twisted like a snake in Connor's grasping waters until its weird face pointed in his direction. And then it exploded.

Connor was already tapping both soapstone and marble, so he caught the flames and deflected them around himself without damage. He was not prepared for the blast of wind that shrieked around him in the creature's death blast. It sounded like the queen.

"No one betrays me or spurns my gifts! Shona, you will suffer tortures beyond your comprehension, and serve as a grim warning to the entire continent. Consider this your last chance to kill yourself. There is no other way to escape my justice."

Connor settled Shona gently to the ground. She was gasping, wide-eyed and badly rattled.

She gasped, "What was that thing?"

That's when Hamish and Kilian arrived with a rush of thrusters and a blast of fire. Growing shouts from the dining hall suggested that the entire community of New Schwinkendorf was turning out to respond to Connor's warning.

They had run regular drills to practice responding to surprise attacks and everyone knew what to do. Within seconds, New Schwinkendorf would transform into a deadly hive of Builder mechanicals, Arishat League weapons, and Petralists ready to fight to the death.

Kilian demanded, "Where's the danger?"

Hamish added, "Her explosion voice was amazing."

He was right. Connor knew how to create autonomous summonings, but had not yet tried to embed within them additional elements that might include secondary abilities, or a death wail message like that one. It was inspiring, but something to study later.

He held up his hands in a calming gesture. "I don't know if there are any more." He gestured at the fallen messenger. "This fellow approached us and attacked with that weird summoned creature. He said he was from the queen, so I assumed there might be more of them."

"There might be. Don't take any chances. Hamish, mobilize everyone," Kilian ordered, his expression grim, his customary laid-back manner gone.

Kilian erupted off the ground in a blast of white-hot flames, soaring across the city. He moved with predatory purpose and looked ready to leap into a death battle with his insane mother at the drop of a sweetbread. Connor was still tapping both soapstone and marble, so he felt Kilian's influence pulsing across the town, seeking additional threats.

The others arrived a moment later, followed by scores of Petralists and Builders, including Nicklaus, who had somehow acquired a full-sized speedsling on a floating platform that he was riding down the street.

The drum full of deadly hornets was already spinning, and he was pointing the weapon everywhere, obviously eager for a chance to unleash a rain of destruction. Luckily Hamish soared over to join him on the platform. By the look of disappointment on Nicklaus' face, Hamish was telling him the danger was past. He did disengage the speedsling, though.

A crowd gathered and as Connor again explained what had happened and relayed Kilian's orders, Verena reached him. She glanced at Shona and her eyes widened. She concealed her glee well, but Connor caught a flash of it before she changed her expression to one of concern.

"Shona, are you all right? What happened to your hair?"

Chapter Sixteen

Pearls Appear in Oysters Lingering Long under the Seas, but Sunlight Reveals Truths Smothered by the Blanket of Night

Late that night, Connor and his close friends met in one of five command rooms in New Schwinkendorf. Other rooms were spread around the city so they could always reach one within moments if they were attacked.

The careful city planning had included far more than well-ordered streets and buildings. It also included many layers of defense. Connor bet any invaders would face far more trouble taking New Schwinkendorf than any other city in Granadure, including Edderitz.

This particular command room was the primary one. It was slightly larger than the others, situated three stories below ground, under the central hall where they had feasted earlier. The room was built like a half dome, and the entire expanse of sloping walls and roof were covered in a gridlike pattern of narrow, steel supports that held dozens of sightstones.

The walls were painted a soft white, which served as the backdrop for the views the many sightstones projected. Three Builders and a dozen assistants worked controls in one corner, managing which of the hundreds of sightstones spread around the city to activate.

The wondrous breakthrough rivaled any of the deeper affinities that Connor could tap. Speakstones had already revolutionized communication, but sightstones promised to revolutionize that revolution. The sloping walls were covered with views projected from paired stones worked into buildings and lamp posts all across the city, the valley, the Arishat enclave, and even into Faulenrost.

The higher grid blocks of the ceiling included images of the sky in every direction. They all showed clear, dark night, broken by brilliant stars and the rising moon, but no airborne threats.

The entire city had mobilized with remarkable swiftness and still remained at a heightened state of alert, even though no additional threats had materialized. It didn't make sense to Connor that the queen would send only a single messenger. Verena had suggested maybe Dreokt was hoping they'd relax, get careless, and lower their guard.

Chances of that were less than Hamish voluntarily abstaining from the next feast.

Verena and Hamish were speaking with the Builders running the sightstone displays, discussing all the views they wanted projected. They were also coordinating speakstone updates from outposts scattered around the valley and farther out into Granadure. They were even in contact with Altkalen to the north and a small outpost at the Badurach Pass border crossing to the south. So far no one had reported any hostilities.

Shona sat in a plush chair near the center of the room, wearing a woolen cap over her charred head, looking shocked. Jean had just arrived with Lord Eberhard after conferring with their Arishat contacts about mutual defense should an attack prove imminent. Connor had no idea where Kilian and Evander had gone. Aifric had said something about finding the queen's spies and left in a hurry.

Ivor entered the room and spread his hands in a helpless gesture when they all looked to him. "The messenger is dead."

Shona scowled. "Did you get anything useful out of him?"

Ivor shook his head, and Shona turned her scowl on Connor. "You didn't have to hit him so hard. I should've interrogated him immediately myself."

Connor was going to protest that he only hit the man so hard because he was trying to save her life, but Ivor interjected. "Don't blame Connor. The fellow seemed to be stabilizing, but couldn't have spoken with that shattered jaw. Before the Healers completed repairs enough to start questioning, his mind simply went dark."

Connor shivered. "The queen can do things like that."

Ivor nodded. "That's what I figure. She could've embedded commands in his mind to kill him once he realized he had failed."

Shona leaned back in the chair, looking like she intended to pout anyway. She had a lot to think about. Sure, they were all risking their lives, but with that messenger the queen had singled out Shona for specific and exceptional revenge.

Shona had risked all in joining the rebellion, but if she hadn't switched sides, she might have died in the fighting or been captured anyway. She definitely would have lost control of Merkland and probably her entire realm. Her bold move had trumped those immediate consequences but set her up to face potentially far worse in the long run.

If they failed, the best they could hope for was to die in battle. Connor hated to think of getting captured, or standing helpless before the queen again, feeling her will brush aside his resistance. Would she destroy him or wipe his mind and rebuild him into a mindless slave? He shivered from a chill sense of horror creeping down his spine.

Getting singled out for prolonged torture had to be disturbing. Shona was used to enjoying a protected status as a high lady.

Verena turned from the controls and said, "We're bringing Merkland online right now. We want to make sure the queen did not launch any coordinated attacks against them tonight too."

She gestured toward the central screen, which was several times larger than any of the others. The sightstone activated and an image appeared on the wall. It showed General Rory's spacious office in the central tower of the Merkland palace. He was dressed in battle leathers, as usual, and of course Anika stood close by his side.

The two looked happy and not too battered from their unique and enthusiastic courtship. Ever since Anika accepted his proposal, the two were inseparable. And repair bills around Merkland had escalated.

Erich, Anika's hulking brother, stood a little to one side with Tomas and Cameron, the captains of the Fast Rollers. The three had been relentless enemies in the initial skirmishes between Obrion and Granadure. Since Merkland had revolted and the Fast Rollers had begun working together with the Crushers, the three had adopted a joint command structure. Connor figured that was just because it gave them more opportunities to bash fight one another.

As soon as the view sharpened, Rory smiled and Anika waved happily. Despite the gravity of the situation, Verena could not help but ask, "How are plans going for the wedding?"

Anika's smile widened until she looked far too much like a blushing bride-to-be and far too little like her normal, deadly warrior maiden self. That change in her always seemed wrong to Connor. Anika was first and foremost a battle maiden, and that's what Rory loved about her. For his part, Rory had started grinning a lot too, an expression that still seemed foreign on his craggy features.

Connor was super happy for them. He had never expected their unusual romance to produce anything but heartbreak. Their impending marriage had instead become an inspiration for the entire revolution.

Rory said, "Anika can talk about wedding plans all night, but I doubt that's why you called."

Hamish said, "Have you suffered any new attacks?"

Rory shook his head. "Nothing of late, not since the last three summoned creatures attacked two weeks ago. Anton discovered and destroyed them before they could do any damage. He's proving as effective a defensive barrier as you ever did, Ivor. Plus he's been working on gradually quelling the lingering instability under the earth in this area."

Ivor grinned. "I'm glad he's taking care of you so well. Don't worry, I'll be returning to Merkland shortly with Lady Shona."

That roused Shona. She stood and joined the rest of them closer to the viewing screen. If they noticed her hat or suspected the reasons for it, they were wise enough not to mention it.

"We were attacked tonight," Connor said.

"You mean, I was attacked tonight," Shona corrected. She gave a brief account of the short but vicious fight with the disgusting summoned creature trying to boil her from the inside out.

Rory grimaced and said, "We haven't seen anything like that here. The other summoned creatures she sent seemed intent on distracting and harrying us. I've been worried she would begin the real assault soon."

"So had we," Connor said.

Hamish looked up from the control station and said, "We found Evander. We're linking him in now."

Another screen on the opposite wall came to life. Evander looked like he was standing in one of their other command centers. Connor wished he had been there to see the surprise on the technicians' faces when Evander rose silently up through the floor or stepped through one of the viewscreen walls. He couldn't imagine the big man doing something as mundane as using the door.

Jean asked, "Have you found anything?"

Evander shook his great head. "Ripples fade quickly in deep waters, but fishermen still ply the depths with experience and skill."

Hearing those confusing sentences always comforted Connor in times of crisis. He really had no idea what Evander was saying. He often pondered the many different possible meanings at night before falling asleep. He was convinced it helped elevate his own Sentry speak.

"It'll be good to have you back," Rory said to Ivor and Shona. "The queen has been stomping out every hint of insurrection among our allies. None of them can make any moves until we win another victory."

Ivor said, "That's why the queen has to be preparing an overwhelming attack against Merkland. Our source in Donleavy suggested that she is adding Petralists to her army daily. Somehow she can share new gifts with those who only have a primary or secondary, like she did with Shona. And she's even helping non-gifted to find primary affinities."

Shona said, "We really need to figure out how she's doing that, or even how Harley temporarily gifted quartzite to me that time."

That was an understatement. They had tried unsuccessfully many times to replicate that amazing feat. They needed a breakthrough, or the queen could simply attack with so many Petralists they'd swarm over the fledgling revolution and the rest of the continent, no matter how clever their defenses.

Evander said, "My research has borne new fruits in that area."

That got everyone's attention. Evander speaking plain Obrioner always did. He must be referring to that vault that he had carried all the way from the Carraig. He guarded it jealously, but it housed all of the hints of deeper secrets that he had pilfered from the destruction of the ancient capital city of Stornoway. It hopefully included nuggets that might help them determine the queen's weakness or learn more about her exotic powers.

Jean especially looked excited to hear about new discoveries in the vault. She was one of the few people Evander trusted to help him in the huge effort of combing through his notes to collate the information and look for clues that he might have missed.

Evander added, "New insights suggest additional tests to perform."

Shona said, "I'd be happy to help. If I had access to a tertiary power, that summoned monster might not have destroyed my hair."

Connor was glad she was thinking positive thoughts. She could have easily fallen into a fit of depression over the loss. It seemed suffering repeated forced baldness helped build resilience.

He was eager for new ideas about how to loan affinities. The possibilities were mind boggling. Think what they could do if they could swell their Petralist numbers, even temporarily.

Rory said, "That would indeed be excellent news, but don't delay too long. We need all the reinforcements we can get. Last reports we received from Donleavy suggest the queen has been creating a lot more summoned creatures than we've seen. If she unleashes a swarm of them against us, they could do serious harm. Ivor, we need you to hold the river. Anton is peerless with earth. Together you're our first line of defense."

Ivor started to respond, but surprisingly Evander spoke up again. "Pearls appear in oysters lingering long under the seas, but sunlight reveals truths smothered by the blanket of night."

Connor loved that one. Excellent Sentry speak included poetic images that helped share vague truths through contradictory comparison. Evander was an artist in that medium.

Most of the rest of the group frowned at the cryptic words, but Jean nodded eagerly. Somehow she always managed to interpret Evander's meaning better than anyone. "You didn't tell me you discovered more secrets about Merkland. We just unearthed that file the other day. I haven't yet had a chance to read through it."

Evander shrugged, but looked a little embarrassed that he had skipped ahead in the research. It was a wonder Jean found any time to spend in that vault.

Evander spoke slowly, as if using too many Obrioner words together was painful. "Indeed, I discovered a hint about Merkland's Builder defenses."

Both Verena and Hamish perked up. She asked, "Builder defenses? You mean more than the famous wall?"

He nodded. "My mother settled Merkland as her summer home. It was she who designed the great wall and laid the foundations for the city that the house of Dougal eventually inherited."

Connor shared a startled look with Verena. He knew the famous Kirstin had been the first-ever Builder. They still held on to the slim hope that something she had done was the cause of the ancient king's madness, the day his wife had to put him down. According to the stories Kilian shared with them, Kirstin might have inadvertently done something to drive him mad and push him to take elfonnel form.

No one knew the specifics, though. Queen Dreokt had wreaked terrible vengeance and launched the Great Purge. She had murdered all the Builders, including her own daughter, and destroyed most of their inventions and research. No wonder Merkland seemed to enjoy more of the ancient Builder inventions. Kirstin had lived there.

Shona looked just as startled. "I never knew."

Connor asked, "Are you surprised? With the decree of death to all Builders, I'm sure your ancestors did everything in their power to distance themselves from her memory."

Evander opened his mouth to speak, but hesitated, his brows creasing. Connor bet he was swallowing the Sentry speak he'd planned to say. "I found a single reference to an additional defense. There is a secret buried in Merkland that may prove a mighty weapon in defending against the attack you fear."

Rory looked thrilled. "Where is it, man? What is it? How do we find it?"

Evander shrugged. "The eager woodpecker bangs his head against many trees in search of a hole, but the dews distill upon the grasses only in the moments before dawn."

Rory looked frustrated. Shona sighed and rolled her eyes.

Jean did not look concerned. "We'll have to make a visit to Merkland soon and see if we can figure out how to unlock it. Verena, Hamish, one of you might have to join us. It might require a Builder."

She was probably right, but Connor would encourage Hamish to make the trip. Better to keep Verena separated from Shona as much as possible. He doubted they'd easily find time for a trip, but if they could discover another powerful Builder relic it might give them another advantage. They desperately needed more of those.

Shona grumbled, "I hate the fact that our entire effort is spent on defense. The queen has every advantage. That's not the way to win this war."

Another good point, but Connor was not sure what she wanted. Attacking Donleavy would only get a lot of good people killed. They were not ready. Shona's comment sparked a discussion anyway. Everyone liked her point, but no one had any idea how to do it.

Then Hamish snapped his fingers and laughed. "Oh, I've got just the thing."

CHAPTER SEVENTEEN

Sculpted Scones!

Verena wasn't sure whether to feel eager or nervous about Hamish's big idea. He was grinning in that way he did when he had eaten himself to the point of self-destruction. That was often when he made truly inspired breakthroughs, but they were talking about attacking the dread queen. She would not allow him to risk precious lives on a half-cooked idea.

"Sculpted scones!" Hamish chortled, looking around as if expecting everyone to understand.

No one did. Verena said, "You can't use that dumb codeword right now. We're not in contact with anyone at the moment."

"No, not that sculpted scone. I'm talking about making real sculpted scones, like we discussed before the Battle of Merkland."

Connor grinned, but Verena rolled her eyes. "There was a reason we didn't try that silly idea."

Hamish looked crestfallen, but the door opened, interrupting his response. Kilian swept into the room, followed by Aifric. She had changed out of her gown and now wore close-fitting leathers. She carried no sword, but wore a pair of long knives on her belt, along with at least a dozen throwing knives of different shapes and sizes strapped everywhere. Her thick, brown hair was braided, and she looked every inch a Mhortair assassin.

"Did you find any other dangers?" Verena asked, her tension returning in a flood at Kilian's grim expression. She'd felt wound up ever since those two had dropped the terrible news of Connor's and Ivor's mind bombs on her.

Kilian pulled off a pair of leather gloves and slapped them down onto the table. "Nothing more from my mother."

Aifric added, "I didn't find any evidence of a coordinated, broader attack either."

Verena hoped she hadn't killed or tortured those spies she'd been keeping an eye on. They needed at least one of them alive for the final piece of their plan to fool the queen into thinking her mind bomb plot had worked. She wanted to ask about them, but wasn't sure if anyone else knew Aifric had left three spies alive. Mentioning it might lead to dangerous questions.

Hamish rubbed his hands together eagerly and said, "I'm glad you're here. We were just talking about my plan to strike back."

"You have a plan?" Kilian asked with a smile. "This I have to hear."

He gestured Aifric to a seat, then sat beside her and leaned back, one leg draped over a nearby desk.

Hamish grinned. "It's perfect. We hit the queen right where it hurts!"

"In her bakery?" Jean asked with a smirk.

"Haven't you ever wanted to punch her in the gut?" Hamish demanded.

Of course they all nodded. Who hadn't dreamed of beating on the terrifying monarch? While she was bound and gagged and bereft of affinity stones, of course.

"Before the Battle of Merkland, I suggested Connor use pastries instead of clay to summon a bunch of little creatures that we could send against Harley's army."

It had been typical Hamish foolery, and Verena had completely forgotten about it.

Connor said, "I think it's possible to do summonings that way. After all the work we've done on autonomous summonings this winter, we could include some pretty advanced commands too. I just don't see how it would accomplish anything."

"She's afraid of Builders. Let's give her a reason to be terrified," Hamish countered.

That was a good point. Verena couldn't believe it, but she was actually warming to the idea.

"To what end?" Kilian asked. "Pastries can't do much damage."

Hamish's eyes were sparkling with enthusiasm. He began pacing as he laid out his idea. "They can show the world that she's not all powerful. We make a few dozen sculpted scones and send them into the kitchens to infiltrate one of her feasts. Everyone eats one. Maybe even the queen eats one. And we set them to wait until they're in everyone's gullets before they unleash fire, or whatever we fill them with."

Connor grinned. "Actually, the queen demonstrated a higher form of summoning with that creature that attacked Shona."

"Don't remind me," Shona muttered, touching her hat and Verena savored the sweet memory of seeing her hair freshly burned off again.

"It attacked you with fire, but when I killed it, I released a second element."

"That awesome threat voice," Hamish agreed with a grin. "What if we filled our sculpted scones with similar things?"

"She'll just laugh if we threaten her," Jean pointed out.

"So we hit her in her pride," Hamish replied.

Connor was grinning in total agreement. "Right. Everyone is so afraid of her, what if the death scream from our scones were just insults?"

Ivor rubbed his hands together and laughed. "I want in. We might not do much real damage, but we can unnerve her and shake her authority a little. It's worth a try."

"And of course we need to include some quickened stones so she knows it's Builders hitting her, not just Connor and Kilian," Hamish added.

Aifric glanced at Kilian, her expression guarded. "It's not a bad idea, Hamish, but we have to be careful with timing. Declaring war on the queen from the Builders will enrage her."

"Maybe make her do something stupid," Connor suggested, sharing a grin with Hamish.

Verena agreed. They faced imminent war with the queen anyway. Why not hit her with an annoyance blow like she'd been sending against them? But she recognized Aifric's concern. The rest of the group didn't understand that they needed to trigger the mind bombs very soon. If they succeeded, they planned to use the queen's own spies to send word back to her that the Builders were dead.

If she then suffered a Builder-sponsored attack when she thought them dead, the entire game would be up.

Evander chuckled, the deep sound like the moving of rocks in the surf. "Hot air rises from every flame, but fear can chill the bravest heart."

"Yeah, let's make her fear us," Hamish agreed. Verena wasn't sure that's what he meant, but the enigmatic Sentry did not correct him.

Kilian finally spoke. "All right, Hamish. Let's turn this sweetbread-induced idea into a concrete plan. If we can make it work and get the timing down right, I'd love to shove a burning pastry down my mother's throat."

While the group chatted excitedly about the idea, Aifric moved to Verena's side and whispered in Student Eighteen's voice, "We can't wait any longer.

I interrogated two of the queen's spies. They knew nothing of tonight's attack, nor anything about any impending assault. They only knew to watch for something important happening soon. After Connor's incident tonight at the feast, we've decided to move forward with the plan tomorrow."

It was time. The thought filled Verena with dread. They were going to risk Connor's life. If they failed, he could very well kill them all. If they were forced to kill him and Ivor, they might be killing all hope for the revolution too. Verena doubted she could live with herself if she was forced to help destroy Connor.

The plan would work. She forced aside her fears and asked, "So there's only one spy left?"

She loved most of the women who shared Aifric's head, but Student Eighteen still unnerved her. Verena would fight and would even kill in battle, if needed. She wasn't sure she could do the things Student Eighteen was called upon to do, but neither could she condemn those actions. The revolution needed her assassin skills if they were to survive. It was an ugly truth, but she couldn't ignore it.

"One is enough for our needs."

"I'll tell Hamish."

The plan she'd discussed with Aifric and Kilian required most of their inner circle of friends to learn the truth the night before they initiated the plan. Hamish and Kilian would separate Ivor, while Verena would lead Connor outside of the city with Aifric and Evander. They would trigger his mind bomb and Aifric would help him defeat it. Then they would meet the others and Connor could help them trigger, then save Ivor. Ilse would manage the city defenses if anything went wrong.

Verena glanced at Shona, who was speaking with Ivor, and hesitated. Shona was the only one who did not have a specific role to play in the dangerous plot. Should she tell her?

"I will inform the others. It will work," Student Eighteen assured her.

"I don't think we need to tell Shona," Verena decided. Connor had believed Shona's unexpected apology, and part of Verena wanted to believe it too, even though that made it harder to despise Shona.

She frowned at the thought of not being able to hate Shona with the same whole-hearted intensity. Shona was incredibly complex, but the attack by the queen's messenger reinforced the fact that Shona was taking a terrible risk breaking with the dread queen.

Usually Verena liked encouraging people to change and to grow. She was a strong believer in everyone's ability to rise above past mistakes, and usually she loved championing the cause of anyone who made the enormous effort to change their life.

Except, this time it was Shona.

Maybe Shona was being sincere, maybe she really had learned vital truths and was struggling to make amends. If so, Verena would have to find a way to reconcile their past animosity. Could they ever be friends? She couldn't see how, especially since they hadn't even dueled once yet.

For the moment, she didn't have to solve that conundrum. Even if Shona was sincere, Verena just couldn't take the risk of sharing the truth about the mind bombs. Shona's presence might confuse Connor at a critical moment.

Student Eighteen said nothing about the choice, but only watched Verena for a couple seconds, one eyebrow raised. Was she trying to read Verena's emotional state? She'd get a basket-load of stress and fear, but hopefully read her determination to do whatever it took to save Connor.

Student Eighteen finally nodded and moved away, but as she passed she placed a hand on Verena's shoulder and pushed a sense of optimism. Verena accepted the gift and embraced it. Chert was a strange and dangerous affinity, but hopefully it could help them save the man she loved.

Verena waited until the conversation was winding down to pull Hamish aside. "Come find me after we finish here. There's something I need to tell you."

Chapter Eighteen

Mind Bomb

Connor strode with Verena along a gently curving path through one of the many parks dotting New Schwinkendorf. Young apple trees marched along either side and would eventually grow to provide shade and fruit. It was a beautiful morning, cool but hinting at approaching warmer days. The trees already had buds beginning to appear, and some of the lower ground cover was starting to turn green.

Verena's hand felt warm in his, and he savored the rare quiet moment, just the two of them enjoying a late morning stroll. She wore her flying leathers, with her satchel hanging over one shoulder. He was just wearing sturdy cotton trousers, cut loose in the thighs in case he decided to frack later. He hadn't bothered with a Boulder jacket since he didn't expect to need much granite, although he had absorbed some earlier. All of his power stones hung at his belt, but he wasn't actively tapping any of them. He'd downed a soapstone mixture after breakfast, but didn't have active connections with any of his other tertiary stones.

It was rare to spend much time without tapping multiple power stones. Usually they were both so busy, they only found brief moments during meals or in the evenings. He'd jumped at the chance to spend the morning together and head south to the foothills for a picnic when she offered. For once, Kilian hadn't assigned him a morning full of training exercises.

So why did he feel strangely grumpy? The more he thought about the beautiful weather and noted signs of impending springtime, the more he felt a growing anger that he struggled to keep out of his voice.

Verena must have noticed anyway, or felt the tension in his hands. While they walked, she had been updating him on all of the developments in their research teams. She seemed to know what everyone was doing, and they were doing a lot.

Her voice trailed off and she glanced at him, suddenly looking nervous. He was such an idiot.

"Connor, will you put your arm around me? I'm chilly. It's still winter, after all," she said.

He was happy to let her snuggle under his arm. She always felt perfect so close, and his grumpy mood faded some. Maybe he hadn't slept enough the night before.

"What do you say we head out early and race to the foothills?" she asked.

"Sounds good to me. Where's the Swift?" He bet she had already packed a lunch, and he seemed to need some quiet time away from the busy city. The park was a patch of calm, but he felt restless and cranky. For the first time he could remember, the thought of time alone with Verena didn't fill him with joy.

She was a filthy Builder, after all.

Connor stopped on the cobblestones in the center of the path. Where had that thought come from? He felt deeply ashamed, but when he glanced at Verena, the thought returned, accompanied by a strange feeling of hostility.

"Connor, is something wrong?" she asked, pulling away and suddenly looking tense.

A bird chirped in a nearby tree and he spotted its nest. Anger bubbled up higher inside of him and he wanted to shout at her that she was the problem. No, what was he thinking?

"I'm not feeling great all of a sudden," he admitted. "Maybe we should push the picnic to tomorrow?"

"No, I think we need to go have the picnic right now," Verena said firmly, but she was looking increasingly nervous. Something was definitely wrong, but he couldn't place it. His thoughts were starting to churn, his grumpiness increasing.

"Hey Verena! Connor, wait up!"

Nicklaus skidded to a halt beside them, his cheeks flushed from running with Wingrunner speed. Connor grinned to see him, but at the same time he wanted to push the boy away.

"Nicklaus, go find Christin," Verena said calmly, but firmly. Connor didn't see the boy's governess anywhere. She was a Wingrunner too, so he must have lost her again. Usually that would make him smile, but he just felt disgusted.

Nicklaus rolled his eyes. "She'll make me study math. Verena, can't I come with you and Connor?"

"Not today," she said, definitely sounding nervous. What was she hiding? What was she planning to do during the picnic? It was probably a vile Builder trick.

Connor paced away, rubbing hands across his face and tugging at his hair, trying to center his mind. What was he thinking? Why was he feeling so angry toward Verena and now toward Nicklaus?

He glanced to the opposite side of the little park and was surprised to see Aifric and Evander approaching fast. Aifric was running, probably with Rith or Mariora in command, while Evander simply slid along the ground beside her. Cobblestones flowed out of his way and returned to their previous position as if they'd never moved. It appeared the quiet morning he was trying to enjoy with Verena was about to end. That just made him grumpier than ever.

"There you are, Connor."

He glanced back in surprise to see Shona jogging toward them. She wore tall, brown leather boots with a green skirt and blue blouse. Her waist-length wool jacket, dyed a slightly darker blue than her blouse, was buttoned only halfway up.

"This is not a good time," Verena said as Shona slowed to a stop nearby.

"Don't be cranky," Shona responded, but her tone was light and friendly. She flashed a dazzling smile at Connor. "It's too beautiful a morning to be angry. I heard the passes are nearly clear. I just love this time of year. Spring thaw is here."

"No, you fool!" Verena shouted, but Connor barely heard.

He staggered as a hurricane-force rage erupted behind his eyes and plunged his mind into chaos. His vision blurred, and for a second his ears were inundated with a tumult of shrieking cries, as if every cat in the city got their tails stepped on at the same time. The scent of charred wood filled his nostrils, and he tasted filth, as if Hamish had offered him a sweetbread that he'd rubbed in a pig sty.

His thoughts raced, but he couldn't seem to hear himself think. He should be afraid, but felt only unbelievable rage. It roared through him like living fires, even though he wasn't tapping marble, and it vaporized his rational thoughts.

All that remained was rage and an unstoppable need to kill.

"Connor! Connor, can you hear me?"

The name should mean something, but it didn't. The woman's voice reached him as if from miles away. The voice seemed familiar, but he couldn't recognize it. The sound of it stoked his rage and he blinked open his eyes. They hurt. His muscles hurt. His mind hurt, and the pain magnified the towering fury consuming him.

She stood before him, her disgusting face twisted in concern. A vile Builder! Somehow he recognized her evil, concealed under that facade of concern. It was like a dark shadow clinging to her. She was a monster who tainted the world with her every breath. The pain was her fault, and it wouldn't end until he killed her.

He shouted so loud his voice cracked. It wasn't loud enough, but he didn't want to waste time reaching for a piece of quartzite. First, snap her filthy neck. He tapped granite, his muscles hardening, and lashed out toward the hated Builder.

Somehow he missed. She was standing right there, her repugnant eyes filled with tears, as if she realized she didn't deserve to live. But he couldn't quite reach her. His hands slid past her neck, so tantalizingly close, but somehow unable to latch on.

Instead of retreating, the Builder slipped under his arm. She drew a tiny knife and slashed at his midsection.

He wanted to laugh at her folly. She could cut him with that useless little knife all day and accomplish nothing. She hesitated for only a second before trying to roll away, but the brief pause was too long.

He snapped a fist out and caught her on the shoulder, knocking her tumbling across the path. She barely missed a tree and slid a dozen feet across the early spring grasses. Only then did he realize in her other hand she held his belt with the pouches of all of his power stones. That's what she'd paused to cut.

"Die, Builder!" he screamed, charging after her. He still had some stones on the necklace tucked inside his shirt. He'd kill her and recover the rest.

Water clubbed him in the side of the head, knocking him right into the tree that she'd missed. The tree cracked, and he rebounded off, spinning to locate the new threat.

A little boy. The same dark shadow of Builder filth clung to him too. He looked frightened but determined, with water and fire crouched protectively beside him like nualls ready to spring.

The boy said, "I won't let you hurt Verena."

Another woman approached, arms raised in a sign of peace, her expression dumbfounded. "What's going on Connor?"

Behind her, two others were approaching fast. They'd reach him in a couple of seconds. None of those three were filled with Builder taint, so he ignored them. He must rid the world of the Builder plague.

"I will purge them," he growled, not taking his eyes from the boy as he tapped soapstone. He felt the boy controlling the elements. Such an abomination to combine a Dawnus with a Builder. He could not allow it to stand.

The boy snapped the water toward him, but he ripped it away. The boy gasped in shock, but he used that water to slam into the boy's chest with so much force he would have shattered every rib if the boy hadn't also been tapping granite. The blow catapulted the boy off his feet and sent him tumbling right out of the garden. He crashed into a cobbler's shop and disappeared inside amid an explosion of shoes.

He would finish him in a moment. First he had to destroy the Builder woman.

Earth seized his feet and locked him in position. He growled with fury. One of the newcomers was interfering. The fool. Friends of Builders had to die too.

The vile Builder might have stolen most of his power stones, but he always kept a piece of slate in his boot. The earth began ripping at his boots, trying to strip the stone away, but he connected with Earth and slammed his will into the ground beneath him.

The man was there, his will like a blazing light. He might be no Builder, but he must die too. Pushing the stranger away, he broke the earth off of his feet and turned to face him.

Just in time for the other woman to crash-tackle him to the ground.

The two of them struck hard, the unexpected blow rattling him enough that the man took control of the earth again. Ground seized his limbs, holding him down while the woman straddled his waist, grabbed his face with her hands, and leaned over him, her big brown eyes wide and glowing with an inner light.

She planned to attack him with chert. So be it.

He tapped chert too. A piece of it was touching the skin of his neck, part of the necklace he always wore. Instantly the connection snapped into place, and she was ready. Her will slammed into him and drove him back into himself. He seized the filthy Builder friend's mind and tore at it as they plunged together into blackness.

From far away, he heard her begin to scream.

CHAPTER NINETEEN

Some Girls Are Downright Scary

Connor seethed with rage. Somehow he recognized his name, and the fact felt important, but he was too angry to focus on it. Fury boiled through him like the purifying fires of the marble threshold. It stripped away all other thoughts, all of his memories, and everything but one overwhelming truth.

The Builders had lied to him.

They were evil, deceptive creatures that had played him like an ignorant linn. Every single one of them had to die.

The problem was, he could no longer see. All of his senses had contracted into his head, and that just made him angrier than ever. He tried to fight whatever that woman had done to him. She seemed familiar somehow, but he couldn't quite place her. It didn't matter. She had to die too.

A splitting headache seared his mind, and Connor cried out. When he blinked open his eyes, the black void was replaced by blinding light. His surroundings seemed to grow out of the air on every side, solidifying in a single, startling heartbeat. He stood in a spacious apartment that seemed incredibly familiar.

A black-garbed figure crouched over a person that he realized with a start looked exactly like him. He was lying on the floor, looking surprised and a little panicked, as he struggled weakly against his assailant.

She leaned over him, dagger poised for the killing blow, and he asked weakly, "Aifric?"

The word tugged at his mind, but slipped away like a fish sliding back into that river he used to know the name of.

She gasped and pulled away the loose flaps of his mask. "Connor?"

"Hi."

"But you're . . ."

"If you don't kill me for a minute, I can explain."

With a start, Connor realized he was seeing a memory, but it was as if he stood in his mind as an observer instead of as himself. Someone was messing with his mind. That was weird, and it made him angrier than ever. The whispers of recognition that had been drifting so close to consciousness faded under the torrent of rage.

The black-garbed woman turned toward him and met his angry gaze. "Connor, remember me. This was the first time I spared your life."

Connor snarled and lunged. This woman was an invader. He wasn't sure how he knew, but he did. She had been in that memory before, but now she was back as an outsider just as he was. If he could snuff the life from her, he'd return to himself.

Before he could cross the distance, another woman appeared beside the first. She looked identical, somehow more identical than if they were twins. She was dressed in a white healer's robe and smiled warmly at him.

"Connor, how many times do I have to heal you?"

Connor tackled her.

He struck so hard that they smashed right through the wall of the apartment. She felt real, but somehow dissolved under his hands, and he stumbled into the next room. That room contained an entirely different memory. He found himself on a vast plain south of Altkalen, facing a river of lava, while opposing armies advancing against each other across a narrow causeway of earth.

In front of him, the same woman, dressed for battle, was touching steel to Connor's memory form. She touched it to his throat, then his bicep, then his inner thigh, and finally pressed the pommel to his eye.

Then she turned to him and said, "Remember me, Connor. I touched steel to every kill location on your body, but chose to spare you."

Connor tried to tap his affinities, but could not seem to reach them. The fact did not bother him tremendously. He would just crush her pretty skull with his bare hands.

He closed on her, but again the white-robed Healer appeared beside the first, looking undamaged, if a little annoyed. Other women started appearing, spreading to either side of the first two.

They were all identical.

They dressed differently, and he could tell some were warriors, while others were academics. They all faced him and said in unison, "Connor, remember me."

It was like he had opened a rat's nest of brown-haired women inside of his mind. He planned to remove them all.

Connor lunged.

The black-garbed version of the legion of women pointed her dagger at him and said, "Okay ladies. We gave him a chance. Take him."

They swarmed at him like a tide of angry cats. They moved fast, without hesitation, and leaped upon him in an overwhelming flood.

Connor met them with all of his fury. He raged and struck with thunderous force. They tried to pin down his arms, but he fought so fiercely, his rage like a living thing driving him on. There in his mind he was the ruler, not her, and he would make her rue the day that she invaded.

With every punch, he knocked women back, but they surged in again every time. He shook his right arm free and clobbered one of the women so hard in the side of the head that her body shuddered and turned to smoke. That woman dissipated from his mind, and the other women around him staggered, as if they somehow shared the pain of her destruction.

That gave him the opening he needed. With a roar, Connor ripped his other arm free and launched into the women, smashing his fists into one pretty face after another. With every blow, another foul enemy collapsed, dissolved into mist, and faded from his mind.

The damage he was inflicting on their companions seemed to rattle and slow them. Their overwhelming numbers no longer mattered as he beat his way through their ranks, aimed toward the white-robed Healer and the black-garbed assassin. Somehow he recognized that much about them, although he still did not care to remember their identities. He would destroy them all.

Those two women shared a worried look as Connor methodically beat down their companions. The Healer said, "This is not working."

"Obviously not."

"Phase two?"

"Phase two," the assassin said with grim resolution.

The two of them launched at Connor, while the other four remaining women seized his arms, struggling with renewed vigor to try to hold him back. He slammed his forehead into the face of one of the women so hard the blow rattled him. It smashed her face and she dissolved. Ripping his left arm out of the momentarily slack grip of the other woman on that side, he beat her head in too.

The Healer lunged, but he tripped her with a kick. With a shout of triumph, he stomped on her face before she could rise. Like the others, she dissolved and disappeared.

The assassin tackled him before he could regain his balance. The two remaining women helped her push him down. He struggled mightily against them, but for a second they held him.

She plunged her dagger into his right eye.

Connor screamed, and everything went black.

CHAPTER TWENTY

A Short Reprieve

Connor blinked and groaned against a splitting headache. He felt sore and wrung out as if the strongest Boulder washerwoman in the world had twisted him like a shirt in the laundry.

The second thing he realized was that he was standing at the edge of the precipitous drop of Badurach Pass. He was lying at the top of the high, steep-sided mountain. He had no idea how he got there and frowned as he glanced out at the panoramic vista on all sides, with clear views into both Granadure and Obrion. Despite the altitude, the sun felt warm, and the land that spread below looked resplendent, draped with summertime greenery.

"I was starting to worry you might not wake up."

Student Eighteen was suddenly crouched beside him, looking like she'd been there all along. Her abrupt appearance startled him, and he just barely caught himself from shuffling away. That would've been a really bad idea. He was only a couple inches from the edge already.

Seeing her opened the floodgates of memories, and Connor gasped as he remembered his insane rage and the battle in his mind.

"I'm so sorry! I didn't mean to hurt all of you!" he cried.

As he thought about it, he realized he had only ever seen all of her personalities together as separate individuals when he had stepped into her mind to help her resurrect Aifric.

Aifric.

As if summoned from his thoughts, she appeared next to Student Eighteen, dressed in her normal Healer's white robe. She looked healthy, although her smile seemed less brilliant than normal. Her hair was a bit disheveled and she grimaced, rubbing one temple.

"You gave us our worst nineteen-fold headache. It's taken me and all the girls with healing affinities every ounce of our power to keep us intact."

Connor breathed a sigh of relief. "So I didn't kill any of you?"

His own pounding headache was still one of the worst he'd experienced, although it seemed to be easing. He could not imagine handling one almost twenty times as bad. Aifric and her mind sisters were tough.

Student Eighteen said, "It was a near thing. If we had pulled you into our minds first, you might have managed it. Luckily, we invaded your mind instead so you were only destroying our mental projections."

The news was so welcome that it took Connor a moment to remember something else. "Hey, you stabbed me in the eye."

She flashed him a quick smile and shrugged. "It was the only option left to us. I'm glad it worked. I don't want to have to change my name to Student Nineteen."

That did sound wrong.

She added, "You were about to drive us from your mind, and I doubt we would've managed to get back in. It was either throw the stones and take that gamble, or admit to everyone else that we failed and you had to be put down."

"How does stabbing me in the eye in my own mind possibly save me? And how am I not dead?"

The memory of beating down their mind sisters was painfully clear, but the rest of the experience was still fuzzy.

"You were there as a mind projection too, although far more intimately connected with your own experiences. However, you're also under the queen's compulsion, which was insulating you from yourself."

Aifric added, "The idea was that as long as we didn't convince you that you were dead, which might have proven fatal even for you, we might be able to trick the queen's compulsion long enough to spirit you away and help you regain control."

"What compulsion?" Connor demanded. That sounded very bad. He didn't feel out of control like he had moments ago. The memory of the queen seizing control over him in Donleavy filled him with remembered horror.

Fears multiplied instantly and he gripped Aifric's hand. "Did the queen attack again?"

"Do you remember the rage?" She asked.

He did. That mindless rage had blocked recognition of his friends. "Was I really trying to kill you?" His voice dropped to an anguished whisper as he remembered more. "And Verena?"

That thought sizzled through his mind like a blast of diorite, filling him with terrible guilt. How could he ever raise a hand against the girl he loved with all his heart?

Student Eighteen and Aifric together quickly sketched out what had happened in Donleavy, how the queen had implanted that murderous order, and then concealed it from him. Connor listened with growing horror. He shivered to think of Queen Dreokt doing such an evil thing to them. He had not thought it possible to hate her more.

As he thought about the queen and her kill order, he became aware of his body. He was not in it. He glanced around at the magnificent view at the top of the pass and realized where he was.

"We're in your mind, aren't we?"

Student Eighteen nodded. "I climbed this peak a few years back. It's a cherished memory, and one that I hoped was distanced enough from your experience that we could hold you here for a time and shield you from the queen's influence."

As soon as she said the words, he felt the connection back to his body solidify, and rage flowed down the conduit."

"It's working, but I can feel the rage. When I return to me, it's going to hit me again, won't it?"

The two women nodded together, but Student Eighteen said, "When you return, you'll be aware of what's going on. That should make a critical difference."

Aifric added, "And we'll be there to help. Together we should be able to throw off that compulsion and break you out of that rage."

"And if we can't?" Connor asked nervously.

The women did not respond, but just stared at him with a grave expression that told him everything. If he could not beat the queen's mind bomb, they might not have any choice but to kill him before he could commit mass murder. He appreciated that they were risking their lives to help him, but he ground his teeth in frustration. Their world was so twisted. Friends shouldn't have to be prepared to kill friends to save each other from worse fates.

Connor shivered to think how close he was right now to that ultimate sacrifice. In his body, he'd fallen completely to the queen's influence. He needed a way to fight back, or he would die. He didn't want to take to the grave the guilt of killing those he loved.

"Any idea what I should do?"

Student Eighteen said, "This is beyond our knowledge. You're the one who's ascended. You have much more control and power in the mindscape than we do, despite our experience. Being self-aware should give you the opportunity to fight back."

Aifric said, "We'll be right beside you."

"Are you sure that's wise? You might not survive if I crush you in the waking world," Connor warned, even though he was deeply moved by their offer.

"If we fail, the queen's going to kill us all anyway. We can't lose this battle, or we'll lose the war. Let's not lose." Student Eighteen rose and extended a hand to haul Connor to his feet.

He wrapped an arm around each of their shoulders in a quick group hug. "Thank you. Let's go kick the grumpy old lady out of my head."

CHAPTER TWENTY-ONE

Nicklaus the Brave

No sooner did he think it than the landscape around them snuffed out like a Solas lantern. Connor blinked as he returned in a rush to the natural world. He again lay on the ground, sealed to the earth by Evander. Trees were waving slightly in a soft breeze overhead, and the sky was brilliant blue, with only wisps of clouds. It was simply too nice of a day to die.

Aifric, who had been crouching over him, slowly collapsed to the side. Her face looked pale, her skin a little clammy and cold, as if she had pushed herself beyond her natural limits. She was breathing fast and shallow, but had not woken up.

The rage was still there, coiled in his mind, and it struck like an avalanche, sweeping away his conscious thoughts. It was like a firestorm of hate that snuffed out any other purpose besides destruction.

It eclipsed his determination to fight it, and he howled with a primal need to kill. His body convulsed as he fought the restraining earth. He tried to tap slate, but Evander had stripped off his boots, leaving him bereft of power stone.

He still had soapstone and he embraced it deeply. He seized a small pond nearby and yanked the waters out of it. Forming the water into a hundred spears of ice, he hurled them across the park in a flood of deadly rage.

Someone screamed, but most of the water was deflected high and away by a shield of air. He couldn't tell if it was generated by a Petralist or by a cursed Builder. He drew water back to himself and drove it into the ground. Surrounding himself in a protective cocoon, he broke contact with earth and lunged to his feet.

The huge Sentry stood barely ten feet away, dark eyes fixed on him. The female Builder flanked him on the left, the blond woman on the other side. Walls of earth erupted around the perimeter of the park, rising to thirty feet and enclosing them all in.

Good. The Builder would not be able to easily escape him this time. He ripped a tiny piece of marble off of his necklace and shoved it under his tongue. The wild euphoria of fire swept through him instantly and he smiled. It fit his need perfectly.

The women were shouting at him, but he couldn't seem to hear them. Rage boiled in his ears, blocking sound, and his mind was filled with a howling cacophony of snarling voices, driving him to destroy the hated Builder now.

He took a single step toward her and started raising his hand to unleash his elemental wrath upon her. The giant Sentry slid forward to intercept him, but the Builder motioned him back. She was vulnerable, exposed, and he would destroy her.

"Connor, I love you," she said simply, her big blue eyes locked on his, her expression earnest. He was still tapping chert, and the connection to her mind snapped into place.

Verena.

That link to her speared through the raging torrent of fury drowning out his thoughts and reached his true core. At that gentle, but powerful touch, he awakened and recognized that his thoughts had been buried under the avalanche of the queen's will. Verena's love wrapped him in a thing, insulating blanket that helped him separate himself from the rage, while her unbreakable determination to save him renewed his strength.

Connor remembered everything, the mind battle with Aifric, the truth she had shared about the queen's mind bomb, and the horrible truth that he had been about to snuff out the life of the woman he loved more than life itself.

The connection lasted for only a second before the murder rage severed it and inundated his mind again with boiling fury. His hand rose again, and crimson flames appeared, wrapping it with the threat of painful death.

This time, Connor recognized what was going on. That contact with Verena had snapped him out of the first shackle. He knew what was happening, but although he fought against the queen's compulsion, he could not stop it.

"Beware," the giant warned, pulling Verena back.

"He was there for a second. I felt it," she protested with tears in her eyes.

Connor tried to scream, "I am here!" but lacked control over his voice. He fought the compulsion with all his strength, but couldn't regain control. He was trapped within his own mind, a passenger shackled inside himself and swept along on the worst living nightmare imaginable.

With growing horror, he felt himself embrace both water and fire and unleash it toward Verena. An incandescent spear of mixed elements erupted from him, aiming for her heart. Evander deflected it aside with an eruption of earth, but Connor swept it back around toward her back.

Tears were sliding down her cheeks now, but she activated a shieldstone, deflecting the elements aside again. Locked in his mind prison, Connor howled with frustration, but he could not break free and take control.

Just like the last time the queen had taken over his mind.

Just like porphyry had consumed him the first few times he unleashed it.

The similarities were unnerving, but he'd beaten porphyry. The queen's murder rage was like a living thing, a monster with a thousand claws driven into his mind. Each claw held another shackle the bound his will.

The thought seemed to give the rage monster tangible form in his mind, and it coalesced into a black nightmare with dozens of eyes like pits of midnight, and claws burrowed into his brain.

Connor recoiled, but couldn't escape. It was like a thousand ticks grasping his mind and sucking at his will, while pouring in hate to replace what it stole. It was disgusting and horrifying, and so very powerful.

But that tangible form gave Connor something to fight. He grappled with it in the silent vault of his mind, but couldn't seem to grasp its claws to pull them free.

"I will rip out you," he growled, but while he struggled to figure out how to resist it, his body continued to fight Verena and Evander. Elemental fire and water swept around them again and again, deflected by earth or Builder shields. Shona even leaped into the fray, trying to tackle him. Connor seized her with intertwined elements and threw her away so hard she smashed through a tree.

The blow infuriated her and she ripped the tree out by the roots and advanced again, holding it like a club. She growled, "I'll knock sense back into your head, Connor."

"I'm surprised you're not encouraging him," Verena said as she ducked another elemental barrage.

"Don't be petty," Shona chided.

Verena scowled, but turned back to Connor, who was busy deflecting a barrage of earthen spears from Evander.

"Connor, wake up!" Verena shouted.

"We are running out of time. We must contain or destroy him," Evander said.

"Don't you dare hurt him. I'll figure it out," she said.

I'm the one who needs to figure it out, Connor shouted as he struggled against the rage monster controlling his mind. He tried seizing his affinities, hoping to block it from using them, but again it defeated his best efforts. He fought it with every bit of willpower, but he simply wasn't strong enough.

Queen Dreokt had wrenched away control over his mind with terrifying ease in Donleavy. How could he defeat her now?

He didn't know.

Evander's attack was little more than a delaying tactic. Connor was grateful for that, but how long before he grew tired of the fight and simply entombed Connor a hundred feet below ground? The thought of getting squashed to death terrified him, but hurting Verena was scarier. He found himself starting to hope Evander didn't hesitate much longer.

As the rage monster forced him to launch his elements at Verena again, they were blocked, but from another source. Nicklaus soared over the earthen wall, gliding on fiery wings like ones Connor had taught him to build. The rage monster in Connor's mind focused on the boy with terrifying intensity, and although Connor fought it with all his strength, it attacked the child with a vengeance.

Flames and water speared toward Nicklaus from every side, overwhelming his defenses and sweeping in, as if to incinerate him and rip his limbs off. He screamed in fear, but activated a powerful shieldstone. It became visible around him as the rage monster surrounded him with elemental fury, tearing at the shielding, trying to break through.

"Evander, help him!" Verena shouted.

Earth buckled under Connor, crashing him to the ground, but somehow the rage monster kept up the blistering attack against the boy. Evander might destroy Connor's body, but the rage monster would commit murder anyway.

Connor screamed and fought desperately, imagining his mind like an arena where he wrestled against the blob-like rage monster. He threw himself against it, tearing at its claws and gouging its many eyes, driven by fear for Nicklaus. For a second, the new approach seemed to work, and the elements battering Nicklaus' shield wavered.

In that second, Nicklaus swept them aside. He hovered in the air, using a quartzite block as a thruster, and lifted a small figurine high. It was a piece of sculpted soapstone. Through the red haze of fury, Connor felt a new kind of fear. What was the boy planning?

His young face set with determination, Nicklaus declared, "You're sick, Connor. This is going to hurt, but I hope it helps."

All of the waters scattered around the earthen prison where they fought rippled and crashed inward toward Nicklaus. Still wrestling with all his might against the rage monster, Connor felt his affinity senses, as if from a great distance. He clearly sensed when Nicklaus tapped soapstone. The boy's will blazed like lightning in Connor's mind, temporarily driving back the rage monster.

Connor started to grin. Whatever Nicklaus was doing, it was working!

Waters gathered under the boy, forming a tall column that stretched down to the ground. He laughed with pure, childlike thrill.

Then Connor felt the soapstone rebound against Nicklaus. It felt like the affinity exploded against the boy, and the air boomed with thunder. The concussion blasted Nicklaus higher, somersaulting over and over as his terrified scream echoed between the buildings. The sculpted soapstone tumbled from Nicklaus' nerveless fingers as his limp body began to fall.

"Nicklaus!" Verena screamed. She rounded on Connor with such an expression of rage, if he had been in control of himself, he would have started running.

He was so shocked at the unexpected event that the rage monster tackled him, pinning his limbs with its claws and restraining him by its sheer mass and size. It seized control over him again and trussed him with bands of hate. He sensed its deep satisfaction that it was succeeding at its mission.

What had happened to Nicklaus? Connor didn't understand it, and that terrified him. Had the rage monster somehow struck him down without Connor feeling it?

Shona cast her tree club aside and ran to catch Nicklaus before he struck the ground. Verena marched toward Connor, her expression as determined as he had ever seen. The rage monster shoved claws deeper into Connor's mind and forced him to strike at her again with water and fire, but Evander deflected his strikes away.

Verena walked through it all, never slowing, never looking away, her stride implacable. She said evenly, "Connor, I will reach you. I will save you. Or we will both die right now."

Chapter Twenty-Two

Sometimes It Takes a Village

Connor would not allow Verena to die. He screamed and fought, seeking for any additional fraction of strength he'd overlooked before.

He found nothing.

Trussed like a helpless child in his own mind, he watched in helpless horror as Verena marched through the firestorm of his rage, protected by Evander and her own mechanicals. She was almost within arm's reach. Once he touched her, he could pour elemental destruction directly into her and nothing would save her. Why didn't she run?

"Run, Verena!" Connor screamed, but no sounds passed his lips.

"Beware!" Evander called.

Verena ignored him and took the last step, reaching toward him as Connor lashed out with one hand already burning with white-hot fire.

Connor lunged against his restraints, howling with the need to save her, but couldn't defeat the rage monster in the arena he'd created in his mind.

He'd created the arena.

In a blink, Connor changed the space, imagining the arena like a fast-spinning ball. The unexpected shifting of force caught the rage monster by surprise as it was flung sideways. Connor threw himself after it, attacking it with all of his fear, his horror, and his love for Verena. He collided with it, and as the two of them bounced and tumbled over and over, he ripped away the claws still grasping him.

It actually felt like he was ripping white-hot slivers of steel from his mind, and he screamed, infuriated by the rage monster's ability to hurt him. He was beyond pain, beyond hesitation, and he tore at the monster in a berserker frenzy. It fought back in a blur of claws and grasping chains. Time seemed to slow as his burning hand extended toward Verena's. He felt the heat beginning to redden her skin, but she did not flinch away.

Without warning, a torrent of strength flooded into him, buttressing his will and smashing through the chains it was using to try imprisoning him again. Connor leaped upon the rage monster and tore at it with all his strength. He wrestled it for his affinities and managed to shackle fire just as his hand grabbed Verena's.

The flames winked out, and the expression of pain already creasing her brows eased. She looked up at him with a flicker of hope.

Connor wanted to shout with joy, but he was too busy fighting for control. The flood of strength had helped, but the rage monster turned against him and tore at his mind with awful intensity. Images of torture and pain flitted past, dragging terror into his mind. He fought it, but felt himself fading after that initial barrage. He was not quite strong enough.

"Hold on, Connor. Love always trumps rage. Loyalty always overcomes destruction."

Aifric.

Her voice spoke into his mind and he realized that burst of strength came from her. Only then did he sense her hand gripping his shoulder.

"Tallan's mercy! I'm so glad you woke up!" he cried.

"We can fight this. Together," she said, and she poured the combined strength of nineteen strong women into his mind.

He sensed them standing around him like a defensive perimeter, shouldering some of the weight of the rage monster's wrath. She was fully committed, risking everything to help him break out of his bonds.

Determination and discipline radiated into him from Student Eighteen. *"Every action must be chosen. The consequences must be accepted. Allow no authority other than your own will to ever drive home one of your blades."*

She spoke the words with reverence, and Connor sensed she was sharing one of the tenets of the Mhortair, a secret her kill instructors had drilled into her. Knowing that she trusted him enough to share something so important, something that had helped define her as a person and an assassin, moved him as deeply as Aifric's joyful support.

With their wills buttressing his own, Connor managed to keep from sinking into oblivion under the mindless rage. His mental space shifted back to the arena, and he battled the blob-like monster with new strength, but he was not able to shake off all of its claws. His body quivered from the strain, and his vision darkened.

"Connor, fight this and I'll fight with you." Verena's words helped him focus on her face. She had stepped close to him, her free hand rising to touch his cheek. Her huge blue eyes seemed to glow with inner light and again the chert connection snapped into place.

His mind lit with the brilliance of her smile, the one that she reserved for him alone. From their connection he felt her heartfelt love. She loved discovery, exploring new knowledge, and fighting to protect her beloved lands. He felt her unbreakable sense of duty, and thankfully he also sensed her deep and abiding love for him.

"Connor, don't let this evil define you. You define you, and you are too stubborn to fall for tricks like this. She may kill us, but she'll never control us."

Connor took a deep breath and redoubled his attack on the rage monster in the arena of his mind. Some of its claws began losing their grip.

"I'm here too," Shona offered, pushing in close beside Verena and gripping Connor's other shoulder. Connor felt her confusion, her fear, and the mutual loathing between her and Verena, but also felt her genuine concern, her determination to help him.

Evander joined them, one huge hand wrapping around Connor's neck. His indomitable strength buttressed their efforts and more rage monster claws fell away. Connor sensed his love of research and a deep and abiding hatred for his mother's domination. He also sensed that if they failed to break him free of the rage monster, Evander was willing to tighten his grip and rip Connor's head right off.

Usually that would make him nervous, but at the moment, Connor found it comforting.

Reinforced by their strength, Connor threw himself at the rage monster, tearing off some of its black claws, driving it back and seizing his affinities from its control. That really angered it, and for a monster made out of pure hate, that was something.

It pressed back against him, blackness oozing past his hands and splattering his face, forming new claws and stabbing into his mind like physical swords.

Connor cried out, his legs buckling. He would have fallen if the others hadn't held him up.

"Fight it, Connor," Verena cried.

"It's trying to kill him. We may have triggered a secondary compulsion," Student Eighteen said.

"How do we help?" Shona asked, looking as worried as Connor had ever seen.

"Give him everything you've got. He needs our strength."

They opened themselves to him, and the flood of strength helped, but the rage monster had gained the upper hand again. It continued attacking, spearing deep into Connor's mind with claws that felt all too real. Aifric poured in healing power, but he writhed in their hands, screaming in pain. His thoughts fled and he felt the rage reasserting itself, knocking him back, forming new chains around him.

Then Hamish landed in a whoosh of thrusters, carrying Jean with him. They raced in and gripped his arms. Hamish brought enthusiasm, love of life, and appetite for learning as much as for eating. Memories of remarkable feasts poured into Connor's mind. With every one of the memories came thoughts of the people who had shared the feasts with Hamish.

Those memories carried a deep and abiding love for friends and family and sharing good things with others. Hamish's unwavering friendship and determination to protect those too weak to stand up for themselves helped ease the pain just a little.

"Are you really going to let some mind-twisting old hag tell you what to do and make you miss lunch?" Hamish asked, his expression incredulous.

Connor laughed, and that seemed to help more than anything else. The new chains that had started wrapping his mental body cracked.

Jean joined them, her brilliant personality like a ray of sunshine piercing the cold black heart of the queen's compulsion. She added limitless determination, love for everyone around her, and such a depth of intelligence and grace that Connor's pain eased further. Her pure willingness to sacrifice herself for others seemed to stymy the rage monster, and Connor ripped away the chains and pulled some of the claws from his head.

Then Ilse slid right through Evander's barrier wall. It melted away to let her pass, her summoned earthen legs holding her upright. She joined them, pouring in iron resolve.

Kilian landed in a rush of water and flames and touched Connor last of all. His will joined theirs with an eruption of diorite that knocked the rage monster right off of him, sending it tumbling across the arena.

Evander's voice spoke loudly in Connor's mind. *"The eel hunts in dark waters, but a pack of nualls can savage even the mighty pedra."*

At the sound of that Sentry speak, the rage monster recoiled and Connor's pain evaporated. With the willpower and energy of all of his closest friends expanding his strength, he charged after the rage monster that was cringing back against the wooden wall of the arena. Connor seized its remaining claws and tore them apart.

It was an ugly thing, loud and mean and deadly. It hissed at him from a dozen gaping mouths and suddenly it smelled like sewer and skunks and terror as it formed new claws and grabbed at him again, but no longer seemed able to find purchase. His skin hardened to impervious granite, and its claws slipped past as if he was wrapped in blind coal.

In that moment he realized that the queen's fury was an empty threat. It battered at him like a sledgehammer, its power in isolating and frightening him. That would weaken his resolve so that she could wield influence over him. Queen Dreokt no longer understood the concepts of true love and friendship, or the strength those bonds provided.

He understood it now, and with that knowledge, he no longer needed to fear her, not within his own mind. As that thought blazed through his soul like a max-tapped Solas, the rage monster imploded and drained away through the sands.

Connor sagged, feeling exhausted but jubilant. With that intense fury gone, the entire world seemed sparkling bright, and he laughed.

His friends laughed with him and Hamish said, "No grumpy old lady will ever take down this group."

They released him, taking their strength with them, but somehow leaving a residue of friendship that glowed in his heart like a heatstone oven set on low. Only Verena stayed close, her arms around his waist, her eyes glittering with fresh tears of joy.

"Wow. Thank you," he told her softly.

She kissed him lightly, but tenderly and said, "I knew we'd reach you."

Student Eighteen said, "Like the queen herself said, you're best motivated by stress. We're proud of you, Connor."

He hugged her. "I don't think I could have survived without you."

"We take care of our friends," she said, somehow imbuing her words with extra depth, as if everyone in her head were speaking together.

Ivor rushed through the gap in Evander's wall that Ilse had made. He skidded to a halt in front of them and glanced around at the battered park. "What happened? Who were you fighting? Why didn't anyone call me? Shona, did you get attacked again?"

"Thankfully not," Shona said. "I'm not sure what happened. Connor went berserk. Some kind of mind bomb implanted from the queen."

Verena nodded, but did not release Connor. Her arms were still quivering against his. The ordeal had drained him, and it looked like it had exhausted Verena too.

"I don't know how she did it. I didn't see anyone hit him," Shona continued. "We were just talking about how wonderful it is that the spring thaw is here and he—"

"Not again!" Verena shouted at the same time Hamish cried, "Look out!"

Ivor's face twisted with rage and twin elements exploded from his hands.

Chapter Twenty-Three

Rage Monsters Aren't the Only Things with Teeth

Connor reacted a second too slow. He still felt drained by his own recent mind bomb ordeal, and it was startling to see Ivor switch from a trusted friend to a murder-crazed maniac so fast.

Had he looked so wild too?

His friends didn't hesitate. They'd already dealt with his insane fury and were ready. As fire and water erupted from Ivor, aimed toward Hamish and Verena, Kilian deflected them away and seized control over them.

Connor was still connected with marble and soapstone so he felt the very brief struggle. Usually Kilian showed great restraint when they sparred together, but at that moment he did not hold back. His will was like another diorite explosion against Connor's mind that totally eclipsed Ivor, and he snatched the elements away like a parent pulling a sweetbread from a toddler.

Ivor staggered forward a step under the onslaught, and the earth erupted around him, sealing him to his neck in a black column that hardened to stone. The air filled with the scent of springtime. Connor tensed, afraid the thought of spring would again trigger a violent reaction, but felt nothing but peace.

Ivor struggled within the prison, tapping granite and straining with all his strength. It was a useless attempt. He howled with rage, screaming curses at the vile Builders in both Obrioner and Grandurian.

"He's been practicing," Verena noted after a particularly fluent torrent.

Hamish had launched into the air at the first sign of Ivor's mind bomb, and slowly settled to the ground beside the raging Dawnus. In his hand he held a tiny glass vial. He glanced at it sadly, sighed, and tucked it into one of his many pockets.

"What were you going to hit him with?" Connor asked.

"A fresh batch of mega stench."

Verena grimaced. "That's vile, Hamish. We all would have gotten dosed."

"Maybe a little, but you never have gotten a true appreciation for what it can do," Hamish retorted.

Ivor was biting the air in Hamish's direction, but couldn't reach the Builder standing so tantalizingly close. Connor approached, flanked by Verena and Aifric. Shona arrived at Ivor's side first, looking deeply concerned.

"Ivor, do you know me?" she asked gently, reaching a hand toward him.

He tried to bite it. She yelped and pulled back. He shouted, "I'll kill you too, Builder friend!"

Verena touched Shona's arm and said, "I'm sorry, Shona."

"For what?" Shona looked more startled by Verena's apology than by Ivor's rage.

"I should have warned you what we were doing. I didn't think you'd be involved today, and I wanted to reduce the number of people who knew about the mind bombs. I made the wrong choice, and a lot of people almost died today. So I'm sorry," Verena said, and she looked like she meant it.

Shona held her gaze for a moment, her expression unreadable, then simply nodded. Connor was sorely tempted to tap chert and read both of their thoughts, but wouldn't do that to them. Hopefully Verena's acceptance of her mistake would help ease some of their hatred.

"My mother sure knows how to bring out the best in people," Kilian said with a grimace as Ivor began shouting more curses.

Shona turned to Connor. "Well, what are you waiting for? Go save him."

Connor glanced at Aifric, but she gestured him forward. "I'm exhausted, Connor. You're ascended so you should be more effective than I was."

"I'd prefer not to have to let him kill me in there," Connor agreed.

"Wait, who did you kill?" Verena asked, suddenly worried.

"It wasn't real. It was traumatic, but not fatal," Aifric assured her.

Verena touched Connor's arm. "Are you all right now?"

He nodded. "I saw everything, but couldn't control it. That was maybe the worst part, knowing I was hurting people but unable to stop myself."

That reminded him of who he might have hurt the most. He glanced around and spotted Nicklaus lying on the ground nearby, tended by Christin, his governess. Connor hadn't even noticed her arrive. The boy looked pale and was still unconscious. He seemed to be panting, and Christin looked close to panic.

"We've summoned Healers," Shona assured him, noting his glance. "Focus on saving Ivor."

Kilian gave Connor a hard look. "And then you're going to explain exactly what you did to Nicklaus."

Connor swallowed a lump of sudden fear. He might not have been in control of himself, but if anything serious had happened to Nicklaus, he wasn't sure what Kilian would do. Kilian seemed to be uncle to half the kingdom, but he had a special place in his heart for Nicklaus. So did most of them. Connor wasn't sure how he'd live with himself if he'd hurt the boy.

First, Ivor.

Connor approached his raging friend, who was struggling so hard against his earthen bonds that he might actually be bruising himself, despite tapping granite. His eyes were burning with white-hot flames, but Kilian was suppressing his elemental powers. Connor hated seeing Ivor in such a state. Somehow, he had to free him.

Connor felt worn out, but he had to make the attempt. He'd crushed one rage monster already. He could do it again.

So he tapped chert and focused on Ivor. As he stepped right in front of his big friend, Ivor glared at him, and the connection snapped into place. Merciless rage boiled up the connection, but Connor understood it, sensed the will of the queen behind the onslaught, and let the emotions slide off his mind.

Seizing that connection, Connor plunged his mind through it and into Ivor. His world went dark, then the mental scape coalesced around him.

He stood outside of a spacious log house perched high on a mountain, with panoramic views down over a community Connor did not recognize. The sky was a breathtakingly blue, and the air held a hint of evergreen.

Ivor stood on a wide deck that wrapped around the entire ground floor of the three story cabin. He was dressed in casual finery, like a high lord lounging at home.

"Hello, Connor. Come on in," Ivor called with a friendly wave.

Connor approached slowly, feeling confused. He'd expected storms of rage like he'd experienced, but the entire scene was serene. Where was the queen? Where was the mind bomb?

Had Ivor's mind broken?

No, Connor refused to accept that. Ivor was one of the strongest people he knew. He would never succumb so fast.

When he climbed the steps to the deck, Ivor grinned and said, "I was hoping you'd come. We need your help to destroy all the Builders."

"Um, about that . . ." Connor said.

"It must be done immediately," Ivor said, his expression ruthless.

"Why?" Connor asked as Ivor led him through an open door into the spacious interior.

They entered a great room with a vaulted ceiling that extended up through the second floor. Exposed beams lent the room a rustic feel, but it was furnished with plush couches and chairs around a thick rug in front of a giant fireplace. The stone chimney was twenty feet thick.

Alyth stood in front of the fire.

She looked poised and graceful and beautiful. She smiled warmly at Connor, and he instantly sensed what Ivor had loved about the girl. The only time he'd seen her was after the queen had mind-wiped her. Alyth's quick mind and free spirit were gone, her body left vacant.

"Connor, thank you for coming. The Builders have betrayed me and they plot the destruction of my realm. We must destroy them to save our people from their evil designs."

She spoke calmly, but steely resolve filled her voice, and something about her eyes was off. Ivor joined her and kissed her. She took his arm and glanced at Connor, a look of absolute assurance on her face.

The scene looked innocent enough, if plotting mass murder could be innocent. As Connor approached Alyth, he quested out with his thoughts, trying to see the truth behind the facade being draped over his mind.

An invisible force resisted his efforts, so he pushed harder and punched through. Instantly he realized what was going on. The queen had implanted the mind bomb in a more subtle way for Ivor. She'd crafted it around the fake Alyth. Ivor was completely enthralled by her, and this vision played upon his lingering sorrow over losing her. She was back and she was his, and he would obey her demands without his usual calculating thoughtfulness.

It was a masterful display of the queen's most terrifying powers.

Except she hadn't planned on Connor. He bowed over Alyth's hand and said, "You overlooked one tiny thing."

"What's that?" she asked, and her eyes turned black, like bottomless pits of fury.

"You're best at breaking people's minds. I'm best at breaking pretty much everything else."

Connor reached up and ripped off her face.

At the same time, he struck with chert, seizing that lie and twisting it. Alyth shrieked and clawed at his hand, but moved too slow. The lie the queen had implanted was subtle, and she had accounted for much, but she hadn't planned for that.

The fake Alyth's face dissolved under Connor's and she stumbled away, screaming, hands over the writhing blackness that had been concealed underneath. It looked like a tiny version of the many-limbed rage monster that had attacked Connor's mind, its little claws waving wildly as it tried to rebuild its false face.

"Connor, what are you doing?" Ivor cried. He grabbed Connor's shoulder and wrenched him back, his expression outraged.

Then he saw the truth and gaped. "Alyth?"

Connor felt deeply satisfied. This was going better than he'd feared.

Except, that's when the rage monster exploded out of Alyth's head. It grew to the size of a pedra as it crossed the space between them and crash-tackled both Connor and Ivor to the ground. Its hundred deadly claws raked against them, tearing at flesh and pinning arms. Two disgusting mouths grew out of the front end of it, extending on fleshy throats and gaping open with dozens of needle-like teeth. One snapped at Connor, and the other at Ivor.

Connor reacted with instincts honed from countless hours of battle training. He tapped granite to harden his skin and raised a hand to seize the disgusting maw. It was squishy and slimy and smelled like rotten pumpkins. The neck compressed under his grip, but somehow continued to slide through, the maw gaping wide toward his face.

So he filled it with water and hardened it to ice. The trick had worked well with rampagers and elfonnel, but did little to slow the disgusting thing. Its neck just swelled around the ice and it lunged at his nose.

"Stop!" he shouted in horror, pushing against it with all his will.

It stopped.

Close enough that its putrid breath filled his nostrils, but it stopped. And that's when Connor realized his mistake.

He'd been fighting it like a physical thing, but they were in Ivor's mind. The struggle was mimicking a physical battle, but it was not.

Ivor shouted and thrashed as the other mouth bit at his chin. Flames exploded out of him with white-hot intensity and washed over the rage monster, but accomplished little.

"It's not real. Fight it with your will," Connor cried. The other mouth was snapping at him, trying to close that last fraction of an inch, but Connor pushed back with all his strength.

It was just barely enough. He hadn't been strong enough in his own mind, but with the help of his friends, he'd beaten the rage monster and resumed mastery over his own mind. He understood the threat Ivor was facing, and that gave him an advantage. Hopefully it would be enough.

"How?" Ivor coughed as he wrestled with the monster. It was still expanding, more nightmare limbs growing out of it and slashing at Ivor. Barbed claws were digging into his stone-hardened skin, and he looked close to panic.

Connor had to change the equation.

"This is a mind bomb that Queen Dreokt implanted in us in Donleavy. Ivor, she destroyed Alyth and she's trying to use us to destroy everyone else we love."

As he fought off the swarm of clawed limbs striking at him, he imagined the visage of Queen Dreokt. Her face appeared on the front of the rage monster, laughing at Ivor, with that disgusting throat and mouth sticking out the front.

That did the trick. Ivor's panic evaporated, replaced by towering rage. His anger was controlled, and all the more deadly for it. His eyes filled with flames and he whispered, "No."

Ignoring the claws raking at his body, Ivor seized the disgusting, slimy throat of the monster mouth chomping at his face.

He bit the throat and ripped the head right off with a savage shake of his teeth, then spit it out with a howl of fury.

Connor gaped. That was disgusting, and awe-inspiring.

The move caught the rage monster totally by surprise. The raking claws shrank back from Ivor, but he pursued, seizing them and ripping them apart, his expression absolutely merciless.

Connor redoubled his own assault, beating on the monster with his mind, tearing at its illusion. He continued talking, reminding Ivor of the queen's plots, of how she'd destroyed Alyth and how she was threatening to torture Shona and kill all the Builders.

"Shona will never be yours," Ivor growled at the fast-shrinking rage monster. He waded through the swarm of clawed limbs and plunged his hands right through the queen's face that was still attached to the creature's front side. Her expression had turned concerned, but now her black eyes opened wide with shock as Ivor ripped her face apart.

The rage monster imploded. A gale force wind rushed in through the open door and swept away the lingering shadows, dragging them up the chimney and away.

Ivor dusted off his hands and said, "I hate that woman."

Connor clapped his friend on one muscled shoulder. "You know, when you're angry, you're downright scary."

"Thanks for helping me out," Ivor said, gripping Connor's hand.

"Any time. I admit I'm a little disappointed, though."

"In what?"

"We have that tradition of curse-punching each other whenever one of us saves the other from guaranteed destruction. I feel a little cheated."

Chapter Twenty-Four

Anything Can Be Broken

Their celebration of Ivor's freedom would have to wait.

When Connor returned to himself, he found Evander watching over him, but the rest of the group were clustered around Nicklaus. Even Aifric had left Connor to free Ivor alone and was crouched beside the boy, her hands on his head, her face bowed.

Connor appreciated their confidence in his abilities, and he didn't blame them. Nicklaus needed help as much as Ivor did. The boy was still unresponsive. His eyes were open, staring in unblinking shock.

Ivor blinked and looked around. "Evander, will you release me, please?"

"It's all right. His mind is normal. Well, as normal as it can be, I guess," Connor said when Evander glanced at him.

"Hey," Ivor objected as the ground melted away from him. Evander turned away, but Connor swore he caught a hint of a smile on the big man's lips.

Connor rushed to the rest of the group. With Aifric's hands on Nicklaus, the boy should have started recovering, but he looked unchanged. Not good.

Connor touched his forehead and tapped sandstone, pouring healing energy into the little boy and questing for damage. He felt Aifric's presence in there too, doing the same. It felt like Nicklaus was panicking. His pulse was pounding so fast it was a wonder his heart had not exploded.

The problem was, Connor sensed no physical damage. That meant the injury might have been mental. That terrified him. Had the queen somehow attacked Nicklaus through Connor's mind rage? What might she be doing to him? He was a clever kid and sometimes acted far more mature than his years, but he was still just a child. He wouldn't stand a chance against a mind attack.

Ilse was gently stroking one of the boy's hands, speaking gentle words. She had taken to watching over Nicklaus as an unofficial guardian, and she glanced at Connor, anguish in her eyes.

"I don't know how to save him, but I can't lose another person under my protection. What do we do?" she asked softly.

"I'm not sure yet," he admitted, deeply moved by her plea. Ilse had thrown herself into that self-assigned protective detail after so many of the Crushers, including her own husband, had died in the battle of Merkland. Protecting others had become one of her primary missions.

Verena crouched beside Nicklaus, her expression worried. "What's wrong with him?"

"I don't know," Connor said.

Jean said, "I've already called for transport. Mender Flight is on the way."

"We shouldn't need them. We have Aifric," Kilian said, crouched beside her, his expression calm, but Connor sensed his tension.

Aifric blinked open her eyes, met Kilian's gaze and shrugged helplessly. "I don't know yet." Then she noticed Connor and said, "I'm glad you're back. Will you join me? I need to check his mind."

"Of course." Just what he was fearing.

Connor braced himself for what they might find, but he was determined to drive the queen's influence from the boy's mind, no matter how much the effort might cost him.

Christin grabbed Connor's hand. "What happened?"

"It's not clear. He was helping Verena stop me." He frowned as he thought back through the hazy memory. "Verena, was he using a sculpted stone?"

That surprised her. "I didn't notice."

"Where would he have gotten a sculpted stone?" Christin asked.

"And what was he trying to do with it?" Kilian added, his expression graver than ever.

Verena turned to Hamish. "See if you can find it. Whatever stone he was using, he dropped it."

"Have Gisela check it out," Connor suggested. "See if there's anything she can sense from it that might give us a clue. Quick."

Hamish looked happy to have something to do, and hurried off.

Aifric shifted closer to Connor and said, "You lead. I'll ride your connection in."

Connor was grateful to have her by his side. He wasn't sure what they would find, but between them, they would figure it out. They both tapped chert and locked gazes for a moment to establish a strong bond. Then Connor leaned over Nicklaus and stared into his blank gaze.

As the connection solidified, he braced himself. He'd spent too much time that day in mental struggles, fighting in a way he barely comprehended. He hoped they were overreacting, but couldn't make himself believe that.

The connection to Nicklaus snapped into place. After a brief disorienting moment, the mindscape coalesced. He and Aifric stood in a large, cheery room that clearly served as a very fine play area. The walls were colored brightly with reds, oranges, and yellows. A soft rug covered the floor, which was piled with toys. A couple of large windows looked out over a majestic castle Connor had never seen before. One was open, a gentle breeze stirring fine white curtains and wafting in the scent of baking bread. He wondered if they were seeing Nicklaus' room in Edderitz.

Connor quested out with every sense, but felt no rage clinging to the scene, no concealed mental trap holding Nicklaus prisoner. That was encouraging, but if there was nothing wrong, why was Nicklaus trapped in there?

In the far corner of the room Connor spied a little cave made by draping curtains over some chairs. Nicklaus sat inside. Connor rushed to him, followed closely by Aifric. They both dropped to their knees to peer inside the little shelter. Nicklaus was sitting there, staring at his hands.

He held piles of mixed stone dust that Connor recognized as affinity stones. He spotted both granite and basalt, as well as sandstone, limestone, marble, and soapstone.

Aifric crawled forward and asked gently, "Nicklaus? Are you okay?"

He sighed and looked up at her, his cheeks streaked with tears. He extended the powdered stone toward her and sobbed. "They're gone. All gone."

"What's gone?" Connor asked.

"My affinities."

Connor shared a shocked look with Aifric. "What do you mean? You can't lose your affinities."

The boy wiped at his eyes and regarded Connor with that too-adult gaze of his. "Not wanting to face bad things won't make them go away."

Connor's mind was racing. He'd feared to find Nicklaus had suffered horrible trauma. The boy looked whole, but could he be right? Connor couldn't believe it.

"Listen, Nicklaus, you were fighting me while I was under the queen's influence. Did I somehow hit you? Could my temporary insanity have caused this?"

He shook his head. "No, Connor. It wasn't anything you did. I was using that stone, and it was so strong." His young face lit up with the memory, then his expression fell and he glanced at the affinity sand and shrugged. "But something happened. I lost control and everything broke."

He started to cry again. Aifric pulled him into her arms and held him, gently stroking his hair and whispering soft words.

Clearly Nicklaus believed his story, but he had to be mistaken. Minds could do weird things, especially for people trapped inside of them. At the same time, symbols were very powerful inside the mind and seeing all of Nicklaus' affinities represented as piles of dust wasn't good.

Connor touched the powdered stone and flicked his affinity senses over them. He sensed no power there. The powder felt empty, useless.

"See if you can help him wake up," Connor suggested.

"What are you going to do?" Aifric asked.

"See if I can figure out what's going on here."

He willed himself awake. The others were still gathered around in a nervous circle. Kilian gripped Connor's shoulder and said, "That was fast. I hope you've got good news."

Christin looked up with pleading eyes. "Is he okay?"

"I think so. Aifric is in there with him. She'll bring him out. He doesn't seem to have suffered any mental harm."

Verena frowned. "What's going on, Connor? You wouldn't have left her just to tell us that. Did the queen hurt him too somehow?"

"I had worried about that too, but it seems totally unrelated. There's something weird with his affinities."

"Weird how?" Jean asked.

"He claims he's lost them all."

The look of shock on their faces matched how he still felt. Kilian's eyes widened and he said, "We need more information."

"Is it possible to lose affinities?" Connor asked.

"Not usually. Sometimes when trying to establish new affinities, or when ascending problems can arise, but it's extremely rare, and none of those situations apply here. Are you sure he's free of my mother's influence?"

"I can check again, but he seemed fine," Connor assured him.

Just then, Aifric took a deep breath and sat up. Nicklaus blinked open his eyes, and groaned. Christin shouted with joy and swept him into her arms, tears sliding unheeded down her cheeks. While the others all leaned closer, eager to speak with Nicklaus, Aifric pulled Connor free of the crowd.

"What is it? Did you sense the queen in there after all?" Connor asked.

"No. Nicklaus' affinity troubles are a mystery, but leave him to the others for now. We have to leave right away."

"Leave? Why?"

Her expression turned predatory. "We have a spy to intercept."

CHAPTER TWENTY-FIVE

The Best Death Scene Ever

A crowd of curious onlookers had gathered around the park, clustered in front of the opening Evander had allowed Ilse to make through his earthen wall. The rest of it still sealed the park away from view.

Connor crouched beside Student Eighteen behind a large bush next to one of the young apple trees. It wasn't great cover since the branches were still bare, but it was better than nothing. He peered through the bush at the hesitant crowd jostling for a glimpse inside. He doubted they could have seen more than brief flashes of elemental fire or water from the battle.

"There," she said, her voice calm and cold, the tone she used when hunting.

"I don't see anyone who looks like a spy." Everyone looked like people he saw every day, a mixture of merchants, workers, and even a handful of children running around the edges.

She glanced at him, her lips twitching into a smile. "And what does a spy look like, Connor?"

"I don't know. Maybe . . ." He trailed off, realizing he was about to say something stupid.

She chuckled. "My job's not that easy, Connor. They don't walk around wearing sinister black masks or carrying signs saying, 'I'm the enemy'. Look closer at the fellow dressed in worker overalls with the blocky face."

Connor spotted him jostling toward the front of the crowd. He did seem motivated to get a glimpse inside, but even knowing his target, he couldn't see anything special about him. Then he tapped chert and opened himself to the crowd.

He kept the connection loose, not looking for specific thoughts, but just feelings. Most of the people gathered were curious or slightly concerned. Their emotions flowed over him like faint warm breezes against his skin.

One part of the breeze was hot, like a wisp of air from a burning candle. It came from the worker, and as Connor centered his focus on the man, his thoughts became clear. "*Curse that filthy brute. Why does he have to conceal my moment of glory? Come on, just one glimpse and I can get out of this Tallan-cursed cesspit of a town and return to my queen.*"

"Is that how you ferret them out, by their emotions?" Connor asked. It made sense, but he'd always thought there was something more to her unerring ability to detect enemy spies.

"It's part of what I do. Some of them are skilled at concealing their true intent, but this one doesn't ever seem to bother."

"Why did you leave him for last, then?" Connor asked.

"Because he's also convinced he's the best spy in the seven kingdoms. That kind of pride serves as wonderful leverage."

"So what do we do? He'll see we're not all dead in a minute," Connor said uneasily. He'd fought many battles and had killed more than once, but what was Aifric planning?

He loved the gaggle of women in her head, but some of what they were called upon to do made him queasy. He didn't think he was strong enough to step into the darkness like she had to do with any confidence he could return and still remain whole.

She flashed a predatory grin. "We give him a show, of course."

"I thought we didn't want the queen learning much about us."

"We can't stop her from gathering some intelligence. I wasn't able to confide in you earlier, but there's a method to how we manage enemy spies. I've worked it all out with Wolfram and Ilse. This one's special, though."

"Because he'll see we defeated her mind bomb."

"On the contrary, Connor. We need to make sure he sees you kill Builders, maybe even Shona too."

Of course. Connor grinned as the idea caught hold and possibilities began flooding in. If the spy witnessed success, he could report that to the queen and . . .

"Wait, if we show him that we succeed, the queen will expect us to report back to her. I don't think sneaking into Donleavy again is a good idea."

"You're right. That would be suicide. No, we're going to show him success, but then you and Ivor need to die. Make it spectacular."

That was such a good idea. He'd nearly died for the cause a few times, and had even been executed once. He hadn't enjoyed the experience, but he found himself growing excited by the prospect of mirage-dying to trick the queen.

She added, "I'll work the emotional pushing part. I'm better at that than you, but you need to handle the mirage."

"Oh, yeah. I've got this," Connor said, rubbing his hands together eagerly. He couldn't fight Queen Dreokt directly, but he could pass misinformation. First he needed materials to work with.

"I'll be right back."

He hurried back to where the others were still gathered around Nicklaus. Kilian raised an eyebrow and asked, "What are you waiting for? Aifric said the spy is in position."

"He is. I need some voices to make it convincing. Can you each say something?"

He tapped serpentinite, and sounds came to life around him. The rustle of small branches triggered little bursts of faint, yellow light. The murmur of the growing crowds outside was like a glow on the horizon.

"Like what?" Verena asked, and the words erupted from her mouth like green butterflies. Connor seized them and set them hovering around his head.

He was going to say, "Anything," but it would be easier if he got them to say the words instead of building them from the shards he captured. Why not tap into their creative brilliance? "Imagine Ivor and I are going crazy again and that you're losing. Hamish, how about some pain? Shona, a good death scream would be amazing."

They rolled with the request with exceptional gusto. Hamish lifted into the air, thrusters roaring, bursts of light exploding off of him as he shouted with rage and then pain, as if he'd seen someone steal an entire tray of fresh sweet-breads, then got clobbered by a hot cast-iron pan. Shona screamed, her rich voice rising into a crescendo of terror and mortal injury. She really knew how to scream. The sound made Connor shiver, even though he knew she was acting.

Not to be outdone, Verena screamed, "Connor, no!" then broke down into such a wrenching cry of despair, Connor almost forgot to capture the sounds. She held his gaze the entire time, and his heart nearly broke, imagining how nearly he'd hurt her just moments ago.

Kilian shouted battle orders, and Ivor raged like a rampager. Even Evander shouted, his deep voice like a mountain preparing to erupt.

Connor gleefully captured everything. Soon words and sounds and screams buzzed around his head like a swarm of really colorful hornets. He fed them enough energy so they didn't fade.

"How about an elemental show to reinforce the mirage I'm building?" he asked.

Kilian and Ivor complied with explosions of varied-colored flames, shooting them high into the air above the earthen walls. Evander shook the ground, and both Verena and Hamish activated mechanicals.

Hamish got a little carried away and fired a diorite missile into one of the apple trees. It exploded, shattering into thousands of deadly shards of wood. Verena blocked the shrapnel with a shieldstone and gave him a disgusted look.

"It's for the revolution," Hamish reminded her, trying to look innocent. It didn't quite work.

"Thanks. Keep it up for a few more seconds," Connor told them, then rushed back to Aifric, who was grinning and slowly shaking her head.

"I shouldn't be surprised. I'm the one who asked you for a spectacular show, but I'm still impressed."

"That's just the opening act," he assured her as he again crouched beside her in the soft ground and peeked through their concealment toward the crowd.

Most of the onlookers had retreated from the fresh sound of fighting. The emotions were growing in intensity and turning more toward fear. They felt like a cold breeze against his arms. Excellent.

The spy alone was creeping closer, daring the dangerous exposure for a chance to witness events for the queen. His thoughts were easy to pick out.

"*Just a few more seconds. Everyone else is gone, probably from that infernal Mhortair. I have to get away before she finds me too.*"

"He knows about you, suspects you've been targeting the other spies. The queen must have warned him," Connor said.

"Good. We can work with that fear," she said.

"Now for the main event."

Connor tapped limestone, and the bright late morning sunlight suddenly sharpened into tangible form around the park. Connor seized the light and twisted it, focusing on the spy and unleashing mirage.

The park exploded. A firestorm blasted in every direction, shredding trees and scorching the grass. Connor mixed in the sounds from the tree Hamish had sacrificed, magnifying them a hundred times. He added in screaming, and Verena's cry for mercy.

The spy stopped, frozen in his tracks, mouth open in terror. It was working! Connor began to smile.

Then the other spectators began to scream and flee.

Tallan blast it all to bacon bits. He hadn't planned on being quite that effective. Aifric glanced at him, and he shrugged. He couldn't stop now.

Within the fiery mirage, he caused Hamish to swoop into the air, protected by a shieldstone. Then mirage-Connor swept through the flames, wielding water and earth like living serpents. He caught Hamish and pierced his battle suit a dozen times. Hamish howled as the elements consumed him and smashed his broken body into the ground.

Verena and Ivor appeared next, fighting a desperate battle, mechanicals against living elements. Ivor burned her face, but Kilian intercepted him, and the two launched into an epic elemental dual.

Verena stumbled away, but mirage-Connor landed right on her head like a thunderclap, smashing her into the ground and seizing her limbs with earth. She screamed, "Connor, no!", but the cry cut off as earth poured down her throat and the ground swallowed her convulsing form.

Even though he was the one controlling the mirage, Connor blanched at the sight of the horrific carnage. He felt tears welling in his eyes, and chided himself for getting too caught up in the show. He had to make it real for the spy in order to keep Verena safe, but his hands started to tremble, and his stomach roiled, as if he was going to throw up. He couldn't spare the time to pace off a line to measure distance either.

So he swallowed down the rising bile, reminding himself that he was doing it to protect Verena. Focusing on that purpose helped, and he released the rest of it. Evander and Ilse circled around Connor on both sides, unleashing an earthen barrage in tandem that momentarily overwhelmed him. Kilian closed on Ivor, diving right through his defensive curtain of mixed fire and water and punched him in the face.

Ivor exploded. Diorite fists seemed the most epic way to finish off a Dawnus out of control, and the spray of gore did Ivor justice.

The few remaining spectators broke and fled, screaming in fear. The spy alone remained in the entrance, eyes wide, so startled by the brutal fight that he couldn't seem to move.

Mirage-Connor burst out of the earthen prison, but Kilian joined in the attack. Between them all, they held Connor down until Evander punched him so hard in the head that his skull cracked and he fell unmoving on the broken, scorched earth.

Silence settled over the park, as if the entire world was stunned by the brutal deaths of the Builders.

"Wow," Student Eighteen whispered. "Now, we make it personal. We need him to run as if death is hot on his heels."

She rose and ran around the bush to join the mirage characters gathered around mirage-Connor. She glanced at the spy and said, "You there, hold!"

His face paled as if someone had hit him with a cream pie. His thoughts shrieked with terror. "*Assassin!*"

He turned and fled, moving with Strider speed. She shouted and gave chase, moving almost as fast. Connor figured she'd stay just close enough to keep him fracked and panicked until she arranged for him to escape in a way that no doubt would convince him he had bested her.

After the spy disappeared, Connor released mirage. He suddenly felt exhausted. The mind bomb battle had taken a lot out of him, and he'd never crafted such a complex mirage. Besides, the sight of Hamish and Verena and Ivor dying had affected him deeply.

When he turned, he found the entire group approaching. They looked impressed, but he ran to Verena and held her tight, savoring the feel of her alive and healthy in his arms.

Hamish pounded him on the back, laughing. "That was amazing, Connor, although I think you killed me off a little too fast to be really convincing."

Ivor wasn't smiling. He gave Connor a disappointed look. "Why did I have to die?"

"The diorite punch was a nice touch. Made it memorable," Kilian commented.

"But Connor only got captured," Ivor pointed out.

"We can't have the queen thinking we'll be showing up in Donleavy soon," Connor explained.

"So why not kill you too?" Ivor asked.

Connor shrugged. "It was my mirage. Someone had to sacrifice for the team."

"I need to make sure no one else sacrifices for the cause," Verena said, pushing away from Connor. "You started a panic."

She activated a speakstone, connecting with Gisela, who was in one of the command centers. She relayed orders to deploy forces to intercept the panicking people and assure them all was well.

"Hold," Ilse said. "I don't like scaring people either, but that spy is still in town. We can't risk him hearing those orders."

Verena sighed. "Well, come on. If we catch them, we can calm them down individually."

"Not you. You're dead," Connor reminded her.

"I'll take care of it," Ilse said, and sped away, sliding over the earth toward the outer wall.

Jean hugged Hamish and handed him a breadstick. "Here. This always cheers you up after you get fake-murdered by Connor."

Hamish laughed and took a big bite. "Yeah, but we used to do it to try to get a kiss from you."

She kissed him, grinning. Verena looked from them to Connor, a question in her eye.

"It's an old tradition from Alasdair," he explained. "Never worked."

"Only won us extra tonic from old Mhairi," Hamish said with a grimace.

Chapter Twenty-Six

Dessert Magic Is the Best

Connor took a huge bite of Hamish's strange, frozen dessert, made of cream, whipped as smooth as honey glaze. Small chunks of Althin chocolate and chopped nuts were scattered through it, adding bursts of flavor that seemed magnified by the cream. Connor sighed and let it melt against his tongue as he savored the remarkable delicacy.

But then the cold seemed to freeze his brain. It was a startling, but not unpleasant sensation. Definitely better than the effects from some of the food Hamish offered. He sucked in a long breath, trying to bring some warmth into his mouth as the cold seized the top of his palate. He was impatient to get onto the next bite, so he tapped a little marble to ease the cold.

The group were gathered in Jean's private dining room, adjacent to her sitting room. Nobility definitely came with perks. The long room was mostly filled with a gleaming oak table, long enough to seat twenty. A delicate blue runner covered the center of the table, holding the insulated bowl of dessert.

The entire group involved in the mind-bomb fight were gathered around the table. They'd all been so ecstatic they hadn't even hesitated before accepting Hamish's offer to share a new dessert.

Hamish was walking up and down the table to read everyone's reaction to his re-creation of one of Schwinkendorf's lost masterpieces. He chuckled when he spotted Connor with his mouth half open, eyes wide, dealing with the brain freeze.

"Connor, you look like you've frozen your will to live."

"At least for once he doesn't look like he's about to spew whatever it is you just fed him," Aifric chuckled.

Connor grinned. "I've got this. Don't worry about me." He took another frozen bite. Delicious. Schwinkendorf had dubbed it Winter's Heart, but Hamish preferred calling it Kiss of the Dessert Fairy.

"I've never tasted anything like this," Verena exclaimed. For a girl who had died a grisly death by mirage just hours ago, she had a great appetite.

Jean said, "I'm still amazed you were already experimenting with chilling cream, Hamish."

Verena chuckled. "Hamish loves experimenting with mechanicals to produce new foods. One of his first projects in the Builder compound was a fantastic jellied pudding mechanical."

Hamish sighed wistfully. "That mountain of pudding was a spectacular moment."

Aifric, who sat on the other side of Connor, had already emptied one bowl. While the others joked about some of Hamish's less spectacular attempts at food crafting, she snuck a second bowl and saluted Hamish's back with her spoon. She seemed to be enjoying the dessert enough that every one of her personalities wanted a bowl of their own. Connor wasn't sure Hamish had made enough.

Ivor sat across from Aifric, beside Shona, engrossed in a hushed discussion with her. She was wearing a stylish green hat with a wide brim that concealed her missing hair, and for a moment seemed to be enjoying herself.

General Wolfram had joined them for the celebration, sitting next to Evander, directly across from Kilian and Aifric. She had reported the spy hadn't stopped running until he leaped aboard a windrider heading south. Even though they didn't expect any other attacks from the queen, Ilse had insisted on remaining on watch.

Hamish was clearly thrilled they all loved Kiss of the Dessert Fairy. "I was experimenting with chilling cream, but wasn't whipping it while it cooled. That's the key."

It was a key that worked wonders. They'd easily consume the rest of his supply. They'd have to arrange a way to make more. A lot more.

Shona gestured with her spoon. "In Merkland we've experimented with chilling juices in the summer, but I've never tried anything like this."

Hamish's eyes widened and he gushed, "Fruit juices. That's a brilliant idea."

Verena sighed. "I don't want to hear about you exploding vats of juice in your workroom, Hamish."

Connor enjoyed the happy banter. That battle of the minds could have easily turned out very differently. Even better, they'd just sent a windrider full of autonomous sculpted scones in a sneak attack against Donleavy. A tiny portion of his mind flew with the tiny creations, but they were so small, they barely distracted him.

He couldn't wait to hear Ailsa's report. They'd sent her a cryptic warning, and he hoped she understood it. If she swallowed one of those deadly little scones, Connor grimaced to think what she might do to them in revenge.

"I want some answers about what happened to Nicklaus," Kilian said firmly.

Connor felt ashamed to realize he'd allowed the little boy's plight to fade to the back of his mind.

"I still barely believe he could have lost his affinities," Verena added softly.

Connor wished he could give them better news. "I can't say for sure either way yet. I'm pretty sure the problem wasn't tied to the mind bomb. It was that soapstone sculpted stone. He had quickened it and was also trying to tap it, but somehow it rebounded against him. I haven't been able to figure out how to prove if he's really lost all of his affinities, or if he's suffering some kind of temporary blockage."

Hamish said, "Gisela inspected the stone. Said it was fine. She had just completed it and sculpted it to higher concentration than most of the sculpted stones we use in mechanicals. Some kind of special new project."

"We were going to use it to test river defenses in case of elfonnel attack from the Nister," Jean explained.

For a moment Kilian looked older than usual. Sometimes it was easy to forget he'd lived more than three centuries. "We're still missing something. He was young to try ascending, but I've seen other Petralists fail. Consequences can be severe, but I've never seen all affinities sundered."

He looked to Connor, and Connor got the message. He needed to ascend the final threshold soon. The third threshold was supposed to be the most difficult.

No way Connor would fail. He'd survived too much to get destroyed in the very act of reaching for the power they needed to finally face the queen as equals.

Verena said, "The part that seems the most unusual was that he was trying to use the sculpted stone when it was quickened."

"We do that all the time, don't we?" Shona asked.

Jean said, "All of the sculpted stones in recent months have been only partially sculpted, and they've all been allocated for Builder use, usually for remotely activating mechanicals."

Hamish added, "Few Petralists try tapping sculpted stones. It's too ingrained into everyone that they're too valuable and should only be tapped by the most powerful Petralists trying to ascend."

"Wait a minute," Connor interjected. "Aunt Ailsa partially sculpted some granite for me at the Carraig. It increased my granite strength like three times."

"But no Builder had touched that," Verena pointed out.

"Oh, yeah." He'd thought he had something there. "The only other sculpted stones I've used was when I was ascending. So yeah, as crazy as it sounds, I don't think any Petralist has tried tapping a quickened sculpted stone."

Kilian was looking thoughtful. "I wish we could test if tapping a quickened sculpted stone would be dangerous for every Petralist."

"Or if the fact that he had quickened it himself just before switching to soapstone had an effect," Jean added.

"Or if he's susceptible because he's also a Builder," Verena said.

Connor hated that they only seemed to find more questions, but no answers.

"One way to test it comes to mind, but I don't like what that would cost us if we proved it true," Ivor said with a grimace.

Neither did Connor. To test it, someone would need a volunteer to potentially lose all of their affinities forever. No one would agree to that.

"Don't we have any prisoners from the battle of Merkland?" Verena asked.

"Would you really try tricking someone into destroying their affinities?" Kilian asked with a raised eyebrow.

She sighed. "Probably not, unless they were criminals."

Kilian shook his head. "No criminals worthy of losing all of their affinities. Minor infractions are handled through regular discipline, but major crimes generally require execution. Justice tends to be carried out quickly in those cases."

Hamish leaned back in his chair and said, "So we can't prove one way or the other what happened."

"I don't know enough about how our affinities work to prove anything," Connor admitted. "He can't activate his affinities right now, although his Builder powers still work."

"That's better than nothing. Monitor him closely and inform me if his condition changes," Kilian ordered.

Hamish added, "We've already issued an order to have everyone double check security of other sculpted stones. If there is a danger, we don't want anyone else getting hurt."

"If only Nicklaus hadn't been so rash!" Verena cried, looking close to tears. Some days the boy's pranks were truly annoying, but he had a good heart, and Verena was related.

"He's a seven year-old boy with earth-shattering powers. Of course he's going to do rash things," Kilian said with the hint of a smile. "I'd be disappointed in him if he didn't. I like to know the dangers to steer him away from, though."

Aifric placed a comforting hand on his shoulder.

Connor wished they could do more for Nicklaus, but couldn't think of what that might be.

Jean said, "Evander, now would be a great time to discuss those new insights about loaning Petralist powers."

Chapter Twenty-Seven

Old Secrets and New Affinities

Connor was eager to learn anything new about loaning powers. It was one of the queen's unique abilities that they desperately needed to understand.

Kilian leaned forward in his chair. "We need a breakthrough, especially after unleashing those sculpted scones. We made a bold statement with that move. Even though the strike should be timed to hit when she thinks the senior Builders are dead, it could trigger an abrupt response."

Aifric grinned. "That last spy will share a convincing story."

Eventually the truth would get out, but Connor hoped the deception would fool the queen for a while.

Kilian said, "If she does buy it, even for a little while, that may give us an advantage when we strike, but it will only embolden her to move against Merkland and Granadure all the sooner."

Verena asked, "Should we have invited one of our Althing counterparts to this meeting then?"

Kilian shook his head. "We'll share that we expect an attack soon, but that's not the main point of today's discussion. They don't need to know the specifics of our efforts to loan powers. Nor do I want them involved as we try to figure out my mother's weakness."

Evander gestured, his bowl of dessert nearly lost in his massive hand. "Butterflies flit about on the wind, but they migrate thousands of miles every year."

It was not his most cryptic bit of Sentry speak, so he must've been trying to make a clear point. Connor figured maybe he was trying to say that they appeared as weak as butterflies compared to the queen. That part made sense, but he struggled with the rest. Was Evander suggesting they migrate somewhere really far away while they still had the chance? He doubted it, although the idea held a certain appeal. They might live a little longer.

Jean smiled. "Beautifully put. We may seem fragile, but together we can accomplish great things. If only we can learn her weakness."

Verena said, "Builders, of course."

Hamish nodded, but Connor said, "We suspect that because of Kirstin's story, but that still doesn't get us any closer to the truth." He looked at Kilian and asked, "Can you tell us any more about what happened with your sister back then?"

Kilian's expression turned thoughtful. Connor was surprised to see Aifric reach out and pat Kilian's hand in a comforting way. He flashed his normal, roguish grin and said, "I've reviewed the memory many times this winter. I still don't know what else I could add."

"It's got to be some kind of mechanical," Hamish insisted.

Kilian shook his head. "My sister would never have designed anything with the intent of hurting my father. As distant as my mother could be, my father doted on Kirstin. He was one of the greatest champions of her work, encouraging her to unlock that brand-new aspect of power. He was the first sculptor, and together with my mother they had pioneered affinity powers. He was a firm believer that other aspects of stone-filtered power had yet to manifest itself."

"You said they were testing something new she'd designed, right?" Connor pressed.

"Indeed. I don't know what it was. I wasn't there until after my father lost control and in a fit of madness raised an elfonnel and tried to lay waste to the city."

Connor shivered to think of an elfonnel in the middle of a city. Even with Kilian and his mother nearby to stop it, the destruction must have been horrible.

Kilian continued. "Whatever triggered his madness, my mother seemed to understand. She didn't explain, but it absolutely terrified her. She was not as close to my sister as my father, but until the Great Purge, I would've sworn that her love for my sister was enough to prevent her from committing violence on her for any reason. Unfortunately, she lost part of her humanity returning from elfonnel form. She executed poor Kirstin, who was so distraught by what happened, I never got a chance to ask her about it."

Connor was struck by a thought. "Your mother tried removing all evidence of Builders, so why didn't she remove the speedcaravan, or Merkland's walls? Wasn't Merkland your sister's summer place?"

Kilian nodded, and Evander said, "Tallan asked her not to."

"I thought he rebelled?" Connor asked.

"Not at first," Kilian said. "She loved him more than anyone. He alone had ascended the third threshold like she and my father. Sometimes she treated him more like her son than she did me. His revolt infuriated her in some ways even more than my sister's accidental destruction of my father." He blew out a breath and added softly, "Those were crazy days."

Aifric patted his hand again, and seemed all too willing to comfort him as much as he wanted. Connor wondered if Cacilia had taken control again.

Verena tapped her spoon on her empty bowl, frowning in frustration. "This isn't getting us anywhere. Your sister made so many new discoveries, some of which we're just now starting to figure out. She was brilliant, and she learned things that we haven't even imagined yet. We wouldn't have figured out keystones or several of the other inventions that have proved critical in advancing our mechanicals without those glimpses into her ancient mechanicals."

Hamish snapped his fingers. "Then we need to find that defensive mechanical buried in Merkland. It might give us hints into another of those higher-level aspects of building that we haven't figured out yet."

Verena grinned. "Give me another bowl of that dessert, Hamish. Clearly it's inspired you, and we need more of that."

She and Hamish looked ready to fly to Merkland that very night, but Jean said, "I think that's a great idea, but we're missing the other point. Evander, you said you had gained additional insights into how we can possibly loan Petralist powers. That could prove as critical as anything else we're trying to do."

Evander nodded. "There was one reference. It suggested that ascension was required to loan an affinity."

If he kept speaking clearly so often, he was going to damage his reputation.

Jean said, "We suspected that much since all of our tests have failed. I wish we knew the next step."

Ivor said, "Maybe we need to think outside of the affinity."

"What do you mean?" General Wolfram asked. He too was looking thoughtful, and the crafty general had proven his brilliance many times. Connor was glad he was there.

"Ascension can only be done by the most powerful Petralists," Ivor said, speaking slowly, brows furrowed in thought. "Usually that means Dawnus, at least. Harley was one of the most powerful ever, but was she somehow combining her powers? We've already shown that combining affinities can produce remarkable effects."

That was a good point, and Connor exclaimed, "Hey, Harley was also the most powerful healer I've ever heard about besides Dreokt the Dreadful herself. Healing helps connect with a target person. Loaning an affinity is a form of connecting, right?"

"That might be the piece we've been missing," Shona said eagerly. "How did you come up with that?"

Connor shrugged and gestured with his bowl. "Brain freeze, maybe? Slow the thoughts so that only the most important ones make it to the surface?"

"That doesn't make any sense," Verena laughed.

"It worked, though, didn't it?"

"Let's hope," Kilian said.

They needed that hope so badly.

Evander spoke slowly, looking pained like he often did when speaking clearly. "Lady Shona, if you will assist, I will attempt again to loan quartzite to you while also connecting with sandstone."

She bowed her head in acknowledgment of the special effort he was making. "I'd be delighted."

General Wolfram said, "I would like to assist too. I have a unique insight into how affinities feel, and might be able to help see connections that the rest of you might miss."

Hamish frowned. "What are you talking about?"

Wolfram glanced to Kilian, who gave him a slight nod. Whatever he was going to share was a closely kept secret. Connor appreciated that they were finally giving a mystery reveal its due dignity. Everyone was leaning forward, eager to learn the secret. So much better than dropping a centuries-kept truth on the floor like a spilled sweetbread.

"I'm actually Agor in my primary affinity. My other affinity is with andesite," Wolfram stated.

Shona chuckled. "I might have known."

Connor shared a surprised look with Verena. "Andesite? I had no that idea that was a power stone."

"It's a closely guarded secret in both Obrion and Granadure," Wolfram explained, tugging on one of his famous mustaches. "Generally only children of some of the highest houses are even tested with it. Andesite is a unique stone, and those who establish affinity with it are known as Seers."

"Seers?" Jean asked, pulling her ever-present notebook out of a pocket.

Verena nodded slowly. "I've heard only a little about Seers."

Shona said, "I guess you weren't considered important enough to know."

She spoke with no hint of malice, but didn't need it for that jab to strike home. Verena did a remarkable job ignoring it. "My other work trumped any secondary distractions."

The rebuttal wasn't as strong as Verena usually managed. Shona seemed pleased as she licked her spoon. "My father used to have a Seer, but I'm not sure if any of the high houses have one at the moment."

Wolfram said, "I have a very minor affinity, barely more than a glimmer, but it's still helpful. Seers have the ability to sense the active affinities and the affinity potential in other people."

Hamish exclaimed, "Wow. That's amazing."

A memory popped into Connor's mind and he said, "That's why the first time we shook hands, your expression changed."

Wolfram nodded. "We had heard rumors that there might be someone with an exceptionally powerful affinity in that region. In addition to spiriting the captured Lady Shona away to barter for Nicklaus, Ilse was also on the lookout for the powerfully gifted, but as-yet unaffiliated person. That's why she showed such restraint in the initial confrontations. Did you never question why she did not tap slate more often? Why she did not simply bury Captain Rory and his forces under the earth?"

"I always wondered about that," Shona said. She looked like she couldn't decide if she was more intrigued by the revelation or insulted that she wasn't the only reason Ilse and her company had risked invading Obrion.

Connor gaped, adjusting his memory of those events to this new truth. At the time, he had not even understood that Ilse had a secondary or tertiary affinity. Now that he thought about it, a number of the Grandurians' actions made much better sense. Ilse and Kilian both had exhibited unusual restraint. It amazed him to think they would take such risks on the simple rumor that maybe there was someone with a gift that they needed to find.

Hamish and Jean were looking equally thunderstruck. Jean said, "You must have heard more than a rumor. Your source must have been extremely credible."

"Ailsa," Connor stated as realization struck. It had to be Ailsa, but he still felt astonished that his aunt Ailsa's spy network had extended into Granadure and beyond even before the first battle of Alasdair.

Kilian nodded. "We met her in Merkland, and she was the one who initially sent us up the wrong branch of the river, suggesting it was vitally important that we discover the Guardian who had not yet won patronage."

"Ailsa has been a central player far longer than I suspected," Shona said, her expression awed. "Every time I think I understand the scope of her influence, I realize I'm still underestimating her."

"Why didn't she just tell you my name? That would've saved us so much trouble," Connor said.

Kilian spread his hands. "I'm not entirely sure, although I have my suspicions. It doesn't matter at the moment. If we all survive to speak with her again, we can talk about all of our secrets and motivations ad nausea."

"I'll hold you to that," Connor grinned. Pulling secrets from Kilian sometimes seemed harder than pulling bacon from Hamish's clenched jaws.

Chapter Twenty-Eight

Time to Set the Board

When they consumed every last scrap of creamy dessert fairy kisses, Hamish produced a huge basket of assorted pastries and sweetbreads, all surrounding a fantastic bienenstich cake. The entire outer layer was coated in a honey-almond mixture of gooey, crunchy sweetness that exploded across Connor's tongue before he even tapped quartzite. The interior was made up of two layers of heaven. A light yellow cake, moist and soft, with a rich creamy filler between layers.

Connor nearly swooned as he ate. The taste was like a golden river pouring down his tongue. For a moment he could only lean back, stare at the ceiling, and savor the moment. He had to keep reminding himself to breathe.

When Jean saw the horde of sweets she exclaimed, "Where did you get all this?"

Hamish spread his hands and grinned. "You're not the only one who's been preparing for difficult times. I have stashes all across New Schwinkendorf. If we're going to suffer a siege, we need to make sure we have enough thinking food."

Connor saluted Hamish with his fork and mumbled, "I concur."

Verena regarded the new pile of sweets in wide-eyed dismay. "I can't eat another bite or I'll explode."

Hamish grinned and grabbed a jelly-filled tart for her, but Connor waved him back. "If you're going to push Verena to the stomach revolt point, we need to do it in a place where we're better prepared to measure the distance."

"You're right. What was I thinking?" Hamish said. "Verena never does anything half way. If she decides to let loose, she'll go for the record."

Jean gave Hamish a playful cuff on the back of the head and said, "Don't be such a brute. Verena does not enjoy distance vomit contests like you guys."

Instead of looking disgusted, Verena's expression turned mischievous. "You never know, Jean. Someone has to show these boys what focused vomiting can really accomplish."

Hamish barked a laugh. "Ha. I love optimistic rookies."

Kilian said, "The vomit-distance championship will have to wait, even though I guarantee I would win."

Verena looked affronted that Kilian would attempt to steal her moment. Jean looked disgusted with them all, and Shona looked like she was ready to bolt from the room.

Kilian continued. "Unfortunately, we need to make plans tonight. Today we set in motion events that guarantee our peace is about to end. The mind bombs are triggered, we've sent her spy running home with reports, and unleashed the sculpted scones. She will hopefully believe most of the Builders are dead and all of us distracted. I have no doubt she will unleash her forces against Merkland."

That snuffed out the good mood. Connor dropped his last sweetbread. The moment they'd dreaded was upon them, and despite the incredible progress they'd made, he could not fool himself into thinking they were ready to face the dread queen.

Aifric declared, "Connor's mind is free. He must ascend."

Her features shivered for a split second and her posture straightened a little as Student Eighteen took over. "That means we need to head to Jagdish, to my people."

That was something Connor was both eager to get on with, and very nervous about. The queen posed such a clear and immediate threat that he believed the Mhortair would embrace him as an ally and assist his ascension with serpentinite. However, there was always a chance they would try to kill him instead. That way they could still remove the lesser threat before he could grow as powerful as the queen, thus making their ultimate mission to purge Blood of the Tallan from the world that much easier.

Shona said, "If you plan to travel to Jagdish, we should stop in Merkland on the way."

"It'll be good to get back to Merkland," Ivor agreed. "Rory will be thrilled to get some more reinforcements. Merkland stands alone against the queen in Obrion. She'll strike with her full might against us there."

Wolfram said, "I'll contact Lady Briet and mobilize the Arishat League forces. We had hoped the roads and passes would be dry by the time we mobilized. We have a lot of equipment to move. Those Tabnit death tubes are very heavy."

Kilian said, "I've already sent word for the mobilization to begin. We knew this would be the next step after triggering the mind bomb. I'll leave it to you to coordinate with them to push the mobilization as fast as possible."

Jean added, "We can send Ilse and a squad of Sappers along with the ground forces. She can keep the roads clear and watch for ambushes."

They spent a few minutes discussing the various forces available to send to Merkland to help defend the city against the queen's armies. Crushing Merkland would clearly be the queen's first military priority. When she stamped out that hotbed of revolution, she could move against Granadure and from there against the rest of the Arishat League.

Granadure had been marshaling their forces throughout the winter. The bulk of the army was gathering outside of Altkalen, and Wolfram assured them those forces could begin to move immediately. The plan called for them to marshal at the pass, prepared for fast deployment via windrider troop carriers before the battle.

Verena and Hamish discussed the status of their research. Ilse's Revenge was not quite ready. With their recent successful tests of Verena's new engine and strum currents, all they needed was final assembly. That would probably take at least a couple of weeks.

The Arishat League had been massing an army outside of Maninder, the capital city of Ravinder. They could move against Obrion from the west, right up the great western trading road into Raineach. Everyone marshaled around New Schwinkendorf could move out as early as the next day. Most of the Petralists in the area would mobilize with them, along with stockpiles of Builder mechanicals.

The problem with moving so many forces burdened down by so much heavy equipment would take a lot of time. Even with the fleet of windrider support, and Jean's flight companies, the mobilization would probably take a matter of weeks.

"What about the battalion deployment platforms?" Kilian asked.

"Not quite finished, but close," Verena assured him.

Connor had spied one of the giant transport platforms from a distance. When finished, it could fly hundreds of soldiers into battle. All together, they could field an impressive host, but he feared they might have delayed too long for deployment.

The queen could hit Merkland on her own in a matter of days, not weeks. Their group, his closest friends, would stand in the vanguard against her. All of their supporting forces and armies would prove vital in countering the queen's armies of Petralists and summoned creatures, but all of that would serve as but the backdrop for the real contest.

Connor and his closest friends would have to somehow defeat the dread queen. If they failed, she could single-handedly destroy everything else they had worked so hard to build. Together his group of close friends represented an amazing concentration of power and brilliance, but would that be enough?

Connor had no idea, but one thing was abundantly clear. If he did not ascend, they were doomed. He had no choice but to risk the trip to the Mhortair.

Student Eighteen interrupted the discussion as they focused on supplies and logistics. As if reading Connor's mind she said, "We have to go to Jagdish. I've given the Kill Council more than enough time to commit to joining our cause. The time for hesitation is past. They must make a choice."

Hamish scowled. "I still can't believe they haven't committed yet. What are they waiting for?"

She shrugged. "It's not easy to throw off three centuries of hatred and tradition. Our mission before the queen rose from the long slumber would have been clear as a drawn dagger. My clan would have instantly united to remove Connor from the face of the planet."

Hamish pointed a sweetbread at her. "But she *is* back. That changes everything."

Ivor added, "I have no doubt your people will see the need to ally with us."

That was easy for him to say. He was not the one that they were going to attack if they decided to be stupid rather than clever.

Kilian said, "I've had a long and unfriendly history with the Mhortair. The fact that I'm allied with Connor no doubt has added to their hesitation." His expression turned grim and his voice hardened. "But my patience is at an end. We will go to Jagdish, and we will make every effort to set the past behind us and reach a joint defense accord with them. If they join us, perhaps together we can stop my crazy mother. If they refuse, if they continue to breathe out threats against us, I will give them war."

As he spoke, tiny specks of white-hot fire danced in his eyes and in that moment, Connor felt immensely grateful that Kilian was on their side. He might have tricked Kilian in their duel the previous morning, but he held no illusions that he'd survive long if Kilian really wanted him dead.

Student Eighteen did not look pleased, and Connor was tempted to tap chert and try to listen to her thoughts. She was extremely good at shielding most of the time, but she might let her guard down. He couldn't do that to such a trusted friend, but he would love to hear the opinions of the many different women in her head.

Student Eighteen was Mhortair and would bristle at any threat against her people, no matter how justified it might be. At the same time, Connor suspected some of the other ladies in her head might view Kilian in a different light. He was suddenly glad he had not tapped chert. That was a complicated situation that he did not want to know more about.

General Wolfram rose, bowed to Jean and to Shona, and said, "Then if you'll excuse me, I will initiate the orders to prepare to move out."

Shona and Ivor followed after him, already talking about what supplies they could bring with them. Connor might be heading to Jagdish with some of his friends, but not everyone could go. Ivor and Shona would join Rory in preparing Merkland for defense. Jean would remain in New Schwinkendorf, supporting the mobilization from her end and ensuring final production of Ilse's Revenge completed soon, along with as many mechanicals as they could finish. No doubt, the already frenzied pace they had maintained through the winter was about to double. Connor had no doubt that the stalwart citizens would prove themselves up to the challenge yet again.

As the group dispersed to their various duties, Connor took Verena's warm hand in his and met her determined gaze. "Here we go again."

She nodded, her expression serious. "Let's hope she gives us just a few more weeks."

Connor doubted they would get that much time. As they headed for the door, he glanced back and was surprised to see Water standing in the air above the table. Her long tresses were blowing gently, like waves in low tide, but her eyes were black like deep pools on a moonless night. Her expression was grave, and she held one hand extended toward him.

He hadn't realized he'd tapped soapstone, and he definitely wasn't drawing from it. Water floated toward him, her mouth opening, her expression intent.

She was trying to tell him something.

"What is it?" he whispered as a feeling of foreboding settled over him. He loved how the elements appeared in his mind when he tapped their affinities and felt he was getting to know them somehow, but this seemed different. She seemed to want to warn him of something.

Water stopped in front of him and extended her hand. Red and green energy mixed across her skin in eye-twisting patterns, and for a second he felt like they were forming letters, but the patterns changed too fast for him to read them.

"Connor, are you okay?" Verena asked, breaking his concentration.

"Yes. Just give me a second."

When he turned back to Water, she was gone. A chill crept across his arm, as if he'd dipped it in the Wick on an autumn day.

Connor shook off the lingering sense of foreboding. His worry about the queen was messing with his head. He rejoined Verena and took her hand. They had tons of work to do, but on a whim he said, "Let's take the Swift up Anika's Gulch for an hour."

She smiled. "Good idea. Might be the last quiet time we get for a while."

Chapter Twenty-Nine

Fear the Scones

Ailsa sat at banquet in the magnificent feasting hall of the central palace. The queen liked taking her meals there, surrounded by lords and ladies and courtiers. On the surface that ensured every feast appeared a grand, festive affair. Queen Dreokt did not seem to care that the hall was always unusually quiet, as people spoke in hushed tones, constantly glancing furtively toward her, terrified they might draw her attention.

The hall was a great, vaulted room, held up by gilded pillars. Enormous paintings on the walls depicted Obrion in its heyday. A bank of windows opposite the queen allowed a panoramic view out over Loch Mealt and the expanse of the city.

Ailsa only lightly sampled each course, but she appreciated the diversity of dishes and the excellent quality. That night they feasted on lamb stew. The thick broth was bursting with delectable chunks of lamb, perfectly seasoned and so soft they seemed to melt as she chewed. Plates of ripe fruit cleansed the palate before the next course of roasted duck and pecan-encrusted chicken, spread on a bed of grilled potatoes.

Other courses followed. Beef and greens, stuffed mushrooms, spicy pasta, and lemon-seasoned fish on yellow rice. It would be so easy to indulge and eat far too much of the excellent food, but she resisted the urge. She sat at the high table, to the left of the queen. Other high level officers and counselors sat to either side, all down the length of the long table.

In addition to offering opinions on any topic the queen might abruptly show an interest in, Ailsa provided the queen's supply of power stones. It wasn't like the queen needed much stone, though. Ailsa still had not figured out how the queen could embrace her affinities so often without needing a far greater supply. She suspected it had to do with the final threshold, but had not managed to figure out a way to broach the subject without drawing too much attention and potential suspicion from her monarch.

As always, she carefully maintained the surface thoughts of her current persona, the queen's advisor, a role that she wore even closer than a concealing blanket. It was more like a second skin. More than just a well-crafted, fake front that she projected in the queen's presence, Ailsa truly became the queen's counselor. The reason the queen never plucked treasonous or improper thoughts from her mind was that when she stepped into that role, none of those thoughts existed.

"*My inner thoughts are mine alone because you will never have a reason to dig deeper.*"

In quiet moments alone, or in her workshop, when she allowed herself to risk stepping into other aspects of herself, Ailsa looked forward to the time when she could interview Aifric in much more depth. The assassin girl was the only person Ailsa had ever met who could assume a different persona even more completely than Ailsa could, but the similarities were striking.

Ailsa was no Petralist, but she understood power stones in some ways better than any Petralist ever could. She would love to understand more how Aifric partitioned her mind, but that was only one of dozens of inquiries she planned to make when the time and opportunity presented itself.

After the main course, several delectable deserts were passed around to all attendees by perfectly silent staff. The selection looked wonderful. Ailsa spied traditional Obrioner puddings, cake sliced into small pieces, and several varieties of sweet cookies. The servers had all been mind-wiped and retrained by the queen to act as perfectly worthy servants.

As usual, everything was cooked to perfection. The cooks in Donleavy had always been exceptional, but after the queen had melted one of them in his own oven for producing a dish she felt unworthy, they triple-checked everything before allowing it to leave the kitchen. Ailsa was not sure how long they could keep it up without cracking, but she had to admit the results were spectacular.

A terrified-looking assistant chef hurried into the room, pushing a large rolling cart. The cooks rarely entered the room, and this fellow looked close to passing out from terror by the fact that he needed to.

His entrance drew the queen's attention. As the chef rushed toward the high table, pushing his multi-leveled cart piled with breads and pastries she demanded, "What is the meaning of this? The bread course was delivered earlier."

The chef blanched, turning as white as his hat, but still continued his advance. He looked like he expected to be murdered, but had decided to die with honor, fulfilling his life's work.

"Forgive me, my queen. Somehow the serving staff failed to deliver this final cart. Since you require that all baked goods be served within the hour of coming out of the oven, I did not wish to anger you by disobeying that command."

"Good move, reminding her of her previous wishes. Sometimes she forgets."

The queen regarded him with a little frown, which usually heralded imminent and violent death. But then with one of her inexplicable mood swings, she grinned, looking delighted. "Well done, young man. You're absolutely correct. It would be a shame to waste so many delicious pastries. I commend your integrity for not concealing the oversight from me. It's unusual for the servers to miss anything, but that's why I have layers of servants to back each other up."

She laughed, as if that was particularly funny. The entire gathered company, who had been bracing to witness a gory murder, instantly erupted into frantic laughter to mimic her current mood.

Looking so relieved he nearly fainted, the young cook beamed as he swept the first silver tray off the top of the cart and presented it with a flourish to the queen. It was covered with muffins, scones, cream-filled tarts, and half a dozen other pastries, all bite-sized so they could be popped into the mouth whole.

The queen did not like watching people gnaw away at large portions. She considered such efforts beneath nobility, reminiscent of the linn rabble who worked to support her existence. She selected a scone and a round, cream-filled puffy pastry.

The cook moved down the high table, offering desserts to everyone. A dozen of the mindless servers converged on the cart and carried other trays full of pastries around the room for the nobles and courtiers to sample. Even though they had started eating dessert, no one would refuse a pastry for fear of somehow offending the queen.

Ailsa selected a small muffin that was still soft and warm from the oven. She placed it on her plate and glanced down the rest of the table. In addition to her and the queen, the high table held Aonghus and Rosslyn, and her father, High Lord Feichin. Several other high-ranking officials, noble men and women, and other chief advisers.

The queen was a stickler for propriety, and she never began consuming a new course until it had been distributed around the entire room. She did not like the distraction of eating while the servers were still moving about. That did not mean she did not insist upon taking the first bite of every course, though.

Soon all the pastries were distributed and the still-beaming cook pushed the empty cart from the room. Queen Dreokt popped the cream-filled tart into her mouth with a happy expression. Instantly, everyone else in the room grabbed a pastry and did the same. Most people did not spend much time savoring their food, but swallowed the small treats as quickly as possible. They seemed more interested in savoring the fact that they still lived.

Ailsa picked up her little muffin and moved it to her mouth, but instead of eating it, she palmed it into her pocket. She did not think about the act as she did it in case the queen noted her deception, but she doubted it would draw anyone's gaze. She was quite skilled at such a simple sleight of hand.

In her deepest thoughts, she risked considering briefly the words of a note she had received earlier that day. The simple, innocuous comment had puzzled her and stuck with her even as she stepped into her counselor persona. "*Your nephew's best friend recommends against partaking of his favorite food. He wants it all for himself.*"

Even in her best-shielded thoughts, she didn't dare name her nephew or his friend. The mention of favorite foods was one she had heard far too often not to recognize. So she could not trust the muffin until she knew more.

One of the lords from southern Obrion, who was sitting at a nearby table, suddenly groaned and clutched at his stomach. He looked like whatever he had eaten had not agreed with him. He cast a terrified glance at the queen, who had noticed his reaction and was frowning in his direction. When he opened his mouth to apologize, panicked words of apology were not what came out.

Instead, he belched with such force that he nearly knocked himself right out of his chair.

The sound reverberated across the room, and shocked silence descended as everyone stared at the unfortunate lord as if he was already dead. He looked completely flabbergasted, his face drained of color. He started shaking his head in denial even as he belched a second time.

Ailsa cringed at what was about to happen. The queen was already leaning forward, her little frown changed into a furious scowl. The man would die within seconds.

Then another belch erupted forth, this one from a demure, elderly noblewoman who the queen had often praised for being an exemplar of perfect etiquette. She looked like she was about to have a heart attack. Four other people lurched in their chairs and belched, long and loud, sounds that no nobleman or noblewoman would ever make.

A second later, the beefy Lord Feichin toppled from his chair and unleashed a fart so explosive it ripped a hole in his breaches. Actual green flames burst from his backside, and he howled in pain.

The queen leaped to her feet and screamed, "Enough! I will not allow such disrespect."

Then she grimaced and clutched at her own stomach. She convulsed, as if trying to keep from vomiting, and wind whistled out of her open mouth. This time it came forth not as a belch, but as the deep, sonorous voice of High Lord Dougal himself.

"Well, paaardon me!"

A couple of people actually laughed, but most of the crowd were too busy clutching at stomachs or trying to clasp hands over faces or backsides in vain attempts to prevent explosive gas from ripping out and embarrassing them too. More voices erupted through some of those gaseous experiences. A few were in High Lord Dougal's voice, but some spoke in the queen's own tones. Ailsa watched in absolute astonishment as complete bedlam descended over the feasting room.

One loud belch whistled around the room like a warm wind, shouting in Dougal's voice. "*I think the reason the queen is so intent on removing all free thought is that she is terrified someone will recognize that she almost always stinks of mulberry wine.*"

Another voice, sounding exactly like the queen shouted, "*Do you realize how extremely difficult it is to appear regal when one possesses the intelligence of a braying mule as I do?*"

Other voices echoed around the room, but the queen suddenly raised her right hand, and all sound ceased. She looked so furious she might simply explode. She must have tapped serpentinite, but it was a wonder she did not cleanse the entire room with purifying fire.

The little pastry she had swallowed suddenly burst out of her mouth, as if she had somehow ejected it from her own stomach. It looked chomped and mangled, but the queen extracted from the center of it two tiny pieces, no bigger than almonds. Ailsa leaned forward, trying to make them out. One of the little things seemed to be struggling, as if it had teeth. The other was emitting tiny jets of fire.

Queen Dreokt gasped and flung the little things away with a terrified shriek. Her face turned ashen, and she pointed a shaking finger at the little pieces of her muffin, "Destroy it!"

Most of the assembled guests simply stared in shock. The queen had never displayed fear before, not even when the Mhortair assassins had cut her into pieces in her throne room. And yet, now she was shrieking at those mangled pieces of dessert the way a common housewife might shriek at a mouse.

General Aonghus vaulted the table and snatched up the two tiny bits of pastry. One of them had started crawling back toward the queen, while the other was just lying there, merrily burning. White-hot flames ignited around Aonghus's hand and he held it there for five long seconds. When the flames winked out, he brushed tiny flecks of cinders from his palm, all that remained of the offending pastry. He bowed to the queen, his expression serious for once, and although his mouth moved, whatever words he spoke did not reach Ailsa's ears.

Queen Dreokt took in a long, shuddering breath and regained her composure. She said in a regal voice, "Thank you, general. I appreciate your quick service defending my honor."

Ailsa marveled as understanding struck. "*My boy, what have you done? You and your friends designed miniature summoned creatures out of bread and dared launch this unprecedented attack against the queen in her own court? Are you mad?*"

"*Combining advanced autonomous summoning with Builder mechanicals is ingenious. It won't do much long-term harm. Not even I know yet what can do that, but you surprised her. Chaos reigns in her court and her perfect little world is damaged. She's afraid. My boy, perhaps this is the break we've been seeking. Well done. I am so proud. I hope you're ready for war.*"

The flood of belching and flatulence seemed to pass, and most of the assembled were rolling around, clutching at their stomachs and screaming silently. Ailsa grimaced to think what it would feel like to have an angry little sculpted creature tearing around inside of her gut.

The queen shouted, somehow making her voice heard even while suppressing all other sound in the room. "Healers! Get in here and rip these abominations from my court."

She did not wait to see her order fulfilled, but swept toward the main exit in a rage. She paused long enough to shout, "Ailsa, attend me now!"

CHAPTER THIRTY

Unintended Consequences

Ailsa rushed after the queen, leaving the dinner disaster behind, not sure what Queen Dreokt might have in mind. Aonghus and Rosslyn came as well. Aonghus was chuckling to himself, looking immensely amused. He had probably incinerated the little sculpted scone he had consumed. Rosslyn was a Healer, so she must be dealing with hers as well because she looked calm and composed. Together they left the chaos of the dining hall behind and followed the queen, who stormed through the palace, her face a thundercloud.

Everyone scurried out of the way, which was a good thing. Ailsa had no doubt the queen would squash anyone foolish enough to stumble in her path. Walking so fast the rest of them had to jog to keep up, she led them outside to a balcony overlooking the loch. She did not speak, but made an impatient gesture with one hand.

Air swept in around them and lifted them rapidly up the front face of the palace to a balcony outside of the queen's own quarters. Ailsa suppressed a grin. The air felt solid underfoot, like a soft carpet. She wished she had time to explore the rare chance to fly with the queen.

"Ailsa, stop fooling around with nonsense," Dreokt snapped, then swept inside.

Her current chief of staff, a wizened old nobleman named Tobson, stood near the queen's throne-like chair, leaning on his staff of office. His bald pate was smooth, but dull. The queen had disliked his wispy hair, but also hated reflective baldness, so he made a point of powdering his head every day.

Beside him stood a blocky-faced man in a travel-stained worker's jumpsuit. His hair was disheveled and lines of exhaustion made him look older, but he stood proudly as he faced the furious queen.

Ailsa expected her to obliterate both men at the interruption. She was amazed when Queen Dreokt's anger evaporated and she exclaimed, "Croir, aren't you a little early?"

"Nay, my queen, I just arrived and came here without even stopping to wash or change."

"*Might not have been the smartest move you ever made. Queen's a stickler for good hygiene.*"

"I tried to encourage him to wait, but he insisted he needed to speak with you instantly, that you had ordered his actions," old Tobson interjected.

He might look like a doddering old fool, but his mind was kept sharp by a strong obsidian affinity. Tobson had lasted a full two weeks as chief of staff, longer than any of the last twelve men and women who held that post. If the queen ordered it, he could literally take Croir apart with that staff of office.

Queen Dreokt settled into her chair and said, "I am in need of good news. Yours had better be excellent."

The man did not appear fazed by the unspoken threat, but made a courtly bow with remarkable grace. He was either far more clever than he looked, or he was a dolt who was about to die.

"My queen, I bring most excellent news from New Schwinkendorf."

Ailsa reinforced her mental defenses around her thoughts at the name. She could not afford even a second of weakness, and not even unexpected news from Granadure could shake her focus.

Croir continued in a rush. "Murder and mayhem in the city. The Blood of the Tallan went berserk, as did that Dawnus fellow, Ivor. They killed the principle Builders, that guy Hamish and the leader girl, Verena. They even fought Kilian and Evander both!"

Despite her reinforced defenses, Ailsa swayed, feeling faint. The words seemed to hammer her mind like piercing daggers. Her thoughts scattered and for a second her inner self was exposed. Luckily she was too shocked to think anything loudly, and Queen Dreokt was far too ecstatic to listen.

"It is done?" she exulted.

"Yes, my liege. I witnessed the end of the fight myself. Took a terrible risk doing it. Nearly got run down by that Mhortair assassin, but I outran her and escaped to bring you word."

He swelled with pride, but the words helped center Ailsa again. She knew much about Aifric, and she found it hard to believe this spy could have escaped the girl if she was indeed intent on pursuit. That suggested many interesting possibilities that she longed to explore. First, she forced her inner thoughts to quiet and reset her surface thoughts, restoring her facade as a devoted advisor.

Queen Dreokt laughed aloud. "He killed Verena? Ha! That's justice for Builders."

"I am sorry to report that the man Ivor was destroyed by Kilian, and it appeared that Connor was captured. I do not know his final fate."

The queen continued laughing, mirth literally boiling off of her in the form of shimmering steam. General Aonghus subtly redirected it away from Ailsa and Rosslyn in an act of unusual chivalry.

Queen Dreokt turned to Ailsa and the generals. "See? You all questioned why I waited so long to strike. I had already struck, and simply waited for my orders to be carried out. Chaos and murder among the vile Builders!" Her expression shifted instantly to seething rage. "They deserve even worse! Those vile Builders touched me with their disgusting creations! I wish I could heal them to kill them again, only slower!"

"Somehow it is their mechanicals you fear. Why?"

Aonghus started to speak, but the queen waved him to silence. "Now we are poised for victory! You and Rosslyn get back to the army. Mobilize everyone to Crann. The time to cleanse this realm once and for all is nearly at hand."

She gestured them away, and Aonghus and Rosslyn bolted from the room. Queen Dreokt turned back to Croir, who was looking immensely pleased with himself. "Tell me everything you saw."

He was happy to oblige and launched into a gory tale of murder and elemental destruction. Queen Dreokt listened intently, her expression giddy, and Ailsa made sure her outer self mimicked her.

"So the walls blocked your view most of the time? Interesting. And Aifric called you out, but allowed you to outrun her?"

The more she heard, the more convinced she felt that Connor and his crafty friends had somehow tricked the spy. Queen Dreokt seemed to believe him, and no doubt she was probing his mind for deceit. If she had found any, she would have immolated him on the spot.

When he finished, he bowed again and said, "Thus I alone of all your servants completed the dangerous assignment and returned with good tidings."

"And you will be rewarded accordingly," Queen Dreokt assured him. "Tobson, arrange for Croir to receive a lordship and appropriate holdings."

That was a wondrous gift. Croir beamed with delight and gushed his thanks. If he was surprised by the order, Tobson didn't show it. He only bowed and said, "At once, my queen."

As he towed Croir from the room, Ailsa allowed a brief inner thought. *"What will you do with him once you realize his report is false?"*

Queen Dreokt turned to her. "Oh, Ailsa, such good news. You're the only person I trust in this fallen kingdom. I need a fresh batch of stones immediately."

Ailsa the advisor felt a flush of pride that she had earned the queen's trust. She curtsied and said, "Of course. I have everything you need right here in my bag."

Instead of taking new stones, the queen paced away, hands clenched at her side. When she spun, her expression had flipped back to furious. "The fools! They don't understand the dangers in what they do."

"Should I call them back?" Ailsa asked, glancing after the generals.

Queen Dreokt crossed back to her throne-like seat and waved away the suggestion. "Not them. I mean the Builders, of course."

"Risking your wrath was foolish," Ailsa agreed carefully, edging closer.

The queen gave her an annoyed look. "Don't pretend to be clueless like everyone else, Ailsa. You possess one of the only truly powerful minds I've encountered since awakening. Why do you think I keep you close but don't work to improve your mind like my other servants?"

"I thought you approved of my counsel," Ailsa said, smoothly shifting along with the unexpected direction of the conversation. She'd trained herself to be flexible, riding the eddies of the queen's focus like a rafter upon turbulent waters, but rarely had the queen's tangents in thought been directed toward her.

"Yes, yes. You provide valuable service," Queen Dreokt said, sounding impatient. "You provide my stones, which is even more important, but Ailsa I keep you beside me to enjoy the presence of an unspoiled mind. You are one who thinks before you speak, you consider before you act, and you are a seeker of truth."

Her gaze held Ailsa, and she seemed more in control, more coherently focused than Ailsa had ever seen. In her inner mind, she shivered. She managed a brief curtsy, which gave her an excuse to break eye contact and shore up her surface thoughts. "I appreciate your confidence, my liege."

"My dinner was ruined!" Queen Dreokt snapped, her expression turning petulant. Witnessing another abrupt switch back to a childlike tantrum was actually comforting after that moment of dangerous lucidity. Queen Dreokt was incredibly powerful, but her instability was one of her weaknesses.

"*If you ever snap out of it, ever recover full control, what might you accomplish then?*" Ailsa forced herself to banish the dangerous thoughts quickly. Even her innermost thoughts might not be fully protected when the queen was so focused on her.

Luckily the queen still seemed distracted. She sighed again, her anger disappearing as quickly as it came. "It's a glorious day, Ailsa. The two most dangerous Builders gone. But the rest will know their research and must be stopped before they tread paths of danger none but I understand. Did you know Merkland was my dear Kirstin's home?"

"I did not," Ailsa admitted.

"Shona and her wicked insurrection have desecrated my only daughter's beloved home, and now the idiotic Builders follow the same mistaken paths she did. Can no one but me see the dangers in using the elements so wantonly?"

She looked honestly sorrowful for the loss of the daughter she had killed, and Ailsa sensed she was sharing something important in that moment of anger.

"I did kill her," Queen Dreokt said with another sigh. She must have siphoned the direction of Ailsa's surface thoughts. "She was my dear, sweet child, and at first her work promised wondrous new ways to access the sylfaen."

"Sylfaen?" Ailsa dared ask. She was not familiar with that word.

The queen ignored the question, her gaze thoughtful and distant. She continued in a soft voice. "But she tread where none should go, somehow sensed the Ramverk itself and stepped to the threshold of danger where the elementals awaited."

She glanced at Ailsa and added, "Even you, with your great mind, understand nothing of the deep secrets or the true dangers we face."

"I am eager to learn how to help you, my queen," Ailsa said, forcing herself to focus on only that thought, not on the scores of questions clamoring for her attention.

"No one can help. No one listens. Not even Kirstin would listen!" She rose, shouting in anger, and fires crackled along her arms.

Ailsa held her ground. Fleeing wouldn't help if the queen decided to strike. "As you said, my queen, I try to listen and I seek truth."

"Some truths are too dangerous. Kirstin walked paths that would have destroyed her and everyone upon these lands. She left me no choice but to destroy her."

Ailsa nodded, but felt confused. She had thought Kirstin had died because of what had happened to King Triath.

Again the queen picked up the thought and said, "I don't want to talk about that. Today I was touched by Builders with elements. The fools have no idea what that might have done!"

Ailsa expected her to announce plans to destroy the rest of them. She loved ranting about wanting to destroy the Builders, but this was the first time she gave any hints about what scared her about them. Instead Queen Dreokt dropped back into her chair, her expression turning thoughtful.

"The risk is too great. My control has never wavered, but if they gained access through another door, could even I stop them?"

"I don't understand. Petralists wield elemental powers every day. Why is it so bad for Builders to release them too?" Ailsa dared ask. She felt too close to gaining critical truths not to take the risk.

"I know what I'm doing! I know how to guard myself, and my Petralists are shielded by thresholds. Builders are not. That is the great danger, Ailsa." She looked angry, but instead of striking out she said, "No, I dare not take the risk. I need another worthy servant."

"Shall I summon someone?" Ailsa offered. She sensed something important was being shared in the conversation, but couldn't quite grasp it.

"No, I alone can summon them, but you will join me. Pack some travel clothing, Ailsa. We leave in half an hour. Today perhaps the most important blow in defense of our lives was struck, but it's time to set the rest of this kingdom right."

"Of course. May I ask where we are going?" Ailsa dared query.

"Harley failed me. I must find another servant."

Chapter Thirty-One

The Simple Lives of Bash Fighters

Merkland's famous white granite walls shone like a beacon of freedom in the early morning light. Connor smiled as he leaned forward in his seat in the front row of the Hawk to better enjoy the expanse of Merkland valley. The city perched atop the bluff above the wide Macantact river like a mighty lord watching over the nearby township.

The township lining the opposite side of the river seemed to be bursting at the seams with people, new roads, and new buildings. The queen's wrath might hang over the valley like an invisible shroud, but Rory, Shona, and Ivor had done a remarkable job inspiring hope for the fledgling revolution.

Connor scanned the wide valley farther to the south. Farmers were already working early spring fields, and that far south the trees were already spreading young green leaves. His gaze instinctively sought the Lower Wick river where it emptied into the great Macantact just a few miles south of Merkland.

In his mind, he followed that river back north, up the long familiar miles to Alasdair. He could still envision Alasdair the way it was when he had visited with Verena after fleeing the Carraig, so many months ago. If he visited today he would see broken mountains and the beautiful valley buried under half a mile of impassable rubble, but in his mind he cherished memories of clean streets and homes freshly rebuilt after the town's first destruction.

Alasdair might be gone, but his family and the rest of the town had survived and were currently thriving in their new homes in Emmerich in southern Granadure. He had not visited them nearly enough that winter, and suddenly wished they had found a way to stop for a visit on the way to Merkland.

Unfortunately, time pressed on them. Every one of his friends shared his unspoken fear. Time was short. They could not afford to waste any of it.

Verena banked the Hawk slightly as they drew closer to Merkland, and Connor glanced out the shielded windows to check the rest of their small flight. The empty Swift was tethered behind the Hawk, its thrusters engaged just enough to allow it to hover weightless on its tow line. It was packed with smaller mechanicals, like every craft in their party. Every inch of space was crammed with so much gear they almost couldn't fit the people.

Nearby, Hamish was piloting a brand new craft. Similar in design to the Hawk, it was a little longer, with an even more streamlined profile, and much longer wings. While the Hawk could bank and turn with almost as much agility as Verena's little Swift, its bigger new sibling was more a battle support platform. Hamish had dubbed it the Albatross before Verena could come up with a better name.

The wagon-like bed in the rear half was a little longer than the Hawk's, and they had crammed in more storage compartments underneath. It also sported several times as many weapons. The long wings proved excellent platforms for deadly missiles and unusually long speedslings. While most of the speedslings, including those on the Hawk and on the Swift were designed to spit forth a staggering swarm of deadly hornets, two of the speedslings on the Albatross had been designed with a different purpose. They fired at a much slower rate, but possessed an advanced acceleration tube that caused the hornets to reach unprecedented speeds.

After the battle with Harley, they had discussed the challenge of dealing with powerful enemies at great distances. Verena's swarm of hornets had not accomplished much against Harley. They had been too obvious, giving Harley too much warning of their approach.

Those new speedslings on the Albatross were designed for longer distance targeting. Hamish had developed sightstones at the tip of each one that projected onto the front window precise aiming pictures. He had even managed to include indicators for distance to help fine-tune the aim. Those speedslings could reach out twice as far as any of the others, and aim with terrifying precision.

The Albatross was loaded down with so many new and upgraded weapons, that it alone could probably devastate entire companies of enemy forces. Hamish had helped with the development and initial testing, but when it came time for battle, one of the other Builders, one of Jean's newly trained pilots, or even Jean herself could take control. The Albatross would stay farther from battle, could glide on the wind currents far longer with remarkably little expenditure of power stone once it reached high altitude, and could unleash destruction from a distance.

Half a dozen long windriders, upgraded versions with enclosed canopies like the Hawk's, followed in formation behind them, stuffed with supplies and mechanicals. They were on loan from Sender Flight, Jean's transport wing, piloted by non-Builders using upgraded keystone controls. They could pilot their craft almost as well as a full Builder. It was truly remarkable, and both Verena and Hamish loved to discuss all the possible ways they could apply those principles to other new mechanicals. If they all survived the war, Builder inventions would transform every aspect of society.

Kilian and Aifric sat behind Connor in the Hawk. The two had chatted all flight, discussing Jagdish, the Mhortair mentality, and the best ways to approach her people. They also spent time discussing Mhortair himself, a topic which Student Eighteen possessed an inexhaustible curiosity about. Connor had listened a little, but had not learned a great deal that Student Eighteen had not already shared with him in the past. He needed to focus on that upcoming meeting with the assassins, but he found his mind wandering a lot during the trip.

He always loved flying with Verena, loved the panoramic vistas of southern Granadure and the Maclachlan mountains from the air. They spent time chatting about her family and memories of the last few times she had visited the family estate outside of Edderitz where she and Connor had recently gone to visit. He liked most of her family immensely, and was even starting to believe that he and her father would eventually become good friends. The next challenge would be to introduce her parents to his.

That would either go extremely well or extremely badly. Connor was hoping for extremely well. If his father ended up having to throw Verena's father out a window, it could seriously damage their courtship.

Shona and Ivor, along with Wolfram and Lady Briet, flew with Hamish in the Albatross. Wolfram was not an enthusiastic flyer and seemed to prefer the more stable flight of the Albatross.

Lady Briet loved flying. In one of the many treaties that the Althing delegation seemed to be constantly pushing, she had managed to include a promise that some of her people would eventually be trained to fly, and that they would receive a squadron of windriders, and at least one craft similar to the Hawk. Luckily Wolfram, Jean, and Verena had managed to avoid committing to a specific timeframe for deliver.

With their close interactions, the secret of the keystone had finally come out. The Arishat League delegates were eager to take possession of a shipment of keystones for their own use and research. That had been one of the other items intensely negotiated as they finalized their joint defense pact.

In return, they shared all of their own research and development. Everyone was benefiting tremendously by the arrangement, and Connor felt optimistic that they would maintain their good relations even after they survived the war. Verena worried about the long-term ramifications of the secrets they were sharing, but Connor could not bring himself to share her concern. He had enough to worry about.

It was far from certain that any of them would survive the upcoming conflict. If they somehow did, how many of them would perish in the process? Worrying about what might or might not happen some years down the road seemed a ridiculous waste of attention. Connor hated to consider losing any of his friends, let alone many, or most, or even all of them, but he could not pretend such disasters were not possible.

They had already lost friends, particularly in the battle of Merkland. He had nearly lost Verena, and he tried to enjoy every moment with her as a result. He had no idea how much more time remained for them to be together, but he was determined to make as many happy memories as possible in the interim.

As they swept in toward Merkland, Connor studied the city within the walls. It looked similar to the last time he had visited, although more soldiers patrolled the wall. Verena had told him a little about the many upgrades they'd designed for the city, but those changes weren't visible from the air. He was glad they'd worked so hard with Rory and his forces through the winter because the hoped-for influx of additional revolutionaries had largely failed to come to pass. They were on their own.

The queen's ruthless efforts to lock down the rest of the country had worked. Apparently some few Guardians had managed to make the arduous journey to Merkland anyway, and he'd heard of more who had been captured trying to do the same. Those captured had all died grisly deaths as a warning, and those warning had produced the desired effects of intimidating others.

The truth was a little disappointing, but not exactly surprising. Obrion as a nation would not revolt until they deposed the queen. They had many secret allies throughout the kingdom, but those allies were forced to conceal their true feelings. Hopefully when the time came, they would rise up and help.

Verena activated a speakstone link to General Rory. "Builder One and Two are on approach, with a contingent of Sender Flight wagons."

Rory responded almost immediately. "We see you. You made good time. We've cleared space in the main square."

They had found ways to link multiple speakstones together, particularly between their flight craft. Hamish's voice spoke over the speakstone. "I still think we should have used the call signs Sculpted Scones instead of Builders. That would've been more appropriate, don't you think?"

"No, I don't think." Verena had always hated that codename, although after their recent secret attack against Donleavy with sculpted scones, she was softening her view a little. Not enough to name their flight group after them, though.

Verena banked over the city, and Connor enjoyed the excellent view of Merkland's famous, octagonal wall. He spotted a couple of hovering windriders farther to the south, elevated scout positions for Pathfinders. They passed over the market area, which looked full of early-morning shoppers, many of whom looked up and raised hands in greeting. Enough shipments of supplies and support had come in from Granadure by windrider that the citizens were getting used the daily flights, and relations between Merkland and Granadure were extremely good. It offered hope that once they resolved the military conflict the peoples of the two nations could find ways to coexist peacefully.

Most of the daily windrider shipments and dispatches landed in a square in the military district, but Verena flew past, headed for the magnificent main palace. It took up most of the eastern quadrant of the city, overlooking the river and the township on the far side. A huge open square faced the palace, and Connor smiled when he saw the enormous fountain in its center.

That was where he had triggered the revolution, the day the devious Craigroy had slipped him a bit of porphyry. Ingesting that stone had forced him to change into a rampager. If Connor had not recently ascended the second threshold, no doubt Craigroy would have succeeded in getting Connor to eliminate Rory and Ivor both, then submit to his will, hopelessly chained to porphyry addiction.

Instead came the revolution. Connor had raced across the city as a rampager, drawing everyone to the square where he had managed to control the beast and shift back to human form. Rory and Ivor had pronounced the revolution, and Craigroy had spent the winter in a prison cell beneath the palace.

A crowd was already gathered, and as Verena slowed and gently touched down, Connor spotted Rory, Anika, Erich, Tomas and Cameron, and many others. He did not spot Anton, the mighty Sapper on loan from Granadure. No doubt Anton was somewhere outside of the city, atop his tower of earth, keeping watch over everyone. He was the only other Petralist Connor knew besides Kilian and Evander who had survived the Tallan wars. He did not possess a Dawnus gift so had not ascended, but was by far the mightiest Petralist to walk with earth beside Evander and his grandmother.

Verena shuttered the thrusters, dropped the shielding windows, and jumped from the Hawk. She rushed to Anika, who was beaming like a happy girl. It was really unnerving. There was no telling what Anika would do next when she was smiling like that.

Aifric followed Verena, already tapping basalt, and reached Anika first. The three ladies embraced, laughing and chattering excitedly in Grandurian. No doubt they were discussing the hundred thousand details that women seemed to insist were necessary for a wedding. Connor had given up trying to understand it all. He was just glad Verena and the ladies did.

Sometimes he dared think about what life might become if they all survived the war and he got an opportunity to officially propose to Verena. His heart sang with joy when he thought about marrying her, but dealing with all that wedding planning would be pure torture.

Verena glanced back at him and their eyes met, and he read the longing in her gaze. She too was eager for their courtship to proceed to a more formal level. The excitement of Anika's impending marriage was like an irresistible cord dragging her toward the day she could begin planning her own wedding.

They'd talked about it, of course. Many times, but Connor still felt the timing wasn't right. What if one of them died in the fighting? No doubt they would talk about it again before lunch.

Rory seemed to be holding up remarkably well. Not surprising. Little fazed the mighty general. Connor and Kilian climbed out of the Hawk and greeted Rory warmly.

Connor asked, "How are things going?"

Rory glanced at his bride-to-be and the ladies chatting so excitedly. Other women joined them, and even Lady Briet was drawn in by the irresistible attraction of wedding planning. Rory smiled at Anika's happy face, but Connor caught a brief flash of near panic in his eyes.

"I'd say defenses are the best we can manage for now. I'll feel a lot more secure when the rest of the reinforcements are staged nearby and ready."

Then Tomas and Cameron arrived. Tomas pounded Connor on the back hard enough to crack ribs. "Not getting soft training without us all winter, are you lad?"

Luckily Connor had seen him coming and tapped a little granite. Seeing his old friends always made him grin and he said, "I train with Kilian most days now."

Cameron punched Connor in the shoulder in greeting, hard enough that even most Boulders would have stumbled back. Connor withstood the blow, and it triggered a wave of happy memories of the intense bash fighting practice he'd enjoyed with those two indomitable and always irreverent warriors.

"Kilian's crafty enough, I wager, but he's not a bash fighter, lad. A man loses his edge when he's forced to think too much," Cameron said in a conspiratorial whisper.

"I train with Aifric too."

Tomas thumbed the side of his nose and nodded in a knowing way. "That girl's deadly enough, but she lacks focus."

"Understanding one woman is impossible. Understanding a whole chorus of them constantly criticizing your choices would make most people crazier than that old widow with no teeth desperate enough to offer to let Tomas court her."

"Says the man so ugly your fleas run away screaming."

"Fleas know when to quit. Smarter than some people," Cameron retorted.

Connor's grin widened. Their constant insults always calmed his nerves. No matter how bad things got, those two would make fun of everything, especially each other.

"You guys haven't managed to consume all the granite in the city with your daily bash fights have you?" he asked.

Tomas rolled his eyes and cast an annoyed look at Rory. "No, lad. Not yet. General seems to think there are other things we should be doing with our time besides max-tapped bash fighting with the Crushers."

Cameron nodded agreement. "Higher ranks always seems to constrict the minds of even the best bash fighters. We had hoped Rory could resist the effects, but not even he's immune."

"If a man like Rory can fail to see the promise of warehouses full of granite at his complete disposal, there may be no hope for any general," Tomas said with a theatrical sigh so loud it was more like a belch.

Rory ignored him. Connor bet he dealt with that argument every single day.

Cameron chuckled, "Of course, there's never been any hope for you."

"Says the man who couldn't even court a blind woman without his ugly driving her away," Tomas retorted.

Cameron laughed. "You can't talk. You thought taking a turn with a woman meant seeing how many times you could make her somersault when you threw her into the air."

Tomas grimaced, looking sheepish. "How was I to know she had such a delicate constitution? We've been training with Anika for months."

"Good point. It's probably good you identified her weaknesses so quickly. She didn't even get good distance when she released all that fine food down the front of her dress."

Connor laughed. They weren't nearly as dumb as they pretended, although sometimes he had to wonder. "It sounds like Anika is keeping you guys busy."

The two nodded, and Erich joined the group. His Obrioner was getting better. "Sister fights good. Beat every other battle maiden two times." Then he grimaced and added, "But many distraction with wedding. Break mind many times."

Connor wasn't surprised. Weddings had that effect.

The other windriders settled down behind them, and Tomas and Cameron moved off with Erich to oversee unloading of supplies and distributing mechanicals.

Rory gestured the rest of them toward the palace. "Come. We have much to discuss."

Chapter Thirty-Two

It's So Hard to Find Good Help

"Stay here," Queen Dreokt ordered.

Ailsa curtsied and said, "Of course, my queen."

The queen marched away across the rocky ground of the bluff they had just landed on in southeastern Obrion. The early afternoon sun sparkled in the bright blue sky, dotted with wisps of soft clouds.

Ailsa shed her heavy jacket as the queen moved away, the hem of her emerald satin dress almost brushing the rocky ground. It was warm standing there in the sun, far warmer than the high elevations they'd just descended from, even though the queen had adjusted the temperature to keep them from freezing.

This was the fourth summoning, and in her deepest thoughts Ailsa allowed herself to wish it might be as unsuccessful as the others.

In each previous case, in quarries far to the north and west, Queen Dreokt had succeeded in raising ancient slumbering elfonnel, but had not been satisfied with what she found within them. She did not explain, but each time banished the giant elemental monsters back into the ground to return to their slumber.

They had traveled the length of Obrion, flying over the land faster than the Builder flying craft, hunting a worthy servant. Despite the danger of standing within a hundred miles of an awakened elfonnel, Ailsa had found the experiences fascinating. She had studied reports suggesting that power-grade stone was created around slumbering elfonnel. Somehow their power seeped into the land around them and infused the stones.

Perhaps that slow leeching of power contributed to whatever weakness the queen found in each of the other elfonnel. The enormous monsters, made of elements come to life, had submitted like docile pups under Queen Dreokt's hand, but that hadn't been enough. After angrily dismissing each of them, Queen Dreokt had swept Ailsa back into the sky to chase the next possible servant.

This one was different. They had not come to a quarry, but flown southeast, down the length of the Macantact river, to the two great twin cities of Freastal and Deifur, at the point where the Saol River, flowing swiftly from the north, joined the Macantact shortly before it emptied into the Sea of Olcan.

Ailsa had never visited that part of the land, and wished for more time to explore. She'd heard Freastal, situated on a bluff just to the north of where the two rivers met, was famous for its art and music. Deifur, on the south side of the Macantact, stretched for miles. It was one of the great trading cities, known as home to the kingdom's best horses, and the knights to match.

They hadn't stopped, but turned south, almost all the way to Chostalan, the second largest city in High Lord Pilib's realm. The lands were wide and open and already lush with spring crops. From the heights, they had spotted the blue expanse of the Sea of Olcan to the east. They had flown over an immense, open pit limestone mine, but Queen Dreokt had not stopped. She continued on several miles before finally landing on the low, rocky bluff, about two miles from a small farming village. Nothing about the location seemed remarkable in any way.

Almost a hundred yards away, Queen Dreokt abruptly stopped walking and raised her hands. From the other summonings, Ailsa understood that the queen was somehow connecting with the slumbering elfonnel and prodding them awake.

High Lord Dougal had been the only other living person Ailsa knew foolish enough to risk raising an elfonnel. He had possessed the ability to seize the mind of an elfonnel through his rare ascension in obsidian. Any other elfonnel might have worked, but he'd accidentally awoken Queen Dreokt instead.

Things hadn't gone well for Dougal after that.

The ground began to shake, and Ailsa dropped to her knees to keep from getting thrown from her feet. She had a good bruise on her backside from the fall that last elfonnel had given her. Earth began erupting upward like a very contained diorite explosion, about a dozen strides in front of Queen Dreokt. She kept her arms raised, and her expression looked exultant as the elemental creature responded to her call.

Ailsa tried to keep her inner thoughts quiet, allowing her surface thoughts to clamor with nervous confidence in her liege, and curiosity about what monster she would raise this time.

"What monster, indeed? Harley nearly single-handedly stopped the revolution. The fight was so close. Who are you raising to take her place? How will anyone stand against them, and your new armies, and your wrath?"

She dared consider the thought that had plagued her the entire trip, but which she only barely allowed herself to think about while in such close proximity with the queen. *"Why do you need another servant at all? You alone could raze Merkland and challenge the might of Kilian, Evander, Connor, and all the Builders together. What is it you fear, and what did you mean with that rant about the elements?"*

With a final explosion of earth that sent dirt geysering three hundred feet into the air, the elfonnel arose. It flowed out of the ground in a billowing cloud of silvery mist that momentarily obscured its form. Ailsa leaned forward, curiosity quelling her nervousness. Elfonnel were unbelievably dangerous, but they were also endlessly fascinating.

She longed to study them more closely, but how could one even attempt such a thing? If she could, she would explore the inexplicable mystery of their existence. They were elements come to life, given form and substance by the Petralists who somehow stepped into the elements to open the pathway for them to rise and temporarily consume them.

How did Petralists like Queen Dreokt or Kilian or Evander survive, retain consciousness, and eventually return? She understood the need for their Dawnus opposite elemental power, but still did not understand why that worked, how it worked, or what other truths lay buried under the awesome creatures they called elfonnel.

This one rose out of the mist that melted into its expanding form. It glowed silver-blue with an inner light as its watery limbs formed and lifted its enormous body off the ground. The monster took the form of a great octopus, with eight tentacles thicker around than a horse. For a moment it towered over the queen, then shrank down until it was only the size of a pair of oxen. Two of those limbs reached for Queen Dreokt, flowing with unnatural grace. No doubt those limbs could rip apart a max-tapped Boulder.

Queen Dreokt seized the tips of each tentacle and danced a little jig, as if the monster was a partner at a ball. Her happy laugh drifted across the still air to Ailsa. She looked thrilled, but she had seemed equally ecstatic at the rising of each of the other elfonnel. She was like a child enjoying the return of a beloved toy, even if that toy would not please her for long.

With each of the other elfonnel, Queen Dreokt had plunged a hand into its head. For the octopus, she drove a hand right through one of its giant, softly glowing eyes. The monster did not cringe or react in any way for a long moment.

Then it shivered, little ripples running down its body and along each limb. Its color darkened to midnight blue, and it shrank by perhaps a third. To Ailsa, it seemed the creature was condensing, even though water could not be compressed.

Queen Dreokt removed her arm from the monster's eye and extracted something long and dark. Had she ripped out its brain, or something? Ailsa frowned, wishing she could see better, that she'd dared approach closer.

With a dismissive gesture, Queen Dreokt sent the monster cascading back into the earth. She strode back to Ailsa, moving with a determined stride, her expression angry. In her hands, she carried the object, bouncing it in her palm like a tiny club. As she neared, Ailsa realized it was a carved rod made of stone.

It took her a moment to recognize the wavy lines of blues and greens and browns that seemed to writhe up the stone's length. Serpentinite. Only recently had she learned of the secret power stone, known to few outside of the Mhortair.

"Does that elfonnel not suit your needs, my queen?" Ailsa asked as Dreokt stomped up to her.

Before answering, the queen sat back, as if settling into a throne. Air swept in around her, forming an invisible seat that caught her weight. More air blew in with a sudden gust that lifted them both into the air. Ailsa had ridden enough with the queen to not panic, although that departure was a bit more extreme than previous ones.

"I don't have time to trifle with niceties," Queen Dreokt huffed in response to the thought.

"Of course, Your Majesty," Ailsa said, her surface thoughts resonating with trust of her liege and disappointment that the queen hadn't found a worthy servant. Inwardly, she was yearning to ask about that piece of serpentinite.

"Oh, Ailsa, I've tried everyone who might have still remained free of the taint, but they're all gone. I cannot trust any of them." She sighed grandly. "Harley was the last to withstand them."

"Surely the revolutionaries are not so strong that your armies cannot defeat them," Ailsa offered, although she doubted that was what the queen was talking about.

"That rabble of fools is more dangerous to themselves than they could ever be to me," the queen snapped, picking up the bait. "The risk they pose is an indirect one, a risk of accidental malice beyond their ability to comprehend."

"*Again you reference risks no one understands. If only I could ask what you mean,*" Ailsa dared think in her innermost, secret self, while her surface thoughts focused on how the queen was impervious to all harm.

"No, they can't hurt me," she said, again responding to Ailsa's surface thoughts. "They could strip my flesh to the bone, but my connection to the sylfaen offers power they cannot comprehend."

"Sylfaen?" Ailsa dared ask. *"If you're so confident in your invulnerability, why fear the Builders?"*

Instead of answering, the queen extended the serpentinite stone rod. "What do you feel?"

At her first touch, Ailsa gasped. The stone was thrumming with such a concentration of energy, it seemed to seize her mind. Without conscious thought, her sculptor senses plunged into the stone. For a moment, she could only stare in wonder.

Vortexes upon vortexes were packed in so tight, they overlapped, creating greater vortexes unlike anything Ailsa had ever felt, beyond imagining. The stone was an octagonal bar of serpentinite about as long as her forearm and as thick as her clenched fist. Each slender, flat side was carved with exquisite detail.

Flowing script in a language she did not recognize covered two sides, while images of monstrous elfonnel covered others. One entire side was engraved with the ancient symbols of Petralist powers. The subtle design only enhanced the master work's beauty.

Ailsa sensed the stone could magnify a Petralist's power a hundredfold, if not more. The higher form of sculpting made her feel inadequate in a way she hadn't felt since her first year studying at the Carraig.

"This is magnificent," she breathed.

"My husband's work," Queen Dreokt said reverently, taking the stone back and tracing one finger down the ancient script, her expression distant, a tiny smile tugging at her lips. "This is a key to the ramverk we built here upon this continent to harness affinity powers. It's been infused in a convergence point for centuries."

More unfamiliar words. Her off-hand revelations were more than Ailsa had hoped for, but the lack of explanations were maddening. Worse, she couldn't demand answers for the hundred questions clamoring in her mind.

"What was its purpose?" Ailsa asked.

Unfortunately the question snapped the queen out of her reverie. Her eyes narrowed in displeasure and she said, "Secrets that should be kept away from foolish children who know no better than to grasp the elements when they should fear them."

Ailsa wasn't sure how to respond, but Queen Dreokt flipped to another topic again. "Did you know I was trapped? Beneath Alasdair I had awakened, but I could not rise, not without losing the last vestiges of who I had been. If I dared rise, I would have opened the pathway for them too." She shivered with apparent dread. Ailsa shuddered internally at the thought of lying awake and conscious, but trapped under all those tons of stone.

"I was trapped within the elements until Dougal's servant offered the lifeline I used to climb free and escape them," the queen added softly.

"I did not know that."

"Of course you didn't! No one did. No one understands the danger. That fool Connor has fallen to the stupidity of my deranged son who knows less than a foolish child. Kirstin gleefully stepped into the gateway of destruction, and he wants to follow! He's leading all those fools to their doom, just as he did my precious Tallan."

"Should we not educate Kilian with the truth?" Ailsa suggested.

"He won't listen. He thinks me mad. Ha! Me? I'm the only one who understands the dangers that he seeks with all his intent. No, I won't allow him to corrupt another."

She gestured with the serpentinite sculpture, her expression intense, her eyes glowing with inner light. "That boy cannot destroy himself if he cannot ascend. I mean to train him, to cure his insanity, and raise him to greatness, but I need time. Time we do not have because everyone is trying to open the gateway to destruction."

Ailsa cowered back from the queen's intensity. She sensed more precious truths in those rantings that she desperately needed to understand, but lacked the ability to process, not with the queen watching her like a starving pedra. Even her inner thoughts might echo just a little too loudly.

Abruptly the queen giggled and her expression turned delighted, her gaze becoming a bit vacant. She stared out over the gently rolling pastureland they were flying over. Their invisible air cushion had lifted them several thousand feet and was accelerating toward the northwest, although Ailsa barely felt the movement. A shield of air blocked the wind, and they sailed through a pocket of absolute calm.

Queen Dreokt leaned closer again, her laughter cutting off abruptly, her expression turning smug. "But I can make time, Ailsa."

"Really?" Ailsa asked, shocked. She had never heard of such an affinity.

The queen burst into a fit of gleeful laughter. "You are such an innocent sometimes, Ailsa. Of course I can't alter time. No one can do that. Well, no one whose work is reproducible, except. . . . Never mind." She pointed a stern finger and warned, "Don't you dare meddle in that."

"I won't," she said quickly, having no idea what they were talking about, and for once feeling relieved that she didn't understand.

"Good. My entire life's work hangs in the balance, as does the fate of this continent. The boy cannot threaten all existence if I prevent his ascension. Then I can take the time to train him properly. After I punish my wicked son, of course."

"How can you prevent his ascension?" The conversation had taken so many weird turns, Ailsa wasn't sure what to expect.

Queen Dreokt gestured with the serpentinite sculpture. "The final threshold is with sound, and with this I own sound. Mhortair's unruly children have plagued the land long enough. They would seek to help that boy usher in our destruction instead of protecting the realm from that bridge. I cannot allow it."

She settled back in her invisible seat and added in a soft, deadly voice. "I mean to wipe them out."

As the full, terrible intent of that simple statement settled over Ailsa, the queen flipped again to a pleasant smile. "My dear Ailsa, did you bring any of that delicious tea from yesterday?"

CHAPTER THIRTY-THREE

Some Problems Only Get Worse with Time

Connor no longer felt intimidated by the great palace of Merkland. He'd spent enough time in some of the grandest palaces of three kingdoms that he felt he could handle it, but even he had to admit Shona's home was impressive. She led the way up the wide, gently curving stairs in the gigantic main hall, with its humongous chandelier lording over vaulted space that rose a full three stories.

The hundreds of crystals in the chandelier were kept perpetually lit by a Solas, with subtly shifting soft hues, playing gentle lights across the walls trimmed in gold, silver, and Shona's house colors of blue and green. The central palace rose a total of five stories, with long wings extending out both sides. The interior was beautiful and spacious. Everywhere Connor looked he spotted carved stone, gilded wood, breathtaking paintings, and sculptures. Even most of the ceilings were covered in frescoes or bright paintings.

They climbed to the third floor and followed a wide corridor back to Rory's office. It was spacious and decorated far more richly than Rory would have ever chosen. It used to belong to one of High Lord Dougal's chief advisors, but Rory had added personal touches to make it his. An armor rack was placed near the door, along with a rack of his personal weapons. A large wooden desk stood at their left side, covered with scrolls and parchments, near one of the big windows overlooking a garden on the rear of the palace.

A fire was already burning in the hearth across from the desk. Several comfortable chairs were situated around it, and by the number of papers on the small table next to the central chair, Connor suspected Rory did a lot of work right there near the fire.

As everyone piled into the office, Shona took a deep breath, looking immensely relieved to be home. "The city looks to be in good order, Rory. What items do we need to focus on first?"

Wolfram showed Lady Briet to one of the chairs. Aifric snagged another before they were all taken. Jean, Verena, and Anika moved to stand near the fire, still clustered together, chatting excitedly, but softly. They'd kept up a running conversation about the wedding through the entire trek through the palace. Hamish wandered toward the desk, peering at papers, probably looking for any snacks Rory had left around. Connor followed him, but Ivor stopped near the door beside Kilian.

Rory remained standing. "Both you and Ivor have stacks of paperwork to attend."

Ivor groaned. "That's one aspect of leadership no one ever talks about."

Rory grunted. "We do have one item that requires our immediate attention. Craigroy has escaped."

Connor had been debating whether to accept a breadstick that Hamish had produced from one of his many pockets. It looked less mangled than most of the food he offered. Rory's pronouncement killed his appetite. Memories of that sly Craigroy trying to destroy him and his friends flashed through his mind. The man could not be allowed to run free.

Shona demanded, "How?"

"We've determined that Lord Torcal arranged his escape three days ago."

"You only discovered it today?" Ivor asked.

Rory nodded, looking disgusted. "Torcal somehow arranged to switch the guards. It seems hefty bribes were involved, and both he and Craigroy are nowhere to be found."

Shona muttered, "I knew we should have disposed of him. Craigroy is too clever by half."

Probably a couple more halves than that, Connor bet. Not only had he tried enslaving Connor with porphyry, he'd orchestrated a revolt during the battle of Merkland and opened the Army gate. It was in the brutal fight to hold that gate that Jean had been so badly injured by Captain Aonghus.

Thinking about it made Connor feel really angry. "We need to find him."

Rory said, "We don't know yet how they escaped the city, but Anton is scanning the countryside. We also have a Spitter checking the river. Striders have been dispatched to Lord Torcal's mansion to see if they fled there."

Shona shook her head. "They'd never go there. Torcal's not stupid enough to think he could hide from us in his own home."

Ivor said, "Torcal always seemed rather unimpressive to me. I'm surprised he had the courage and cunning to orchestrate such an escape."

Shona said, "Torcal would never do it. Craigroy, however, is clever enough to come up with the plan and to convince Torcal it was a good idea."

Rory said, "He was always the one local lord least supportive of the revolution, but I had thought him content with staying on the sidelines until this was resolved."

General Wolfram said, "Apparently he is no longer content."

Lady Briet asked, "How does this affect our defensive plans?"

Rory looked like he had been considering that already because he did not hesitate. "Not as much as you may fear. Torcal was never in our inner circle."

Ivor said, "If Craigroy could orchestrate an escape like this, at a time when we're expecting an imminent attack, I wonder if he has other informants we don't know about."

That was a disturbing thought. They'd found spies all the way north in New Schwinkendorf. Student Eighteen felt confident she'd found them all, but Rory did not have access to her assistance in Merkland. Until now.

As if reading his thoughts Aifric said, "When we're done here, I'll see what I can find."

"I appreciate that," Shona said. She looked as grim as Connor felt. No one liked a spy. Except for the spies that worked for them, of course.

General Wolfram said, "We must assume that more of our plans are known to Craigroy then we would like."

Lady Briet added, "It's good in a way that he fled now rather than a week from now since we are here to finalize arrangements for reinforcements. He may not know they're on the way, and he would definitely not know how we plan to allocate them."

Rory nodded. "In the interim, we've tightened security on all the gates and we will limit access to information to only those who need to know."

Shona asked, "Is that why Lord Nevan has not joined us yet?"

Rory nodded. "I like Nevan, and I want to trust him, but we have to be careful. I underestimated him before the battle of Merkland, and I won't do that again."

Shona gave him an apologetic smile. "His loyalty to me and to my father has always remained unwavering. He betrayed you on our orders, but since I joined the revolution I'm confident that he supports us one hundred percent."

Lady Briet asked softly, "Are you willing to risk all of our lives on that faith?"

Shona actually hesitated. That was enough. They already faced long odds to successfully defend Merkland. They could not afford throwing away any advantage by letting the enemy know what they were planning.

Instead of answering directly Shona said, "One thing is clear, Torcal has committed treason against me in my realm. As a result, I will issue a formal proclamation stripping him of rank and title and property. All he possesses is now property of the realm."

Usually Connor hated the idea of lords and ladies of Obrion having the right to seize what they wanted when they wanted it. Lady Isobel in Alasdair had proven endlessly frustrating with her petty ways, culminating in her blatant theft of the heatstone oven that Ailsa had gifted to Connor's family and which they had decided to share with the entire town.

However, in this case Shona's actions seemed appropriate. Of course, she had now adroitly assumed ownership of one of the richest holdings in her realm. Torcal's city of Curadh managed a very important quarry, and as a result Torcal possessed vast wealth. Now all of that belonged to Shona.

Hopefully she would live long enough to enjoy it.

General Wolfram said, "I propose we get to work. We need to begin hammering out final plans for distribution of our forces and defensive measures."

Ivor said, "Then we should move to the conference room directly below us. I'll order in some breakfast."

Verena said, "While you get started, Hamish and I are going to search for Lady Kirstin's Builder defenses that Evander suggested might still exist. Given the situation and the fact that Craigroy may be compromising some of our intelligence, we could really use that advantage."

CHAPTER THIRTY-FOUR

Second Place Is Just Not Acceptable Sometimes

While most of the group headed downstairs to the conference room, Verena lingered near Rory's fire with Hamish and Connor. She hated to do it but could think of no other option but to turn to Shona and ask, "Shona, could we have a moment?"

Shona smiled graciously, no doubt savoring the moment. Verena couldn't blame her. She savored each of the rare moments when Shona had to ask her for a favor.

"You seek information about Lady Kirstin, don't you?" Shona asked.

Verena nodded and Hamish said, "This is your home. Where do you think she might've hidden a top-secret Builder defense mechanical?"

Shona paced over to the fire and extended her hands to its warmth. "I've been wondering that same thing ever since Evander brought it up. I had not even known this was Kirstin's home. She couldn't have concealed it anywhere in the main palace because my great grandfather heavily renovated the previous palace over a hundred years ago. He's the one who constructed the palace as we know it today."

Verena hadn't known that much. She had originally been thinking it would be best to start in whatever apartments Kirstin might have lived in.

Connor stepped up beside Verena and said, "So either she never concealed it here in the palace, or it might have been destroyed accidentally by workers doing the renovation who would not know what it was."

Verena shuddered. That would be such a tragically stupid way to lose vital Builder secrets. So much had been lost since that great age of discovery. Verena and her teams, with the assistance of Hamish, Jean, and all the resources of Faulenrost and New Schwinkendorf, were struggling to accomplish a fraction of what Kirstin had done.

Many of their most amazing breakthroughs had come only because they had discovered ancient mechanicals still functioning after centuries, and had learned higher aspects of Builder powers that might have taken them years or decades to rediscover on their own.

"Where else would a Builder conceal an important defensive mechanical? She must have feared for her safety to spend so much effort reinforcing Merkland," Verena said.

Connor said, "We'll have to ask Kilian about that again. I always got the sense that the kingdom was pretty stable until that day when the king went crazy and had to be put down. It sounds like the queen murdered Kirstin pretty soon after that. She would have had to build the mechanical before all that happened."

That was a good point. Verena had asked Kilian about the event more than once, but maybe now they knew better questions to help focus his memories.

Hamish was slowly chewing on a couple of smashpacked cakes that he had pulled from a pocket. He offered Verena one, but she refused out of habit. He then offered Shona one. She looked at the little cube askance for a second, then glanced at Verena. She took the cube.

"Thank you, Hamish. I don't get to eat these nearly often enough," Shona said graciously, making a show of chewing and savoring the food. Then her eyes widened and she added in a more honest tone, "Wow. That's a lot of flavor."

"Wait 'till you try the pot roast," Hamish said with a grin and started rummaging around in his pouch for one.

"Perhaps later," Shona said, glancing again at Verena with that smug look she couldn't seem to help adopting whenever they spent much time together.

"Okay," Hamish said with a shrug, totally oblivious to the silent exchange happening under his nose. He popped another cube into his mouth.

"I'll take one," Connor offered, and squeezed Verena's hand as he stepped past to accept the cube. He understood Shona's childish ploy and supported Verena. She loved him so much.

Shona switched back to the main topic as if she hadn't interrupted it in the first place. "There might've been other dangers Kirstin would have worried about. Even though her parents had conquered the entire continent, there might've been hotbeds of revolution back then, just like today. Merkland is far enough from Donleavy that it would've taken a while for help to come."

"You mean Stornoway. That's where her parents lived," Connor corrected.

Hamish said, "Either way, she had a couple of kids to take care of, right?"

"A couple of crazy kids. Evander and Tallan himself," Verena said.

Shona grimaced. "I can't imagine Evander as a child."

Verena hated agreeing with Shona too often, but she was right. When Verena tried, she could only picture a miniature version of Evander, sliding around on the earth, spouting ridiculous Sentry speak when his mother said it was time for bed.

Hamish chuckled and added, "So she probably spent a lot of time in the kitchens."

Verena rolled her eyes. "We're not stopping in the kitchens so you can grab another breakfast."

"If Evander and Tallan were anything like normal boys, they would've been hungry all the time. So if she wanted to spend time with them, it only makes sense she would have to spend time in the kitchens. Maybe she hid the defensive mechanical there," Hamish insisted.

Shona shook her head. "The kitchens were also heavily renovated. If she hid anything down there, it would be gone now."

Verena started to pace, trying to place herself in ancient Merkland. No doubt the city would've been smaller then, but still impressive. It was an area that had not been heavily settled until later, from what she understood, which would explain the great wall of Merkland. That alone was an impressive defensive construct. That Kirstin could look beyond that and build additional layers of defense spoke highly of her mind, and Verena wished she had known the woman.

She glanced up and asked, "Kirstin built the wall. Why wasn't that enough?"

Shona said, "It always has been. Merkland has been attacked on several occasions during the height of the Tallan wars. No one ever breached the walls."

"But she wouldn't have known that. She died before the Tallan wars," Connor pointed out.

"But she had already built the wall," Hamish reminded him.

Verena snapped her fingers. "Yes, she did. What if she planned the additional defenses at the same time she was building the wall, just like we've been working multiple layers of defense around New Schwinkendorf?"

Shona nodded, looking excited by the thought, and Connor took up the idea. "So if she planned for additional defenses while she was building the wall, where would she expect to be standing in a time where she might have to trigger that defense?"

Verena and Hamish answered together. "On the wall!"

They all turned to face Shona, who looked lost in thought. They waited in breathless anticipation for several seconds until Shona's eyes lit up. "On the wall. Of course, that's it! The wall is all made of Alasdair White. However, in the watchtower above the Lord's gate, where the speedcaravan enters the city through the wall, there's an inscription. I haven't thought about it in years."

"It says, *For family, for country, and for all we love.*"

Verena said, "That's beautiful but I don't—"

"It's inscribed in obsidian," Shona declared triumphantly. "It's the only obsidian engraving I know about. It always seemed strange, but not strange enough to think about except when I'm standing right there on the watchtower, looking out over the valley and the river."

Verena exchanged excited glances with Hamish. Obsidian was the key to remotely activate other mechanicals. They'd learned the trick from Kirstin's old mechanicals.

Hamish exclaimed, "That has to be it. Let's go."

Verena turned toward the door, but Connor held back. "I think it's a good idea, but maybe we're jumping to conclusions."

Verena paused, halfway to the door. "What do you mean?"

Connor took her hand. She loved that he did that in front of Shona, and did not even look self-conscious about it. "You told me that when you access sculpted obsidian, it allows you to connect with other pieces of obsidian, wherever they might be, right?"

Verena nodded. "We can sense them like candles on a dark night."

"So why didn't you sense a huge piece of obsidian in the wall above Merkland while we were here during the battle? Didn't you use remote activation quite a few times?"

Verena frowned. He was right.

"There has to be a reason," Hamish insisted. He stood in the doorway, impatiently waving them on. "It's too good of a clue not to go check out."

Verena gripped Connor's hand tighter. "Let's go find out."

Together they rushed down through the palace, and even Shona kept up with them, despite some odd looks from some of her subjects. Shona was a high lady and rarely did she sprint through her own palace unless something really bad was happening. She did not seem to care, but was caught up with the rest of them in the frenzy of discovery.

It was a little annoying that she could be so much like them sometimes. It was easier when Verena could just hate her. Shona might have told them about the obsidian, but Verena didn't plan to let her reach it first and try to steal their discovery.

They rushed up onto the huge expanse of Merkland's famous octagonal city wall, then jogged along the wide upper causeway. The top of the wall was more than a dozen feet wide, providing plenty of room for troops to move or to marshal for battle. A lot of soldiers were stationed on the wall, and they looked alert. The sight of their high lady and the Builders rushing along the wall triggered calls from officers asking if there was an alarm.

Shona assured them all was well, but they still picked up an escort of a score of heavily armed soldiers, led by an enthusiastic captain who insisted it was his duty to see his high lady safe. His high lady nearly threw him off the wall in annoyance, but eventually decided it wasn't worth the hassle.

"If it's unbecoming for you to run, you can take your time and catch up later," Verena offered.

"Don't worry about me," Shona retorted and sped up. She was trying to reach the obsidian first. Verena sped up too, and was tempted to ask Hamish to pick her up and fly them there.

Clueless to the competition between the girls, Hamish ignited thrusters and rose into the air. "Why run when I can fly? See you there."

He accelerated toward the tower. Verena and Shona exchanged glances and Verena read the same dismay in Shona's eyes. Hamish was going to get there first. They both shouted at the same time, "Wait!"

Connor accelerated past them, clearly tapping basalt. "Come on slowpokes. Are you racing to see who reaches the inscription last?"

Verena was tempted to ask him to carry her, or to dig into her satchel for a piece of quartzite to use as a makeshift thruster, but resisted the urge. She would beat Shona without any enhancement.

She ran faster.

Shona matched her step for step, her expression determined. The captain looked surprised by their pace, and some of his men struggled to keep up, burdened as they were by armor. "My lady, is such a rush necessary?" he panted.

"For me it is."

"Then it is for all of us," the man replied grandly and called to his men for greater speed, to not dishonor their lady with weakness.

Verena felt bad for the puffing soldiers, but she refused to slow. Shona was in excellent condition, but so was Verena. She gritted her teeth and dug deep for more speed.

Shona kept pace. Although she was breathing heavier than Verena, she never slowed, never faltered. In anyone else, such determination would be inspiring. In Shona it was just annoying.

Together they reached the Lord's gate at the far southern end of Merkland, overlooking the ruins of the speedcaravan track. She had completely forgotten that during the battle of Merkland, Harley had ripped up huge sections of track to use as clubs against Hamish and his Juggernaut mechanical.

The wreckage had been removed, but there had been no time or need to rebuild the graceful bridge that used to arc up from the plain to the gate. The speedcaravan no longer traveled all the way to Merkland, and Rory and Shona and Ivor had been too busy with more important needs.

They burst into the guard room, surprising the guards who called out, asking for the cause of the alarm. Neither of them paused to answer, but raced for the narrow stairway up to the top. Only one of them could ascend at a time.

Verena sprinted, managing to pull slightly ahead, and started to grin. She would beat Shona after all.

Shona grabbed Verena's leather satchel that was bouncing against her back and yanked with granite strength, pulling Verena backward. The move surprised her and she stumbled. Shona rushed past and called, "Be careful. The stones can be slippery."

"You cheater," Verena mumbled, fuming and chasing Shona, but now she was stuck behind on the narrow steps. Shona was going to win.

So as Verena raced up the steps after Shona, she plunged a hand into her satchel and extracted a piece of quartzite. Clutching it to her chest, she threw wide the release rate. Air blasted out of it and catapulted Verena forward. She hoped to soar right over Shona's shoulder and reach the doorway to the open roof level first.

She missed.

And plowed into Shona's back. Shona had released granite, and the impact blasted the air out of her lungs in a surprised, "Oof!"

Shona fell and Verena tumbled down on top of her. She tried to use the quartzite to pull herself off and away, but Shona grabbed her hands and together they whisked up the stairs and through the door, air blasting both of them in the face.

Verena cut the flow of air before the stone pulled them right over the outer edge of the wall, and the two of them dropped to the stone floor in a tangled heap.

Shona pushed Verena off, and they both scrambled to their feet at the same time. Verena was fuming, and Shona looked equally upset. Maybe this would offer the excuse they both had been seeking to finally issue a formal duel.

"You should have seen yourselves!" Connor chortled. He clapped Verena on the back, laughing so hard he seemed to be having trouble breathing. Hamish stood leaning against the outer parapet, also laughing.

She wanted to glare at Connor, but his laughter was infectious. When she glanced at Shona, she noted the disheveled hair and clothing twisted and wrinkled from their wild tumble up the stairs, and it really was funny. She probably looked as bad.

Verena started to laugh. Shona's glare faded and she joined in. There really wasn't any other choice without looking like a buffoon. Verena wished she'd chosen the buffoon option.

The laughter helped clear her head and remind her of the real mission.

Verena moved to the parapet overlooking the outer edge of the wall and the panoramic view across the southern end of the valley, with the Macantact river flowing south, the highway on the western bank, and farmlands on the east. The obsidian was set into the granite stone parapet, and it gleamed with reflected light, as if someone's job was to polish it every day. The inscription was a little smaller than Verena had expected, barely the length of her forearm.

Hamish tapped it with a finger. "I win."

Then his eyes widened, and he exclaimed, "This is it!"

Verena placed her hand on the inscription too and gasped, instantly sensing the power in the stone. It blazed in her mind like a torch.

Obsidian was mostly pretty useless to Builders, and for the most part she found it a fairly unremarkable stone. The sculpted pieces they had used for their remote activation were generally crafted quickly by Gisela, and were rough and unfinished. They were sculpted though, magnifying the innate power in the stones four or five times, enough to act as remote activation sources.

They served critical functions, but still seemed pretty bland. This stone was not.

For the first time she sensed incredible power, and far more potential than she had ever imagined. That piece of obsidian was sculpted by a master, concentrating its inner power at least a dozen times over. It was a master work, easily rivaling Ailsa's best, and the subtle elegance of the script only served to highlight the incredible workmanship concealed within the stone.

As soon as she touched it, pinpoints of light blazed in her mind. Like she told Connor, when they activated other sculpted obsidian, the pieces it allowed them to connect to were like candles in a dark night, visible and easy to navigate to. While touching that engraving, the lights that she sensed were more like bonfires than candles. There were eight of them and they were spread around the city, nearly a mile out, coinciding with the junctures of the corners of the great city wall.

"Can you feel it?" Connor asked.

"It's amazing!" Verena laughed and forced herself to release the stone for a second to wrap her arms around Connor. She kissed him enthusiastically on the lips. Kissing Connor was always great. Kissing him in front of Shona felt like a victory every time.

Shona refused to give her the satisfaction of scowling, but stepped past them and traced her fingers across the engraving. "So this is power grade stone too?"

"Hamish said, "More than that, it's sculpted to perfection."

Shona whistled softly. A fully sculpted stone was worth a fortune. Most high nobles only possessed a couple and considered themselves vastly wealthy when they did. High Lord Dougal had amassed a dozen of them, an unprecedented fortune, prior to the invasion of Granadure. He had planned to use them to push some of his Petralists through the first threshold and force them to raise an elfonnel. That would sacrifice the Petralists, but offered Dougal enough power to threaten the full might of Granadure. The plan had almost worked.

Verena again touched the stone, and again the eight bonfires ignited in her mind. She reached out to the first one and touched it.

Soapstone. The obsidian that she connected through was linked to an incredibly powerful piece of soapstone. From the vast rush of power that she sensed in it, she suspected it too was sculpted.

Hamish realized that a second later. In an awed tone he said, "Eight sculpted soapstone. That's more than I imagined we'd find."

Shona gaped. "Eight?"

Verena nodded. It was an awesome treasure. Both Obrion and Granadure regulated production of sculpted stones and kept the numbers extremely low. Neither country wanted unsanctioned stones floating around where a powerful Petralist, ignorant of the dangers of elfonnel, might attempt to ascend.

She explained how they were arrayed around the city, and Connor asked, "What do you think they do?"

Hamish shrugged, so Verena said, "I'm not sure. There's something about their positioning and the way they're linked together, but I don't understand yet. This seems to be another higher aspect of Builder powers that we don't know."

"We should take them up," Shona said, glancing out over the countryside toward the first one, which was concealed in the river, a mile to the south.

Verena shook her head. "I think that would be a mistake. That might break the greater mechanical they're forming, and we don't know enough yet to know if we could restore it."

Shona didn't look happy about that, but she also didn't want to potentially destroy a legendary Builder defensive mechanical. Those concealed sculpted stones offered the promise of salvation for her beloved city, and Verena doubted she would risk that just because she wanted to collect eight more sculpted stones.

"We need to tell Kilian about this, and see if he can shed any light on what she was trying to do here," Connor said.

A Strider shot up the stairs and landed in front of them. He saluted. "Lady Shona, you are all summoned by General Rory to return immediately. He has received news, and he requires your presence."

Verena exchanged a worried look with Connor, her enthusiasm fading to new worry.

Hamish grimaced. "That can't be good. Let's go."

Chapter Thirty-Five

It's Annoying to Have Motivated Enemies

Connor entered the conference room close on the heels of Shona, with Hamish and Verena right behind. Their friends already gathered around the table looked worried. Anika grinned at Verena, but that was the only happy sign Connor saw. Several junior officers and other aides were rushing in and out, bringing papers and scrolls to Rory and Ivor, and getting new orders from them.

"What happened?" Shona demanded.

Rory gestured them to take seats. "I'm glad you came quickly. We have word from our asset in Donleavy."

The conference table was packed, not only with their core team, but with several other high ranking officers, and even hawk-nosed Lord Nevan. Not everyone in the room new Ailsa's identity, and Connor did not miss Rory's choice of words. Ailsa's position was critical to their cause, but incredibly dangerous. It was a miracle the queen had not yet discovered her true allegiance, but if she ever did Connor did not doubt Ailsa would die a gruesome death.

Or worse, she would be mind wiped and reeducated. The queen could pull far too much information about their activities in Obrion from her, including her vast network of spies, informants, and secret allies. Ailsa's fall could strike a mortal wound to the revolution even before a single soldier took a step toward Merkland.

They seated themselves and Kilian said, "The report suggests the queen does believe at least Verena, Hamish, and Ivor are dead, and Connor captured and nullified. The sculpted scone attack also succeeded in terrifying her."

Connor exchanged a victory fist bump with Hamish who said, "Told you sculpted scones would prevail."

"They did no real damage, but terrified her like nothing anyone has seen since her awakening."

"Is there a clue what she fears about Builders?" Verena asked, and Connor leaned forward eagerly. That vital bit of information would be worth more than all the armies they had massed for war.

Kilian dashed that hope by shaking his head. "Only vague clues. Our asset suggests they will keep digging. However, the sculpted scones attack also drove her into a towering fury. Generals Aonghus and Rosslyn were dispatched to join her main army massing at Crann."

Hamish growled, "Aonghus." His expression turned furious and his fists clenched the edge of the table. Connor shared his rage, and for a moment saw the horribly disfigured Jean lying outside the Army gate, burned almost beyond recognizing, on the brink of death.

"Crann's not too far from here," Connor said softly, his mind full of sweet images of gruesome revenge.

"We could get there tonight," Hamish agreed with a truly malicious glint in his eyes.

"Table that idea," Kilian said, his voice soft but somehow piercing. His eyes were glinting with points of ice, and Connor's objection died in his throat as he meet Kilian's steady gaze.

"But . . ." Hamish protested.

"The time for vengeance will come, but it's not today. Don't get distracted. Aonghus is not our problem right now. The army is, as is the fact that my mother left with one advisor to raise another worthy servant."

The words were like a slap to the face. Connor looked to Verena, whose face had paled. Shona looked terrified. Hamish asked, "Another Harley?"

Connor tried to wrap his head around the grim news, Aonghus forgotten, along with the joy he'd been feeling from discovering the ancient super-mechanical.

General Wolfram said, "The good news is that it sounds like although she raised at least three elfonnel from slumber in locations across Obrion, she has so far failed to find one she considers worthy."

Hamish dropped a smashpacked dessert he was preparing to pop into his mouth. "I really hate that woman. She has ruined my appetite more days than I can count."

Verena snatched up the smashpacked cube and popped it into her mouth. "I wish the only thing we had to worry about was your appetite."

Connor appreciated her attempt at humor, but wished he'd reacted faster. The dessert she'd just stolen looked like one of those Althing chocolate cakes.

Kilian said, "The report suggests the elfonnel she raised had lost too much of their humanity and could not be restored."

"She could still send those elfonnel against us, right?" Lady Briet asked. She looked as worried as the rest of them, even though she had never seen an elfonnel. She had read the reports, and obviously believed them, but the reality of elements come to life had to be experienced in order to feel the appropriate level of abject terror.

Kilian said, "It is possible, but unlikely. The elements are still rather unstable, particularly up here near the border. Elfonnel are very powerful, but extremely difficult to control once released. I doubt she would risk unleashing one here and potentially destabilizing the area like happened at the Carraig. My mother is ruthless, but she wants an intact kingdom to rule, not a wasteland. Besides, she alone is more dangerous than a handful of elfonnel."

He was right. And of course those words made almost everyone turn to look at Connor, their expressions a mixture of desperate hope or outright fear. It was no secret that he would have to face the queen. Even though his powerful friends would fight at his side, his responsibility would be the greatest. They had to be wondering the same thing he was. Could he do it?

His fear whispered that she'd obliterate him. Then she'd kill Verena and everyone around the table. Then his family. Then lay waste to the rest of the continent.

No. Somehow he had to stop her. He focused on that determination to protect the ones he loved, and it helped displace some of his fear. He simply could not fail. No one had ever figured out how to destroy the queen, but he and his friends had to.

So he said, "That's why I have to get the Jagdish right away."

"That's not the only reason," Kilian added solemnly. "This latest report suggests that the queen plans to move personally against Jagdish too."

Connor rocked back in his seat, as if the words had struck physical blows. Jagdish, the home of the Mhortair, was the one place he needed to reach before the queen. "How soon?"

Kilian shrugged. "She's already on the move. I don't know if she's planning on attempting to raise any other servants, or if she's abandoned that effort entirely."

Verena grimaced. "I want to say I hope she abandons her attempt to raise another Harley, but if she does, she could already be heading for Jagdish."

"And if she does find a new mighty Petralist to restore, that could fundamentally change the war," General Rory said with a grimace.

"Either way, the threat is imminent. My mother can cover a lot of distance when she wants to," Kilian said.

Aifric nodded. "She won't wait long. No doubt she understands that by removing them, she removes Connor's opportunity to ascend and become a real threat."

Hamish dug a cream-filled pastry out of one of his pockets. "Then what are we waiting for? We have to get to Jagdish before she does."

The pastry looked remarkably intact. He'd talked about experimenting with pocket-sized shielding. If he started doing that more often, Connor might actually consider accepting some of the sweets that he proffered from those pockets.

They had always assumed when the queen moved against Jagdish she would bring with her the army that had been marshaling in Raineach all winter. Moving with an army would slow her down dramatically.

Lady Briet must have been thinking along those lines because she said, "Our forces outside of Maninder were supposed to help intercept any invading army, but they can't face the queen."

She would wipe them out. Connor shuddered to think of the resulting slaughter if Queen Dreokt focused her wrath on that army and the helpless population of the great Ravinder city.

Kilian said, "I doubt she'll deign to deal with a mundane Arishat League army. Even the Mhortair pose little real threat to her, but they dared attack her on her throne. She will raze Jagdish to rubble when she arrives."

Student Eighteen looked sick with fear. "For so many reasons, my people are in grave danger."

Hamish muttered, "I still can't believe that attempt against her failed. They were so close."

"I doubt they were as close as you thought," Kilian said. "I know they cut her into pieces, but that's never stopped her before. I've seen her dismembered, burned, and crushed. She recovered from *all* of it. Those kind of wounds tend to just really irritate her."

"How do we stop her?" Connor asked in a small voice. He possessed a strong healing affinity, but the thought of getting dismembered and trying to fight on made him feel sick.

"We can't until you ascend," Kilian said simply.

He knew that was true, but hearing it still made his mouth suddenly dry.

"You'll get there in time. You have to," Shona said, giving him an encouraging smile. "And at least if her army is marshaling to come against us here, they won't have her with them."

That offered a slim ray of hope. Ailsa had reported on how the queen had swelled her army with hundreds of new Petralists. Even without the queen, they would prove a daunting force.

General Wolfram added, "Knowing that Dreokt is on the move changes everything. Imagine the risk if we had no advanced warning?"

As usual, Wolfram was right. Ailsa's work was vital, but Connor still felt terrified for his aunt. It sounded like she'd risked a lot to even get that much intelligence to them. He loved her brilliant mind, her daring courage, and her dedication to their cause despite the unprecedented risks she took. He just did not like to think about anyone else he cared about getting hurt.

Shona's expression remained remarkably calm in the face of the news that her beloved city was finally going to face battle again. "Generals, we need to initiate our defensive plans at once."

Ivor gestured at the papers on the table in front of him. "Our forces are well prepared. I believe we can stop the army, but not if we all travel to Jagdish."

Verena said, "Many of those defenses need Builders to run them. Most of the Builders are still en route with the reinforcements."

General Wolfram said, "We've already dispatched messages via speakstone to encourage them to accelerate the march. Windriders were dispatched just prior to this meeting to bring in some of the Builders and most powerful Petralists. Chances are good the rest of the army will arrive before the queen's forces."

Shona still looked worried. "But there's a chance they won't. We cannot abandon the defenses of my city. Merkland is too important to allow it to fall."

Rory and Ivor nodded agreement and Kilian said, "Agreed. We have to prove that one city can remain free."

Verena spoke up. "And don't forget the powerful new weapon we just discovered."

"What weapon?" Rory and Ivor asked together.

Verena declared proudly, "With Shona's help, we discovered the keystone Kirstin set up to activate a remarkable super-mechanical we've dubbed Kirstin's Defense."

Connor gripped Verena's hand. Her enthusiasm was back, and he loved how her eyes glowed when she spoke of Builder discoveries. He appreciated that she'd given Shona some of the credit, especially after that hilarious race to the tower.

Hamish added, "It links to eight sculpted soapstone, arrayed around Merkland in a ring about a mile out."

They looked exuberant about that find, although Connor did not doubt they also felt incredibly annoyed by the queen's bad timing. They needed time to study it.

As if reading his thoughts Shona said, "We did find it, but we don't yet know what it does."

Hamish added quickly, "That doesn't mean we couldn't activate it if we had to. That would be the best way to tell what it does. Right in the queen's face."

Verena said, "But that's not the ideal solution. Better to understand it first. It appears to utilize additional higher-level Builder skills that we do not yet understand. It would be a tragedy to waste this opportunity to learn."

Shona said gravely, "War requires hard choices. If it comes to choosing between saving that mechanical for research or using it to save the city, we must be prepared to unleash it."

Verena looked like she wanted to argue, and the two held each other's gazes for a moment. Connor bet they were communicating all sorts of things with that look, but he didn't feel even a little tempted to tap chert. He knew they hated each other, and only hoped they could avoid coming to blows.

General Wolfram said, "I like that we have a secret weapon as a last resort, although with the additional defenses we've already implemented, hopefully we won't need it."

Connor hated the idea of leaving some of his friends in Merkland to face danger without him, but he could see no way around it. "I still need to head to Jagdish."

Kilian nodded. "Without question, and I must come with you."

Student Eighteen did not entirely look convinced that was a good idea but said, "It's best if we keep our group as small as possible. We've been in touch with my people, but we don't want them to think we're an invading force."

Kilian gave her a wink and that roguish smile. "It would be unfortunate if I had to kill a few of them before you could convince them we meant no harm."

Student Eighteen opened her mouth to object, but the door opened and Tomas and Cameron rushed inside. Connor was surprised to see them. He had figured they would be assigned to rouse the garrison and review defensive preparations from the Fast Rollers. Then he noticed they were carrying a piece of quartzite.

The two men threw quick salutes to Rory and Ivor and nodded toward Shona in what Connor expected was the only bow she ever received. Then they rushed to Rory and presented the speakstone.

Tomas said, "Urgent news from Anton, General."

Cameron added, "Much better receiving it this way, Sir. Last time he rose up out of the floor without warning, nearly gave us heart stomps."

Connor had feared time was short. Suddenly he felt a growing conviction that they were simply out of time.

CHAPTER THIRTY-SIX

Nothing Is Ever Easy

Connor leaned forward, listening intently as Rory held up the speakstone and said, "Anton, this is Rory. You have news?"

Anton's deep voice echoed through the room. "The pedra rules over life and death while in the skies, but even the mighty warrior can be smothered by a pillow in his sleep."

The news couldn't be all that bad if he was speaking in Sentry speak. Connor felt a little of his worries subside, even though the words seemed unusually grim from the great Sapper.

Rory seemed used to dealing with Sentries and he did not miss a beat. "We're in battle conference right now. Is this immediate?"

"As immediate as a swarm of summoned creatures moving against Merkland at speed, barely ten miles out."

Connor's sense of security evaporated. He scowled at the speakstone. It was a rotten trick to lull him like that. Now he could never trust that any indecipherable Sentry speak was not critical intelligence.

Rory clenched one fist, his expression making it clear he wanted to throttle Anton for not speaking plainly earlier, but he refrained.

Kilian interjected. "If you sense them ten miles out, she's not even trying to shield them."

"I doubt even she could shield this host. They cover the land like a plague of locusts for at least half a mile downriver."

Connor felt a chill of fear creeping down his spine. They'd heard the queen was creating summoned monsters, but who could imagine even she could create so many?

Looking grim, Wolfram asked, "Can you estimate a number?"

"Thousands at minimum, and those are only the ones I can sense through the earth."

"Thousands," Connor whispered, exchanging a worried look with Verena. During the battle of Merkland, they had fought Harley's summoned hounds with their own small army of summoned creatures that Connor had dubbed the Famcakes, but they'd barely created a hundred. How could Queen Dreokt have summoned thousands, let alone control them?

"Can you summon creatures to intercept?" Verena asked Connor.

"Not enough to make a difference. Not in time," he told her, hating that he couldn't give her better news.

She muttered a soft curse, brows furrowing. No doubt she was already calculating how to best apply their layered defenses. She had overseen many aspects of their design and knew them better than anyone, but they'd never imagined dealing with such a host.

Lady Briet asked, "Can you sense if the army is on their heels?"

"Negative."

That was two clear sentences in a row. The day was shaping up to be terrible.

Verena said, "I wonder why she didn't save them until the army was in position? A double strike like that would probably crush us."

Kilian said, "She most likely assumes her swarm will breach the walls and wreck Merkland. She has never really considered her armies more than status symbols, forces best utilized for occupying territory she has already conquered."

Rory grimaced. "On any other day, she might be right. We're lucky we have all of you here, but we don't have much time." He turned to Tomas and Cameron. "Issue the general alert. Activate all defensive measures."

Verena added, "Shona, I recommend we initiate the Tomb Protocol."

Everyone turned to her and Shona's already pale face whitened further. "You have such little faith in the defenses you designed?"

"Not at all, but we've got twenty thousand civilians in the city. You heard Anton. Thousands of summoned creatures. We can't afford to underestimate them."

Shona held Verena's gaze for a moment, and Connor silently willed them to set their differences aside for the sake of the city. Shona nodded. "You're right. See it done and add the Overrun Directive to it."

They weren't holding back. Everyone hoped for victory, but with such a swarm closing on them, even the famous walls of Merkland might not be enough. Verena nodded and said softly, "We'll spare all we can."

"If my people survive, we can rebuild the rest," Shona stated. She glanced around the table at everyone watching the two of them and added sharply, "Let's move, people!"

Tomas and Cameron rushed out, along with most of the military officers. Connor heard Tomas say, "That boy always brings the fun with him."

"Barely landed this morning too," Cameron added.

Sometimes Connor wished he could see the world through the lens of how good a bash fight each challenge presented. Maybe the two of them were right and thinking was overrated. His thoughts were just making him scared.

Anika rose, kissed Rory's cheek and said, "I go help Erich prepare the Crushers." She chased after the other two, her expression eager, as if she didn't get to bash fight with Rory every single day.

Verena said, "I'll order the Albatross into the air. They can provide air support and scan for additional threats, like any flying monsters."

That was a good idea, but Connor hoped they wouldn't see any flyers. The ground swarm sounded like more than enough.

General Wolfram turned to Lady Briet. "I recommend you ascend with the Albatross."

"So I'm not a liability here on the ground?" she asked with a half-smile.

"Not at all. I need a skilled observer to monitor from the air and relay intelligence to me."

It was a good idea, and she appeared to accept it at face value. She excused herself to find the Builder Verena told her would take the Albatross up. Connor appreciated Wolfram's cleverness. No doubt both he and Lady Briet had already considered the ramifications to their alliance if the battle went poorly.

If summoned monsters breached the walls, they might wreak terrible destruction. Lady Briet was the overall leader of the Arishat League alliance, and if she was killed, her death could hamper or even shatter the recently formed defensive pact.

Ivor rose. "I'm off to the river. If the queen is sending so many by land, she may be sending water-bound creatures as well."

Shona said, "As we rouse the rest of our forces, we'll send our Spitters to assist."

Battle had come to Merkland too soon. They weren't quite ready, and as Connor watched his friends rushing off to face the deadly threat, he couldn't imagine leaving them. He glanced from Verena to Student Eighteen, and then to Kilian. "We have to stay and help."

Kilian shook his head. "You said yourself, it's most vital that we get you to Jagdish immediately. If we stay here and get distracted, those extra hours might prove the difference between arriving in time to meet with the Mhortair or arriving to find their city a smoking ruin."

Connor started to protest but Verena placed a hand over his. "They're right, Connor. You have to go. No matter what happens to Merkland, it does not change the fact that the knowledge you need from the Mhortair is more important than any of us."

He hated the fact that she was right. Connor always felt driven to step into the heart of danger. Not only because he was uniquely gifted to fight it, but if he did not do it that meant one of his friends would be forced to take the risk in his stead.

Hamish had nearly died keeping Harley distracted during the battle of Merkland, Verena had nearly died supporting Kilian when her second Swift crashed, and Ilse had been brutally crushed. Her husband Lukas, Mattias, and many others had paid the ultimate price, and of course Jean's terrible injuries served as a daily reminder of the risks they all faced.

Verena shook her head, dashing his hope that at least she would be spared having to go into battle without him again. "I'm staying here."

"Verena—" he started protesting, but she tilted her chin in that way he found adorable, her expression challenging.

She gripped his hand as his words failed him and said, "We don't have enough Builders to activate all of our defenses. We lack time to fly in those reinforcements. Besides, I know them better and can manage more of them than anyone else."

"She's right," Hamish said simply.

Connor scowled at him and even Verena looked incredulous. He grinned and added, "Not about the fact that you can do more. That's just a little Grandurian-noble pride that you haven't worked through yet. You're still the one who should stay and take care of it." He added to Connor, "Don't look at me like that. You know she's right. Verena in battle fury even gives you pause before you try to kiss her."

He had a point, but Connor still didn't like it.

Hamish continued. "I'll fly you to Jagdish in the Hawk. I have more experience with the Mhortair than Verena does. Student Eighteen and I were there when her dad almost killed old Dreokt. Together we can share that story. From what Student Eighteen has told me, a good death battle story will win them over better than even Althing chocolate."

Rory rose. "Figure it out. I'll expect one of you Builders to run the mechanicals. We have work to do. Anton, we'll prepare our Sentries to support you, but how far out can you begin initiating defensive measures?"

"I have already begun. Keep the other Sappers and Sentries closer to Merkland. I will do what I can to slow the swarm."

Connor stared at the speakstone, mouth agape. He knew how devastating autonomous summoned creatures could be. He, Kilian, Ivor, and Ilse all together had fought to support their Famcakes against Harley's hounds. Connor couldn't imagine standing alone against thousands.

Verena said, "Anton, I advise you to retreat to the one mile point. I'll be able to provide support at that range."

"Negative, Builder. I will maintain a buffer at two miles. You will have time to prepare for the swarm that passes."

"Be careful," she urged, looking close to tears. Connor did not know Anton terribly well, but Verena had known him all her life. Connor knew Verena hated seeing friends step into danger as much as he did.

He took her face in his hands and said, "You be careful."

She kissed him quickly and flashed that predatory grin of hers that she usually wore right before a fight. Luckily he no longer feared her punching him in the face after kissing him, but he still enjoyed the thrill he felt knowing he was courting such a dangerous woman.

"Go. Hurry, or you'll waste your chance." Then she rose and hurried after the others. Connor watched her go, feeling that heart-freezing terror that he'd felt during her coma. He'd feared he would never see her awaken again. Now he wondered if he was watching her walk away for the last time. He should tell her a thousand more things, but he couldn't seem to find any words.

The door closed behind her with a finality that made him cringe, leaving him alone with Hamish, Aifric, and Kilian.

Kilian was scowling, and Hamish wasn't even chewing on anything. They were as worried as Connor. Kilian said, "Let's move out. We have a lot of ground to cover."

As they headed outside, the palace buzzed with energy as soldiers raced in every direction, shouting commands and donning armor. The swarm was coming fast, but Merkland would be fully mobilized in moments.

"I wish I had a couple of Juggernauts here," Hamish muttered as they all climbed into the Hawk and strapped in.

"Me too," Connor said.

Hamish activated the window shielding, opened the release rate on the thrusters, and lifted the Hawk smoothly into the air. As they ascended vertically over the city, Connor leaned out to study the view.

Soldiers were streaming from barracks up onto the wall. Teams of engineers were assembling catapults, ballistae, and some of the new siege mechanicals around the city. Once they reached a thousand feet, Hamish activated the rear thrusters and accelerated rapidly south, along the river.

"Ravinder is farther to the east," Student Eighteen pointed out.

"I know, but I want to see the swarm and forward it to Verena via sightstone so she can have a visual."

"Just don't get distracted," Kilian warned, but he made no other objections. Connor was glad of that. He wanted to see the swarm, although he feared that seeing it would only make him fear for Verena's safety even more.

Hamish had activated speakstones that paired with Verena, Ivor, and Rory. As they flew, they listened to the rapid mobilization effort.

"Contact," Ivor suddenly called from his position sliding along the surface of the river, just south of the bridge between Merkland and the township. "I sense at least several hundred more water-bound creatures." He whistled softly, his tone turning awed. "The entire river is full of them, closing on the two mile mark from the city."

Shona must have been linked into the conversation through one of the others because she responded. "Can you stop them?"

"I've already engaged, but there's no way I can stop them all." Ivor sounded tense and a little distracted, suggesting he was already fighting a long-distance battle.

Connor's tension grew and he gripped the rail in front of his seat, wishing he could do more than look down at the river. Ivor was fighting for his life, but from their height he could not see the danger. Hamish did not slow or bank the Hawk to magnify the view, so Connor tapped quartzite to his eyes. The view swept closer, as if he was diving on the back of a pedra instead of riding level in the Hawk.

A couple miles south of Merkland, he caught sight of the swarm in the river. The entire surface of the water churned and boiled. He saw glimpses of limbs and tentacles and enormously fanged mouths. They seemed to vary dramatically in size and shape.

Some of the creatures lunged out of the water, looking like fish, but with legs and sickle-like arms. Others galloped along the surface, like enormous horses, hooves crackling with fire. Many of them sported the deadly jaws of pedras or many-tentacled arms with suckers. Others carried scorpion-like stingers.

"I have visual," Hamish declared in the remarkably calm voice he usually assumed during a fight.

Connor was struggling to find his fighting calm. He glanced forward and had to release quartzite because Hamish had activated the long-vision aspect of the front viewscreen and the double magnification effect gave Connor an instant headache. The swarm of land creatures was even more dense than the river swarm had been.

The land seemed to writhe under the dense tangle of hideous summoned creatures, flowing north like a deadly tide. Monsters clawed over each other in their single-minded drive to reach the walls of Merkland. Whatever Anton had been doing did not seem to have accomplished much.

Thousands upon thousands of monsters remained. Some were small, shaped like sleek nualls or thick-jawed hunting hounds. Others were fashioned like armored torcs or even larger creatures that Connor couldn't identify. They seemed to be bursting with long fangs, deadly claws, or burning breath.

Aifric whispered, "Creeping blade of death, there are so many!"

Connor did not see Anton. He wouldn't be surprised if the mighty Sapper had sunk into the earth to protect himself from the swarm as they passed, but as he studied the road, he suddenly spotted Anton's work.

A series of walls erupted out of the ground in front of the leading ranks of the monsters. A dozen feet wide, they reared over twenty feet in just a couple heartbeats. For a second Connor was not sure what Anton was doing because a staggered series of short walls like that would not slow that swarm at all.

Then the walls started to move. As the swarm of creatures boiled over and around them, some toppled forward with tremendous force, smashing to pieces any creatures caught beneath them. New walls rose immediately behind the first and slammed down in turn, like a giant waterwheel half sunken in the earth. Other walls smashed together, crushing monsters between them.

It was an excellent display of earth mastery, but did not seem to slow or even significantly thin the horde. With sinking dread, Connor realized that maybe they had underestimated the danger. "We have to help."

Hamish reached for one of the controls, clearly in agreement, but Kilian grabbed their shoulders from his seat behind them. He spoke in a kind but firm tone. "Don't get distracted."

"But," Connor and Hamish said in unison.

"Our friends are indeed facing danger, but they are prepared. Trust them just as they trust us. If they fail, people will die. If we fail, everything is lost. Keep that in mind. We cannot afford to waver, not now."

Connor twisted in his seat, seething with fear and a driving desire to do something, anything. "They're going to die. You realize that, don't you?"

"Every battle is dangerous. If we delay, we might save a few lives for a few days, or even weeks, but might guarantee the death of everyone we know. Are you willing to take that chance?"

Connor wanted to smash something. He *needed* to help, but Kilian was right. He spun back around to face out the viewscreen at the tide of destruction rushing in its unstoppable wave toward Merkland and Verena. His hands shook with the need to unleash his affinities and he trembled with the barely suppressed urge to leap out of the Hawk and plunge down into that seething mass of monsters and rain destruction upon every monster that dared threaten the woman he loved.

But all he could do was watch, hating himself, hating Kilian, and most of all hating the Queen for forcing him to gamble with the lives of his loved ones.

Hamish blew out a breath and activated a sightstone set in the front panel of the Hawk. "Verena, are you seeing this?"

She gasped. "So many."

Aifric suddenly cried, "Contact! We have flying monsters."

She pointed a little bit to the left, and only then did Connor notice the dark, fast-moving clouds churning through the air in their direction. The entire horizon was blackened by their numbers. He'd been too distracted by the land and water swarms and had thought the dark clouds were a storm blowing in.

As Hamish magnified the view, Connor's heart sank. The sky was filled with hundreds of flying monsters. Some of them looked like enormous pedras that made the great stone pedra that Kilian and Ilse had summoned so long ago seem like a baby. Others looked like giant eagles, while others were weird creations of nightmare.

Some looked made from leather like that strange inflatable-bag elemental monster that attacked Shona, while others sported long torsos with many limbs, capped in razor claws. Still others had multiple heads, with enormous, fang-filled jaws, many of which spurted flames.

Verena muttered a Grandurian curse that Connor had learned from her that winter. "I'm glad you spotted them. We weren't looking into the air at all yet."

"Do you want us to engage?" Hamish asked, hand again reaching for the controls.

Kilian started to speak but Verena said, "No. Get out of there. You have your own job to do. We'll activate the shielding. The siege mechanical operators haven't had nearly enough target practice. Looks like they'll get all they can handle today."

Connor appreciated her optimism, but she wasn't fooling anyone. The city-wide shielding was not designed to stop a swarm like that.

"Roger. Disengaging," Hamish said, but pivoted the Hawk in the air to face the distant swarm. Every missile packed under the Hawk's stubby wings leaped away, driven by marble thrusters. Connor silently wished them on, but even if every one of the dozen missiles killed a monster, they wouldn't make a dent in that swarm.

"Well done," he told Hamish anyway. Seeing those missiles away helped ease some of his towering frustration at running while Verena and everyone inside Merkland fought for their lives.

Lady Briet spoke, connected to them through Rory's line. "We have visual from the Albatross. These long vision viewports are incredible. We will begin targeting from here."

"Thank you," Verena said.

Connor had forgotten all about the Albatross, but knowing that they were already engaging helped a little.

"I approve the missiles," Kilian said as Hamish banked the Hawk in a long turn to the west. "They won't make much difference, but thank you for giving us that much."

Hamish said, "Aifric, I hope your people understand the risk we're taking today. If they don't help us, they will regret it."

She gripped his shoulder and said softly, "We'll make them listen."

Connor hoped she was right because he agreed with Hamish. As they accelerated toward the west, he turned in his seat and watched the swarms closing on Merkland with terrible fear eating at his heart and a heart-wrenching certainty growing in his mind.

He was leaving Verena behind to die.

CHAPTER THIRTY-SEVEN

Desperate Times Call for Desperate Measures

Verena rushed onto the great wall of Merkland, which was already crowded with soldiers. The mobilization was progressing as well as she had dared hope. Everyone knew the danger and understood that when the queen struck, they would receive the hammer blow of her fury. Rory, Ivor, Shona, and their officers had worked hard through the winter to prepare everyone to leap to their stations and duties without needing orders when the alarm was raised.

She pressed through the crowds of soldiers, heading toward the gatehouse over Army gate. The morning air was cool and calm, the sky bright. So different than the blizzard they had fought in the last time an army attacked Merkland. It was loud. Sergeants bellowed orders, soldiers called out statuses, and their armor creaked as they made last minute adjustments.

Sirens wailed across the city, rising and falling in the pattern that warned all citizens to get below ground. Forty-seven giant caverns had been excavated beneath the city and heavily fortified by Sentries and Sappers. They could each hold two thousand people and included food and water for two weeks, as well as Builder lightstones.

Once each filled with their allotment of civilians, Sentries would seal them shut, and a Builder team would activate every possible type of shielding available. They should remain impervious to all but relentless assaults by experienced Sentries. Verena dearly hoped the mindless summoned creatures would fail to sense them.

She planned to give the monsters plenty of more active targets to focus on.

Time was short, but Verena paused at the platform of one of the new Builder siege-defense weapons. The sight of the amazing invention gave her hope. It looked rather unassuming, just a padded chair on a swivel base that allowed the Builder operator to rotate in any direction and angle back nearly prone.

The chair sat on a heavily reinforced steel cube. That's where the magic happened. A basalt tube a full six feet long and six inches in diameter, reinforced with steel and quickened granite, rose from the cube. That was the launch tube, and it rotated with the operator seat, giving it an unparalleled field of fire.

Six smaller, squat tubes, three on each side, filled with ammunition, acted as feeders into the cube. Each round of ammunition looked like a cylinder with a rounded top. The ordinance was driven by a blast of compressed air.

It acted on similar principles to the speedslings, only with much bigger ammunition. The operator would set the triple-layered basalt acceleration drum contained within the cube rotating. Each round of ammunition would be inserted into the drum for initial acceleration. When it released up the acceleration ramp, driven by compressed air, its speed would double again. The launch tube, lined with basalt doubled the speed yet again so that the shells shot away at shocking speeds.

The weapons had only been delivered to Merkland a couple weeks prior, and Verena was glad the shipment had not been delayed. A young Builder named Marwin was already strapping in as the operator. Several assistants were working to load different types of ammunition into feeder tubes.

They were not nearly as destructive as the enormous elfonnel-busting Last Word bombs they had developed before the battle of Altkalen. These were smaller, designed with the intention of blasting max-tapped Boulders to splinters. Should work equally well on summoned creatures.

"Are you ready?" she asked.

Marwin nodded eagerly, looking nervous and excited at the same time. He patted the long delivery tube. "Show me a target."

The ammunition fed into the acceleration cube included high explosive rounds, reinforced quickened granite penetrator rounds, and others. The mechanical could release thirty rounds per minute.

Verena gestured into the sky. "Your primary duty will be to defend against airborne attackers."

"Really?" Marwin asked, his grin fading.

She nodded. "We have visual confirmation of a swarm of flying monsters. Those of you not facing directly south or over the river will be tasked with defending the city from aerial attack. I'm heading inside to activate the shield before we trigger the sentinel stands."

Marwin gripped his controls. "We'll be ready."

They had all better be, because from what she'd seen of those swarms, they would be challenged to the breaking point. She concealed her worries, patted his shoulder, and rushed inside.

Behind her, she heard the low humming as Marwin activated the shielding around his mechanical. Those shields had been another recent breakthrough. They would protect the entire mechanical but leave a tiny gap where the ammunition could fire through.

Verena still struggled to make those selective gaps in shields. It was one of the few mechanicals that challenged her creative abilities. Hamish had figured out the concept, and he was the one who had created the shielding for all of those siege weapons. His mind worked in a twisted enough way that the mind-bending process seemed natural for him.

In the guardhouse she found a number of officers and technicians manning one of four banks of speakstones distributed around the wall. They were connected to officers all across the city, and could coordinate immediate information sharing. The room already buzzed with dozens of conversations. Most of the officers spoke calmly, but she could read their emotions, ranging from eager anticipation to barely suppressed fear.

They would hold. There was no other choice. Summoned creatures would show no mercy. The men and women stationed in the guardhouse waved, but Verena did not stop to chat. She descended a ladder through a hole in the floor to a reinforced bunker under the tower.

It consisted of a small, round chamber with a padded command chair on a swivel column in the center. Verena settled into the chair, which always seemed a little too comfortable for the deadly tasks it allowed her to perform. The arms of the chair included a series of controls. Small sculpted obsidian stones allowed her to connect to most of the mechanical defenses scattered around the city.

Verena scanned them with her Builder senses, feeling her confidence grow as she sensed all those mechanicals ready to come alive at her will. The sight of those swarms of monsters closing on the city had shaken her, but she settled into her battle calm. She knew autonomous summoned creatures could not think or feel emotions, but if they could they would soon regret invading during her watch.

First she activated a couple of remote sightstones, projecting their views onto the walls in front of her. Her command chair included tiny quartzite thrusters that allowed her to rotate so that she could use the entire curved wall for projecting viewscreens. The ones she activated gave her excellent views over the southern approaches to the city.

The monsters were still about two miles out, so those views were still secondary. Next she activated a piece of quartzite, connected to the most complex shielding array they had yet attempted. As soon as it activated, she rotated her chair and projected a view onto the blank wall behind her to watch it deploy.

Set in the top of the military command tower, that sightstone looked straight up. Hamish had thought it a silly place to put a sightstone, but Verena was glad now that she had insisted. The view showed her the sky above Merkland and clearly outlined the shimmering, amber glow of the shield she had just activated. The half dome was extending high above Merkland, stretching over the entire city.

Verena had depended upon shieldstones since the very first clash with Captain Rory's Fast Rollers in Alasdair, but they were a weird invention. One of the quirks of quartzite was that it allowed her to compress air in very defined areas, somehow forming a physical barrier that even Petralists struggled to penetrate. Shieldstones had saved her life more than once.

Now hopefully they could help save the city.

The enormous Merkland shield was powered by a complex array of linked quartzite, anchored to more quartzite pieces set just inside the walls. All together, they spread a softly glowing dome of protection over the entire city, anchored to the inside edges of the walls. That allowed the soldiers and Petralists to fight without getting stuck inside the shield.

They had debated if they should extend the shielding to the outer edge of the walls, but had finally decided that it made more sense to shield the inner city but not interfere with the work of the Petralists. She began to wonder if that had been such a good idea, but it was too late to change it now.

While Verena monitored the huge shield, she activated secondary shields that made up part of the Overrun Directive. Angled shields appeared a dozen feet above the walls, anchored to each watchtower, spreading canopies of protection a hundred feet in both directions. They would help a little against aerial attack, but not block the Petralists' abilities to respond. Those shields were mobile so if the wall was overrun, soldiers could carry with them the quartzite powering each section as they retreated to secondary fighting locations.

Even a few months ago, she would have scoffed at the idea of shielding an entire city, but they'd made so many breakthroughs that things that had seemed beyond miraculous were becoming reality. It was a marvelous time to be alive and to be a Builder.

Today she would need every trick, every ounce of power she could muster to protect her people from harm.

Once Verena confirmed the shield was up and active, she rotated her chair back around to the front wall and activated a speakstone linked to Ivor, and another one to Anton.

"Status?" she asked.

Ivor answered immediately, his tone tense, his words clipped. "Kind of busy. Water-born swarm has closed to almost the one mile mark. I'm doing everything I can, but there are so many of them, and they've got some kind of shielding along the front edge that makes it hard to target them."

"I've got a squad of six more Spitters moving downriver to reinforce you."

"Thanks. We're going to need all the help we can get." He hesitated, then added, "Unless I'm sensing this all wrong, it seems the queen created the water-bound summoned within bodies of water."

"Can she do that?" Verena asked, surprised, and really not happy about that. They couldn't deal with more surprises at the moment.

"We know it's possible to house the elements within different types of bodies. I just hadn't considered housing water-bound within water. It's going to make killing them a lot harder."

Verena muttered a curse as Anton spoke, his deep voice calm as always. "The mountain shakes under the mindless violence of the avalanche, but the rough stone is only smoothed by the passage of the waters."

"I take it you're still fighting them too," she said, allowing a little smile of relief. She had worried Anton would do something foolish or be swarmed under and destroyed by those monsters.

"The bonfire may pose less risk than a forest fire, but the hand thrust into its flames is burned just as severely," he replied, his tone tenser than usual.

"So I'm assuming that means you killed a bunch of them, but they still pose a dire threat." She loved Anton, but part of her wanted to reach through that speakstone and slap him.

The inventor part of her immediately started wondering if it was possible to invent a slapstone. She vowed never to voice that idea anywhere in Hamish's company.

"Sculpted scone," Anton responded, and actually sounded like he was smiling.

Verena groaned. "We got rid of that ridiculous codeword, you know?"

"Hamish informed me how much you loved it."

Ivor laughed and said, "If you can joke a time like this, things are either not as bad as I feared or they're so bad that I might as well stop worrying because we're all going to die."

"The swarm comes, and monsters of earth and fire have almost reached the one-mile mark," Anton said.

That was a critical point. Kirstin's Defense was located a mile out. Verena had no idea why it was situated so far, but it was possible any closer to the city might destabilize Merkland. She could still activate it, but did she dare?

Did she dare not?

"I still think we should send a squad of Sentries to support you," she offered.

"Negative. They will be more effective working from the wall. The land swarm just sensed my presence and are actively targeting me."

"Get out of there," Verena said instantly, her fear spiking again. She'd seen the swarm from a distance. Not even Anton could stand against it.

"They are employing a new form of shielding. Warn the others. I will continue to do what I can from here."

"Don't do anything rash," she cried, hating that her voice shook with her growing fear. Anton was legendarily powerful, but even he had limits. She couldn't bear to think of losing him as the first casualty to the swarm.

"I am activating the sentinels," she added.

Ivor said, "Good hunting."

Anton said, "Preparation places the hunter in the path of the charging torc, but the heart who fights for love wields a mightier blade."

Ivor grunted. "Like I said, good—"

His voice abruptly cut off with a cry of surprise.

"Ivor!" Verena cried, silently cursing as she scrambled to activate the sentinels. She needed to see what was going on.

"Some of them came in along the riverbed ahead of the others. Totally shielded." Ivor's voice sounded hoarse, still calm, but she could tell he was rattled. "They're smarter than they should be. They—"

Again his voice cut out.

"Ivor? No! Get out of there!" Verena screamed as the sentinels activated in her mind like distant candles.

Her first line of defense was situated three quarters of a mile south of the city. Four tall pedestals rose from the depths where they had been concealed.

Three rose in a line near the road, while the other rose up in the center of the river. As soon as they reached the surface, Verena activated the sightstones embedded within each one. The views appeared half a second later on the wall in front of her, replacing the previous ones.

The four views showed similar scenes, all facing south toward hordes of onrushing monsters. Verena gulped in rising fear as she stared at all of those summoned creatures tearing up the road and the river with single-minded purpose to kill everyone inside of Merkland.

She spotted a crenelated tower of earth standing near the road, already overrun by the front ranks of the land swarm. Monsters of all shapes and sizes were boiling over it in a tide of destruction. Even as Verena focused on it, the monsters ripped the tower apart, spraying dirt fifty yards in every direction. She saw no sign of Anton as the tide of destruction continued north, not even slowed.

"Anton? Tell me you got out of there!"

No response.

"Ivor? Ivor, talk to me."

No response.

She felt cold with fear, but could not allow the terror to control her. Verena had faced difficult battles before. "Stay calm," she urged herself, but staring at that fast-approaching swarm, her usual calm nearly cracked.

Then the rage hit.

Those monsters wanted to destroy everyone she had vowed to protect. And they would. Unless she killed them first.

"Spitter team one, fall back!" she ordered, switching to another speakstone line.

"Tallan's fury, look at that," one of them breathed. It was a woman's voice, mature, but shaken. At the moment, Verena couldn't remember her name.

"Get back to the city! Fortify the defenses and prepare for shielded monsters attacking from a quarter mile ahead of the main host."

"What about General Ivor?" the woman asked.

"Don't worry about Ivor. Just go. Now!"

Verena didn't wait for a reply, but switched to the main commander line. "The swarm is almost to the one mile mark. Ivor and Anton reported elevated intelligence and tactics. The front ranks of the swarms are protected by shielding. Pass the word and prepare."

"Can they retreat?" Rory asked, his voice grave, as if he already sensed the answer.

Verena refused to accept that Anton and Ivor might have died, but still had to report, "Communication was lost."

"It's happening too fast," Shona breathed.

"Focus! I am preparing to engage with the sentinels," Verena said, then switched off the line. She couldn't deal with any distractions.

Verena prepared to unleash the devastation poised within the sentinels, but the sight of those swarms, still numbering in the thousands, boiling toward her viewscreens gave her pause.

There were simply too many. Even if every round from every sentinel destroyed a monster, she would barely make a dent in the hordes stretching back as far as the viewscreens allowed her to see.

Merkland would never survive that tide of destruction. No wonder the queen hadn't sent her human armies with them. She didn't need them.

That thought infuriated Verena. No. She would not allow the city to fall. She could not hold back any possible weapon.

She had to activate Kirstin's Defense.

Chapter Thirty-Eight

An Unexpected Meeting

With lingering doubts whispering that she was making a terrible mistake, Verena launched herself out of her command chair and up the ladder to the tower command room.

"Builder Verena, what are you doing up here?" the officer in charge asked, looking worried.

"Spread the word that at least parts of the swarm are shielded. Prepare all forces for unrestricted engagement," she cried, but didn't slow. She tore across the room and up the stone stairs toward the roof, taking them three at a time.

The rooftop was crowded with soldiers and officers, all staring south toward the distant swarm. Even at over a mile away, Verena could clearly see the swarm covering the land in an undulating, black mass. The air was heavy with fearful whisperings and she felt the mood turning grim. Even a fool could see that they were doomed.

Not if she could help it.

Ignoring the calls from officers asking her what she was doing, Verena pushed through the crowd to the crenelated outer wall to the obsidian plaque. She paused for a second, staring at the inscription, her doubts rising again. She was about to destroy perhaps the most powerful link to higher forms of Builder power in existence. Activating that mechanical was no guarantee of survival, but it guaranteed the loss of critical knowledge.

She glanced over the wall at the distant swarm and her doubts wilted under simple truth. If she did not activate the mechanical, she and everyone in Merkland would die. No truths concealed within the mechanical could help them then.

"I hope you knew what you were doing," she whispered to Kirstin's memory.

Then Verena pressed her hand to the sculpted obsidian plaque and plunged her Builder senses into it.

The eight sculpted soapstone roared to life in her mind like distant bonfires. Verena reached for the one due south, situated in the river. It was the keystone of the entire higher mechanical. As soon as her mind touched it, Verena activated the first command to initiate the mechanical.

She wasn't sure what to expect, and now that she had committed to action, she felt a rising sense of excitement. Hamish would be so disappointed he wasn't there to experience it too, but she hoped the mission to Jagdish proved easier than her fight was about to be.

Her mind was swept into the super-mechanical as it activated. The eightfold matrix of master-sculpted soapstone linked together. In Verena's mind it was like sheets of silvery fire exploding from each stone and shooting across the space to the next stone, linking them all in an unbroken octagon of invisible power surrounding the city.

Then the entire landscape glowed silver in her mind, as if the sun had risen in her thoughts. Vast amounts of energy poured through that linked matrix of stones, more than even such a collection of sculpted stones should be able to produce.

Linked to the mechanical, Verena felt herself rising above the city in that silvery cloud, and for the first time in her life she sensed a gateway hovering unseen just above her. She gasped as understanding struck like a jolt of diorite.

A Builder threshold.

Thresholds only existed for Petralists, but she felt it as clearly as she'd ever felt Connor's strong hand in hers. She wanted to laugh with delight. It was awe inspiring. Dozens of questions arose in her mind, but she realized with a new sense of dread that she didn't understand how that higher mechanical was pushing her to that threshold. She might never again experience it.

So she had to reach it today.

Verena embraced the flow of power. Connor had said that to ascend, he had to unite with the element. She had never understood what that meant until now. She cast herself into the current of raw power, and it filled her in a way she'd never felt before. It was exhilarating!

Activating mechanicals was always a more external act for Builders than walking with elements or tapping other affinities was for Petralists, but this was different. Verena was one with the mechanical, infused with power that flooded her mind and filled her with peace.

It accelerated her thoughts, but her mind raced so fast she couldn't focus on the new ideas flashing through her mind. She sensed marvelous inventions, just out of reach, but if she paused to focus on any one of them, she sensed she would lose momentum and never make it to the threshold.

So she somehow lunged upward, swimming up through the silvery cloud of raw power and reached the threshold. She struggled to pull herself up through it, but her progress stopped right at the cusp of it. Something was missing, but she couldn't comprehend what it might be.

In that second a fresh wave of pure energy flooded down through the threshold in a torrent so mighty she scarce comprehended it. It swept her down into the matrix, carrying her mind along with it as that power plunged into the river, seized the great Macantact, and gave the waters a savage twist.

The river south of Merkland exploded a quarter mile into the air in a geyser so insanely huge it sucked all the water out of a hundred yard section. As if from a great distance, she heard the soldiers around her shouting in amazement. She wanted to tell them what was happening, but her body felt distant and inaccessible. That should bother her, but she was one with the water, and it filled her with joy and a sense of power unlike anything she'd ever known.

The swarm of summoned monsters paused as it neared the new barrier. They might be mindless killing machines, but even they could sense the threat of that mighty wall of water.

The waters did not plunge back into the river, but swept eastward, as if blown by an invisible hurricane. The cascading, blue tide boiled across the landscape, aimed directly at the spot where the next sculpted soapstone was buried. It picked up speed, sucking more and more water out of the Macantact, and Verena sensed even more water, buried deep underground erupting upward as it was caught in the pull of Kirstin's Defense.

When the flood reached the second sculpted soapstone, it again exploded high into the air, and the underground river joined the flood, doubling it. Waters rose over two hundred feet in a solid wall a full fifty feet thick. It continued to move, rapidly encircling the city, plowing across the landscape through trees and hills and roads, scraping a perfectly level furrow through everything as it circumnavigated Merkland.

It completed the circuit in moments, an eight-sided mega-manifestation of elemental water that mirrored the famous Merkland walls, only magnified a thousandfold. It was glorious, and it rivaled anything Verena had ever heard from the mightiest Petralists.

For a second, Verena feared the swarm would not dare the waters, that they would simply wait for the mechanical to exhaust itself. She sensed it could run for a long time, but would eventually peter out. Those soapstone sculptures were imbued with incredibly concentrated amounts of power, but staggering quantities were being consumed to keep the construct alive.

After their initial hesitation, the land swarm seemed to build upon itself as monsters piled atop monsters until they reared almost as high as the water barrier. Then one huge creature that looked like a rocky hill with squat legs that could plow right through Merkland without slowing, broke ranks and charged.

That triggered the entire swarm. Hundreds of monsters erupted into motion. The ones on top were flung high into the air, soaring right over the wall, some howling with blood lust, while others shot gouts of flame in front of them.

Verena blanched. She had never imagined the swarm might figure out how to leap the barrier wall. If they were that smart, Merkland was indeed in trouble.

In the river, the monsters had also massed, and they surged forward in a tight formation, attempting to spear right through the barrier wall.

Something seemed to click in Verena's mind as an additional stage of defense kicked in. The waters of Kirstin's Defense boiled higher, tendrils snatching at monsters attempting to leap over it. Those tendrils seized many of the monsters and yanked them down into the swirling depths.

It ate them.

Verena gasped in shock. With her mind connected to the mega-mechanical, she sensed the waters within the wall transform into icy spikes, arranged like interlinked gears in the most complex machine in the world. The ropy tendrils of water yanked earth and fire elemental monsters into those fast-spinning gears that tore them apart with unimaginable savagery.

Monsters exploded into muddy chunks or fiery clouds, but the gears of ice kept spinning, churning through more and more monsters. Feeling those many monstrous bodies torn apart in such an intimate way sickened her, but she still wanted to cheer.

Within the river, the first ranks of monsters that plunged into the swirling defensive wall met a similar fate. Churning gears of ice sucked them in and ripped them apart. The waters that gave them life were consumed and used to buttress the wall so that their demise only made the defenses stronger.

Verena wondered with sick horror what would have happened to any mortal army charging into that maelstrom of mechanical destruction.

The monsters kept coming, driven by their single-minded need to kill, to destroy, and to obey their master. At first the wall defenses stopped them all, and Verena lost count of how many of the swarm were ripped apart.

"Yes!" she exulted, surprising herself with the sound of her own voice, as if from a great distance. She'd been drawn in so deep, she was more part of the mechanical than separate from it. The experience was amazing, but as she recognized what was happening to her, she felt a growing sense of unease. If she lost herself in there, could she ever escape?

"*Wisdom in one so young is as rare as it is vital for survival,*" said a smooth female voice directly into her mind.

All of a sudden, Verena found herself standing in the midst of the watery wall. For a second she nearly panicked, but when she concentrated, she could still feel her body standing on the rooftop, one hand pressed to the plaque.

It was a strange experience. Her mind was somehow projecting into that space, as if the mechanical was forming a vision in her mind and she stepped into it. That was the kind of weirdness she'd expect from Connor.

An elegant woman appeared before her. Her face was flawless, but still somehow old. Her blue eyes seemed as deep as the ocean, and her long, greenish-blue tresses swayed behind her as if driven by gentle waves. She wore a shimmering, silvery gown that glittered like a thousand diamonds. No, it was as if she was wearing a gown of brightly polished scales. Ignoring the carnage around her, the woman approached through the waters.

"What is going on?" Verena asked, looking around nervously at the waters churning all around them, monsters getting ripped to elemental bits on all sides. She no longer felt it, as if she was standing in the midst of a sightstone viewscreen.

"*You have approached a threshold only one other has ever accessed. I wish I had sensed your coming sooner. Perhaps I could have prepared a more fitting greeting to one who walks the gateways to the sylfaen.*"

"Please, I don't know what that means. Who are you?" Verena asked. She sensed great power in the woman.

"*My name would mean nothing to you, but you may think of me as Water. That's how your friend Connor sees me.*"

For a second, Verena could only stare as the ramifications of those words resounded through her mind like ever-multiplying whispers. Finally she managed to blurt, "How? Connor said he sees you, but he never said anything about speaking with you like this."

"We have not yet spoken, but I hope he will succeed in crossing the final threshold to a bridge where my words can finally reach his ears."

"Tallan's mercy, this is hard to believe," Verena whispered.

Water surprised her by frowning. *"Tallan wasted his chance, but we have high hopes that Connor will finally prove a worthy candidate."*

"For what?"

"To act as our champion, of course," Water said with a wide smile.

Verena wanted to ask a thousand questions. Connor had started speaking of the elements as if they were people. At first Verena had thought that weird, but he seemed convinced they had personalities, and that those insights were helping him walk with them better.

Now she was speaking with Water? Could the elements really walk and talk like people? She'd always thought the term 'walking with the elements' more poetic than real, but what if it wasn't? The elements were so powerful, they might know how to stop Queen Dreokt.

She opened her mouth to speak, but in that second, Kirstin's Defense reached its limit. So many monsters plunged into it through the river or boiled up over the top of it from the land side that not even that mighty mechanical could stop them all. Thousands of summoned monsters were attacking Kirstin's Defense.

Hundreds got through.

Some were missing limbs or dripped fire in their wake like blood, but they resumed their charge toward Merkland. If Verena hadn't triggered Kirstin's Defense, Merkland would have been swarmed under for sure.

Even though she had, they still might not survive.

Kirstin's Defense had become so saturated with monsters that its power became overwhelmed. Verena sensed it reaching its upper limit and wanted to scream with frustration. Why couldn't it last just a few more minutes? She needed the information Water could provide as badly as she needed those monsters destroyed.

Water sensed it too. She cocked her head to the side and sighed, looking so sad that Verena wanted to weep. What truths could the elemental share with her?

"Go, daughter of men. Perhaps Builders will once again learn to step through this threshold and across the final bridge. Know that we hope for your success."

"Wait!" Verena cried, but Water saluted, and an invisible force cast Verena's mind out of the mechanical. She came to herself in a rush and staggered back from the plaque. The smooth obsidian cracked with a loud report, its power also spent.

Verena swayed and would have fallen, but a strong soldier caught her. "Easy, Lady Verena. What's wrong?"

"Was that you're doing?" Another woman asked. She wore the insignia of a Spitter, and her expression looked awed.

"It's coming down!" A soldier cried, and they all turned to look.

Kirstin's Defense collapsed. Waters cascaded down all around the city in a tidal wave miles in circumference. Verena imagined she could feel the ground shaking beneath the city like a death knell.

There were still too many summoned monsters. They could never stop them all.

"Prepare!" she shouted and pushed away from the soldier supporting her. She still felt weak, but couldn't waste time. She ignored shouted questions and plunged back down into the tower. She nearly fell on the steps, and had to lean on the stone wall for support.

"What's going on out there?" one of the officers inside called.

"We slowed them, but they're coming. All units prepare to engage."

Verena slid down the ladder, missing most of the rungs, but managed not to fall off. She dropped into her chair, her mind still reeling from the vision of Water and the incredible experience of feeling so immersed in that unbelievable mechanical.

She allowed herself one heartfelt shriek of frustration that the wall hadn't held longer. The sound reverberated many times in the tiny, enclosed command room. She'd been so close to learning so much! Was that why Kirstin had discovered so many Builder secrets? Had she learned the secret of a Builder threshold and crossed it?

Verena needed time to write down everything she'd experienced and time to try recreating that link, but she didn't have time. Merkland was still about to be overrun by a monstrous swarm that they could not stop.

So she reactivated the sentinels. Time to hunt.

Chapter Thirty-Nine

The Most Dangerous Predators Are the Smart Ones

Verena linked to the four sentinel towers, somehow sensing their various Builder parts more clearly than before. Was that because of what she'd just experienced, or just a side effect of greater focus forced upon her by the sight of hundreds of monsters already swarming past the towers?

Each of the sentinels acted as a remotely controlled siege weapon, similar in concept to the ones around the city, like the one being operated by Marwin. Frazier, the maze lord, had helped design the ingenious mechanicals. Instead of feeder tubes, all the ammunition was preloaded inside of each pedestal in a winding magazine built over powerful springs. Fully loaded with two hundred explosive rounds each, they were each capable of delivering devastating destruction upon any enemy foolish enough to close on Merkland.

Verena took a deep breath as the acceleration drums sped up. She activated a speakstone linked to the Albatross, high above the city. "This is Builder One. Status?"

Lady Briet answered. "Albatross here. We have engaged the flying swarm. Missiles and hornets do appear effective, but there are so many of them we're increasing our attack rate. We will exhaust our ammunition long before we significantly damage this horde."

"Do not return to the city to rearm. Keep your distance. Hopefully they'll ignore you. I recommend you reserve some rounds in case we need close support."

"Sculpted scone," she acknowledged.

Verena grimaced. She really needed to talk with Hamish about that codeword.

The monsters were proving far more resourceful than the few they'd dispatched through the winter. Time to thin their ranks.

The leading edge of both the earthen swarm and the water swarm were already passing the sentinels. They had ignored the towers, so that offered some hope. If their mission was to destroy Merkland, maybe they would focus on destroying the wall and the buildings instead of the people. From their work with Jean's summoned arm, she knew that commands needed to be specific, and miscommunication was easy.

All four weapons spooled up, and Verena grinned. It was a heady thing to control so much destruction with so little effort. Sometimes she worried how such an enormous power could be misused, but remotely activating weapons had saved her life at the battle of Merkland, and today she expected the mechanicals would save many more.

Each sentinel included a sighting reticle positioned just above the end of the barrel, but Verena did not need them. There were so many monsters, it would be impossible to miss. Even if she tried aiming straight up, she'd probably hit some of the flyers.

Verena activated all four Sentinels.

The deadly mechanicals began spewing destruction, and the highly explosive rounds blasted into the ranks of monsters on land and on the river. They produced instant and marvelous effects against the monsters on the land. Both earth-bound and fire-bound monsters disintegrated under the onslaught. Unfortunately, other fire-bound in the later ranks of the monsters seemed to absorb the flames from the explosions and only grow stronger.

Uh oh. They had not expected anything like that. There was nothing Verena could do about it though, and destroying all the earth-bound monsters would still give them a significant advantage so she kept the sentinels working.

The effects on the river were harder to judge. The sentinel tower in the river fired a different type of ammunition. Instead of high explosive rounds, it fired a penetrator round that could pierce deep into the water.

Many of the monsters remained underwater, while most of the monsters visible on the surface slipped beneath the waters when she opened fire. Verena could not tell if they were reforming, or dissipating. She wished Ivor could tell her if she was hurting them.

Then one of the views abruptly spun crazily. A second later it winked out.

"No!" Verena cried as she realized what was happening.

The monsters were attacking the sentinels.

She kept the others firing, but within seconds the other sentinels were ripped apart and she lost connection. She stared at the blank wall where the viewscreens had been for a moment, fighting a fresh wave of fear.

The monsters were smarter. They had sensed the danger and reacted to it.

She switched to viewscreens closer to the city to see the swarms closing to within half a mile. Kirstin's Defense had slaughtered thousands of them, but hundreds more remained. And when she glanced upward, her heart sank. The sky was blackened by the largely unchallenged flying horde. That swarm was almost upon Merkland and would rain destruction from above upon the walls.

She activated a speakstone linked to all of the siege weapons placed around the city. "All units, prepare to engage."

As a chorus of acknowledgments sounded in return she added, "Units seven through twelve along the river wall prepare your teams to repel water-bound invaders. The explosive rounds may work better once they leave the river, but units eight and eleven, I advise switching to harpoon penetrators."

Even if they lacked time to switch over the ammunition before the first wave swarmed out of the river, they would fast exhaust the ammunition in the feeder tubes. They could then reload whatever rounds they needed. They might well exhaust every round available.

That was assuming all of the siege platforms remained operable and weren't overrun, and that the reloading assistants were not killed.

No, she refused to think such negative thoughts. Verena switched to the command channel that was already buzzing with warnings from her team. "This is Verena. The sentinel towers are down. Preparing to transition mobile command to the Swift."

"Any word from Ivor or Anton?" Rory asked immediately.

"Negative," she said softly, the words catching in her throat. She hadn't even had time to mourn their loss. She feared before the day ended the list of brave soldiers they needed to mourn would grow terrifyingly long.

Shona spoke, her voice strong, her tone confident. "All forces are ready. We will give them no quarter. Prepare to defend the walls!"

"We will hold," Rory said with unshakable confidence. "We have to."

Verena appreciated the boost to her courage his words offered. If they were going to fight an overwhelming foe, she was proud to fight them in such mighty company.

Verena rose from her command chair. She'd activated everything she could from there. She had to get up on the wall. As she scrambled up the ladder, she allowed herself to think of Connor and hope he reached the Mhortair before Queen Dreokt.

They had to hold the walls. She couldn't imagine Connor returning victorious from ascending only to find Merkland a smashed ruin. She could not do that to him, could not leave him to face Queen Dreokt alone.

Verena reached the main floor of the Army gate just as every siege weapon began firing. In addition to the fast firing mechanicals, Merkland possessed a full complement of ballistae, catapults, and trebuchet. They fired much slower, but their huge missiles did tremendous damage, and the wall shook with the shuddering of heavy timbers as they delivered their deadly payloads.

The air thrummed with the rapid-fire whooshing sound of the siege mechanicals spitting projectiles and the staccato thunder of detonations. Soldiers were shouting and pointing, while reloading crews moved new ammunition into place as fast as they could move.

The swarm of earth and fire-bound monsters was pouring up the gently curving road, and the rain of destruction smashed into them with awesome force. Explosions rent lumbering monsters to pieces, but the swarm swallowed up the dead without seeming diminished, and more monsters poured over the remains, unhindered.

Other monsters were leaping straight up the cliff and walls of Merkland, tearing into hardened granite with claws strong enough to pierce the reinforced stone. Flames billowed up in vast clouds toward the defenders, and the air spiked twenty degrees hotter.

Flameweavers and Firetongues deflected the fires and worked to seize the flames from the monsters, while Spitters swept creatures from the wall with long, whipping tendrils of silvery liquid.

The ground outside rumbled, and grasping tendrils of earth shot up to trip monsters and rip them to pieces. As the swarm clawed through opposition toward the gate, Verena frowned. Their Sentries did not seem to be causing nearly enough damage. She spotted one weird, whip-thin monster that looked like a wolf's shadow somehow slip through grasping fingers of earth without damage.

The bank of speakstones behind her in the tower was squawking with officers shouting warnings of some kind of shielding blocking Petralist efforts.

"Tallan preserve us," Verena whispered as she stared down at the seething mass of wildly charging monsters. Their eyes glowed red with flame or stared with dead, black earthen pupils, hungry for blood.

The cacophony of shouting soldiers and howling monsters, crackling fires and hissing steam intensified as the swarm charged the last fifty yards toward the wall right at Army gate.

"Brace!" General Rory shouted from his position a little way down the wall, flanked by Anika and a full contingent of Fast Rollers and Crushers. Erich was grinning, and it looked like Tomas and Cameron were betting on something as they prepared for an epic fight.

To her left, along the southernmost tip of the wall, the first monsters reached the top. A sinewy monster, like a long snake, its earthen body eight feet in diameter, propelled by a dozen short, powerful legs, flowed up over the wall. Its huge jaws gaped open impossibly wide and it lunged at the company of plate-armored Boulders stationed there, already charging to repel it.

And with blood and steel and fury, the battle for the wall was joined.

CHAPTER FORTY

When the Best-laid Plans Don't Account for a Swarm

A wave of nightmare creatures clawed and tore their way up Merkland's famous walls. Tertiary Petralists battered dozens of them down, but more scrambled past even as the front ranks of monsters fell. Verena feared there were simply too many, coming too fast.

Siege weapons fired a continuous stream of destruction down into the mass of summoned monsters, but the hundreds of explosions seemed to do nothing to thin the horde. Verena stood at one of the widows in the Army gate tower and stared, dumbstruck by the incredible ferocity of the swarm.

Somehow it seemed as if more of the monsters remained than she thought. Was that possible? Could the queen be regenerating them somehow?

She didn't think so, but there was no time to think. The wave of monsters was all consuming, a tide of destruction and terror, heat and howling fangs.

Verena switched to the siege weapon operators channel. Operators were shouting reports, many sounding awed or nearly panicked. Water-bound monsters were swarming up the eastern wall too, and the siege weapons had less effect against them.

She shouted, "Units along the river, aim for the monsters' heads. Might have better luck. Everyone else, change focus to clearing the top of the wall. Give the defenders support!"

Instantly Marwin pivoted his siege weapon. He couldn't shoot straight down, but could angle his fire downward to help the soldiers near the Lord gate. He fired explosive rounds perilously close over the heads of soldiers fighting monsters nearby, targeting creatures clambering up the wall to their south.

Ballistae began casting enormous spears and exploding missiles at point blank range, almost straight down, but it was not enough.

A huge creature, like a giant torc, but ringed in flames, boiled up over the wall about a hundred yards away from Verena, and its legs split open, spraying fire over the soldiers rushing in to fight it. They fell back, some screaming, but others activating personal shielding devices.

Verena breathed a sigh of relief, even though she felt so tense it was hard to breathe. Those personal defensive mechanicals might prove critical in helping turn the tide in their favor.

A Firetongue swept the monster's flames away a second later, and the Boulders charged in, smashing the creature apart.

It exploded.

The shockwave knocked soldiers flying and cleared a section of wall for several smaller monsters to scramble up and leap upon the disoriented defenders. The fighting was vicious and close, and Verena felt an overriding need to do something to help.

She clutched at her satchel, but the stones in there weren't powerful enough. Through a piece of quickened sculpted obsidian in her glove, she connected with the Swift and activated its thrusters.

She wore the battle armor that Connor loved so much, with her sword and throwing daggers belted on her waist, and her satchel filled to bursting with deadly mechanicals. Against any human foes, Verena would feel confident, and she hated how helpless she felt in the face of that swarm.

In the Swift, she could fight them as an equal.

As she remotely piloted her deadly personal craft up from the courtyard below, where she'd left it hovering, she calculated the best ways to use her armament of weapons to support the intense struggle.

In that moment, the sun darkened as the flying swarm blackened the sky over Merkland and dove at the city. Scores of monsters slammed into the glowing dome of the shield, and it shook under the tremendous force. Other airborne monsters swept along the walls, raking at exposed soldiers with tooth and claw.

The men and women of Merkland responded with barrages of slung stones and with handheld speedslings. The explosive rounds traced the paths of the monsters targeted by the deadly streams of hornets, ripping out chunks of flesh, and tearing off limbs.

The rapid-fire mechanicals took up the fight, targeting the flying monsters swarming around the shield, battering it relentlessly. Unless they could drive off those monsters quickly, the shield would not survive very long.

All of that force battering it drew deeper and deeper from the quartzite stones powering the shield. The massive construct consumed enormous amounts of power already, despite the incredible advances they had made in fine-tuning the shapes of the cut stones to magnify the resulting power and reduce drain.

Verena watched carefully as the siege weapons tracked the monsters, pouring explosive rounds up into the sky. With a growing sense of dread, she realized they would fail.

At that close range, with the monsters zipping back and forth, banking hard, and plunging down toward the exposed soldiers on the wall, the rapid-fire mechanicals were just too slow. There were hundreds of flying monsters, so they hit some, but not nearly enough.

The operators were already shouting to each other to try leading the monsters to get a hit, but that was extremely difficult. The monsters shifted flight paths so fast it was almost like they anticipated the rounds.

It was a bad time for the distraction of the flying swarm. With defenders and siege weapons turning to fight them off, the land-bound swarm attacked again. A new wave of terrible creatures swept up onto the wall. For a moment it looked like the defenders would be totally overrun.

"Reinforcements!" Verena shouted into the officer channel.

As more soldiers pounded up stairs to assist, the Sentries responded. They might have struggled to fight off the earth-bound swarm through their shielding, but now they were on home turf.

A cresting wave of earth erupted from the courtyard below. Wide, but thin, it arced just above soldiers' heads and smashed monsters off the wall by the dozen. As the wave of earth avalanched down onto the swarm below, it erupted back up onto the wall, spreading in a thin sheet across the white stone.

As more monsters tried swarming up the stone, the earth swept their claws aside, denying them purchase. Verena laughed, impressed and so very relieved. She hadn't seen that particular trick employed before.

With the wall momentarily clear, defenders regrouped and set themselves again. The earthen slippery barrier wouldn't hold for long, but those precious seconds might have saved that section of the wall from getting completely overrun. From what Verena could hear from other gates, the situation was dire, but no section had fallen yet.

Denied access to the city via climbing the stones, the swarm redoubled its efforts to breach the gate. Somehow they seemed to sense it was a weakness.

Some of the bigger monsters smashed into the gates, shaking them despite the heavily reinforced timbers and complex locking mechanism. They were led by some of the biggest monsters Verena had seen so far. Some looked like giant, armored torcs, as big as oxen, while others walked on two legs, roughly humanoid, but vastly larger than people.

They were armed.

Those giants carried clubs a full ten feet long, spiked and studied with steel. Verena shuddered to think what those clubs could do to a person. Even a personal defensive shield might not be strong enough to protect against a blow from one of those.

She felt a growing conviction that the queen had been playing with them all winter. She'd sent relatively weak summoned creatures against them, dumb creatures that were easily identified and dispatched. They'd grown confident, assuming they could defeat any monsters she created.

They were wrong, and that misplaced pride might kill them all today.

No, she refused to believe it and drove the thoughts away. Still, they clung to the back of her mind, whispering that she would fail, that all of her work would prove insufficient, that Builders could never stop a fully ascended Petralist, that she was a fool. If she listened to those fears, they would weaken her and steal her courage.

She might fail, but it wouldn't be for lack of trying.

The entire tower shuddered from the impacts as the monsters battered the gates with awesome strength. The soldiers manning the communications glanced down nervously, but did not abandon their posts.

Those magically enhanced monsters would batter through the gates in less than a minute. Other monsters continued trying to swarm up the walls, clawing through the earthen defenses by sheer volume.

"Call for Sentries to try buttressing Army gate," Verena told the lead officer in the tower, who nodded and moved to relay the order. She hoped it would buy them some more time.

As the monsters began reaching the top again, the soldiers charged in to knock them free. Now that they'd survived the first wave, the brave men and women of Merkland began quickly adapting to the unique challenges of the siege.

Battle joined along the walls with incredible ferocity. Soldiers charged in with axes and maces, led by Boulders, while tertiary Petralists slung elements at the monsters and strove to deflect the creatures' blasts of fire and water that they spat in deadly waves.

For the moment, the defenders held and Verena allowed herself to hope they might actually do this.

"Help! The water-bound are cascading up the wall like an upside-down waterfall," a panicked female voice shouted over one of the speakstones behind Verena.

She turned to listen as the operator tried to ask for details. The woman wasn't listening, but continued shouting. "Adrian and Dunbar tried to stop them, but they were. . . . It ripped. . . . Oh, Tallan's Fury! Run!"

The voice trailed away in a scream of terrified pain that sent a shiver of dread racing down Verena's spine. She doubted that unknown woman had survived.

More reports poured in, nearly overwhelming the bank of speakstones.

"Section four overrun. The siege weapons are gone, most of the defenders swept off the wall. The water is smashing everything!"

Another voice shouted, "Spitters retreating from sections two through five. Hostile forces are pouring through the breach. Flooding in the eastern reaches of the city. Monsters are reforming inside the walls!"

Verena rushed to the communications officers as they scrambled to relay messages and coordinate routing reinforcements to that sector of the city. The problem was, every Spitter and Water Moccasin was already committed. It would take too long to plug the gap.

She grabbed the senior officer's shoulder and asked, "The shield! Find out if they've targeted the stones that form the shield."

The woman's eyes widened in understanding. Verena did not know her name, but could see she understood the danger. If enough quartzite blocks were broken out of the mechanical matrix fueling the city-wide shield, it would collapse.

Using obsidian, she linked remotely to the shield, and when she flickered her Builder senses across it, she grimaced. The flying monsters were still battering it relentlessly, with several of them high atop the peak of the dome, out of effective range of the defensive mechanicals. They were rapidly draining the shield's reserves, which did seem much lower than they should be.

She didn't need to wait for the officer to report on what the water-bound monsters were doing. Somehow they understood to disable defenses. The shield was about to fail. The city would lie defenseless beneath the aerial swarm.

"The citywide shielding will collapse in a moment," she stated, switching back to the officers line.

"Those flyers are too fast," General Wolfram stated. He spoke fast, and behind him Verena heard screams and shouts of battle, mingled with the deep roaring of angry monsters. He was positioned atop the southern stretch of the wall, above Lord's gate, right in the midst of the heaviest fighting.

Verena said, "Prepare your forces to defend against aerial attacks throughout the city. I will activate the Draw."

"Can you do anything else?" Lady Briet asked.

"Yes. I'm headed for the Swift."

She did not wait for their reply, but linked via obsidian to a series of backup mechanicals positioned around the city.

She activated them all.

Then she headed for the Swift. She emerged from the gatehouse and stepped into pandemonium.

Soldiers everywhere were shouting and cursing and pressing forward against horrific monsters. Explosions of elemental fire and water battled back and forth, sometimes catching soldiers and catapulting them from the wall. Enormous monsters were constantly lunging over the parapet and snapping at soldiers.

She felt immensely grateful they had shipped so many personal defensive mechanicals to Merkland. Again they saved dozens of lives. Most of the soldiers flung from the wall activated personal shielding, surrounding themselves in temporary, shimmering spheres that protected them from the brutal impacts. Others managed to activate blind coal gauntlets that allowed them to slip through otherwise deadly attacks from snapping jaws and raking claws.

For the moment they seemed to be holding their own, but those personal defenses only worked a couple times before running out. She hoped they would last long enough.

General Rory charged past Verena, shouting a wordless battle cry. He tackled a gigantic monster with arms as big around as his torso just as it lumbered up over the parapet. Rory plowed into the beast and with a mighty heave of his stone-hardened muscles, lifted it right over his head, then slammed it to the stones.

Tomas and Cameron attacked it instantly, each wielding a pair of heavy battle hammers that had to weigh thirty pounds each. They smashed the monster's skull flat within three heartbeats, even as it raked deadly claws across Rory's stone-hardened skin, shredding his already tattered battle armor and scraping gouges in his granite-like flesh.

The injuries did not bleed, although Verena knew they would when he released granite. Hopefully Healers would be ready to assist immediately, or he would suffer greatly. Rory lunged to his feet and threw aside his destroyed battle jacket, revealing his muscled torso, perfectly defined in rippling, living stone.

He glanced at Verena and saluted. "Don't dawdle, lass. Those flying monsters are making a mess of my men."

As if to punctuate his words, a long, leathery monster swept past overhead, its long body undulating through the air like a snake, propelled by wings that seemed far too small to keep its bulk aloft. It sported a dozen stout limbs, with deadly claws, and it spewed a gout of orange flames toward Verena and Rory.

Even as Verena moved to activate a personal shield, the flames rebounded away from them, caught by a nearby Firetongue. Laughing like a maniac, with orange flames dancing in her long, black hair, the slender woman drew the flames into a white-hot spear that she then plunged into the face of another earth-bound monster climbing over the wall. It erupted with a hideous death shriek, air blasting in every direction, and the queen's voice rang out all around them.

"*Feel my fury, unworthy servants! You will all die miserable, painful deaths.*"

Verena grimaced. Hearing the queen's angry voice above the din of desperate battle sent a shiver of cold fear trickling down her spine. It also firmed her resolve. Wow, she hated that woman. She moved toward the inner edge of the wall, above the courtyard.

The battle raged all around her, men and monsters crashing together in desperate struggle, with elements blasting all around them, punctuated by screams of men and summoned creatures. She smelled blood and fire, scorched hair, and a strange musky scent from the dead creature that Rory and his captains had just shattered. She needed to get into the fight.

The Swift rocketed toward her and she adjusted the controls for it to slow to a hover next to the inner edge of the wall. As she leaped aboard and quickly fastened her safety harness, the gate nearby shattered and huge monsters the size of oxen charged inside, bearing down on the defenders already massed to meet them.

Other monsters followed in a wave, at least twenty of them, among the largest and strongest of the entire horde, including the huge humanoid ones she'd spotted earlier with the clubs. A pair of fire-bound monsters roared through the gap also, wreathed in living flames.

Only then did Verena realize that Shona herself, flanked by Erich and Anika, led a full company of mixed Crushers and Fast Rollers charging to meet them. Shona wielded a heavy mace, reinforced for use by Boulders.

She max-tapped granite, raised the mace high, and shouted, "Merkland forever!"

CHAPTER FORTY-ONE

A Target-rich Environment

Shona charged the huge monsters pressing in through the shattered gate, and Verena had to admit she was an inspiring sight, rushing into battle at the head of her small force, showing no fear in the face of the terrifying horde. Her forces surged into the breach behind her, shouting battle cries and leaping into deadly peril.

At the same time, the shielding over the city flickered and crumbled. Hundreds of flying monsters screeched in victory and plunged down toward the unprotected city.

Even though Verena knew the shield was about to fail, she softly cursed the timing. They were facing breaches from too many sides. She could sense the tide of battle beginning to turn against them. They had to turn it back fast, or momentum would sweep them all away with it.

A few of the rapid-fire siege weapons that had not run out of ammunition opened fire on the plunging monsters. They had heard the warning that the shield was about to collapse, so had plenty of time to aim, correctly reading the path the flying monsters would take when the shield gave way.

The exultant monsters flew right into a barrage of high explosives that shattered half a dozen of them in the first volley. The rest of them banked away, scattering like a flock of giant, deadly sparrows, diving and twisting so aggressively that the siege weapons could not hope to keep up.

Those were the ones Verena had to deal with.

She activated her window shielding and banked away from the wall, but glanced back once to check on Anika. She was fighting one of the giant, lumbering humanoid monsters with her usual flair, dodging a downward blow that shattered cobblestones and sank a foot into the ground beneath. Max-tapping granite and laughing with the thrill of battle, Anika looked every inch a legendary battle maiden.

But it was Shona who raced right between the monster's legs, smashing one knee with her mace before plunging even deeper into the melee.

There was much Verena did not like about Shona, but even she had to admit Shona did not lack courage. If she was not such a cold-hearted wench, she could be quite inspiring some of the time.

Despite their bravery, the swarm of monsters was just too thick, and the tide swept right over the defenders, knocking many of them back and simply overrunning others.

The monsters met the furious onslaught of the mighty Petralists with horrifying brutality, smashing aside dozens of dauntless warriors with enormous sweeps of their weapons and claws.

Most of those plate-armored Boulders of Shona's personal guard recovered quickly and plunged back into the fight with fresh battle cries. Reinforced by four-man squads of Crushers, they fought to drag monsters down, often beating at their limbs to reduce mobility. Most of the monsters towered over the soldiers, so they had a huge advantage.

The fight was so vicious that Verena swung back around and fired a missile down into the face of a huge, rock-like monster that was shrugging off Boulder hammers and stomping soldiers flat. It was just opening its craggy jaws full of craggy teeth when the missile whooshed right into its mouth and detonated.

The monster's head exploded and it collapsed into a pile of rocks that began dissolving as the elemental power fueling it fled. Its death wail shrieked over the square, a cackling laugh in the queen's voice that shouted, "*You're all going to die and no one will mourn you!*"

Shona alone had continued pushing deep into the monster horde, shouting curses at the monsters that dared invade her home. She ended up in the middle of the invading horde, separated from support, and was buried under an avalanche of raging summoned monsters.

They swarmed over her, a brown and crimson tide of terrible fury, raking and biting and trying to rip her to pieces. The other soldiers of her company fought valiantly to reach her side, but they would arrive too late.

Singing a boisterous battle song, Erich heaved one of the enormous monsters in his path high overhead and smashed it down onto one of its companions so hard that both monsters exploded. Anika rushed past and dove right into the enormous open maw of another huge creature before ripping its head off from the inside. Their remarkable bravery was inspiring, but it would not help Shona.

Verena needed to fight off those flying monsters. That swarm was already plunging down into the city, largely unopposed, and she almost banked away. Shona had chosen to lead the charge and she would live or die by the strength of her own hand.

Only, she could not do it.

Shona was still a companion, one of the leaders of the revolution. So as Verena fired another missile at a huge monster that was leaping high into the air, aiming for the inner edge of the wall, she activated the speakstone paired with Shona's direct line. "Shona, can you hear me?"

The missile exploded into the back of the jumping monster, ripping it to pieces. Shona's only response was a gasp, then a scream. Verena also heard sounds of chomping and grinding, as if from huge teeth sawing at Shona's granite-hard torso.

"Do you have any blind coal?" Verena demanded as she pivoted around for an attack pass.

"I'm kind of busy right now," Shona cried, then screamed in rage. "You Tallan-cursed servants of a psycho hag. Give that back!"

It was a good sign that she could still curse at the monsters, but idiotic bravery could only get her so far.

"I can help, but it'll hurt if you don't have blind coal," Verena pressed. She'd give Shona one more chance, but if the haughty noblewoman continued to refuse her help, she'd leave her to her fate.

"I have one little piece, but it will only last for a second or two."

"That should be enough. Activate it on my mark." Verena did not wait for acknowledgment. A fire-bound monster was rushing toward the pack, and while the others held Shona down, it might succeed in pouring living flames down her throat and crisping her from the inside like the one had tried to do in New Schwinkendorf.

"Hurry."

"On three . . ." Verena triggered another diorite-tipped missile.

"Two . . . one . . ."

The missile shot away from the Swift.

"Now!"

The missile accelerated to blinding speed as it shot across the short distance down to the pile of monsters and Shona.

It struck in a glorious explosion of fire and destruction. It shattered several of the monsters instantly, and catapulted several more back. It also knocked Erich flying. Verena had not even seen him closing on the pinned Shona.

The fire-bound monster seemed to grow, morphing into the shape of an enormous nuall hunting cat. It tipped back his head and roared with newfound strength. Just in time for a dozen spears of ice to punch through its head and torso from the walls up above. The monster exploded in a second wave of fiery destruction, charring the melting corpses of the other destroyed monsters.

Shona emerged from the firestorm, with her recovered mace in hand, raised in victory. Wreathed in flames like that, she embodied the image of a high lady battle maiden perfectly.

Verena grimaced and banked away. Just like Shona to turn a potential disaster into an opportunity to awe her followers yet again. She had courage and class, and knew how to use both of them.

It was super annoying.

Time to get to work. Verena accelerated into the sky. Her delay might have saved Shona, but it might have cost other lives in the meantime. Flying monsters raced back and forth across the city, targeting anyone that moved, although they seemed smart enough to focus on soldiers.

The rapid-fire siege weapons were mostly focusing on slower monsters breaching the gates or still swarming up the walls. She turned on a speakstone linking to the main communications hub to listen to reports of the rest of the fighting.

It wasn't encouraging. The river-facing wall was breached almost down its entire length, and the eastern reaches of the city were being savaged by water-bound monsters, despite every effort by defenders to plug the gap.

The rest of the wall was holding, but just barely. Defenders were spread thin, and now they were exposed to attacks from the air on all sides.

They were about to be overrun.

Verena hated doing it, but she activated the link to the commander line. Just in time to hear General Wolfram's panting voice shout, "We have to fall back."

"We can hold!" Shona protested, but when Verena glanced back she saw even Shona and her small force fighting for their lives as they were steadily driven farther back from the gate. More monsters were pouring through the breach and already climbing up the inside of the wall to attack defenders from behind.

"The wall is lost. Fall back to secondary defenses," Verena said.

Shona muttered a curse, punctuated by a scream of one of her companions then said, "You're right. Issue the orders, Wolfram. Fall back!"

Verena left them to coordinate the retreat. "Lady Briet, if you have any missiles left, target Army gate. Fire everything you've got. It might delay the advance long enough for our people to get away."

"Roger. Sending everything," she responded instantly.

Verena didn't have time to help the retreat. She had ascended into the air to get a better view of the city and the damage being done. She entered the domain of the flying horde and monsters swept in from every side, shrieking bloodlust, some spitting flames.

Verena's worries and tension evaporated as battle rage swept through her. She shouted a wordless challenge, mimicking Rory's earlier cry as she activated full thrust and rushed up to meet the nearest monster.

They outnumbered her hundreds to one, but she was the hunter, and she opened up with twin streams of hornets from her speedslings. The nearest monster was a magnificent pedra, bigger than her Swift, wings spread wide as it raked toward her.

Verena blasted it right across the face and neck. Hornets chewed into the monster, while the explosive rounds blasted its head into pieces. It erupted in a spray of muddy water that Verena shot right through.

Her shields shuddered as she plunged through the corpse, already spinning the Swift horizontally in a full circle. She fired two missiles at birdlike monsters swooping in from either side, smashing them out of the sky.

But dozens more were swooping in. The explosions and death shrieks of the other flyers drew more monsters, howling for blood. Not even Verena could shoot down so many.

So she rolled the Swift upside down and activated the Puking Dooms on the underside of the craft. Flames erupted forth, shooting into the sky and crisping a winged monstrosity Verena could not name.

The pressure hurled the Swift toward the ground, pressing Verena into her seat so hard she felt the skin of her face stretching. She pointed the Swift straight down and activated full thrust.

She shot downward with terrifying speed, momentarily outpacing her pursuers. The swarm gave chase, wings flapping, snakelike bodies undulating like mad as they swam through the air.

Verena pulled up and activated additional thrusters under the front side of the Swift to help her make the turn to horizontal just before smashing into the ground. She leveled out barely six feet above the ground and shot down one of the main streets into the military district.

Buildings blurred past and she grinned with the thrill of such awesome speed in such a tight space. One mistake, and she would shatter to bits, despite her reinforced shielding.

To her right, she glimpsed the soldiers that had been manning Army gate rushing down a parallel street toward the castle-like military command building. It would serve as one of the secondary defensive sites, along with the palace itself, and other rally positions scattered around the city.

The flying swarm could wreak terrible havoc among the fleeing defenders, but it looked like Verena had distracted at least a hundred of them.

She glanced back, impressed by how fast the monsters could fly. Some were winging down the street behind her, while others dove from above, cutting the corner and closing with astonishing speed.

"Let's see how maneuverable you are," she growled as she focused on the first turn. The road split into two smaller thoroughfares. She banked the Swift to the left, easily making the first turn, now following the street toward Market gate.

A flood of earth and fire-bound monsters was already pouring over the distant wall toward her, so she banked right and entered a warren of smaller streets.

Instincts kicked in as Verena flashed through the city, banking, turning, firing thrusters and Puking Dooms on every surface of the Swift to make the turns. It was hard to breathe, hard to see as each turn came faster than the last.

Monsters poured down the streets behind her, a wall of flapping, howling, deadly destruction. More monsters plunged down from above, raking at the Swift as the monsters dove at her.

She dodged most of them. A couple raked her shields glancing blows that nearly sent her spinning into buildings, but she managed to hold on, shouting curses at her foes the entire time.

Then one huge monster dove out of the sky directly on top of her. It didn't bother raking at her as she sped past like the others had, but plunged down on an intercept course. Too late, Verena realized the monster planned to simply collide with her and smash her into the cobblestones.

She threw the Swift into a barrel roll, firing thrusters out every side just before impact. The monstrous body smashed into the Swift, momentarily blocking her view as it bashed her down toward the cobblestones.

The spin helped her slip past it a fraction of a second faster, and the maxed thrusters helped soften the impact with the monster as well as the impact with the ground, but could not avoid it.

The Swift shuddered as it crashed down, and Verena maxed her double-layer shielding. The impact strained the shield's limits, but they held, and she bounced back up.

But the impact threw her into a spin that momentarily knocked the Swift out of control. The world spun wildly around Verena, filled with monsters and stone buildings. One warehouse seemed to rush toward her, its huge oak doors closed.

Verena screamed, unable to avoid the impact.

She activated blind coal.

The world seemed to shimmer as Verena and the Swift turned somehow slightly incorporeal and slid right through the warehouse. It was packed with grain, and Verena caught a glimpse of it as she slid through before passing out the far side.

Blind coal never lasted long, and she feared she might need it again soon, so as soon as she passed through the warehouse, she released it and activated the main thrusters.

The Swift shot into the air, and Verena regained control, using every secondary thruster. Behind her the warehouse exploded under a barrage of monstrous bodies that plunged into it, heedless of danger to themselves.

Verena didn't know if any of the monsters died in the collision, but it didn't seem like it. The sky was full of monsters, diving from every direction. She felt rising panic as she sought a way out.

Then she recognized a street and banked down into it, plunging almost to ground level, shooting east as fast as the Swift could fly.

Time to fly the Draw.

Chapter Forty-Two

Hope Is Fragile but Hard to Kill

"Come on. Just a little faster," Verena urged the Swift as she rocketed toward the main city market, a huge, open square usually filled with shops and stalls, and packed with shoppers.

Today it would be empty. Scores of nightmare monsters raced after her, driven by elemental power as much as by the flapping of their wings. She glimpsed other monsters plunging out of the sky into the city, attacking defenders or just wrecking things.

Some were being drawn into traps that Verena had set. They were part of the Draw, a last-ditch defensive measure she'd designed with Hamish. She was about to plunge right into the heart of the Draw herself.

That was not something she would usually recommend, but she needed an edge, a way to break away from pursuit and rejoin the other defenders.

She activated a speakstone, linking her to the teams working the Draw. "This is Verena. Closing fast on Draw site One. I'm bringing the party with me."

"Builder Verena, do not enter the Draw," a harried-sounding officer responded. "Every station is active. You'll fly right into a death trap."

"I know the configuration. I can make it. When I arrive, do not hesitate, but hit them with everything."

He paused for a second before saying, "Roger, Builder. I hope you know what you're doing."

So did she, but she lacked time to reply. Another huge flyer tried crushing her from above, but she'd learned her lesson. She spotted it diving, but waited until the last second to respond.

Once she was sure it was committed and unable to swerve, she rotated the Swift ninety degrees, pointing the nose directly upward, even while continuing down the street at breakneck speed.

As soon as her sights lined up on the huge, scaly monstrosity, she fired both speedslings.

Streams of deadly hornets erupted from the front of the Swift and ripped apart the monster, but it was too big and moving too fast and would still splatter her into the ground.

Verena couldn't afford to get knocked off track again, not that close to the market. So she again activated blind coal.

Again the world seemed to darken as she passed right through the huge body's shell, then right through the boiling fire filling the center of its torso.

It struck the ground and exploded right behind her as she slipped out the far side of it. She released blind coal, even though the flames of the monster's explosion roiled over the Swift, shaking it so hard her teeth rattled and the controls sputtered.

Her shields held, and she still had enough blind coal for maybe one more deployment, as long as it was a short one. Verena allowed a fierce grin as she leveled out just in time to shoot into the market square.

It was teeming with people.

Even though Verena knew the view was fake, generated by a clever array of sightstone screens, for a second her heart skipped a beat as she plunged right into a crowd of soldiers, standing in battle formation. She passed right through since it was just a projection. It would look especially real from above, and she spotted several flying monsters diving toward the square, shrieking for blood.

They might be chasing her or aiming for the projections, but either way, they'd strike in seconds.

"Activate!" she cried as she threw her nimble craft into a series of acrobatic turns she'd calculated in advance.

She moved too fast to react to the Draw, and hoped she'd calculated correctly. She spun, twisted, and rolled through the square, punching through more projections, flying scant feet above the paving stones. Behind her, monsters boiled into the square.

The Draw activated.

Spikes erupted from between every paving stone, ripping into the underside of monsters. Spears longer than grown men erupted from concealed ballistae stations set into the buildings along the perimeter. Some were tipped with diorite, others with mechanicals that sucked heat out of any monster they struck, freezing them from the inside.

Other paving stones erupted into the air, revealing nests of speedslings already spun up and ready to fire. Grouped in nests of two dozen, the speedslings spewed walls of hornets into the air, ripping monsters apart by the dozen.

All around Verena, death and destruction erupted from the ground and from every side. Projectiles passed within inches of the Swift, and she couldn't help screaming with exhilaration and fear as she plunged right through the heart of it all.

Then she was through, shooting along a narrow street, hemmed in by three-story houses, packed close together along both sides. Her rearview sightscreen revealed no monsters immediately following her. She'd left the pack behind, mired down in the death traps of the Draw.

Laughing with relief, she eased the Swift to roof level and glanced around. Most of the horde of monsters that had been following her were still distracted by the Draw and seemed intent on destroying the soldiers they thought were responsible for wreaking such havoc among their brethren.

The city was getting wrecked, though. Everywhere she looked, she spotted flying monsters smashing buildings or flocking around the few heavily defended positions manned by Merkland's brave defenders.

She risked banking east, drawing closer to the flooded neighborhoods closest to the river. Entire streets were underwater, buildings smashed apart as the floods spread. It was a sickening sight. Had the water-bound monsters discovered the nearest underground civilian caverns?

She hoped not. She headed back toward the palace, keeping low and trying to avoid monsters instead of engaging. She couldn't afford to draw another horde around her. She might not escape again.

Verena opened the communication link to the leader channel. It was buzzing with rapid-fire reports of casualties and defensive position statuses. She was relieved to hear General Wolfram's voice, reporting from the palace, but the news was not good.

"We've got flying summoned attacking every window, but shields are holding for now. We've allowed some to break into the trap rooms and our forces are engaging with relative success. If we could keep the numbers low enough, we could eventually defeat them all."

"That's not going to happen," General Rory said, his voice grim. He sounded exhausted, but undeterred by the dire circumstances. "Here in the military command building we're also holding for now, but we've got a column of heavy earth-bound closing on our position. I spotted another column heading toward the palace. Prepare ground floor personnel to repel an attack against the main gate."

Wolfram muttered a soft Grandurian curse, and Verena felt her recent hope dwindling again. They'd killed thousands of the monsters, but still Merkland was being overrun.

"This is Verena. I led a horde into the Draw, but there are too many."

"Verena, Tallan be praised," Wolfram said, relief in his voice. "We thought we'd lost you."

"Not yet."

"Are there other mechanicals you can activate?" Shona asked. Verena suspected she was in the palace, but wasn't sure and didn't have time to ask.

"No. We've committed everything," Verena said as she banked down to street level and sped below a row of overhanging buildings to avoid getting spotted by a trio of slow-flying monsters that looked like huge, burning blobs. She had no idea if missiles or hornets would do anything against those, and was too low on ammo to waste it finding out.

Shona cursed. "My city is overrun. We need more."

She was right. They were in a desperate situation, defenders separated into small, isolated groups, swarmed by monsters. If any of those groups fell, no one could help.

Verena struggled to find an answer, to figure out a way to leverage their fast-dwindling resources to new advantage. Slightly distracted, she flew around a tall government building and almost flew directly into a huge eagle-like monster, winging straight at her.

Verena screamed and banked into a rolling turn, scraping along the side of the eagle as its long, deadly beak snapped down with such force it pierced the outer layer of her shielding and knocked the Swift ten feet sideways in the air.

"Verena, are you okay?" Wolfram demanded, but his connection cut out as the speakstone was overwhelmed by the sudden sounds of battle and abruptly winked out.

Verena hoped he was okay, but didn't have time to even ask. She was too busy trying to stay alive. Half a dozen other flying monsters, also looking like giant raptors, were following the huge eagle and they all attacked. She spun down toward the ground and tried her escape tactic again.

The giant eagle got their first. It was like the creature had seen her escape like that once before and anticipated the move.

As Verena shot downward, driven by every thruster, the eagle struck from the side, shaking her shields and nearly overwhelming them, driving Verena right into the stone facade of another building.

She lacked time to even activate blind coal, but punched through the building so hard her shields temporarily winked out. Dust and debris filled the air around her, and Verena banked sideways, barely spinning the Swift in time to fit through the door on the opposite side of the room she'd crashed into.

Wood scraped one wing, and the doorframe ripped off the tip off the other. One of her remaining missiles fell free, and Verena activated it remotely just as another monster bird landed in the opening she'd made.

The explosion tore off the monster's face and tossed the Swift down the corridor. She struck the carpet and slid down it, using secondary thrusters to avoid tumbling into a roll that would have ripped the Swift apart.

Panting with fear, Verena managed to turn the Swift on the carpet, aiming for the big window at the far end of the hall. She desperately reset the shield mechanical and reactivated it.

One of the big bird-like monsters descended into a hover right in front of the window, its beak open, fire dripping out.

Verena shot it with both speedslings.

The monster exploded in a fantastic fireball that consumed part of the wall and sent flames boiling down the corridor toward Verena.

The Swift plunged into them just as the shield reignited. Verena gasped from the searing heat and activated the rear thrusters. She shot out the window and blasted through the disintegrating remains of the bird's carcass that left long, crimson smears across her shield.

That was too close. Her outer shield was inoperable, even though she tried three times to reignite it. She was almost out of hornets, and only had two missiles left. The Swift was flying well still, but another hit like that would kill her.

Verena tried for altitude, shooting into the air on full boost trying to leave the deadly monsters behind. Three bird monsters were winging after her, led by the giant eagle, and other monsters caught sight of her as she rose into the sky. They seemed to be closing from every direction.

She tried to control her rising panic. She couldn't lose focus, had to think, but no option felt good. Verena glanced to her right, toward the military command building, but instantly discarded that idea. It was too far, and even if she fought through all the monsters between her and that possible safety, she'd never punch through the swarm of monsters already attacking the building.

The palace was also too far, and equally swarmed with scores of deadly monsters.

With no better option, Verena banked to her left and applied maximum thrust. She was burning through her thrusters with scary speed. They were enhanced versions, but such intense maneuvers consumed quartzite so much faster than normal flight. She was running out of time.

"Verena, what's going on?" Rory demanded, his voice tight with concern. She had forgotten she'd left the line open.

"I'm under attack from all sides. Running out of options here," she said, scanning the skies in every direction and checking the sightscreens positioned all around the Swift.

"Can you reach us?" Rory asked.

"Negative." She was flying east, right into the flooded section of the city. At first it seemed the direction with the fewest direct threats. Fewer flyers were swarming over that area that was already mostly destroyed.

Water started erupting off the flooded streets, forming into slender water-bound monsters that extended grasping fingers of water so much farther than Verena thought possible.

Tallan help her, she was doomed.

Verena banked hard, spinning aggressively, and managed to avoid several watery tendrils, but more and more kept rising. She tried angling into the air, but flyers were closing from above. They'd rip her apart.

With a sinking feeling of dread, she realized there was no way out.

That made her angry, and she rotated the swift back down, aiming at a huge, water-bound monster that was rising on two dozen legs into the air toward her. Its entire torso opened into a jagged maw to swallow the entire Swift.

Verena fired her last missile.

It exploded inside the monster, shredding its watery torso into millions of glittering droplets. Verena shot through, grinning with what might be her final victory. They wouldn't take her easily.

But the droplets didn't blow off the outer edge of her shield. Instead they began to coalesce, gathering, joining, and reforming.

"You've got to be kidding me," Verena groaned. She risked dropping the shield, and most of the water blew away, but some of it struck her in the face.

She yelped and brushed it away, reforming the shield, hoping that the water that landed inside the Swift was just water and not a mini summoned creature that would try biting her face as it reformed.

More water-bound rose into the air all around her, so she banked toward the eastern wall. If she could get past the wall, she could escape out over Merkland township and figure out how to best succor those trapped within the besieged city.

Except the wall was covered in water, and as she sped toward it, the entire expanse transformed into summoned creatures.

Verena screamed, unable to turn in time, and unleashed the last of her hornets. The little projectiles tore into the watery monsters, and she applied full thrust, hoping to burst through the hole.

She struck the wall of water with terrific force and it gave way. She plunged through and over the wall, shouting with victory.

Her cry died on her lips as her forward momentum slowed dramatically. The waters that she'd plunged through hadn't bled away from her shield, but held on, like long fingers. More water was coursing up those fingers, reinforcing them and surrounding the Swift in a thin coating of impending death.

The speedslings were empty, her missiles gone. Verena activated the Puking Dooms. Flames tore through the waters beneath the Swift, and the entire craft shuddered, but did not break free.

She cut out the Puking Dooms and twisted the ship, trying to dive down through the hole she'd just blasted in the water, but the water returned too fast. It caught her and drew her back toward the wall where more monsters were forming.

Verena panted with fear, her hands shaking with cold panic. She blinked away tears, desperately scanning her diminished arsenal, trying to figure out how to escape.

She couldn't think of anything.

The monsters were going to rip through her shield and tear her apart.

"Builder One is down. I don't think I can escape this time," she said, her voice hoarse and soft.

"Where are you? We'll send reinforcements," Rory offered, but it was a false hope and they all knew it.

"Don't you dare give up," Shona ordered sharply. That surprised Verena. She had expected Shona to gloat. She'd wanted Verena dead almost since the first time they met.

"My city is overrun. Don't think you can avoid responsibility to help that easily, Builder. Fight, Tallan curse you. We all have to keep fighting!"

That rallied Verena a little, but as the watery fingers dragged her inexorably back toward the wall, she still couldn't figure out what to do.

"Wait, maybe I can reshape my shielding in a way to allow me to escape through the hole," she suggested.

"That's the spirit. Do it," Shona said.

It was a brilliant idea, offering one tiny hope, but Verena had waited a few seconds too long. The water holding her prisoner yanked her harder, ripping the Swift right out of the air and into the midst of the watery horde. Water slammed into the Swift from every side, shaking the shields and rattling the ship.

Verena screamed as the shield gave way and water plunged inside, ripping at her, tearing at her clenched lips, trying to pour down her throat and drown her. She thrashed within the grip of the waters, barely biting back a scream.

She activated a tiny personal shield. It sealed around her like a form-fitting second skin, driving the waters back for a second. It wouldn't hold for long, but Verena would not surrender and let the monsters kill her.

Water slammed into her from every side. She couldn't breathe, couldn't see, and felt like every muscle was getting pummeled.

"*Oh, Connor, I'm so sorry,*" she thought as crimson flames exploded through the waters all around the Swift. One of the other fire-bound monsters must have arrived to broil her.

Verena sat up straight and reached for her satchel, determined to fight to the end.

Abruptly the waters drained away and the Swift was tossed up into the clear air.

Verena was so shocked by the abrupt release that she almost forgot to activate thrusters. When she did, she accelerated away on full burn, racing away from the city. She didn't stop until she flew out over the Merkland township on the far side of the river.

So far the township looked undamaged by the attack. When the monsters finished destroying Merkland, would they turn on the town too? Probably.

Only there, finally feeling safe enough to think she might survive after all, Verena ascended to five hundred feet and banked back around toward Merkland.

Instantly her eyes were drawn to the river wall that she'd just escaped. A man stood atop the wall, wreathed in full Dawnus glory. White-hot flames and ropy tendrils of deep blue water ringed him in a rippling, fast-spinning sphere.

He was striding down the wall, wielding fire and water like enormous blades as he systematically hacked apart all of the water-bound monsters clustered atop the wall.

Monsters swarmed him from every side, but he tore them all apart in a display of elemental mastery that rivaled anything Verena had ever seen.

He spoke, his voice coming through a speakstone in her cockpit. "Hey, did you miss me?"

"Ivor?"

Chapter Forty-Three

Up the Creek, and It's Burning

Verena cheered, despair washed away by the sight of Ivor's return. "I thought we'd lost you."

"I've been busy. Sorry it took so long to fight through to Merkland. You have no idea how many of these creatures I've had to dispatch," he said, his voice calm even as he tore through elemental monsters charging in from every side.

Flames pierced monsters and they erupted into shrieking steam. Water harder than steel slashed through monsters' heads, severed limbs, and simply ripped elementals apart. It was awe inspiring.

"I never imagined water could be wielded against water-bound like that," she breathed.

Ivor chuckled as a big, blob-like monster exploded in front of him. "Neither did I until today. How's the rest of the fighting?"

"Not good."

"Well, I've got this side covered," he said, and she exulted at his confident tone.

Then more water exploded up from the Macantact in an inverted waterfall. At first, Verena thought it was Ivor's doing, but the wave plunged down over him and swept him right off his feet.

"Ivor!" Verena screamed as he tumbled, but continued fighting. His combined elements tore and ripped in every direction, but monsters were piling in like waves of an insane sea.

"Might take me longer than I thought," he gasped.

Verena wanted to help, but she was mostly out of weapons. What could she do? She hated feeling helpless.

"Are you safe, Verena? Was that Ivor?" General Rory demanded. Behind him, the sounds of fighting were intensifying again.

"It was. He's trying to regain the eastern wall."

"Let's hope he manages it soon. We need help. We're under severe attack here.

"Here too. Palace main gates are breached. Intense fighting inside," Shona said, sounding breathless.

Sounds of battle echoed through her line. Screams and shouts and monster roaring suddenly swelled. Shona shouted her battle cry and abruptly her connection cut out.

Verena couldn't sit as an idle witness while all her friends faced annihilation. She needed more mechanicals, but all of the stores were in the city.

Wait, there might be some in the township. Verena banked around and plunged toward one of the huge, earthen warehouses that some of the Builders had used that winter.

"Lady Briet, do you have any ammunition remaining?"

"Negative. I wish there was more we could do," came the immediate reply. Lady Briet sounded close to tears.

"There may be. Return to the township. We might be able to rearm from one of the warehouses."

"On our way!"

Verena grinned as she plummeted toward the city. She only needed moments to rearm. Then she could rejoin the fight.

"Help! Is anyone there?" A desperate voice broke over the line.

"Who is that?" Verena demanded. She had thought she knew everyone on that line.

"Our commander is dead. I found this on his body. I'm with the Draw team. We've been overrun. Almost everyone is dead. The rest of us are trying to reach the citadel, but our last Sentry just reported that the monsters discovered civilian cavern sixteen. They're breaking in!"

"Can you render aid?" Verena asked, horrified by the news. So far all the destruction of Merkland was mostly superficial. Buildings could be replaced, but she couldn't stomach the idea of those monsters tearing into the masses of unarmed civilians.

"Negative. Every one of us is wounded and we're under heavy attack. We can't—"

The voice abruptly cut off in a scream. Verena briefly heard a monster roar, followed by a sickening crunching sound, then the connection broke.

Verena was only seconds away from the warehouse, only minutes from fully rearming. She stared longingly at the huge building and the promise of aid it offered.

If she took the time to rearm, she could better defend the cavern. How many civilians would die in those minutes?

Maybe the situation wasn't as bad as she feared. She tried to link to the speakstones used in cavern sixteen, but got no reply. Was she already too late?

Verena banked the Swift and accelerated back toward the city. She simply couldn't take the risk that her delay would seal their fate.

"I'm coming," she whispered as she rocketed into the air to pass high above the embattled figure of Ivor.

Merkland spread below her, sections flooded, many buildings smashed to pieces, fires raging in dozens of locations. Dead littered the walls, while monsters roamed in destructive packs. At least a couple hundred monsters remained, most of them focused on attacking the few defender strongholds.

That fact offered Verena her one hope. Maybe only one monster had discovered the cavern. The Swift might be out of weapons, but she still had her satchel. She'd figure a way to destroy it and secure the cavern. Then she could return to the township to rearm.

Luckily no flyers seemed to have noticed her return to the city, and she dove toward the square on the southeastern quadrant of the city where cavern sixteen was concealed.

When she swooped around a tall, square tower, her heart sank. Three enormous earth-bound monsters were digging into the ground right above cavern sixteen. They were shaped like giant hounds, as big as wagons, with eight legs and fiery eyes.

Verena slowed to a hover, trying to figure out what to do. She doubted she could destroy those monsters if she landed, but she was currently useless from the air.

Without warning, something crashed into the top of the Swift, swatting it toward the ground so hard, Verena screamed. The restraints holding her into her chair tore at her shoulders. She fired the Puking Dooms, slowing her descent, but again the Swift was struck from above.

She finally glanced upward and groaned in new fear. It looked like the same huge eagle monster had returned to finish her off. It was directly above her, enormous talons gripping the Swift's shield as it drove her down to the ground.

She crashed down hard, but the shield held. The earth-bound monsters nearby paused their work to glance in her direction. Verena wished they'd come fight the eagle for the right to eat her first.

They didn't, but returned to digging. It looked like they'd encountered the first layer of shielding. It wouldn't stop them long.

The eagle monster plunged its beak down and pierced right through the shield. The Swift seemed to scream as the monster ripped the roof right off and Verena stared up into the huge maw as it gaped wide that beak and shrieked so loud Verena screamed.

And she released a piece of quartzite that she placed beneath a piece of diorite.

Air exploded from the bottom of the quartzite, shooting it and the diorite up into that open beak in a makeshift missile.

It streaked right down the monster's gullet before exploding.

That monster was filled with fire, so as the explosion ripped holes in the monster, flames poured out in a firestorm of destruction that tore the monster apart and boiled down over the Swift.

Verena activated her personal shielding and tapped blind coal. Flames filled the cabin, melting her controls and setting everything aflame. For a couple seconds, it passed harmlessly through her. She could feel it like a distant breeze, sliding somehow through her body but not quite able to gain purchase.

Then blind coal expired and Verena returned to herself.

Searing heat enveloped her, threatening to suck out her life, despite her last personal shielding. Blinded by fire and heat, unable to breathe, barely able to think, Verena pulled another piece of quartzite out of her satchel just as it disintegrated under her hand.

She activated the quartzite and air erupted from it. The makeshift thruster dragged her up out of the shredded remains of the Swift. Her restraints fell away, burning to tatters and she soared fifty feet before tumbling to the blessedly cool cobblestones of the plaza.

Behind her, the explosion exhausted itself and faded away, leaving her beloved Swift a blackened wreck.

Verena wanted to cry, but she was too busy staring at the eight legs of the nearest earth-bound monster as it turned toward her and fixed its glowing red eyes on her.

"That is so unfair," she whispered.

The monster charged.

Chapter Forty-Four

Some Days You Need a Friend with Bigger Guns

Verena was exhausted, winded, sore, and shell-shocked from nearly getting incinerated. Her personal shield was nearly spent, she was out of blind coal, and her satchel was gone.

So she struggled to her knees, her soot-covered hand grasping for the hilt of her sword. It might be a pitiful gesture, but she would not just lie there and let a monster eat her for breakfast.

The giant monster seemed as big as a house as it charged her, its eight thick legs shaking the ground like an avalanche. The square was empty, devoid of anything she could use as a weapon or as cover. All she could smell was smoke, her mouth was filled with it, and her ears didn't seem to be working.

Her hand shook as she drew her sword and staggered to her feet. Raising it high she screamed, "Come on!"

The monster skidded to a halt, barely fifty feet away and turned in a surprisingly agile move, spinning in the other direction and charging back the way it had come.

Verena frowned. No way she'd scared it. She glanced back behind her, but saw nothing intimidating.

She turned back toward the retreating monster just in time to see it explode into a million bits of dirt.

She gaped as a figure burst right through the monster, their entire body blazing as if they'd swallowed the sun. Had she already died, but not realized it yet? Then she recognized the figure as he slid to a stop beside her.

Connor.

"Verena, are you all right?" Connor shouted.

"Connor? What are you doing here?" was all she managed to ask. She felt befuddled, in shock. The thought of sheathing her sword was more than she could manage, so she dropped it and stepped forward to throw her arms around his waist.

Connor held her tight, and the feel of his strong arms helped wash away the horror of battle and the fear of death still clinging to her. She shuddered under a spring of new hope and gazed up at him, daring to smile.

He looked so concerned. "Are you all right? Did they hurt you?"

"No. I'm fine. What are you doing here?"

He kissed her briefly, and his lips quivered against hers. In fact, his entire body was wracked with tremors. She realized he was shaking with relief. He'd been convinced he was going to lose her. The level of emotion radiating off of him brought tears to her eyes.

Connor said simply, "I couldn't leave you to face this alone."

"But your mission," she protested, even though she was so relieved he'd returned that it was hard to speak.

"We'll deal with that. First, we'll deal with these monsters." His tone turned grim and his expression merciless. He glanced back to the monsters and only then did she realize he'd destroyed the other two earth-bound too.

"The queen tried to hurt you. I'll make her pay for that. Today her army pays," he growled in a furious tone, and fires danced in his eyes.

Connor leaped straight into the air and elements gathered around him. Crimson flames, silvery water, and black earth. The sounds of battle trumpets bugled around him as he shot into the air, hands extended.

Verena cheered. She hadn't expected to live, let alone feel content within minutes of nearly dying, but seeing Connor wield elements with such skill bolstered her hope. The siege was broken. The monsters were about to realize it. She loved having such a handy boyfriend.

Seven flying monsters, drawn by the movement and bright light, swept in from every direction, closing on Connor, shrieking with bloodlust.

Connor destroyed them.

Two of them just exploded. Verena had no idea what he did to them. The others were ripped to shreds under elemental fury. Their death shrieks were cut short, and Connor drew in the flames from one of them, enveloping him in a shroud of destruction.

Verena rushed back to the charred cockpit of the Swift and settled into the remains of her chair. The smell of ash hung heavy around her. Most of the padding on her chair was gone, leaving it a lumpy, uncomfortable frame. The wooden interior had burned away, exposing the skeleton of her Swift, and the sight made her want to weep.

Connor's return filled her with hope, but she refused to remain trapped in the square. "I know you're not dead," she muttered to her beloved Swift, flicking her Builder senses across it. She found the basic flight controls still working, and grinned, patting the charred front dash.

It wouldn't perform nearly so nimbly, but it would fly. Verena activated thrusters and carefully ascended. The Swift groaned, but she believed if it was a person, it would insist it could still carry her, and not complain about the abuse. It rattled, as if on the verge of simply falling apart.

As she rose slowly into the sky, thrusters sputtering, craft shaking, she activated the speakstone to the commanders. "Connor is back!"

"Are you sure?" Rory demanded. Sounds of battle reverberated through the connection. He was the only one to respond.

"Yes. He's coming!" she assured him.

Rory laughed and shouted, "Reinforcements! Come on you lot, fight like you mean it!"

He broke into a hearty battle song just before the connection cut out. Verena smiled. With Rory's hope renewed, they'd hold until Connor could help.

She spotted Connor easily, crossing the city like a whirlwind of destruction. Everywhere he passed, monsters exploded or were ripped to shreds by elemental fury. He was heading toward the embattled military command building.

A flash of light drew her gaze to the east. Something moved across the city so fast it looked like a shooting star, only it skipped across rooftops. Ringed in white-hot flames, the living meteor slammed into the mass of water-bound monsters swarming Ivor.

The impact detonated like a Last Word bomb, scattering monsters and ripping them into shrieking steam. Verena activated the long-vision capability of the Swift. The viewscreen appeared, crackled a few times, but finally the sight magnified. The view was a little distorted and far less clear than usual, but it worked and she recognized the newcomer.

Kilian.

He had landed crouched on one knee, one fist pressed to the stone at the top of the wall. The stone looked cracked and blackened. Ivor was sprawled nearby, looking rattled by the blast.

Kilian rose and sauntered over to him, flames pulsing across his shoulders. He hauled Ivor to his feet and Verena easily read Ivor's relief. He looked battered and exhausted. He probably wouldn't have lasted much longer.

Kilian gestured toward the flooded section of the city. Ivor grinned, his expression turning predatory. Together the two of them jumped off the wall. Verena lost sight of them, but suddenly felt convinced the water-bound swarm was about to be terminated.

"Verena!"

She turned to see the Hawk flaring to hover nearby. Hamish sat at the controls alone. He stared at the battered Swift. "How are you even flying that wreck?"

"Skill," she said with a happy grin.

He laughed. "I can't wait to hear the story of how much skill it took to wreck it."

"I'll land and join you," she told him, happy to switch to an air-worthy flyer. The Swift was just about dead. She had enough parts in one of the warehouses to rebuild it, but that would take a few days.

In seconds they ascended over Merkland and Verena asked, "What about Aifric?"

Hamish gestured toward the southern end of the city. "She jumped out to help Anton break the siege on the palace."

"Anton is alive?" she exclaimed, feeling immensely relieved. She'd feared she'd lost him.

"Alive and really angry. Dressed in an earthen suit like that one Harley used to spank the Althins last fall. He charged into a horde of monsters and just ripped them apart. Seems motivated to finish the fight before lunch."

Verena laughed. "Oh, Hamish. I'm so happy to see you."

His smile faded as he glanced out over the devastated city. "We almost didn't return."

She placed a hand on his arm. "I'm so glad you did. I don't think any of us would have survived."

"We almost didn't," he repeated softly, his expression haunted. "Verena, we were going to leave you all. Connor's mission is that important, but . . ."

He trailed off and focused on her, his eyes clearing. "But we don't leave friends behind to die."

Chapter Forty-Five

Time Waits for No Man

Connor landed in the huge square in front of the main palace. The cobblestones were blackened in places, but mostly intact, although the huge fountain that had stood in the center of the square was smashed.

The palace had suffered terrible damage from the summoned horde. The inner wall surrounding the palace was simply gone, and the entire front facade was cracked and pockmarked with two dozen gaping holes. The giant double doors at the main entrance had buckled, and pieces of one swung slowly, askew on only one hinge. From the glimpses he caught of the wrecked interior, fighting had been intense.

Rows of injured were being gathered along the opposite side of the square. Hundreds of soldiers lay on cots or blankets or coats, or only on hard stone, groaning, crying, or trying to comfort each other. Two dozen white-robed Healers were tending them, assisted by scores of assistants.

Shona stood nearby, conferring with General Rory and other senior officers. Anika stood close to Rory, with a very battered Erich hovering protectively nearby. Connor didn't see Tomas and Cameron, but had heard they survived the fighting with their usual unflappable enthusiasm.

Like most of the others, Shona was covered in blood and monster gore, her hair tangled, her face dirty, but she still clutched a wicked-looking battle mace in one hand and carried herself with her usual grace.

Rory was missing most of his armor. His thick chest still rippled with stone-hardened muscle, and almost every inch of him was covered in white scratch marks where monster claws and teeth had scored him. If he ran out of granite, he'd bleed out so fast, Connor doubted anyone could save him, but he still moved with vigor.

Anika, who looked more energized than exhausted by the recent near-death battle, was monitoring him closely, holding an extra portion of granite in case he needed it. One Healer approached him, but he gestured the woman toward the more severely injured.

Connor felt so relieved to see his friends alive. He'd broken the siege on the military command building just as the monster horde was breaking through in five different places. The defenders had fought valiantly, but were at the point of getting overrun.

Connor had torn into the monsters with a towering fury. He'd tapped obsidian, chert, and a little porphyry to help improve his connection to the elements. The emotions of the defenders had swept through him like a raw torrent, full of despair and fear, but also determination. The rampager in his heart had howled with approval as he'd embraced battle rage in a way he never had without transforming. He was glad there had still been so many summoned creatures left because he'd needed a lot of targets for his rage.

The sight of Verena standing defiant in that square next to the blackened Swift, sword raised in the face of that charging monster, still filled Connor with fury. She'd never looked so beautiful, and perhaps he'd never come so close to losing her.

The fact that he and the others in the Hawk had almost chosen not to return filled him with icy terror. He'd almost left Verena to die.

His hands shook with anger at Queen Dreokt for threatening those he loved, and he glanced back across the battered city, hoping to see a monster he'd missed in his last circuit. There were none.

After destroying the monsters attacking the military command center, Rory had rallied his forces to charge back to the palace to assist Anton and Aifric in breaking the siege there. Connor had crossed the city, descending on every knot of monsters he could find.

He'd eradicated them all. Even caught up in the battle rage, he'd noticed that the elements seemed to respond to his call better than ever. He had enjoyed the exceptional level of elemental mastery while he liberated Merkland and slaughtered more summoned monsters than he could count, but now he wondered at that close link.

The elemental manifestations had walked in his mind, seeming so real he could almost hear them talk. They had not resisted his calls for power, and seemed to approve of his vengeful assault. Was he really getting better, or was it just the towering rage that drove him? Or maybe the fact that they'd beaten the queen's mind bomb? Had her mental commands been somehow limiting his access? Was that possible?

"Connor!"

The Hawk landed nearby and Verena leaped out. Connor rushed to her and lifted her off the ground in an enthusiastic embrace. He savored the feel of her alive and healthy in his arms.

"I'm so glad you're safe," he said.

"You timed that grand entrance pretty tight, Connor," she said lightly and kissed him on the lips. He could read in her eyes that she'd thought she was going to die.

She tried brushing her hair, but it was a mess, tangled from her wild fight, slightly singed, and never more beautiful. Verena looked battered, her clothing charred, her armor dented, her face blackened, but her spirit unbroken.

Hamish jumped out of the Hawk as the Albatross swept in over the square, flaring for a landing. Every one of its missiles had been fired, but it looked undamaged.

"We made the right choice," Hamish said, clapping Connor on the shoulder. "But you barely left anything for me to do."

"You made sure the civilians are all okay," Connor pointed out.

"Yeah, but they were fine. No monsters in there. Everyone is returning to the surface to help clean up, but I doubt anyone will get much for lunch. Should be able to make a decent dinner, if they're lucky. I'll suggest Shona distribute some of the smashpacked stockpile."

Hamish was consistent. Over the past few months, he'd led a huge team of bakers and cooks tasked with preparing half a million meals and smashpacking them. Merkland had several reinforced warehouses filled to bursting with enough easily transportable meals to feed the entire army for months.

Ivor and Kilian raced into the square on fracked legs and skidded to a halt nearby. Ivor looked exhausted, but exultant. Kilian looked grim, but satisfied. They trotted over, and Aifric raced across the square from where she'd been tending patients and fell into step beside Kilian.

Connor had heard accounts of Aifric's heroics as the gaggle of women in her head had worked together to destroy dozens of summoned. They'd flowed from one affinity to the next so smoothly, some people were starting to whisper that she might be another Blood of the Tallan.

If only. She smiled at Connor, looking pleased even though her clothing was covered in gore. Her hands were clean, though, and Aifric had taken over as soon as the monsters were destroyed, shifting to healing.

"We've cleared the eastern reaches of the city and verified the river is clear," Kilian said.

"I can't imagine the queen's got a second wave, not after sending so many against us, but I've already ordered Spitters and Sentries to return to watch, and I've sent windriders with Pathfinders ten miles south, just in case," Ivor reported.

That was good thinking. Connor hadn't even thought about additional enemies. Merkland had survived, but if the queen had more forces to send against them, they'd find the defenders already exhausted and most of their mechanicals either destroyed or out of ammo.

He needed to leave soon with his small team, race for Jagdish with all speed. They were hours behind schedule. Even before turning back, they'd worried they might not arrive before the queen. They couldn't afford to wait to see if more enemies were coming.

"I think we'll be fine," Verena assured him. "We're rolling out every replacement mechanical, and we've got enough stores to rearm the ones that still function. Merkland's defenses will be ready should another attack come."

Shona and Rory moved to join them. Lady Briet exited the Albatross. General Wolfram greeted her there, then the two of them also jogged over. Wolfram looked almost as battered as Rory, and Lady Briet kept reaching out as if wanting to support him.

Connor draped one arm over Verena's shoulders, feeling a deep sense of contentment to see his friends gathered and alive.

Hamish said, "I just heard from Ilse. She's en route with a couple hundred reinforcements from the main army moving south from Granadure. She's got Petralists and Builders and supplies. They'll arrive within half an hour."

Verena looked relieved. "Good. She can oversee the outer defenses while Anton rests."

"He deserves to sleep as long as he wants," Aifric said, her expression turning awed.

Connor had heard about the mighty Sapper's underground running battle with the earth-bound swarm. He'd killed hundreds of the creatures and nearly been overwhelmed, but borrowed Harley's trick of wrapping himself in an earthen battle suit. He'd broken the siege against the palace, and with Aifric's help had destroyed that swarm.

Kilian greeted Verena with a hug and kissed her forehead, not hiding his relief. "You all had us worried."

"We're so glad you came back when you did," Verena told him.

"We don't have much time, but I want to hear about the battle," Kilian said.

Verena and the others took turns relating the incredible siege. Connor felt more and more awed by their heroic efforts to protect the city from the unbelievable swarm.

"Whoa! You activated Kirstin's Defense?" he exclaimed.

Hamish looked disappointed. "I knew we shouldn't have left! I wanted to be here when we used it."

"I'm sorry, but I couldn't wait," Verena said, then related the incredible effects of the mechanical. Connor had seen the line of devastation a mile south of the city where the watery wall had stood, but hadn't seen the corpses of any of the monsters. They were simply gone. Even the ones killed inside the city were melting into muddy sludge.

Hamish whistled softly and handed a smashpacked dessert to Verena. It looked like an entire dozen sweetbreads smashpacked together. "You're going to have to tell me everything about it when we have more time. I bet we can figure out more of Kirstin's secrets."

"Not now, though. We have to leave immediately," Kilian said.

He was right. Connor felt convinced they'd made the right choice in returning, but if they didn't reach Jagdish before the queen, they might have sacrificed the success of the greater war in order to win one battle.

"We'll keep you posted on any other developments via speakstone," Rory said as they headed for the Hawk.

Connor hated to leave so soon. He kept Verena's hand in his as they walked, wanting to keep that connection as long as possible.

"Connor, there's something else you need to know," she said, pulling him to a stop. Kilian glanced back, and Connor gestured that he was coming.

"What is it?" Her big blue eyes seemed to swallow his. He expected her to offer reassurance that she'd be all right. Instead she grinned, looking excited.

"Connor, I spoke with Water!"

He blinked. "What?"

"Water! She appeared to me when I activated Kirstin's Defense."

That was astonishing. "I thought I was the only one who saw them like people."

"I know. It was completely unexpected. She's beautiful. I can sense so much power in her. I only wish we had more time to talk. I sensed she had a lot more to share."

"Wait, you spoke with her?" He had thought the manifestation of the elements in his mind was a way he'd invented to establish a better relationship with them, but if Verena had also seen Water, what did that mean? Was she really alive as a tangible being? Was that possible?

Verena nodded, her grip tight on his arms. "I didn't understand a lot of what she said. It was so unexpected and things were happening so fast, but she mentioned you and said she hopes to be able to speak with you soon."

"I hope so! This is amazing. I never imagined they could actually talk. Did she seem like a real person?"

"Real in my mind, at least." Verena paused and leaned closer. "Connor, I think I discovered that there's a Builder threshold."

"What?" he exclaimed again. He hadn't thought anything could surprise him more.

She laughed with delight. "I sensed it, Connor. Kirstin's Defense took me right to the gateway. It unlocked so much more power than I've ever imagined possible. Connor, if there's a threshold we can ascend through too, that might change so much!"

The possibilities were mind boggling, and if Verena was right, a Builder threshold challenged their fundamental understanding of the makeup of Builder powers. "I wonder if Kirstin ascended. Was that how she pushed the limits of Builder mechanicals so much farther than anyone else?"

"Maybe."

The others had reached the Hawk and Kilian shouted back, "Connor, come on!"

"We need to share this with everyone else," Connor said as he and Verena broke into a run toward the rest of the group.

"You don't have time. Tell Hamish and Kilian about it while you travel. See if Kilian has any insights. We can discuss it when you return."

They reached the Hawk and Connor paused to sweep Verena into his arms one last time, holding her tight. She clung to him for a couple seconds and whispered, "Be safe, Connor. I know you'll get there in time and ascend. I'll see you soon."

He kissed her, then waved to the others and jumped aboard the Hawk just as Hamish activated thrusters and lifted rapidly into the air. He applied rear thrusters before they even rose above the wall, and accelerated fast. They shot over the heads of waving soldiers already returning to man the wall, and sped southeast on full throttle.

Connor settled into his seat and glanced back at Verena, standing in the square that fell away behind them. Verena touched two of her fingers to her lips in a sign she used sometimes instead of blowing a kiss. He grinned and returned the gesture, happy that she was okay.

Then he said, "You guys aren't going to believe what Verena just told me."

Hamish glanced over and said, "I knew it. Lunch *was* ready."

Chapter Forty-Six

History Gets Twisted in Funny Ways

"Verena saw water as a living being?" Kilian asked incredulously.

"And she sensed a threshold for Builders?" Hamish exclaimed.

"That's what she said," Connor repeated.

He wished Verena was there to explain it to them in more detail. She would have loved to see the looks on their faces. They had tried connecting with her via speakstone, but she hadn't responded. They'd reached Rory, and he said she was already working on rebuilding the Swift. He had promised to send someone to request she contact them as soon as possible.

They were flying high, speeding for Jagdish. Hamish had pushed the Hawk so high that if not for the shielding around the windows, coupled with some quartzite air to stabilize the pressure, they might have asphyxiated. He had also activated the marble stoves in the cabin to ward off the bitter chill.

The land spread beneath them for miles in every direction. Mountains looked tiny, and somehow flattened. With the help of Air, Connor had found a powerful wind rushing in the direction they needed to go and they'd ascended to it. Through his quartzite senses, he could feel how the air around the Hawk grew so thin the thrusters began struggling to find sufficient purchase.

Driven by those powerful thrusters and the roaring wind, they were hurtling over the land at speeds that would have seemed impossible only months ago. At the moment it still felt too slow. Connor had coaxed Air to help reduce wind drag to gain even more speed.

Air seemed a little offended as she pranced about in his mind. She did not seem to like the fact that they wanted to fly faster than her mighty wind, but Connor spent some time praising her, and that seemed to help. As a result, they shot across western Obrion and into Ravinder faster than anyone had probably ever traveled.

Even Kilian looked impressed as he gazed out the window. "And you see the elements like living beings in your mind?"

Connor nodded. He hadn't shared that fact with anyone but Verena, and it felt strange discussing it aloud. He'd worried they would laugh at him, but Kilian only looked thoughtful.

Connor said, "I started seeing them as people after my first ascension, and they seemed even more solid after the second. Seeing them like that helps me feel more connected."

"I encouraged you to visualize your connections, but hadn't expected you to take it so far," Kilian admitted with a grin.

"What are they like?" Aifric asked from where she reclined on cushions across the second row of seats.

"I see Water as a mature woman with long, flowing tresses like gentle waves."

"And Verena saw something similar?" Kilian asked.

Connor nodded and Aifric asked, "Do you think she's inventing an elemental person like that just because you told her about it?"

"I don't know. She hadn't planned to see anyone, but said Water just appeared to her when she activated Kirstin's Defense."

Kilian said thoughtfully, "Kirstin had started speaking of the elements as if they had personalities in the last days before my mother executed her. I thought she was just waxing poetic."

"You've never seen them like people in your mind?" Hamish asked.

He shook his head. "Never."

That seemed weird to Connor. Kilian was so much more experienced. If the elements were really were somehow real, why not manifest themselves to Kilian?

"Did your parents ever speak of the elements like living beings?" Connor asked.

"No, and honestly they urged extreme caution when tapping tertiary powers."

"Really? I thought you said they focused more on tertiaries than any other power," Connor said.

"They did. Especially my mother. I always thought she was just jealous that anyone else could access the same affinities, but maybe there was more. She once told me I wasn't ready to learn the deeper secrets because I didn't respect the dangers enough."

"I wish she'd told you more about the dangers," Aifric said. "Then maybe you'd know more about what Kirstin did to hurt your father."

"Me too," Kilian said softly.

"Did Kirstin ever talk about a Builder threshold?" Hamish asked.

Kilian shook his head. "I'm as astonished as you to hear about it. Kirstin and I were close, but she grew more distant when she moved to Merkland. I thought she was just grieving for the loss of her husband and focused on raising her boys."

Connor felt deeply frustrated. "We need to know more."

"We'll learn a few things when we get to Jagdish," Aifric assured him.

"We'd better," Connor said glumly.

"Well, we already learned we can travel a lot faster than we'd realized," Hamish said happily.

Kilian grinned as he looked out at the land scrolling past. "I can move very fast when I need to, but this . . ." He gestured at their comfortable cabin. It was warm and calm, although the entire vehicle thrummed from the quartzite thrusters. "I believe this will revolutionize how we think of travel."

Hamish started and reached for one of the speakstone controls. "I've got a connection coming online. Hold on."

Verena's voice sounded through the cabin, but it was crackly, her words indistinct. ". . . Connor . . . Talk."

"What's wrong?" Connor asked, leaning forward, frowning as he tried to make out the garbled transmission. "Are they under attack again?" The thought filled him with dread. If they suffered another attack, could the weary defenders really fight off another wave of monsters, or an army? Could Connor's team risk turning around to help again?

Hamish frowned as he concentrated over the speakstone. "I think it's the distance."

A moment later, Verena's voice faded away. If she really was trying to ask for help, and if they didn't turn back again, would he ever hear her voice again?

"Are you sure?" Kilian asked, also looking concerned.

Hamish nodded. "We're pretty far away already and we're moving away really fast. We haven't set up signal boosters out this way yet."

"Something to consider for the future," Kilian said.

"Can we boost the signal to make sure they're all right?" Connor asked, feeling tense.

"I could try linking in our spare thruster blocks. That would probably do it," Hamish offered.

Connor liked that idea, but Kilian said, "I doubt they're under attack again so soon. Besides, Ilse and her reinforcements should be almost there. With how much power we're consuming, we'll need those spare thrusters. No, let's wait until our return."

"I think we should try anyway," Connor said. He didn't like not knowing.

Kilian held his gaze and said simply, "If we did, and if we confirmed they are indeed under attack again, what would you have us do?"

The question hung in the air and Connor hesitated. Of course he wanted to know, and if Verena and the others were in danger again, he would want to help.

Could they risk it again?

He leaned back in his seat, folded his arms, and scowled at the panoramic view. "I know we can't turn back, but I hate not knowing."

"Trust our friends. Trust Ilse and her reinforcements," Kilian said. "Our mission is fraught with enough danger, and we already took one calculated risk. We cannot afford to get distracted."

He was right, Tallan take it. Connor still didn't like it. Aifric placed a comforting hand on his shoulder. "They'll be fine."

Kilian said, "Where exactly is Jagdish?"

Connor pushed aside his lingering worries and decided that focusing on his mission to ascend was the fastest way to return to Verena. Besides, he really was eager to prepare for the attempt.

Aifric shifted to Student Eighteen, sitting up a little straighter, her features shifting subtly. She gestured slightly left of their current heading. "I've never approached it from this angle, but I think we're on track to pass it a little to the north. It lies northeast of Maninder and east of the trading road from Granadure."

"Okay. We can follow this wind stream for another half hour, and then we'll probably have to drop lower and bank south," Hamish said.

Student Eighteen added, "We'll be looking for some rough, uneven hills, broken by a couple of mountains. Jagdish is located on the eastern side of the taller peak. It's very difficult to access from the ground, and almost impossible to see until one has already passed through the outer defenses."

That only made Connor want to see it even more. Keeping secrets was difficult. Keeping an entire community secret for three centuries seemed impossible, yet the Mhortair had somehow managed it. No doubt, they removed anyone who was unfortunate enough to stumble upon their stronghold. He hoped they didn't try anything like that today.

"What else can you tell us about your people?" Connor asked.

"Jagdish has always remained fairly small. If the population grows too much, the kill council sends families out to infiltrate other parts of the continent and establish satellite bases for our assassins, spies, and informants."

Hamish looked impressed. "That's really smart. How many outposts do you have in Obrion?"

She only raised a single eyebrow. Hamish assumed that "I'm innocent" look that never worked on anyone Connor had ever seen and exclaimed, "You don't trust me?"

She barked a laugh. "It's not a matter of trust. I don't even know all of the locations. Even if I did, and I shared them with you, what would happen if the queen picked them out of your mind the next time we faced her?"

Hamish shrugged. "I doubt she would bother. She hates Builders so much she would be too busy boiling me to sludge."

"Even if that was true, the kill council wouldn't be happy you knew too much."

"Who are the kill council?" Connor asked. She had mentioned them before, but he knew too little about her people, and suddenly that worried him. They were on their way to try negotiating a peace accord.

"They rule every aspect of Jagdish life." She explained how the Kill Academy was the premier school, where every child was tested and taught their first lessons, and where their ranks were winnowed down to the few skilled enough to eventually become assassins. The rest of the community was dedicated to supporting the mission of the assassins, providing the food, weapons, power stone, and everything else they needed to succeed.

Every other aspect of life was considered secondary to that mission. Such single-minded dedication to a cause would have been inspirational if the cause was perfecting omelets or fine-tuning recipes to maximize belch potential instead of killing.

Connor had been forced to fight a lot, and even to kill more than once, but he could not imagine dedicating his life to nothing but death. Then again, hadn't they all dedicated all of their resources and pulled in vast support from Granadure and the Arishat League with the specific mission of killing? They had to kill the queen, and everything else in their lives was sacrificed as secondary to that mission.

He didn't like the idea that his current life resembled the Mhortair so closely. What choice did they have, though?

"What do your people fear would happen if they lost focus a little?" He asked.

"What do you mean?"

"Your entire community is totally focused on the mission of murder, infiltration, and destruction. Why? What would happen if you lightened up a little?"

She opened her mouth to respond, but hesitated, her expression thoughtful. "We do a few other things too, you know. It's not just a murder fest every day."

"That's good to hear. I bet you eat overcooked bacon just to toughen yourselves up," Hamish said with a chuckle.

"Actually, one aspect of our missions to perfectly infiltrate other countries is to know their food. We've been compiling a master list of the best recipes from across the continent for over two centuries. Mister One, the supreme leader of the kill council, always encourages us to find more."

Hamish turned in his seat, his expression eager. "Really? Your leader sounds really wise. I'll share Schwinkendorf's recipes with him."

"Just like that?" Connor asked, surprised. Those recipes were probably Hamish's greatest treasure beside his battle suit. Maybe he'd develop ways to incorporate some of the recipes into his suit. The idea made him smile to himself, imagining clever mechanicals built into the suit to rapid-fire produce omelets.

Student Eighteen chuckled. "I am sure he would love to trade recipes with you. He's ancient and extremely powerful, and he loves good food."

"He'd have to. A wise man like that understands that the more we share good recipes, the better we'll all eat. And people who feast together are far more likely to focus on creating better desserts than trying to kill each other."

Kilian chuckled. "When you speak with your stomach, you show uncommon wisdom."

"I'm just a guy with an uncommon stomach affinity," Hamish responded, patting his belly.

Connor laughed, hoping Hamish could help keep the mood light when they met the Mhortair. There was a very real chance the meeting could go badly, and he hated that he had to prepare to fight the people he so desperately needed to ally with.

Kilian chuckled. "Let's hope Mister One responds positively. He's descended from a long line of sometimes foolish men."

"Please don't speak to the kill council members like that," Student Eighteen said carefully.

"I have a long history with the Mhortair. It wasn't always friendly, but I'm willing to let the past remain in the past in order to deal with the present," Kilian replied calmly.

Connor hoped so. He wasn't sure if the kill council understood that Kilian had known Mhortair, had been trained personally by him in battle tactics, and knew him as the queen's most trusted bodyguard.

"Mhortair is revered as our great and first leader, and any insult to his memory will likely result in a fight to the death," Student Eighteen added.

"I won't reveal things that might upset your people's memory of old Mhortair. Sometimes secrets are kept for a good reason."

He would know. Kilian knew more secrets than anyone Connor had ever met.

"Can you explain how your society is structured and why you use such ridiculous titles?" Hamish asked.

Student Eighteen bristled. "They aren't ridiculous. They date back to the great Mhortair himself."

Kilian smiled. "He might not have been as great as you're led to believe."

She gave him a warning look, but Hamish said, "Seriously, why are your leaders called Mister One, Mister Five, and things like that? And you said your commanders are numbered too. And your kill instructors are called Sir. I thought at first maybe the purpose was to mask your true numbers from any potential enemies, but your titles actually accomplish the opposite."

Kilian chuckled. "That's one mystery I can answer for you. Mhortair was a great fighter, master of many of the subtle arts of assassination, deception, and murder. He also considered himself quite the poet, so he routinely came up with tongue-twisters and bits of poetry that he loved to recite during lessons. He was convinced they would help me and his other students internalize the lessons and master the skills he taught."

"We use similar techniques in the kill academy," Student Eighteen said proudly.

Kilian responded with a smile. "Some of old Mhortair's were pretty bad. The one in question went like this:

One little Mister always draws a knife.
Two little Misters take the target's life.
Three little Misters creeping in like a dream.
Four little Misters leave no time to scream.
Five little Misters clear the food from your plate.
Six little Misters strike with overwhelming weight.
Seven little Misters touch steel to every kill point.
Eight little Misters take the heart and not the joint.
Nine little Misters draw secrets using screws.
Ten little Misters kill them while they snooze."

That wasn't actually too bad, although the line about clearing food from a plate sounded more like a truth Hamish would teach. The mental image made Connor smile. What other courses would he teach if he ran an academy? Pocket hoarding, food diplomacy, and practical joke fundamentals immediately came to mind.

Student Eighteen looked shocked, and exclaimed, "The great and first leader would not institute the sacred titles based on such a silly rhyme."

Kilian shrugged. "You know I never lie. Mhortair was your first and great leader. Fine, I won't argue that point. However, I knew him in earlier days when he pursued a different life. Arguing about why he experienced a change of heart, reversed the direction of his life, and established your community the way he did would be a waste of time."

While she considered that, Hamish said, "I think it's time to bank south."

He descended from the fast-moving air current and made the turn. Soon they spotted the peaks and swooped down in that direction. Most of that part of Ravinder was comprised of flat plains, broken only by gently rolling hills. It already looked green with spring grasses, and Connor could see why Ravinder was renowned as the grain-growing capital of the world.

A cluster of mountains broke the otherwise unremarkable plain. A group of low hills surrounded a smaller number of larger hills, almost big enough to be called mountains. Two tall peaks reared out of the center, rising several thousand feet higher. They were rather narrow, like giant stone spears driven up from underground.

The tops of the peaks were sheer stone cliffs, close together like two tines of a giant fork. They reminded him a little of Badurach Pass. Lower down, they expanded into a series of shoulders and canyons, with steep valleys clogged with lots of broken stone and debris. He spotted few signs that anything green or living grew anywhere on the desolate peaks. Any other time traveling past, he would have felt no desire to explore the grim peaks.

The afternoon shadows were beginning to settle heavy over the canyons to the east of the mountains, and even when Hamish activated the long vision viewscreen, Connor didn't see anything that looked like a city.

"Are you sure these are the right mountains?" Hamish asked, peering forward intently.

Student Eighteen smiled. "Do you think it would be easy to spot a secret city?"

"From way up here I did," Hamish admitted.

The fact that they were having so much trouble finding the city helped ease Connor's fears. If they struggled to find Jagdish, surely Queen Dreokt wouldn't know exactly where to find it either. She'd fallen to the long sleep before Mhortair transitioned to his new life as the great and first Mhortair.

"There!" Connor said, pointing. He wouldn't have spotted the subtle signs of human habitation in one of the high, rocky canyons if not for movement. Scores of soldiers were rushing along the top of what looked like a sheer cliff high up one of the canyons. Only as he focused on the area did he realize it was a wall, cleverly worked into the natural landscape to look like a rock face.

The top of the wall was more than a dozen feet thick, but the flat walkway was hidden by a three foot wall of rock that blended in with the cliff face. Squat guard towers were worked into the slopes at either end, and even with his enhanced vision he almost missed them.

The wall blocked a steep, narrow canyon that wound down through the lower reaches of the mountain to the foothills and plain beyond. It looked like a difficult climb, and the city would be invisible to anyone approaching from the land. Now that Connor recognized the wall, he spotted the angles and straight edges of buildings of a city clustered in the deep canyon behind it. At first, they had looked like boulders and debris. If not for Student Eighteen's guidance, they could have searched for weeks without finding Jagdish.

"They must have spotted us," Hamish said with a frown. "I had hoped to surprise them."

Connor's tension grew as he gazed down on the fast assembling soldiers. He sought peace with the dangerous assassins and vital knowledge to ascend. With Student Eighteen's help, he hoped to make the Mhortair powerful allies, but their response suggested they might not be as accommodating as he had hoped.

Kilian glanced at Student Eighteen. "Did you warn them we were coming?"

"Of course not. I've been actively suppressing the noise from our thrusters to keep them from noticing us."

"Pathfinders might have spotted us descending, but why would they be scanning this high? With our paint scheme, we're hard to see unless they were specifically looking for us," Hamish said.

He was right. It didn't make sense that they'd been spotted so soon. Connor scanned the area beyond the mountain, trying to figure out what was going on. At the edge of his vision, movement miles to the south drew his gaze. He focused on a solitary figure sliding across the land upon a glittering throne of ice.

Sudden fear chilled him as he recognized the figure.

"They're not mobilizing because of us. Look! Queen Dreokt is already here."

Chapter Forty-Seven

If Only We Had a Month to Plan

Connor's hope wilted as he stared down at the queen. At least she wasn't flying, but that offered little consolation. For some reason she had chosen to approach Jagdish by land. Maybe she was questing out for the city through slate, although Connor would be surprised if the Mhortair city wasn't heavily shielded.

If it was, she'd pierced the illusion because she looked like she knew exactly where she was going. Queen Dreokt moved at speed, sitting on a glittering throne of ice, carried along by a boiling platform of blue-green waters. She slid north, moving fast, but not as fast as Connor suspected she could. It was almost as if she wanted to give the inhabitants of the doomed city time to recognize their fate.

Harley had acted in similar arrogant fashion in her assault on Althing. It had been extremely annoying, although ultimately they had managed to use the time to turn the tide against her.

Kilian grimaced and muttered a curse under his breath. "That's her, all right. She'll reach Jagdish in less than half an hour."

"Oh, no," Student Eighteen breathed, her face ashen with fear. "We're too late."

That's what Connor feared. He couldn't help think that if they hadn't turned back to help their friends in Merkland they would have arrived in time to learn vital information and hopefully gain some help in preparing him to ascend. Just as he had feared, saving Verena and the others might have just cost them the war.

He hated thinking that, and refused to accept the idea that sacrificing Verena to that summoned horde might have been the right thing to do.

"What can we do?" Hamish asked nervously. He had slowed their descent. They were still a couple miles in the air, a few miles northeast of Jagdish.

"We have to help them," Connor said.

"Yes," Student Eighteen said eagerly. They all turned to Kilian, who was scowling down at his mother, small in the distance even through the enhanced viewscreen.

"We're not ready to fight her yet," he said gravely.

Connor opened his mouth to protest, but Kilian flashed a predatory grin and added, "But we can't afford not to. Student Eighteen, can you contact your people without her hearing?"

She nodded and leaned forward, focusing on her distant home. Connor tapped serpentinite and reached for the other elements too. He was nervous, not angry, so the connections came a little slower this time and he had to tap a little porphyry to help stabilize them.

Porphyry awoke in his heart and he felt the beast reacting to his fear with a growl, and sensed its desire to transform and hunt whatever dared scare him. That feeling eased his fear a little, and the elements appeared in his mind. Water appeared first, looking beautiful and regal, as always. She wore a shimmering gown that glittered like ten thousand points of light reflecting off of crystal droplets of water.

Strangely, porphyry reacted to her appearance with another growl. Connor pushed it back out of the way. He didn't have time for porphyry's out-of-control rage problems. He'd thought he was past all that.

Connor addressed Water in his mind. *Can you hear me? Are you real? Verena told me she met you. Thank you for helping her.*

She inclined her head toward him and smiled. He sensed that she wanted to communicate more, but for some reason did not. If she was only a figment of his imagination, then he was giving her those attributes, but he hoped she was something more, and wished he had time to explore the mystery.

Fire appeared beside Water, dressed in a fancy doublet made of flickering, multi-colored flames. As always, the red and green energy frequencies flowed across his clothing, but did not diminish the brilliant colors of his wardrobe. His hair looked longer, full of crimson and yellow flames, and he winked at Connor, then strode around Water, appraising her elegant gown with an appreciative eye.

Earth rose up from the depths to stand beside the others, his expression a bit troubled as he glanced out toward Queen Dreokt. Air flitted down from above, her gown made up of dozens of strips of light blue cloth, their detached ends floating around her like clouds. Her hair was loose, and it hung long and dark around her oval face, blown constantly by an invisible, gentle breeze. Her eyes were filled with tiny tornadoes, and she winked at Connor, then danced lightly around Earth, who tried to look unimpressed, but turned to follow her.

Serpentinite entered his mind with the sound of Verena's laughter, echoing endlessly around the other elements. They ignored the formless late-comer, and Connor sensed for the first time that they somehow considered serpentinite unworthy of their company.

Where had that come from? Was that another figment of his imagination, or a glimmer of truth from real beings that chose to walk with him?

His musings were interrupted by a brilliant beam of pure, white light streaking away from the Hawk. It originated with Aifric, who had opened her mouth to speak. Connor heard nothing as she caught her words and cast them down that beam of light that acted like an insulating tube, preventing anyone else from eavesdropping.

The beam of sound touched down upon the wall and bounced back and forth between the guard houses for a few seconds before one of the soldiers reached out a hand and caught it.

"They have received my message," Student Eighteen said happily.

"What did you tell them?" Hamish asked.

"I told them we're here, who we are, that we spotted Queen Dreokt approaching, and wish to help."

"That's a good start," Kilian said.

Connor hoped so. The Mhortair could have easily interpreted their arrival at the same time as Queen Dreokt as a threat. They all had too much to deal with to fight each other over a misunderstanding.

Another beam of light erupted off the ground and shot for the Hawk. Connor tensed to defend them if the light proved dangerous, but Student Eighteen extended a hand, and he felt her pulling at the light. It struck her hand and rolled up her arm.

The light disappeared into her ears. She sighed, a little tension easing from her posture. "They know she's coming. They had received warning from an unknown source of an imminent attack."

"Ailsa," Connor guessed.

"How can she do all that?" Hamish asked incredulously. "She's traveling with the queen, after all."

"I don't know, but I bet it's her," Connor said. The terrible risks she took to send warnings scared him, but he felt inspired by her bravery and her ability to somehow remain right under the queen's nose without being discovered.

Student Eighteen continued, looking pleased. "They've chosen to accept our offer of aid. Much of the population is already concealed in heavily shielded caverns beneath the mountains. They've marshaled all of the strength of Jagdish to repel the queen's attack. Flanking parties are already moving out onto the plain. They want to know what we can do to aid."

Connor welcomed the news. It suggested the Mhortair had already decided to ally with them. If only they'd arrived a little sooner! He liked hearing that they were trying to conceal some of their people. Chances were good that everyone who openly stood against the dread queen would die, unless he and his friends could find a way to drive her off.

Kilian glanced out the window, looking from the city to the distant queen. "I'm surprised they shared so much with us."

"Well, they shared it with me and cautioned me to keep some of it secret, but . . ." She shrugged.

"We can help. She doesn't know we're here," Hamish said eagerly, and Connor agreed. He didn't want to fight Queen Dreokt before ascending, but surely they could do something.

He said, "Maybe we can hit her from behind, from the air, surprise her, distract her, make her retreat, or something."

After a couple seconds deep in thought, Kilian nodded, his expression serious. "Very well. We'll fly out wide. We'll have to give her a lot of space to not draw her attention. Once the battle starts, we'll make our move."

"What move?" Connor asked, licking suddenly dry lips. Helping Merkland had been the right thing to do, and he didn't regret it. Helping Jagdish was the right thing too. Surely they could figure out how to save the Mhortair. The alternative made him sick.

Kilian said, "The only one we can try with so little time to plan. My mother is focused on Jagdish. Look at her, how she sits on that ridiculous throne. She knows she'll win, and she is planning to enjoy the destruction. Connor, shield us with every trick you know. Hamish, you too, and swing us out wide."

Hamish immediately complied, banking the Hawk away from the mountain and gently increasing thruster. Without needing to be told, Student Eighteen seized all the sounds they made and squashed them.

"Not quartzite shielding yet. It glows and she might notice," Connor cautioned. "I can shield us with air almost as well, but keep it invisible."

"Good idea. Activating pumice," Hamish said, his hands flicking across various controls on the front panel.

Connor reached for Air, who hovered over to him and slid her warm hand into his. She and the other elements were starting to look a bit troubled. He wondered if that was because they recognized Queen Dreokt, and knew she was far more their master than he ever could be.

"Help me. We can defeat her together," he urged.

Air seemed to like that idea and flashed a dazzling smile. At her touch, he sensed all the air currents flowing past. He carefully parted them around the Hawk, forming a protected bubble within the air that would hopefully deflect Queen Dreokt's air senses from noticing them.

"Nice and easy," Kilian urged Hamish in a soft tone, even though Student Eighteen was shielding their words. Little points of light had ignited within his eyes. "We'll fly out wide and hit her from behind while she's distracted."

"Hit her how?" Connor asked.

"I've got missiles and hornets, but will those do any damage?" Hamish asked.

"Not really, but they're great distractions. When the battle starts, I'll have you make a pass over her, then hit her with everything you've got. The three of us will bail out on that first pass." He glanced at Connor. "Find one of those Builder descent jackets for Aifric."

Connor scrambled to one of the storage hatches set in the floor of the Hawk and pulled it open. They'd packed in lots of supplies, including power stone, mechanicals, and the clever jackets. Similar jackets had been used to great effect at the battle of Altkalen.

"We can activate pumice on the way down to shield ourselves from her until we reach the ground," he suggested.

"When we hit her, don't hold back," Kilian said grimly. "She's a lot stronger than we are, but together we should be able to distract her for a while. If the Mhortair strike teams can join us, we might be able to drive her off."

"How do we kill her?" Connor asked, trying not to think about how crazy the plan sounded. Kilian was terrifying when he wanted to be, but he'd just admitted the best they could hope to accomplish all together was to distract his mother, maybe injure her or force her to retreat for a while.

What would happen if they failed? He usually thought of Kilian as too powerful to die, but Queen Dreokt could destroy him. What about the rest of them? She could kill them all.

He suddenly wished he'd taken more time to say goodbye to Verena.

Student Eighteen's expression had turned predatory. "The kill squads will include champion sword masters and some of our most powerful tertiary Petralists and kill instructors. They are masters of every possible form of death."

"But can they kill her?" Hamish asked nervously.

"I've seen her injured before, hurt so badly that she retreated to heal," Kilian said.

That was probably supposed to be reassuring, but Connor glanced at Hamish, who was starting to look a little sick.

"I've seen her cut in half. That only seemed to annoy her," Hamish reminded them, his eyes a bit wild from the terrible memory.

Kilian placed a calming hand on his shoulder. "We can do this. It's not ideal, but we can do it. If we can distract her, get enough kill leaders in close, we might have a chance."

Student Eighteen said, "We can. We saw her cut in half, Hamish, but that wasn't enough. Maybe if we can cut her into even more pieces we might be able to destroy each of those pieces before she can heal."

Connor swallowed, trying to focus on that small chance. "Hit her with everything you can think of, Hamish. You're a Builder and she fears Builders. Maybe you can scare her."

Hamish tried to laugh, but couldn't quite make the sounds come out. "Sure. I'll scare the scariest person on the planet."

"That's the spirit," Kilian said. "It's a daring plan. She won't expect it."

It was insane, but Connor couldn't think of anything to add to it. If things went well, they might be able to surprise the queen and turn her expected murder spree into a victory. If they won the day, could they win the war before it really got started?

Connor hated the cold fear that kept whispering to him that they were doomed.

Chapter Forty-Eight

A Glimpse into the Heart of Evil

Student Eighteen sent another beam of light with another message, outlining their plan. Hopefully the Mhortair strike teams could coordinate supporting their strike.

The Mhortair sent a reply, and Student Eighteen gasped when she received it.

"What?" Connor and Hamish demanded together. Connor feared the Mhortair were betraying them or something, but Student Eighteen smiled, looking happier than Connor had ever seen her.

In an awed tone she said, "The message came from Mister One himself."

Hamish muttered under his breath, "I still think those titles are stupid."

She ignored him. "He sends greeting to each of you and a message. Today we face our greatest threat, but will emerge with our greatest victory. The entire purpose of our people culminates this day, and we will live up to the purpose of our creation. May the great and first leader smile upon us all."

Connor appreciated his optimism. He hoped Mister One was right. All winter they had been preparing for this fight, but he'd always assumed the final showdown with the queen would take place surrounded by brutal struggle and desperate battle between enormous armies. If they could defeat her, they would save so many lives.

"Let's hope we all live to thank him for his warm greeting," Kilian said, then turned to face the distant figure of his mother, still sliding implacably across the land toward Jagdish. They rode in silence for a few minutes as they banked miles around the dread queen.

Student Eighteen eventually whispered, "Today I will avenge my father."

Hamish muttered, "I wish we had Ilse's Revenge with us."

Connor wished they had thousands more mechanicals, but that would mean Verena would be there too. Verena was as deadly as she was beautiful, and part of him longed to see her flying nearby in the Swift, but part of him was grateful she had been spared this fight. Even if things went badly, at least she would not be one of the people who might die there that day.

Kilian said, "She definitely knows where she's going."

"I hope she found it in someone's mind and didn't decide to lay waste to Maninder to learn it," Connor said.

Hamish grimaced, looking sick by the idea. The capital city of Ravinder would have been helpless before the queen even though a large Arishat League army was marshaling around Maninder. If she'd traveled that far south, he didn't doubt she would have destroyed the army and maybe the city in a fit of anger.

The thought helped firm his resolve to fight. Battlefield creativity was one of his strengths, and they were going to need every bit of it before they beat the dread queen.

As they flew, Connor sensed no indication that the queen had noticed them. He felt no movement through the air, no foreign will tugging at his. Shielding air was kind of similar to shielding earth, but very difficult until Connor had ascended the second threshold. Only then did Air seem to pay him much attention and not just look for ways to make his life difficult. If the queen decided to fight him with air, would she abandon him and submit to the more powerful Petralist?

With serpentinite, the landscape brightened with subtle sounds of early morning. Connor enjoyed looking out at the sights as Hamish banked farther to the east until the distant mountains of Jagdish became tiny. They'd begin to come around behind the queen any second.

Hamish had activated a small sightstone, projected on the side window, showing the queen below them. He did a great job keeping the view centered on her and zoomed in close even as he banked wide around her. She was sliding north toward the mountains of Jagdish, her expression regally stern, and did not seem to have noticed them.

As Connor focused on her, studying her regal gown of silver and gold, he noticed that she was holding something in her hand. It looked like some kind of stone. He tried focusing on it, but the distance was so great that even with the viewscreen zoomed in so far, it was hard to make out details.

"What is that thing she's carrying? Is it a sculpted stone?" he asked.

Kilian frowned and leaned closer to the viewscreen. "She doesn't need anything. She's already at the pinnacle of her power. What is she up to? Hamish see if you can magnify this view any more."

The fact that he looked nervous made Connor terrified.

Hamish said, "It's zoomed in on max power. I'm beginning our turn. Give me a minute and I'll be able to focus the front window on her. The magnification is better. Maybe we can figure out what she's doing before we start our attack run.

Hamish began banking in a long, gentle turn.

Queen Dreokt stopped.

She stood, and her icy throne melted away behind her. She raised one hand, finger extended as if to chastise the wicked city of Jagdish.

"What is she doing?" Connor cried. She was still at least three miles from the mountain.

"Too soon," Student Eighteen whispered.

The ground beneath the queen buckled under an explosive concussion. But it wasn't a blast of earth.

It was a blast of sound.

It blazed in Connor's serpentinite senses like a hundred suns concentrated together. He blinked and cried out, turning away, unable to look at it, even though he was seeing it with serpentinite eyes and not his natural ones. The blast was so bright and overpowering that he felt stark terror replace his previous cautious optimism.

In his mind, the elements recoiled, as if in horror. Earth looked deeply offended and swung his arms out wide. Connor realized with shock that he was striking out at the invisible echoes of serpentinite. What?

Aifric screamed, "I don't understand. . . . Oh no!"

Hamish oriented the Hawk directly at the queen and magnified the view. Connor was already tapping quartzite to see better. Despite the disorienting twist of the double-enhanced vision, Connor gritted his teeth and magnified his gaze. What he saw through quartzite did not matter. It was what he saw through serpentinite that horrified him.

That concussive blast of sound was spreading like lightning across the land, and the earth was buckling and reverberating like a giant drum struck by an enormous mallet. Vibrations of earth and sound radiated north toward Jagdish, moving so fast Connor did not even have time to shout a warning.

It was like the queen had triggered an earthquake with sound. It struck Jagdish and the mountains above the city like a hammer from the heavens. Sound blasted soldiers from the walls, shattering their bodies before they even struck the stones. Buildings crumbled, and the shockwave blasted up through the canyon like a hundred thousand thunderclaps.

In Connor's mind, Earth dropped to one knee, his initial shock turning to a towering fury. Air flitted toward him, but he glared at her then sank down out of sight. Connor's connection with him faded away.

Down on the ground, the shaking of the earth continued, the landscape undulating like a sheet on a line, blown by a strong wind. Every ripple blasted through the foothills, shattering them into loose piles of rubble that cascaded down.

Then the waves of destruction struck the city. The entire canyon buckled like an unruly stallion. The cliff face of the outer wall shivered apart in the first wave, and the mountain peaks swayed like drunkards. As more destructive waves of earth and punishing sound poured in with relentless, unstoppable force, the shaking grew worse and worse. Buildings shattered or shook apart, then as the shaking continued to intensify, they were flung into the air.

Connor watched in horror at the devastation unfolding. He felt cold, couldn't seem to breathe, and gripped the front dash of the Hawk so hard it splintered. Down in the doomed lands, the entire mountain shuddered as the two majestic peaks smashed into each other. Vast stones exploding apart, as if made out of tiny blocks sitting on a table that someone kicked over.

A single beam of light shot away from the city as it fell. Student Eighteen was screaming, and Connor realized he was too as he watched Jagdish fall. In seconds the entire community was sundered and broken into piles of shattered rubble.

He caught the beam of light and drew it in. It was a message in an elderly man's voice that he instinctively recognized as Mister One's. It was ancient and wise and immensely powerful, and far too calm to have spoken in the midst of that catastrophe.

"*We are fallen! You alone must stop this insanity. I entrusted the treasure you need here. Find it and—*" The message cut off abruptly, and Connor knew with a sense of cold horror that in that second, Mister One had died. So had every living soul who had stood to defend their home.

They were all gone, lives snuffed out like ten thousand candles dropped into the sea. The magnitude of the queen's murder left Connor feeling numb and sick with horror.

Waves of sound and earth continued to beat the broken mountains until millions of tons of stone shook apart. Both peaks collapsed, their deaths concealed by billowing clouds of debris, as if the very world was ashamed of what had happened and sought to conceal the horrific details. Thunderclaps of stones smashing against each other rumbled across the land, like brilliant gold streamers to Connor's serpentinite view.

He stared, dumbfounded, unable to process the magnitude of what had just happened. He had seen incredible elemental powers unleashed by Petralists, but with that single stroke, Queen Dreokt had revealed a level of power he had not dreamed possible.

A few seconds later, Hamish managed to increase the magnification of the front window to maximum and bank the Hawk toward the broken city. All they saw were billowing clouds of destruction. They waited in silence, while Student Eighteen wept, until the cloud began to disperse.

Absolute destruction. The two proud mountains had been reduced to hills of broken rubble. Jagdish was simply gone.

"I don't understand," Student Eighteen wailed.

"It had to be that stone," Connor said, his voice sounding hollow. He felt shocked, as if he was living a nightmare, but couldn't wake up.

Hamish pivoted the craft back around toward the queen.

She had dropped to one knee.

In that magnified view, she looked utterly spent. A trickle of new hope burned away some of the despair Connor was feeling. Whatever she had done, it had taxed even her incredible strength to the max. If she was suffering exhaustion similar to what he'd felt rising through a threshold, this might be their best time to attack her.

The others spotted it too and Kilian barked, "She's down! Hamish—"

Queen Dreokt slowly turned her head and looked straight at them.

Everyone in the cabin gasped, and Kilian muttered a soft curse, one Connor had never heard before.

He placed a hand on Hamish's shoulder and ordered in a tense voice, "Turn this thing around and get us out of here."

Chapter Forty-Nine

Make Time for the Important Things First

"We will send everything we can at once," Jean assured Verena.

Jean and her flight leaders, along with a dozen other officials and military officers were assembled in her private conference room in her residential palace in New Schwinkendorf. The men and women gathered for the call were somber as they stared at the view of battered Merkland visible behind Verena.

"Thank you," Verena said with a tired smile. She still wore her dirty, battered armor, her hair a mess, her face streaked with grime. She looked exhausted, as had Rory, who had joined the call briefly.

"Let us know if you need anything else," Jean offered.

"Thanks," Verena said again. "I have to get back to work. We have a lot to do before dark."

The connection faded away and Jean turned from the whitewashed wall where the viewscreen had been projected. Facing her team, she switched to Grandurian and asked, "What can we offer for immediate aid?"

"We have a dozen healthbeds," Gisela said after scanning a list of supplies she already had handy. Jean always found it fascinating that she spoke Grandurian far more fluently than Obrioner.

"Good. It sounded like those siege mechanicals worked wonderfully, but too many were destroyed. Can we get replacements?" Jean asked, turning to Bruno.

The huge blacksmith, who now oversaw all manufacturing in New Schwinkendorf grimaced. "All units were shipped to Merkland. We are building more, but most will not be ready for a week."

"We need to send supplies by tomorrow morning. How many can we have ready?"

"Five," he said after a moment's thought, then added, "Along with two thousand rounds of ammunition."

"So many?" she breathed. Five rapid-fire mechanicals were far too few, but that much ammunition could help turn the tide of any new battle.

Bruno grinned. "We've got motivated teams."

Jean glanced to her right, toward the leader of Sender Flight, her transport corps. Vanora was a solid, dependable Builder of late middle age. She was Dierk's widow and had arrived in New Schwinkendorf a few weeks back, determined to avenge him. She had taken to flying almost as well as Verena, far more quickly than Dierk ever had. She had proven an excellent choice to head up the new Sender Flight and had helped develop the training program for non-Builder pilots.

"Vanora, I want every available craft prepped for lift-off at dawn, packed with everything we can squeeze into them."

"If the battalions were ready, we could easily transport everything they need," she said, glancing at Admiral Forfar.

He replied, "Another couple weeks should do it. I can make some of our elongated transport windriders available, if needed."

"Thank you," Vanora said. "We may have enough. I'll let you know."

Jean appreciated the offer and was glad the two were focusing on helping instead of their growing rivalry. Jean's Sender Flight had grown quickly to a very capable transport corps of two dozen heavy windriders, among other craft available as needed. Admiral Forfar led the newly christened Grandurian Flying Army.

They might be new on the scene, but they were extremely well funded and their ranks were growing fast. It was becoming clear that any army that could own the skies would gain a vast advantage, and the Grandurian high prince Theodor had personally committed to building the new flying force.

It was a great idea, but Admiral Forfar didn't like the fact that Jean owned a private flying force not yet rolled into his broader army. He'd begun pressuring her to fold her flights into his army, but now that she was the lady of New Schwinkendorf it wasn't as easy for him to argue that her legion needed a legitimate chain of command. Hopefully he'd drop his quest to control all flying corps. The Builders would always have their own independent flyers, and so would Jean.

"Dulax, I want a contingent from Defender Flight as escorts. We don't know if the queen has any other summoned creatures assigned to harry reinforcements," Jean said, turning to the huge Boulder who led her fighting forces.

He saluted and said in his deep, resonant voice, "I will see it done, my lady."

Dulax had been one of her first recruits during the Battle of Merkland. She'd chosen him as her first caller, and his powerful voice and commanding presence had helped win over the rest of the forces she'd taken control of. During the terrible battle at Army gate, he'd been badly burned by Captain Aonghus and still bore scars across his face. He was one of her most devoted troops and had proven an excellent leader.

Advie, the Healer who led Mender Flight spoke up. "They have many wounded. We'll send a contingent of Healers to assist." Jean had won her loyalty during the Battle of Merkland too. Advie was one of the Healers who had helped save her life after Aonghus' fires had nearly ripped the life out of her.

Jean resisted the urge to touch her scarred face or the patch over her bad eye. She'd lost much that day, but preferred to focus on the positive that had resulted since then.

"I recommend we send some of our new semi-autonomous summonings to assist as well," Rafford added. "The tender shoot trampled by careless tread may yet rise to greet the new dawn."

The Sapper tried hard to limit his confusing speech. Jean wasn't sure if it was to make communicating easier with the members of Render Flight, which he led, or if it was simply because Captain Ilse tended to speak more plainly than any other Sapper Jean had ever met. Rafford was slender for a Sapper, and even with only one good eye, Jean could see how devoted he was to Ilse.

"You'll have to accompany them too. Ilse might be too busy rebuilding defenses to oversee applying them," Jean said. Rafford grinned enthusiastically. She hoped he was wise enough to wait a lot longer before professing any feelings for Ilse. Lukas' death had deeply affected her and was still far too fresh.

"Please have your teams review available stockpiles for any supplies that might prove helpful. I want a list of every item we can send. We'll reconvene to make final decisions this evening. Thank you all," Jean said.

As everyone filed out of the long room, she finally allowed herself to worry. Verena had said none of their close friends had died, but they'd all faced terrible danger. Verena had looked so battered, it was clear the fighting had been brutal. Jean was so grateful Hamish and Connor had returned in time to save the city, but she worried for them. It sounded like time was short. Their mission was so critical, she couldn't help worrying.

Jean felt grateful that she could marshal so much aid to send to Merkland. She was still adjusting to her new position as Grandurian nobility. She often felt uncomfortable with how some of her people treated her, as if suddenly she was somehow better than they were. She was gently trying to teach them that she was no different than always, but it didn't seem to be working.

She did appreciate her authority to mold the city and the focus of their work even more than before. Her time was full with so many responsibilities that she'd been forced to promote more well-deserving people and delegate ownership of some of her projects to them. Bruno's appointment to oversee manufacturing was one, as was Artur's appointment over the city construction. Lady Carolin oversaw most of the social and educational aspects of the city, and was preparing plans for a wonderful new theater and arts center.

Danhildur, the lead Althing scientist, now served as acting head of the Schwinkendorf Academy, which was still growing fast. Scientists, researchers, and academics from every realm were pouring in, eager to participate in the academy, which was already recognized as an important center of learning.

They were all extremely capable, and Jean trusted their decisions completely, but she still felt a slight sense of loss that she hadn't figured out how to utilize her time efficiently enough to still participate in every aspect of all of those efforts. She loved hearing their daily reports, but already felt more removed from the actual day to day work of her beloved teams.

Worrying for Hamish and Connor was not productive, so she rose and headed for the exit, humming softly to keep her summoned arm swinging correctly. She had already grown so used to the summoned limb that she didn't have to think about the notes she needed, and it responded so smoothly, she could almost forget that she'd lost an arm. Bruno's leg brace reinforced her weak leg wonderfully. In fact, some days grew so busy she was sometimes tempted to ask him for another brace for the other leg so she could keep up with herself.

Gisela fell into step beside her, carrying the leather tome of Jean's daily schedule and updates from every team. So much of their current effort was focused on churning out mechanicals and weapons, but not every aspect of her life was consumed by the threat of war.

"You are due to meet with the Builder teams in one hour," Gisela reminded her.

"Let's stop by the hospital on the way," Jean said. She collected a small bag containing her healing herbs and draped the strap over her shoulder. It was warm enough that she didn't need a jacket over her blue dress.

"Stopping at the hospital usually makes you late."

"I'll be quick," Jean promised.

Gisela wasn't fooled, but knew better than to try convincing her to skip the hospital. Together they left the opulent palace and headed down the main thoroughfare toward the wonderful new hospital just three blocks away.

The streets were crowded with people, from military officers to workers to researchers to housewives, with children running around everyone. Most people walked, while some rode horses or drove wagons. Striders rushed past, using special lanes marked in the middle of the streets that allowed them to move fast while minimizing the risk of colliding with other pedestrians.

Everyone knew her, and many of them waved or bowed. She greeted them all warmly and knew most of their names. She only wished she had more time to ask them how they were doing. New Schwinkendorf was bustling and alive, despite how their numbers were depleted after the departure of the army. To Jean the city pulsed with its own spirit, like a lifeblood of vibrant energy that enlivened her. She loved being a part of it, and still scarce believed she'd been entrusted with its governance.

The hospital was actually a group of buildings, packed within a low fence around an entire city block. The main treatment areas were located in the large, three story central building. The entire top floor was one huge, airy room with lots of windows, all open to let in the warm spring air. A dozen healthbeds clustered on one end of the room, while observation beds marched down either wall.

There were not many patients at the moment, but Jean still found old Healer Karlmann making the rounds. He was immensely old and frail, but his blue eyes still glowed with enthusiasm. A score of other doctors and assistants trailed him. They did most of the work while he observed or took the hand of each patient, asking about their health in that comforting voice of his.

When he spotted Jean, he rose from the side of a mature woman who had fallen down a flight of steps. She looked bruised, but nothing a little time on a healthbed wouldn't cure.

Jean gently hugged the kindly old Healer. "How are your patients?"

"Most of them are recovering well. I hear there is need for healers in Merkland."

She wasn't surprised he'd already heard. He might be old, but his mind was sharp, and he had a way of knowing what was going on. "I think we have enough people available. We shouldn't need to pull any of your staff."

"We are willing to go, if needed," He assured her, then winked. "But I am grateful we may not need to interrupt our work so soon. We seem to make new discoveries every day."

Together they headed toward the wide stairs leading to the lower levels. The second floor held offices for staff, while the first floor was used for surgery and treating serious trauma.

Karlmann led the growing team of Healers and medical staff researching diseases, particularly infection. Using the latest generation of the near-vision goggles Hamish and one of his teams had developed, they could peer deep into tiny secrets of the little molecules that made up the basic building blocks of life.

An entire score of Althing scientists had recently arrived, excited to participate in those efforts. Jean hoped they would uncover secrets to battling infection and other diseases that resisted Healers. That understanding could lead to medicines that could save thousands of lives every year.

Even more exciting, secretly she hoped one day to discover the physiological effects that resulted from powerful Petralist affinities. Why was it that some Petralists could defy aging and live for centuries? If they could identify the changes those affinities gifted to those special individuals, could they figure out how to replicate those benefits? Perhaps the Builders could produce a mechanical to similarly slow aging. The possibility thrilled her.

When they reached the second floor, Karlmann gestured toward his office, located at the end of the wide hallway. "I would like to share my most recent notes."

She wanted nothing more than to spend half a day poring over that research with him. She was still more a healer than nobility, but she sighed. "Perhaps tomorrow. I want to visit the long-term residents before my next meeting."

"Tomorrow then," he said.

Feeling refreshed by even that short visit, Jean led Gisela to one of the other buildings in the compound. It was long and low, built of honey-colored wood, with a friendly feel. Inside lived several patients recovering from terrible wounds that had left them paralyzed or crippled. Most people liked to pretend wars didn't produce so many victims of lost limbs, lost eyes, broken hearing, or other handicaps.

With the help of Rafford and Render Flight she was trying to build semi-autonomous summonings to assist. Unfortunately, with Ilse gone the work had slowed. Still, the team had made tremendous progress and Rafford was working hard to apply the techniques he'd learned from Ilse.

So far they had built a dozen summoned arms, although none of them included the sophisticated sound-controlled movements of Jean's. At least one patient possessed the vocal range to possibly succeed like Jean, so the upgrade was planned for the following week. For the others, they were exploring related concepts to improve mobility, and she expected many marvelous breakthroughs in the coming months.

They had produced eight summoned legs with varying levels of success. When Ilse returned, Jean hoped to work with her to explore ways to reproduce the miraculous summoning she'd crafted for herself that allowed her to walk and move, despite her crushed spine and paralyzed legs.

She spent twenty minutes visiting the patients, encouraging them, and listening to their enthusiastic reports of progress made with the summoned limbs. Even though none of them had resumed full mobility yet, they were optimistic about the future.

Eventually Gisela made a discrete gesture toward the door. They were already late for her next meeting. As the lady governess of New Schwinkendorf, Jean could skip a meeting if she chose, but that would result in extra work for her people, so she didn't like letting them down.

So she reluctantly excused herself. As they headed across the campus she said, "Almost ready. One more stop to make."

"I can reschedule," Gisela offered, but Jean shook her head and gestured toward another cottage nearby.

"I just want to check in on Nicklaus."

CHAPTER FIFTY

You Can't Walk through a Closed Door

Hamish pushed the Hawk to its limits and they tore through the air, fleeing the dread queen. Beside Connor, Kilian looked outwardly calm, but he spotted little telltale signs that even he was nervous. For his part, Connor couldn't help constantly glancing behind them. He kept imagining the queen rising into the air to chase them down. He sensed nothing, but could he really penetrate her shielding?

Student Eighteen had remained in stunned silence for the past several minutes, tears dripping down her cheeks. Connor didn't blame her. He struggled to process what they had just witnessed. Somehow the queen had unleashed unprecedented destruction upon Jagdish. He doubted he'd ever forget the sight of the city shattering, bodies blasted to pieces, and the mountain collapsing over everything in the biggest mass grave in all of history.

He felt a chill of dread thinking of all the people. Had the citizens of Jagdish survived the implosion of the mountains in those shielded caverns, or had they all collapsed too?

He was amazed the queen had not yet attacked them in the Hawk. No doubt she could reach far with her elemental powers, farther than he could, and make their life difficult. Why hadn't she?

Hamish was flying fast, and the Hawk could outrace even many air currents. Air seemed nervous when Connor reached out to her, but she did not flee his mind. With her help, he identified a strong wind at a slightly lower elevation, and guided Hamish down to it to increase their speed.

Eventually Student Eighteen sniffled loudly and wiped her nose. Her eyes were red, but her expression determined. "We have to go back."

"Not today," Kilian said calmly.

"She's weak. You saw her," she insisted.

Hamish glanced over from the controls. "She saw us. She would know we were coming. We wouldn't last long enough to get within a mile of her, let alone within striking range."

"You don't know that."

"We're lucky she hasn't attacked already," Connor said.

Student Eighteen shook her head. "That she hasn't proves she's weakened. So she sensed us? Does that mean she could still fight us? You saw her. She looked exhausted. Perhaps she frightened us away only because she is too weak to fight us."

Kilian looked unfazed. "Or she was trying to lure us into attacking so she didn't have to chase us halfway across the continent."

"If she wanted to draw us in, why look at us?" Student Eighteen asked.

It was a good point, but the only way of knowing was to go back and see who was right. If they got it wrong, they would all die. If they got it right, some of them might live. Then Connor remembered something. "Hey, doesn't she think we're dead?"

They all exchanged surprised looks and Hamish said, "Well, she thinks at least some of the Builders are dead, but she'll know some of us survived now that she's seen the Hawk."

"She thinks you're dead or captured," Student Eighteen said to Connor.

"So who did she think was in the Hawk?" Kilian asked.

Hamish said, "We had shielding up, so I doubt she could reliably scan us, and with the angle of our approach, I doubt she could have seen us in the windows."

"What does that change?" Kilian asked.

"I don't know," Connor admitted. "Maybe that's why she didn't attack us. Maybe she figured we were just random Builders."

"Random Builders who just happened to be flying to Jagdish?" Student Eighteen asked.

Connor shrugged. "We could turn around and go ask her."

"Not funny," Hamish said with a shiver.

Kilian said, "We can't risk turning back, not yet."

"We do need to risk it, though," Connor said, even though all he wanted to do was keep running as fast and as far as possible.

"Connor . . ." Kilian started, but Connor cut him off.

"Mister One sent a final message."

Student Eighteen looked shocked. She'd been so distraught she hadn't even noticed the message. Connor explained. "He only got part of it out before he died."

She leaned back in her chair, fresh tears in her eyes, and couldn't suppress a sob. Her features shivered and tough Tresta took over. Her voice became rougher. "We need to avenge her people."

Connor wondered if the other ladies were all gathered in their common mental space, comforting Student Eighteen as she mourned the loss of her leader and her people. He'd been almost overwhelmed by the sight of Merkland swarmed and the knowledge that he almost lost Verena and so many of their friends. What must it feel like to witness the total destruction of your home?

He said, "In the message, he said that the treasure I needed was with someone. It sounded like somehow he thought they could still help us."

Kilian blew out a breath and glanced back the way they'd come. "If she does attack us, we'd be in serious trouble. We have to learn how she struck Jagdish like that. Not even I understand and that worries me."

"I need to ascend, and whatever Mister One left for me might be vital in making that happen," Connor reminded him.

"We have to go back, find out if anyone survived," Tresta insisted. "What if they're trapped under that rubble?"

That was a scary thought. Connor realized that if the kill squads out on the plain had been identified and killed by the queen too, and if the people hiding under the mountain had died, Student Eighteen might now be only one of very few living Mhortair. Sure, there were small groups scattered around the rest of the continent, but all together how many could there be?

"Slow down, Hamish," Kilian said after a moment. "Take up a circular flight path at high elevation. If we can verify my mother has left the area, we'll make an attempt to land tonight after dark."

"Thank you," Tresta said.

Connor felt it was the right decision, but as Hamish slowed, gently banked to the left, and began climbing, his tension rose. Would the queen really leave, or was she hiding somewhere, waiting to attack?

He leaned forward, calling upon his elemental affinities again to scan for any sign of the queen. He also tapped serpentinite. His connection with it had faded as they fled from the disaster. He couldn't afford to get distracted like that. Any sounds the queen made might be the one clue he'd get before she attacked.

He felt nothing from serpentinite.

Frowning, Connor tried again, focusing on the little stone, but still felt nothing. He pulled it out of his pocket, just to make sure it had not broken or wasted away when he was not paying attention. Holding it in his hand, he felt power in it, but somehow could not reach it.

He looked to Tresta. "Has Student Eighteen used serpentinite lately?"

She shook her head. "Not since the queen destroyed Jagdish. The blast was so overwhelming, it felt like she nearly burned out our serpentinite eyes."

Connor nodded. "I felt that way too, but now I can't get anything."

That drew Hamish's and Kilian's attention. They watched curiously as Student Eighteen resumed the control position and tried to connect to serpentinite too. After a moment her brows furrowed and she said, "I can't either. I sense power in the stone, but somehow I'm locked out from the sounds."

"Do you know what's going on?" Connor asked Kilian.

He shook his head. "I've never heard of affinities getting blocked, not to multiple people at the same time. Individuals can have an affinity sundered under certain circumstances, but this is different."

Hamish asked, "Is serpentinite somehow tied to Jagdish?"

"Are you asking if the destruction of our home and the collapse of the mountains would somehow affect our affinities, I would have said definitely not," Student Eighteen said. "But at the moment, I have no explanation."

Hamish said, "We never had much serpentinite, so we never did much with it as Builders. I was hoping to see if we could combine it with quartzite speakstones and one of those diamond recording crystals of yours to see if we could record messages we receive via speakstone, but I haven't had the chance."

Connor handed him the piece of serpentinite. "See if you can release any of it."

Hamish took it and concentrated over it. "I feel power for sure, but it's like the crack I usually pry open to release a stone's power has been welded shut."

Connor took the stone back. "Can she do that? Can she seal us away from our affinities?"

Just saying the words terrified him. Their Petralist powers were the key to their hope of meeting the queen in battle. If she could sunder their affinities, she would have no need to fear anything.

Aifric shook her head. "If she could do that, why hasn't she done it before? She could have marched into Merkland and Granadure with no resistance and taken everyone."

Kilian said, "No, I suspect this is something new."

Hamish asked, "But is it new to the queen too?"

The thought that the queen might have discovered a way to break their affinities terrified Connor. The thought that she had stumbled upon that truth by accident seemed even scarier, and very offensive. She was already more powerful than any of them. It was so unfair to think she might accidentally discover a higher order of power just when they were hoping to catch up.

Then the full weight of their problems hit him like a fresh collapse of Jagdish mountain.

"If I can't tap serpentinite, how am I going to ascend?"

CHAPTER FIFTY-ONE

Usually It's a Bad Thing for Kids to Hear Voices

Christin opened the door to the cottage and smiled. Nicklaus' governess looked relieved to see Jean, and gestured her and Gisela inside.

The cottage was cozy, designed for long-term rehabilitation. Nicklaus and Christin were the only residents at the moment. The boy jumped up from the table spread with scrolls and heavy, leather tomes where he'd obviously been studying. He looked ecstatic for a chance to take a break.

"Jean!" he shouted, taking two quick steps, then jumping. He came down with legs locked straight, leaning back a little. He slid fast across the floor, and Jean side-stepped to avoid a collision.

The boy cut off the power and with a couple of quick steps stopped right in front of her. He grinned and hugged her.

"What was that?" Jean asked with a smile, relieved to see his energy and enthusiasm returned.

"Slipping shoes," he said proudly, lifting one shoe to reveal little pieces of basalt embedded into the sole. "I borrowed the idea from Verena, although she usually likes to ride basalt on her knees. Don't understand why she does that. Maybe she doesn't want to fall. You know Verena, she's better in the sky than anywhere."

He was just as bubbly as ever, talking fast. Jean ruffled his hair and said, "I'm glad you're feeling better."

"Much better," Christin said, giving the boy a stern look. "Slipped out before lessons again. I didn't catch him until he was halfway to Faulenrost."

Nicklaus shrugged, looking unaffected by her reproof. "They're making that new secret suit of Hamish's there. I wanted to see it."

"How do you know about that?" Jean asked. They had moved that project to Faulenrost to keep it secret from Hamish until they finished the new model."

Instead of answering, Nicklaus asked eagerly, "I'm happy you came. Are you releasing me today?"

"Not yet. I just stopped by to see how you're doing."

Nicklaus slumped, looking dejected. He gestured toward the table and sighed. "Terrible."

"We still have a lot of catching up to do. You prefer skipping more lessons than studying," Christin said.

"Like I said, terrible," Nicklaus groaned. Then his eyes brightened and he grabbed Jean's hand. "Unless you need me to come test shooting soldiers again!"

"Hopefully soon, but not today, I'm afraid." He sighed again and she suppressed a smile, then asked, "Have you felt anything from your affinities yet?"

Nicklaus shook his head. "Nothing. They're gone, Jean. I broke them." He seemed to notice Gisela for the first time and scowled at her. "You should have told me you made a bad stone and maybe I wouldn't have."

Gisela tried stammering an apology, her fair skin reddening as she blushed.

"You know Gisela didn't mean to hurt anyone," Christin chided Nicklaus.

"I know, but it's really frustrating," he admitted. He gave Gisela an apologetic smile and wandered back to his seat. He perched on the edge of it, and his expression brightened again.

"At least my Builder powers didn't get wrecked. They're stronger than ever."

"Really?" Jean asked. She and Gisela followed him.

Beyond the table was a sitting area with a comfortable couch and several chairs arranged near a fireplace and bookshelf. A warm fire was burning in the grate. Several Builder mechanicals in various states of disassembly were scattered across the hardwood floor or the square piece of carpeting set in front of the couch.

Nicklaus led them to the mechanicals. One looked like a miniature windrider, another like parts of a personal defensive mechanical vest, while a third was a jumble of parts she couldn't define. Pieces of stone lay scattered everywhere. Jean circled the carpet, keeping away from the fire, inspecting the half-built mechanicals.

Christin picked her way through the mess and sat on one of the chairs. "Master Nicklaus has been very busy tinkering with mechanicals during his convalescence."

"Have you discovered anything new?" Jean asked, happy to see that the boy was using his time well and focusing on the powers that remained to him instead of pining about what he'd lost. That kind of attitude was one of the most important aspects of healing from deep trauma.

He nodded and dropped to the floor next to the defensive mechanical. "See? I figured that if we pair two smaller quartzite stones like this, we can improve the coverage and duration of the defensive vests nearly twenty percent."

"Wow." Jean exchanged a surprised look with Gisela, who immediately produced a pad and pencil and began jotting notes. Jean's hand itched for her own notebook, but she'd been training herself to let others take notes for her. It was one of the unexpected prices for leadership that she didn't like. "That previous design was already so much better than the last one."

"Mine's better," Nicklaus said simply. He gestured toward the partially assembled mechanical she hadn't recognized. "I started building a water purifier too."

"A what?" Jean asked. That was new.

"Water sometimes gets messy. I figured people like to drink clean water, but sometimes can't get it. This pulls in water through this feeder tube and separates out the bad parts."

Impressed, Jean settled to her knees beside the boy. The ramifications of such an invention were wonderful. She glanced at Christin, who beamed at her ward and nodded at the unspoken question. "It seems to work remarkably well."

"How did you come up with such an amazing idea?" Jean asked.

Nicklaus shrugged. "Like I said, after I broke my affinities, my Builder powers seem stronger than ever. Especially with mechanicals that use elemental powers." He leaned closer and his voice dropped to a conspiratorial whisper. "Sometimes I can hear them."

"Who?" Jean asked.

"The elements."

She blinked in surprise, then glanced again at Christin, who looked troubled. "What do you mean?"

He shrugged again, regarding her with those too-mature eyes. "I broke my affinities with water. You'd think she'd be angry about that, but she wasn't."

"She?" Jean asked.

He nodded. "I'm pretty sure Water is a girl. She sounds real nice, although I can only just barely hear her. Sometimes I can't hear anything, but sometimes the whispers are really clear. She's the one who suggested I purify the water. I think that makes her happy."

Jean frowned, puzzled. She had no idea what he was talking about. She glanced at Gisela, who looked equally puzzled.

Christin said, "I've asked Nicklaus to repeat everything he hears from those whispers. I've started writing them down." She held up a small notebook and Jean eagerly scanned the one page covered with writing.

Most of it seemed gibberish, but a few bits and pieces stood out like the line that said, "*Your sundered bridges blocked vital access.*" Another included the tantalizing bit, "*The gateway to unlocking vast powers.*" And a third, "*Walk with me and I can teach you.*"

A couple of the lines seemed more complete, like one that stated, "*Activate a counter current to the one that draws the water. Utilize the junction of pressures to siphon the impurities through the screening barrier.*"

"This is amazing," Jean breathed, her mind whirling as she considered the possible meanings.

"So you believe me?" Nicklaus asked, again studying her with eyes that seemed to read her doubts.

"Why wouldn't I? You've always possessed a remarkably strong Builder power. This is unusual, and we need time to understand what you're experiencing."

"I bet I could hear the whispers better if I got to use more explosives," he declared.

Jean smiled, but Christin quietly made a "Definitely not!" signal with her hand behind him, looking terrified by the idea. "Perhaps under the right circumstances, and with the right protections in place."

"Great! Let me know when we can blow up some stuff. Can we have lunch now?"

"We'll leave you to it. I'll check in with you tomorrow," Jean promised. She and Gisela excused themselves.

"What does it mean?" Gisela asked as they walked through the hospital campus.

Jean said slowly, "I'm not sure, but it might be an important breakthrough. I'll send word to Verena and see if she has any insights."

Chapter Fifty-Two

You May Have to Fail a Hundred Times Just to Figure Out the Right Questions to Ask

Verena entered Shona's private apartments, situated at the top of one of the two central towers of the palace of Merkland. She really liked the sumptuously appointed apartments, ever since that day when she and her small company kidnapped Shona with the weakening powder.

She had also assumed those apartments temporarily before the battle of Merkland, and although Shona had taken them back when she switched sides and joined the revolution, Verena still felt a small sense of ownership. Shona's quarters were some of the very few rooms that hadn't gotten trashed by the recent fighting.

Shona was there already, along with Ivor and Wolfram. Even Ilse had made it. Verena had thought she was still out patrolling the outer defenses, but greeted her with an enthusiastic hug. Ilse and her small contingent of reinforcements had bolstered everyone's spirits.

There were still weeks of work ahead of them to rebuild Merkland, but they couldn't ignore other priorities. They were gathering to continue testing in the effort to figure out the secret to loaning Petralist powers.

Verena had volunteered to join the effort to see if she could sense any connections as a Builder that they might have overlooked. Plus, she appreciated having a tough mental puzzle to occupy her mind. Otherwise she'd probably end up worrying about Connor. She hated to think that she might be sitting in luxurious comfort while Connor and the others might be battling for their very lives.

There was nothing she could do to help him, so she forced herself to focus on the current task. The recent attack on Merkland by that swarm only highlighted how badly they needed to succeed. She'd used Kirstin's Defense and needed to figure out how to find that threshold again. So much to do, and time was desperately short.

Evander, who Verena had somehow not even noticed sitting in a gigantic chair slightly apart from the others said, "Smiles of greeting warm the heart, while thoughts race upon the wings of light."

"I'm glad to see you too," she said with a grin.

Evander had arrived in Merkland just hours earlier, shortly after Ilse. He had slid up to Merkland on his signature earthen chair. For such a giant man, sometimes it seemed that he could shield himself from view as readily as he shield himself from earth powers.

He pressed his enormous hands to his eyes as the rest of them settled into the comfortable chairs drawn in a circle. A moment later, he pulled his hands away from his eyes. He held a tiny bit of white lamacal powder.

Verena was impressed. All Petralists could purge primary affinities, but she doubted more than a handful of people outside of that room understood that it was possible to purge secondary and tertiary affinities too. Harley had somehow loaned quartzite to Shona through her lamacal.

Evander said, "Flowers open at the touch of gentle sunlight, and the whisper of a child at times confounds the wisest."

Verena loved the images of that Sentry speak, but didn't get a clear sense of how to interpret it. Shona and Ivor looked equally nonplussed, but Ilse nodded and smiled. "Excellent way of putting it. Some of the hints we've received from your account, Lady Shona, have helped open our minds to new ideas, and the research Evander has been reviewing clarifies some of the assumptions we've long held inviolate."

Evander passed half of the powder to Shona. Verena leaned closer, fascinating. Usually lamacal was considered a waste product and brushed away, but Harley had made Shona consume it. That had been a key to loaning the affinity, although Evander hadn't managed to produce the same effect.

Grimacing, Shona licked the tiny bit of lamacal off her palm, then chased it down with a swig of water. "I hope we figure this out, because I still think lamacal is disgusting."

Shona might be complaining, but any number of people would eagerly volunteer for the opportunity to take her place in the testing. The promise of gaining one of the coveted tertiary affinities was a dream normally far beyond the hope of most people. Verena doubted Shona would ever cede her position to anyone else.

Not only was she the only person alive who had experienced the effects of a loaned Petralist power, but she would never grant anyone else the potential glory of becoming the one who figured out how to make it work. Verena only hoped that her past experience helped facilitate success.

They waited expectantly as Shona closed her eyes, opened them, rubbed them, and glanced around the room. After a moment, she sighed and shook her head. "No different than last time. I feel nothing."

Verena asked, "What variants have you tried?"

Wolfram said, "We've used different strains of stone, with various affinities tapped. Nothing seems to affect the resulting lamacal or Shona's ability to tap its powers." He extended a hand and added, "May I inspect this batch?"

Evander passed the last little bit of lamacal to Wolfram. He poked and pried at it with his fingers, his expression intent. Verena took the opportunity to reach out and touch the powder too. She flicked her Builder senses across it, and felt something.

Sitting up straighter she grinned. "I can feel power in this lamacal."

"Really?" Shona asked, looking excited. "Can you activate it?"

Verena tried. Reaching out with her Builder senses, she sought the invisible crack that she could pry open to unlock Petralist powers. There. She felt the crack, but could not seem to pry it open.

With a frown she said, "There is power there, for sure, but something's blocking me from reaching it."

She loved research and the wonders of exploring, but she preferred to have a sense of what she was doing. Many of their best inventions had come more as accidents than intention in the early days of their research, but recently she felt more and more like they were working on proven methods and principles.

This research was casting them back to the early days of just throwing ideas into the dark. At some point they would succeed, but there was no way of knowing when.

Wolfram continued prodding at the powder, looking thoughtful. "I sense a whisper of your intent, Evander. I still feel that combining your elemental power with sandstone and focusing on your intended target helps you connect with Shona, but there's something missing."

"Obviously," Shona said with a frown.

"What could be missing?" Ilse asked calmly. She had displayed extraordinary patience and a methodical mind as she helped Jean work through the myriad iterations of her summoned limb.

Verena asked, "Have you tried touching Shona as you prepare the lamacal? Maybe one hand on her shoulder the way you might if you were healing her?"

Shona rolled her eyes, looking impatient. As a high lady she was not used to having to wait for what she wanted. She made a dismissive gesture. "Yes, yes. We've done that. No difference. When Harley loaned me quartzite, she did not touch me, so I don't think that's a requirement."

Verena nodded, nonplussed. "We may want to retest it again at some point, because the contact might facilitate the initial breakthrough."

Ilse repeated, "So what else is needed? We have the power, Evander can expel it. We had the intended target, and sandstone is applied to help facilitate connection with that target and transition authority to tap that affinity."

Wolfram looked up from the lamacal and asked softly, "But what of the connection to the affinity itself?"

Verena was not sure what he meant, and by the frowns of the others they felt the same. Shona said, "You're holding it. The affinity itself is the connection to the affinity."

Verena snapped her fingers as the concept slipped into place. "Perhaps not. We can remotely trigger power stones that we cannot otherwise access. The secret to that ability lies in obsidian."

Wolfram nodded, a slow smile spreading on his face. "Obsidian. That may be it."

"How so?" Shona asked, shuffling forward in her seat, expression eager.

Wolfram said, "Obsidian is a unique power stone. Not only does it allow Builders to connect to remote obsidian and from there to other power stones, but it plays a unique role for Petralists too. As High Lord Dougal demonstrated, it is possible for one tapping obsidian who has ascended the proper thresholds to connect to another Petralist also tapping obsidian, and through that connection exert influence over their mind."

Verena took up the train of thought. "So if we add obsidian to the mix, it might add that missing piece, the connection to the affinity, and from there to the mind. Coupled with the sandstone connection that facilitates the targeting of the individual, that might complete the loop and allow it to work."

Ilse looked to Evander, who was slowly nodding, his brows furrowed in thought. "Harley did possess affinity with obsidian. She rarely used it, seemed to never trust it, but she had it. Obsidian was the first-ever power stone, and she was one of my grandmother's chief assistants, so she established affinity with obsidian first."

That was perhaps the longest plain speech Verena had ever heard Evander make, which reinforced the importance of their train of thought. She loved the feeling of knowing they stood on the cusp of a great discovery, but her good humor faded with a new thought.

"How have we not considered obsidian before?" Verena asked.

Evander shrugged, his expression pained as he again spoke plainly. "Like I said, Harley almost never used it and I lack an obsidian affinity."

Verena appreciated his effort to speak clearly. "So if we're right, in order to loan a Petralist power, the person loaning it needs to be ascended and have affinities with both sandstone and obsidian."

Shona grimaced and glanced at her palm where she'd licked the lamacal a moment ago. "So we can't test our new theory until Connor returns."

Verena repeated softly, "We need Connor."

She needed Connor on so many levels, and she hated knowing he was on a dangerous mission without her. She decided that when she saw him again, they needed to talk very seriously about formalizing their courtship. She needed Connor and felt a growing need to publicly announce their betrothal. Either of them, or both of them, might die in the coming war. That fact made Connor hesitate, but it made her feel more anxious than ever to bind their futures together.

As soon as he returned.

CHAPTER FIFTY-THREE

A Glimmer of Light

Connor tried to match Kilian's relaxed pose as Hamish carefully guided the Hawk down toward the huge pile of shadowy rubble that had been the Jagdish mountains. They were half a mile out and still a mile above the rubble, moving slowly, scanning constantly.

Night had fallen, and although the sky was clear, a pall of dust still hung over the destroyed area, leaving it in a hazy darkness that was hard to penetrate, even with quartzite-enhanced vision.

Connor felt so tense, it was hard to breathe. He was tapping every tertiary affinity except for serpentinite, which he still couldn't reach. He tried not to focus on that loss. Every time he did, he felt like panicking. He clung to the thin hope that they could find something useful in the ruins of the Mhortair city that could help them understand the mystery.

His granite curse skittered along his torso, a comforting, constant itch. He'd also absorbed some pumice, which might offer a critical advantage if they found the queen lurking in wait. Obsidian and basalt powder were stuck to his thigh battle plates, so he could switch to those almost instantly if he needed to.

He was also tapping chert as a secondary and was ready to add blind coal if needed. He was primed for battle and ready to throw everything at the queen if she showed herself. The fact that the elements in his mind seemed calm helped him believe that maybe the queen had left after all.

"Nice and easy," Kilian whispered, the tension in his voice belying his outward calm.

They had circled high and slow and wide around Jagdish all afternoon, scanning for the queen or any other threat. They had seen nothing.

She might have left. If she'd flown away, she would have been long gone before they began their turn and started scanning for her. She also could have moved into the rubble to search for survivors, to murder anyone who might have survived in the shielded caverns beneath the mountains.

Student Eighteen had agonized over the fact that they might be leaving the last of her people to die with their slow, cautious approach, but Kilian would not change the plan without good reason. Connor agreed. Rushing in blindly would most likely get them all killed.

They hadn't spotted her, nor had they spied any signs of life among the rubble. If people had survived, they would be trapped underneath tons of debris. Even if they had Sentries with them, Connor doubted they would risk emerging any time soon.

If the queen had remained in the area, she would surely find and destroy any survivors. Had she spotted the Hawk, realized their intended purpose? She could have concealed herself among the rubble, heavily shielded, waiting to strike when they finally ventured within range.

"Go now," Student Eighteen urged. She was peering out the left side window. Her tears had faded to simmering anger. A couple times, Connor heard her growling softly under her breath, her lips moving silently, as if her head crew were holding a conference. She looked eager for a chance to strike at the monster who had destroyed her people.

"We're almost there," Kilian said, not tearing his eyes from the viewscreen. "All shields active?" he asked Hamish for the fifth time.

"Quartzite and pumice, with blind coal on standby," He said instantly, his face tense, hands flickering across various controls as he brought them in slowly. He was prepared to unleash every weapon if the queen appeared, but this close, their primary defense would lie with Connor and Kilian.

Even though the Hawk was surrounded by a softly glowing nimbus of their quartzite shielding, Hamish had dropped the inner window shields so they could use their tertiary affinities without hindrance, if needed.

They had risked landing half an hour ago, five miles out, and Connor had scanned the area with earth senses. He'd been surprised when Aifric joined him. One of the few women in her head that he hadn't gotten to know very well had assumed the control position.

Ennlin was a skilled Sapper. He realized with a shock that of all the women he knew in that head, he hadn't met any Sentries before. The other women tended toward tertiaries with quartzite, marble, and soapstone.

Unlike most other earth walkers, Ennlin seemed extremely high-strung. She also had an exceptional dependence on cheese, and had exited the Hawk already munching on a piece of extra sharp cheddar.

When he asked her about it, she gave him a cool look and said, "Mister Five lost focus while giving me life with Student Eighteen. The process proved . . . difficult. This is how I cope. Have a problem with that?"

He'd wisely said, "No. I love cheese."

Neither of them had sensed the queen or any overt signs of life, but had been too far out to search for subtle shields. Ennlin had said, "Curds hold the seeds of life, but a stone flung from a high hill still disappears into a pond."

He still hadn't figured out that one, but was happy the convoluted Sentry speak had seemed to calm her nerves. With a little more confidence, they'd decided to attempt to land on the rubble.

Now in the Hawk, Kilian rose to a crouch and said, "Hover here. Once Connor and I go, prepare to engage if she attacks."

"Sculpted scone," Hamish acknowledged instantly, not looking away from his instruments and the big front window. Three separate viewscreens were active, showing views in front, directly beneath, and slightly behind them.

"Ready?" Connor asked Student Eighteen, who was donning the descent vest they'd pulled from storage earlier.

"I'll hit her from above while you distract her," she promised, her hand moving to the hilt of one of her daggers.

"Let's hope it doesn't come to that."

Kilian glanced at Connor, who nodded. It was time. He took a deep breath, and his tension faded to deep concentration, as it so often did when the moment for action arrived. The waiting was worse. Now the tension would just get in the way.

Without another word, Kilian rolled forward right through the unshielded window. Connor jumped after, and the two of them fell toward the shadowy mountain of rubble.

For several long seconds, they dropped silently, the only sound the rush of wind in Connor's ears. He was wearing a pair of Builder flying goggles to help shield his eyes from the dust, with a mini-hub strapped to his armored right forearm, already set to a paired speakstone in the Hawk. He breathed shallow, not wanting to draw in too much of the dust-laden air and start coughing.

The dust smelled of broken stone, which was usually a scent that reminded him of happy memories in Alasdair visiting the quarry or his father in the Powder House. It seemed wrong that such a familiar scent should now be associated with devastation and mass murder.

The weight of his custom armor didn't help as much as usual. No amount of armor would help if the queen was lying in wait. Still, wearing the armor that Verena had given him helped him feel close to her, and that helped calm his nerves even more. He would not fail her.

About a hundred feet above the jumbled pile of broken rubble, Connor drew upon Air. She responded instantly, and winds rushed in around him, slowing him to a stately descent.

Dropping through the swirling clouds of debris gave the scene a surreal appearance. Separated from the hum of the Hawk's thrusters, for the first time Connor could hear the disaster. The entire mountain seemed to groan as stones and earth continued to settle and shift. Occasional sharp reports of rocks falling or wood snapping punctuated the darkness with foreboding reports. He shivered.

Kilian waited until the last possible second. Just before getting splattered on the rocks, twin jets of white-hot fire erupted from his feet. He slowed enough to land on the tallest rock in a crouch. Kilian kept the flames whirling around him, ready to strike.

Connor landed fifty feet away and instantly tapped slate, questing out for enemies. He didn't find one.

He found four.

Connor spun to his left. "Contact!"

Kilian cast flames in the indicated direction, illuminating the broken landscape of jumbled stones. Four figures emerged from behind large fragments of rubble. They were spread out in a loose semi-circle among the rubble, slightly lower than Connor's position. About ten yards apart, they all dressed in leathers colored with blends of tans and grays that seemed to meld with the shadows.

"It's not the queen," Connor said, elemental affinities poised to strike.

Student Eighteen landed on a fairly flat chunk of stone between him and Kilian, slightly closer to the unknown people. Her voice was filled with joy. "Wait! They're Mhortair!"

Connor relaxed, but then wondered if that was such a good idea. The Mhortair looked stern, dangerous. Their leader was a mature woman, tall and slender, who radiated confidence like a Blade. Her straight, brown hair fell only to her shoulders and was pulled back from her face by simple leather cord.

The other men, standing deeper in the shadows, were harder to make out. The leader stepped closer and raised a hand in a sign of peace.

"Is that you, daughter of the hidden people?"

That was a title Connor had not heard. It was very good. He took it as a good sign that they were speaking instead of attacking.

"Mistress Four, we came to help." Student Eighteen dropped to one knee and spoke rapidly in a beautiful, singsong language that Connor recognized as Havaen, which the Mhortair called the language of breezes. He had heard it spoken only a couple of times and had no idea what she was saying.

Mistress Four, another of those odd titles. It suggested she was a member of the kill council. She deliberately turned toward Kilian, who still stood wreathed in flames, and gave him a formal, short bow.

Kilian nodded in response and spoke briefly in Havaen. Mistress Four and her men couldn't conceal their surprise. She said, "We received no reports that you spoke our language."

"I was there when Mhortair developed it."

By the shocked looks on the other three soldiers' faces, the knowledge that Kilian had known and trained under Mhortair was not a well-known fact.

Hamish brought the Hawk in low, flaring nearby, weapons pointed at the Mhortair. He waved from his seat and called, "Glad to see some of you survived."

Mistress Four said, "We know you, Builder. You are a friend of the Mhortair, one who has stood in battle against the Dread Queen, the one who saved our daughter from destruction. If only we could have saved our people today in like manner."

Her expression clouded with grief. The other three soldiers shifted along the rough terrain to draw closer to her.

Hamish gasped and exclaimed, "Daulah?"

One of the soldiers, a short, stocky fellow who radiated confidence, took a step forward and spoke in perfect Obrioner. "I am Commander Six. Daulah was my younger brother."

"He could've been your twin. I still have nightmares sometimes about that day in Donleavy when he attacked the queen with that whip sword of his. Snick snick snick, and just like that she was falling in pieces." Hamish snapped his fingers to punctuate the words.

"If only we could have closed with her today, we could have cut her into smaller pieces," Commander Six promised.

Kilian dropped off the stone he'd been standing on and approached them a few paces. "We don't know how she struck your people, but we came to look for survivors."

"And for the key to ascension," Mistress Four added, looking at Connor. "On any other day, the presence of Blood of the Tallan among us would be met with battle." As she spoke, her men regarded Connor coldly. He recognized the look of killers deciding whether or not to strike.

So he interjected, "Then perhaps some good can come of our meeting today. I am not your enemy."

Mistress Four regarded him for a long moment, and his tension grew. It was insane to think they might have to fight to the death against these few survivors.

Finally she nodded. "We need every ally in these difficult times. Jagdish is gone, the kill council sundered, so the decision falls to me. I welcome you to our cause."

Connor relaxed, but felt a flicker against his mind. Mistress Four was touching him with chert. His own affinity was already active, so he felt the connection.

Instead of fighting it, he met her gaze and lowered his defenses. *"See my thoughts. I am not your enemy. Queen Dreokt threatens all of us, and we represent a great coalition assembled to destroy her."*

She spoke aloud. "Very well, Mister Connor. We will join your effort to destroy the dread queen."

He grinned. "Just call me Connor."

Commander Six and the other Mhortair stiffened, and Student Eighteen gasped. "Connor! Don't ever correct a member of the kill council. She just paid you great honor."

"I don't need honor. I need help, and together we need to see if anyone else survived."

Mistress Four surprised him by smiling and gesturing her men to relax. "We only recently returned. From what I've seen, all other kill squads were located and destroyed by Queen Dreokt before she left."

"You saw her leave?" Kilian asked.

She nodded. "Flew away to the south hours ago."

"Cackling like a lunatic," Commander Six added with a growl.

"Do you know if anyone survived under the mountain?" Student Eighteen asked.

"We have not investigated yet. We spotted your craft and waited in case you were allied with the dread queen. She can pick truths from even well-trained minds, and we could not risk knowledge of survivors getting stolen from us."

"Did Mister One contact you before the queen struck? We were in communication with him, trying to coordinate a counter-attack," Connor said.

She nodded. "That he chose to ally with you was part of why we did not attack when you first landed."

"That would have been a bad move," Kilian said simply. "Are any of you Sentries?"

The men looked like they'd rather fight Kilian than share information, but Mistress Four said, "One of my men and I are both Sappers."

Connor figured at least one of them had to be. Otherwise they would not have been able to hide from the queen or conceal themselves from his earlier scan.

He was relieved that they hadn't landed in the middle of a death battle. He said, "Let's see if we can find your people."

Hopefully they would not only find mass graves.

CHAPTER FIFTY-FOUR

Focus on What You Have Left, Not What You've Lost

Connor tapped slate. Earth looked annoyed as he surveyed the broken landscape. He seemed to be sulking about the fact that so much damage was done to his domain by a lesser element. Connor wished he could ask him about it.

Earth didn't resist Connor's call, and the connection came immediately. Standing there on top of the pile of broken rubble, questing down into it with his earth senses, everything felt wrong. Ancient stone was shattered, mixed with earth, jumbled together in an unruly mess. He could sense Earth's displeasure.

The first priority was to make sure none of them broke a leg on the uneven terrain, and to provide a level landing platform for the Hawk. Connor grasped the earth around them and gave it a tug.

The ground shifted beneath them, bits of stone realigning and earth compacting. A fresh cloud of dust rose off the ground, and the earth groaned as it shifted.

"What's going on?" Commander Six exclaimed, hands going to his belt.

"Connor is securing this area. Stand down," Mistress Four said calmly.

"Sorry. Should have warned you," Connor said. They were still barely allies, and any misunderstanding could result in precipitous violence.

It took only another moment to flatten and settle the ground at the top of the rubble mountain. Connor formed a level area about fifty yards square. It would probably hold for a while, but would no doubt get broken up as the rest of the mountain continued to settle.

Hamish lowered the Hawk to the ground as Connor focused his earth senses deeper. Far beneath them, he sensed bits and pieces of the city. Every building had shattered, then tons of debris cascaded down over it, but he still felt vestiges of the human construction, like ghosts languishing underground.

Every time he walked with the earth, he picked up hints of taste. Good, solid earth often tasted like fresh bread, flavored with spices from plants and minerals. The broken Jagdish mountain tasted like burnt toast, old and dry and brittle.

Surprisingly, he found a couple sizable open pockets within the rubble, formed when large stones had fallen together. Nothing living had survived in them, and he started fearing that he'd find only bones of the dead in his search.

As his senses spread farther through the broken mountain, he found a couple underground streams, their passage blocked, waters pooling and seeking release from imprisonment. He quested farther still, pushing his senses deeper.

He rarely pushed so deep into the earth. Most of his practice with slate was for fighting, so usually he focused on the top layers of the ground. He had never realized that since his ascension he could extend his senses far deeper than before. In any other circumstance, it would have been really fun.

Eventually he slid his thoughts beneath the piles of broken mountain to the solid earth beneath. Or maybe not quite so solid. Even down there the ground was not spared from the brutal shaking of the serpentinite super bomb. The earth was already packed, so it couldn't exactly collapse, but it felt rattled, like a pudding flung around a room in a sock.

Connor almost missed the first cavern. The heavy shielding was still in place. It was subtle, made of more than a dozen layers carefully woven together to gently deflect his senses away. He might not have picked up on it if not for the fact that part of the huge cavern had collapsed, which broke the seamless angles of the shield.

Once he understood what he was feeling, he pushed through the shielding. The cavern had started collapsing, and still felt unstable. Two Sappers were among the hundreds of refugees stranded down there. They were employing all their might in keeping the cavern intact, but had not yet managed to stabilize it. There was just so much weight pressing down on them. Connor doubted they would last much longer.

"I've got a cavern full of people!" he shouted happily.

Ennlin rushed over. "I haven't sensed anyone yet."

"It's very deep." He glanced at Mistress Four and added, "Excellent shields."

"We've worked on them for centuries." She looked proud of that and ecstatic that he'd found survivors, but he sensed she wasn't happy he'd pierced the shielding so quickly.

"The cavern is unstable, though. They're holding it together, but only barely. I'm going to see if I can help. Then I'll open a passage."

"Do you need help?" she asked.

"How many caverns were people hiding in?"

"Seven."

"Better if you focus on finding the others. They may be in trouble too."

He turned his attention back to the first cavern. He touched its floor and with a little concentrated effort, raised letters in Obrioner, writing a brief note to the people stranded down there.

"The queen is gone. I'm here to help."

Hopefully they'd believe him and not fight his efforts. That might destabilize the area and seal their fates.

The earth above the cavern had collapsed under the weight of a huge pile of heavy stones that had fallen directly above it.

Moving that much weight would be difficult, but he didn't have to move it all. He just had to deflect it. Like Kilian liked to say, it didn't matter how much force he brought to bear, but how he applied it for best effect.

Focusing on the earth beneath those heavy stones, Connor compressed it, forming reinforced buttresses in long arcs over the cavern. He pulled earth up from below to compress into the new structures, creating a narrow void above the cavern. As the arches formed, they deflected the vast pressures down their lengths to either side.

As they assumed the incredible weight, their ends sank deeper on either side until that narrow void Connor had created was almost totally consumed. He reinforced the ends, fusing them into the earth, forming wide bases to distribute the weight.

Working with such heavy weights at such a distance strained his earth abilities, and he felt a sense of triumph when he managed it. Before his second ascension, he doubted he would have succeeded.

In his mind, Earth smiled approval, and seemed to want to speak, although Connor couldn't hear any words. Unexpectedly, Water appeared beside Earth. He'd released his other tertiary affinities, and didn't expect to see her again until he reestablished the connection.

She gave Connor a warm smile, but seemed annoyed with Earth. That was so strange. Usually she only got annoyed with Fire's constant flirting. She and

Earth weren't opposites, so they usually coexisted fine, with neither any great show of affection or disaffection.

For his part, Earth folded his arms and glowered. He was good at that. Connor had no idea what they were arguing about, but didn't like it.

"*Cut it out,*" he willed to them. "*I don't have time right now for drama. Can't we all just get along?*"

Earth gave Water a look that screamed, "*This is your fault.*"

She turned her back on him and smiled warmly at Connor again before striding purposefully out of his mind. She disappeared and his connection to soapstone again faded.

What was that all about?

Connor returned to work. He monitored his new supports for another minute. When he was convinced they'd hold, he scanned the cavern again. The two Sappers seemed to recognize what he'd done and had withdrawn their influence.

One of them drew on the floor of the cavern, "*Who are you?*"

He was tempted to reply that he was Blood of the Tallan, recently arrived with Kilian, but that might start a panic.

So he only said, "*A friend. Mistress Four is with me. Let's get you out of there.*"

Then he concentrated on the ground nearby and began opening a winding stair down toward the cavern. Earth exploded out of the hole as he pulled it out of the way. Five minutes and seventeen gentle spirals down into the ground later, he reached the stairway the two Sappers had begun creating from their side.

Once the connection stabilize, he tapped limestone and formed points of light on every spiral, illuminating the long stair so they could navigate up.

A few minutes later, refugees began emerging from the stair. Led by one of the Sappers and two dozen soldiers, they formed a defensive perimeter around the hole.

Mistress Four called greetings to them, and Connor joined her. Together they approached the Sapper, a heavyset woman with lots of gray in her hair, but who still seemed as solid as the Jagdish mountains had been.

The Sapper bowed, banged her right fist to her chest, then moved it to her chin before dropping it. Student Eighteen had told them about that gesture on the flight over. It was a sign of respect that was more formal than the usual salutes.

Mistress Four beckoned the woman to rise, then hugged her. That seemed to surprise and please the other soldiers. Connor doubted they showed such emotion publicly very often, but he approved. They were survivors of a terrible catastrophe, and seeing hundreds of Mhortair emerge from that pile of rubble must have seemed miraculous.

Mistress Four's thoughts touched Connor's. "*Exactly. We will all remember this day for the duration of our lives. I wish to ensure we create some cherished memories to soften the edges of the tragedy.*"

The Sapper looked close to tears by the show of outward affection. She gripped Mistress Four's arms and said, "You are truly a master of earth. Saving this people was beyond our strength."

"I did not save you," she said and gestured toward Connor.

He waved. "Hi. I'm Connor."

The woman bowed to him and gripped his hands in both of hers. Looking nearly overwhelmed with emotion, she said, "Thank you!"

"It was my pleasure. I'm happy you're so willing to trust the Blood of the Tallan."

She gasped, dropping his hands, looking confused. The other soldiers retreated a step, hands moving to weapons. Mistress Four sighed and gave Connor a long-suffering look exactly like what his mother might have.

She said, "I'll explain later. He's an ally."

Hamish landed nearby with a rush of thrusters. He was carrying a large sack that Connor recognized from the stores they'd packed on the Hawk. It was full of smashpacked meals.

He made the bowing, fist-to-chest-then-chin move to Mistress Four and waved cheerily to the newly emerged citizens. "You must be starving. Here. Try these. Special recipes from a very old cookbook."

The Sapper took the first smashpacked meal with clear reservations, but at Hamish's urgings, she took a careful bite.

"No, put the whole thing in your mouth. So much better that way," Hamish said, demonstrating by tossing two cubes into his own mouth.

The Sapper glanced at Mistress Four, who nodded approval. She followed Hamish's example, and a moment later her eyes widened as the smashpacked meal began softening and expanding.

She whispered something in Havaen that made Kilian chuckle, then exclaimed in Obrioner, "What magic is this? An entire meal in one tiny cube?"

Hamish looked thrilled. "The son of the Matron of Evil herself has declared that I have an exceptional food affinity."

He then started passing out smashpacked cubes to everyone. Soon word spread about how good they were, and people pressed in, eager to try the unique treat.

Hamish made a point of sharing dessert cubes with the many children. That seemed to rekindle their joy, and the first sounds of laughter echoed through the dark ruin. Somehow the situation felt less terrible.

Smiling, Connor joined Ennlin, who was standing near Commander Six and his companions. One of them, a bulky fellow who was clearly the Sapper, had his eyes closed, his expression intense.

Ennlin's features shifted to Student Eighteen, and instantly her eyes filled with unshed tears. "We found another cavern, but it collapsed. Three hundred people crushed."

Connor hugged her. "Let's find the others."

He plunged back into the hunt with her and together they scoured the area under the broken mountain. It took another half hour to find the other five caverns. Two were untouched by the disaster and they quickly opened stairways for the refugees to escape.

One was partially collapsed onto fifty more hapless victims, but Connor rescued the other two hundred survivors. The people emerged into the dust-filled rubble heap with exclamations of joy, and many tears. They'd been convinced they would all die down there.

The final two caverns were crushed flat. Hundreds more dead lay buried under tons of earth and stone.

In all, more than ninety percent of the population of Jagdish were killed, and their city totally destroyed. It was heartbreaking, and Connor found himself nearly overwhelmed by emotion.

If they hadn't turned back to save Verena and the others in Merkland, they would have arrived hours earlier. Would that have been enough to turn the tide or help more people escape? Or would they have simply become more victims to the queen's assault?

He'd felt convinced that helping Merkland was the right thing to do, but he'd arrived too late to save Jagdish. He felt more convinced than ever that Queen Dreokt needed to be destroyed, but how could they fight her now that she'd broken serpentinite?

He tried to focus on the joy of the hundreds who had survived, but it was hard. The survivors had some supplies and quickly set up a makeshift camp for the night.

Connor found Kilian leaning against the Hawk, expression unreadable as he surveyed the refugees.

"I hate that we arrived so late," Connor said.

Kilian nodded. "I spoke with Mistress Four while you were saving the others. She also has affinity with serpentinite, as do at least three others of her people. None of them can reach it either."

"Do they have any idea how your mother broke our connections?"

Kilian shook his head. "She said she has something for you. Mister One had entrusted it to one of the Sappers in that first group you rescued."

"Do you know what it is?" Connor hoped it would help, but couldn't see how. Mister One had said he had some kind of treasure to help, but Connor doubted he understood the full scope of the disaster before he died.

"I think we're about to find out." Kilian gestured to where Mistress Four was approaching with Commander Six and Student Eighteen. She was carrying a small, wrapped package in her hands.

CHAPTER FIFTY-FIVE

Truths Revealed through a Well-cooked Steak

"I'm sorry we couldn't save more of your people," Connor said when Mistress Four reached them.

"Without your help, more would have died," she said. Behind her, the glow of a small campfire illuminated some children playing. It was refreshing to see how resilient children could be.

Kilian said, "We will avenge your people."

"And we'll help," Commander Six promised.

"Your people need you," Kilian said.

"They will not be safe until the dread queen is dead. Our kill team will join you," Commander Six insisted.

Mistress Four nodded. "Our people have enough soldiers to protect them."

"Where will you go?" Connor asked.

"We will split into smaller groups and disperse among our other satellite communities for now," she said. Connor was glad they had places to go.

Mistress Four added, "Right now we must focus on helping prepare you in every way possible to face her."

She held up her small package. It was wrapped in soft, white leather, which she removed to reveal a beautiful sculpture. Connor recognized the snakelike pattern of serpentinite. The sculpture was simple, but finished in exquisite detail. It was shaped like a double-edged Mhortair dagger, which seemed extremely appropriate.

She presented it to him. Connor wasn't sure what good it would do. Queen Dreokt had somehow broken serpentinite, but he wouldn't refuse such a priceless gift, so he reverently accepted it.

Out of habit, he focused on the stone. It thrummed with a vast amount of power, and for a second he sensed a flicker of response. It faded away so fast, he wondered if he'd imagined it.

"It's beautiful," he said as he studied the sculpted dagger. The edges were even razor sharp. Made sense. Even a stone dagger could kill, and the Mhortair would never allow a weapon to become dull when it could be kept sharp.

Mistress Four was watching him carefully. "The third threshold has only ever been crossed by three people that we know of. It is an arduous task, and one not to be tempted lightly."

"It should never be attempted again," Commander Six muttered. He was glaring at the dagger in Connor's hand and didn't even try to conceal his thoughts when Connor tapped chert.

"You may be an ally, but all blood that rises through the third threshold becomes tainted."

Connor met his glare and said, "I hear your people like to cook."

That surprised him. "What does that have to do with anything?"

"Do you believe that a tough cut of meat can only produce a tough steak?"

He scowled. "You make no sense."

"Just answer the question," Connor prodded.

Commander Six hooked his thumbs on his belt and said in an annoyed tone. "Of course not. Even tough meat can be tenderized if prepared properly."

"Exactly. With all of your help, I hope to prepare properly so I don't end up corrupted like Queen Dreokt."

He stared at Connor like he'd lost his mind, but Mistress Four's lips twitched into an almost smile. Kilian chuckled, and Aifric laughed. "Connor, you didn't just compare ascending to cooking steak!"

He shrugged. "It's been a weird day. I guess I'm hungry."

Commander Six scowled. "Only a fool mocks a threshold."

"And only a greater fool assumes defeat before they even arrive at the battlefield," Connor retorted.

"Mistress Four has decided to allow you to proceed. I hope she's right," the warrior stated in an unfriendly tone.

"So do I," Connor said with a smile.

"Peace," Mistress Four said to Commander Six. He obediently retreated a step, but Connor could see he still had reservations. That was fine, as long as he didn't act on them.

Mistress Four held up a small leather book. "This contains the few records we have compiled about ascending with serpentinite."

"Wait, some of you have ascended with serpentinite, right?" Connor asked.

"No. Serpentinite is always the final threshold. It has no opposing elements as the others do. We have attempted to ascend with serpentinite, but none have succeeded. We do not possess the full range of affinities."

That was disappointing, but not entirely surprising. Serpentinite was a strange stone. He had hoped the Mhortair had discovered other secrets about it. He wished he could still access the vital affinity. He bet she could teach him much about using it.

He accepted the slender, leather book. "Thank you. I'll study every word."

She added, "I can say that successful ascension apparently culminates with the sound of a giant bell that will be heard for miles around."

"Makes sense," Aifric said.

Hopefully that would be the worst part about ascending. Connor liked bells. Maybe it would sound like a dinner bell. No one would complain about that.

He again studied the exquisite sculpture. He turned the dagger over in his hands, trying to find a connection to it. He felt something there, just barely out of reach. It was so frustrating!

That stone was the key to ascension, and that ascension offered their best hope of surviving the war and defeating the queen. How could he reach it?

He needed stronger connection. So he tapped pumice. Pumice was one of the stones that he regularly tapped to help him improve his connection with tertiary stones, so it couldn't hurt.

As soon as he activated pumice, the sense of power in the stone magnified sharply. He sensed it flowing just past his mental fingers, like wind rushing past a thin door, but still it eluded his grasp.

The others began discussing logistics of the groups of refugees that would begin their long journeys in the morning, but Connor didn't listen. He felt so close, and wanted to scream with frustration as the connection eluded him.

Connor purged granite. He hated pushing away his first-ever affinity, but he could only tap two primary affinities at the same time, and he needed obsidian.

Obsidian was the second stone that helped him strengthen connections with tertiary affinities. The final one was porphyry, which often helped the most. He didn't have much porphyry left, but he'd use it if he had to.

He absorbed some obsidian through his thigh, and it rippled up to his heart like a breath of fresh air. As soon as he tapped it, Verena's laughter sounded in his mind. He didn't know why he heard her with obsidian, but he loved that he did. As usual, that sound helped him relax and strengthened his bond to obsidian.

When he focused on the serpentinite again, it was there, a vast power ready to answer his call!

He gasped as power thundered through him. It had been crafted by a master sculptor, and for a second he could only marvel at the magnitude of it. The night erupted with the bright lights of visible sounds, and he laughed with joy, then laughed again as his laughter erupted from his mouth like a flock of yellow butterflies.

"I did it! I can feel serpentinite!"

The others clusters around him, calling out a hundred questions. He gestured with the stone dagger and added, "I couldn't do it before, but the combination of this sculpture's power, combined with pumice and obsidian bridged the gap."

"Praise the first and great one, but I still can't access my power. Why did you try that combination?" Mistress Four asked.

"They help me stabilize my connection with the tertiary powers," Connor said. He focused again on his serpentinite connection, and only then realized why.

He sensed no red energy flowing through serpentinite, but only green. Pumice and obsidian helped stabilize his connection to the tertiary powers because they were stones attuned to green energy more than red. They were both odd stones, unlike the other primary affinities, and it wasn't until his second ascension that he'd begun understanding why.

He interrupted another barrage of questions. "Listen. The link to serpentinite is broken for everyone under the first two thresholds. I can reach it because with the second ascension I can access a different variant of the power that fuels affinities."

"Really?" Mistress Four asked. She looked amazed. "I know nothing of different variations in power."

"It's something few people know," Kilian said. Connor could tell he didn't like sharing that secret, but Connor didn't care. They were allies now, and if sharing a secret would help secure that alliance, it was well worth it.

"You're sure the connection is solid, despite only accessing it with this variant?" Mistress Four asked.

In answer, Connor seized the sounds of her words. Using the techniques Student Eighteen had taught him and that he had practiced through the winter, he split apart the words, reordered them, and filled in the missing pieces with other sounds in her same voice. Then he released them.

They heard her voice say, "The connection is as solid as Commander Six's skull."

Aifric laughed, Kilian chuckled, and Mistress Four actually smiled. Commander Six scowled, so Connor shrugged and added, "I bet you believe me now."

"So you can ascend?" Aifric asked.

"I think maybe I can," Connor said with a happy grin. He felt weak with relief. The queen might have somehow broken serpentinite, but he could get around that!

"Not here, not now," Mistress Four cautioned. "We witnessed the queen leave, but the sound of your ascension might still reach her ears. We cannot risk her return."

That was fine with Connor. He didn't want to try ascending until he read their little book anyway.

Kilian clapped Connor on the shoulder, his expression deeply relieved. "Well done."

Then he added, "We'll make the attempt tomorrow. Tonight, we'll see to your people and make plans. There is one other point I need to address before I consent to allow you and your team to join us. I need to know how Tallan was killed."

That squashed the good humor. Mistress Four frowned, and Commander Six took a step back, his hands again going to his belt. The belt was wide, made of cloth. Did he have one of those whip swords wrapped around his waist like Daulah had? If so, they would need to take him down fast if a fight broke out. That weapon had sounded particularly dangerous.

Kilian added, "Let me make one thing clear. I am not interested in fighting you. We've come to terms for peace, and I welcome that. You've made it clear that you do not hold me culpable of the crimes of my bloodline. You have chosen not to hold Connor culpable of the atrocities committed by my mother simply because he shares the same affinity set. I am willing to offer you the same courtesy. I will hold you and yours responsible for the crimes you commit, but not for the crimes committed by your forebears. I need to know what happened to Tallan, not because I seek revenge, but because we seek knowledge. Any weakness that might have been exploited to destroy him is a weakness we might be able to exploit to destroy my evil mother."

Connor was impressed. He had feared Kilian still harbored resentment over the loss of Tallan all those years ago. He probably still did, but he was wise enough to put their future success ahead of vengeance.

Mistress Four inclined her head to Kilian in a sign of respect. "We are not strangers to revenge. It is sometimes necessary, but never as effective in blotting out offenses of the past as looking to the future. I accept your conditions of treaty, and agree to abide by them with my people."

Commander Six looked like he wanted to protest, but she continued. "Mhortair himself assassinated Tallan."

Kilian took a long, deep breath, his expression resigned and a little sorrowful. For a moment, Connor glimpsed ancient pain in his eyes. "No doubt your community considers that murder a great victory. I ask you not to speak about that. We will disagree on that point."

She said, "I fear your hope in gleaning secret weaknesses will prove unfruitful. Mhortair administered a powerful sedative to Tallan. Only while sleeping was he completely detached from his affinities and therefore vulnerable."

That made so much sense, Connor felt like an idiot that they had not considered the idea. He exchanged an excited look with Student Eighteen. Although murdering Tallan in his sleep after drugging him had been such an act of cowardice, Connor felt no compunction about attempting the same with the queen. She was so deadly, there might be no other way to defeat her.

He also decided to be very wary of accepting any food or drink offered to him by the Mhortair, particularly Commander Six.

Kilian nodded, his expression unreadable. "I suspected it might have been something like that. Why is this information not helpful?"

"Because we've already tried to destroy the dread queen this way more than a dozen times."

Student Eighteen gasped. "You attacked her again? It was my right to join the kill team assigned that mission."

Commander Six snapped, "It is also you're right to be executed for questioning the decisions of the kill council."

Mistress Four raised a calming hand. "I will forgive the lapse. Student Eighteen, you were already providing critical intelligence and performing a service that no other Mhortair could. There are others far more talented than yourself in administering poison, those who are not known in Donleavy."

"Did the queen kill them all?" Connor asked. She had killed so many, he could not imagine anyone surviving a failed assassination attempt.

"Every one of them escaped after administering the poisons and sedatives when it became clear they had no effect."

"How is that possible?" Student Eighteen asked.

Mistress Four shrugged. "We have no idea."

Commander Six spoke. "I made one of the attempts. I infiltrated the kitchens and laced the queen's plate with enough poisons to have killed half of the capital, and enough sedative to have probably sent an elfonnel into the long slumber. She consumed the meal with no ill effect I could identify."

Connor struggled to believe that. Sure, the queen possessed an even more powerful healing affinity than Harley had, but how could she ignore poison?

Mistress Four said, "We are prepared to share all the intelligence we have gathered. Perhaps we can discover a weakness on our journey."

Kilian nodded. "Agreed. Let's get some sleep. Connor, tomorrow you need to ascend."

Chapter Fifty-Six

Mind Killers

Just after dawn, they rose above the ruins of Jagdish. Connor looked out over the broken landscape at the bands of refugees already wending their way through the rubble at the start of very long journeys. Even in the soft light of early morning, the mountain of rubble looked desolate, and the view left him feeling melancholy.

He had no idea how many hundreds or thousands of people had died and were buried under that rubble, but he felt a lingering sorrow that if he had somehow arrived a little earlier, some of them might have survived.

"We will grow into a mighty people again some day," Mistress Four vowed softly from the middle row of seats where she sat with Aifric and Commander Six. Two other soldiers sat in the last row.

The rest of the Mhortair team were quiet, although Commander Six was looking around in wide-eyed wonder. None of them had flown before, and Connor suppressed the urge to ask Hamish to demonstrate some of the more aggressive maneuvers they could manage in the Hawk.

At some point they should, just to make sure the entire team understood their full capabilities. He'd told Mistress Four they would share information. That would be one piece of information he'd love to share with Commander Six.

"You are part of our alliance. We can offer aid in rebuilding," Kilian said.

She inclined her head in thanks. "I believe the resources we have invested in the various kingdoms should suffice, but I may take you up on the offer. For now it is enough to know our survivors will find safety."

"Then the fighters will join us for the war," Commander Six promised.

Connor welcomed as many fighting men and women as they could get. Most people distrusted the Mhortair for good reason, but no one could argue they weren't great killers.

"Where to?" Hamish asked.

"North. Head for Badurach Pass," Connor said.

Hamish banked in that direction, but Kilian asked, "You don't want to return to Merkland immediately?"

"Not yet. Ascensions can be rather traumatic. I don't want thousands of people nearby who might accidentally get hurt when I try it."

Kilian nodded approval. "Badurach Pass it is, then. The reinforcement army should arrive there shortly."

"I thought they were heading for Merkland," Hamish said as he increased thrust and the Hawk shot into the sky, ascending toward the clouds.

Mistress Four began grinning widely, craning her head to look at the fast-receding ground. Commander Six was pressed back into his seat, hands gripping the arm rests so hard his knuckles whitened. Connor found that strangely satisfying.

"Eventually they may, but the initial staging ground will be the pass. The flying army should have the battalions online soon, right?" Kilian asked.

Hamish nodded. "Last I heard they were barely weeks away. I bet they'll finish early."

"Good. With that work completed, they can stage out of almost anywhere," Kilian said.

"What are these battalions?" Mistress Four asked.

"Enormous flying platforms, capable of transporting hundreds of troops, flying fighting craft like this one, and other battle mechanicals to the battlefield," Hamish said proudly. He'd helped develop them. Connor hoped they worked as planned. He still wasn't convinced anything so huge, carrying so much weight could actually lift off the ground, despite the size of the many thrusters they planned to install.

"I am eager to see these new inventions you speak of. We know much of the work you've done, but seeing it is so much better," she said.

Connor glanced back at Student Eighteen. He'd known she was sending reports to her people as part of her efforts to secure the alliance. He wondered how much she'd shared with them. He trusted her completely, but didn't necessarily want the Mhortair knowing everything they could do.

She winked at him. He hoped that meant she understood his concern and was reassuring him that she'd been careful. He didn't dare ask about it with Mistress Four nearby. In fact, he reminded himself to keep his mental shields reinforced. She had already demonstrated a powerful affinity with chert.

"*Even the best of friends should keep some secrets safe,*" Mistress Four's mental voice spoke to him. "*So yes, I recommend you practice your shielding. Your technique is a little rustic. I will teach you.*"

"*Thank you. First, allow me to study the book you shared with me. Then I'm happy to practice with you,*" he responded.

After helping Hamish find the best current flowing north to bolster their speed, Connor extracted the little book and eagerly read it.

The pages were thin and fine, but only a handful of them held any writing. Some of it was in Obrioner, and he quickly scanned its contents. It didn't offer nearly as much as he had hoped. Apparently some of the notes had been written by Mhortair himself after interviews with Tallan.

That was incredible. He looked at the little book with new respect. It had been written by people living centuries ago. He tried to imagine those days, and found it was pretty easy. Mhortair and Tallan had lived in times of terrible strife and brutal warfare, not dissimilar to their day. He glanced at Kilian, who had turned in his seat to chat with Student Eighteen and the rest of the Mhortair in Havaen.

Kilian had lived through those long years. It seemed marvelous that he had survived that terrible war, witnessed the sundering of the original Obrioner empire and the creation of Granadure and the Arishat League. He'd lost most of his family, including Tallan to war or murder. Why hadn't he assumed the throne? How had he maintained purpose through the long intervening years?

Connor knew much about Kilian, but suddenly felt like maybe he didn't know as much as he thought. The man was a mighty Petralist, a trusted mentor, but still in some ways an impenetrable mystery.

Kilian glanced over and noticed him looking. "What is it?"

Connor felt embarrassed, but held up the book. "Some of this is written in a language I can't read."

Student Eighteen extended a hand, and he passed over the book. "It's written in Havaen."

She scanned the pages and read aloud from notes that Mhortair had jotted down about ascension, serpentinite, thresholds, and higher forms of affinity powers.

"What does he mean, *the queen often warned of the dangers of ascending*." Connor asked at one point.

Mistress Four and Kilian both craned around to read along with her. She said, "It's not clear. He just adds that although greater powers can be unlocked through the thresholds, as the bridges are strengthened, so too grows the risk of opening the gateway to destruction."

"I don't like the sound of that," Connor muttered.

Commander Six, who had taken to staring at the ceiling as he clutched the arms of his chair, looked down long enough to say, "Too much power corrupts. That's what he means."

"Perhaps," Kilian said, scanning the rest of the page. He shrugged. "There's no explanation. Most of the rest of the page is filled with bits and pieces of wisdom that he heard my mother say. She never elaborated and was not taken to sharing deeper secrets. I did hear her warn of the dangers of ascending, but she never explained in detail since I could not ascend the third threshold."

"Did she share it with Tallan?" Hamish asked.

"She loved Tallan more like a son than me sometimes," Kilian said softly. "He was a good boy, and she did give him private lessons. I don't know any other great secrets that I have not shared, but as I think on it I do remember Tallan seeming hesitant to embrace the elements too deeply."

"That's weird. Your mother loves using elements," Connor said.

He nodded. "I thought so too, figured maybe she was trying to scare him so he didn't ever threaten her dominance, but maybe there was something else going on that he hadn't shared with me."

They read through the remainder of the little book three times, but found little concrete information. Just lots of warnings to approach thresholds carefully and not become overly dependent upon the elements. One cryptic line warned of keeping the bridge to humanity strong and never to cross to the other side. Connor wished the queen had followed that advice. He'd sensed her mind, and she'd seemed more like an alien than a human.

As far as the third threshold, Mhortair's notes made Connor more nervous than ever. He spoke of it as a terrible trial that pushed the ascending Petralist to the ultimate edge of existence. He described it as standing in the threshold of life itself, on a knife's edge between the greatest power and ultimate destruction.

Hamish whistled softly when they read that part again. "We'd better break out the full cooking gear and make sure you get a real meal, not just smash-packed cubes before you make the attempt."

Connor appreciated his friend's thoughtfulness. Last meals should be meaningful. But he refused to give in to the fear and said, "Better to prepare a big celebration feast."

"Just to be safe, we should do both," Hamish said with a grin.

Mistress Four frowned. "You two seem to focus on eating a lot."

"I do have a highly developed food affinity to feed," Hamish said with a straight face.

Connor shrugged. "And friends should help their friends develop their talents, right?"

She chuckled. Commander Six was starting to look a little green at the talk of food. Connor smiled. He'd known a few people that got sick flying. He didn't understand it, but then again some people got sick after eating four helpings of dinner. There was no explaining it.

"Will you practice chert with me?" Connor asked Mistress Four.

"Of course."

"May I join you?" Student Eighteen asked eagerly.

"Of course," she said again. "You have lacked a mind killer instructor for too long, daughter."

While Hamish kept the Hawk powering north at best speed, Connor practiced with the two Mhortair. Mistress Four was a senior mind killer, versed in all the secrets of using chert, and she shared much with him.

First she taught him how to better shield his mind. "Unlike shielding with earth, you cannot make a mind killer think you have no mind or pretend you don't have thoughts. Instead you must insulate them, wrap them in a blanket of obscurity that will protect you and warn you of foreign tampering."

Connor listened eagerly. Student Eighteen had helped him develop a solid foundation, and now he practiced higher forms of shielding. It helped when he thought of it like wrapping his mind in sweetbread dough, then cooking the dough, forming a sweet shielding layer that anyone trying to breach could get distracted chewing on.

"That's very good," Mistress Four commented after he got the new shields in place. "I've never felt a well-shielded mind that distracts me so well. Somehow I started thinking of breakfast."

They went on to study techniques for pulling thoughts from other minds, and the time passed quickly. They lacked time to break out the full cooking gear for lunch, but Hamish unveiled a secret stash of cookies and sweetbreads. He warmed them on one of the little cockpit heater stoves, and somehow managed to make them taste like they were fresh from the oven.

Connor ate eleven.

Commander Six waved away the food, but the others all partook heartily, then chased the desserts down with smashpacked dinners from Schwinkendorf's cookbook. The meal might not have rated really high on the last meals measurement scale, but for any other day, it was excellent.

By midafternoon, Hamish slowed and started their descent toward the split peaks of Badurach Pass. The mountain reminded Connor of the broken Jagdish peaks, and he wondered if he'd made a mistake leading them there.

Mistress Four saluted the peaks solemnly. "Thank you for bringing us here, Connor. This pass will always remind me of our home when it still stood proud against the evil that walks our world."

So he decided he'd definitely chosen the spot on purpose.

"Where do you want to land?" Hamish asked.

The two plateaus on either side of the pass were still only occupied by small encampments, although some work was being done to prepare the Grandurian side for the arrival of the army. Long rows of earthen barracks and warehouses had been carefully raised. The area was still pretty unstable, so any work with slate had to be performed with agonizing slowness and delicate control.

Connor pointed to the peak. "Set us down on top."

Chapter Fifty-Seven

An Unexpected Friend

Connor jumped out of the Hawk as soon as Hamish touched down. The others followed, led by Commander Six, who exited with the frantic haste of a drowning man escaping the river. He dropped to his knees and touched the snow-covered stone, looking ecstatic to return to solid ground, even if it was the top of the high, narrow peak.

"Are you sure this is the best place to do this?" Hamish asked, grinning as he watched Commander Six.

Connor nodded, slowly turning a full circle to appreciate the panoramic view atop one side of the broken peak of Badurach Pass. The air was clear and cold, the sun bright. He smelled nothing but mountain breezes and a hint of snow. It was refreshing after the dust-filled ruin of Jagdish.

Mistress Four took in a deep breath. "I like it. Ascension should not be taken lightly, and I can think of few locations more appropriate than this."

He grinned at Aifric. "I wouldn't have thought of it if you hadn't brought me here while trying to free my mind. Today I need to free a lot more than that."

Hamish shrugged. "Works for me. If you get all fainty like you've done after the other thresholds and fall off the cliff, at least I'll have time to catch you before you splatter on the rocks."

Aifric rolled her eyes. "Do you have so little faith?"

Hamish grinned and offered her a smashpacked dessert, which she took. The other Mhortair soldiers climbed out of the Hawk and lined up for cubes of their own. Like Hamish always said, food diplomacy crossed all boundaries.

Kilian remained near the Hawk, leaning against one of the window supports, arms crossed and looking satisfied. "This should work. Let's hope your connection is strong enough."

"I'll make it work," Connor promised as he surveyed the wild landscape and the rugged Maclachlan mountains that inspired a sense of homecoming. The choice felt right, like the first cookie snatched from a still-warm tray.

On a whim he tapped the elements and they stepped into his mind without hesitation. Earth tapped his foot, glancing down at the majestic spire of the broken peak with a satisfied expression. The location also worked for Air. She flitted around, hands outstretched as she twirled, and seemed to be petting each of the eager currents that whistled around the peak.

Water looked content to see the mountains covered in snow, while Fire grinned as he considered the smoking vents in the plains below, broken open by the clashing of elements during the initial battles of Dougal's invasion force. From that position, Connor could easily tap into any of the elements. It seemed a fitting choice to ascend with the fifth.

He extracted the sculpted stone dagger, gripped the hilt with both hands, and said to the expectant company, "Here we go."

Hamish grunted. "As far as last words go, that was pretty weak."

Connor chuckled, happy for a joke to help him avoid thinking about how nervous he felt. Ascending was hard enough without worrying about the fact that he was trying to ascend while accessing only half of the frequencies that usually fueled the power stone.

What would happen if the ascension failed? Kilian had said sometimes it was possible to sunder one's affinities. According to Mhortair's notes, failure to ascend with serpentinite would likely result in death. That would definitely ruin his plans.

He decided not to ask about it. Better not to know for sure. Usually he seemed to do better blundering into situations slightly clueless and having to come up with a response on the spur of the moment. He chose pumice and porphyry to maximize his connection to the green power frequency. Obsidian might be enough with pumice, but porphyry created the strongest link to the green, and he felt that the ascension was important enough to risk some of his dwindling supply of precious porphyry.

His friends watched expectantly, but the Mhortair were harder to read. He felt that Mistress Four was committed to the alliance, but wasn't so sure about the others, particularly Commander Six. It would make him feel less nervous if they weren't right there watching while he made the attempt, but he sensed that he'd offend them deeply by asking them to withdraw.

He decided to trust them. Even if they chose to betray him and revert to old habits of trying to murder Blood of the Tallan, he could count on Aifric, Kilian, and Hamish to watch his back.

So he took a deep breath, tapped the serpentinite sculpted dagger, and willed the connection wide open.

Sound thundered into him, so strong that his entire body shook. The haunting, jubilant melody of the Carraig gargoyles blasted through his mind, mixed with the sounds of distant thunderclaps and low murmurings, as if from thousands of excited voices.

As the connection deepened, Connor sought to unite with serpentinite as he had with soapstone and marble on his previous ascensions, deeply grateful that for once he was making the attempt in a calm moment instead of the middle of a battle.

His other senses began to fade. He barely felt his hands on the sculpted dagger, and the scent of the high mountains slipped from his mind. Even his vision and hearing contracted until all he saw were the lights of living sound radiating around him, and their murmur echoing in his ears.

In his other ascensions he had lifted off the ground, but now he couldn't tell if he was still standing, or if he'd stumbled right over the edge. Billowing gray mist consumed the world around him, filled with brilliant flashes of light and sound. He could not tell if what he saw was happening only in his mind, or if it was filling the physical world. It didn't really matter.

Connor drew deeper from the dagger until the sounds crashing through his mind overwhelmed all other thought. Only sound existed. The chorus swelled into a crescendo of blaring, crashing tones that made up an almost-melody that he struggled to understand. He watched, mesmerized, as the noise boiled around him in brilliant flashes of light.

Every piece of the song, every explosive report of thunder bounced around him in vibrant, rainbow colors. They reminded him of how light split into its various frequencies when he tapped quartzite to his eyes. He lacked the focus to wonder for more than a fraction of a second about how light and sound might be connected. He'd get back to it. Maybe.

Now all he could do was stare at the brilliant cacophony in mesmerized wonder. The murmuring of voices seemed to creep along the ground near his feet, colored shades of red. Those sounds moved slower, with lower frequencies, but seemed able to continue rolling on far longer. Meanwhile, thunderclaps echoed back and forth, bright blues and violets that raced with abundant energy. The other sounds of the melody twisted together in oranges, yellows, and greens, all moving in individual harmony that formed a bedlam of sight and sound.

Connor extended his hands, feeling the sounds moving around him, and for each one he sensed their frequency and origin. As he touched each sound, it fused to him, becoming part of him. He could re-create any of them again whenever he willed it.

Cherished sounds from memories began pouring out through his ears to join the growing tumult, energizing the entire colorful cloud. Of course Verena's laughter raced in endless loops around his head. His parents' voices, the sound of his siblings laughing, and thousands of other sounds that he had absorbed and internalized over the years all poured forth and gathered around him in a thickening whirlwind of color and noise.

It should have created a cacophony of confusion, indistinguishable as individual sounds, but it didn't. Connor heard everything, recalled with vivid clarity the memories associated with every one of those sounds. He grinned in wonder, hands extended as he slowly turned through the cloud of bright lights and re-lived all those memories.

The marvelous experience reminded him of that remarkable moment when all of his friends had united around him to fight the mind bomb. Each friend had carried with them precious memories like the ones he was experiencing again. Those memories, those sounds, had helped form him into who he was. They were integral parts of him, the pieces of his life and character that he had chosen to cling to. Now they wrapped around him, reinforcing his identity and infusing him with marvelous strength.

In that moment, Connor sensed the threshold, like a great, double doorway forming in front of him, filled with rainbow light and with every bit of laughter he had ever heard.

Connor eagerly stepped forward.

As he passed into the doorway, it was like plunging again into the invisible barrier of the Varvakin lightning energy. Only, this time the experience wasn't nearly as much fun.

Connor gasped as his limbs shook, his arms shot out to either side, and his back arched in an agonizing spasm. The sounds that had rippled around him now plunged back into him, piercing him through every pore, like a million tiny darts burrowing into his skin.

He tried to scream, but the sounds refused to come forth. They boiled in his throat and plunged back down his gullet. He gagged as panic rose like a black cloud. He was drowning in sound and couldn't spit them out.

More and more sounds pierced through his muscles, then deep into his bones. The pain eclipsed his ability to comprehend it, and for an unknowable amount of time Connor simply stood in the threshold shaking as the terrible sounds consumed him and welded to every fiber of his being.

He began to tremble as each piece of him vibrated at different frequencies, tuned to the various sounds consuming him. The shaking rattled him violently, and for a moment he feared he'd tear himself apart, each piece of bone or muscle dancing away from his corpse to a different tune.

His thoughts evaporated, his ability to understand what was happening vanished, and for a moment Connor was convinced he simply ceased to exist.

Only one thought rose through the tumult.

He was not going to make it. This threshold was going to kill him.

Connor lacked the ability to feel fear or regret, but as that single thought reverberated through him, he wanted to scream with denial. He couldn't fail, couldn't end like this. He refused to simply disintegrate.

But even though he threw every ounce of willpower, every bit of his hunger to live into the effort of stepping out the far side of the threshold, he couldn't move.

He simply wasn't strong enough.

Then a gentle hand slipped into his and pulled him the final step. Connor stumbled through the threshold and feeling returned in a flood.

Ow.

Connor groaned and for a moment regretted he'd taken that last step. He felt like Erich and Anika had beaten him with that tree for a year without letting him tap granite or porphyry first. Every tiny bit of him felt raw, as if he had exercised every particle of himself to exhaustion, then burned it for good measure.

The hand holding his pulled again, and he took another faltering step. Only then did he feel like maybe he'd live. He blinked a couple of times, tightening his grip on the warm hand holding his.

Hope blossomed. Somehow it had to be Verena. Had she realized where they were going, come to meet them in the Swift? He longed to see her and take her into his arms and thank her. She'd saved him again.

His eyes cleared. He once more stood in the billowing gray of the serpentinite world, with a single figure standing in front of him. It was not Verena.

It was Water.

She looked as real as anyone Connor had ever known. Her skin was warm, although he could feel the coolness of ocean currents rippling just under the surface. She brushed tendrils of hair from her face, and they flowed back around her head like retreating waves.

"Am I dead?" Connor asked. His voice was hoarse, his throat sore, and the effort of speaking made him cough.

Water placed a finger to his lips, and a trickle of cool liquid seeped through, eased the hurt, and settled his coughing.

She smiled again and spoke in a gentle voice like the murmur of low tide. "You're not dead, Connor. We have waited longer than you can comprehend to greet one like you into our company. Welcome to the real world."

Chapter Fifty-Eight

Is It Bad When Imaginary Friends Talk Back?

Connor blinked in surprise. "Did you just talk to me?"

"Maybe you're more dead than I thought," she said, frowning and touching his forehead. Cool air gently stirred his hair, like a breeze flowing just over the surface of the Wick on a hot summer day. She was acting like a real person, not just an images he'd created to help him relate to his affinities.

"I'm a little muddled. My mind is hiding down in my feet, I think. You've never spoken to me before, although Verena told me you spoke to her in Merkland."

She laughed, the sound like a bubbling brook. "After your first ascension we sensed the potential in you and we chose to manifest into your mind. We hoped it would encourage you to continue your journey."

"I don't understand. Aren't you just an affinity?"

Water laughed again, but her eyes turned gray like the sea before a storm. "Your affinities allow you to connect with the tiniest part of who we are through your connection to the various frequencies of power. We are not defined by them, nor they defined by us, but we have discovered ways to walk together."

Connor still felt sore, shaken to the roots by the brutal ascension. The appearance of Water as an intelligent being seemed too amazing to really believe. Had he actually failed and just not yet realized he was dead? Was he lying on his back, staring up at the sky with a broken mind? He wondered what Aifric would find when she ventured in there. Instead of Alasdair on a Sogail day, would she only see Alasdair buried under tons of rubble?

He decided he liked the idea that Water really was speaking with him. Death-by-ascension didn't really fit his life strategy.

"This is kind of a lot to take in right now," he managed.

"I believe you are finally one who we can help understand," she said, her eyes changing to clear blue like Loch Sholto on a bright summer day.

Fire suddenly stepped through the billowing gray of the mindscape where they stood and spoke. He too looked more real than ever. He again wore his fancy, fiery doublet, his unruly hair shifting between shades of dancing flames. He laughed, and his voice was deeper than Connor expected. Instead of the childlike crackling of a cheery campfire, his voice was more like the deep rumbling of an inferno.

He clapped Connor on the shoulder, and in that brief contact Connor felt heat pouring off him that somehow did not hurt. "Well done, Connor. You're the first who's made it this far in a very long time. We've stoked the feeble little flame of yours with nothing but desperate hope that you would set the fuel ablaze. And now look at you. We finally have one who could become our champion."

"I figured you'd sound crazier," Connor admitted before he could catch himself.

Instead of flying into an explosive rage, Fire merely laughed. Connor asked, "Aren't you really good friends with Kilian? You actually look a lot like him."

Fire shrugged. "Kilian is a true brother of the flame, but if we tried to manifest through him like we hope to do with you, we'd crisp him to cinders."

That was more than a little freaky. Kilian was powerful enough to fry Connor to tiny bits any day he chose to. If Fire and Water wanted to do something with him that they feared would destroy Kilian, he was pretty sure he didn't want anything to do with it.

Earth rose up from the depths to Connor's left. He towered over the rest of them, a huge man with shoulders twice as wide as Connor's and hands the size of frying pans. He reminded Connor so much of Evander that he said, "And what about you? I thought Evander was your champion."

Earth's voice was gentler than Connor expected. He still radiated the same permanence as always, his thick, brown hair reminding Connor of freshly tilled earth, while his eyes now seemed far deeper and greener. Looking into them was like looking across the Maclachlan mountains in the height of summer, their peaks and valleys filled with a dense mixture of greens.

He said, "Evander is a friend, and we have walked together many times, but he has never responded to my call through these many years. I'm afraid he lacks the strength to step into our world."

Connor shuddered. He didn't know anyone stronger than Evander. The queen might be freakishly powerful, but was she actually stronger? He wasn't sure. Evander had thrown a mountain. He doubted she'd added that feat to her resume.

Air arrived then, settling out of the gray sky as gracefully as a swallow. Her dress billowed around her, hair flowing like the sighing of afternoon breezes, and she grinned at Connor like a delighted child. Her voice was like the rushing of winds through evergreens. "Connor, I am so happy you made it. Finally we have someone to play with who can see past their own petty needs."

She settled to the ground near Earth and strutted past, tracing one hand along his broad shoulders. He turned to watch, and she winked and blew a kiss. She noticed Connor watching and laughed again, the sounds moving around him like dust devils. "Earth and I love to flirt, but he'll never fly like you and I."

Earth grunted, his expression a little wistful. "And you'll never grow roots or make anything permanent."

She shrugged and blew him another kiss. "You make things, I wear them down. That's the price you pay when you reach for the skies, muddy britches."

Water rolled her eyes. "Don't mix me in. You two are incorrigible."

Connor was so fascinated by their interchange that he'd almost forgotten about his ascension. His pains had faded as he focused on the elemental beings and the incredible insights he was gaining into their nature. He said, "What about you and Fire?"

Fire chuckled, his expression turning hungry. "Yeah, what about us?"

Water tilted her nose up just a little but couldn't help smiling. "You love what you can't have."

Fire laughed. "Exactly why we're so thrilled to have you with us, Connor. We've rarely succeeded in manifesting so openly to any little human. We don't understand what you are, but we need to."

Water nodded, her expression serious. "You've managed to touch us with a finger, to draw upon our powers, but not quite step into our world. The Builder girl, Verena, represents a potential avenue of contact, so similar to Kirstin."

"That girl had potential," Fire agreed enthusiastically, his eyes flashing in a way that reminded Connor too much of General Aonghus. It was weird that feeling nervous around Fire actually helped reassure him that he wasn't hallucinating.

"And the boy offers perhaps another bridge, but you Connor are here," Water added with a warm smile that filled Connor with joy. "The mystery of who you are and to what extent we can connect with you is a mystery we cannot settle without your help."

Connor grinned. "I'm happy to help. I need to understand you too. I've sensed there had to be more to our connection, and when Verena said she spoke with you, I hoped we could find a way to talk. I need help to stop the queen."

Fire snorted, and flames burst from his nostrils. Water said, "She represents a great mystery and a great disappointment. Somehow she bridged the gap from humanity to the sylfaen where we have remained imprisoned since our birth, but she rejected us and refuses our counsel."

Air twirled, and her dress continued to whirl around her after she stopped, a mini tornado that she did not seem to notice. "We had such high hopes for her, but she refuses to see us as anything but slaves waiting at her beck and call."

Earth added, "She breaks when she could create, she thinks she has reached the pinnacle of power, but she is a babe in the real world."

That was encouraging. Babes could be destroyed, and if the elementals could help Connor understand how to see the dread queen as a babe, he would gladly help them understand his people in return.

"You mentioned sylfaen. What is that?" he asked.

"Sylfaen are the great powers encircling the world. You touch upon a miniscule fraction of the sylfaen as it is filtered through your affinities," Water said.

"You're talking about the red and green frequency powers, right?" he asked eagerly. He sensed they knew so much more than even Kilian or Evander had ever understood. Finally, he could get some answers.

Earth said, "The filtered powers that you so quaintly refer to as red and green are distilled effects of the sylfaen."

"Are there other frequencies? How do we access them? You said you're separate from the sylfaen, but we access your power through affinities too. How does that work?" Connor asked, trying to give voice to the thousand questions their words triggered in his mind.

Fire laughed heartily, blue flames puffing from his mouth. "Your new bridges are barely set and you wish to leap into the void already?"

"At least he is curious," Water responded, her voice a gentle rebuke. Fire shrugged, and Water added, "You cannot understand everything at once. You have now crossed to a place where we can communicate, but the final crossing to step into our realm still lies ahead, and is fraught with much danger. We will guide you and prepare you for that final crossing."

"Another threshold?" Connor asked, amazed. No one ever spoke of a fourth threshold.

"If you wish. Let us understand you better, and we will find the best way to teach the path to you," she assured him.

He wanted to know so many things, but forced himself to refrain. He was speaking with them. That was such a huge step forward, more than he'd even considered possible until recently. "What about sound? I don't see sound as a person?"

Air huffed. "She is not one of us. At least not yet. She has existed as part of the sylfaen, but did not rise when we did."

"I don't understand," Connor said, frowning.

Fire interjected. "These are things that you are not yet ready to understand." He gave Air a look that seemed like a warning. Connor wondered what she'd started to say, and why Fire didn't want him to understand.

Earth said, "For today it is sufficient for you to understand that when Dreokt started making bridges, Sound began to find herself. She hasn't completed the journey, and we're not sure if she ever will. It is a different route than we traveled, but maybe with your help she'll become self-aware enough to join us."

Fire snorted again, and Air didn't look pleased by the idea. Water's expression remained neutral and she said, "Those bridges are the key to our discussion, for they offer a link from us back to you. Just like the people of Queen Dreokt were limited by the fact that they could not directly tap the sylfaen without some kind of filter, you cannot walk among the elements without similar filters. The bridges of your affinities can access sound. Your bridges also link to us. Thus it may be possible once you complete your journey that your bridges might offer a roundabout path for Sound to arise and join us."

"I don't understand the bridges you speak of," Connor said, feeling like he was missing important information.

"Understanding flows as one walks the path through the dawn of new growth," Earth said, sounding so much like Evander that Connor smiled. It seemed appropriate for Earth to make less sense than anyone else.

If he was understanding correctly, it sounded like maybe Sound could figure out how to manifest in full form like the other elements. That would be amazing, although he wondered if she'd be incessantly chatty like Hamish's sisters.

Water took Connor's hand. "There is much that you need to learn, but we can only manifest to you using forms of things you can understand. Human minds break far too easily."

Air floated over to him and took his other hand. She gave him a reassuring smile. "But we need to show you some things. Are you ready?"

"Definitely ready to learn. Not really eager to break my mind, though."

Water smiled. "We will attempt the first, and try to avoid the second."

CHAPTER FIFTY-NINE

Welcome to the New World

Air laughed and kissed Connor's cheek. At the touch, a violent gust of wind caught him and would have thrown him head over heels if the two elemental women had not been holding him steady. When he recovered, blinking his eyes from the sudden gust, the gray expanse had shifted into a familiar sight. He now stood with the elementals above Alasdair valley as it had existed before getting destroyed.

The town lay in the distance, but they stood above the two ancient flooded quarries, Loch Sholto and Loch Ladhar. Strangely, the waters of Loch Sholto glowed brilliant crimson, while Loch Ladhar had turned a deep, emerald green. The surfaces of the lochs were rippling. With a start Connor realized those ripples matched the frequencies of the two energy sources that fueled affinity stones.

As he peered closer, he noticed shapes in the water that slowly clarified into the ancient symbols of the various affinities. The red pool of Loch Sholto contained most of them. He easily recognized granite, basalt, sandstone, and limestone. He spotted one tiny piece that he thought might be obsidian, but the symbol was incomplete. When he glanced in the green pool, he saw the rest of it. In the green pool he also noticed most of pumice and porphyry.

Intrigued, Connor willed himself closer. He'd experienced enough weird dream visions that he understood he couldn't physically walk, but as he focused on moving, it just sort of happened. It was a lot of fun, actually. Well, as long as he didn't think about the fact that he was stuck in a living dream with imaginary beings that had started talking to him like real people who claimed they could share the secrets of deep magic with him.

He realized the pools were showing how the different affinities connected with the two energy sources. Most of the primary and secondary affinities were fueled from the red power source. However, when he studied the green pool, he noticed those same symbols, but reversed, as if they were reflections seen in a mirror. Somehow he sensed those must be the higher-level aspects of those affinities, accessible by ascended Petralists.

Sandstone was clearly a red-energy affinity, but *sandstorm* was green. Limestone might be red, but *mirage*, *death beam*, and *sensory deprivation* were green. The two elemental ladies hovered in the air beside him, watching him closely. He sensed great excitement from Air, and a more restrained eagerness from Water. He wondered if she feared they were pushing him too far. He didn't want to break his mind, but he didn't feel strained to the limits. In fact, he was deeply fascinated by the vision they were sharing.

He willed himself even closer until he could dip hands into the lochs. Somehow in that mindscape, he could touch both at the same time. As he touched a finger to each pool, the affinities there snapped into focus. He smiled at the wonder of it.

Glancing up at his companions he said, "We sensed a lot of this. It's nice to know we got so much right."

Water gave him an encouraging smile. "You are like a child taking your first faltering steps. They are perhaps the most important, but pale against what awaits."

Air rolled onto her back, reclining in the air like she was lounging in a hammock. "But like most children you think your living room is the extent of the world."

She blew him a kiss, and it struck him in the face like a whirlwind. His vision blurred and for a second he saw additional pools of water surrounding and even somehow squeezing in between the red and green pools. He caught glimpses of orange, yellow, and blue, but sensed nothing else about them before the vision disappeared.

"What was that?" he exclaimed.

Air only laughed, and Water said, "Hopefully a future lesson. Like I said, if we fill your mind with too much truth it'll snap and we'll lose the one champion we have finally led this far."

Connor wanted to ask a thousand questions, but Fire appeared in front of him, standing with one leg in each pool. Red and green energy flowed up his legs and mingled in his jacket and across his skin.

"What you need to know today is that we are not defined by either frequency of the sylfaen. You reach us through your filtered connection, and we choose to walk with you, but you need to get to know us as distinct in a way that no one else has, or you will never reach your potential."

"How do I do that?" Connor asked.

"Come visit us often, and we will continue to teach and mold you," Water said.

Air flipped over and plunged behind Connor, grabbing his legs, and yanking him down so one foot sank into each pool. The familiar frequencies of the red and green power sources rippled up through him and mingled across his skin like it did across the elementals.

With a start he realized the two frequencies were not canceling each other out. They both flowed over and through him, like different waves pulsing to different tunes. They no longer crashed into each other, but slid past as if they were running in different invisible conduits through the same space.

Air said, "First lesson. You have crossed a vital bridge that allows you to draw upon either fraction of the sylfaen, or both, without the interference you struggled with in the past. With this new connection in place, you can begin learning how the world works."

"Don't let us down, dear Connor," Water said. She took Connor's face in her hands that were now as cool as river stones and kissed his forehead. An invisible wave crashed through his mind, snapping him out of that strange vision world where they had been speaking.

He blinked open his eyes, and groaned as every muscle protested, clamoring for his attention, as if frustrated that he hadn't noticed how much he was hurting. He was lying on his back on the stone slab at the top of Badurach Pass, staring into the clear blue sky. For a second he glimpsed Air hovering above him, twirling like a dancer before she faded from view.

The experience felt like an extremely vivid dream. He wasn't sure what to make of it. But first he needed to understand why his chest was hurting so badly.

He tried to rise, but Kilian, who was kneeling by his head, pressed his shoulders back down and ordered tersely, "Don't move."

His surroundings came into focus and Connor noticed the entire team kneeling around him, looking worried. Aifric had both of her hands pressed to his chest, her face set in a mask of absolute concentration.

That was not a reassuring sight.

Hamish was standing over him, leaning forward with one hand clasped around the hilt of the sculpted serpentinite dagger. The point had been driven into Connor's chest.

Definitely not good.

Connor looked up at Hamish and blinked in confusion. "You stabbed me?"

His voice was weak, and trying to speak triggered a wave of pain through his entire torso that left him breathless. What was happening? He was totally exhausted from the brutal ascension, his mind whirling from the vision with the elementals. He simply couldn't comprehend why his best friend had chosen to stab him. Had he attacked Hamish while in that trance, insulted Schwinkendorf's memory or something?

Aifric cried, "Now!"

Hamish yanked the dagger free.

Connor gasped, but wasn't wracked by as much pain as he should have. Getting stabbed in the center of the chest was supposed to be fatal, or at least make for a really bad day. He felt extremely sore, and his chest definitely hurt, but he didn't feel like he was dying. That was either a good sign or very very bad sign. The dagger in Hamish's hand looked much smaller, barely a thin sliver of stone. Even as Connor watched, it crumbled to dust.

Hamish stared down at him, looking more frightened than Connor had seen since the terrible day Jean was injured. "What were you thinking, Connor? I didn't stab you. You stabbed yourself."

"What?" Shouldn't he remember such poor knife handling? Usually he had a much better sense of self-preservation.

Connor glanced from Hamish to Mistress Four and added, "If he didn't stab me, and I don't remember stabbing me, did the Mhortair sculptor who crafted that dagger somehow imbue it with a sense of purpose?"

She seemed to like that mental image. Her mouth twitched into a half smile. "I have no idea, but it would be tragic for any Mhortair blade to reach the end of its useful life without tasting any blood."

Hamish said, "Almost as bad as a fresh-baked sweetbread falling off a tray and getting stomped flat before anyone can eat it."

"So will I be okay?" Connor asked, feeling annoyed that they were joking while he might be dying. It seemed disrespectful.

Aifric leaned back, blew out a breath, and gave him a weary smile. "You'll live." Her expression turned exasperated and she added, "I'm glad you retained the sense of mind to tap sandstone. Without your help, things might not have gone well."

Connor didn't remember tapping sandstone either. Wow, he was having a really bad day.

So he said, "Thanks for helping. I was kind of out of my mind there for a while."

Mistress Four leaned closer. "We're assuming it worked. The entire mountain shuddered. Even though we still can't tap serpentinite, we all clearly heard a giant bell."

Hamish chuckled, clearly relieved. "Like a huge gong. We figured you either finished the ascension, or your mind just snapped in the most epic way anyone's ever imagined."

Connor groaned. He still felt terribly weak and sore all over. He tapped sandstone. The affinity came instantly, and he could feel both the green and red power sources flowing through the stone now. They did not interfere, but seemed to reinforce each other in a way that magnified the power available to him and supercharged it.

Vast amounts of healing flowed through sandstone now, even more than when he was using one of his aunt's amazing sculpted pendants. He pushed healing energy through his body, and it washed away the pains. He flickered his healer senses across his chest, and everything seemed fine. Aifric had done an amazing job.

Aifric leaned forward, her eyes widening. "Connor, how are you tapping so much healing without your sculpted pendant? I can feel it without even having to touch you."

"I'm not sure. I think it's a result of the ascension."

Hamish lifted a fist in victory. "Excellent! You're triple-ascended, Connor! We need a huge celebration feast."

Chapter Sixty

Simple-mental

As soon as Hamish set the Hawk down outside of the battered central palace of Merkland, Connor joined the others rushing to exit. He couldn't wait to see Verena.

A remarkable amount of cleanup had already been accomplished. Debris had been removed, the broken main doors to the palace replaced by far simpler ones made of heavy timbers, reinforced with steel.

He ignored the crowd of friends gathered to greet them, his entire focus on Verena, who was rushing toward him, her smile like a Solas beacon. He was not actively tapping his tertiary affinities, but they seemed to remain subtly active anyway.

It was kind of unnerving, actually. He figured it must be a lingering effect of the ascension, coupled with his exhaustion, but for the first time in his life he struggled to turn off his affinities. He could feel people moving all around him, both because of his connection to earth as well as air. All of his normal senses were hyper acute, as if he kept a low-level connection with quartzite attuned to all of them. Even though he was not actively tapping chert, a low murmuring of voices echoed in his ears. Whenever he focused on them, thoughts snapped clearly into his mind.

He didn't want to become like Queen Dreokt, who abused other people's minds. Chert was very helpful sometimes, but the realization that he could easily invade his friends' minds and pilfer their deepest secrets made him uneasy. They had all practiced techniques for shielding their thoughts, and prior to his ascension those efforts had worked pretty well unless he focused hard. Now it was like they were screaming thoughts at him. He had to figure out how to control it.

First, kiss Verena.

His heart sang to see her. He could sense her moving through space toward him, could map every inch of her if he wanted to, and he smiled when he realized it. He had long thought he'd memorized her adorable face. Now he could actually do it in minute detail. She'd washed away the grime of battle, and her armor gleamed in the sunlight. She hadn't gotten the dents repaired, and they remained a mute testament to how nearly he'd lost her.

Connor did not try reading her mind, but couldn't help feeling her emotions. She was thrilled to see him, eager to hear about his ascension that Hamish had only mentioned briefly when he called in to warn her they would soon return. She also felt a little annoyed that he had not waited for her to join them before making the attempt.

Connor swept her into his arms, exulting in the feel of her as he spun her in a circle and kissed her warm, minty lips.

Others pressed in around them. Rory pounded Hamish on the back in an enthusiastic greeting while Shona, Ivor, and Anika greeted Aifric and asked about the journey. Everyone was still wearing armor, although Shona sported a bright red hat with an enormous, floppy brim. Wolfram and Lady Briet greeted Kilian warmly, and even Ilse slid toward them from across the square, standing poised and calm, a little smile on her lips.

She manipulated the earth with such a subtle touch that the paving stones didn't even ripple as she slid across them. Erich waved at Connor, but remained with the soldiers forming a perimeter against a larger crowd of curious locals who had come to see who had landed.

"You don't look any different," Ivor said when Connor set Verena down. "I half assumed that after your third ascension something about you would've changed."

Hamish chuckled. "Well, he managed to stab himself and survive. Although I guess that's nothing new. Maybe just an enhanced clumsiness ability. Is that a thing?"

Connor laughed. He was really looking forward to exploring the full ramifications of his ascension. He still felt wasted, but his strength was returning quickly, especially with Verena snuggled under his arm.

Tomas and Cameron left the perimeter group to jog over and greet Connor with their usual good-natured pounding that rattled his eyes in his skull, even though he tapped granite when he saw them coming.

"Heard you broke Jagdish before even setting foot on the mountain," Tomas commented.

Cameron fixed him with a reproving look. "I know we trained you to always try to improve, but lad, we were talking about bash fighting."

"I didn't destroy Jagdish," Connor protested.

"It was the queen's fault," Verena added.

Tomas looked impressed. "Getting the queen involved was a brilliant twist, laddie."

"Just be careful. She likes destroying just to be mean," Cameron added, tapping his nose with a wink in a move Connor wasn't quite sure how to interpret.

Verena looked exasperated, but Connor just chuckled. Those two were far brighter than they pretended, and they'd never let simple logic destroy one of their arguments.

He noticed a new insignia on the lapels of their battle jackets. It was a simple spherical design, surrounding a lightning bolt. "What's this?"

Both of the Fast Roller captains swelled with pride. Tomas tapped the design and said, "General Rory assigned us as the first two simple-mental replacement pilots for them huge Juggernaut beasties Hamish and his Builder teams are cobbling together."

Cameron punched his partner in the shoulder hard enough to have staggered any other man, but Tomas barely shifted. "Not simple-mental, the word is supple-something-grand."

Verena was looking from one to the other in absolute astonishment. "You can't be serious. You're the supplemental pilots?"

Tomas grinned. "Yes ma'am. Like I said, simple-mental."

"What are you talking about?" Connor asked, not sure he could believe what he was hearing.

Hamish joined them, trading shoulder punches with the two big warriors. Verena demanded, "I thought you were looking for the best possible supplemental pilot candidates."

"Right, and Rory decided to give us his Fast Roller captains," Hamish said with a grin.

"Why?" Connor asked. He didn't want to be rude, but what was Rory thinking? Tomas and Cameron were brilliant bash fighters, but the thought of those two piloting a couple Juggernaut mechanicals made him shiver with visions of the absolute mayhem they could unleash upon the world.

Rory had noticed them talking and joined them. His men saluted smartly. Connor was impressed. Usually their idea of discipline was pretty lax until the bash fighting started.

Rory said, "Most of the pilot spots are filled with Builders and some of Lady Jean's flight pilots. Good folks, but not a real warrior in the bunch."

"Piloting those mechanicals will be a unique challenge," Verena protested.

Rory nodded. "We've got simulators set up in the basement of the command castle. A team updates the controls daily to match any changes made on the real thing. My men will know how to pilot them, and they'll know how to take Ilse's Revenge to battle in a way no other pilots could be taught in time."

Ilse smiled, just a little, at the mention of the name Hamish had dubbed the super-mechanical all those Juggernauts could become when linked together. Connor loved the name, but still struggled to wrap his mind around those two bash fighters riding into battle inside two enormous Juggernauts.

He bet they'd crash right into the biggest concentration of enemy forces just to get the bash fighting started sooner. Then again, maybe that was what Rory was planning on. They might need that exact level of brilliant devastation if they hoped to win the day. Rory had proven many times that he was far more devious than people usually gave him credit for. Connor just hoped he was right this time.

Tomas and Cameron looked thrilled by their general's confidence. Tomas said, "We've been training hard. The instructor Builder knows the controls, but he's never actually been in a fight."

"He's a good man at his job, but did you know he can actually tickle his own feet?" Cameron said, leaning forward, his voice dropping to a conspiratorial whisper.

Tomas grunted and said seriously, "Not a good sign, that."

"Might help keep a man awake during watch, though. Might want to try it," Cameron said.

"You usually just hit yourself in the head with a frying pan."

Cameron nodded, a wistful smile on his face. "Got that frying pan from the blind girl I dated all those years ago. She was something."

Verena had that incredulous look on her face that so many experienced when speaking with Tomas and Cameron for long. Connor just smiled. Their banter always helped put him in a good mood.

Rory wasn't rattled by them. "Just practice hard. I've heard good reports that you've taken to the Juggernauts better than anyone expected. Let's not waste that advantage. I want you ready if we need you."

"Aye, General. Easier than walking on our hands," Tomas assured him.

"Never did learn to walk on my hands," Cameron admitted with a frown.

Tomas grunted. "You have a hard enough time walking on two feet and breathing at the same time."

Cameron grunted. "Complex thinking is for officers."

"So are forks."

"Leave forks to those who know how to handle them," Rory ordered, barely holding back a smile. "Back to your duties."

They saluted and trotted off, discussing the dangers of washing socks too often.

Shona approached, her expression eager. Connor appreciated that she was so happy to see him, and was willing to greet him so warmly with Verena standing right beside him. She had seemed in earnest when she apologized back in New Schwinkendorf and they had agreed to try forging a path forward as friends. Of course, he had helped break the siege of Merkland and save all of their lives. That tended to help strengthen friendships.

She held up a piece of quartzite. "We think we've figured out how you can loan me quartzite. We should test it immediately."

Shona was nothing if not motivated. Connor didn't blame her. He really wanted to find out if he could actually loan affinities. Could he loan other things too? He'd love to loan Shona double-tap sickness when she got especially annoying.

He smiled and asked, "Do you want me to test quartzite first, or would you rather I try fixing your hair?"

Shona gasped, hands rising to her hat.

Hamish dropped a breadstick he was just about to pop into his mouth and exclaimed, "That's right! I can't believe I didn't think of it before. You should be able to do the same things the queen can."

Verena's eyes lit with understanding and gripped Connor tighter around the waist. "You might be able to heal Jean more."

"I certainly hope so," Connor said, and then turned toward Captain Ilse. He gestured toward her summoned limbs that allowed her to walk and move despite her crippling injury. "I'm thinking first we should try to fix your legs."

Captain Ilse glanced down at her marvelous summoned limbs and suddenly looked nervous, an expression so foreign to her. She always had an answer, a clever response to any situation, no matter how difficult. She had created those summoned limbs after Harley had crushed her legs and hips and murdered her husband. Now she glanced from Connor to her withered legs with a mixture of hope and fear.

Connor grinned. "Come on, Captain. Don't you trust me?"

"You've never made such an attempt," she pointed out, recovering her calm.

Hamish chuckled. "Maybe you should start with Shona after all."

Shona clutched her hat again and withdrew half a step before she could catch herself. She glanced at Ilse guiltily and surprised Connor by saying, "You're right. My hair is already gone. Maybe you should test the process with me."

Hamish said, "It's not like he can make things worse, unless maybe he made your nose fall off or something."

Shona suddenly looked like she wished she hadn't made the offer, and Verena slugged Hamish in the shoulder then yelped from punching his armored suit. "Don't be a beast."

Even though Connor was not actively tapping chert he clearly sensed how much Verena would love to see Shona's nose fall off in a freak accident. One day maybe the two of them could become, well, not exactly friends, but maybe less enthusiastic enemies. That feat would be even more amazing in its own right than a new enhanced healing ability.

General Rory said, "Before we jump into more testing, will you introduce your guests?"

Connor had forgotten all about the Mhortair survivors, who stood behind him, outwardly calm, but he could read their tension. Mistress Four's emotions were blanketed by excellent shielding, but he still picked up glimmers. If he focused, he could pierce her shielding.

And then she'd probably stab him through the heart. He decided to resist the urge.

Assassins weren't often high on everyone's Sogail invitation list. They probably half expected to be met with nooses. Most days that would probably be the right response too.

Student Eighteen made introductions. Captain Rory bowed to Mistress Four and said, "I heard about Jagdish. You have our condolences."

Anika looked like she wanted to offer to wrestle Commander Six, probably figuring that a solid beating would help him feel more at home, but Rory moved on and introduced High Lady Shona. Mistress Four and the other Mhortair made their bow of respect.

Shona smiled warmly. "We welcome all allies as we prepare for the great battle of our day."

She was very good at high lady stuff like that. Sometimes it amazed Connor that he'd managed to escape her plans for him. He credited Verena.

"It is our pleasure to join the cause of freedom," Mistress Four said in perfect Obrioner. She stood as regally as Shona and spoke as an equal forming a mutual pact of defense instead of as a refugee from a broken city.

Ivor extended a hand and shook hers, then each of the others in turn. Shona radiated grace and regal grandeur, but Ivor simply showed genuine friendship and that would probably win them over even more. "Welcome. We're a little short on formality here, so come join us. I've got enough space in my office for all to witness Connor's attempt to heal our friends."

Ivor then bowed to Shona and extended his arm. "Shall we?"

Together they all traipsed into the palace and up to Ivor's office. As they walked, Connor managed to turn off chert with some focused effort. He vowed to exercise extreme caution with that affinity. Everyone deserved to keep their thoughts private. The queen's invasion of his mind was one of the things that had bothered him the most, but now he saw how easy it would be to slip into similar habits.

That thought made him distinctly uncomfortable. He liked thinking of the queen as an intentionally evil despot, not a woman who had simply gotten sloppy managing her affinities.

He had brought up the idea of fixing Shona's hair and Ilse's legs on a whim. He probably should have tested it first, but how better to test an enhanced healing ability than by actually trying to heal someone?

First he had to share some exciting news. So when they reached Ivor's quarters Connor said, "Before we proceed, I want to tell you all about something amazing I experienced during my ascension." He held Mistress Four's gaze and added, "Including you and your people. You're part of our team now, so we don't keep secrets."

She inclined her head in thanks and said, "I appreciate your confidence in us." Her mind voice added, "*Thank you for not forcing me to choose between respecting your thoughts and curiosity about this announcement.*"

"*Friends don't eavesdrop on friends' minds. Please refrain from using chert on my people,*" Connor replied.

She nodded slightly again, for him alone.

"You never did explain what happened. Must have been bad if you tried to kill yourself to get it over with," Hamish said as he wandered over to Ivor's desk and peeked inside an earthen jar where Ivor often kept snacks. With a smile he snagged a sweetbread. Ivor sighed.

Connor gestured them to take seats, but remained standing near the cold fireplace. He tried to explain what it felt like to ascend and the strange experience with the sounds. He doubted he could share just how wonderful and terrible it had been. Mistress Four produced a small notebook and started jotting notes. It was so similar to what Jean would have done that Connor smiled.

When he got to the truly amazing news, Verena exclaimed, "You met Water?"

Connor grinned. "Just like you did when you activated Kirstin's Defense."

"This is unprecedented," Kilian breathed.

"Yeah, since I met all of the elementals," Connor said. "Although Verena met Water, and they mentioned they've met your mother."

"I wish she'd told me more about those experiences," Kilian said.

"You did say she liked keeping secrets," Shona pointed out.

That habit ran in the family.

Kilian nodded, but still looked troubled. "There must have been a reason, though. If the elements truly are self-aware and we're accessing pieces of their power, our relationship with our affinities is fundamentally different than we thought."

"What's Water like?" Hamish asked eagerly.

Anika asked, "What of other affinities, Connor boy? Is granite alive as strong man in sky powers?"

Her Obrioner was improving immensely. Connor hadn't considered that question before. He shrugged. "I haven't met any other affinities, and I don't think they exist in the same way as the elements. The elementals consider themselves different. They spoke of other affinities as filtering the available power in a way we can access it." To Hamish he said, "Water is something. She's like a queen. Regal and beautiful and powerful."

Shona's lips curved into a wistful smile. "I wish I could meet her."

"They said it's hard to connect with humans. I don't think Petralists can speak with them until they've ascended the third threshold."

"How come Verena could?" Ivor asked.

Verena glanced at Connor, a question in her eyes. He nodded slightly and she said, "It was Kirstin's Defense. It was so powerful, it lifted me right up to what I believe is a Builder threshold. That's when she appeared to me."

"What?" Ilse exclaimed, voicing the shock reflected on everyone's faces. Apparently Verena had been waiting for their return to share the amazing discovery.

Connor said, "Please keep the fact that there might be a Builder threshold secret. We don't know for sure, and it might offer us a potential huge advantage against the queen."

"Especially since she thinks most of the Builders are dead, or at least the most important of us," Hamish added.

Kilian made a calming gesture as several of the group began asking questions at the same time. "This is all new. We'll explore these concepts and try to figure out the advantages and potential dangers to these revelations. For now Connor, tell us about the elements. What is Fire like?"

"He's seems to be a lot like you," Connor said, and Kilian smiled.

Hamish said, "Figures. You're so old, it's probably one of those less understood effects of elemental powers that they start affecting your face."

"Except Kilian also walks with water. He doesn't look like a regal, beautiful woman," Verena chuckled.

Hamish grinned. "Glad you picked the right mentor. Could have gotten weird otherwise. I think we need more sweetbread if we're going to start delving into deep questions of the arcane, though."

He glanced at Ivor hopefully. Ivor made a grand gesture toward the little stash of sweetbreads on his desk. "Help yourself, but there's not enough thinking food in that jar for all of us."

"We'd better order in more," Hamish suggested.

Shona gave him an exasperated look. "Merkland was just half destroyed by a summoned army, remember? We barely have enough kitchens working to feed everyone as it is. We don't have buckets of extra sweetbreads."

Hamish turned to Ilse with a reproachful look. "I thought you said you were bringing critical supplies."

She chuckled and raised one eyebrow, as if challenging him to discount her efforts. He was wise enough to sigh and settle back into his seat with Ivor's jar of sweetbreads in his lap.

Connor briefly recounted what he'd heard from the elementals and described each of them in turn. Everyone listened in rapt fascination. Kilian in particular looked thrilled to learn about them, but also troubled.

"So Water and Fire have forbidden attraction?" Anika asked, winking at Rory. "I am liking them more than before."

"I never imagined Earth tempted by Air, but they are opposites and there's always an attraction between opposites," Ilse acknowledged with a little smile.

Connor loved seeing that. She'd smiled far too little in recent months. She was too focused on fulfilling her duty and protecting her people. She considered it the ultimate way of honoring her late husband.

"We will have to discuss this new discovery in depth, and find Evander. His research vault might offer important insights now that we know some new questions to ask," Kilian said.

Connor liked that idea. He asked, "How about it, Captain Ilse? Want to be the first test case to see if my healing affinity is really better?"

She smiled, her eyes twinkling with challenge like they had so often in the past. "Let's do this."

Chapter Sixty-One

Un-deadly-captain-ish Behavior

Shona looked like she couldn't decide if she should be relieved or insulted that he'd chosen Ilse first. Connor was just glad she didn't protest. She'd lost her hair more than once, usually because of Connor, and it would eventually regrow. Ilse had fashioned a marvelous summoning to overcome her handicap, but as powerful as she was with earth, she could not permanently heal herself.

Now maybe Connor could.

He felt eager and nervous at the same time. The queen's miraculous healing abilities still seemed beyond human comprehension, and the thought that he might be able to duplicate at least in part that same level of healing awed him. At the same time, if he failed, how would Ilse react?

She had dealt with her crippling injury with such indomitable bravery she'd inspired everyone who heard the tale. Now he was giving her hope, but if he failed, would the new loss be the stone that broke the cart? He doubted anything could really break her spirit, but felt terrified that he might be the cause of new pain for her.

It was too late to turn back now, so he vowed to find a way. He was a Tallan-grouted fool for offering to heal such an injury without practicing first, but all he had to do was find a way to pull off a miracle.

He wished he'd snagged one of those sweetbreads before Hamish consumed them all.

Connor kept his worries from his face as Ilse adjusted her chair and released her summoned limbs. He had grown so used to seeing her legs and hips encased in that thin sheathing of living earth that it came as a shock when it melted away to reveal her withered, twisted legs and crushed lower body. Although he and other healers had worked hard to help her, had stripped away her pain and done what they could to fix the broken flesh, he still shuddered to see again the extent of her injuries.

Since she always wore that concealing covering of earth, she only wore a pair of short pants that barely extended halfway down her thighs. A tiny flush of embarrassment rose in her cheeks. They had all seen her injury, though. They knew it, and the fact that she had risen above it to join in battle again against Harley eclipsed any pity anyone might feel for her. She was one of the bravest women Connor had ever met.

He tapped sandstone as easily as thought, crouched beside her, and laid one hand on one withered thigh. He might not need direct contact any more. The queen had altered people around her without physical contact, but he didn't need any additional challenges, and he suspected the contact would help her understand what he was doing.

Her legs felt cool, the atrophied muscles having shrunk almost to nonexistence. Her rough scar tissue felt hard, while the rest of her skin hung a little loose over her bones, which he clearly felt underneath.

Connor cast his sandstone healing senses into her legs like he had many times before, and the bones, muscles, and skin sharpened into view in his mind. As he extended his feelers into her hips and spine, he clearly felt the broken connections that had defied his best attempts to heal.

Now as he tapped sandstone he willed himself to connect with both the red and green frequencies at the same time. He had never been able to consciously manipulate which power sources he drew from before. Now the dual connection came easily, and he felt that thrill of discovery so similar to when he established new affinities.

As soon as he connected with both red and green power, he felt a deeper pool of healing available than he ever had before. It was as if he had always worked with sandstone healing by sipping only the top of a huge goblet of power. Now he could plunge his hand into the goblet and absorb it directly through his skin like he did with primary affinities.

As soon as he connected to that deeper source of healing, the warmth of sandstone intensified into penetrating heat. Ilse gasped, eyes wide in astonishment. "I feel something!"

Connor poured that heat into the broken bones and along her spine, willing the pieces back together. His concentration deepened as his sandstone senses consumed his mind. It was as if he stepped into Ilse's spine, with the broken connections clearly visible to him like snapped branches of a tree ripped to pieces by a mighty storm.

He seized those pieces and fused them back together, welding them with the heat of pure energy. As he worked, he sensed how the pieces needed to connect, and quickly realigned them.

But Ilse had lost a lot of mass. The queen had changed people's sizes and shapes so it should be possible to build new flesh. Connor willed her muscles to rebuild, to return to their former size. The healing power flowed through him and fused to her bones. In his healer sight, it appeared like glowing embers that he could mold into whatever shape he envisioned.

Under his hands, he felt her skin ripple as the muscles grew and reformed, that pure energy converting into living flesh. It was a marvelous experience that awed him.

So he continued on with renewed optimism, forming muscles, repairing bone, reshaping her legs from top to bottom. While he worked, he noticed the healing energy shift subtly. It was still pouring through him, then into her, but it seemed to flow down through his legs and hips, mimicking the work he was doing on Ilse. He sensed something getting drawn from deep inside of his own legs, a critical essence that he sensed was inaccessible to him before, but was vital to succeed in rebuilding such devastating injuries.

He didn't yet understand what he was doing, didn't comprehend what he was having to give to make the healing work, but he did not hesitate. The process didn't hurt, and although something about it made him a little uneasy, he refused to hold back. Ilse had risked her life for him many times, had lost her husband and many of her troops and had been crushed almost to death fighting Harley. If he'd arrived to help her sooner, she might not have been hurt. Now he could help her, and no matter the cost, he would.

Connor tried to ignore his worries and focus on the thrill of helping her. The elements had confirmed he knew less than he thought he did about his abilities. That didn't bother him as much as it probably should have. As long as it worked.

As the final pieces came together, the entire whole fused into her system and Ilse gasped again, her body rocked with a violent spasm that almost shook her out of her seat. She convulsed right up out of her chair, stumbling, but caught herself and straightened on quivering legs. Her own flesh and blood! Looking down at her reformed body, she cried out in joy, with tears streaming down her face.

Connor blew out a breath, feeling tired but jubilant. "I guess maybe it worked."

Ilse pulled him to his feet and embraced him hard enough that he nearly needed to tap granite. Ilse sobbed in that un-deadly-captain-ish way she had sometimes shown around her husband, making Connor feel distinctly uncomfortable. He was overjoyed that he could help her, but he definitely looked forward to her returning to her normal unflappableness.

Hamish commented, "Probably won't let you cut to the front of the lunch line any more."

Ilse laughed and released Connor. She danced around the room, exulting in her restored health, hugging everyone, even the Mhortair who she didn't even know. They accepted it with stoic good grace.

Verena hugged Connor tight and gave him a tender kiss. "Well done, Connor."

Hamish slapped him on the back, grinning. "I'm very impressed."

"You think I couldn't do it?" Connor challenged, although he too was grinning.

"It's not that. It's just, Ilse's got some of the toughest looking legs I've ever seen on a woman. I bet she could squat lift the entire palace."

Ilse heard him. She glanced down at her legs, and of course everyone else did too. Her short pants were indeed straining to contain her new impressive thighs. Every muscle stood out in perfect detail, even though she did not seem to be tapping granite. She laughed again and saluted Connor.

He shrugged. "Maybe I got a little carried away."

Then he felt a wave of weariness clobber him. His legs buckled and he collapsed into Ilse's recently vacated chair. His head swam, and he nearly fell to the floor. Verena and Hamish caught his shoulders. She started speaking urgently to him, but he found it hard to hear. The words sounded like distant buzzing, and he groaned.

Instinctively, he reached for granite to reinforce his muscles, but his affinity also felt distant and weak, almost as bad as that time Aifric had hit him with gabbro, the secret Mhortair weakening powder that blocked all primary affinities.

The shock of not feeling granite skitter up his arms struck him with far more fear than the momentary weakness, which was already passing. Others were gathering around, calling out questions about what had happened. Aifric dropped to her knees beside Connor and placed a hand on his arm. He felt her healing power flicker through him, seeking the problem.

"I'm okay," he assured them, but his voice sounded strained even to him, and he barely listened to their questions. He was too busy trying to figure out what had happened.

"You seem physically whole," Aifric said.

Ilse dropped to her knees beside him, her expression worried. "What happened to you, Connor? Did you draw too deep?"

"I'm not sure." He hated seeing the worry in her gaze, and he could not block her emotions, which seemed to boil off her. She felt a powerful sense of guilt that she'd caused him injury. He also sensed a fierce determination to protect him from harm. It was like a fire burning through her core, so intense he could not entirely block it.

"I'm fine. This is not your fault," he told her, and felt relieved to sense her anxiety diminish.

"So what happened?" Kilian asked.

Connor glanced up at his friends. Their obvious concern touched him. "Give me a second."

Granite still felt shaky and remote, so he tried basalt. Nothing. The connection was weaker than granite. His fear grew, and he switched to obsidian. He felt a flicker, and his mind accelerated briefly before fading again. The influx of obsidian-enhanced speed thinking helped, and he got an idea.

"You suffered a deep injury, Ilse. To heal you I had to draw upon some of my own strength. But it's only temporary and it's a price I'm more than willing to pay."

Verena didn't look convinced. "Kilian, you've probably seen your mother perform more miraculous healings than anyone. Has she exhibited symptoms like this?"

He hesitated for a moment, brows furrowed in thought as he reviewed his memories. "I don't remember seeing such an overt reaction, but then again she had decades of practice before I was old enough to pay attention to things like that. Connor, do you sense any effect on your primary affinities?"

"Yes," Connor exclaimed, surprised by the question. "How did you know?"

"My mother always favored the tertiaries, despite her cryptic warnings of dangers inherent in using them. I remember one time she brought Harley back from the brink of death. She'd suffered such trauma that even her incredible healing affinity was taxed beyond her abilities. My mother healed her, crafted a new body for her, and mentioned something like, 'Good thing I didn't need my primaries today.'"

Mistress Four said, "I have read notes from the First and Great One himself that suggested deep healing carried consequences, but his notes were pure conjecture."

"You should have shared that conjecture with us before Connor tried this," Verena said sharply.

Connor placed a calming hand on her shoulder. "It's okay. I would have done it anyway. Good thing I don't need my primaries today."

"Don't start quoting the mad queen," Verena said, then sighed and touched his face. "I'm glad you're going to be okay."

"Any other conjecture we should know about?" Shona asked.

Mistress Four hesitated before saying, "The rest made less sense. Something about a bridge and the price of humanity. Not even Mister One understood the reference."

The reference to bridges was interesting. The elementals had mentioned bridges too. Connor sat back, enjoying Verena's warm hand in his. He was already feeling a little better, although his legs still felt unusually weak. He didn't want to worry Ilse so he said, "Give me a minute, and I'll be fine."

As everyone returned to their seats, Anika entered the room. Connor hadn't even seen her leave. She carried a pair of uniform trousers, which Ilse gratefully accepted and donned. They were a little tight in the thigh, which only made Ilse smile again.

"Everything seems to work, right?" Connor asked Ilse to help draw attention away from himself.

"Better than even in my dreams," she admitted with a wide smile, and a tear glinted in her eyes again. She blinked it away, which Connor appreciated. Seeing Ilse fully in control helped him feel like all was right with the world.

After another moment, Shona asked, "Connor, how are you feeling?"

He didn't need chert to sense her impatient eagerness, but she suppressed the urge to ask. She was enough of a lady to know that it wasn't appropriate to badger him for cosmetic fixes while they were still celebrating the miraculous healing of a dear friend. Especially since he'd weakened himself in the process.

"I'm feeling better, thanks, Shona. I appreciate it a lot."

As he talked, Connor reached out to her with sandstone. He still felt unsteady, and he should probably wait, but he needed to understand how much healing might affect him, and to what degree. Ilse's injury was deep and severe, Shona's need cosmetic. Surely there was a difference. The queen had mastered advanced healing without severe consequences. He needed to master it too.

Besides, he really wanted to experience healing someone without first touching them. That was such an incredible ability, he couldn't wait to try it. Shona's charred hair and burned skin mapped clearly to his healing senses. Now that he understood the trick to drawing deeply from both power sources, it took only a moment to heal her scalp, restore the roots under the skin, and encourage them to begin to grow.

Thick, golden hair sprouted from Shona's head. She absently reached a hand up to scratch as if feeling an itch, and gasped. Eyes wide with wonder, she snatched her hat away and felt her hair as it grew more than an inch every second. Connor noticed the healing power flow up around his own head before crossing over to Shona. His scalp itched, and he felt a powerful urge to check to see if his own hair started falling out.

He doubted it would. The queen had regrown Shona's hair without losing her own, and this healing drew far less from him. It was barely a glimmer of loss. The excited chatter of the others faded away as they all turned to watch Shona's gorgeous hair extend out from her head and cascade in a slow-motion waterfall.

"Connor, I thought you needed to rest," Verena protested from her seat drawn close beside his.

"I need to understand the limits of my affinity," he said, but she crossed her arms, looking displeased. He decided not to wonder if she was unhappy that he was taking more risks, or unhappy that he was helping Shona restore her famous hair. He could pick the thought from her mind, but really didn't want to know.

Connor stopped the hair growth just as it reached Shona's shoulders. "Feeling better?"

Shona patted her new hair, expression filled with wonder. Tears shone in her big, hazel eyes, and she laughed. Her rich voice seemed to fill the room. She rose and crossed to him.

"Thank you, Connor. This is a marvelous gift, especially when you were still not recovered from your last healing."

Then she leaned in and kissed his cheek. Not like the seductive attempts she had tried the previous year, but simply a sign of appreciation from a friend. She gave him a dazzling smile, then returned to her seat. He clearly sensed her joy, her desire to shout and twirl and show off her new tresses, but she was a well-trained high lady and she would never show off when they were still celebrating Ilse's recovery.

Anika and Aifric both joined her and made a point of congratulating her on her new hair. Verena leaned in close and asked softly, "Are you all right?"

He nodded. She said, "I'm glad you didn't hurt yourself to heal her pride." He started to smile, but her expression hardened. "But if she ever tries kissing you again, you're gonna need to regrow her another set of lips."

Connor started to protest, but Hamish grabbed him by the arm and exclaimed, "If you can heal without touching, can you heal Jean from here?"

"I don't know the range, but I doubt I could reach all the way to New Schwinkendorf."

"Even if we get her on a sightstone?" He pressed.

"I can't extend my senses through a sightstone connection," Connor told him, then frowned. "At least, I don't think so."

"If you could do that, wouldn't the queen have already tried sabotaging us from Donleavy?" Verena asked.

Hamish didn't look worried. He gestured toward the door. "Come on! If we hurry, we can get back to Jean by dinnertime."

Chapter Sixty-Two

Something Nutty

Ailsa sat on a comfortable cushion of air next to Queen Dreokt. She had grown probably too comfortable flying with the queen, and she enjoyed the panoramic view of eastern Ravinder from several thousand feet up. Queen Dreokt had remained unusually quiet for most of the trip after picking up Ailsa along the great western trading road earlier that afternoon. She looked tired but extremely pleased with herself.

Queen Dreokt smiled and said, "Of course I am. You would be too if you had such a busy day."

It did not surprise Ailsa that the queen was reading her thoughts. She'd come to expect it and sometimes it did make communication easier.

"*Especially when I'm this tired,*" the queen spoke directly into Ailsa's mind.

Ailsa didn't want to get too comfortable sharing thoughts with her liege, but couldn't even allow herself to think about why with the queen already sipping from her mind, so she said aloud, "If you're exhausted, we could land and procure a carriage or something to give you time to rest."

She did not sense that the queen was struggling to maintain their comfortable seats in the air, and they were hurtling over the landscape as fast as they had in any of their previous excursions together.

Queen Dreokt made a dismissive gesture. "That would be far more of a bother than just flying. Maintaining such a simple connection with air is not taxing. I could keep us aloft in my sleep."

Ailsa hoped she didn't decide to test that theory.

Queen Dreokt laughed with delight. "Oh, Ailsa. It can be so refreshing to travel with one not burdened by the cares of conquest and rule, deeper magic, or the responsibility to maintain the ramverk."

Another new word. Ailsa's inner person wanted to howl with the need to ask questions, but she shuttered those deep thoughts. The conversation was far too intimate to risk it. So she inclined her head and said, "Indeed, Your Majesty. I'm a simple sculptress, who only needs to worry about producing my best work and hoping for the ultimate success of our kingdom."

The queen chuckled and again spoke directly into her mind. "*That's one of the reasons I keep you close, Ailsa. You know your place and you are content with it. But don't pretend to more humility than you possess. We both know you provide perhaps the most penetrating insights of any of my counselors. Most are so burdened by pride, ambition, and self-doubt that I cannot confide in any of them.*"

She smiled at the praise. Her surface self, devoted counselor to the queen, was immensely pleased that the queen appreciated her hard work. "I'm sorry my scouting mission to Maninder proved unfruitful. I feel like I let you down."

The queen had kept her close in their whirlwind journey around Obrion while she attempted to raise another worthy servant, but had insisted on dealing with Jagdish alone. Soon after entering Ravinder, she'd dropped Ailsa off on the great trading road with orders to investigate reports of a large army massing around Maninder.

That was unusual in the extreme. Usually the queen would have simply destroyed any army that dared oppose her, but she had insisted she could not be distracted by vermin. She had continued north alone, shifting to riding on a great ice throne, carried along by a churning platform of water.

Ailsa had changed mental hats to her persona of Ailsa the revolutionary. She had contacted her network immediately and warned them that the army must disband and flee with all possible speed. That was so much easier than the very risky warning messages she'd managed to send to both Jagdish and Merkland during the trip across Obrion.

Switching back to her persona of Ailsa the sculptress and advisor to the queen, she'd been annoyed to learn about the army's sudden flight. She had dutifully shared that report with the queen when she returned to pick her up. Queen Dreokt had appeared too tired and distracted to really care.

Now Queen Dreokt said, "I don't have time to chase down rabble. I'll send Aonghus or Rosslyn to mop them up after we destroy Merkland."

Ailsa dared allow her surface thoughts to feel subtly surprised that attacking the remote, isolated outpost of Jagdish could so exhaust her liege. The queen plucked the half-concealed thought instantly.

"Mhortair's unruly children are an annoyance, not a threat. I could have destroyed them the old-fashioned way, but I told you I needed to not only punish them but also block the misguided child Connor from ascending until I am ready to assist him."

"Do you mind if I inquire if your elegant plan indeed required the use of the serpentinite sculpture you showed to me earlier?" It was a daring question, and one that could easily trigger the queen's volatile and unpredictable wrath.

The queen only sighed, a happy smile playing across her lips. "It was a brilliant stroke, Ailsa. It's been so long since I've meddled with the delicate ramverk we established over Obrion. I'm glad I did, because it felt so good, and honestly I feel more alive than perhaps I have in all the time since I awakened from the long sleep."

"I'm so glad to hear that. I too find great joy and fulfillment by working on the most challenging of projects," Ailsa said. In her deepest thoughts, she yearned to ask more about that ramverk. Understanding those cryptic terms might help her understand the queen better, might help her discover the weakness she still dared to hope must exist.

"Perhaps you of all my counselors can appreciate my brilliance. Yes, my dear Triath's sculpture played a critical role." Her gaze sharpened and she added in a warning tone, "I don't need any stones to command my affinities, mind you."

"Of course not," Ailsa agreed instantly, filling her surface thoughts with absolute confidence in her monarch's unrivaled powers, tinged with a bit of fear.

That mollified her and Dreokt settle back, looking up into the scattered clouds. Her voice grew soft in a way it often did when she trod old memories. "Even the elements must do my bidding. I buried that sculpted stone soon after arriving on these foreign shores. This land was wild and unruly, populated by belligerent and uneducated barbarians. The magic was completely untamed. No one even seemed to understand that power streamed past, close enough to taste! Our ramverk was the first grand effort to begin filtering the sylfaen in order to secure our enduring dynasty. We created the filters that produced affinity stones as we had begun doing in our homeland. That began the great journey toward crafting real power."

Ailsa listened raptly, astonished by the casual revelations. She knew nothing of how the power of affinities were infused within stones. She knew of no records of Petralists prior to the rise of Queen Dreokt and King Triath, so as incredible as it sounded, they might very well have been the first Petralists.

She said, "I had always assumed affinity stones always existed but that we did not know how to access them."

Queen Dreokt laughed, a delighted sound. "It's rare that anything catches you by surprise, Ailsa. I love it. No, my dear Triath and I . . ." She trailed off, her expression softening, and Ailsa was startled to see the glint of a tear in her eyes. The queen sighed deeply and said, "Some days his loss is almost more than I can bear."

Such a display of humanity was rare from her monarch. Ailsa's surface persona felt moved by the privilege of witnessing it.

Queen Dreokt snapped out of the reverie, her expression hardening. "I had to destroy him because fools overreached their knowledge! I will not allow it to happen again."

"Of course not," Ailsa agreed, recoiling deeper into her seat from the abrupt change.

The queen's emotion flipped again just as fast, and she sighed, her expression turning thoughtful. "As I was saying, with our research team, we created the first filters of sylfaen powers through stones and established the first affinities."

"I am awed by your achievement, but I do not understand sylfaen," Ailsa dared say when the queen paused.

"Of course you don't," Queen Dreokt snapped, looking annoyed. "No one understands. No one on this backwater continent has access to the deeper learning of my lands."

"I know nothing of other lands," Ailsa said, allowing her surface thoughts to hold curiosity about them.

The queen snorted. "Probably for the best. They're a pack of pompous, self-important know-it-alls who reject true advancement into the mysteries when we dropped it right in their laps."

"That must have been frustrating," Ailsa said.

"More than you know. Everyone wanted to access the sylfaen." She rolled her eyes like a child and added, "Sylfaen is the name of the great powers of magic that encircle our planet. They fuel and support life, but raw sylfaen is beyond human capacity to control. Our people knew about it for centuries, and great men and women had attempted many times to harness it, with few successes and some remarkable failures."

Ailsa listened, fascinated and eager to learn more. She doubted anyone else on the continent knew the secrets she was learning. Queen Dreokt suddenly wagged a warning finger at Ailsa, her tone turning dangerously quiet. "Don't you dare explore those failures. The elements weren't the only consequence of their foolishness."

"I won't," Ailsa promised, wondering what she meant.

But her mood switched again and she leaned back in her invisible chair, gaze growing distant with memories. "We attempted a novel way to filter the sylfaen. My husband discovered how to see vortexes of power that got caught in stones."

"The first-ever sculptor," Ailsa breathed, wondering how it had all begun, marveling that he figured out how to magnify and mold those powers. Despite her great skill at sculpting, she was not sure she could ever have developed her abilities without the critical training she received at the Carraig.

"He was a genius among men," Dreokt said, a wistful smile playing across her face. "He was the one who began concentrating enough power in the stones to prove it might be possible. The sylfaen cannot be managed by humanity, but we worked out how to filter it into lesser bands that could pool in stones. Those stones became fuel cells that we could tap. When we arrived here in Obrion, we moved quickly to bury various sculpted stones at locations where the sylfaen converged."

"World-level convergence points," Ailsa breathed, so caught up by the amazing tale that she almost forgot to shield her deeper thoughts. Luckily Queen Dreokt was so distracted by her memories that she didn't seem to notice.

"Exactly. We called our efforts the ramverk. The sylfaen encircle the world, high above the clouds, like a great, invisible shell around the planet. The energy contained within it is vast, and it plunges down into the planet at convergence points, like streams falling through the holes of a giant colander. Through those points of contact, energy flows into the planet, fueling life. The energy is raw and vast, but disperses through the planet until the basic elements of life can feed from it. That gave us the idea of using filters."

If what she was saying was true, Queen Dreokt had come from a land of vastly advanced learning. No wonder she considered the rest of them little more than barbarians.

The queen had settled into a trance-like state, similar to other walks through old memories, only deeper than usual. Most of the time Ailsa only gleaned a couple of fragments of those memories before the queen lost her train of thought and returned to the present. Perhaps her exceptional exhaustion helped her see deeper into the past. Ailsa was grateful for it. She couldn't imagine any other way to learn such fascinating insights into the queen's past.

Queen Dreokt continued, her voice barely above a whisper. "We discovered that by sending a worthy servant who had established higher affinities into the earth in elfonnel form right at a point of sylfaen convergence, bearing with them one of Triath's highest-form sculpted stones, their presence helped connect their stone to the flow of sylfaen. That stone facilitated dispersing the sylfaen more aggressively. The lowest frequency of sylfaen power could radiate across the land in a form naturally drawn to power-grade stones, particularly those situated near slumbering elfonnel."

Ailsa wanted to ask a thousand questions, but did not dare interrupt. The queen's trance was deep. She looked half asleep. Ailsa was not even sure she was conscious that she'd spoken aloud. Ailsa wished she had known the queen in her younger days before the long sleep had corrupted her. Her tale suggested she and her husband had been truly remarkable people, and they had brought affinity magic to an entire continent. How much good could they have done if things had turned out differently?

The queen's gaze snapped into focus and she growled, "Of course it's a tragedy. Poor Triath died too young and my wicked son blinded my precious grandson with foolish words of treason. That war destroyed almost everything we had created, and now he has even cost us serpentinite."

"What do you mean?" Ailsa asked before she could stop herself.

Queen Dreokt rolled her eyes in annoyance. "I thought you were listening. You're usually smarter than this, Ailsa. I told you that burying that stone with my servant created the affinity."

"So by burying that sculpted serpentinite stone with an elfonnel at a convergence of sylfaen, you created the serpentinite affinity that others could then access?"

"Like I said," the queen said with a curt nod. "My decision to retrieve the serpentinite stone was indeed a master stroke in the short term, but does carry a heavy price. I struck down Jagdish with that stone. It granted me elevated access to serpentinite and I believe a permanent increase in my power, for all of my other affinities feel stronger. Unfortunately, in the process I shattered the filter between the sylfaen and the serpentinite affinity."

"You broke serpentinite?" Ailsa demanded, aghast. To create affinities in the first place was mind bending enough. To now break those affinities was nothing short of terrifying.

The queen made another dismissive gesture. "Oh, don't be so melodramatic, Ailsa. It's broken, yes. Broken for the sorry fools who are stuck in the lower thresholds. Even for me, it's all but useless. But it's only a short-term loss. Few Petralists can use serpentinite anyway, and nearly all of them died in the rubble of Jagdish. But as we created the affinity before, we can create it again."

She gestured at an earthen box that she had carried along since her return from her mission of destruction. "I collected enough samples of serpentinite that at least one should prove a fitting specimen for your next master work. Ailsa, I need you to craft me a superb serpentinite sculpture. After we bring this continent to heel, we'll return it to my servant again, and the affinity will be restored in a few short years."

Then her expression shifted to eager happiness, like a small child preparing to attend a Sogail celebration. Her eyes sparkled as she said, "When we return to the palace, I would like roasted duck for dinner. And maybe some banana bread. Something nutty sounds splendid."

Chapter Sixty-Three

Miracles

Jean looked up from production reports of Builder mechanicals at a knock on the door. Her private study was but one of the many rooms of her suite, which she still felt was far too vast for a single person, even the lady governess of the city.

"Come in," she called and dropped the last report onto her desk. It was a large, wooden expanse, much grander than the simple desk she had used for so long in Lord Eberhard's manor house in Faulenrost. She loved the new desk, especially the many drawers. They were full of mechanicals, healing supplies, and piles of her notebooks and pencils.

The room was large enough that even with floor-to-ceiling bookcases along most of the walls, there was still room for a fireplace, although she rarely used it. She did use the comfortable chairs and couches that faced it, often holding informal brainstorming meetings. She loved the free flow of information. Sometimes she felt the very walls must be soaking up the dense cloud of fresh ideas. It helped the room smell good.

Gisela entered and made a brief curtsy, a habit that Jean was trying to get her to stop with little success. The people of New Schwinkendorf had celebrated Jean's appointment as their lady governess with remarkable enthusiasm and they universally insisted on strictly observing all of the social norms. She thought it foolish.

"What is it?" she asked.

It was not yet time for dinner, at least she didn't think it was. She often got so distracted by her work that Gisela had to remind her to go eat with her people. Jean preferred mingling through the various eating halls, greeting friends and asking for updates on their many projects. Some of them seemed to prefer her to sit at the high table, but most of them had accepted that she wouldn't change. More than one commented that people needed to be flexible when dealing with the idiosyncrasies of nobility.

Gisela approached and held up a speakstone. "Hamish is asking for you, my lady."

Jean hummed a few barely audible notes in a sequence that was becoming as natural as breathing. Her summoned arm extended, wrist turning, fingers opening to accept the speakstone. With another soft humming melody, Jean closed the fingers around the stone and lifted it to her mouth. "Hamish?"

"There you are. You left your speakstone in your other dress again, didn't you?"

There was laughter in his voice, and it sounded stronger than it often did when passed through the booster relays between New Schwinkendorf and Merkland. "Have you already returned from Ravinder? How did things go with the assassins? How are the poor people of Merkland doing? Have you seen Anika's dress?"

Hamish laughed, and she smiled to hear his good humor. Things must've gone better than she had feared. She was happy to receive some good news. Her heart still ached to think of the many killed and wounded in the dreadful attack by that army of summoned creatures. So many more people could have been hurt if Hamish and Connor hadn't returned to help. She was eager to get to Merkland soon herself and see the success of her flights' efforts to aid, particularly with their summonings.

"Have we got stories to tell you. Connor and I are almost there. Quick, open your balcony doors."

Jean frowned and exchanged a worried look with Gisela. "Don't you dare try landing the Hawk in my rooms," Jean chided as she moved toward her balcony doors. Her office might feel large, but it wasn't that big. She might feel her quarters were a bit ostentatious, but she preferred they not get trashed so soon.

"We're not in the Hawk," Hamish replied with another laugh. Whatever he and Connor had concocted, he was thoroughly enjoying it.

That made Jean more nervous than ever and she increased her pace to the doors. As she drew them open she said, "You didn't carry Connor all the way on your back again, did you?"

"I don't think I'll ever have to carry Connor on my back again."

Jean stepped onto her balcony, with its panoramic view over New Schwinkendorf. The night air was cool and clear, and she immediately heard the sound of

Hamish's thrusters. She grinned, flooded with excitement to see him again. He had indeed flown from Merkland in his battle suit, or maybe parked the Hawk somewhere to complete the journey in the suit. He liked flying up to visit her that way, and she heartily approved. They were forced to spend far too much time apart, so she appreciated every second he could save returning to her.

Seeing Connor flying confidently through the air beside Hamish without a Builder suit did surprise her. Hamish twisted and fired thrusters to slow and make a perfect landing. Connor merely stepped out of the air and onto her balcony as if it was as easy as rising from the dinner table and heading for the dessert tray. He looked happy, and excited about something. She was so glad they both looked healthy.

Gisela gasped. "Connor, I am never seeing you flying so well."

He grinned. "One of the funnest new side effects of ascending that I've discovered so far."

Jean gripped Connor's hand with hers, humming softly to move her new arm in the appropriate sequence. "You ascended! Tell me all about it. How was Jagdish?"

"Rather tragic, actually," Hamish said with a grimace.

Jean released Connor and eagerly stepped close, quickly humming a soft tune, moving her arm around to hug Hamish before he cut off the sound with a kiss. She loved his enthusiasm. She felt safer and more confident of the future when they held each other than at any other time. She was thrilled beyond measure to see him again so soon. She had feared it would be weeks before he returned, and had worried about what might have happened to them in Jagdish.

When he released her she said, "Come in and take a seat."

She led them inside, humming softly the tune to move her summoned arm in sequence as she walked. It felt better to have it swinging by her side instead of hanging limp. She liked to hum, so adding just a little more music to her daily life had been such a tiny price to pay for use of another arm.

They stepped inside and Gisela closed the doors behind them. Jean led them to the sitting area and Connor ignited a fire in the hearth with a flick of his finger. The sudden flames made Jean start, and she couldn't help touch the side of her face with her good hand and sidle farther away. She hated that she couldn't control the impulse, and forced herself to relax and move toward the chair closest to the fire.

Connor did not even seem to notice that he had done it. He did not look different, but he moved with new confidence. Those tiny glimpses into his abilities suggested he had indeed gained significant enhancements. She could not wait to test them all out, and glanced at the little table next to her chair to verify one of her notebooks and pencils were there waiting for her.

Instead of sitting, Hamish and Connor followed her to her chair. Jean raised an inquisitive eyebrow as she sat. They were up to something, but she doubted they would spring one of their pranks so soon after returning. Hamish dropped to his knees beside her, eyes glowing with powerful emotion. She began to fear what might've happened to the poor people of Jagdish.

Connor began smiling, which helped settle her nerves a little, but they were both acting so strange.

"Out with it. You two are going to burst if you don't tell me something, and I don't want a mess on my new carpet."

Hamish actually looked like he was close to tears. Maybe the news really was tragic. But if it was so bad, why did they look so happy?

Connor placed a hand on her shoulder, his eyes twinkling with flickers of limestone light. "I've ascended the third threshold, Jean."

Warmth spread from his hand, and she recognized the effects of healing. He, Aifric, and far too many other healers had spent far too much effort trying to heal her injuries. Then that familiar warmth intensified into a deep, penetrating heat. It spread to her injured leg, and she gasped in astonishment as the constant dull pain that had remained despite everything the healers could do vanished. She reflexively straightened it, and it flexed perfectly.

"What?" she gasped, touching her leg in wonder. It seemed completely healed. With trembling fingers, she fumbled at the straps holding the leg brace in place. Hamish gently took over, and within seconds set the brace aside. She stood and laughed as she felt her leg support her fully for the first time since Aonghus struck her down.

"This is incredible," she laughed and hugged Connor so tight he grunted. "Your ascension improved your healing so much so fast?"

"It sure did," he said with a grin. "Now if you'll please resume your seat, I'm not quite finished yet."

Jean sank back into her seat, nearly overwhelmed by joy and gratitude. That's why they had returned to Merkland so soon. She bet Hamish had used up an entire set of thruster blocks in his haste.

Connor touched her shoulder, and the penetrating heat of his healing flowed up to her face, then seeped into her damaged eye under her patch. Healing warmth flowed into it like hot water, and she placed her good hand over the patch to feel what was happening. Under her fingers, the shrunken, misshapen orb that was all that remained of her sightless eye swelled back into shape. Barely believing the wonder of it, Jean pulled the patch away and gasped again. She stared at her study in full, living color.

"Tallan's mercy," she breathed, blinking rapidly to see through a flood of tears that welled from both eyes.

Both eyes!

For a moment all she could do was look around, marveling at the colors, at the sudden depth of everything. She hadn't even realized how flat her world had become when viewed through only one eye. Jean laughed through her tears and looked up at Connor, a hundred questions on her lips.

He was also blinking rapidly. At first she thought he was blinking back tears, and felt moved that he was so affected by seeing her whole. Hamish wasn't even trying to hold back, and a tear of joy was trickling down his cheek. But then Jean realized Connor seemed to be having trouble focusing on her face. That was so strange, like the opposite of what she was experiencing.

She reached out to touch his face with her good hand and asked, "Are you all right?"

Connor nodded and took her hand in his. "I'm fine. It's nothing. It'll pass soon. Let's not get distracted. We're not done yet."

Her hair began to itch. That was not uncommon. The scattered patches that were starting to regrow itched pretty constantly, but this was different. The heat of healing magic flowed across her scalp, and the itching intensified. Jean reached up and removed her hat to feel her head.

Her hair was growing back.

The wonder of it filled her with speechless astonishment. Jean had witnessed many miracles as she worked with Builders to push the limits of their science magic and help her various research teams delve into previously inaccessible aspects of the natural world. But this was personal and affected her at a primal level.

Her hair quickly grew, expanding like a living thing. As it reached her shoulders, she pulled some of the thick, golden locks around to stare at them in amazement. Her hair continued to grow until it reached down to the center of her back. She was not sure what to say, was not sure she could say anything. She glanced from the grinning Connor to Hamish, who was gripping her good arm in both hands, smiling brighter than a Solas.

"Connor, this is amazing," she whispered, her voice thick with emotion. She wanted to chide herself for feeling so moved about her hair. The healing of her leg was far more significant, but she couldn't help it. Knowing she wouldn't look like a hairless freak eased a knot of tension deep in her heart that she hadn't been consciously aware existed.

"We can't have the Lady of New Schwinkendorf looking less than regal," Connor said with a grin. He began idly scratching at his scalp, and Jean spotted several strands of hair wilt under his fingers. If she hadn't been looking at it, she wouldn't have noticed.

"And of course, we always save the best for last, just like dessert," Connor said, again reaching for her. He missed her arm by a couple inches.

Jean grabbed his hand, filled with sudden worry. "What's happening to you, Connor?"

"I'm healing a friend," he said, but his eyes shifted away from her face, and he still didn't seem to be able to focus properly.

"What you're doing to me is hurting you somehow, isn't it?" she demanded.

Connor looked chagrined, and Hamish shrugged. "She's a quick study, as always. Might as well tell her."

"Tell me what?" Jean demanded, glancing from one to the other.

"Let me finish, and then I'll explain," Connor said.

"Finish what? Explain what?" she asked. He'd already healed her leg, her eye, and her hair.

"Do you trust me?" he asked.

She gave him 'the look' and hummed softly, crossing her arms in that way that used to intimidate them. At the moment, it had no effect.

"Please, Jean. Let him do this," Hamish said, and the emotion in his eyes moved her.

She sighed and hummed to uncross her arms. "Fine, but only if you won't hurt yourself any more."

Connor nodded, and Hamish placed hands on her earthen arm and said, "First we need to take this off for a minute."

Jean glanced from her earthen arm to Hamish, then to Connor, who was again grinning. She suddenly found it hard to breathe, a wild hope blossoming in her heart, but she didn't dare say it aloud.

She glanced down at her earthen arm in wordless wonder as Hamish helped her unfasten it. He set it aside with barely a glance, and anticipation mounted in her until she found it hard to remain calm. That earthen arm had accomplished more than she'd ever dreamed possible. Now was Connor really offering her something more than she could allow herself to dream?

Connor took her good hand, and healing power rolled through her and down into her stump.

Jean stared in open-mouthed awe as her arm began to grow. First the upper arm, lengthening out from her short stump, glowing softly as if it was a mirage. Then her elbow formed, then her forearm, her wrist, hand, and fingers. When the entire limb was rebuilt, it flared for a second, and then solidified.

Feeling flooded up the arm, a rush of connection ten thousand times more intense than those occasional moments when an arm or hand went numb. She gasped, rocking back in her seat, grasping her new arm with her other hand as every inch of the new limb tingled.

She felt it all!

Jean wept, feeling complete for the first time since that terrible day.

Laughing with delight, Hamish gripped her re-formed hand in his, and his touch drove home the wonder of the miracle. Jean couldn't speak, could barely breathe as she reached up with her healed hand and touched Hamish's face. She traced the track of his tear, marveling at the wonder of feeling his warm skin. She cupped his cheek and laughed, filled with more joy than she could express.

With trembling lips, she leaned forward and kissed him. She felt his answering emotion radiating through his lips. He pressed her to him, and she hugged him, laughing again at the feel of his battle suit and his tangled hair. She exulted in the sight of his handsome face in both of her restored eyes.

Connor was grinning like a fool. "Not bad, eh? You'll have to measure them together to make sure I didn't give you a gorilla arm or something."

Laughing, Jean leaped to her feet and embraced him. "Thank you!"

That was not nearly enough, and she was not sure there was any way to express the depth of her feelings, but Connor's grin made it clear that he understood.

Hamish stood and Jean threw herself into his arms again. As he held her, she started to sob. She cried with joy, relief, and with a sense of awakening from a permanent nightmare. As she clung to Hamish, she realized the extent to which her injuries had damaged her.

She had refused to allow them to define her, but every day had been a challenge. Every time she looked in the mirror, or walked into a crowded room where she could not hide her deformities, she had faced the decision anew. Should she cringe and run away, or force herself to move forward with faith and confidence? So many of her patients failed to overcome their injuries, but let those injuries define them.

She could not allow herself to do that. Their need had bolstered her courage and she had forced herself to move forward, beyond her injuries, and define herself as more than her limitations. She had refused to admit the awful gulf of dread and remorse and guilt still lingering deep in her heart.

Now the trial was over and she could scarce believe it. All of that pain and horror that she had refused to acknowledge erupted through her now that she could finally release it. For a long moment, she clung to Hamish as emotions racked her and sobs ripped from her lips.

She forced herself to feel it, to acknowledge it. That was the only way to truly release it, and she yearned to feel whole again. Hamish seemed startled by the intensity of her reaction, but held her until the storm of emotion passed, whispering words of comfort.

When she finally released him he said, "If you really preferred that summoned arm, I'm sure Connor can undo what he just did."

Jean laughed, and that helped wash away the last vestiges of the horrors of those recent months. "Don't be silly." She turned to Connor and said, "Please tell me how you did this, and what it cost you."

"It's nothing," he insisted, but as he stepped toward the nearest couch, his right leg buckled and he collapsed to the floor. He caught himself on one arm. The other, his right, the same one he'd healed on her, just flopped at his side. He didn't seem to be able to control it.

A terrible fear grew in Jean as she rushed to help him sit up. "Don't you lie to me, Connor. You never could when we were kids, and you definitely can't tell me nothing is wrong now."

Connor sighed, and a gust of air blew in through the still-open balcony doors. It encircled him and lifted him to the couch. Jean stared in fresh wonder. She'd never seen anyone command air so easily.

He looked up at her with that slightly off-focused expression and said, "The short answer is everything has a price."

CHAPTER SIXTY-FOUR

Bridges to Affinities

Connor hated that Jean saw the effects of using his new, higher-level healing ability so soon. He didn't mind paying the price of temporary personal limitation, or even the temporary loss of his primary affinities for her. He would pay far more to see her healed, but he did hate that those consequences were dampening her joy.

He tried not to show how exhausted he felt, or the fact that he couldn't see out of one eye. His right leg lacked strength, and he couldn't seem to move his right arm. The effects were only temporary. Hopefully.

Jean was watching him expectantly, and Hamish was glancing toward her desk where no doubt he somehow sensed a stash of sweetbreads. Connor was about to explain what they knew about the effects, but Air appeared in his mind.

He was already tapping quartzite, and she tended to flit in and out of his mental view when he wasn't drawing heavily from her. She dove into view, as if she had leaped off a high cliff and dove headfirst into his mind like a loch. Before plunging out of view beneath his feet, she abruptly stopped, hanging upside down, but somehow her long hair and her dress stayed in place. Her dress looked like it was fashioned from reflections of a rainbow through high clouds.

She rotated to face him, still upside down, but apparently unaffected by her orientation. Her eyes glittered, full or brilliant oranges and reds, as if they contained the final moment of a glorious sunset.

She spoke calmly, but her voice held echoes like a flock of a hundred sparrows. "To fly, a baby bird must cast itself out of the nest. Sometimes early lessons are painful."

"You sound like Earth," he said a bit grumpily. He hurt too much to decipher air-speech.

"He's not the only one who speaks deeper truths through imagery," she said brightly, rotating face-up and starting to float slowly around him.

"Usually I don't mind. I'm just not feeling too well," he explained, happy she hadn't taken offense. Air was responding to him better than ever. He'd marveled at how easily he'd flown with her after they landed the Hawk at the main landing field and decided to fly directly to Jean's balcony.

Air had seemed giddy to have someone able to fly so well with her. She'd complained that the queen never wanted to chat when she flew, and Air enjoyed talking about the many spectacular sights she saw flying around the world. In their short flight up to Jean's tower, Air had hinted that she could tell him about the many lands she knew.

She'd crossed them all, from the vast oceans to endless prairies to giant mountains that put the Maclachlans to shame, and every other possible landscape. She knew hundreds of countries, full of people so varied she doubted he could comprehend them. Connor was looking forward to learning more about them.

Water stepped into view in Connor's mindscape. He'd downed a soapstone mixture earlier, but was not actively tapping it. The fact that the elementals could initiate contact with him still surprised him. There was so much he needed to learn. She wore a long gown of deep blue satin, with a train that rippled behind her along the gray expanse that served as the floor. Her long, dark tresses were worked into a complex braid, and her eyes were perfectly clear, like the Lower Wick on a summer evening.

"You have already grown much since your ascension," she said approvingly. "But you lack much understanding."

"No better way to learn than by doing, right?" he asked. Water's presence always helped reassure him. She was so dependable.

Her lips turned up in the beginning of a smile. "You have healed. Are you enjoying the consequences?"

"I'm willing to pay the price for my friend," he assured her.

"But what if you didn't have to pay that price?" she asked.

"There's a way to avoid it?" That was great news.

Her smile widened. "That's why I am here. You have much to learn and very little time."

"Wow. I hadn't realized you were interested in teaching me more so soon," he admitted.

"You must progress in order to survive. Your survival is important to us."

"Really?" He liked the elementals, loved that he could communicate with them, but hearing her say she cared made him feel really good.

Air laughed, the sound like the wind rushing through tall grasses. "Of course, you silly boy. You can't help us without proper training."

"How can I help you?" Connor asked.

"Don't jump ahead," Water told Air. She sounded like a school teacher warning a student to stick to the lesson material. Air shrugged, waved to Connor, and shot up through the gray of the mindscape and out of sight.

"What did she mean?" Connor asked.

Water made a dismissive gesture and smiled reassuringly. "You cannot understand everything today, but I can show you how to release the weakness you suffer as consequence of your healing."

"I'd love that," Connor said. He was eager to learn how he could repay the elements for all their help, but was willing to wait until they shared more.

"Are you all right?" Jean asked, leaning forward in her chair, brows furrowed. She couldn't hear his mental conversation, and conversing with the elements seemed to take only a fraction of the time it would take to talk with someone not standing inside his head, but something in his expression must have looked weird.

"Just figuring a couple things out," he said, tapping the side of his head.

His eyes clouded and the view of Jean's luxurious quarters faded away, replaced by a strange, empty landscape. Connor stood with Water on the center of a simple rope bridge with wooden plank treads, connecting two cliffs about fifty feet apart. The empty space under the bridge roiled with gray fog. The land behind her was rocky and bare, ending in a sheer cliff that looked like it was made out of white soapstone. The distant sound of crashing waves echoed out of the darkness far below.

She gestured behind him. "Your last ascension allowed you to cross to this point, which is why we can finally speak together. This is the farthest I can tread into the domain of your mind. Your journey to reach this point has crossed all of those bridges."

At her gesture, he rose into the air and turned to see the landscape spreading wide behind him. Stranger things had happened in his mind so he did not stress over it.

The land that connected his bridge to the soapstone cliff was but a small island, barely ten paces across, with several other bridges connected to it. Other small islands drifted in the gray abyss nearby, each linked by more bridges. All of the islands were eventually connected back to a larger mainland that appeared hazy and indistinct.

Connor drifted over to the nearest island and touched each of the bridges connecting to it, finally understanding what they meant. That island represented his tertiary affinity with water. It was constructed of fine soapstone blocks, and anchored the end of the bridge where Water stood.

Four other small islands hovered in the gray fog to either side, roughly parallel to the one where he stood. He recognized the stones used in their construction. Marble, Slate, Quartzite, and Serpentinite. Those were his other tertiary affinities.

Each of those islands were connected by bridges back to a group of four more floating islands that had to be his secondary affinities. They were in turn connected to another row of islands closest to the mainland, which would be the primaries.

So fascinating. Connor floated over to the islands representing his secondary affinities, studying them with a growing sense of wonder. Huge brown sandstone blocks formed one island, while softly glowing green limestone formed another. The strangely metallic hue of blind coal made up a third, while flint-like gray chert seemed to whisper to him from its spot in the distance.

"This is amazing," he grinned as he studied the visual representation of his affinity connections. As he slowly spun in the still air above limestone, he noticed for the first time that each of his affinity islands was built with three tiers of stones, like steps in really short pyramids. The bridges connecting to them were actually made up of three tiers too, each bridge connecting to a different tier.

He floated closer to the bridges linking limestone to soapstone and landed beside the reinforced foundation that secured the end of the topmost bridge at the topmost tier of the island. Connecting bridges to the corresponding tier on the opposite island made sense, but Connor wondered why he had three bridges for each connection. They were built directly above each other, making it possible to traverse only the topmost bridge between the topmost tiers.

Stranger still, he noticed that his tertiary affinity islands were taller than the rest, but the top tiers of slate and quartzite were shorter than soapstone and marble. Seemed a waste of effort to construct tiers of bridges like that. Was there more purpose behind that construction, or was it a flaw in Water's attempt to translate the concepts for him? Or maybe it was a weird twist his own mind created in the vision.

Water had remained standing in the center of the final bridge from soapstone while Connor explored his islands and bridges. She called, "Traverse your bridges back to your mainland. There you will see the final bridge, and the key to today's lesson."

"Don't you want to come?"

"I cannot cross to your side of this bridge yet," she said, a hint of longing in her voice.

It seemed unfair that she couldn't come closer even when he invited her. "Is that how I can help you, by inviting you across these bridges?" Connor guessed.

"That is part of the assistance we hope you can offer," she admitted, her expression turning eager, one foot raising as if to take another step, but she lowered it again.

"How can I do that?" he asked. If his connection to the elements was so strong when they could only cross halfway, how much more power could he unlock if he could invite them all the way in?

"By studying and practicing, and by obeying my counsel to return to your mainland."

Connor floated along the bridges of his affinities back to the expansive mainland that anchored them all. He might have gotten there faster by floating out over the roiling gray abyss, but something about that empty space made him nervous, so he followed the zigzag course between the islands to reach the mainland.

As soon as he stepped down on the mainland, it sharpened into focus, and he smiled with instant recognition.

Alasdair.

He stood at the top of the switchback road near the lochs, overlooking the beautiful expanse of Alasdair valley as it still existed in his dreams. Lord Gavin's manor stood on the plateau below, with the Wick flowing past on the other side. The township was just visible, peeking around the curve of the mountain to his right. He grinned, feeling a sense of homecoming. Behind him, the gray abyss obscured most of Wick Torr and Lookout Rock, which meant his affinity islands and bridges stretched back toward the quarry. That felt right.

As he studied the cherished vista, a new bridge materialized. It was a single-layer bridge, not triple-stacked like the ones spanning his affinities. It anchored to the top of the cliff right next to where the switchback road began its steep descent, and extended in a long, graceful arc down toward Alasdair. It too was made of wooden planks, but they were attached to solid, white granite trusses. Slender rails, also made of Alasdair White held aloft a polished wooden handrail. He sensed the far side of the bridge anchored in the living room of his home. It was the only bridge that formed more of a ramp, and he bet if he coated it with ice he could get fantastic speed sliding down its long length.

Water's voice reached him clearly from where she waited on her bridge. "Focus on the pain and weakness you suffered from your healing and cast them upon this final bridge. It will take the weight of those consequences for you."

"Really?" The idea seemed somehow wrong.

Then he chided himself. He needed to show more flexibility. If this bridge anchored to Alasdair, it most likely represented the security and support of his family and community. They would definitely help ease any burdens they could.

So Connor focused on the phantom pains he felt in his face, eye, leg, and arm. As soon as he did, they seemed to flare, and he groaned. His right leg suddenly felt weak. He hobbled over to where the bridge was anchored and leaned on the rail for support. That did seem to help. Good thing, because suddenly his right eye grew dim, his vision fading to black, and his right arm lost strength, feeling suddenly deadened and useless, just like when he slept on it wrong and cut off the blood flow, only he couldn't get it working again by shaking it back and forth.

"Cast the pains upon the bridge and be healed," Water urged, her voice intense. She was really motivated to help him recover. He appreciated that.

Connor drew all that pain and weakness together like he did his affinities when preparing to purge them, then drove it all out through his chest. The pain intensified, and he gasped, clutching at his heart. The flash of pain passed quickly and he cast it all away onto that long bridge to Alasdair like an indistinct ball of shadows.

Instantly he felt better, the pain gone, his weakness evaporating as if it had never been. He laughed and shouted, "It worked!"

"Well done. You have taken an important step forward in your journey," she said, sounding very pleased.

His happiness faded when he noticed that the ball of shadowy pain had splashed down onto the bridge and flowed across it. He had expected it to evaporate, but instead it seeped into the wood, leaving a black stain, like early rot. The left side rail of that bridge, right where he had gripped it for support, also looked worn.

He leaned closer to study it, his frown deepening. Before the granite of that first rail support had gleamed with the healthy shine of polished Alasdair White.

Now it looked dull and cankered, as if it had aged a century. The first six inches of the wooden railing also looked worn and cracked.

"What happened here?" he asked softly.

Water said, "As you told your friend, miraculous healing comes with a price. The cost was paid by your body until it could replenish itself. Now you have transferred that cost to this final bridge."

"Can I fix it?" he asked, feeling a strange sense of loss to see the bridge disfigured by his pain.

"You don't have time to worry about such trivialities. That bridge is long and secure. It can withstand many more transferals. You have more important matters to worry about, such as mastering other new aspects to your affinities."

That made sense, and he did love the feeling of renewed health he was enjoying. He rose and began traversing the topmost layer of bridges toward Water. He traced his fingers along the rails of each one, sensing their power, which helped restore his good humor. He'd only caused a tiny bit of damage to that bridge, which wasn't even real. It was just an image in his mind. Water was right. He needed to focus on more important things.

When he returned to her he asked, "Is this how Queen Dreokt manages her healing too?"

"We will not speak of her today," Water said with a scowl. "Return to your friends and practice your healing. We will begin your next lesson soon."

The mindscape vision of his bridges faded, and Connor blinked, returning to Jean's study. She had risen and was crossing toward him, looking concerned. When their eyes met, she asked, "What happened? You sort of faded out for a moment."

"I'm all right," he assured her with a wide smile. "Like I said, I was figuring out some things. I was having trouble with the healing because I didn't understand how to do it right, but I'm good now."

She didn't look convinced, so he jumped to his feet and lifted his arms to show everything was all right.

Hamish looked surprised. "How did you do that?"

"You expected him to be affected, didn't you?" Jean demanded. "And you let him heal me anyway."

"Of course," Hamish said simply. He took her hands in his and looked deep into her eyes. "We would both suffer a lot more than temporary discomfort to heal you, Jean."

"He's right. I was more than willing to pay the price, but turns out it was a shorter price than I'd feared."

She sighed with relief and smiled that radiant smile that seemed to light up the room. She gripped one of each of their hands, her expression turning excited. "Then what are we waiting for? I have some more people for you to heal!"

Hamish sighed. "I knew we'd miss dinner."

Chapter Sixty-Five

Everything Has a Price

Hamish was right. They completely missed dinner. Jean kept them busy, rushing from one sickbed to another, and from there to visit everyone she knew with any type of handicap.

She seemed to know everyone.

Connor was thrilled to share his remarkable new abilities with so many, particularly with the patients in the long-term rehabilitation building on the hospital campus. It was obvious that Jean visited often. She and her medical teams were already working with many of them to provide replacement limbs that were almost as advanced as the earthen arm she had worn.

Most of the patients exclaimed in wonder at seeing Jean with a restored eye, face free of lingering scars, arm regrown, and leg restored to strength. They loved her and celebrated her miraculous healing with her. Of course they also eagerly asked how they could get healed too. Jean promised Connor could help them all, and set aside a semi-private area in the common room for him to visit with each patient and heal them.

Connor was acutely aware of the attention, the heavy weight of responsibility, and the desperate hope the patients clung to as they each visited him. He still felt uncomfortable with the solution Water had shared with him for side-stepping the consequences of using his higher healing powers, but he could not deny the need of those patients.

Even if he was tempted to, he could never deny Jean. She'd already done everything in her power for those people. He could tell many of them were already dealing with their disabilities with courage, even when the hope of full healing was impossible. He read Jean's influence in every face. That she could accomplish so much without a single affinity or special power awed him. The amazing efforts she expended for those people meant he could do nothing less than his best to help.

Besides, Water had said he needed to practice, and he loved exploring new abilities. His new healing power amazed him. He scarce believed he was the one accomplishing so much. Good thing he had Verena, Hamish, and Jean around to help keep him humble. He could see why the queen and even Harley had developed such bloated heads and overdeveloped senses of their own importance. His ability with sandstone was now nothing short of miraculous.

The first nervously eager patient was a middle-aged woman who said she was a baker until her hands were crushed under a falling oven. They hadn't been amputated, but she could barely move them. They looked like skeletal claws more than human hands. Connor held them in his own, and the fact that he didn't cringe at her touch moved her nearly to tears, even before he began healing her.

Again Connor's enhanced healing powers helped him see how the bones, sinews, and joints needed to be formed, and what was wrong with them. His experience healing over the past few months, training with old Marcus and then with Aifric, had given him a strong foundation, but his new healing abilities eclipsed all of that.

Within moments, he restored her hands, and the woman shrieked with joy, jumping up and down with glee, nearly crushing his ribs as she hugged him. She promised to bake him every one of his favorite foods in thanks.

Hamish smoothly stepped in to share ideas for dishes she could cook since Connor was busy tending other patients. News of the woman's miraculous recovery bolstered the hope of other patients, and they each eagerly took the chair beside Connor, or were wheeled in on chairs or rolling beds, depending on their infirmities.

Connor healed them all.

As he poured his healing power into the bodies of his patients, he learned to understand the different nuances of how each body reacted to the energy. Bodies were fascinating things, filled with such a delicate balance of blood and tissue and muscle, all mixed together in marvelous ways. His sensitivity to those systems was deeper now, and as he removed scars and fixed crushed or missing limbs, it deepened even more. Soon he was able to understand with a single flick of his healer senses what each patient needed. The broken or incomplete systems in their bodies tugged at his mind like splinters in his own skin, drawing his attention without needing to seek them out.

That understanding helped him fine-tune control, which reduced the impact the healing had on him, which he deeply appreciated. Several times he had to pause to return to the mindscape with his affinity bridges and cast those effects onto that final bridge back to Alasdair. It wasn't an affinity bridge, but he sensed it was somehow vital, and he hated weakening it.

He didn't like referring to it as 'that bridge back to Alasdair', so decided to call it his Family Bridge.

What choice did he have but use it, though? He couldn't stop, not now that he'd given those people hope, not when Jean was counting on him. But he also realized he didn't have to cast the entire burden upon the family bridge. He held back, releasing only enough of the consequences so that he could keep working. As a result, he began to feel deeply exhausted. Every limb ached with phantom pain, his vision deteriorated, his hearing turned inconsistent, and he nearly fell several times.

He didn't think anyone but Jean noticed. The patients were too distracted by the healing, and Hamish was distracted by the baker, but Jean watched Connor with concern that she tried to conceal. Luckily she didn't interrupt or force him to explain what was going on. Connor had survived battle and danger many times without shrinking from it. He would not shrink from healing.

As he poured the healing power into people, he could now direct it at a microscopic level, fostering growth and connections that had been previously invisible. One thing that surprised him was feeling flashes of pulsing energy flowing through nerves. He'd never felt that before. He sensed it was used to control muscle movement, but the little pulses felt so much like flickers of strum that he'd felt from the Varvakins. Was that a coincidence, or a deeper connection than anyone had yet made? The idea was fascinating.

As Connor moved from healing terrible injuries to helping regrow burned or scarred flesh, or even entire limbs like he had with Jean, he grew to understand the process better and better. Growing new limbs became more a process of stimulating the body's innate abilities to grow and heal than it was adding foreign matter to their systems. By the time he had regrown his fifth limb, he could direct the work far more efficiently and with far less expenditure of energy.

That fifth patient was a seven-year-old boy, crippled since birth. He was one of the patients that Jean had been planning to help with one of the semi-autonomous summoned limbs. Connor could feel how nerves and tissues and even some of the bone structure had grown incorrectly, preventing the boy's legs from ever working. As he guided the healing power, he exulted to feel the misaligned pieces slide into their correct positions, and he loved the look of wonder on the little boy's face.

Almost before he finished, the boy began shouting. "I can feel my legs!"

Despite cautions from Jean that he take it slowly, he bounded off the bed to his newly strengthened feet.

And of course fell flat on his face.

He had not yet developed balance, and it would take some time, but he did not let that slow him down. He leaped back to his feet again, exclaiming at the wonder of being able to move so quickly. And when he again toppled over and rolled onto his back he laughed so hard that tears shone in his eyes.

Connor laughed too. As the boy's jubilant parents helped him to stand again, Jean hugged them all, tears of joy in her eyes. That moment burned itself into Connor's mind. He knew he'd never forget how happy he felt.

They did not finish the work until nearly midnight. Jean looked like she could have continued for days. Her eyes were glowing with overflowing joy, and she kept randomly kissing Hamish. That helped him stay focused too, although as much as he liked to grumble that they had missed the feast he did not urge them to stop.

Jean coined a new term for Connor's new healing power. Flesh crafting.

That was very good, as good as one Verena might come up with. It was a pretty accurate depiction of what he did too.

Finally Connor leaned back in his chair, barely suppressing a groan. He felt like a crippled old man and just wanted to lie down to sleep for a year. He could cast all that pain away, but stubbornly refused to do so. Even holding back like he had, he'd cankered the left-hand rail of his family bridge for a hundred yards, and the right-hand rail for fifty. He needed to understand better what he was doing before he would do it more.

"Is that everyone?" he asked, glancing up to where Jean stood, looking more like a blurry ghost than herself.

She pressed a mug of soup into his hands. "Just one more patient. Drink this, and we'll go see him."

Connor gladly sipped the warm soup. It filled him with warmth and seemed to ease some of his aches. Was that why the old gaffers in Alasdair always liked soup so much? Connor had assumed it was because they'd lost most of their teeth.

As he lowered the soup, he spied a padded rocking chair, empty now that he'd healed the man who'd occupied it. It called to him in a way no rocking chair ever had, and he couldn't resist the urge to rise and cross to it. He tried to conceal how much he hurt, but groaned softly, rubbing at his lower back.

"You should rest," Jean suggested, not hiding her concern.

"I'll be fine," he assured her as he settled into the rocking chair with a sigh of bliss. It fit perfectly, and that gentle rocking motion eased his aches wonderfully.

Hamish wandered over, chuckling. "Never thought I'd see you enjoying a rocking chair."

"I'll have you know, in my day I've been a . . ." Connor trailed off, shocked. Had he really started a sentence that way?

Hamish chortled, and even Jean laughed, although she looked even more worried. Connor concealed his embarrassment by slurping down the rest of his soup and asked, "Why do we have to visit the last one? Is he confined to a bed with no wheels?"

"No. He . . . doesn't want us to visit," she said softly.

"He doesn't want to be healed?" Connor asked softly, his own pains fading as he considered the strange idea.

"Of course he does, but . . ." She sighed, and even with his blurry vision, he could tell she looked grieved. "He's given in to despair and doesn't have the hope left to believe he can be healed."

That was so sad, Connor immediately rose. He had never felt that level of despair, but how would he have reacted if he'd suffered a debilitating illness or injury with no hope of relief? "Where is he?"

Jean led the way. Just the two of them followed the central hallway to the last door on the left. Connor wobbled a little as he walked. Jean took his hand to lead him and said, "Thank you for sacrificing so much for strangers, Connor."

"I'm doing only a fraction of what you do every day," he said honestly.

She gripped his hand, but made no further comment. When they reached the right door, Jean knocked softly and entered. Connor followed her into a comfortable room. His knees creaked audibly, and his back hurt, but he suppressed another groan.

The walls were bare, the room completely unadorned. A man sat in a rocking chair facing away from the small window, staring at one blank wall. His body looked fairly fit, maybe in his thirties, but his eyes looked old, and he didn't look up when they entered.

"Why do you torment me, Lady Jean?" he asked in a forlorn voice, surprising Connor by speaking near perfect Obrioner.

She crouched beside him and said in a cheery voice, "Because I want to hear your music, Golssen. I want to hear you sing."

Golssen gestured with the stump of his left arm, which ended at the wrist. "Don't mock me. Without my hand, I cannot play my lute. Without my lute, my voice is but a mockery."

Jean glanced back at Connor, looking anguished. Connor stepped closer and placed a hand on the man's shoulder. He could simply start healing, but felt Golssen needed a little more of a push. "What if I told you I could heal your hand?"

"No one can," Golssen said with simple finality.

"What if I could? What would you do with your restored life?" he pressed.

The man gave him an annoyed look, but Connor held his gaze, and he must have sensed his earnestness because he hesitated, glanced at Jean, then back at Connor. He spoke softly, but with the first strength Connor had seen from him. "If you are mocking me, I will find a way to make you pay."

"Good man. And if I'm telling the truth?"

"Connor, what—" Jean began with a frown.

"Trust me," he told her, not breaking eye contact.

"If you can heal me . . ." Golssen hesitated, as if really considering the question for the first time. "I'll dedicate my life to helping others find hope."

"Works for me," Connor said with a smile.

He tapped sandstone, and healing power again roared through him. He focused his fleshcrafting down into Golssen, whose eyes widened at the feeling of intense heat. Other than his hand, the man was whole. His depression had crippled him more than his injury. Connor fixed the first handicap in a moment.

The rest was up to Golssen.

The man stared at his restored hand, a look of wonder on his face. His eyes slowly lit with hope as he realized he was really seeing his hand again, really feeling it. He laughed aloud, threw back his head, and burst into song. It was a Grandurian tune, and Connor couldn't make out most of the words, but he didn't need to. The song was full of heartfelt joy.

It took a few minutes to get away from Golssen, who pumped Connor's hand more times than he could count. His own hand wasn't feeling well and he couldn't seem to grip, but Golssen didn't seem to care. He sang another Grandurian song, and his voice really was excellent. By the time they left the joyous group, Golssen had found his lute and started playing a foot-stomping tune for the other patients.

Usually Connor would love to stay and enjoy the music, but at the moment he felt cranky and longed for a little quiet, a soft blanket, and a long nap.

Chapter Sixty-Six

Glutton Crafting

Connor felt so happy that he managed to make it back to Jean's quarters before collapsing. Jean worried over him, but he assured her he just needed rest and to eat.

She immediately rang for a servant to bring them lots of food.

He felt horrible, but happy at the same time. With all the danger in the world, all the terrible threats they faced, it was wonderful to see some good come from Petralist powers. The queen might have used her unmatched abilities to destroy the entire city of Jagdish, but he had just restored normal life to scores of people. For the first time he began to glimpse Jean's drive to dedicate her life to healing.

"That was pretty amazing," Connor admitted.

Hamish grinned. "I bet that baker will have the first batch of pfefferneusse here within the hour. Did you know she was the personal baker of Lord Eberhard?"

Jean looked completely content. "You worked miracles tonight, Connor. I know it cost you more than you want to admit, but you saved their lives."

Hamish said, "You'd think the queen would spend more time healing. I bet if she did that instead of destroying everyone's minds, she'd own Obrion. No one would revolt if she helped them like this."

That was a good point, but Connor doubted she would ever consider it. The queen's powers were for her use and her glory, not for serving others. And by getting so caught up in that, she missed the true potential of her greatness.

Besides, he doubted she'd willingly sacrifice so much for anyone else. Glancing at Jean, Connor could imagine her as queen of Obrion. She would spend her life toiling endlessly to help improve the situation of all of her subjects, and as a result they would follow her through any danger. He could already see it among the citizens of New Schwinkendorf and even Faulenrost. He did not doubt her influence would only continue to grow because she used her new station as a way to find even broader opportunities to serve.

That gave him hope for the future.

Jean said, "If you're willing, and once you're recovered, I'd like to prepare a list of other severe cases. Maybe when we have time we can visit them one at a time."

Connor smiled. It felt a little lopsided. "I think that's a great idea."

"Once you understand how to manage the side-effects better," she said sternly. Then she added, "There's one other thing I would like you to take a look at as soon as possible, and one thing I need both of your thoughts on."

Connor chuckled. "I don't think even I could find a way to fill Hamish's head with anything other than thoughts of food."

"And thoughts of Jean," he added. That won him a happy smile from her.

She said, "First, Connor we've been studying infection and trying to determine why healers sometimes struggle curing it. We've been fine-tuning our special super-near-vision goggles, which we now call micro-vision goggles."

"That last model is working, then?" Hamish asked between bites of an entire nut-crusted muffin he'd produced from somewhere.

She nodded with a grin. "Wonderfully. We're seeing down into tiny structures that the Althins think are the basic building blocks of life. They call them molecules."

Hamish chuckled. "Sounds like that skin condition Stuart caught when we were ten."

Connor grinned at the memory. Old Mhairi had mixed up a particularly foul ointment to spread over the rash. She'd insisted the rash was infectious and that Cinead and Keith rub it over their faces and arms too. Connor had always suspected she'd made up that part just to humble them. They had been exceptionally troublesome that year until that vile lotion treatment.

Jean gave Hamish an annoyed look and stole part of his muffin. She popped it into her mouth, despite his protest, then brushed crumbs from her fingers. "As I was saying, we're still trying to understand what we're looking at. My teams are documenting their finds, but I'm realizing this is a process that's going to take years. I'm hoping with your help we can understand more. That could cut months or years off the research and eventual cures."

That was a good idea and Connor immediately agreed. He hadn't gotten to peer through those new micro-vision goggles yet. They sounded fun. He wondered if her teams had looked up each other's noses with it yet. That had been the first thing he and Hamish had done with one of the earlier models. He smiled at the memory.

"What's the other thing you need from both of us? More of my muffin?" Hamish asked, gesturing with the mostly-finished confection as if daring her to try snagging another piece.

"It's Nicklaus," she said.

"Is he all right?" Connor asked, instantly concerned.

"He's recovering well. Still can't access his affinities," she answered before he could ask. "I'd like you to check in on him to see if you can sense what happened."

"Good idea," Connor said. With his new sensitivities, maybe he could figure out how to heal Nicklaus' affinities. That would be something.

"And I'd like you both to speak with him about the conversations he's been having with elementals."

"What?" Connor and Hamish exclaimed together.

Hamish added, "You mean, just like Verena and just like Connor?"

Jean nodded. "Verena mentioned something about a threshold and speaking with Water the last time we talked, and you had mentioned you see elementals."

"I speak with them now too," he told her with a grin.

"Good. Nicklaus claims he hears them, particularly Water. She taught him how to purify water."

She didn't sound pleased. Hamish asked, "Why does that worry you?"

"Have you heard elemental people speak to you?"

"No, but I'd love to."

"Nicklaus is just a boy."

"I think the elementals want to help. They've been teaching me things, like how to handle the effects of my fleshcrafting," Connor told her.

"So why aren't you using that technique?" Jean asked simply.

He hesitated before saying, "Well, I'm still figuring it out."

She gave him that look that told him she knew he was holding something back. She repeated, "Nicklaus is a boy. I don't know what the elementals want. I just want you to speak with him and encourage him to talk with you before following their instructions again."

Hamish chuckled. "I'm impressed he listened at all. He doesn't like obeying anyone."

Connor loved speaking with the elementals and learning from them, but it did seem strange that they would reach out to Nicklaus. He hadn't approached that threshold, so how did they make contact? Was it somehow tied to his lost affinities, or the fact that he had possessed affinities as well as Builder powers?

He said, "Sure, we'll speak with him before we head back to Merkland tomorrow."

The food arrived and interrupted their discussion. A long procession of staff entered, each pushing a rolling trolley filled with mouthwatering dishes. All of the main dishes served in the dining halls that night were included, along with samples of all of the desserts, plus an entire trolley of Hamish's favorites.

A pot of savory sauerbraten stew accompanied a tray piled with thin-sliced cuts of pork, grilled, and drizzled with gravy. Connor spotted mashed potatoes, baked potatoes, and fried strips of potatoes. Sixteen types of sausages were cooked into all sorts of dishes, including three different casseroles.

Connor recognized some of the Grandurian dishes by name, like roasted schweinshaxe. The pork was cooked to perfection, the skin crisp, but the juicy meat falling from the thick bone. Rinderroulade was a kind of beef roll, with the thin-sliced beef strips wrapped with sausage, bacon, onions, pickles, and mustard. They were served with small roasted potatoes and a type of dumpling that Hamish tried to monopolize.

They also enjoyed Obrioner meals like breaded fish, hearty meat pies, and entire roasted grouse slow-cooked in a delicious honey glaze.

Hamish eagerly grabbed the first cart and looked like he planned to consume everything on it right there. Jean made him wait until they moved into her private dining room, large enough to seat more than a dozen people. They dug in and for quite a while Connor let himself get lost in the simple pleasure of eating.

He consumed several plates of the main dishes, interspersed with eight different types of breads, then sampled bunches of the desserts. Cranachan and almond cake and shortbread petticoat tails from Obrion, along with Grandurian lebkuchen, dipped in Althing chocolate, followed by jelly-filled linzer cookies and plum-apple crisp still warm from the oven.

That's when he discovered another new aspect of his enhanced healing abilities. As his stomach grew so full he felt like he might burst, he instinctively tapped sandstone again and connected with his overfull tummy. Distracted by a cream-filled pastry, he absently tugged at the food in his stomach, hoping to ease some of the hurt.

The food dissolved into energy that absorbed straight into his body, nourishing and strengthening him without the need for the long process of digestion. That flood of food energy poured right into his aches and pains, as if they were holes inside of him that the food energy partially filled. He rocked back, astonished as his pains noticeably faded and his vision cleared a lot.

Connor laughed and exclaimed, "No way! This is amazing."

"I'm glad you like it. I'll be sure to tell the cooks," Jean said between bites of a huge, fluffy pastry dripping with nuts and honey. Somehow she had consumed it without getting any on her face.

"The food is delicious, but that's not what's amazing."

He patted his stomach that was no longer bulging dangerously. "I just discovered that I can instantly digest my food."

Hamish gaped. He glanced from Connor to the food spread around the table. "Can you do that for me too?"

"There's one way to find out."

Hamish vaulted right over the table, activating thrusters to avoid crashing down on a beef stew, and landed beside Connor. Connor yelped as the air blast from the thrusters threatened to knock food from the table. He caught a couple of cookies blown right off their plate and stuffed them into his mouth so he could save the fish from sliding over the edge. The stew pot rattled, little waves of gravy whipping across the top, but did not topple.

"Be careful," he cried.

"Sorry," Hamish said, cutting off thrusters and helping set the dishes right. He grabbed Connor's hand and pressed it to his stomach. "Come on then. Test it."

Connor shared his enthusiasm and extended sandstone senses. Sure enough, he could feel the mountain of food Hamish had already consumed. He glanced at his friend, newly impressed by his abilities. Hamish had eaten at least twice as much as Connor had. Without the protective layer of his suit holding in his stomach, it might've already ruptured.

Connor touched that food and willed it to dissolve. It did so, and pure energy flowed all through Hamish's body. He whooped and started to leap into the air, but Connor caught him and said, "No thrusters!"

"Sorry," Hamish said again and retreated several feet from the table before jumping into the air and triggering thrusters. Connor tapped air and deflected the blast away from the table, just to be safe. Hovering with arms thrown wide, Hamish laughed with pure joy. "I knew your ascension was going to be awesome, but this is revolutionary."

Jean groaned. "Are you telling me you can seriously eat without ever having to stop?"

Connor shared a grin with Hamish and they shrugged in unison.

"There's only one way to find out."

Chapter Sixty-Seven

Flipping the World Coin

The next morning Connor awoke feeling completely refreshed. He should. He'd consumed enough food that he probably could have fueled himself for weeks, but instead all of that food energy had poured into the holes that his fleshcrafting left inside of him, replenishing his inner self. He loved that he'd discovered an alternative to casting that price onto his family bridge.

He was tempted to try eating that much again some time just to see if he could really live off of that converted energy in lieu of eating. Then again, he wasn't a fan of long-term fasting, so he would make sure not to share the idea with Jean. He loved research, but not starvation research.

At the moment he felt as good as if he'd been tapping granite and slate all night. He and Hamish had eaten everything, and had been tempted to sneak down and break into one of the pantries to test the limits of his newfound ability, which Jean had dubbed glutton crafting.

She had ordered them not to, even though Hamish had insisted it was purely for research purposes. She wasn't fooled. As if they'd ever actually fooled Jean.

Despite Hamish's loud protestations, Connor had let Jean overrule them. He didn't usually like acting like a glutton, but glutton crafting was a heady thing. He would have to watch Hamish because over-eating could easily to go to his head. And if Connor stopped helping him fast-digest, it would definitely also go to his stomach.

He had work to do. Time was short, and although the previous night's achievements had restored his sense of optimism, he needed to study what else the ascension had accomplished. So he skipped breakfast, tapped basalt, and raced out of New Schwinkendorf and onto the plain to the north.

He spent some time simply running at full fracked speed, circling the plain again and again. He loved the freedom of basalt speed and couldn't help simply enjoying that fracked sprint for a while. He felt convinced his top speed had improved again, even though he hadn't believed that was possible. He flew more than ran, and if he turned too sharply, sometimes he slid whooping for fifty yards across the grasses, still damp from early morning dew.

Luckily he had the space all to himself. Most of the Builders and Petralists had left with the reinforcements, along with the vast majority of the Arishat League forces. Those who remained were focused on building additional mechanicals and Arishat League weapons, particularly the ambitious Ilse's Revenge project.

Connor eventually slowed and tapped his elemental powers. He found that he no longer needed to tap porphyry, obsidian, or pumice to help stabilize his tertiary affinities. He was loving this ascension. It felt like somehow he was linked tighter to his affinities, as if they were a part of him more than external connections to foreign sources of strength. Tapping his affinities felt *right* at a fundamental level. Water appeared in the air beside him, looking stately and beautiful as ever, although she looked rather cross. Before he could ask her about it, Fire joined them, and he too looked grumpy.

"What's going on?" Connor asked uneasily. He had big plans to explore the effects of his ascension. He hadn't expected they might have wanted to sleep in.

"You spurned my counsel last night," Water stated, her tone definitely annoyed, hands on hips exactly the way his mother used to do when scolding him as a child.

"I don't understand. Last night I healed a lot of people, just like you told me to."

"Why did you not cast the burden of that healing across your final bridge?" she demanded. Fire paced around them, scowling, little explosions of crimson fire erupting out of his ears at every step.

Connor blinked in surprise, then grinned. "I didn't need to. I discovered how to use food energy to deal with the consequences."

"Food energy," she repeated, sounding disgusted. "You have no concept of the difficulties your ignorance creates for us."

"I thought it was a good thing. I didn't like what I was doing to that bridge," he told her, feeling confused, which made him feel angry in turn. He had never heard of elements chiding their Petralists.

She fixed him with a stare that mesmerized him. Her eyes were filled with enormous, cresting waves, the foam whipped off the tops by an invisible wind.

The waves looked far too big to remain constrained within her eyes, as if he was somehow looking through portals at a scene of a stormy sea somewhere. It reminded him that the elements were not human. They were more than he ever assumed, and he needed to tread carefully until he understood them better.

Fire said, "You assume the bridges Water showed you should always remain in place."

That surprised him. "Actually, I did. Those were bridges to my affinities. I can't lose those, or I'd lose my affinities, wouldn't I?"

"The final bridge contains no affinities," Water told him.

"What is it? It seemed to stretch back to my old home." He chose not to tell them the name he'd given it. It felt too personal.

"That is a truth for another day," Fire said quickly.

Water added, "You called us to inquire about additional truths this morning, is that not true?"

He nodded, happy for the turn in the conversation. "I sensed energy flowing through my patients' nerves last night. It reminded me of the Varvakin strum. Do you know anything about that?"

"Perhaps, but should I risk sharing additional truth if you won't take my counsel to heart?" Water asked.

Not good. He was finally able to speak with them, and he sensed he could learn so much. He hadn't imagined they might refuse to answer his questions. "I need to practice, to explore, and to understand what I'm learning. You said yourself that you are trying to understand humans. Did you know that I could use food like I did?" Connor replied, keeping his voice respectful. He couldn't afford to offend the elements. It still felt weird to consider that he might.

She didn't answer immediately, and he wished he could read her expression. It was calm, like the surface of a loch at dawn, but he sensed invisible turbulence below. Fire continued pacing, but his expression seemed less annoyed. Connor took that as a good sign. The two shared a look, and Connor sensed they were communicating, but he couldn't read it.

Water's expression cleared and she smiled warmly. "Never mind that. Perhaps there was something lost in translation. Let us move on to the next lesson."

"Great." Connor was happy that little misunderstanding seemed to have been resolved. He needed to be careful, but how could he have known using food would annoy them?

Then he realized they couldn't eat. How would he feel if people ate mountains of food around him that he couldn't partake of? The idea was really depressing.

He'd have to be careful not to remind them constantly that they couldn't enjoy the benefits of humanity.

Fire spoke first and surprised Connor by asking, "Have you realized yet that you can tap all of your primary affinities at the same time?"

"What? Really?" Connor exclaimed. It made sense, and he should have realized it, but he'd been mostly focused on his miraculous fleshcrafting.

"Don't get so distracted by one new bridge you've crossed that you fail to see the rest," Fire chided.

"I'll practice with them today," Connor promised eagerly. After his second threshold he had no longer needed to fear double-tap sickness, but he'd still been limited to only two of his primaries. He couldn't wait to try granite, basalt, obsidian, and pumice all together.

Water said, "Make sure you do. Now, your question leads us to a pair of principles that are vital for you to understand."

"Wonderful. Thank you," Connor said sincerely.

Fire laughed, and flames twirled around him like a glittering shroud. "We can share some of the things the queen discovered, but why limit yourself? Now that you can walk with us as our champion, you don't have to share her limitations."

"What do you mean by your champion?" Connor asked.

He had never imagined the queen as limited. What could he possibly tap that she might have overlooked? He needed every possible advantage, but that was not the first time one of the elementals had mentioned a service they required in return. He still had no idea what they intended, and he'd spent enough time around nobility to learn that one couldn't leave an undefined debt hanging around too long.

Water took his hand and the landscape around him faded to a mindscape Connor didn't recognize. He stood atop the vast bulk of a great mountain at night. The sky was clear, and snow covered the landscape. The air smelled clean in that way that he'd only ever smelled during fresh winter snows. It was bitterly cold, but he felt unaffected by it.

Water and Fire stood to either side of him, with Water still holding his hand. Fire gestured into the air toward sheets of soft light flowing high overhead. Green, blue, and shades in between flickered like immense curtains in the sky, flapping in an invisible breeze. In that moment he realized where he must be and what he must be looking at.

"Those lights are what the Varvakins call the Merry Dancers, right?" They were awe inspiring.

Water nodded. "Take Fire's hand also."

He did, surprised to feel Fire's skin cool to the touch, despite little flames dancing along his arm. As soon as he connected with both of them, Connor suddenly felt the glowing sheets of light overhead flickering in his mind as much as in his vision. That had to be the power of strum that the Varvakins had learned to harness.

Connor grinned. "How can I feel that energy so clearly?"

"Because you walk with both of us at the same time," Fire said. "Now you have gained the sensitivity to access this, one of nature's great forces."

Connor reached out fingers of thought to touch the Merry Dancers. He expected to feel the lightning-like power that had struck him when he ran into the invisible field on the plain. He did sense some of it, but mostly felt a different type of force. Invisible, but powerful, it seemed to tug at his core and pull upon the very fabric of the earth beneath him.

"That's magnis, the grip force that pulls on steel, right?" he guessed.

Fire nodded. "The Merry Dancers that fill the night sky are made up of a combination of two types of energy that are closely intertwined. The Varvakins have discovered these forces and have begun to learn how to manipulate them, but they don't understand them. These two energies are fundamental forces of the natural world and they offer tremendous power."

Water said, "These powers are found in the movement of the earth, the shifting of the seas, and the strength of raging storms. They generate the lightning and can exert remarkable influence upon all the natural world."

"Their potential for destruction rivals our own, so of course we felt it appropriate to help you connect with these energies first," Fire added with a wink.

"The Varvakins call them strum and magnis, but they are two halves of one coin," Water said.

"So it's kind of like a world coin, then?" Connor asked.

Water chuckled, the sound like the bubbling of the Upper Wick in springtime. "World coins. A unique turn of phrase, but apt."

Connor loved that sense of discovery. It was one of the things he enjoyed most about exploring new affinities and new aspects to his powers after ascending. He wished he could share more discoveries with his friends. No one else got to feel that unrivaled thrill as often as he did.

"Teach me," he urged.

Water smiled and said, "The key to accessing these fundamental forces of nature is to recognize that they pull matter out of its neutral state into a charged state."

Connor frowned. "So I can only access magnis and strum when I'm charging at someone? What if they're charging at me?"

He thought back to the time he faced the torc, so long ago when he had virtually no concept of his curse. He bet a charging monster like that could generate a lot of strum. Was that why they were so terrifying?

Fire laughed. "His brains are going to leak if you're not careful." Water scowled, and he added to Connor, "Haven't you ever noticed sometimes if you drag your feet over a carpet, then touch something, especially metal, sometimes you feel a little spark?"

Connor grinned. That was such a fun game. He and Hamish had often tried to out shock each other in the winter. They had worn right through one of his mother's favorite rugs. That's when she insisted they find other things to do, more productive things, like catching rats and releasing them into Cinead's kitchen.

"That's what Water was trying to say. The rug, your feet, and that metal don't usually shock each other. All of you, and most things in the world, naturally tend to a neutral state where shocking things doesn't happen."

He obviously didn't know Hamish very well, or most teenage boys for that matter.

Water took up the train of thought. "The force you call strum is a movement of tiny bits of energy attached to every bit of matter. Generally that energy moves between points where one side has built up a charge, a concentration of power. It may be a static charge like Fire just mentioned, which is caused by friction. It causes the little charges on the carpet to wake up and shake themselves out of their neutral state and collect together so they can accomplish something. Living beings like you humans use tiny bits of that energy in your bodies, as you sensed last night."

That was fascinating, and the explanation did sort of make sense. Most people Connor knew liked to end up in a neutral state too. Preferably gorged on a big meal, sitting on a comfortable chair in front of a warm fire. He could stay in a neutral state like that for hours. But when they were motivated to get active and get together they could really get a good charge started.

Fire said, "So one of the easiest ways that you can access the power of strum is to generate friction."

Connor frowned. "I'm afraid I don't understand how to do that." He imagined luring the queen onto a giant carpet to zap her, but sensed that wasn't what Fire was talking about.

Water said, "You can reach out with your senses and sweep them across the nearby area. People, buildings, the air itself, and even the earth. They all can be swept for tiny bits of strum energy. Collecting those together builds what we call a positive charge. Then you can release that built-up charge toward a target. Ideally you've pulled charges away from it, leaving it short of strum, in a state of negative charge. That increases the attraction between your charge and your target."

That seemed to make sense, but Connor wasn't sure he really understood. Fire recognized his expression and said, "Think of it this way. If you are in a great hall eating breakfast with all of your friends and you took one bite of each of their meals, you could collect a great deal of food without affecting everyone else very much. Everyone that you took pieces of food from are now missing a tiny bit. They now have a slightly empty plate, or in terms of what we're discussing, a slightly negative charge."

Water added, "And just as you can concentrate small charges of strum together, there are ways to strip more energy from your target, making their negative greater. The greater the buildup in charges, and the greater the difference between the positive and the negative, the more powerful the release of energy will become, and the more impact it will have."

Finally things started to make sense. If he collected enough bacon from everyone in an entire feasting hall, the resulting pile of bacon would hold tremendous potential. If he could also strip all the food off of someone else's plate, the difference between their breakfasts would be overwhelming. It sounded like deep arcane powers understood breakfast balancing better than he had ever imagined. If he threw an entire overflowing plate of bacon at someone whose plate was empty, the impact would definitely have a lot more effect than if they already had tons of food to begin with.

"How do I practice it?" he asked eagerly.

"Focus on the world around you, seek the charges, and draw them to you. Then release them," Water said, as if that was the simplest thing in the world.

"But don't give yourself the negative charge, or you'll end up hitting yourself," Fire added quickly.

"Why would you caution him against something so dumb?" Water asked with a frown.

"Because he's human," Fire said simply.

Connor was glad for the warning. He didn't want to accidentally hit himself with lightning.

Water said, "You can draw more power from the movement of the air and clouds, particularly during storms."

"Movement of air, transfer of heat, and the friction of great clouds generates lots of strum. That's where lightning comes from," Fire added with a grin.

"The queen has mastered the art of calling forth lightning when needed, and you'll need to be able to do so too, as well as sense when she's preparing to unleash such a blast against you."

"Can I stop lightning?" Connor asked, thrilled by the idea.

"Deflecting it more likely," Fire said. "By mastering magnis."

Water said, "When we showed you the Merry Dancers, those lights are the result of many strum charges flowing around a giant worldwide field of magnis."

Connor gaped. "Our entire planet is a huge lodestone?"

"At its core, yes. It generates a vast but rather weak field of magnis. You can see its effects in the properties of lodestones."

Connor thought about the directional compass that Hamish had started installing in all the flying vehicles. They had learned the trick from the Tabnit mariners. The key was a tiny piece of lodestone in each one that pointed north.

"Why do lodestones affect iron, but not much else?" Connor asked.

Water smiled. "Good question. Iron naturally reacts to magnis because of how the strum contained within it is structured."

Fire said, "But most things don't have a structure that react as well to weak magnis fields. More important for today's lesson is the relationship between strum and magnis."

"So magnis can move strum?" Connor asked, starting to feel like he was getting a sense of why magnis might be important.

"Yes, although the relationship works both ways. The movement of strum generates temporary magnis fields too."

Connor was intrigued, but starting to get a headache. He bet Jean would love the lesson. He usually just liked to tap his affinities and see what he could break with them, but he needed to understand, so he forced himself to resist the urge to just try to create lightning.

Instead he imagined a piece of iron and a lodestone into his hands. The iron instantly stuck fast to the lodestone, drawn by the invisible magnis. He gestured with the items and asked, "Show me."

Fire showed him how by moving the lodestone along the iron, it generated a tiny flow of charged energy. "Remember that magnis affects nearby strum, and if the magnis field is moving, it affects it more. The opposite is true."

"So if the queen tries to hit me with lightning, I could create a magnis field like this lodestone to move it away?" Connor asked.

"Indeed. That is the first step to mastering these forces of nature," Water said.

He couldn't wait to practice with them.

Water added, "But you are not limited to moving energy through tangible objects. Most things allow charges to move, even water when it has impurities in it, although pure water does not transmit charges easily, and air also insulates against moving charges most of the time."

"Then how does lightning happen?" Connor asked with a frown.

Fire grinned. "When the charge is great enough, you can break some of the rules. Lightning carries so much energy that it actually punches a hole through air and transforms the air in the path it travels into a different state called plasma."

"We'll practice with it some time," Water promised before Connor could ask. "Think of plasma like making a hole in the air for lightning to slide through, like soup sliding down your throat is easier than a big chunk of meat."

Connor had never heard of plasma, but it sounded fun. He decided he needed a lot of soup.

"This is a lot to take in." He envisioned a piece of Althing chocolate cake into his hands. He consumed it instantly, followed by a couple of enormous cookies that were the specialty of one of the bakers on Jean's staff. The imaginary influx of sweets and sugar helped settle his mind.

"These are the fuel to elevate your mind to a higher state," Fire said as the landscape around them changed back to the gray expanse of his own mindscape. He definitely needed to practice with both strum and magnis. He hadn't yet truly grasped the potential in them. Fire had suggested that the queen hadn't either.

Fire saluted and faded out of his mind. Water remained, her expression serious. "Study hard, Connor, but I must caution you against sharing our visits with anyone else, especially with your close friends and with Evander or Kilian."

"Why? You've already visited Verena, and Jean just told me you've been speaking with Nicklaus. I wanted to ask you about that."

"The Builders offer another avenue of hope for us, but you remain our primary focus. Your friends are not ready to attempt crossing additional bridges, but knowing that you have done so and by following the guideposts of your words, they may feel obliged to make the attempt. In so doing, they would most likely destroy themselves."

Connor grimaced. He hated that knowledge-can-kill-you-sometimes aspect of higher level affinities. If it was so dangerous, why was she reaching out to them, though? Something seemed missing from her argument, but he couldn't risk offending her again.

So he said, "Thanks for the warning. I'm looking for ways to help, not new ways to kill people."

She gave him a benevolent smile. "Train hard, Connor, and you will become our champion."

Chapter Sixty-Eight

If You Could Blow Yourself to the Moon, Wouldn't You Try It, Too?

Water faded from Connor's mind before he could ask her about that cryptic 'champion' thing again. He definitely needed to understand that. At the moment, he had plenty to think about, though. He blinked his eyes open and found himself lying in the grasses of the plain north of New Schwinkendorf.

He sat up, feeling mentally exhausted, but also energized. He'd learned that he could now access strum and magnis by walking with Water and Fire together. The potential for wielding lightning excited him, and he suspected he could probably use those forces to do even more. In their training session, he'd sensed things about strum and magnis, the movement of tiny charges and how to manipulate them that were hard to explain. It was as if knowledge had poured into his subconscious, and he needed time to let it settle and congeal, like a fresh pudding.

In the meantime, he couldn't wait to try tapping all of his primary affinities together. Connor jumped to his feet and tapped a little basalt. Sometimes it was easier to act than to think.

As he resumed jogging across the new green springtime grasses of the Schwinkendorf valley, he felt his head clear. He had small supplies of all of his primary affinities in tiny pouches secured to his belt. He decided to absorb a little of each of them and prove Fire was right. He was already tapping the wild freedom of basalt, and in seconds the itchy-crawly feel of granite skittered up his arm, followed by the bubbly feel of pumice.

He added a tiny bit of porphyry, and loved the fact that it no longer felt like getting bitten by a thousand tiny monsters as it absorbed into his skin. Obsidian came next with its acceleration of mind and body and the sound of Verena's laughter. That sound bolstered his confidence, and he absorbed a bit of diorite. It rippled through him, like living strum, filling him with exhilaration and a hint of danger.

With a growing sense of excitement, he tapped a little blind coal and swallowed the snake, applying the blind coal slippery protection to his bones. After making sure he felt a strong connection to sandstone, just in case this was one of those things Fire didn't understand about humans, Connor tapped all of his primary affinities.

He expected to feel his muscles strengthened by granite, maybe a bit of additional grace and control through obsidian, perhaps a hint of the beast of porphyry flexing in his heart, and pumice helping blind coal protect him from an eruption of diorite.

What he got was so much more.

As soon as Connor's primary affinities all activated, they melded together into a whirlwind of energy that eclipsed any individual power. Each affinity seemed to snap into place with his already-activated basalt, magnifying and reinforcing it. Granite strengthened his muscles and made it easier to run. He'd experienced that when he'd double tapped before.

Obsidian linked into the mix and his movements became more fluid and graceful, his mind expanding so he could anticipate his movements. He laughed with the thrill of it. He bet he could win any running battle now. No regular Striders would stand a chance, and he might even hold his own against Kilian for once.

Pumice snapped into place and he felt the well of his affinity powers seem to deepen, but the drain on his power stones eased until he barely needed any powder to maintain a full, max-tapped connection to his affinities. Awesome!

Then porphyry activated and the beast in his heart roared with the desire to hunt. That need filled him and he felt his senses expand, similar to when he tapped quartzite, but with a much more predatory feel. He sniffed scents on the breeze and noted tiny animals cowering in the thick grasses nearby, their tiny hearts thundering loud in his ears while the sound of their blood pumping tempted him to snatch up one of them and consume it.

That was a bit freaky, but then diorite activated and lightning-like energy erupted through him. He could have held it in, ridden the wave on the cusp of destruction for a few delicious seconds, but that wouldn't be nearly enough fun.

Connor released it.

Since basalt was the first primary affinity he'd tapped, the explosion blasted through him and out his feet. Grass vaporized, along with a huge chunk of earth, forming a deep crater over fifty yards across. Connor barely noticed. He was too busy whooping as the blast catapulted him into the air like a meteor falling upward.

He'd ascended quickly with air or by using the force of fire, but they paled against the raw power of explosive diorite. Connor hurtled over a thousand feet into the air, a tail of smoke sucked into the air after him. The force of the blast would have crushed his spine if not for the reinforcing protection of his other affinities. He tapped air enough to keep from suffocating from the incredible speed, or having the wind rip off his clothes and scour off his skin.

At the apex of his ascent, he hung in the air for a second, completely untethered, looking out over the valley and the city to the south. He spotted a Longseer on a windrider not far away and waved. The woman, who had been staring at him in obvious astonishment waved weakly in reply.

As Connor began to fall, he released his primary affinities and tapped fire, forming crimson wings to help him glide back toward the city. He could have simply tapped air, but sometimes gliding was more fun. He still couldn't explain why fire could act as a tangible substance when he tapped it, but he loved that it could.

He couldn't wait to try combining his primaries in different sequences. If he activated different stones first, would the combined effect produce different results?

He hoped so.

Connor aimed his approach to land at the northern edge of the city. As he touched down he noticed a babble of voices. At first he thought he had tapped chert and was hearing the thoughts of the multitudes, but when he double checked, he confirmed that he had not. He had maintained a slight connection with all of the elements, though. Ever since his ascension, connecting with the elements was as easy as breathing, and he had to really focus to remove that connection completely. It did not feel like that light touch even consumed any of his power stones.

With a start, Connor realized the babble of distant voices was reaching him through his connection with quartzite. He had not actively tapped it to his ears, but now did so. The usual flood of sounds burst into his ears. He let it pour through without trying to understand it, just leaving himself open to pick up any conversations that might be of interest.

Hamish's voice drew his attention. "No, I haven't seen Connor this morning. I'm going to go look for him in all the dining halls."

Connor was surprised to hear Verena respond. "Don't get distracted, Hamish. It's late enough that I'm sure you had at least one or two breakfasts already."

"Third breakfast never hurt anyone."

"Well, when you find him have him contact me. Shona is going crazy clamoring for his return so we can test loaning Petralist powers."

"Will do. We should be able to head back by tomorrow."

Connor stopped to stare at nothing in particular, completely startled by the realization of what he was hearing. He was listening to Hamish speaking with Verena, but she was still in Merkland?

He was eavesdropping on their speakstone conversation.

That was not something he'd expected, hadn't even thought it might be possible. He resumed jogging slowly, puzzling over the astounding realization. Other conversations drew his attention. He picked up on words from people that sounded like they were in different parts of the city, and even a few conversations between residents of New Schwinkendorf and coworkers in Faulenrost.

Somehow he could hear the words being cast between paired speakstones. It was wondrous, but his good humor vanished under the full ramifications of the discovery. He tapped basalt and rushed through town as quick as he could without running over anyone. He found Hamish in one of the dining halls, carrying a tray heaped with food. Hamish waved and set the tray on an empty table.

"Connor, I figured you'd come to your senses and meet me here."

Connor ignored the food, although it did look really good. "Were you just speaking with Verena via speakstone?"

"Yeah. How did you know that?" Hamish asked, with a ham-and-cheese filled croissant halfway to his mouth.

Connor snatched the pastry out of his hands and pointed at him. "Because I heard you."

He consumed the pastry in two bites, barely tasting the excellent blend of smoked ham and smooth, tangy cheese.

Hamish started to protest the theft of the pastry, but then frowned. "If you were close enough to hear us, why did you wait so long to come find me? We could've grabbed two trays from the food line."

“I was halfway across the city.”

Connor dropped into one of the chairs and pulled the tray closer. He began to eat rapidly as he considered the ramifications of the discovery.

Hamish actually just watched, frowning. “How can you hear a speakstone conversation from across town? You don’t have a speakstone linked to mine that I forgot about, do you?”

Connor shook his head. “I was tapping quartzite.”

“That would mean—” Hamish’s draw dropped open.

Connor nodded and grimaced. “Yeah. It means I can eavesdrop on speakstones. I bet the queen can too. Does Ailsa ever use them?”

Hamish paled at the thought, but thankfully shook his head. “I don’t think so.”

“We’ll have to get word to her not to use one ever.”

“And we need to tell everyone else. If we have anyone going anywhere near the queen, we can’t communicate through speakstones or she’ll hear every word.”

CHAPTER SIXTY-NINE

Some Problems Taste Worse Than Others

As Connor pushed open the door to the cavern-like work area where Ilse's Revenge was being built, Hamish followed close behind and grumbled, "I don't see why we have to stop here first. We need to get to Jean and warn everyone about the speakstones."

They did have to deal with that, but they had a little time. The boosters that pushed the signal between New Schwinkendorf and Merkland couldn't push signals all the way to Donleavy for the queen to eavesdrop.

"I want to double check something. I learned this morning that I can now sense strum and magnis."

"Really?" Hamish's worried frown changed to that inquisitive look he wore when exploring new mechanicals or new recipes.

"I don't understand most of it yet, but they're definitely related forces, and I want to see if I can feel what the Varvakins are doing." Connor didn't think revealing that he could manipulate those forces broke Water's warning not to speak more of them. He still wasn't sure why she would insist on that since she had already revealed herself to Verena and Nicklaus, but planned to tread cautiously until he understood better.

Hamish rushed past Connor to the observation deck overlooking the huge workspace. He gestured at the army of workers scurrying in and around and over the dozen enormous Juggernaut spheres. "Well, this is the perfect time to explore that. They're almost finished, and if you can sense something about them, I'm sure the queen could too. Better to know now."

Connor nodded agreement as he reached out to Fire and Water. He might be the only one who could see them, but it was still really cool to see them appear beside him, floating in the air.

Water said, "The facilities here are rudimentary, but it is remarkable they have progressed as far as they have, given how little they understand what they're dealing with."

Connor grasped their hands, easily combining both affinities. As soon as he did, he felt the rippling current of strum running through the circuits from the Varvakin generator and through the various Juggernaut shells. He also felt the waves of magnis binding mechanicals together and tugging subtly on his body.

"I feel something. Let's get closer," he told Hamish with a grin.

A long stair zigzagged down the length of the wall to the ground floor, but stairs were boring. Connor vaulted over the rail. Air appeared beside him as he also tapped quartzite, and currents whistled in to support him, and he sailed across the room on a stable, sure platform. He grinned anew at how reliably she now responded to his call.

Hamish jumped over the rail too, thrusters firing. It was so fun finally flying as equals. He really looked forward to flying with Verena soon too.

They crossed the great space and dropped to about thirty feet. Workers waved in casual greeting to Hamish, used to his flying suit, although more than a few looked startled to see Connor flying beside him. They accepted the change quickly, though. Working in that remarkable location helped people develop great mental flexibility.

As Connor hovered over the Juggernauts, he marveled at the feeling of all that energy coursing through the room. The wires glowed faintly to him, and he touched them with affinity senses. The energy flowing through those wires was more concentrated, more refined than the vast, raw power he'd sensed in the mindscape vision. The Varvakins had managed to corral a bit of that natural energy. It flowed like water and he could see how they applied it to activate mechanicals, engines, and other components. It was brilliant, but he sensed that if any of those circuits were broken, the strum would leak away in an instant. It was an obedient animal, but like the rampager caged in his heart, once released it might do terrible things.

Magnis was more subtle, but it called to Connor powerfully. He descended until he could touch one of the Juggernauts that was coupled to a second one as the scientists tested the linking mechanism. They used magnis to move great clamps to lock and unlock the huge mechanicals at the touch of a button. It was clever, but a mere baby step to what he could sense that magnis could really do.

Fyodor, the head Varvakin researcher, approached and shouted over the din, "What brings you here today, Builder? We're not running any new tests, but just calibrating the systems before final assembly."

Hamish shrugged. "As if I need a reason to come in and check on this miracle factory of yours." The burly, bearded fellow laughed heartily but added, "Tests are going well except for one sphere. One of the circuits won't close and we're trying to isolate the leak." He gestured toward the third juggernaut down the line.

Hamish glanced at Connor and said, "Let's take a look."

The two of them floated over. As Hamish tipped completely upside down to stick his head through the open top panel to chat with the researchers inside, Connor touched the outer shell and quested through the mechanical.

It was similar in a way to casting his senses through a living body before healing. In this case, the huge sphere of the Juggernaut was a dead thing of steel and stone, with a heart fashioned from one of Verena's engines. That engine was dormant at the moment, the only power provided by the wires connecting the sphere back to the generator.

The strum current radiated through the juggernaut shell like an invisible bloodstream, and Connor could feel it pulsing all around. Except for one point. His attention was drawn to a connection near where wires coupled to the engine. That connection was loose and energy was draining out and dissipating into the steel nearby.

He tapped on the shell and said, "Check behind the engine."

A moment later heard excited exclamations. Hamish pulled his head back out and asked, "How did you know it was there?"

"I can feel that some of the energy wasn't moving properly," Connor explained. He did not want everyone understanding he could manipulate strum, but did want to help.

Hamish's face was turning red from hanging upside down so long, and he seemed to be enjoying it. "Can you feel anything else?"

"Yeah, and that worries me. If I can feel the energy powering these things, the queen probably can too."

Hamish grimaced. "If she can feel it, can she change it?"

Excellent question. Connor reached back into the Juggernaut shell with his enhanced senses and again felt the rippling currents. He scanned the Juggernaut and noticed a circuit near the top of the sphere that controlled the activation of a mechanical. With a thought, he tugged on the strum current just enough for it to cross the closed connection. Energy instantly flowed into the mechanical and activated it.

With a clank, the octagonal panel in the outer shell next to Hamish whisked open and a blast of pedra's spittle foam erupted into his face, covering him in an instant. As the foam sealed around him, it snuffed out his thrusters and he fell face first into the Juggernaut.

He would've landed on top of the researchers, but Connor caught him by the ankle and lifted them back out. Laughing, he tapped fire to melt away the thick covering of pedra's spittle that had formed over Hamish's face.

Hamish coughed and spat a couple of times. "This stuff tastes awful. I can't believe we didn't add better flavoring."

Grinning, Connor set Hamish down on top of the Juggernaut. The workers inside were shouting at each other, trying to figure out how they had accidentally activated that mechanical. Fyodor rushed over to find out what happened, and apologized repeatedly to Hamish.

Connor said, "Relax, Fyodor, I triggered that mechanical. I needed to test a theory."

"I can think of a better way to verify that foam tastes terrible," Hamish said, purposefully missing the point.

"What theory?" Fyodor asked with a frown. "How did you activate that mechanical? My men say the circuit was closed."

"I can feel strum, and I can manipulate it. That means the queen could too."

Hamish grimaced. "Since we're planning to use it to fight her, that's not exactly good news."

Fyodor threw his hands into the air and exclaimed, "It's a disaster! Our entire mission is to create a battle platform that can take the fight to the dread queen. If she can manipulate our mechanicals, we're doomed."

He was right. Connor glanced across the vast space and the scores of men and women toiling so hard to construct the Builder miracle attack mechanicals. They'd accomplished so much, but they were powering it using forces that the queen could control.

Could they use something else? He thought of the elemental powers he could draw upon. Other Petralists could wield those too, but when applied right, one could still surprise an enemy.

By shielding.

He grinned and interrupted Hamish and Fyodor, who were chattering with the other men inside the Juggernaut in rapid-fire Grandurian that he couldn't keep up with. "Hold on. It might still work if we can find a way to shield it."

They stopped arguing as the idea sank in. Hamish grinned. "Brilliant! That way we wouldn't have to rip out all the Varvakin pieces. That would force us to go back to the design phase. It wouldn't be done for months."

By his expression, Connor could easily read that Hamish shared his fear. "And we don't have months."

Fyodor rubbed his hands through his thick, dark hair, heavy brows furrowing as he considered the problem before glancing back at Connor. "Do you have any suggestions?" He looked super frustrated, and Connor did not blame him. If he had just learned that his masterwork might be turned against him and used for evil he would've been desperate for ideas too.

Connor gestured toward the nearest Juggernaut. "You're running strum through copper wiring. It looks like you're encasing it in something."

Fyodor nodded. "Otherwise the energy would dissipate. We started testing various insulators, and one of the best is a Tabnit material that they harvest from trees in the southern parts of their kingdom. They call it rubber."

He moved to an open panel in the side of the Juggernaut and gestured at black-coated wires running along one of the support beams. He tapped it with a finger and said, "Can touch without danger, as long as the sheathing is not broken. Rubber is amazing, but supplies are limited. More is being shipped, but probably will not arrive in time."

Hamish asked, "What's the best alternate material?"

With his active affinities, Connor clearly saw strum flowing through the Juggernaut, although it seemed much dimmer in the sections coated by rubber. That confirmed his suspicions that if they insulated the wires well enough the queen probably wouldn't even realize what energy they were using, or that she could mess with it.

Fyodor said, "One of the best is Sehrazad steel glass. It's very strong, it seems to insulate well, and it can be formed into almost any shape. They shipped in an entire fabrication team that is very skilled at making custom pieces, including tiny tubes for the wires." He gestured at another section inside the Juggernaut nearby where the wires were indeed encased in narrow tubes of clear steel-hardened glass. Those cases also seemed to help insulate against Connor's affinities, but not enough. He could still sense and reach out to the flow of charges moving along the wires.

"It's a good start, but we need more."

Fyodor ran his hands through his thick hair and considered the challenge. "We could make the sheathing thicker, I suppose. Would that do it?"

"Maybe. How long would it take to put a small sample together so we could test it?"

"I'll assign a team to work on it through the night," Fyodor promised. "Rewiring all the Juggernauts will be difficult, but easier than redesigning the entire platform."

"Better that than letting the queen take control of them," Hamish agreed.

Connor doubted she'd ever consider using them. Builder powers were filthy to her and she'd focus on destroying them.

"We'll come back in the morning to test it with you," Connor promised.

Chapter Seventy

Don't Mope over Spilled Affinities

The next morning after breakfast, Connor and Hamish visited Nicklaus in the little cottage where he was still under observation. His governess looked relieved to see them, and ushered them inside. Nicklaus was flying around the small living room on one of the dining chairs. He had tied sofa cushions to it using what looked like curtains, and had attached a spatula, two large spoons, and a rolling pin to the sides.

The quartzite blocks acting as thrusters worked well enough, and he had even set up a softly glowing shield dome around himself. Connor exchanged a surprised look with Hamish and stepped into the room, wondering at the boy's creativity.

Hamish shouted, "Hey, Nicklaus! What are you doing?"“

The boy rotated and spotted them. Grinning, he swooped over and settled into a hover. He released the window shielding, waved, and said proudly, "What do you think of my Swift?"

Connor laughed, recognizing the boy's attempts to recreate Verena's deadly flying craft. He'd done a remarkable job with the materials at hand. Where had he gotten the quartzite?

"Very impressive," Hamish said, activating his own thrusters and rising to hover around the makeshift flyer. He spent a moment inspecting it seriously and discussing with Nicklaus the best ways to attach more thrusters to the cushions for improved somersaults.

"It doesn't have real weapons," Nicklaus pointed out with a disappointed sigh. "I could go get some. I know where Verena keeps her spares, but Christin won't let me."

Connor was surprised Nicklaus had obeyed that order. They'd found some pretty advanced weaponry concealed beneath Nicklaus' bed more than once. As if reading his thoughts, Christin shook her head and said, "No equipping weapons to living room furniture, or I will arrange a holiday for you back in Edderitz."

Nicklaus groaned and made his little craft roll a complete backward somersault. "You're so mean!"

"I am not mean. I simply won't allow you to wreck this beautiful cottage Lady Jean has allowed us to stay in," she responded calmly.

Connor silently wished her luck in enforcing her orders. Hamish and Nicklaus settled back to the floor, and Nicklaus jumped out. "When are we going to build me a suit like yours, Hamish? We could fly together. I bet I could fly faster. I'm smaller and I don't eat nearly as much."

Connor chuckled, and Hamish patted his trim stomach with a mock look of outrage. "I eat to fuel my work."

"If your work is trying to get fat," Nicklaus said with a laugh. He scooted away before Hamish could grab him, and said, "Hey, Connor, I heard you ascended. Can you read my mind? Can you make me taller? Can you change Christin's hair to blonde? She thinks her boyfriend would ask her to marry him if she was blonde."

Christin blushed deeply, looking shocked. "How did you . . . ?"

Connor laughed again. He enjoyed the boy's energy and felt relieved that Nicklaus seemed to have recovered so well. "I don't think I'll try changing anything today. It's better if you grow at a normal rate."

"That's slow," Nicklaus muttered.

"Since my ascension, I can feel affinities better. I'd like to see if I can feel yours," Connor said. He made a point of not suggesting he hoped he could fix them. He wasn't sure if that was possible.

Nicklaus plopped onto a padded chair in the living room and regarded Connor with that too-mature look of his. "Connor, I broke them. Why does no one else want to accept that? Bad things happen sometimes. I'm still the best Builder my age, right Hamish?"

"Absolutely," Hamish agreed with a smile. Connor doubted there were any other Builders Nicklaus' age, but that didn't matter.

He said, "I'd like to check anyway. I know you broke them, but maybe by understanding what happened to you we can better understand how affinities work for everyone and avoid anyone else breaking theirs."

"That's a good idea," Nicklaus said. "And then you can tell me about Water. She said she talks with you and that you're helping them. What do elementals need help with, Connor? She seems nice. I bet she's pretty. Is she as big as a river?"

Connor sat on the carpeted floor near Nicklaus' chair. Water had told him not to speak about them to others, but she'd already spoken with Nicklaus, and Hamish and Christin both knew that, so he decided to risk it. "I do speak with her and the other elements. They're teaching me things."

"Me too!" Nicklaus interrupted, bolting off the chair and literally flying across the room, using a piece of quartzite as a makeshift thruster. He landed on a high shelf next to the chimney and pointed at an odd-looking device full of tubes and large globes of glass. "She taught me how to purify water. I think we can help a lot of people. It's sad that sometimes people don't have clean water to drink. Usually in the palace we get clean water, but not everyone has the same privilege, do they?"

Hamish lifted into the air to inspect the device more closely, but Connor waved Nicklaus back down. He was interested in learning about that device, but didn't want to get sidetracked. "Do you hear the others?"

"Not usually. Just Water. She's nice, like a governess who encourages you to try new things." He glanced pointedly at Christin, who crossed her arms and raised one eyebrow, as if challenging him to say more. Wisely he turned back to Connor and added, "Mostly her voice is very soft, like she's far away. Sometimes the words are clearer. She's teaching me how to build new things."

"Why?" Connor asked.

"Because we need them, I think," Nicklaus said with a shrug.

"And she started speaking with you around the same time she spoke with Verena, right?" Hamish asked.

Nicklaus nodded. "I want to ask Verena about that. Maybe we can work together. Water's been teaching me how to build a higher-level mechanical. I thought I was building a replacement for Kristin's Defense, but it didn't work like that when I tested it."

"Wait, what test?" Connor asked, exchanging a surprised look with Hamish.

Nicklaus kicked a stone, looking suddenly sad. "It didn't work."

Christin said, "It's a remarkable invention. We tested it by the small pond here on the hospital grounds yesterday."

"I thought it would make a big wall of water, but it didn't make anything."

"Nothing?" Hamish asked with a frown.

"I think poor Nicklaus must have misunderstood one of the instructions," Christin said, looking at her charge with compassion. "He repeats everything she tells to him, and I write it down." She gestured at a small notebook lying on a nearby table.

"We reviewed every word, and I did it right. It just didn't work!" Nicklaus said, pouting.

"What did you feel?" Hamish asked. Connor was glad he was around. He wouldn't have known what to ask about.

Nicklaus shrugged. "It seemed to be messing with a lot of energy, but it didn't work."

"We didn't have much time to practice," Christin explained. "A Water Moccasin working on the pond asked us to stop. The mechanical was interfering with his affinity."

"Really? How?" Connor asked. Some mechanicals would mess with a Petralist's access to their element, but Nicklaus' work seemed different. He glanced at Hamish, who shrugged.

"I don't know. I think he was just lazy," Nicklaus said. Then he brightened and asked, "Hamish, can I borrow a missile?"

"Ah, don't get distracted," Hamish said.

Connor told Christin, "Can you make me a copy of your notes? I'd like to review them with Verena."

"I've already duplicated everything for Lady Jean. I'll give you her copy and make another for her," Christin said.

"Thanks. Please keep recording everything Water says, and send us copies regularly. It might be really important." He was deeply intrigued why Water would start reaching out to the boy instead of to Verena again, or to Hamish.

Those two were the lead Builders. He didn't understand yet what the elements wanted, so he couldn't grasp the reasons for their actions, but he did not doubt everything they did had a purpose.

They seemed eager to reassure him that their purposes coincided with his own, but he didn't know enough yet to know for sure. Hearing Nicklaus' tale made him think he needed to press the elements more for an explanation.

Christin said, "We're being released this afternoon."

"Yes!" Nicklaus cried.

She continued. "Lady Jean has offered to house us in her palace."

"And let me keep shooting soldiers," Nicklaus added enthusiastically. "I'll have to add weapons to my flyer, though, unless you make me a suit." He looked meaningfully at Hamish. Christin looked terrified by the idea, and Connor agreed. Nicklaus with his own battle suite would be an unparalleled force of destruction.

Hamish said, "We've submitted the request to your parents. Once we receive permission, we'll schedule a time." Connor doubted that would happen for another ten years.

Nicklaus seemed to wilt with disappointment, and Hamish sighed. "But how about I take you up with me for a spin around the city later?"

He brightened instantly. "Can I bring a speedsling and shoot at the floating targets Defender Flight uses?"

"We'll, see," Hamish said with a grin.

"But first I need to take a look at your affinities," Connor added.

Nicklaus sighed. "If you have to."

Connor tapped chert and focused on the boy. Instantly he felt a connection snap into place between them. Nicklaus was remarkably calm, given his outward enthusiasm. Connor sensed a very methodical mind, coupled with a bottomless sense of curiosity. Great characteristics for a Builder.

Nicklaus' thoughts flowed into his mind. "*Connor had better propose to Verena soon, or she's going to get mad. Not even Connor would like it if Verena got mad at him.*"

Connor suppressed a groan. Figuring out their timeline for a formal proposal and eventual wedding date was a huge task weighing him down, but it was something he needed to figure out with Verena. If Nicklaus was thinking about it, how many other people were?

He was glad most of them kept the questions to themselves. Life was busy enough already, but he reminded himself to find a time to talk with her about it. Nicklaus was right. She did seem to be growing impatient. He was eager to bind himself to her, but could he do so in good faith with the threat of war hanging over them?

Something to figure out later. Connor pushed aside the distracting thoughts and focused on the connection to the boy. As it intensified, he felt himself drawn into Nicklaus' mind. He sensed the boy's thoughts, but did not feel his affinities. He'd hoped to view them like he had his own, but sensed nothing.

Maybe he needed a slightly different type of connection. Chert connected him to a mind, but he needed to connect to Nicklaus' affinities. Verena had explained their reasoning about how he might be able to loan an affinity, and it made a lot of sense. Obsidian could help connect to the mind via affinities, and sandstone helped link to a patient. Maybe something similar was needed to feel the affinities in another?

He didn't have anything to lose. Nicklaus was growing bored, staring into Connor's eyes, and his thoughts were turning to how much easier it would be to sneak out of Lady Jean's big palace than it had been to sneak out of the little cottage. He loved exploring the city when Christin thought him studying or sleeping. He particularly enjoyed secretly visiting all the Builder workshops.

Connor didn't want to pry into all the boy's secrets, but he enjoyed the glimpse into Nicklaus' life. Connor and Hamish had found many ways to entertain themselves in Alasdair as kids, but they hadn't understood their powers, so lacked many of the unique opportunities that Nicklaus was taking advantage of.

Connor tapped obsidian and sandstone and instantly felt the connection to Nicklaus deepening. His vision blurred, and he appeared inside a mindscape. The land solidified around Connor and he found himself standing on the plain north of New Schwinkendorf. He sensed the community somewhere behind him, but when he turned in that direction he could not see that far. The grasses ended at the edge of a cliff, the area beyond filled with slowly roiling, gray mist. That's where Connor's mindscape depicted affinity islands floating, connected by bridges, but he saw nothing like that for Nicklaus.

It surprised him that he landed in a local scene. The boy had formed his affinities in Edderitz and in Altkalen, so Connor had expected to see a scene from one of those locations. Then again, Nicklaus had enjoyed his affinities far more working with the Builders and researchers in New Schwinkendorf. His connection to Verena and Hamish was powerful, so that might have played into it too.

"Connor, what are you doing?"

He jumped, startled to see Nicklaus standing beside him, looking curiously out over the mist-filled abyss.

"I didn't expect to pull you into this mindscape," Connor admitted.

"We are looking at my affinities, after all," Nicklaus pointed out. "Mindscape is a fun word. Did Verena come up with it? She names almost everything because she's so smart. But we're looking for affinities, so shouldn't we call this my affinityscape?"

Connor smiled. "Perhaps. Your affinities should look like little islands over that abyss, with bridges attached to them."

"Why?"

"Um, well, because that's how mine looked," he offered. Maybe other people's minds worked differently.

He cautiously approached the edge of the cliff to peer over, and spotted two sets of anchor stones right at the outer edge. They looked like the ones in his mind that had secured the ends of the lowest tier of the bridges that extended to his primary affinities. One pair was made of granite blocks, while the other was basalt. The granite blocks were broken into a mass of tiny pieces, while the basalt blocks were charred. When he touched one, it crumbled under his finger.

Nicklaus poked it with his foot and sighed, looking sad but not surprised. "Looks like you were right, Connor. I had bridges here, but they're busted."

Those blocks had suffered severe damage, as if they had shattered under violent force. How had Nicklaus managed to shatter his affinities? Connor was starting to learn some startling things about affinities, but the thought of destroying them really bothered him and he shivered, with goosebumps rising along his arms.

"It's not healthy to mope about something you can't fix," Nicklaus said. He lifted a small hand, which Connor took reflexively. Nicklaus turned them both around and pointed. "Let's go see what's over there!"

Together they headed into the grassy land north of New Schwinkendorf. After walking for a moment, Connor noticed something different. Not far ahead, just visible above the gently waving grasses, was a low, stone well.

"What's that?" Nicklaus exclaimed, noticing it at the same time. He dropped Connor's hand and raced ahead. Connor gave chase, about to call out a warning to Nicklaus to be careful, but then he realized that was silly. They were walking inside Nicklaus' mind. He doubted the boy could hurt himself in there.

The low stone wall turned out to be a well, and Nicklaus rushed right up to it, leaning dangerously far over to peer down. They might be in his mind, but if he jumped down a well, what would that mean?

Connor ran faster. The grasses around the well were shorter, allowing him to see farther. He noticed other wells scattered around nearby. When he reached Nicklaus and the first well, he touched it, and immediately understood.

Quartzite. The well was constructed with rectangular quartzite blocks about the size of his head, and a gentle flow of quartzite energy was rising from the depths, like smoke from a small fire. Connor's touch solidified the connection and he cast his affinity senses down into the opening.

He finally felt an island, a quartzite island, but instead of floating near the cliff, he sensed it far out in the mists, far below where he stood, with quartzite energy radiating off it. Some of that energy flowed up to that well and drifted up into Nicklaus' mind. Just like bridges were the mental representation of affinities, the well must be the mental interpretation of Nicklaus' Builder powers.

Nicklaus produced a pebble from somewhere and tossed it into the well. It disappeared from view, and the boy frowned. "No splash."

"I think this is the well of your Builder access to quartzite," Connor said, fascinated. Builders did access the power of stones differently, and a well elegantly suggested the way Builders could access energy but not actively control it.

Nicklaus nodded seriously and turned a slow circle, studying the other wells. He grinned and pointed behind Connor. "Is that why that soapstone well is so big?"

Connor turned and noticed for the first time a much bigger well in the distance. They ran over to it, and sure enough it was made of soapstone. When Connor touched it, he sensed far more energy flowing through it. "I wonder why this one is so much bigger."

"I think Water wants it that way," Nicklaus said proudly.

"Maybe," Connor said. The idea was intriguing. Could Water affect how much Nicklaus could access her powers? Why would she? The idea made him slightly uneasy, although he couldn't identify why.

He planned to check Hamish's and Verena's minds to see if their representation of their powers were similar to Nicklaus'. Did either of them have islands that might allow him to help them create bridges to form affinities? Or were all Builders missing that critical piece?

They had learned something, maybe something important. He just needed to figure out what it all meant.

Chapter Seventy-One

It's One Bridge in front of Another

Connor soared over Badurach Pass and drank in the vista of northern Obrion. When he magnified his Pathfinder vision he could see Merkland gleaming white in the distance. He accelerated.

Hamish powered through the air beside him, flying backward in a half-reclined position that made it easier for him to shield the little travel stove he had crafted for cooking his meals while flying. He was making some kind of omelet with egg, cheese, bacon, and a bunch of spices. He had actually mixed it all up before they left and was now heating it in a sealed ceramic container.

"You know, I'm sure we'll get to Merkland before lunch," Connor chuckled as he drifted closer to his friend.

"Good thing too. I only brought enough for each of us to get four or five of these."

Connor appreciated having a friend who was always prepared. "I'm surprised Nicklaus didn't find a way to convince you to leave your spare battle suit with him. Flying with him might not have been the best idea, you know."

Hamish grinned. "But it sure was a lot of fun. That kid is going to be an amazing flyer, and probably amazing at whatever he puts his mind to. I want to make sure he puts his mind on positive things."

Connor couldn't argue with that.

Hamish added, "I'm just glad we figured out that wire shielding before we left."

He tossed the completed omelet container to Connor who caught it and pried open the top. The ceramic jar held the heat extremely well, although heat no longer harmed Connor even when he was not actively tapping marble. The omelet was delicious and luckily Hamish had brought along a couple of forks. Tomas and Cameron might not approve of forks, but Connor was willing to take the risk sometimes.

He sat back on the air, imagining it like a comfortable chair that just happened to be hurtling over the landscape at incredible speeds. The air parted in front of him so the only wind he felt was wind that he wanted to feel. Being ascended was so much fun.

It didn't help with making his schedule easier, though. He needed to make time to train more, but the rest of their morning had been packed. After leaving Nicklaus, they'd joined Jean for a second breakfast. The feasting hall had been packed to overflowing with citizens eager to see her restored health, and many had thanked Connor as enthusiastically as if he had healed their own daughter.

Jean had insisted they visit her medical team with the micro-vision goggles too. The latest model indeed allowed them to view deep into the tiny structures that made up tissues, bone, and blood. Using his fleshcrafting sensitivities, he'd studied a sample of diseased tissue they were studying and managed to give them some pointers on how to interpret what they were seeing.

That group of serious researchers had been chattering like giddy children when he left. He hoped he'd helped, and that they could indeed develop new breakthroughs to help healers better treat their patients. He was only one person and could not hope to treat everyone.

Although Shona had sent seventeen messages urging them to hurry back to Merkland to test loaning Petralist powers, they still needed to stop to visit Fyodor too. The man had been more than true to his word. His team had produced several different iterations of enhanced shielding for the wires.

They started by simply doubling the thickness of the rubber and of the glass sheathing, but had not stopped there. Next they tried combining the two, first sheathing the copper wires in rubber and then encasing that in steel glass. All three attempts had demonstrated significant improvements in insulating the wires, but did not block Connor's ability to easily sense and even manipulate them.

Fyodor had been extremely frustrated by that and complained that if they added too many more layers the wires would become too bulky to be of use. Connor had spent time the previous evening considering the words of the elementals about strum and magnis, so he had some additional ideas.

Both Air and Water had said their elements could effectively insulate if they did not contain impurities. He and Fyodor's team had experimented with those ideas. After several different attempts, they discovered that sheathing the wire between two layers of glass with a small gap between them increased the insulating factor significantly. When he then filled that tiny gap with purified water, he could barely feel the current.

Air had proven a little trickier, but he learned that if he could draw out most of the air between the two layers, forming an empty space with negative pressure, it also proved extremely effective. Ensuring that the vacuum space remained properly sealed proved challenging. Since working with water was simpler, they'd focused on that.

They'd filled a large tank and Connor had stripped it clean of impurities, then sealed it to keep it pure. If they were careful, they could use that water to fill the double layer of glass tubes. That should do enough. He doubted the queen would notice the strum and magnis, at least not in time to alter the outcome of the conflict.

Then they'd taken to the air, leaving the Hawk for more of Jean's Mender Flight personnel to bring to Merkland later. Reviewing the busy morning made Connor suddenly glad Hamish had thought to bring food. He saluted with his now-empty omelet jar and said, "Here's to trouncing old hags with Juggernauts."

Hamish tossed him a second omelet just coming off the burner and saluted with his own. "To trouncing old hags. May they never return."

Then he held up his canteen. "How about giving me something better to go with this than plain water?"

"What would you like?"

"How about some of that Althing heated chocolate?" Hamish asked eagerly.

Connor grinned and swallowed the rest of his omelet in one huge gulp so he could concentrate. "I'll see what I can do."

While purifying water for the Varvakins, he'd learned something about his affinity with water. Since he'd been studying tiny particles in iron to learn about magnis and strum, he recognized that he could sense the particles of water at that same molecular level. While he waited for Hamish to say good-bye to Jean, he'd studied the structure of some fresh-squeezed juice he was drinking. While idly messing around with it, he rearranged the molecules and transformed it into water.

That was so much fun that he'd immediately tried other options. He'd discovered that he could transform liquid into pretty much whatever other type of liquid he wanted, and he'd shared the amazing discovery with Hamish before they took off. Now he studied his and Hamish's canteens. He hadn't studied hot chocolate at a molecular level, but how hard could it be?

Tapping water, he messed with the molecules in his canteen, envisioning delicious chocolate. The water thickened and darkened and he grinned. "I think I've got it."

Hamish tried a sip, then coughed and spat it out. "Ugh! This tastes like liquid dirt."

So of course Connor had to try a sip too. He grimaced. That really was bad. He and Hamish had tasted enough dirt over the years to know. So he went back to work on the liquid, but the best he managed was a weak tea.

Hamish chuckled. "Just change it back to water. I wouldn't have thought triple-ascended Petralists might be bad cooks."

"I'll study hot chocolate next time we drink it. I'll be able to make it work then. Messing with particles is tough."

"Yeah, looking through the micro-vision goggles, I realized tiny stuff is kind of scary," Hamish agreed as he finished cooking another omelet and tossed it to Connor.

While Connor ate, Hamish called ahead to inform the others of their arrival. Connor wondered if he could send voice messages to speakstones directly, even if he didn't have a paired speakstone himself. It would be a handy trick. One more item to add to his training plan.

A tiny shape lifted off the ground from distant Merkland and accelerated rapidly to meet them. Connor did not need quartzite to recognize Verena's graceful flying style. She met them several miles out and the three of them hovered together.

Verena had mostly restored the Swift. It looked complete, the broken components replaced, although she hadn't managed to paint over the scorch marks and signs of recent repair. It flew as good as new, though. Connor drew in close and Verena dropped the shielding from her windows.

She was dressed in flying leathers, but had left her goggles behind. Her black hair was pulled from her face by a blue, silken cord that perfectly matched her eyes and seemed to make them shine. Connor drank in the sight of her, marveling anew that she'd chosen him.

Hamish waved and said, "I'll meet you back at the palace. Don't wait too long or Shona might just pop her gullet or something."

Connor chuckled. "That's not really a thing, you know?"

"If only it could be," Verena grinned.

Hamish shrugged and accelerated away. Verena sighed as Connor cupped her face in one hand. "I don't really like to encourage Shona too much, but I do hope this works. We need it for all of us."

Connor started to reply, but an idea struck from out of nowhere. A lot of times those ideas proved to be some of his best. He grinned and said, "Hold on."

He absorbed a little obsidian and tapped it, then added sandstone, and then quartzite. He could've tried any of the elements, but Shona had been working so hard to make quartzite work that it felt natural.

Air appeared in his mind, dressed in flying leathers to mimic Shona. She shook her head. "Your girl is not ready for this."

"We won't know until we try," Connor protested.

"I can't walk with someone who hasn't crossed even the first bridge."

"What do you mean?"

Verena looked at him, a question in her eyes. He hadn't realized he'd responded aloud. Speaking with mental projections could be tricky sometimes. He tapped the side of his head. "Kind of busy in here."

"Sometimes I worry about you, Connor."

"Only sometimes?"

Air drifted closer and said, "Don't you remember talking about bridges?"

Connor nodded and replied only to her inside his mind. "Of course. I'm trying to loan a bridge to Verena right now, right?"

She gave him a long-suffering look. "How can you plan to ask her to cross the third bridge if she hasn't crossed the first?"

Connor blinked as understanding struck like an unexpected curse punch. He exclaimed aloud, "So Shona was able to accept a tertiary power loaned from Harley because she already had a secondary?"

Verena's eyes widened, looking as astonished as he felt. "How do you know that?"

Connor decided he wouldn't keep secrets from Verena. Water had appeared to her, so she must trust her some. "Air was just explaining some things to me."

"She's here?" Verena asked, looking around eagerly.

"Can you allow her to see you too?" Connor asked Air. To him, she was hovering outside of the Swift right next to him.

She shook her head. "She's not yet ready to converse with us, but her research into higher forms of Builder mechanicals may gain her access to the bridge she needs."

He relayed the message, and Verena grinned. "I've already started trying to work out how to recreate a higher mechanical like Kristin's. Oh, Connor, it's so exciting to know we're on the right track!"

He agreed. They needed the power that greater access to the elementals offered. "I was going to try loaning you quartzite, but it's not going to work. Air explained I can't loan a tertiary to someone who doesn't have a secondary."

He thanked Air and switched to granite. He'd made it a habit to wear battle plates on his thighs with basalt and granite stuck to the inside edges of each one so absorbing granite was as easy as concentrating to pull it into his skin. The itchy crawling of his lifelong curse bolstered his confidence. If he could make this work with anything it would be granite.

He had never purged a tertiary power before, but had purged granite many times so the effort was simple. Tapping obsidian and sandstone, he connected with Verena like he had just done with Nicklaus, but not deeply enough to step into her mind. At the same time, he concentrated some of the granite power into his chest and willed it out through the skin. Lamacal formed on his shirt and he scraped a small handful free before it could blow away.

Extending it to Verena he said, "Want to help me make a new discovery?"

She did not hesitate, even though it meant eating lamacal. She threw the small handful of white powder into her mouth and took a drink from a water bottle she extracted from a tiny compartment near her right leg. After swallowing a few gulps she grimaced. "Shona was right. It tastes terrible."

"Feel any different?"

Verena started to shake her head, then her eyes widened. A second later her skin faded to gray and her shape altered slightly to perfectly sculpted lines. She laughed with joy, and Connor laughed with her. It actually works!

She exclaimed, "This is how it feels to be a Rumbler? I understand now. I want to hit something."

That didn't surprise Connor at all. Verena liked hitting things right after smiling. So he tapped granite too and made a beckoning gesture. "Come on. Knowing me has only encouraged you in the past."

Her right fist struck in an excellent curse punch that knocked Connor right over backward in an aerial somersault. Verena had always been a good puncher, and reinforced by granite she was nothing short of amazing.

Verena gasped. "Are you okay?"

Connor laughed and flew in close to steal a quick kiss. "Never better. Come on. Let's go share this with everyone."

Verena grinned and said with a mischievous look in her eye, "I'll race you back."

She seized the control levers, but did not yet understand her strength and managed to rip them right out of their bases.

Verena groaned in dismay and Connor laughed. "Granite takes a little getting used to. Don't worry, I can still help you land. Although crashing your Swift again without the excuse of a giant monster would definitely help you gain even more legendary status."

She grimaced. "I don't want that kind of legend. Better to be known as the second Builder Petralist after Nicklaus, even if it's just for an hour."

"We need to talk about Nicklaus. We stopped to visit him. Water's been speaking with him," Connor told her.

She nodded, her expression thoughtful. "I heard. I'm glad you spoke with him. I haven't been able to get Water to respond to me again. I'd love to understand how his connection works."

"Me too."

Connor helped turn the Swift and push it back toward Merkland while Verena worked to reattach her control levers.

"This is so much fun," Verena exclaimed again, flexing her arms.

"Am I going to have to deal with you pestering me to loan you my powers all the time now?" he teased.

She turned in her seat and gave him an innocent look, pretty blue eyes wide and inviting. "You wouldn't deny me, would you?"

He sighed. "Never."

"That's why I love you. Now, fly faster."

Chapter Seventy-Two

Walking the Razor's Edge

Ailsa arrived at Queen Dreokt's personal apartments in the central palace of Donleavy breathing a bit fast from the exertion. She might be the queen's closest and most trusted advisor, but it would never do to dally when summoned unexpectedly. She'd stood in the queen's presence all afternoon during her normal audience session. Usually the queen did not require her presence again until the evening feast.

Even before she knocked, the ornately carved door to the queen's suite opened and a silent, handsome attendant beckoned her inside. The man had been one of the royal family, reeducated into a mindless, efficient servant.

Ailsa was growing so accustomed to the mind-wiped servants that she no longer even shuddered around them. It might be an effective self-defense mechanism, but deep in her protected inner thoughts, she hoped she never became so jaded to the realities of life in the palace that she started thinking of it as normal.

The queen waited in her large sitting room, with its panoramic view over the expanse of Donleavy. The seven levels of the tiered city spread below, sparkling in the late afternoon sunlight. Queen Dreokt was not alone. Ailsa instantly recognized the man standing before her, and her heart skipped a beat.

Craigroy. High Lord Dougal's chief spymaster. The last she had known, he was still prisoner in Merkland.

As she approached, she schooled her features into her normal façade. She would weather the storm as she did all others, but she could not quite suppress a thought deep in her inner self that perhaps this storm would prove deadly. She knew Craigroy a little, had met him briefly in Merkland before the crazy events occurred around Alasdair that started Connor on his adventures.

They had not parted as friends.

"Ailsa, there you are." Queen Dreokt gestured her closer. "I have been interviewing the most interesting servant. He brings word from Merkland. Isn't that wonderful?"

"Wonderful indeed," Ailsa confirmed, forcing her surface thoughts to reflect pleasure, but tinted with reservation.

When Craigroy turned to greet her, she nodded, her expression neutral. "Craigroy, is it not?"

Craigroy was too good a spy and an actor to betray any outward emotion. No doubt he was on careful guard, as were everyone who wanted to survive long in the queen's presence. He did not look like he expected to see her, which suggested he had not dared tap quartzite in the queen's presence. Wise choice.

He inclined his head in return and asked, "Ailsa, is it?"

Queen Dreokt's bright smile faltered. "You two have met."

Craigroy quickly said, "We have indeed, Your Majesty. I met this woman under questionable circumstances last year in Merkland."

"Indeed?" Queen Dreokt asked, one eyebrow raised in question. Craigroy looked pleased with himself, but Ailsa was not about to let him control the conversation so she said, "I agree. Your actions were indeed questionable."

"My people found you rooting around in High Lord Dougal's personal apartment, and when I attempted to question you, you supplied only vague answers." He added to the queen, "She escaped her cell without ever satisfying my curiosity."

Queen Dreokt laughed, looking delighted. "Ailsa escaped the very dungeons that held you for months? How long did it take?"

Ailsa shrugged, her surface thoughts reflecting distrust for Craigroy and pride in her accomplishment. "Perhaps an hour."

The queen laughed again and slapped her knee. "From all accounts, you're reported to be an exceptionally clever fellow, Craigroy. How did it take you so long to escape?"

Craigroy maintained perfect control, although in her inner self, Ails wished she could sense his thoughts like the queen could. She hoped her liege was reading him, and didn't doubt she was learning much.

He said, "I was known already and kept under significantly tighter guard. Besides, I used my time wisely. When I left Merkland, I brought with me much useful intelligence."

"And what might that be?" Ailsa asked in a slightly bored tone, as if not expecting anything to prove quite as useful as he claimed. She kept her surface thoughts calm, slightly distrustful of him. In her inner self, she forced aside the fear that perhaps he had discovered something about her.

"I know much about the inner workings of the revolution, drawn from their own mouths." Craigroy smiled as he lifted a small box from a satchel he wore over one shoulder.

"And what's in there? Your lunch?" Ailsa asked light heartedly. Queen Dreokt started to chuckle along with her. That was a good sign.

"This contains a speakstone, one of the marvelous Builder inventions—"

He never got a chance to finish. Queen Dreokt's good humor vanished as she leaped to her feet, her expression enraged. She made no gesture, but an invisible force hurled Craigroy across the room. He struck the wall hard enough to snap bones, and the breath exploded from his lungs. He slid to the floor in an unconscious heap.

The box also hurled away, but never struck the wall. Instead it remained hovering in the air, held aloft by a tiny whirlwind.

Queen Dreokt regarded the box like it contained a deadly viper. Actually hissing in rage, she snarled, "How dare he bring filthy Builder mechanicals into my rooms? I will make him pay for such folly."

"Should I dispose of it, Your Majesty?" Ailsa asked. In her persona as the queen's trusted advisor, she allowed herself to feel great pride in her majesty's bold defense of her person against devilish Builders.

Queen Dreokt hesitated, staring in rage at the harmless box. "I would crush it to dust this very instant, as well as that foolish man, but he brought disturbing news that I must understand before meting out justice."

That was not good. Usually the queen's wrath was an uncontrollable thing, and in a fit of rage she rarely showed so much control. "What news could be worth risking a Builder mechanical in your presence?"

"Word that a spy resides among us." Her wrath intensified, if that was possible, and she stomped a foot in frustration, cracking the floor. "How can a filthy spy remain in my household? Have I not purged the unworthy, reeducated the foolish, and surrounded myself with the very best?"

"I have no idea. Perhaps the spy is another concealed mechanical, listening in on our communications?"

The queen considered that, and ground her teeth so hard they actually started crumbling from the force. She did not seem to notice, and the teeth reformed instantly.

"Take the filthy thing, Ailsa. Drag that idiot from my presence. I suppose you should have him healed so he may answer my questions before I decide his fate. Search the palace. Employ whoever you need. Find the concealed mechanical, if one exists. If not, I will scour the minds of all who enter my presence to identify the spy. When I find them, they will suffer such torments the world has never imagined."

Ailsa curtsied, grateful for the chance to look down and compose her expression. She kept her surface thoughts full of confidence in the queen's ability to root out evil, and outrage that the pitiful revolution could sneak a spy into the palace. Deep in her inner self, she fought to suppress a shiver of fear. She was playing the ultimate game of catch-the-devil. She couldn't imagine retreating from it, but one second of lost concentration could trip her up. Or one new player in the mix. And if the queen realized she was the spy, she had no doubt she'd suffer more than any living person ever had.

Better not fail, then.

Ailsa grabbed the box and gestured one of the silent servants to take Craigroy and drag him into the hallway. She was tempted to put him out of his misery, but she wasn't sure she could conceal such a lie from the queen. She might not be able to kill him, but that did not mean she had to show him loving attention either.

She was tempted next to have the servant simply drag him up and down flights of stairs until the jarring finished him off. She could probably justify that, but what if he did not die? Then again, why not change the situation? He might have a previous reason to suspect her, but if she saved his life, not even he could ignore such a debt.

Especially if he continued living only as long as she allowed him to.

So she ordered the servant to deposit Craigroy in a nearby empty parlor, then go with all speed and bring a Healer. In the meantime, she pillowed Craigroy's cracked skull in her own sweater. Then with tender care she extracted three vials of chemicals from a pocket. Used for etching stone, when mixed in specific ratios they proved deadly if ingested. But they did not kill immediately and the effects could be delayed using small doses of antidote.

She'd perfected the chemical mix, and not even the queen would wonder why she carried them with her. They were for her job, after all.

Ailsa carefully mixed the chemicals in a tiny cup of water and fed it drop by drop into Craigroy's unconscious mouth. He instinctively swallowed every drop. Humming softly to herself, she tended to him as best she could while she waited for the Healer. She passed a few minutes considering how best to turn the very dangerous man into her most profitable servant.

Then her thoughts turned to the little box and the speakstone it contained, as well as the queen's charge to root out the spy among them. The challenging development could indeed be turned into an opportunity. The hammer had fallen, but no critical fault line had been exposed.

The resulting piece would reflect her will, and would serve Obrion, not Craigroy.

Chapter Seventy-Three

A Perfect Excuse

Merkland still looked battered, the famous white walls, normally pristine and sparkling in the noonday sun, scarred and scorched, but Connor spotted signs of rebuilding everywhere. Merkland had bent but not broken under the weight of the queen's summoned horde.

"I think I've got control," Verena said as Connor pushed the disabled Swift over the city, aiming for the huge square in front of the palace.

Connor released his grip, and the Swift banked slightly. He accelerated to fly right next to Verena's cockpit. She had kept the shielding lowered, and some of her hair had pulled free of the band she was using to keep it back. Connor had decided he really loved how she looked with her hair that deep, black color that she'd awakened with after her coma. She looked adorable with her brows furrowed, biting at her lip the way she did when concentration.

Verena glanced over and said, "I reattached the control rods enough to manage landing on my own, but they still need work."

She had reduced her tap rate to make sure she didn't accidentally break anything else, but every few seconds her skin faded to gray momentarily, and she couldn't stop grinning. Connor loved that they could finally share the wonder of granite and that she was enjoying it so much.

Hamish had already landed, so everyone knew they were coming. A crowd of their close friends waited in the plaza. Rory and Anika stood together, surrounded by a gaggle of other women that seemed always to press in around Anika, chattering about the thousand details of the upcoming wedding. Tomas and Cameron stood nearby, along with Ivor, General Wolfram, and Kilian. Connor figured that if Aifric joined them, she'd probably appear right behind him with a dagger before he could see her. Evander would just ascend through the paving stones.

Of course Shona was already there, one finger tapping at her thigh. She rushed to meet Connor and Verena, so close to their landing site that Verena nearly touched down on her head. Connor wasn't actively tapping chert, but he still clearly sensed her temptation to shift over a bit and clobber Shona, or ignite the Puking Dooms and vaporize Shona's recently-restored hair.

Luckily she did neither, but of course she did tap granite right when Shona opened her mouth to speak. Verena's skin faded to gray and her body hardened. She was already in excellent shape, so the transformation did not change her as much as it did some people, but everyone noticed it.

Shona in particular. She was standing closest, and she gasped, eyes wide. The depth of the hurt he saw in her eyes shocked him.

"How dare you steal my honor?" she cried.

That was actually a pretty nice way to say it. There was no love lost between Shona and Verena, and she could've easily used the moment to insult Verena again. The fact that she didn't gave Connor a little hope that they could resolve the issue without violence.

He should have known better.

Verena assumed a surprised look. "Connor has given no honor of yours to anyone. The honor of loaning a power stone is his alone."

Their other friends gathered closer, eager to see, and Connor was startled when Rory frowned and said, "Should have waited, lad."

Several of the others looked displeased by what he'd done too. That rattled Connor. He'd expected them all to react with joy that he'd managed to loan a power at all. They'd been hunting that ability for months.

"The honor of receiving that loaned power first was mine," Shona said angrily.

Connor glanced at Kilian, who shrugged and nodded. He couldn't believe it, but felt a new worry growing within him. He hadn't intended any insult, but had only wanted to explore his new abilities.

Shona looked to Connor with anguish in her eyes. "How could you?"

His good humor withered under Shona's glare, pained by her open hurt. She did have a point, but how could he admit that in front of everyone? He didn't want Shona angry with him but neither would he ever be party to slighting Verena, especially not in public, especially not in front of Shona.

So he said, "No slight was intended, Shona. I just realized as I was talking with Verena that I can't loan a tertiary power to someone who has no secondary."

That surprised them.

"How did you—" Ivor started at the same time Wolfram exclaimed, "Of course!"

Kilian spoke over both of them. "How did you come to that conclusion?"

"Think about it. The queen helped Shona gain a secondary power. It was only after that when Harley loaned her quartzite."

Kilian nodded slowly. "That makes sense, but it's not exactly conclusive, is it?"

Connor shrugged. "Ever since my ascension I have a far greater sensitivity to affinities and the power sources that fuel them. It just makes sense that loaning powers has to follow the same rules as gaining new affinities, doesn't it?"

"Perhaps," was all Kilian said, his expression thoughtful, and Connor wondered if he suspected there was more he wasn't saying.

Everyone knew he was speaking with the elements, but Water had warned him about sharing too much about them. He'd been mostly ignoring that counsel, but the crowd around them was growing, so he couldn't risk it, not without understanding the consequences better.

"That may be an important discovery, but it does not change the fact that you then tested your theory with Verena instead of waiting to give me an opportunity first," Shona reiterated angrily.

"You can still test receiving a tertiary power first," Verena offered, completely calm in the face of Shona's wrath.

Connor made a point to not even think about tapping chert. He didn't want their thoughts screaming into his mind and distracting him. He appreciated Verena's attempt to smooth things over, but Shona did not.

She glared at Verena and shook her head. "That's not nearly good enough. This is an intentional slight on my honor, one which I cannot allow to go unanswered as a high lady wronged in my own realm."

Rory said, "Now, Lady Shona—"

"Don't '*Now Lady Shona*' me."

General Wolfram said, "Let's remain calm. You are correct, Lady Shona. You were slighted, but we cannot condone violence among ourselves."

Shona scowled at Wolfram and started to argue. Verena interrupted. "I think the solution is obvious, isn't it?"

She tapped her stone-hardened skin. "Some of you participate in fantastic bash fights every day. If Shona feels slighted, I propose we do the same."

Definitely not the direction Connor wanted the conversation to go. The two girls had been eager to fight almost since the first moment they met. An eventual duel between the two of them had been one of the things Connor had feared the most.

Ivor started to protest too, but Shona waved him to silence, her expression turning eager. “I accept your proposed solution, Verena. What better way to test the effectiveness of a loaned granite affinity than trial by combat?”

Verena mimicked her predatory expression. “Research demands we make the attempt.”

“Research and honor,” Shona agreed with a grin.

Sure, granite did offer more protection than Verena would enjoy otherwise, but she couldn’t hope to face Shona in a one-on-one bash fight. Shona was one of the most skilled bash fighters in all of Obrion. She understood every nuance of her power and how to apply it in a fight. Verena had already demonstrated that she had no concept of her own strength or how to control it.

“This loaned power is so new, we shouldn’t jump straight into bash fighting,” Connor tried.

“Course you should,” Tomas said. He and Cameron had joined the group, drawn by the argument, probably hoping to get some bash fighting of their won.

Cameron nodded, his brutish face split in a wide grin. “Best way to test pretty much everything.”

Aifric added, “Sounds good to me. You cannot resolve an honor debt in a better way.”

Connor blinked. Where had she come from? He glanced around, but didn’t see the other Mhortair. He wondered where they were quartered, or if Wolfram had devised an assignment to keep them busy. That would have been wise.

He tried to protest again, but Shona gave him an imperious look and said, “It is decided, Connor.”

Verena placed a hand on his shoulder. “Don’t worry, Connor. I’ve got this.”

Even Kilian was grinning at the idea of the two girls bash fighting. Tomas and Cameron immediately started betting on the outcome. Of course they each choose a different champion. That way at least one of them would always be disappointed. Ivor and Aifric both quietly added their own bets, and Connor didn’t doubt everyone else would get drawn in too. He appreciated that they seemed to be giving both girls pretty even odds.

Kilian clapped Connor on the back and winked, eyes dancing with mirth. “We’ll keep an eye on things. I’m sure the ladies will stay in control.”

Both Shona and Verena nodded immediately, but continued watching each other like pedras preparing to fight over their territory. Connor had no doubt they would both commit everything to the duel.

"But I only loaned Verena a tiny bit of granite."

"Well, you'd better loan me some more then," she said matter-of-factly.

Shona added, "And since we're so focused on research today, you'd better loan me a tertiary power while you're at it."

Anika, who did not seem to share Connor's concerns said, "Is very good. Train together make us better friends." She winked at Rory who couldn't help grinning like a fool in return.

General Wolfram gestured toward the palace. "I suggest we retire to a more private venue to conduct our research."

The entire group eagerly agreed and headed that way. Connor walked with Verena, who was grinning with anticipation. She said, "This is going to be so much fun."

"Verena, don't you think you should wait? Shona has years of training with granite. You've only had it for moments. You know she'll have an advantage." Bash fighting when they were both protected by granite was probably the safest way for them to finally work through their lingering resentment, but he didn't want to watch Verena get pounded.

Verena shrugged. "As if I'd face her with only granite. She'll have a tertiary power, so I'll have mine too."

"I don't think it's wise to try loaning you additional powers so soon."

He did need to practice, but didn't think that was the best way. He felt a heavy weight of anxiety to spend as much time practicing with his affinities and exploring the nuances of what he could now do, but using Verena as his test subject was not what he had in mind.

"No, silly. My tertiary powers are my mechanicals. Granite strength is Shona's defining characteristic. Builder mechanicals are mine. Do you think I would ever duel without them?"

CHAPTER SEVENTY-FOUR

A Moment Worth Waiting For

Verena stepped into the officers' training courtyard in the southern wing of the palace, feeling as excited as she had the first day she tried flying her little hovering chair that eventually became the Swift. That same sense of eager anticipation filled her, a sense that she was about to make history.

She was so grateful Connor had chosen to loan her a Petralist affinity. As a Builder, Verena was powerful, and confident in her own skills, but as much as she knew power stones, she had not truly understood how amazing it was to tap granite internally.

Connor had always described granite as an itchy crawly feeling under his skin, but that's not how she felt it. For her, the feeling of granite sliding up her limbs and across her torso was a feeling of freedom that rivaled flight. She always kept herself in excellent condition, but no physical strength could match the wonder of granite. She might be new to it, but she felt a deep connection to it already.

On top of all of that, she would finally get a chance to pound Shona's haughty face with the full approval of everyone, and not worry that she would break her own fist in the process.

She did feel bad for Shona. Connor hadn't intentionally slighted her, but how else could Shona interpret his decision to test his ideas with Verena first? Verena would have felt guilty for stealing that honor from her if not for the fact that the accidental slight had finally given them the chance to fight.

All of their friends came to witness the historic duel, including Ilse and Evander. Ilse wore snug-fitting trousers on her muscular legs, as if to celebrate her recent healing, and Verena had hugged her, feeling a rush of emotion. Connor's fleshcrafting ability was simply miraculous.

Luckily most of their friends seemed enthusiastic about the duel, and Tomas and Cameron were working a lively betting circle. She knew Connor worried, but he should thank her for coming up with such a great solution. She and Shona had needed a duel to help settle things between them for months, but they had both avoided it because they sensed that one of them would not walk away.

Now that they could both bash fight, chances were more even that neither of them would be critically injured. For a long time, Verena would have happily accepted responsibility for killing Shona, but life had gotten complicated. Shona had switched sides, had shown remarkable bravery, and had kept her word as far as Verena knew to not attempt to seduce Connor back to her. As much as Verena still resented her for all of the problems she had caused for them, she had to respect Shona's dedication to changing.

She would still punch her and hopefully disfigure her face. Connor could heal her, after all.

Verena walked with Shona to the center of the courtyard, while the rest of their friends spread out along the wall to watch. The space was not huge, about fifty paces to each side, ringed by a ten-foot stone wall, with the ground covered with packed dirt. It was situated at the rear of the palace, not far from the southern sweep of the great wall. Towers of the palace reared high overhead, and Verena caught glimpses of faces pressed against the glass.

They hadn't exactly kept this research bout a secret, and word had spread faster than Hamish finding the nearest eating hall at dinnertime. Far more soldiers than normal clustered along the high wall too, with an excellent view down into the courtyard. Verena loved the idea of hundreds of Shona's subjects witnessing her get pummeled.

She also loved how Rumbler battle leathers felt. She had been tempted to wear her custom armor, but it did not shift properly for a Rumbler. Besides, this was the one time she was justified in wearing the signature battle plates. She had left her sword and daggers behind and wore small power stones strapped to her arms and in pouches hanging from a wide leather belt at her waist.

Shona had not protested her bringing mechanicals. She had tried to get Connor to loan her marble, but he had refused. She'd tried for soapstone next, but he had insisted that she had always said she wanted to try quartzite first. She couldn't deny those words, so she had agreed. Verena appreciated Connor's concern. Quartzite was perhaps the least effective battle stone, but Shona had insisted he loan her external quartzite instead of internal. Verena was not concerned. Let her tap whatever affinity she wanted, Verena would still curse-punch that face.

Shona looked just as eager. She moved with deadly grace, her recently regrown hair braided to keep it out of the way, projecting absolute confidence in her battle leathers. She hadn't even bothered tapping granite yet, at least not enough to change her skin or transform her body into rock-hard, sculpted perfection.

The two of them stopped together, the smooth sand crunching slightly under their feet. They faced each other, just out of lunging range, and when they locked gazes, Shona mirrored Verena's eager smile.

Kilian alone joined them in the center, acting as referee. He said simply, "This is a friendly match. Remember that." He held Verena's gaze until she nodded, then did the same to Shona. With the message given and received, he asked, "Any questions?"

They shook their heads in unison, so Kilian lifted his hands high and said simply, "Then have fun."

Despite his warning, Verena knew Shona understood as perfectly as she did what the match was really about. It was payback time.

Verena couldn't help it. She rushed forward, crossing the distance to her foe in a flash, striking with a granite-hardened fist at Shona's face. She would love to knock her opponent onto her backside in the first second of the match.

As if expecting the move, Shona smoothly pivoted aside, grabbed Verena's wrist, and heaved.

Verena understood the move, had practiced it many times in her martial training, but was still unprepared for the brutal reality of Shona's raw strength. Her arm was nearly torn out of the socket as Shona yanked her off her feet and hurled her toward the outer wall. Striking the wall at that speed might have cracked her, even max-tapping.

Battle fury swept aside a flicker of fear, replacing it with an intense, burning need to strike back at the woman who dared mistreat her so. Verena activated the quartzite stones on her upraised forearms and her waist. Air blasted out, slowing her to a halt just before she struck the wall. She grinned, feeling her confidence grow. She could do this!

She shuttered the stones, dropped to the earth, and turned back to face Shona.

Just in time for Shona to lunge at her, fist whipping toward her face. Shona had given chase, and clearly intended to finish her off as fast as Verena had hoped to do to her.

Verena activated blind coal on her left forearm.

Somehow Shona's fist slipped past her face, just missing, and she stumbled forward into the wall. Verena was too close for a good punch, so she twisted and slammed her elbow into Shona's cheek, intending to smash it against the wall again.

She had forgotten to increase her tap rate.

Granite was still so new that she had to focus to adjust the tap rate. Although she was tapping enough granite to avoid cracking her elbow against Shona's stone-hardened cheekbone, she still felt a flash of pain and yelped. The blow knocked Shona's head sideways, but it was not the satisfying smack Verena had hoped for.

She hesitated a fraction of a second to increase her tap rate. Shona took advantage of the delay to push back from the wall and backhand Verena across the sternum. The blow was like a sledgehammer and it catapulted Verena backward forty feet. She was so strong!

Verena again caught herself with quartzite thrusters and landed in a battle stance facing Shona, who this time pursued her at a confident stroll. Verena's heart was racing and she was breathing faster than she should have. She'd always thought bash fighters seemed ponderous, but Shona was deadly fast. Again she squashed a flicker of fear, replacing it with a renewed determination to win.

"Not bad, but you can't master tap rate in the middle of a fight. It takes practice." Shona clearly expected to continue dominating the match.

Verena hated that she had given Shona such satisfaction in the opening moments, and willed herself to settle down and enter the battle calm she usually sought during a fight. Knowing that anger and impatience would get her hurt was different than actually exercising patience, and she felt another flash of irritation that Shona could push her like that.

Most of their friends were enthusiastically cheering, as were scores of soldiers along the wall. Connor looked concerned, but raised a fist in encouragement, which she appreciated. Tomas and Cameron were laughing and gesturing excitedly as they chattered back and forth, no doubt altering their bets. Verena assumed they were betting against her, and that helped firm her resolve to make them lose all their money. She should've taken a bet of her own before the bout commenced.

"I can see why you held the top standings for Boulders at the Carraig," Verena told Shona.

Shona look surprised by the compliment as she drew almost within striking range. She started to nod acceptance but Verena added, "Fighting untrained children must be really nice. When you lose today, I expect you'll find the experience educational."

As she intended, the insult enraged Shona and she rushed in, right fist cocked to deliver a mighty blow. Her initial dominance of the match gave her just enough overconfidence to fall into the trap.

Verena dropped straight down to her side, using quartzite to catch herself just above the sand. As Shona rushed past, surprised by the move, Verena kicked with all of her granite strength at Shona's leading foot.

She connected! The blow knocked Shona's foot right out from under her. With a squawk of outrage, Shona tripped to the ground, but did not have the decency to land on her face. She caught herself on her hands.

Verena slid forward, using a gust of quartzite and kicked at Shona's face, but Shona was too fast and rolled aside.

The move wasn't a surprise. Shona was fast and graceful, but Verena was quickly gaining a feel for her opponent. As nimble as Shona might be, Verena could still return to her feet faster with an explosive blast of air. In fact, she released enough air to lift her right off her feet, and she applied all that force into another might kick just as Shona rolled to a crouching position.

Verena's stone-hardened foot caught her in the chin, and Verena exulted with the sense of profound *rightness* she felt at that moment.

The look of surprise on Shona's face was priceless. The blow struck her so hard that Verena's foot ached, despite her high tap rate, and Shona catapulted right over backward.

As Shona tumbled away, Verena rushed after her just like Shona had done to her earlier, intending to smash Shona down when she tried rising again. Bash fighting was so much fun.

But Shona would not fall for the same trick twice. As soon as she crashed to the ground, she hurled herself back to her feet with one mighty, convulsive heave of her entire body. It was an incredibly acrobatic move, one that most Petralists burdened by ponderous granite bodies would never attempt. Shona was far more graceful than any other Boulder, and she knew exactly how and when to tap her strength.

She managed to set herself just before Verena reached her, but Verena still fired a hard, but controlled punch. Shona blocked it with a forearm and returned with a punch of her own. She might be superhumanly powerful, but Verena knew hand-to-hand fighting just as well.

She blocked Shona's return, twisting her elbow around Shona's forearm to deliver a backhand across her cheek. Her satisfaction at landing a blow against

Shona's hated face fizzled when Shona didn't even grunt, didn't acknowledge the blow, but threw another punch.

Verena refused to back up, and neither did Shona. For the next several seconds they stood toe to toe, raining mighty blows over each other, slamming sledgehammer strikes into each other's faces and torsos.

Verena managed to block or avoid more of the blows than Shona did, something that she felt proud about for a few seconds until she realized that blocking or dodging was not nearly as important in a bash fight. All of her training had taught her to avoid taking damage, but Boulders didn't need to worry about that.

Shona was grinning as she fought, the picture of Obrioner nobility. Verena grinned in turn, matching her punch for punch. It was an exhilarating feeling, and she finally understood why Boulders always whined when their bash fights got cut short.

She'd never experienced anything that quite matched the brutal, wild freedom of it. She still loved flying more, but in a different way. Bash fighting answered a primal part of her that she usually refused to admit existed.

So she threw herself into the fight with every ounce of skill and newly won granite strength, and for a moment held her own. She could tell that annoyed Shona, and it reinforced her battle lust. But Shona adjusted quickly, and demonstrated again her experience by slowly beginning to drive Verena back, despite everything Verena did. In a force-on-force bash fight, Shona was going to win.

Then Shona tapped limestone. Her entire body blazed with such brilliant light that it blinded Verena momentarily, and Shona connected with a brutal uppercut that knocked her right off her feet.

Verena did not need to see Shona to understand that Shona was about to grab her legs and either throw her against the wall or simply slam her into the ground. The heavy bash fight had been a joy, but if Shona wanted to bring in their other weapons, Verena was happy to oblige. She tapped quartzite shielding.

Shona's fist struck the shielding along her ankles, just as she expected. Shona was not able to grab her, but still knocked Verena horizontal. So Verena triggered a tiny jet of marble from her extended forearms, aimed at Shona's face.

Shona had nothing to fear from such a tiny bit of marble, but as Verena expected, she couldn't help yelping and pulling back, hands instinctively rising to protect her precious, recently restored hair.

Verena released the shielding and dropped to the ground. She wasn't proud of using the hair trick. Every woman understood the primal need to defend her hair, but she wouldn't hold back. Shona was still glowing like the sun, and air came whistling in around them, but not strong enough to pull Verena away. Verena lunged and slammed her knee into Shona's midsection so hard that it was Shona's turn to get lifted into the air.

Verena grabbed her ankles and spun mightily, hurling Shona with all her strength at the nearest wall, about twenty feet away.

Shouting an angry curse, Shona slammed into the wall and bounced off, landing on her feet, unhurt.

The momentary reprieve gave Verena a chance to snatch a stone from the pouches at her waist and activate the mechanical. She felt the bout shifting to her favor, and she was not about to let up. Shona stopped glowing, and approached, glaring again.

Verena assumed a nonchalant pose. "Thanks for suggesting that move. It's very effective. How did you enjoy it?"

"I plan to demonstrate a few more," Shona said, breaking into a run. She glanced up at the many onlookers, plainly annoyed that they had seen her take that hit. She had long claimed she could easily destroy Verena if ever given the chance, but now those claims were being proven nothing but empty air, like the tertiary power she was still tapping uselessly. It was starting to whip sand into the air, but Verena could easily ignore that.

Shona did not need to know that though. Getting a fun idea, Verena stepped back a pace, raising one hand to shield her eyes and grimacing as if she had gotten sand in one of her few vulnerable parts.

The wind intensified as Shona laughed and charged. Verena took another stumbling step back, raising her other hand toward her face too, as if momentarily disoriented. Shona took the bait and rushed in, her right fist already cocked back to deliver a mighty curse punch to end the match.

Connor shouted, "Verena, look out!"

He was a dear, but he should know her better. She let Shona close, blinking her eyes wildly and shaking her head to reinforce the illusion.

Shona should know her better too.

As Shona rushed in to deliver a punch strong enough to crack her stone-hardened skin, Verena dropped her hand and stared Shona in the face, smiling.

Shona blanched, realizing too late that she'd been duped. Before she could skid to a stop or change course, Verena dropped a stone.

When the tiny piece of slate landed, a wallstone erupted out of the ground. The earth covering the floor was not extremely thick, but she didn't need much for such a focused wall. Only two feet wide, it erupted from the sands at a forty-five degree angle and caught the still-charging Shona in the chest with brutal force.

It reminded Verena of that first fight in Alasdair when Captain Rory had led his ignorant army right into Ilse's trap. They had known nothing of Builder powers and had been caught completely by surprise. It was even more satisfying to catch Shona with the same trick months later when she knew exactly what Verena could do.

The brutal impact blasted all the air from Shona's lungs and catapulted her back in the other direction. The impact was so hard it looked like she might have gotten neck whip-snap, despite her granite-hardened muscles and bones. In any other moment, Verena would have cringed to unleash such overwhelming force against an opponent, but the months of pent-up loathing for Shona made her grin.

Shona had apologized to Connor, but had never apologized to Verena. That crushing blow was exactly the penance Shona needed to pay to help Verena accept the idea of reconciliation.

Feeling remarkably content, Verena gave chase by jumping and landing on her knees where she had affixed a couple pieces of basalt. Activating the stones' sliding properties, she shot across the ground after Shona as fast as a Strider.

Shona crashed into the wall of the courtyard so hard that she cracked the stones and left a Shona-sized indentation. When she stumbled free, she fell to her back, momentarily stunned. Seeing her like that reinforced Verena's sense of catharsis. She'd never seen Shona unable to immediately shake off a hit. She appreciated that Shona gave her plenty of time to slap two more pieces of basalt onto the soles of her feet.

Shona blinked open her eyes and Verena punched her right between them, striking with every ounce of might she could generate. The blow jarred Verena all the way up to her shoulder, and it drove Shona's head three inches into the dense ground.

It felt so good!

Verena was tempted to kneel on Shona's arms and pummel her unconscious, but she didn't need to. So she rose, stepped back a pace, and gestured Shona to rise. It took a couple seconds for Shona to recover her senses, but she was a fighter. She growled angrily, her expression determined, and she lunged back to her feet.

And of course her feet instantly went out from under her as if they started to run before she was ready. They shot up, nearly clipping Verena as Shona crashed onto her backside hard enough to grunt.

Verena chuckled. "What's the matter? Too tired to continue?"

The blows to her head must have rattled her thinking because Shona immediately leaped back to her feet. They again slipped out from under her, this time sliding sideways in opposite directions and dropping Shona into a full split.

She actually wasn't that limber, and clutched at her thighs with a groan as she toppled backward again. Connor and Hamish both grimaced. Verena couldn't help laughing, and she felt gratified when Ilse did too. Anika clapped loudly, whistling.

Shona glared up at her and snapped, "What did you do, vixen wench?"

Verena crouched, careful to stay out of Shona's reach and said calmly, "What did you expect me to do? I'm a Builder."

Shona tried lunging again, but every time she planted a foot it immediately slipped out from under her. Verena retreated and watched, enjoying every moment of it until Shona realized what she had done and ripped the bits of basalt off her shoes. She threw them at Verena, and Verena caught them, eliciting another scowl.

Shona jumped back to her feet, showing remarkable resilience, but Kilian stepped between them. Verena had not even noticed him crossing the floor. "I'd say that's enough for today."

"I can keep fighting," Shona insisted.

"That's never the problem with Boulders, is it? Fight's over. I call the test a success."

So did Verena. She had thoroughly enjoyed it. But Shona looked so crestfallen that Verena could not help but saying, "Excellent match, Lady Shona. I appreciate you demonstrating the strengths and weaknesses of bash fighting. I think we'll have to do additional research regularly."

Shona brightened. "Absolutely. No research is completed in a single day." She was taking the beating with better grace than Verena had expected, and she was grateful for it. It left the door open for them to beat on each other far more often.

She surprised herself by extending a hand and smiling at her long-hated enemy. Shona took it with a firm, but not overpowering grip and said softly for just Verena to hear, "We should have begun punching each other a long time ago."

"I agree. It opens a whole new aspect to our friendship."

Had she actually said the word friendship to Shona? She felt shocked, confused, but somehow pleased by it. She was sure her expression reflected her surprise. Shona looked just as startled, but gripped Verena's hand for another second, her expression turning thoughtful. "We shall see."

That was good enough for Verena. She chuckled at a sudden thought. When Shona arched an eyebrow in question she said, "Who would have thought Anika was so wise?"

They laughed together. So weird!

Connor jogged up and gave her a fierce hug. He looked relieved, but was careful to keep his joy restrained. "I'm not sure I want to loan you granite every day so you two can beat on each other."

Verena gave him a charming smile and said, "Excellent point. We should try basalt next time."

Connor groaned.

Chapter Seventy-Five

New Limits and New Opportunities

Connor felt immensely relieved that neither Verena nor Shona had been badly hurt. He grinned as he stood next to Verena, facing Shona, so relieved that they both seemed to be in such good humor. He should have foreseen that they'd insist on dueling more. He loved bash fighting as much as anyone, and his initial reservations about those two fighting more often were softened by their reactions to their first fight.

"You're taking to granite really well," Connor told Verena. He appreciated how both of them had fought hard and creatively, and he loved seeing Verena wielding a Petralist power. With training, she could become a force to be reckoned with on the battlefield. She was already incredibly deadly, but add superhuman strength and nearly impervious skin, and he started wondering if he had accidentally unleashed a monster.

A super-cute adorable deadly monster.

"Thanks," Verena said, flashing that special smile that melted him on the inside.

Shona actually nodded. "Daily dueling will help work out your hesitation."

She seemed to be taking her loss with remarkable grace, and Connor appreciated that. She had gotten in a number of excellent strikes against Verena too, and no doubt every single one of those were already cherished memories. What pleased him the most was how they had shaken hands at the end and even seemed to share a private joke.

Either Shona had gotten rattled a lot worse by that wall smash than he thought, or finally getting to beat on each other was actually proving beneficial. Combat therapy. Who knew?

"I noticed you tapping quartzite. How did it feel?" he asked Shona.

She grinned, a look of wonder on her face. He knew that expression all too well. He felt it every time he tried a new affinity.

"It's amazing. I need to learn how to fly."

"Flying is difficult until you've ascended. Air is very fickle and doesn't seem to like responding to a Petralist's call."

"Will you tell me more about her?" Shona asked.

He wanted to, but what about Water's caution that he not share too much? "Soon."

Shona accepted that with grace and said, "Now that I've tried quartzite, I'll need to try each of the others too."

He did not blame her. Trying new affinities could be very addicting. The rest of the group gathered around. Tomas and Cameron were already exchanging money. He'd have to ask them later what the final wagers were. They owed him a sizable chunk for his bet on Verena.

"I actually do need to train with loaning powers; and I need someone to help me. I don't think I can loan powers to myself."

Hamish chuckled. "You'd need to split your head like Aifric does."

"We don't actually work that way," Aifric protested.

"I'm just glad you girls don't get into slap fights all together," he replied with a grin, then added, "Let me go next, Connor. Shona already had a turn."

"That doesn't mean I shouldn't get to try another," Shona protested.

Verena chimed in. "I'd like to try another one too."

That elicited a round of enthusiastic calls from everyone else to help Connor train. Most of the group started debating loudly about which Petralist power they wanted to try first. Connor grinned at their enthusiasm. Usually only he could enjoy the effects of his ascension. Getting to share his training and exploration of marvelous new discoveries with them was a wonderful treat.

Most of the group settled on affinity choices quickly, but Hamish struggled before grinning and saying, "Got it. Diorite. This way we can hold that puking competition on fair terms."

Shona grimaced. "You are not going to spew flaming vomit all across my palace."

"You're the one who was just touting how important research is," Hamish countered.

Kilian stepped in. "No diorite. You'll only blow yourself up."

Luckily Hamish had a flexible mind and he moved on from that disappointment by requesting porphyry.

Connor laughed, but Kilian only stared, his gaze literally turning icy as frost crept across his eyes. Not even Hamish could maintain his "I'm innocent" look in the face of that cold, gray stare.

So he sighed and said, "Fine. How about obsidian?"

Connor had expected Hamish to try granite or basalt, but it made sense. In that battle suit, Hamish was already deadly. Amplified by obsidian, Connor wasn't sure if Hamish would have any limits.

General Wolfram requested basalt, claiming that he'd always wanted to feel the speed of Wingrunners. Knowing it could help him better understand their capabilities and therefore more effectively deploy his troops. Captain Ilse requested basalt too, and challenged Wolfram to a running battle. He instantly accepted.

Neither Tomas nor Cameron wanted any different primary affinity. They spent their entire careers laughing at Striders and avoiding Blades so there was little appeal in joining either camp. They were excited to try a secondary affinity, though. Cameron had never managed one, and although Tomas could tap limestone, it was such a weak affinity it might as well not exist.

Neither Kilian nor Evander opted to try any additional affinities. Kilian simply shrugged and said, "I know my limits, and my affinities are such a part of me I couldn't imagine changing them."

Evander had said, "The Evergreen never loses its leaves, but the sturgeon best appreciates the deep cold of the abyss."

Too bad Jean wasn't around to help decipher that one. Connor couldn't decide if it meant Evander was content as he was, or if he was threatening to throw Connor into the nearest loch if he tried tampering with his affinities.

It took only a few minutes to gather the stones and powders they needed. Connor told his eager friends, "Remember, this is a loan. Pay attention to your tap rates. We need to understand how effective the affinities work for each of you, and how long the loaned power lasts."

Wolfram nodded approval. "We should also test if we would suffer double-tap sickness by tapping double primaries."

"Test that if you want. I've seen the effects and don't want to disable myself for a day or two," Shona said with a grimace.

Connor said, "I agree. I suspect you'd hurt yourself, but we can test it at the end, when your loaned power is almost spent."

With a sense of anticipation, Connor turned to Wolfram, who had stepped closer as they talked. "You first, General."

"I am honored."

"While you're working with basalt, I'd like to try it too," Verena said.

"Me too," Shona added. "Joining Wolfram and Ilse in that running battle should be fun."

Plus it would give them another chance to hit each other.

Kilian said, "I'll referee the match. No doubt you'll need some pointers. Running battles are not as simple as they seem."

They had never looked simple. Running battles were as much the ultimate test of Striders and Wingrunners as bash fighting was for Boulders and Rumblers. The intricate, beautiful patterns of a running battle sometimes masked their deadly intent. Connor decided he'd follow them too. That group in a running battle would be amazing to watch.

Loaning basalt to Wolfram went well. Using the same stone combination of obsidian and sandstone to establish the connection, then purging basalt while focused on his target produced instant results. Wolfram grinned as he raced around the courtyard, and Connor felt relieved that the process seemed to work consistently.

Loaning basalt to Ilse also went well, and he felt so happy to see Ilse smile a genuine smile. That was something she still did too rarely. He loved that she could experience basalt speed on her newly restored legs. It seemed appropriate, and he felt a new sense of wonder at his amazing fleshcrafting abilities when he looked at her powerful legs.

Connor then focused on the next batch of basalt to create lamacal for Shona, but his connection to basalt felt strangely weak. He still managed to create enough lamacal, but had to struggle to complete the process. While Shona eagerly licked the lamacal from her hand, barely grimacing at the chalky taste this time, Connor turned to Verena. He found that he could barely absorb any basalt. Frowning, he explained the problem to the others.

"What do you mean, you can't connect with basalt?" Verena asked, looking worried as the others gathered around.

Still frowning, Connor focused over the basalt, willing it into his hand. "It's weird. I can feel it, but can't seem to absorb more. It feels the way I might when I've already absorbed a full measure, except right now I'm empty."

General Wolfram said thoughtfully, "I had not considered the possibility."

"What possibility?" Connor and Verena asked together.

"We're talking about loaning powers. You have already loaned a significant portion of your basalt to three of us. You assume you can loan your powers to as many people as you want, but perhaps there is a finite limit."

"Are you saying that when I loan a power, I'm actually giving away part of the power that I would otherwise be using?" Connor asked.

"Precisely."

That made sense. If he was sharing breakfast, he'd have to accept the fact that he wouldn't have as much to eat himself. But somehow he'd imagined he could just keep sharing powers as long as he had affinity stones to replenish what he'd used.

Hamish sighed. "So much for the idea of loaning granite to a thousand regulars. That would have been too easy. Connor is sharing a single tray of affinity desserts, but we'd all assumed he had the entire kitchen available to keep making more."

Kilian chuckled. "Sometimes I marvel at how many truths you can wrap in a single sweetbread."

"All truth can be connected to dessert if you just leave yourself open to the possibilities," Hamish quipped.

"Or if you snort sugar in your sleep," Verena joked.

Hamish looked thrilled by the idea, but she gave him a serious look and said, "Don't."

Captain Ilse said, "We can test the hypothesis easily enough. Wolfram and I can each purge some of our basalt. See if that allows you to then loan more."

That was a good idea and would help establish how his access to more basalt was linked to their consumption rate. The two Grandurians quickly purged some of the basalt, and sure enough Connor managed to then absorb enough to loan to Verena.

"What if you need a power you loan to us after you've loaned it?" Verena asked as she held the white lamacal. "I'd hate to think you might get hurt because you needed an affinity that we were using."

Another excellent question. Connor tried simply willing the power back to himself, taking back the loan early, but it didn't seem to work. He said, "We'll have to test that, but if I loan you a power I think it's yours until you consume it all."

"We'll explore the idea, but not now," Wolfram said with a grin. "I simply can't stand still any longer."

He bolted from the practice yard, heading for the nearest gate. Ilse and Shona gave chase, laughing with the freedom of basalt. Verena hesitated long enough to kiss Connor and grin excitedly before tearing off after the others.

Hamish eagerly accepted some obsidian and erupted into the air with a blast of quartzite thrusters to test his reflexes. Cameron took his place in front of Connor and said, "Can you really help me activate limestone, lad?"

"Let's find out," Connor said with a smile. Cameron looked so eager, almost nervous.

Then he realized he had a problem. Secondary affinity stones like limestone and sandstone didn't need to be absorbed, so how could he purge lamacal for Cameron to consume?

"Maybe I should eat it," Cameron offered.

A small stone wouldn't hurt. Hamish had accidentally swallowed enough rocks growing up that Connor wasn't worried about that, but the solution didn't feel right. "We'll reserve that for a last resort."

He tried simply focusing on Cameron, holding limestone while tapping obsidian and sandstone, but got nothing when he handed the stone to Cameron. As Cameron returned the stone, Connor felt a flash of connection and said excitedly, "Wait! Don't let go."

It took only a moment to establish the deep connection required. The small piece of limestone ignited like a hundred lanterns, and Connor envisioned the affinity transfer like sliding part of a dessert tray halfway across a table for Cameron to pick up a piece of his cake. The glowing piece.

The connection slid across, and Cameron laughed like a child as he lifted the still-blazing stone high. "I'm tapping limestone!" he chortled, his ugly face looking far less hideous under an expression of pure joy. He strode around the courtyard, glowing like a sun, exclaiming at the wonder of it.

He shouted, "If I'd been this bright a little sooner, not even that blind woman could've denied me."

Tomas laughed. "You may be bright, but you're still dimwitted."

"Let's see you do better," Cameron challenged.

Tomas stepped close to Connor and whispered, "Come on, lad. I don't need a tertiary. I just need to light more than a candle, or Cameron will never let me live this down."

"I'm not sure if it works that way. We're loaning new powers to people, but you've already got a limestone affinity."

Tomas gave him such an imploring look that he said, "Okay. I'll see what I can do."

Connor tried the same trick he'd used to loan limestone to Cameron. He easily connected with Tomas, and once he felt the connection, he activated the limestone. It ignited with brilliant light.

"Now you try keeping it active," he said as he slipped his hand free.

Tomas gripped the little stone hard, squinting up his face with his concentration. Despite his mighty effort, the light dimmed to barely a flicker. Connor had never seen such a weak affinity.

Cameron chortled. "If you keep twisting your face that hard, you might get permanently uglier."

"No worry that I'd ever challenge you for that title," Tomas snapped, still concentrating.

"Or title for brightest of the Fast Rollers," Cameron agreed with a gap-toothed smile.

"Come on, laddie," Tomas urged Connor quietly. "I'm doing the work. Help a mate out, will you?"

Connor hated to let Tomas down. The two Fast Rollers had taken him under their wing when he was clueless, barely able to tap granite. They'd taught him some of his first lessons, taught him to fight, and believed in him enough to ignore the order to capture him when he'd gone to free Verena and Nicklaus from that cave. They'd stood by him through all of his dangerous adventures, always encouraging him in their bantering way. He had to find a way to help Tomas now.

So he again touched the limestone and felt Tomas' affinity. It was like a gossamer thread connecting him to the stone. Connor marveled that he could feel the connection so clearly. He hadn't sensed it in any of the others, but then again he hadn't been trying to loan them an affinity they already possessed.

He focused on that connection, trying to feel that affinity within Tomas. The queen had activated a permanent new affinity for Shona, so there was a way to do it. He didn't actually need to duplicate that feat, although he hoped through his training and rigorous practice that he could figure it out. At the moment, he didn't need that much. Tomas had already established a connection. It was weak, but maybe by helping Tomas strengthen his affinity, he might better understand how the process worked.

Connor closed his eyes and focused entirely on that feeble connection. He could sense Tomas' tension, but the connection to the affinity was so weak, he didn't clearly feel it through obsidian yet. There had to be something else. He needed to see it.

He thought back to the vision the elements had shown him of his own affinities, as well as what he had witnessed in Nicklaus' mind. So he tapped chert too, and a strong connection to Tomas instantly snapped into place.

His vision darkened as he plunged into Tomas' affinityscape.

Chapter Seventy-Six

Building Bridges

Connor found himself standing on a beautiful, grassy knoll, overlooking a forest with a small village in the distance. It was not a location he recognized. It felt calm and peaceful, not something he would've expected to find in Tomas' head.

Then he turned around and grinned with relief. Behind him the grassy knoll abruptly ended in a dark chasm with a bridge to a floating island. It appeared similar to the affinityscape of his own mind, except there was only one bridge out to one of the islands.

That closest floating island was made of only a single tier, formed from enormous blocks of granite, stacked together in a complex interlocking pattern, with the wooden rope bridge securely fastened to it by a heavy iron framework. Tomas might only have one primary affinity, but he was linked to it very securely.

The bridge was wide and seemed solid so Connor jogged across. Like all rope plank bridges, it wobbled, but not too severely. Once he stepped onto the island he sensed the power of granite flowing up through his feet. A single frayed rope extended from the opposite side, about ten paces away, toward another low, single-tiered island that glowed faintly in the darkness.

That was Tomas' connection to limestone. Where his first bridge was broad and strong, that rope was all the bridge he had to limestone. To cross, one would have to move hand over hand, hanging over that bottomless abyss.

The representation of his weak affinity was perfect. Connor wondered if he'd projected his concept of islands and bridges into Tomas' mind, or if everyone at some fundamental level understood their affinity connections like that.

He wondered why Tomas' affinityscape only depicted singled bridges connecting to single-tiered islands. Did it represent the fact that he had only established good primary affinities, but Connor had established strong tertiaries? After a moment's thought, he decided maybe they represented his ascensions. He was triple ascended, so why not have triple-layered bridges?

The idea seemed important, and he sensed he might be right on the verge of understanding something else important, but the harder he tried to grasp the concept that floated just out of reach, the more it receded, until it faded away. That was annoying. If he wasn't already traipsing around in Tomas' head, he'd use obsidian to accelerate his thoughts and try figuring it out. He wasn't sure if that would interrupt his connection to Tomas, so decided to try it later.

At the moment, he needed to figure out how to solidify Tomas' affinity bridge. If that visual representation of Tomas' affinity actually tied to his powers, the logical solution would be to figure out how to strengthen the bridge. If he could build a better bridge, would Tomas enjoy a better affinity?

It was worth a try. Besides, he didn't feel like tempting that sketchy looking rope. He was in Tomas' mind, and he did not want to get lost there.

So he jogged back across the first bridge to the grassy knoll and descended from there to the forest. He was tempted to summon an ax, but it didn't feel right. So he tapped granite and ripped a couple of tall but slender trees out of the ground by the roots. Then he heaved them onto his shoulders and jogged back across the rope bridge to Tomas' granite affinity island. After stripping the branches from the trees, he considered the long gap between the granite and limestone islands.

The trees should be long enough. "Here we go," he whispered as he hefted the first tree, gripping the thick base firmly and dropping the top toward the limestone island, willing it to connect. He was linked to Tomas' mind through the obsidian, chert, and sandstone. He drew upon those connections, trying to reinforce the bond as he worked to build something new for Tomas.

As the tree fell, the wood transformed in his hands from a rough, rounded trunk to a thick beam, uniform in width. The end thudded solidly onto the softly glowing green limestone island and iron bands rose up from the stone to secure it in place.

"Yes!" Connor exulted. "Mental construction sure beats using hammer and chisel in the real world."

Feeling more hopeful by the second, Connor pressed his end down onto the granite island beside the frayed rope. Again, iron bands rose out of the granite and locked the end of the trunk into position.

Connor felt energy flowing along the tree trunk when he touched it. He took that as a good sign, and dropped the second tree into position just like the first. It also transformed and locked into place.

Not bad. His efforts seemed to be working. He had done some creative building in Aifric's mind to help resurrect her after the queen had snuffed out her life, so he was comfortable with the intangible process. He'd taken some liberties recreating the walls of her mind, and her affinities had strengthened as a result. He hoped to accomplish the same result for Tomas.

It took only a few minutes to return to the forest and collect more trees. Connor hoped he was not causing Tomas any mental pain from the effort, but somehow doubted it. Tomas liked to claim that thinking was for officers and he was better off doing none of it, so hopefully he wouldn't even notice that Connor was in there mucking around.

He returned with the additional wood and snapped it to the appropriate length for treads between the two trees-turned-beams that formed the trusses of the new bridge he was constructing. He placed the sections of tree in position between the trusses, and each piece transformed into thick, finished planks that slid out along the trusses when he pushed them. They each locked into place at the end of the fast-growing bridge.

Mind construction was so much fun. In the real world he was not exactly a great carpenter. If Tomas had to wait for him to figure out how to cut and plane each of those planks, they'd probably both die of old age.

Instead he completed the bridge in short order, including polished hand rails, supported by gracefully turned balusters. He surveyed his work, feeling satisfied. "Too bad mom can't see this."

He'd apprenticed with the local carpenter before taking the apprentice with old Tam, the Alasdair town hunter. He'd taken to carpentry exactly opposite to how he'd taken to hunting. He'd proudly built a pot-hanging rack for his mother, only to have it collapse as soon as she hung her pots and pans from it. The entire rack had fallen on Blair's head with a spectacular, crashing din. Connor chuckled at the memory of Blair stumbling around the room with the biggest cast-iron pot stuck over his face.

He confidently crossed to the limestone side to survey his work from there. It looked good. Maybe he should have created a bridge using ropes, but Tomas was hard on delicate things. Connor's bridge could stand the test of time, and Connor liked adding a personal touch to his mental construction work.

The glow of the limestone island began to increase until Connor felt like he was standing on top of one of the amazing prism lanterns from the Rhidorroch. His work was done. With a thought, he willed himself back to his own head and blinked open his eyes.

Tomas stood in front of him, mouth agape in wonder, light pouring off him in waves.

Connor laughed. "Wow. Looks like it worked."

Tomas seized his hands and shook them so hard he nearly dislocated Connor's shoulder. "I don't know what you did, lad, but I've never felt anything like this. Limestone is a part of me, as much as granite ever was."

He laughed and spun away, hands outstretched, light blazing from him as bright as any Solas Connor had ever seen.

Cameron approached, scowling, and shuttered his own limestone with a sigh. "Why did you have to go and do that? Now he's going to get a swelled head."

Tomas laughed again and multicolored waves of light erupted out of his mouth. He didn't even seem to realize he was doing it.

Cameron groaned. "Swelled head, sure as latrine duty. I'll have to pound it flat every day for a month."

"As if you could," Tomas laughed, teeth glowing. He was really taking to limestone, as if making up for lost time.

Cameron charged his partner, and the two launched into a brutal bash fight, both of them blazing with light, lending their usual brutal fighting an epic air. Connor laughed, thrilled he'd made it work. He'd just helped Tomas dramatically improve his limestone affinity, just as he had accidentally helped Aifric improve her affinities. Could he apply the same concepts to establishing brand new ones?

The thought of it maybe working sent chills of excitement shivering down his spine. Creating new affinities was one of the queen's abilities that might most heavily affect the war effort. If Connor could duplicate that . . .

Tomas interrupted Connor's reverie by throwing Cameron into him, knocking him right off his feet. Tomas laughed and shouted, "We taught you better than to get dough-headed during a fight. Come on, laddie!"

Connor tapped granite and plunged into the bash fight with the two mighty warriors. For a few minutes, he let himself get lost in max-tapped pummeling. It felt good to forget about all the mind-bending affinities and worries about the queen's plans and simply beat on a couple of good friends.

CHAPTER SEVENTY-SEVEN

Old Truths and New Lessons

Connor flew southeast from Merkland, several hundred feet in the air, marveling at the vista of the lush Merkland valley in springtime, and thoroughly enjoying the wonder of stable flight. He imagined the cushion of air carrying him as a soft mattress that he could just sprawl on while he soared. The cool air smelled fresh and carried scents of budding leaves and eager spring growth.

He spotted Kilian and the others crisscrossing the pasturelands in the middle of a running battle. Herds of curious cows and oblivious sheep meandered through the battlefield, and luckily it looked like no one had collided with any of them yet. Connor slowed to watch. He'd always enjoyed the graceful, deadly movements of the intricate duels between fast movers.

His friends still had a long way to go before they looked anything like that. It took time to understand how to bank and turn by shifting one's weight and to grasp the intricate moves a running battle required because of the enormous speed of the combatants. No doubt in their minds Shona, Verena, Ilse, and Wolfram envisioned themselves making those moves perfectly. What they were actually accomplishing was a whole lot less, with varying degrees of hilarious failure.

They were all experienced enough warriors, with excellent balance, that they didn't just trip over their own feet like Connor had done many times when first practicing with basalt. However, more than one of them turned too abruptly and fell, rolling end over end before coming to a painful stop. They looked to be accumulating an impressive number of bruises. He expected calls for loaned sandstone next.

Once they did get moving properly, they still had to actually hit each other with their borrowed practice weapons, coated with bright-colored powder. Moving that fast, one had to anticipate strikes sooner, and most of the blows they attempted missed because they swung a second too late.

Kilian spent his time trying to give instruction and advice, zipping between the others like a frantic coach. As Connor drew closer, he noticed Verena trying to chase down General Wolfram, grinning with the thrill of speed.

Wolfram abruptly skidded to a halt and turned to face her, powder-coated weapon raised high. Verena tried to stop instead of simply swerving wide. She stumbled directly at Wolfram, who was too surprised to move. Connor cringed, expecting a brutal impact.

Earth rose up to block Verena, and she plowed into it, sinking half a foot before the earth spat her out onto her backside. Captain Ilse arrived, laughing so hard she almost fell over herself. Wolfram started laughing too, his long mustaches wagging. Verena grinned up at them from the ground and rubbed dirt out of her hair.

Then they spotted Connor and gathered as he came in for a landing. He clapped as he drew closer, grinning to see them having so much fun.

"It's harder than it looks," Verena admitted.

"Some of us pick it up faster than others," Connor admitted with a wink.

Shona rolled her eyes. "I can remember lots of things you didn't pick up so quick."

"Well, today I picked up how to help strengthen affinities," he replied with a triumphant grin. "Well, at least one, and it was pretty weak to begin with. But I think I might have a clue about how to try building brand new affinities."

Their shocked expressions made him smile even wider. Sharing affinities with them was wonderful, but sometimes it was fun to drop surprises on them too.

"How?" Verena cried as she rushed toward him with super speed and almost slid right past before she could stop. He caught her arm and pulled her around, her legs lifting right off the ground as he pulled her into his arms. They both laughed and he kissed her cheek.

He set her down and said, "Tomas. I helped him establish a much stronger connection to limestone."

Shona frowned. "How does that help with creating permanent new affinities?"

"It might not, but when I connected with his mind, I saw how his affinities were structured."

Verena chuckled. "What did you see in there? I imagine his mind looked like a never-ending bash fight."

"He's a lot more capable than he pretends," Connor said, but still smiled at the joke. He told them about how he saw affinities as islands and bridges and how he'd created a better bridge for Tomas, resulting in his much improved affinity.

Verena started nodding immediately, and Shona said, "So you think you can create new bridges for us too?"

"Is it that simple?" Ilse asked with a frown.

"In a way, I think it might be. The complexity is connecting to the mind the right way, just like we had to figure out with loaning affinities. "We'll still have to test it, but I think it might work. There has to be a way. The queen's been adding hundreds of new Petralists to her army. What if we could do the same?"

The others chatted excitedly about the possibility, but Kilian said, "I need to have a talk with you, Connor."

He looked unexpectedly serious. That discovery promised to make a huge impact on the success of the revolution. If they could field as many Petralists as the queen, they could defeat any army she sent against them. With so many Petralists, Connor could only imagine what chaos the clever Wolfram and Ilse could unleash, supported as they were by the Arishat League and the Builders. The queen's armies would never know what hit them.

"We need to start testing Connor's ideas immediately," Shona insisted.

"Soon," Kilian promised as he towed Connor away from the rest. "We'll all get a chance soon, I promise."

Connor could not tap basalt yet because the others were still using it. So Kilian gestured into the sky. Connor wrapped them in a supportive bubble of air, envisioning it like a couple of comfortable chairs that lifted them high above the valley. Beneath them, the rest of the group accelerated back toward Merkland, exchanging the running duel for a race. He was happy he had not granted any of them enough basalt to frack. He doubted they were ready to handle that experience.

Once he and Kilian rose several hundred feet, Kilian leaned back and regarded Connor seriously. "You've shown remarkable progress since your ascension, Connor."

"Thanks. I'm enjoying the process a lot more than the last one," he admitted. The third threshold was as wondrous as those early days when he started establishing his first affinities.

"So what else are you not telling me?" Kilian asked.

"What do you mean?" Connor suddenly felt less thrilled that he was stuck in the air alone with Kilian.

"Everyone's experience is a little different, but I spent a great deal of time with Tallan after his ascension and during the war. He was a brilliant lad, not unlike yourself in many ways, but he never mastered the trick to loaning affinities, let alone granting new ones. I was convinced no one but my mother would ever figure it out, but here you get it within days of ascending. You're clever Connor, but no one's that clever. What's going on?"

He shouldn't have been surprised that Kilian wasn't fooled. Kilian was too good at keeping secrets and had far too many of his own not to recognize that Connor now had a few.

When he hesitated, Kilian asked, "You've been speaking with the elementals again, haven't you?"

He wanted to protect Kilian from the vague dangers that Water had warned him about, wanted to honor his word to her not to share too much about them with others, but he could not lie to Kilian. So he sighed, rubbed one hand through his hair and said, "Things are getting complicated."

Kilian didn't look surprised. "That's why I felt we needed to talk. So talk."

"I'm not sure I should."

"Why not?" Kilian prodded gently.

"I have been speaking with them. They've been teaching me about some new aspects to my affinities and helping me understand the ascension. The insights I gained about islands and bridges were from a vision they showed me. Without that, I don't know if I could have figured it out."

"What else have they told you?" Kilian urged, leaning forward, looking intrigued.

"They said I shouldn't tell any of you more of what they're teaching me," Connor admitted, trying not to cringe as he said it.

Kilian cocked his head in surprise. "Why would they say that?"

"They fear that if I share too much, you or Evander or someone might get ideas about how to try ascending or connecting with them, and it could be dangerous for you."

That made him think. Kilian leaned back, thoughtful. "And yet they appeared to Verena."

"And Water is speaking with Nicklaus," Connor added.

"What?" Kilian exclaimed, looking more shocked by that than any of the mind-bending new abilities Connor had exhibited so far. His eyes ignited with rippling flames, and Connor suddenly felt nervous. Kilian had a protective streak for Nicklaus wider than Hamish's love for sweetbreads.

So he added quickly, "I just learned about it when we visited him in New Schwinkendorf."

"What has she been telling him?" Kilian asked, his voice soft, even, and very dangerous.

"She taught him to build a water purifier, and he said he thinks she wants to teach him how to build something important."

"Why?" Kilian asked, his anger evaporating under a look of guarded concern.

"I don't know. Verena said she hasn't been able to reach Water since triggering Kristin's Defense. I don't know why Nicklaus has been hearing her, or what they want with him."

Kilian's gaze sharpened. "And what do they want from you?"

"I'm not sure yet," Connor admitted.

"There must be something. My mother spoke of unknown dangers associated with the elements, but never elaborated. My sister spoke of them a little, but seemed excited rather than worried. I appreciate that they've begun teaching you, that they warned you about dangers on the road you're following, but I don't believe they are helping out of pure charity."

Connor agreed. "They've made a couple of comments in passing, something about needing a champion, but won't elaborate."

Kilian frowned as he considered that.

Connor added, "They were clear about me not sharing too much, but I've probably broken that charge already. I don't know enough yet to tell you their purpose, but if I offend them, I'll never know. I have to ask you to trust me with figuring it out."

"I don't like it," Kilian said with a grimace. "You know I carry many secrets, but I know why I carry them, and when I must share their truths with you and the others. You lack that understanding, which leaves you in a potentially dangerous position."

"We're all in dangerous positions. I can't afford not to pursue every potential avenue for learning, can I?"

Kilian sighed. "Sometimes a lifeline can become an anchor instead and drag us down instead of lifting us to safety."

"Do heights make you wax poetic, or have you been spending too much time with Evander?" Connor asked with a smile.

The attempt at levity failed to lighten the mood. Kilian's eyes changed to a dull slate color, like the sea during a heavy storm. His expression was serious, but not angry and he surprised Connor by asking, "Do you remember when I told you of the Treaty of Baltray?"

"Um, yes," Connor said, shifting gears. "That was the treaty between all the nations swearing to never use elfonnel again."

Kilian nodded and said softly, "Because of the Battle of Vallanes."

"I don't know anything about that." Connor always wished Kilian would share more of his past, and hoped that he was about to get a glimpse into a piece he'd never heard of before.

"That was the battle where it all happened. The Tallan Wars had dragged on a long time, with great loss of life on both sides. Tallan was convinced that if we could draw out my mother and defeat her, we could win the war."

"Kind of what we're hoping to do now," Connor noted.

"Elfonnel were always the ultimate weapon, and a few had been used, but the cost was always high. More often than not, the Petralist summoning them was consumed in the process. But we staked everything on a bold plan to lure my mother into battle, each raise an elfonnel, and destroy her together."

"That's where you did it, at Vallanes?" Connor guessed. He could easily imagine how they reached that conclusion, although he shuddered to think of planning to summon multiple elfonnel. He'd seen the destruction they caused. Parts of southern Granadure, from the broken Badurach Pass all the way up past the ruins of Harz, and almost to Altkalen, was still dangerously unstable.

Kilian nodded. "We went to Vallanes. It was a sturdy fortress on a remote stretch of the east coast. The population was sparse, and it seemed perfect. We let word leak through my mother's spies that we were there, exploring a leftover mechanical of Kirstin's."

"I bet that got her attention," Connor guessed.

"Immediately. She flew straight there to confront us, but brought Harley along too."

"That's how there were so many elfonnel," Connor said, trying to imagine such a battle.

"Five of us," Kilian said with a grimace. "My mother and Harley raised earth-bound, so Tallan and I both embraced Water. We had brought another powerful Dawnus with us. General Sterkur raised the fifth. Fire-bound. We met in titanic battle, flinging elements at each other without restraint, and you already know we broke the land so severely that an entire section of the continent collapsed and the Sea of Olcan rushed in."

"Creating the Broken Waters," Connor said, chilled by the thought of such overwhelming destruction.

"My mother disappeared, and we all know now that she fell victim to the long sleep as a result. Harley escaped, as did Tallan and I. General Sterkur was consumed by the waters," Kilian said, looking tired, with old sorrow reflecting in his eyes that had turned a brilliant blue.

They hovered in silence for a moment as the tragic history weighed on them. Connor felt moved by the story, reminded of the grim and deadly task they were engaged in. "I'm not sure why you shared that with me," he ventured finally.

Kilian fixed him with a steady gaze. "Because we were so convinced we needed to pursue every possible avenue to find advantage, we unleashed more than we could control, and killed hundreds, if not thousands of innocents in our arrogance."

"I don't . . ." Connor started to protest, but paused. He'd said those exact same words. Was he rushing headlong into disaster too? The idea scared him, but did it scare him more than the idea of losing to Queen Dreokt?

"I promise I'll be careful, and I'll share what I learn, as soon as I understand enough to know what I'm sharing with you," Connor said.

Kilian grimaced, then chuckled. "How often do you understand what you're doing ahead of time?"

Connor shrugged. "Not as often as I'd prefer."

"As much as I hate to admit it, I'm afraid I agree, and I'm willing to trust those instincts of yours. Sometimes they serve you well."

Connor was grateful he didn't point out the times that Connor's instincts hadn't been exactly productive. One of his talents was creative battlefield strategies, and with the elements assisting him, he hoped he could develop an actual plan for victory.

They rode in silence, floating toward Merkland, deep in thought until Connor spotted Hamish rise into the sky from the city. He was moving fast and angled to intercept them about half a mile out.

"What's up?" Connor asked as Hamish slowed and stepped onto the invisible floor supporting the two of them.

He pushed open his visor, looking a bit annoyed and said, "You're not tapping quartzite internally, and you don't have any speakstones, do you?"

"Why? What's wrong?" Kilian asked.

"We just received a note from Ailsa. Sounds serious. We need you guys back in the conference room right away."

Chapter Seventy-Eight

If Only Problems Could Be Solved with Marshmallows

The conference room one floor below Ivor's office in the palace was already packed with their entire core group, plus Mistress Four and Commander Six of the Mhortair, who sat beside Aifric. She had saved a seat for Kilian. Connor took the open seat next to Verena.

She squeezed his hand and flashed a happy smile. "I love granite, but basalt was so much fun!"

"I agree." He loved that she finally understood how it felt. He scanned the room of friends, all anxious to hear the latest news from Ailsa. Evander took up most of the foot end of the table, with Hamish and Wolfram flanking him. Ilse sat next to Wolfram, one muscular leg crossed over the other, smiling every time she glanced down at them.

Shona sat at the opposite end, with Rory and Ivor at either side, and Anika close beside Rory. Many of the group looked windblown from their recent sprint, and Connor wanted to ask who won the race. Despite the crazy world they lived in and the terrible danger looming over them, at least they'd gotten one really fun training together.

Ivor called the meeting to order and said, "Our recent communique includes much to discuss, including the alarming news that before Craigroy escaped Merkland he arranged with one of his supporters to conceal a speakstone in my office."

Startled murmurs rippled around the table. That was terrible news. Connor glanced at Verena. "So he's been able to listen in on all of the discussions there?"

Ivor nodded. "It appears so."

Verena looked really annoyed. "We should have noted a missing speakstone, but we've been using them so extensively, our tracking has gotten a bit loose.

Wolfram said, "I recommend we find ways to improve our accounting methods."

"I'll get on it right after this meeting," Hamish promised.

Shona said, "Craigroy served my father with great distinction for years, which is why I insisted we keep him alive, despite understanding how dangerous he could be."

Rory grunted. "That stone has already fallen. At least we've done most of our meetings in recent days here instead of your office, Ivor. Verena scan the tower and the rest of the palace to identify the location of the concealed speakstone and to make sure there aren't any others."

Connor said, "I might be able to help with that too. I discovered that I'm now able to overhear speakstone conversations."

Most of the team had heard that disturbing news, although the Mhortair had not. They quickly grasped the potential security risks of having the queen overhear what they were saying.

General Wolfram, who was still running fingers through his windblown mustaches to straighten them said, "When you discover the speakstones, I request taking charge of them. They offer a significant opportunity to pass carefully prepared misinformation."

Shona said, "Of course, General. Such an intelligence windfall is too good an opportunity to miss."

"Especially if the enemy has learned enough through them to consider the information trustworthy," Wolfram said with a predatory smile.

Rory said, "I don't have a mind for those games. Part of me still wants to be a simple bash fighter."

Verena said, "I now understand your love of bash fighting. I wish the worst challenge we faced was coordinating the world's biggest bash fight."

Rory smiled wistfully. "Aye, lass, that would be grand indeed."

Wolfram said, "Until that day arrives, we'll deal with what we have. We will most likely call upon each of you to participate in our misinformation campaign. For this to work we need Craigroy or whoever is listening for him to believe the stones are as yet undiscovered."

Connor was impressed but not surprised that Wolfram would immediately begin planning such an elaborate hoax. No doubt Ilse would assist. Even back around Alasdair they had demonstrated the importance of gathering intelligence and using it against their enemies.

Verena had gifted to Connor a speakstone and asked him to keep it with him to remind him of her. She had failed to inform him that in the meantime it was capturing all of the conversations he had with Shona, General Carbrey, and everyone else. The Grandurians had known everything they were planning.

Shona tapped a parchment on the table in front of her and said, "Our informant also shared insights into how the queen unleashed such terrible destruction upon Jagdish."

The Mhortair perked up at that, and Ivor said, "I hope it'll help, because we're very short on time. The part of the message I've read so far also shared news that the various cohorts of the queen's armies have been gathering in Crann and orders have just been issued for them to marshal and prepare to move against Merkland in force."

The announcement was not a surprise, but it still blanketed the room in a new somber quiet. Connor felt deeply frustrated that they didn't have just a little more time. He felt convinced that he was close to proving he could help people establish new affinities. If he could, then they could swell their army significantly in a matter of weeks.

They would still need to train those new Petralists. Without that training they would face battle at a significant disadvantage. Verena had demonstrated that in her recent duel with Shona. Although she had performed remarkably well, without all of her mechanicals to assist, Shona would have pounded her. Any other new Petralist he helped would not have the benefits of her mechanicals and experience.

Shona added, "Our report suggests the queen herself may be journeying to Crann to take command of her forces and lead them against us."

The already somber mood in the room turned grim. Facing a much larger and more powerful army was pretty much standard practice for them. If not for the queen leading her people, Connor felt pretty confident they could defeat her army, no matter their size and makeup.

Aifric and the other Mhortair did not share his worry. They exchanged excited murmurs, their expressions turning eager.

Mistress Four said, "This will be our opportunity to strike."

"Perhaps," Kilian said but his expression was more thoughtful than enthusiastic. He knew better than anyone the challenges of confronting his mother.

General Rory raised a hand to calm the swell in conversation around the table. "Before we get bogged down in detailed battle planning, let's discuss the other information provided in the communique. With any luck it'll shed some much-needed light on what the queen did to Jagdish. We need to prevent her from doing the same to Merkland."

Everyone listened intently to Shona. "Apparently the queen did utilize a sculpted serpentinite stone in that attack."

It was good to get confirmation that what he had seen was indeed a sculpted stone, but Connor glanced at Aifric and her two Mhortair companions and asked, "I still don't understand how that allowed her to destroy everything. Have you come up with any new ideas?"

They shook their heads. Shona pointed at the paper. "There's more here, but it does not exactly make sense to me. See if any of you understand it. I'm hoping you, Master Evander, at least can gleam useful insights. Apparently, the stone had been buried along with one of her powerful ancient servants in elfonnel form, who's been slumbering for centuries at a convergence of something called the sylfaen."

Verena perked up. "I heard Water mention that term, but don't understand it."

"She mentioned it to me too," Connor said. "Explained that it's some kind of vast energy that encircles the planet."

"What's the convergence?" Hamish asked.

"I don't know," Connor admitted.

Evander started nodding slowly, as if he was making connections in that big head of his. Connor dearly hoped so.

Shona said, "Your explanation helps, Connor, and there's more about convergence here." She frowned and added, "But this part still gets a little weird."

"Let's see if we can work through it," Kilian suggested.

Shona scanned the page and read, "Apparently the sylfaen touches down onto the world at these convergence points. They're scattered around the globe and funnel energy that sustains and supports life." She looked up, frowning, but Kilian gestured her to continue.

"That energy is dispersed through the planet. Okay, here's the part I don't get. By burying slumbering elfonnel at these convergence points with master-sculpted stones, she claims they filter some of that power into frequencies accessible to Petralists. The power gathers in quarries where it's absorbed by power-grade stone to be tapped by Petralists. Have any of you heard of anything like this before?"

It made sense to Connor. He'd seen the red and green energies, as had Kilian and Evander, but he hadn't understood how the energy of the sylfaen was filtered at convergence points by elfonnel and sculpted stones. That part was brilliant, although he couldn't imagine how anyone had figured that out.

"Did your mother build that system to create Petralists?" Connor asked in an awed tone.

Kilian was also nodding slowly, his expression amazed. "I think so. Some of the off-hand comments she made now make sense.

"Why did she never teach you any of this?" Aifric asked, placing a hand on his.

"I can only guess she feared I might have messed with it." He smiled, his eyes flashing for a second with white flames. "I was known to act impulsively at times in my youth."

Evander guffawed, laughing louder than Connor had imagined he could. "That's an understatement big enough to swallow Donleavy."

Connor exchanged grins with Verena. He bet Kilian had been wild. With such powerful parents, the greatest Builder as his younger sister, and both Evander and Tallan as nephews, he'd almost have to be. He really wanted to ask Evander to share some tales.

Kilian scowled at the red-faced, laughing Evander, whose mirth was spreading around the table despite the very serious nature of the conversation. It seemed impolite not to join in while Evander's deep, booming laughter shook the room like muffled thunder.

"Enough, or I'll share the story of when you and Tallan tried rerouting the Macantact to avoid taking baths," Kilian warned.

Evander actually managed to look chagrined, an expression that Connor had never seen on his face. While the big man coughed, trying to swallow his laughter, Kilian seemed to think pretending the outburst hadn't happened would make everyone forget about it.

He looked to Connor and asked, "Have you sensed these convergence points? I have no direct experience with them."

Connor had witnessed many amazing new things, and as he considered the list, he felt anew a deep sense of wonder. His affinities were such an integral part of him that he couldn't imagine living without them, and yet as much as he knew about them, he was still learning more. He marveled that so much truth could be woven together into layer after layer that had resisted their efforts to peel back for so long. Maybe they were finally getting to the deepest secrets.

He asked, "Any idea what a convergence of sylfaen would feel like? I've felt the red and green frequencies of power, but haven't sensed where they might be coming from."

Evander spoke softly, his brows furrowed and his expression one of deep concentration. "The first glimmer of dawn, filtered through the clouds, is sufficient to cast back the blankets of even the darkest night, and the greatest secrets begin to yield their fruit when the lock is turned and the door of the vault cracks open."

That was excellent Sentry speak, but not as indecipherable as most. Connor actually felt like he grasped the heart of what Evander was trying to say.

Most of the rest of the team merely stared at Evander with long-suffering looks, but Captain Ilse looked excited. "You've made new connections between items from your vault research, haven't you?"

Hamish muttered, "It's so good to have a translator."

Evander nodded and spoke in the slow, deliberate way he used when using unfiltered words. "Indeed, Captain. I am thinking of a reference heretofore obscure. A rare page written in my grandmother's own hand. She stated, '*The great duty of the monarch is not in managing an unruly populace and dragging them ever resistant toward enlightenment, but the maintenance of the ramverk. Only its stable filters ensure access to the sylfaen. It must be maintained at all costs or my dynasty will fail*.'"

"Ramverk?" Verena asked, glancing at Connor, who shrugged and looked to Kilian, whose expression had turned thoughtful again.

"I've heard my mother mention ramverk, although she never explained it. In the context of our conversation, my guess is that ramverk is what she calls the process of harvesting power from these convergence points."

"Almost like a higher form of Builder construct," Verena exclaimed excitedly. "Don't you see, what she's doing with stones and elfonnel to harness power, to filter it and make it available is so similar to what Builders do. I bet Kristin started figuring it out."

"That may be possible," Kilian said. "She seemed to understand things about wielding Petralist powers that she should not have."

"And she built the higher constructs like Kirstin's Defense that pushed the limits. What if she was trying to access one of those convergence points?"

"Would that be good or bad?" Connor asked.

Her good humor faded and she shrugged. "I don't know, but I feel like we're right on the verge of finally understanding important truths."

"Me too," he agreed, taking her hand and squeezing it.

"I wonder if that factored into my mother's decision to execute her," Kilian said.

"That would reinforce how important these facts are," Verena said eagerly.

"I hope they're important, but I don't see how it helps us stop the queen and her army," Hamish said with a frown. He gestured at Evander with a hard breadstick he'd produced from a pocket. "No offense, but I had sort of hoped your next breakthrough would be something like, *'I finally understand. My mother's weakness is toasted mallows.'* or something like that."

"Mallows?" Evander asked, curious.

"Don't get him started," Verena warned.

Shona said, "Back to the matter at hand. This may help. Apparently by utilizing that serpentinite stone, the queen tapped elevated levels of power beyond what even she can normally achieve. Something about rising into the green. Apparently she believes all of her affinities are permanently enhanced as a result."

General Wolfram blew out his mustaches and muttered, "The last thing we need is for her to continue growing stronger."

Shona continued reading. "And apparently by using and consuming that stone she did indeed somehow sever the serpentinite affinity."

Mistress Four looked like she thought that made sense, but Connor frowned. "She severed it from the lower power source, but not from the green."

Shona shrugged and gestured with the parchment. "According to this, the queen considers serpentinite all but useless even to her until she can get another stone sculpted and bury it again with her servant. That's supposed to restore the affinity over a period of years."

The look of hope on Mistress Four's face faded to dejection as she realized there would be no restoration of her affinity in the near term. Connor wondered what her bridges and islands would look like in her affinityscape. If his attempt to make new bridges failed to help establish new affinities, maybe her broken affinity might give him additional insights.

"I'm amazed that our contact gleaned so much information," Ivor said, saluting the parchment in Shona's hand. "Her contributions might prove the deciding edge in this war."

Connor agreed. He loved his Aunt Ailsa and marveled at her success. He couldn't imagine standing right in the queen's presence for months but remaining undiscovered.

"So how does this help us?" Hamish asked again, looking frustrated.

Shona only looked at Connor and raised one fine eyebrow. "Any thoughts?"

Everyone looked at him expectantly, as if he could pull the answer out of his hat. He should've worn a hat. That might've helped.

"I think we should figure out how to find this ramverk. Maybe that will help us figure something out," he offered.

"Good idea," Kilian said.

Ivor added, "So, how do you propose to do that?"

They continued watching him, waiting expectantly, as if the fact that he'd ascended again gave him all the answers. Even Kilian and Evander were looking to him. No doubt Evander had more things to say, but seemed willing to wait until Connor made the attempt to find the ramverk or a convergence point.

Connor was actually excited to give it a try but could not waste such an opportunity. "To make this work I'm going to need some bacon. And a tub of winter's heart."

CHAPTER SEVENTY-NINE

The Power of Thinking Food

No one actually believed Connor needed more food before beginning the hunt for the ramverk, but it was mid-afternoon, and Hamish reminded them that they needed sustenance to properly enjoy dinner in a few hours. Shona protested, but was overruled by Rory and Ivor, so she finally relented and ordered platters of food from the kitchens.

Merkland was still too battered to be cooking many desserts, so Ivor ordered a couple cases of smashpacked sweetbreads. No one in Merkland had started making Winter's Heart, and Hamish promised to rectify that by asking Jean to send a flight with one of his spare research kitchens.

"Research kitchens?" Ilse asked with a laugh. "How did you justify that?"

"And how are you still able to fit into your battle suit?" Wolfram added with a grin.

Hamish tried to look properly offended as he exclaimed, "Hey, without my research, we wouldn't have delivered so many smashpacked meals to Merkland."

"He has a point," Shona offered.

Rory added with a smile, "Although in reviewing the lists, I couldn't help but notice that you sent twice as many sweetbreads and desserts as you did main courses."

"Of course. Fighting troops need energy and hope. Desserts and sweetbreads deliver both."

Smiling, Kilian said, "While we await refreshments, are there any other points we need to discuss from our latest intelligence report?"

Ivor shook his head, and Rory said, "Wasn't that enough?"

"More than enough," Connor agreed.

He spent a few minutes discussing with Kilian and Evander where they'd felt the red and greed energies strongest, but none of them could pinpoint where they might have sensed a convergence of power.

Verena circled the table to join Anika. She asked something, and Anika grinned very girlishly and produced several small pieces of white cloth. Verena gushed over them, and Ilse rose to join them. Shona scooted her chair closer, and even Mistress Four rose to join the women. Connor frowned at Kilian, nodding to the knot of women who began chatting excitedly in hushed tones.

"Samples of bridal veil cloth," Kilian explained.

Evander surprised Connor by adding, "Autumn breezes warn of the journey of seasons, but no day contains enough light to witness the bride's work complete."

Connor frowned, but Hamish chuckled. "I think I get that one." At Connor's surprised look he shrugged. "Jean's in touch with Anika daily to talk about the wedding. Her dress is long finished, but there's only weeks before the wedding, and there's still so many details, it's good Rory's got access to an entire army to help get it all done."

Wedding planning seemed to affect even the most warrior-minded women in ways that Connor didn't understand. Seeing Verena so excited about Anika's wedding, made him happy, but also a bit nervous. She glanced up to meet his gaze, and lifted one eyebrow for a second before returning to her conversation. That look communicated volumes.

She definitely wanted to have 'the talk' soon. He felt powerful, conflicting emotions about that. He wanted to wed Verena more than anything, but would that expose her to even more danger from Queen Dreokt or her agents?

Besides, the thought of planning a wedding was overwhelming. He had not ascended through nearly enough thresholds to figure out that incomprehensible jumble of tradition and social norms.

Luckily the food arrived before she could return to his side and start that conversation. The Merkland cooks might not have winter's heart, but they had a lot of bacon. They even managed to include a couple trays of huge cookies. The main dishes were simple, but well seasoned. One platter held long strips of thin-cut beef, marinated in a delicious spicy honey sauce. Another dish included pork cutlets baked in thick gravy. They'd been slow-cooked to perfection, so tender each bite seemed to melt in Connor's mouth.

A venison roast came next, but Connor almost didn't get any of it. By the time it passed Shona and the generals, then Hamish, it was already half gone. Ilse took a huge serving, and the Mhortair dug in with so much gusto, Connor barely snatched one thick slice. It had been roasted on a spit and basted with gravy and a subtle mixture of spices that made the taste seem to erupt through his mouth, even though he wasn't tapping quartzite to his tongue.

He managed to grab the cookie tray while the others were distracted by a platter full of small, roasted hens. After munching down seven still-warm cookies, he began wishing for some chilled milk to go with them. That's when he noted Mistress Four staring at him and Hamish with open-mouthed awe. Hamish was happily consuming half a loaf of bread, while grasping a roasted hen in his other hand.

Connor was feeling full and discreetly tapped his newfound glutton crafting talent. He wasn't sure when he'd have to fleshcraft again, but he didn't doubt he would need to, and he needed to store up extra energy. He applied glutton crafting to Hamish's stomach too.

Hamish grinned and saluted with the half-eaten hen. "That is the best affinity I've ever heard of."

"Don't overdo it. I've got work to do and can't save your stomach again," Connor told him.

Hamish sighed, looking disappointed. He stared longingly at the last huge piece of Althing chocolate cake sitting alone and unclaimed on a nearby platter.

Verena didn't miss the exchange. She leaned close to Connor and asked, "What are you not telling me?"

"I'll tell you later."

"If you tell me now, can I finish off that piece of cake Hamish is making moon eyes over?"

"Give me a kiss and I'll eat that cake for you."

"No, I want it."

"How about a kiss for a cake," he replied. They'd both get something they wanted then.

She did not look like she entirely believed him and made sure to slide the large piece of cake a little farther out of his reach before kissing him lightly on the lips. Through that contact, he reached through to her stomach and converted her food into energy.

She sat back, eyes wide in wonder, glancing down at herself. He could feel the energy coursing through her and grinned at her surprise. "Like Hamish always says, sometimes you have to eat yourself to the point of no return in order to learn something new."

Verena saluted Hamish with her fork, then plunged it into the soft cake. He watched in pitiful silence as she closed her eyes, chewing slowly, and didn't even offer to share a bite with Connor.

"That was the only fresh cake," Hamish said.

"You've got an entire crate full of smashpacked desserts," Ilse said with a laugh.

Hamish grinned. "Yes we do."

He stood and went to the crate of smashpacked desserts and selected six of them.

"How is such feasting possible?" Commander Six asked.

Aifric grinned and said, "Don't ever accept a food challenge from those two."

"Don't stuff yourself into a stupor, Connor," Kilian warned.

Hamish chuckled. "I think that's actually impossible for Connor now."

Connor wasn't about to share the glutton crafting secret with the rest of them. There wasn't enough food left for them all to try it. Besides, he had work to do. So he said, "I'm going to see if I can find the convergence point."

"Where are you going to go?" Verena asked as she licked the last of the chocolate from her fork, somehow making the very unladylike move seem dignified.

Connor tapped the side of his head. "Nowhere physically, but hopefully pretty far using my elemental senses."

"Good luck," she said, kissing him again. Her lips tasted like chocolate.

Smiling, he closed his eyes and tapped his tertiary affinities. As the connections became strong, he appeared within the gray, formless expanse of his own mindscape. Surprisingly Earth appeared first, rising from the insubstantial mist of the floor with as much epic grandeur as Evander could ever muster.

"Are you sure you and Evander aren't related?"

Earth grinned. "Evander is a talented child and although I cannot walk openly with him as I do with you, he has grasped many truths with remarkable clarity."

"Then how do you know he's not ready to see more of you?"

"Sometimes wisdom lies in silence."

Connor could understand that, but still felt convinced they could find a way around the elemental hesitation. Evander and Kilian both knew so much more than he did. Surely they wouldn't do something stupid with more knowledge.

"Do you know why I reached out to you now?" he asked.

Earth nodded, again confirming that somehow the elementals seemed to understand his thoughts as clearly as if they were tapping chert. Maybe it was because he was inviting them into his mind. He was not sure how to prevent them from doing so, and didn't want to risk offending them by asking about it. He needed their help too much to risk it.

Water appeared next to Earth then, materializing in an instant. She wore a beautiful gown of midnight blue, with a subtle pattern of waves flowing across its fabric. Her long hair had turned a deep green and hung in an unrestrained sheet down her back. Her expression looked stern, her eyes gray, like the sea before a storm.

Fire appeared on the other side of Earth, wearing black trousers and a linen shirt that looked charred. Tiny flames flickered all over his torso, and his eyes were pools of white heat. Air settled down from above, her gown a soft blue, like late afternoon sky if seen through a sheen of wispy clouds.

Connor started to smile in greeting, but Water said sternly, "You return seeking boons of knowledge, yet you spurned our latest counsel immediately after promising to temper your tongue."

"We have given much that has been treated with contempt," Fire added, little blue flames leaking out his mouth before evaporating with tiny hisses.

Not the reception Connor had hoped for. He'd worried they would be upset that he'd shared information about them with Kilian and the others, but how could he not have? He felt a stirring of frustration and said, "I'm trying, but I don't understand the reasons why you placed those restrictions on me, and my friends needed to know."

"I told you his mind would leak," Fire said to Water.

She made a shushing gesture, her intimidating gaze holding Connor's. "Understanding comes through study and experience, and by trust."

"I'm trying to study. I trust you, and I hope you trust me," Connor replied.

"You have not demonstrated reasons for our trust," Fire said, still frowning.

"And you haven't entrusted me with what you need from me," Connor retorted. He probably shouldn't push, but he lacked time for subtlety.

"Why should we share this our dire need with one who will not hold our confidence?" Water demanded.

Connor felt so frustrated that they were placing those restrictions on him, but he was not in a bargaining position of strength. They claimed they wanted his help, but he desperately needed theirs.

So he took a deep breath and said as humbly as he could, "I am very sorry I broke your confidence. I promise not to share with anyone, not even Verena or Kilian, anything else you teach me until you give me leave to do so. Please, I need your help, and I need to understand how I can help you in return."

Earth slid slowly around Connor, his legs not moving, his thick arms folded over his enormous chest. He was dressed in a long, leather jacket, much like Evander often wore. "Insanity for humans is repeating an action again, but expecting different results. Insanity for us is giving without receiving."

That he chose to speak in a convoluted way that reminded Connor so much of Evander offered Connor a flicker of hope. "Please give me another chance."

"A chance with a test," Fire said, crimson and orange flames billowing around his face, casting his eyes into deep shadow. The effect was both mesmerizing and intimidating.

"Very well," Water said with a nod. "You are a child who must grow quickly for your own survival and for ours. We can guide you, but you must allow us to do so."

"How is your survival at stake?" Connor asked. He couldn't imagine anything actually harming the elementals. They were forces of nature, weren't they?

"Survival is more than existence," Air said, her long tresses beginning to billow around her head from an invisible wind. Beautiful silvery streaks began sliding through her hair, as if slender clouds were passing through it.

"I don't understand," Connor admitted. He felt lost, and that frustrated him. He'd finally ascended, finally established a bridge to communicate with these incredible beings, but he felt like he was missing entire layers to the conversation that were vital for him to grasp.

Water said, "We are prisoner, Connor, held fast with shackles that lock us between the sylfaen and your world. Human attempts to access the sylfaen prompted our awakening, but humans have failed us every time we attempted to walk among them, and thus we languish in eternal prison, unable to accomplish the potential of our existence."

For a moment, Connor wasn't sure what to say. He wanted to ask about that awakening process, but didn't want to distract them. The elements were so amazing, so powerful, he struggled to imagine them imprisoned. What could do that to them?

"How can Petralists access your power, then? And what can I do to help?" he asked.

"We are not powerless, but we are restrained from walking freely," Water said, as if that made perfect sense. "We can share drops of our power with humans, but none have grasped our true forms. Not even you can yet see all that we are."

"I'm glad I've gotten to meet you," he said truthfully.

She smiled, looking so beautiful, so regal, he was filled with pride to be considered their friend. She said, "If you allow us to prepare you, we can show you how to help free us."

That was still far too vague, and some of his earlier unease returned, but he squashed it. He couldn't further damage the frail trust he was building with them. So he said, "I am eager to learn more. Will you help me find the ramverk and the convergence of sylfaen?"

She dashed his hopes by shaking her head. The other elements moved behind her, watching him with pleasant but unrelenting expressions. "We shared part of our secret with you, but can do no more until you prove yourself by protecting it from all others."

"I promise I will, but I need help."

"The road without mountains is soon despised for its ease," Earth said.

That wasn't helpful. "How can I find it when not even Kilian knows what it is?"

"You have the tools before you, and the resources for success," Water said with an encouraging smile that somehow eased some of his frustration, even though it was a pretty useless answer.

"Good luck. Don't waste too much time. You don't have that much left," Fire said, saluting then fading from his mindscape. The others followed, leaving Connor alone.

When he opened his eyes, he found Verena leaning close, one hand on his, expression concerned. "What's wrong? Why are you frowning?"

The rest of the company was still gathered close, watching intently. Connor hated giving them bad news, but sighed and said, "I spoke with the elementals, but they either can't or won't show me the ramverk. We're on our own."

"That's not very helpful," Hamish said, popping a pair of smashpacked cubes into his mouth. One was black, and Connor recognized it as a full Althing chocolate cake. The other was a mottled mixture of tans, browns, and yellows, a newly developed meal made from smashpacking thin-crusted breads, with layers of cheeses and meats between. That one was best when heated for a moment in one of Hamish's tiny stoves before eating.

"What exactly did they say?" Kilian asked.

Connor hesitated. He couldn't share the intriguing revelation that the elements considered themselves somehow prisoners. He bet Kilian and Evander could help him decipher that one, but sensed that if he shared it the elementals would refuse to teach him more.

So he only said, "They told me that I already have the resources to find the ramverk."

"What resources?" Verena asked.

"We already finished eating," Hamish agreed.

"I know, but there's got to be a way," Connor insisted.

"We know the ramverk is out there, that those convergence points exist," General Wolfram pointed out.

"We just need to figure out how to sense them," Kilian said.

Connor nodded, deep in thought. "I can sense the red and green frequencies when I focus on them, but I've never actually tried extending my senses along the currents to try figuring out where they came from. I'm not sure I can reach that far or that I'd recognize a convergence point."

"Maybe we need to think about it differently," Verena suggested.

Hamish saluted her with another dessert cube. "Right! Sort of like when you're a kid, you believe the propaganda that desserts can only be eaten after dinner. Eventually you realize desserts are always out there, and you don't have to limit yourself just because it's the normal approach to food."

Verena laughed. "You're the only one who can explain the deepest arcane mysteries through dessert."

Hamish shrugged. "Like that really smart guy says in that book Jean told me about a few weeks ago, *All truth can be kneaded into one giant sweetbread.*"

"That is not what she quoted," Verena protested with a laugh. Connor smiled. He appreciated Hamish's ability to misremember things so remarkably.

Evander said through a smile, "A child is never satisfied until it succeeds in walking on its own, but it is a rare yearling colt that approaches its first rider as an opportunity to reach freedom."

Connor glanced at Verena, who looked as confused as he felt, then at Kilian, who simply shrugged. Connor had started thinking he was mastering the trick to interpreting Evander's Sentry speak, but he wasn't sure what the big man was going for.

Ilse leaned forward, her expression thoughtful. "I might not have phrased it that way. Hamish's argument is indeed a bit doughy, but he has a point."

"Please don't encourage him by speaking bakery-talk," Verena warned.

Ilse smiled. "I'll tread carefully. Hamish's attempt to consider desserts in a deeper way reminded me of how we can use summoned creatures to improve our own senses."

"I did notice when I summoned that squirrel that my senses were sharper," Connor admitted.

"Exactly," she said. "What if we could sharpen our energy-discerning senses through a summoning?"

"What animal can you summon that senses energy?" Verena asked.

"Not an animal, but a different approach to tapping elemental energy," Kilian said, giving Ilse a little salute of respect. "Very clever, Captain."

Connor had gotten so used to needing the elements in his mind to access their power that he had overlooked the fact that he could probably still draw upon some of it without calling them into his mind. That's what he'd done before his second threshold.

"So you're suggesting I summon a creature entirely out of elements?" The idea sounded sort of like what Harley had done when she summoned that mini-elfonnel serpent that had killed Lukas and crippled Ilse, but he'd never bring that memory up in Ilse's presence.

"All summonings include the elements. We just wrap them in the illusion of flesh. When you summoned the squirrel, you gave it form using clay, but it was your mind that assumed it must have better senses than your own," Ilse said. "Somehow you molded it in that way."

"Fascinating point," Wolfram said, stroking his mustaches.

"Or I tapped quartzite to my senses without realizing it," Connor suggested. "That would have improved my senses too."

"Perhaps, but I suggest you create a summoning with a focus that will improve your ability to see energy," she said.

Connor loved the unorthodox approach. Ilse was so clever, she didn't need to rely on thresholds to accelerate her mind.

How to make it happen, though? While he mulled over the idea, he absorbed a little obsidian and tapped it. Verena's laughter sounded through his mind, easing his tension as his thoughts accelerated. He also gestured at the half-empty crate of smashpacked desserts. "I need thinking food."

Hamish didn't even need to reach for the crate, but produced eight smashpacked desserts from various pockets. After considering them for a couple seconds, he selected one and handed it over. "This is an entire batch of cookie dough, smashpacked and then baked."

Connor popped it into his mouth and tapped a little quartzite to his tongue. His taste buds awakened and flavor burst across his mouth like the rising of the sun. The dessert was made from his favorite shortbread cookies, with a touch of honey and nuts, and the taste was magnified a hundredfold by so much of it being smashpacked together before baking.

Under the rush of sugar euphoria, his obsidian-enhanced thoughts accelerated even further, pushing him into the realm of pure inspiration. Suddenly he knew what he had to do.

He chewed slowly, savoring the sweet, crunchy, sugary perfection of that smashpacked cookie cube as he considered the new ideas filtering through the sugar haze. "I've got it."

Hamish nodded approval. "The way of the cookie for the win every time."

As Connor closed his eyes he heard Ivor say softly, "Send a dozen of those up to my office."

Chapter Eighty

Sometimes You Need to Look at Your Problems in a Different Light

Connor popped a fresh piece of marble into his mouth and wedged it under his tongue with a practiced motion. He still had plenty of soapstone in his bloodstream. He tapped both affinities, but just a tiny bit, envisioning them the way he used to, as doors set back to back, facing opposite directions. Water was filled with a tiny tempest, while Fire's door was rimmed with orange flame.

"Why do you attempt to limit us like this?" Water asked in Connor's mind, although she did not appear in his mindscape.

"You told me I'm on my own. I need to access some of your power, but don't want to disturb you."

"Very well," she said, but her tone suggested she didn't entirely like the idea of him tapping their power without the close connection they'd enjoyed lately. Maybe she shouldn't have told him to figure it out on his own, then. Luckily she did not protest. Fire said nothing, so Connor figured he was okay with the arrangement.

As the sure, steady strength of water flowed through him, spicy flavor grew in his mouth. He was grateful that tapping marble no longer burned, and enjoyed its vibrant spicy taste. He'd overlooked that of late, so distracted by conversations with the living elementals.

Tapping both, he combined them and sought the raw, fundamental powers of strum and magnis. His senses expanded and he felt faint currents of strum around him. He sensed no strong magnis fields anywhere nearby, but could pinpoint the location of every steel item in the room.

Gathering the power of strum and magnis into a small, intense ball of energy in his chest, he drove it out exactly the same way he always did when summoning. This time, instead of directing that energy into a pile of clay using granite, he tapped limestone and called forth a globe of absolute darkness. He drove the dual power of strum and magnis into that globe and willed it to life.

The air above the table in front of him burst into light, with hundreds of tiny rainbows erupting into view, one atop another so fast they hung in the air, the colors building and deepening beyond anything he'd seen without quartzite. Hamish gaped, dropping a fork he'd stuck in his mouth in lieu of another sweetbread. The others gasped, and Verena breathed, "Beautiful."

It was beautiful, but it wasn't working. The construct fought him, pushing against his control like an unruly animal, refusing to enter a cage. Connor pushed harder, but the energy rippled around his mental fingers, threatening to slip away entirely. Bits of light erupted across the room, bouncing wildly and sending his friends ducking, their expressions of wonder fading to concern.

The process was just so weird, so unfocused. Trying to combine limestone with strum and magnis was unusual enough, but doing it in an amorphous sphere was just too much. He realized he was going to fail.

So he envisioned the globe of darkness as a miniature pedra.

Immediately the wild light show winked out, replaced by absolute darkness that flowed into the shape of a double-jawed flying monster, no longer than Connor's forearm. It was so dark, it seemed to suck light into it, and the room noticeably darkened. As it took shape, the forces of strum and magnis poured into it and bonded with it, becoming the most unique summoning Connor had ever heard of.

The air cracked with a tiny thunderbolt, and Connor smelled a faint scent of cool breezes through evergreens. The black pedra settled to the tabletop and crouched, eyeing the crowd of gaping people.

Connor laughed, exulting. "Yes!"

He petted the pedra. Its skin was slick, as if coated with a thin layer of oil, and he grinned, but had to look away. Staring at the summoned pedra too long made his eyes ache.

"Wow," Hamish grinned, leaning close to study the pedra. It opened its big outer jaw flaps to reveal the smaller inner jaws with razor-sharp fangs and growled. He poked at sweetbread at it, and it snapped its jaws closed over the bread, cleanly severing half of it.

"What affinities did you use?" Verena asked, her eyes glowing with wonder.

"Strum and magnis, wrapped in limestone." Connor felt a surge of pride at the approving looks from his friends.

Even Evander looked pleased and said, "May we find illumination of truth upon the wings of darkness."

Kilian reached out to stroke one sable wing. "Very good, Connor. A clever choice."

"I hope so. In my last ascension I noticed I can see light no one else can. I'm hoping through the senses of this creature I can see the sylfaen and the convergence points."

"And feel them through their interaction with strum and magnis," Ilse said with a nod.

"Well, give it a go," Ivor encouraged.

Hamish said, "And I'll track it with one of mini sightscreen flyers from the Bumblebee."

"Good idea," Verena said. "Project the image onto the wall."

"Bumblebee?" Mistress Four asked with a frown.

Connor let Verena explain about their flock of tiny, remotely controlled flying craft that could project views onto nearby walls through paired stones that she and Hamish controlled. He closed his eyes and focused on the invisible link tethering the summoned pedra to him. His consciousness rushed into it, and suddenly he was that creature.

The world lurched to his new point of view, staring up at the huge humans gathered around the flat wooden table. Pedra-Connor's senses expanded many times, but did not threaten to overwhelm him like when he tapped quartzite. He tasted hundreds of scents, including his friends, and cataloged them without having to think about it. He could have listed the contents of the crates of smashpacked cubes, and knew exactly what everyone had eaten from the scents still clinging to their faces and clothing.

Sounds seemed exceptionally sharp, but he couldn't hear as far as he could with quartzite. That didn't bother him, because he was more focused on what he could see. Light streamed past in stunning colors. The air was full to bursting with the spectrum of light far broader than any living pedra, any living person, or even any other Pathfinder could see. In addition to the visible spectrum, he noted streams of light ranging deep into realms beyond any physical sight.

Strum and magnis filled him, giving him life and fueling his senses as fully as limestone. Through those primal forces, he recognized streams of charged light in various frequencies pouring past. Physical light bounced around the room until it reached him. None of it bounced away, but was absorbed by his absolutely black skin, its energy drawn into his body to replenish him. The stronger, invisible streams of light passed right through people and objects, and often right through walls, although most bounced off of the heavy stones.

He absorbed it all, and that process helped him understand it. He sensed how strum and magnis influenced those various wavelengths of light and energy, and gained vital insights into how to reproduce those wavelengths should he need to. He sensed great power in them, and grasped how to increase power by increasing the energy but decreasing the wavelength of any light he chose to emit. If he pushed the limits far enough, he sensed vast potential.

That unique view of the world was fascinating, but not what he sought. While the humans talked in their slow way, he gathered himself and leaped into the air, tiny wings flapping powerfully. He circled the room a couple of times and roared with the joy of flight.

Okay, that was one aspect of being a tiny flying creature that wasn't nearly as epic as everything else he was experiencing. His voice came out as a high-pitched squeak that made some of the humans chuckle, and at least one of the females exclaim, "Oh, it's so cute!"

One of the humans noticed that the window was closed and drew it open. He flashed through it, restraining the urge to try roaring again. Next time, he'd apply a little quartzite to the mix too so he could control his voice. He'd roar so loud he'd shatter windows.

As Pedra-Connor ascended rapidly above the great palace and the sprawling expanse of the city, he forgot about the wonders of flight, the miracle of sensing wind currents and riding them. His eyes were drawn upward so far he would have fallen over backward if not for the benefit of his long, serpentine neck.

The sky was ablaze with light, packed even denser than in that conference room. And high above the tangled mass of beams of light bouncing all around shone pure white brilliance. He absorbed all wavelengths, but a vast river of energy high above emitted more than he could ever consume. In frequencies beyond the ken of mortal men, light filled the expanse. It rushed overhead, but remained aloft and aloof from the surface.

The sylfaen.

Pedra-Connor roared again, not caring how squeaky it sounded. He couldn't restrain his glee. His gamble had paid off! He could see it.

The sylfaen really existed, like a vast river of energy flowing high above the planet. It was beautiful and enticing. If he could reach it, how much power could he absorb? How many secrets could he understand?

He beat his little wings as hard and fast as he could, grateful that he was not limited to the frailty of flesh and blood. While elemental force filled him and fresh energy absorbed into his jet-black skin, he could fly with all his might without ever growing tired. So he drew deep from his reserves and shot into the sky like a living black arrow.

In seconds he left Merkland far behind, rising thousands, then tens of thousands of feet. The land fell away beneath him, but he continued to climb. The air became thin, but he didn't need air, and his wings could still find purchase, pulling against the invisible frequencies of light and energy that fueled him. So he continued, higher and higher, far beyond the limit of even the most powerful Builder mechanical.

As if from a great distance, he heard Hamish's voice. "I've lost him. He's just too fast, climbing too high."

The rest of the conversation faded away. A tiny part of him wondered if he should return to explain what he was seeing, but he decided they could wait. Reaching the sylfaen was all that mattered.

As he continued to climb, the land spread below him like an enormous map on General Wolfram's table. He flapped his outer jaws with the wonder of seeing the land so open. Not even in the Hawk had they seen so much. He picked out mountains that he recognized, from Donleavy far to the south to the gleaming white walls of Merkland directly beneath him, shrunk to a tiny glowing pearl.

Looking north, he spotted the vast trading city of Altkalen in Granadure. Farther still, he could see all the way up into Varvakis, to a lake so vast it seemed like an inland sea. At the eastern edges of his vision he noticed the mountains of Althing, with Dagmanson nestled in the arms of one of them and the Three Sisters flowing south. To the west he could look far into Ravinder and even down into the endless sands of the Sehrazad desert. Nearly the entire continent spread below him, but the sylfaen seemed just as far above him as when he started his climb.

So Pedra-Connor paused, sensing he'd never reach it that way. He felt a deep sense of frustration, but a bright point of pure white light drew his eye. It was centered over the ruins of the Carraig. Other points of light began to appear, spreading across the continent like glowing pins. One was situated in southern Obrion, and Connor guessed that was the quarry where Evander mentioned he had defeated a slumbering elfonnel and taken a stone from him.

Another was far closer, appearing between Crann and Merkland, while several more appeared in Granadure. One was located near Altkalen, while another was located in the mountains near the capital of Edderitz. Still others were spread into the nations of the Arishat League, but as he studied the various points of light he noticed slight differences.

The ones in the Arishat League were all pure white, but several of those scattered throughout Obrion and Granadure actually emitted faint variations in color.

"The convergence points," Connor guessed. He heard his own voice from his far-distant body speak the words in a faint whisper.

Verena's voice sounded close to his human ears, and despite the distance he heard every syllable. "Where are you? What are you seeing?"

It was too hard to speak that way. He sensed that if he got distracted by a conversation he could easily lose his connection to the pedra, so said, "Soon."

Then focused entirely on his pedra form. Now that he was hovering, concentrating, he noticed that the pure-white sylfaen river of energy was made up of bands of every color, mixed together into that white whole. It flowed slowly past, far overhead, filling the expanse of the heavens, but he sensed its power like the hints of a distant breeze. The sight was awe-inspiring and a little intimidating. He'd never imagined everything surrounded by a vast blanket of raw energy.

Rainbow-colored whirlwinds of light extended down from that unbroken blanket of sylfaen like funnel clouds in an enormous storm. Narrow and delicate-looking but clearly containing vast energy, they touched down upon the ground. The connections at those convergence points seemed as dainty as ballerinas dancing on their toes.

He had to see.

Pedra-Connor tipped into a dive. With gravity assisting the powerful driving of his wings, he dove faster and faster, shooting back into thicker air like a pure black meteor. Friction against the air heated his skin, but could not harm him, so he plunged ever faster. In seconds, he crossed miles, trailing thunder, aiming for the convergence point situated south of Merkland.

Finally he had to slow, or he'd risk smashing himself flat against the ground. Ten thousand feet above the mountainous terrain, he flared his wings. The strain was intense and would have ripped any flesh-and-blood creature asunder. Speed bled away, but he only barely managed to slow to a hover about five hundred feet from the ground.

Invigorated by the experience, he slowly winged closer to the pillar of the convergence. There he noticed other faint energy fields flowing horizontally out from it, coursing along the surface of the ground like water. The first was red. The second, a little higher above the earth, green.

Streaks of brown marred those energy fields like swirls of paint. Intrigued, he landed near where the convergence touched down to the earth, a high plateau several miles from the Macantact river. The huge, rocky expense appeared void of human habitation. That close, the convergence of sylfaen energy blazed like a white-hot pillar, a quarter of a mile in diameter. His entire pedra body shook from the dense sheets of light plunging into it. He felt super-filled with power, and suddenly wished he was bigger.

Even though he stood on solid ground, his senses extended down through the earth. Those highest-energy wavelengths of light were not limited by earth, but plunged through and he could sense them. Deep in the earth, he finally spotted what he'd hoped to find.

An enormous elfonnel, shaped like the world's biggest pedra, lay slumbering around the glowing pillar of the convergence. Clasped in its paws was a sculpted stone. Even from that distance, Connor sensed the condensed energy barely contained within the stone. It was full to bursting with . . . Healing power.

Understanding dawned as he studied the wavelengths of energy radiating through him. The elfonnel was earth-bound, and it was clutching a long rod of sculpted sandstone in its claws.

Pedra-Connor roared his pitiful roar again, laughing inside with the wonder of the discovery. Just like Ailsa had mentioned in her letter. Somehow she'd learned from the queen the amazing secret to powering affinities. That stone filtered the raw sylfaen power. Now that he understood, he recognized the undercurrent of healing power flowing past, mingled within the red and green frequencies. That sculpted stone was creating the power that fueled all Healers.

It was awe inspiring. He wished he didn't have to fight the queen, to rid the world of her insanity. If only she could be restored, he yearned to ask how she and her husband had figured out the remarkable idea of using those stones to create affinities.

Wishes like that were like sweetbreads left unattended in Hamish's house. Simply gone.

As much as he loved the experience of flying and exploring as Pedra-Connor, his friends needed to know what he'd learned. So he released the energy that bound the summoned creature and returned in a flash to his own body so many miles away.

Rocking back in his chair, he blinked open his eyes against brilliant sunlight. It might pale against the lights he'd been able to see in summoned form, but it still took a moment to recognize Verena sitting close beside him. The rest of his friends sat where he'd last seen them, looking impatient for news.

Verena shuffled even closer, her leg pressed against his. "You mentioned something. It sounded amazing."

Connor grinned and touched her cheek. "It was, but not as amazing as you."

Anika laughed and punched Rory on the shoulder. "Is good boy. Teach you how give happy words when see."

"Hey, I tell you I love you all the time," Rory protested.

"Yes, you strong hands. Train hard. Kiss many good, but sometimes you words many simple."

Chapter Eighty-One

In Order to Win, Great Sacrifices Might Be Necessary

Connor had only been gone for about an hour. During that time, additional platters of food and drinks had arrived. Lady Briet had joined the group, sitting beside General Wolfram. She was dressed in a brightly colored Althin dress of blue and gold and had dived in to help everyone consume most of the food.

Hamish had saved some and pushed a plate of beef, potatoes, and carrots over to Connor. It was cold, but still tasty. A second plate included a mound of fruit, cut into chunks. Connor dug in, feeling ravenous, despite everything he'd eaten earlier. Bonding so close to Pedra-Connor had taxed him more than he realized.

Hamish said, "Sorry we couldn't get more desserts. Lady Shona seemed to think you needed the rest of this too."

"We do need solid food," Shona protested.

Verena rolled her eyes and added, "You can't live on sweets alone."

"After everything I've taught you about the proper appreciation of brain power, you still believe that?" Hamish exclaimed with a look of mock horror.

Evander arrived then, rising right up through the floor. Connor hadn't even realized he'd stepped out, and silently saluted with a fork full of beef. It was reassuring to see Evander act true to the legend. He was still dressed in his great, black leather duster, but this time he carried in one hand a sheaf of parchment papers and in the other hand an enormous mug the size of Connor's head. It looked like it held beef stew, and it smelled delicious.

Hamish glanced at Connor and grinned, gesturing at that enormous mug. Connor nodded understanding. They had to figure out how to get mugs like that too.

Kilian put down the wine he'd been sipping and asked, "Did you find anything useful?"

"I did." Connor tried to explain what he had seen of the continent, the sylfaen, and the convergence points. Verena and Hamish both nodded knowingly as he tried describing the wonder of untethered flight. Even though he'd flown with Air since his ascension, flying as that pedra had been remarkable. He doubted he successfully communicated the vast scope of what he saw, but they seemed to understand at least some of it.

Lady Briet said thoughtfully, "So you spotted convergence points in Arishat lands, yes? I wonder why we don't enjoy as many affinity powers."

"Good question, and I think I saw the reason," Connor said, explaining how only a few of the various convergences included sculpted stones. "Each sculpted stone filters a different affinity, as was suggested in that communique, so maybe it's that filtered power infusing our lands that actually trigger Petralist abilities among the people who live here."

General Wolfram said, "That's an interesting point. It suggests that if we decided to add more stones at additional convergence points that we could spread Petralist powers across the rest of the continent."

"If we can figure out how to do it without having to sacrifice a Petralist-turned-elfonnel at every one," Verena said with a frown.

"Of course," he agreed immediately.

The idea was fascinating, and Connor hoped they got a chance to try it. He wondered if they'd run into political resistance from Obrion and Granadure, though. Granting new Petralist powers to other nations would probably take a while to show much effect, but when it did, the great advantage that Obrion and Granadure enjoyed over their neighbors would disappear. How much would that change the balance of power?

Kilian breathed, "This is amazing. I wish my mother had explained more. This is the foundation of everything that we know."

"She was so messed up even then," Hamish said with a frown.

Aifric said, "Perhaps there was more to her reasoning than that. What if truths of the convergence points and this ramverk of creating affinities actually holds the key to her weakness."

Connor glanced at Evander. "Does this help at all?"

After taking an enormous gulp of his steaming stew, Evander nodded. "It may. Coupled with the notes I shared earlier, this does indeed shed new light upon the construct of my grandmother's life."

He drew from the pocket of his huge coat a sculpted stone made of slate. Like the sandstone piece that Connor had sensed in pedra form, it was much larger than most sculpted stones. Even sitting ten feet away from it, Connor could sense its power radiating like invisible waves of heat.

"That's what you took from the elfonnel that you defeated in southern Obrion last fall, right?" Verena guessed.

Evander nodded. "I did not expect to find such a stone, but when I defeated him it fell from his grasp. It contains far more power than any stone I have ever held, and I have studied it, trying to determine why that is so. At first I thought perhaps the elfonnel had somehow poured some of his essence into it before expiring, but I cannot discover how he might have done so."

Hamish grinned. "And now we know better. That stone's been a filter at the nexus of power for hundreds of years. If it absorbs even a tiny bit of the energy that's flowed through it, it must be thousands of times more powerful than any other sculpted stone."

Evander nodded, but Ilse suddenly gasped. "You took it from a convergence point. With it removed from the ramverk, does that mean we're going to lose our slate affinity?"

That was an excellent and very scary point.

Evander said, "I have not experienced a withdrawal of earth yet, although if we do not eventually return the stone a drought may occur."

General Wolfram said, "Then again, it wasn't until the queen consumed the serpentinite stone that she broke the affinity. Might the sylfaen still be filtering through that stone somehow even though it's no longer at the convergence point?"

They all glanced at Connor and he shrugged. "I have no idea. I can study it to try to find out."

Kilian said, "Later. We haven't noticed problems with slate yet. Let's not get distracted. You noticed other things, and we need to know them."

Connor told them about the convergence point between Merkland and Crann, as well as how he'd sensed an earthbound elfonnel there and the sculpted sandstone.

Aifric looked extremely excited to get her hands on that stone, but Kilian reminded her if they removed it, they might break her healing ability. That dampened her enthusiasm a lot.

Evander said, "These truths enter the mind like a lantern cast open in a dark cave."

"So you think this can help us somehow?" Shona asked.

Ivor added, "I hope so. The queen and her army will be on the way soon. We're out of time. We need to figure out a strategy for attack."

Evander asked, "What is the great need of our cause?"

Connor considered that for a moment. They needed a lot of things. More Petralists, more time, more power stone, and more desserts.

Verena did not hesitate. "We need to understand the queen's weakness, of course."

Oh yeah. That. That was such an overriding concern that he'd totally overlooked it. It was as if he'd asked the people of Alasdair what defined them as a village and no one mentioning the quarry.

Kilian leaned forward and asked, "Have you figured it out?"

Evander shook his head, dashing Connor's newly reborn hope before it could take its first breath. "And yet while not understanding the physics that command a great ship to float upon deep waters, one can still figure out how to sink it."

"What are you saying?" Shona asked.

Evander flashed a rare smile. "What is the queen's great strength that we have yet to overcome?"

Connor was ready this time. But Hamish blurted first, "Growing new hair."

Verena chuckled, and Shona instinctively patted her head. Hamish flushed and added, "I mean, you know, her freakish ability to heal." He gestured at Commander Six. "Even when your brother cut her into pieces that only seemed to annoy her."

He was right. The queen's healing ability was their great challenge. Evander nodded and spoke yet again in plain speech. "Exactly. We may not yet understand how to slay her outright, but what if we could diminish her capacity to heal?"

Whoa. The idea was like a diorite explosion in Connor's mind. He exclaimed, "Are you suggesting we go retrieve the sandstone filter from that convergence point and destroy it?"

Most of the group looked shocked by the suggestion, and Aifric paled and looked like she was about to swoon. Her expression shuddered as Student Eighteen took the control position. Connor could imagine inside her mind Aifric lying on a cot with the other ladies gathered around fanning her face or throwing buckets of icy water at her.

Student Eighteen said, "That would destroy all of our healing abilities too."

Could they really risk such a drastic move? The idea of it seemed impossible, even though they had already experienced it with serpentinite. Affinities had always seemed a constant in the world, like the sun rising and setting or the inexorable movement of the tides. The loss of serpentinite had shaken the absolute of affinities, but few Petralist established that affinity, so the pain was isolated.

Sandstone was a totally different matter. Healers were a vital part of the national identity and armed forces strategies of both Granadure and Obrion.

Lady Briet said, "If such a thing could be possible, the Arishat League have proven that we can field an army without healers."

Verena said, "But so many would die. We would lose the healthbeds as well as the healers."

Shona asked, "But what if it was possible? If we chose to assume such a dire cost, would it grant us the power to defeat the dread queen?"

Connor raised a hand to draw their attention. "One other point to consider. We know now that it's possible to break an affinity. Terrifying, but possible. When the queen broke serpentinite she severed only the red energy source. I can still access it when focused exclusively on green. We might be able to do the same with healing."

"But then only you and the queen herself might be able to heal consistently," Ivor pointed out. "The rest of us would pay such an enormous cost and potentially not even block her."

Kilian, whose expression had turned thoughtful said, "But what if she did not realize she still had access to it? From that note, it appears she believes serpentinite is beyond her grasp, or at least that it's not productive for her to pursue it. If we could sever sandstone long enough to attack her, might the distraction of that loss prevent her from recognizing the possibility that she might still be able to access it?"

Verena added, "As much as I hate the idea, if we did survive and defeat her, we could craft another sculpted stone and bury it again. That would restore healing eventually."

Student Eighteen was still scowling, and no doubt several of the women in her head had to forcibly hold Aifric back from assuming control and shouting at all of them that they were insane. Connor understood her fear. He would've died many times over without the miraculous power of sandstone. The thought of sacrificing healing across the entire continent for the slim chance of just maybe defeating the queen seemed an awfully high risk to take.

But they could not ignore the possibility.

"Could we even take the stone without awakening the elfonnel, or would we have to fight it before getting a chance to destroy the stone?" Ivor asked.

"If we could, would it be possible to restore another stone to it as well?" Wolfram asked.

"Or would we have to sacrifice someone in elfonnel form to restore it then?" Shona asked with a grimace.

No one had an answer.

"If we did awaken it, would the queen sense its rising?" Verena asked.

Excellent question. Connor bet she would. The rising of an elfonnel rippled across the continent. Someone as powerful as the queen would surely notice it.

Kilian nodded. "She would, and most likely would rush to investigate anything tampering with her ramverk."

"Could we use that against her?" Connor asked.

"Perhaps," Kilian said, lapsing into thought.

The conversation faded as they considered the myriad questions. They faced too many unknowns. There was no way to know for sure. Any one answer they got wrong would most likely destroy the attempt and waste the effort, leaving them weakened instead of the queen.

Connor thought back to all the uses of sandstone. He considered the precious sculpted sandstone pendants that Aunt Ailsa had sent to him. They had saved many lives. He thought of the healthbeds and all the great work the Builders were doing to push science, led by Jean and her fixation on the tiny world of molds and rot and infection. Could she still pursue her research without the power of sandstone? If only she had years to make new discoveries before they considered destroying that power.

As he thought of Jean and the marvelous work that she and her teams were doing, he thought about the recent visit with Nicklaus and got an idea. He snapped his fingers and exclaimed, "Nicklaus!"

Everyone turned to him, clearly not understanding the reference. Kilian asked, "What about him?"

Connor turned to Hamish. "Remember when we visited him?"

"Sure. I want to study that water purification mechanical."

"Remember the other part, about the higher level mechanical he was building that didn't work?"

"Oh, yeah. Sort of forgot about that with everything else going on," Hamish admitted.

"What higher level mechanical?" Verena asked.

"Something he was working on that Water was teaching him. I was going to discuss it with you, but with loaning powers and everything, I totally forgot. Actually, loaning powers plays into what I'm thinking too."

"How?" Ivor asked.

He grinned, struggling to make a concrete idea out of that flash of inspiration. "Two things just came together for me that might help us. First, loaning powers. I could only loan so much. Once I spread my affinity far enough, there was nothing left for me."

General Wolfram asked, "Are you suggesting we find a way to convince the queen to loan her powers to others to leave herself vulnerable?"

"She'd never do it," Kilian said.

"I know, and that's where Nicklaus' failed mechanical comes in. Hamish, remember he said when he turned it on it only seemed to be messing with a lot of energy?"

"Yeah," Hamish said, still not getting it.

"And a Water Moccasin asked him to turn it off because it was interfering with his affinity?" Connor pressed.

"What?" Verena exclaimed as Hamish nodded, a look of dawning understanding on his face.

Connor was growing more excited by the second. "I have a copy of everything Water told him in a book in my room. Christin wrote it all down. What if that higher-level mechanical gathers affinity power, sort of like how my summoned pedra absorbed light?"

"What if it could?" Shona asked, looking confused. "No mechanical could absorb all the healing magic everywhere."

"Not everywhere. At the convergence point," Connor said triumphantly. "It's where healing power comes from, right? There's a lot of healing power available, but not an infinite amount. What if we could divert it somehow through a mechanical?"

Verena's eyes lit with that thrill she always got when exploring new concepts. "When I activated Kristin's Defense, I saw how the stones were linked, how the commands were layered. If that notebook does have some clues, I'm confident I could build a higher mechanical to suck in all healing power in a concentrated area."

Hamish grinned. "If we could leave the queen temporarily without full access to healing, that might accomplish the same thing as destroying the affinity altogether, right?"

Verena said, "I like that idea a lot better, if we can build it."

Kilian said, "I've never considered exhausting all of the available affinity power. Before now I would've said it wasn't possible, but maybe there's a way."

"There's a great deal of power imbuing affinity stones already. How would we use all that?" Mistress Four asked.

Connor wasn't sure, but the idea excited him more than anything else they had considered. It finally offered a chance to move beyond conjecture and wild dreams. This idea might actually have a slim chance of success. He glanced at Evander who did not look convinced, then at Kilian who was looking thoughtful.

Kilian said, "My greatest concern is how short we are on time."

Shona said, "If no one has any better ideas, we have to try something. How fast can we build something to test?"

"How fast can you get me that notebook?" Verena asked.

"Two minutes," he promised. He wished he had an affinity for calling objects to him from a distance. That would be a neat trick.

Kilian nodded. "Get on it. If we can indeed make it work, there's no reason not to try. Destroying sandstone affinity is definitely not the preferred option, but if we can't come up with anything better we might have to make the attempt. We're facing the fight that could very well define all of our lives and the very future of our nations. We cannot fail."

He held each of their gazes in turn, little points of white-hot flame in his eyes. Kilian was extremely good at motivating his people, and Connor felt his resolve stiffening.

Kilian added, "Evander and I can challenge her elemental dominance."

"Hamish and I can distract her," Verena promised. "Maybe we'll even get a glimpse into why she fears us so much."

Connor was feeling pretty confident in the plan until Ivor declared, "Then we activate our healing drought, and Connor goes in for the kill."

Chapter Eighty-Two

Sugar-saturated Creativity

Verena exited her bedroom, carrying the leather-bound notebook where she'd recorded everything she could remember from the amazing experience activating Kirstin's Defense. Hamish waited for her in her plush sitting room. Verena liked the suite assigned to her by General Rory. Situated in Dougal's tower, it had once belonged to Craigroy. The master spy might be an evil, conniving villain, but he hired excellent decorators.

"Do you really think we can create a mechanical to suck up all the healing power?" Hamish asked, glancing up from the notebook that Christin had given to Connor.

She settled into one of the plush chairs beside the one where he sat close to the warm fire and tucked her hair behind one ear. "You were there, you talked with Nicklaus. What do you think?"

"I'm not sure," he admitted after a moment's thought. "I wish we'd looked into it more right away, but I hadn't realized it might be so important."

"We didn't know about convergence points or the queen's ramverk construct that filters sylfaen to create affinities. It's crazy how much this knowledge changes things." Usually she loved to savor the sense of wonder she experienced when learning new things, but this time they were just too rushed. Why couldn't they have learned about these deeper truths three months ago?

"I wish I'd gotten to experience Kirstin's Defense with you," Hamish said with a sigh. "I feel like I'm trying to build a new sightstone when I'm blind."

She held up her notebook. "How about we swap? You study my notes and I'll study the instructions Water gave Nicklaus. Then we'll compare."

"Deal." He took her notes and began reading, absently pulling a hard breadstick from a chest pocket. He'd left his battle suit in his rooms and wore trousers and a cotton shirt, with a many-pocketed denim jacket over it.

"Have any more of those?" she asked.

"Silly question," he grinned. "You should have asked how many varieties I've got handy."

He extracted another one and handed it over. She took a bite and was surprised by the rich, honey flavor. He wasn't holding back the good stuff. She appreciated that Hamish understood the importance of proper encouragement.

She eagerly opened Christin's notebook and began reading. Nicklaus had repeated everything he heard from Water, and many of the lines were short and rather cryptic. She wondered if Nicklaus had accidentally spoken aloud some of his own random thoughts, like the line that only said, "No missiles on the pantry door."

Or, "No one's awake after the second midnight bell."

She ignored the random or gibberish-sounding commands, scanning the pages to pick out the meatier communications. She's spoken with Water and immediately recognized the different tone from Nicklaus' other rambling. At first they were short, sounding more like Water was probing the communication channel, trying to understand the boy she was speaking with, almost as if she was surprised he could hear her.

The directions for building the water purifier were the first meaningful messages, and Verena instantly recognized the brilliance of the suggestions. Water had communicated a very clever use of Builder powers in simple terms that the boy could grasp. Verena longed to establish another connection with Water herself. What more could she learn from the elemental personage?

"Did you read this," she asked Hamish after turning the page and reading another line. "*You are a child of exceptional perception, thus I will teach you higher truths.*"

"Yeah. Water seems to like Nicklaus. I'm just impressed that he actually took her advice. He doesn't like obeying commands."

"He does like learning new things," Verena pointed out.

"And he was pretty bored in that cottage. Christin really enjoyed collaring him for regular schooling. He must have hopped at the chance to build something new."

"I was hoping to understand how he speaks with her, but I get the sense the connection surprised Water, as if it was more an accident than anything," she said, feeling frustrated.

"Me too. I wonder if breaking his affinities heightened his Builder powers or something?"

"Maybe. Connor speaks of affinities like bridges, and Water mentioned a bridge when I spoke with her. Maybe his mind was prepared for the connection better than ours."

Hamish tapped Verena's notebook. "I just read that bit. She actually said there's some kind of bridge we can establish if we can reach that threshold that will allow us to connect with them more like how Connor does?"

Verena smiled at the awesome memory. "She was magnificent, but hadn't expected to speak with me. When I activated Kirstin's Defense, it unleashed so much power it pushed me right to the threshold, but something blocked me from getting through it."

"What?" he asked eagerly.

"I have no idea." If only she'd figured it out! Ascending through that threshold might have unlocked even more truths that they needed so desperately. She sighed and added, "We're right on the verge of so much, Hamish! I was starting to feel proud of how much we accomplished this past winter, but we're barely scratching the surface."

He nodded. "In here you said you felt multi-layered commands in Kirstin's Defense. Water's instructions to Nicklaus include some complex structure too, but it's way beyond what we usually use."

She wasn't surprised Hamish had picked up on that. Verena felt it held the key to making their new, ambitious attempt possible. "There was a lot about what I sensed in there that I didn't fully understand, dozens of ideas and insights that flashed through my mind in an instant. They were like fragments of a remembered dream. Those notes are my attempt to piece them back together."

"I noticed," he said with a grin. "You jump around so much, I suspected you might have taken my advice to sugar saturate yourself more often, but forgot you also need to give all that energy physical outlets too."

"I'd be willing to try sugar saturation if it would help us figure this out," she admitted.

Without a word, he pulled a cream-filled pastry out of another pocket. It was still soft. "How do you keep it warm?" she exclaimed.

"I drop tiny pieces of marble in my pockets and activate them just a bit. Sort of like mini heatstone ovens. Pretty neat, huh?"

She couldn't argue with that and saluted with the pastry before consuming it. It was delicious.

"Tell me about the layered commands," Hamish urged.

Verena took a moment to gather her thoughts. Christin's notes helped, since Nicklaus had used similar principles, if on a far simpler scale. "Some things I still can't explain, like how those soapstone sculpted stones were already partially activated, but hadn't run out of power despite remaining active for three centuries. Or the fact that there were no pieces of active obsidian placed beside each one."

"I didn't even notice that when we first touched it," Hamish admitted.

"Those eight stones were linked together by those complex commands, which were triggered and controlled by the keystone of the construct, the stone due south of Merkland."

Hamish nodded. "I get that part. Even Nicklaus' water-hogging mechanical used a keystone concept like that. I'd thought we were getting pretty complex in our mechanicals, but I'd never realized we could layer commands over each other."

She hadn't either. The easiest way to release a stone's power was to simply reach into it and wrench open the crack, allowing its power to flood forth in a wave. Every Builder could do that instinctively. Next came more subtle applications that pushed a stone's power out through the mechanical or out to the rest of the world in a more controlled manner.

The most complex mechanicals they'd built to date included commands to link to additional stones, or to release a stone's power in a focused way, like the new shieldstones they used, crafted to generate shields of specific size, shape, duration, and intensity. Sightstones were even more complex, combining image and sound transmission, but were still pretty straightforward.

Hamish added, "Water's instructions to Nicklaus made it seem so simple, as if creating higher forms of commands was as easy as layering various flavors of cake over one another."

She smiled at the analogy. "To me, it felt more like invisible parchments, each containing a single command, built upon each other. Only when I activated Kirstin's Defense did I understand. It was like flipping each page past my mind, one after another, and only together did the entire plan make sense."

Hamish nodded thoughtfully, glancing back down at her notes. "It's making more sense now. So we need to define the full scope of what we want and figure out how to break it down into a string of simple commands that we then have to layer together to create the final program."

"I think so," she agreed, impressed that he could grasp it so quickly when he hadn't experienced it. "I like that word for it. Programming sounds right.

Kirstin's Defense included secondary command groups that didn't activate until the first set was finished and the defenses were in place. I'm not completely sure how to do that, but I don't think for what we're trying to do we'll need that."

"I can't wait for the time to practice the whole process," Hamish said, voice soft with wonder. "Kirstin was amazing. Sometimes I wonder what else we've lost from her that we may never get back."

Deep thoughts like that from Hamish often caught Verena by surprise, even though she knew him so well. He loved to project a goofy persona, but she shouldn't get fooled by that. Under that goofy exterior and bottomless appetite was a brilliant, creative mind.

So of course he added, "I just got a great idea how to build a higher-level mechanical to deliver sweetbreads to my rooms every twenty seconds, all day long."

Verena laughed, feeling her confidence growing. With Hamish's help, she felt convinced they could build a mechanical to absorb healing power.

She turned to a blank page and extracted a pencil from her satchel. "Then let's get to work."

Chapter Eighty-Three

Bash Fighting for a Good Cause

Connor landed on a flat, rocky plateau a few miles northwest of Merkland where the rest of the team waited. As he touched down and he released Air, the two invisible chairs faded away, rousing Kilian from the doze he'd fallen into on the return trip.

Connor couldn't blame him. He felt exhausted, despite the noticeable increase in his strength and endurance, even when not tapping any affinities. The ascension had changed him at a fundamental level, but he'd been pushing the limits in the last couple days. While Verena and Hamish were busy creating new mechanicals, he'd spent every waking hour training hard with Kilian, Evander, Aifric, and Ivor, exploring every aspect of his altered affinities that he could.

He'd learned some fun things, like the fact that he could hold his breath almost indefinitely when tapping pumice, and he'd dueled both Kilian and Evander together and actually held his own. He still couldn't touch Kilian with a blade, but his elemental powers were noticeably stronger. He only hoped the huge improvements he'd made would be enough. He wished he could spend another year training that hard.

Verena jogged over from the Swift that she'd been tinkering with. She'd gotten it repainted, and it looked fully restored from that battering it suffered fighting the swarm. Hamish stood nearby in his battle suit, talking with Evander and Ilse. General Wolfram and Lady Briet exited the Albatross parked nearby, while Rory raised a fist to signal the halt to the bash fight he'd been enjoying with Anika, Erich, Ivor, Shona, and Tomas and Cameron. Aifric raced up on fracked legs from around a pile of boulders. The other Mhortair followed, the entire group sliding across the hardscrabble ground.

"Did you find a good spot?" Verena asked after greeting Connor with a kiss. Her black hair was braided for flying, and she wore flying leathers. He loved how cute she looked snuggled into that fur-lined jacket.

"We did," he said loudly so all could hear.

"Good. We're ready for the test," she told him happily, pointing toward a cluster of three windriders parked in a loose circle nearby. Each one held a large, square block of sandstone as tall as Connor. They were committing enormous resources to the attempt to destroy Queen Dreokt. If they succeeded, it would be a tiny price to pay.

"Perfect timing," Kilian said, giving Verena a hug and a warm smile. "We'll lay our trap on the opposite side of the river from the convergence point Connor sensed."

"It's about a dozen miles upriver from Crann and another ten inland to the east," Connor explained. "It's rough, with no population to speak of."

"Good. I'm glad we can try this without putting a lot of people at risk," Verena said.

"Just us," Hamish pointed out.

"We know the risks, and if today's test is successful, we'll have a better chance than maybe anyone has ever had," Kilian said.

Everyone turned to Verena and Hamish expectantly. Hamish gestured toward the parked windriders with their sandstone loads. "Those blocks are twenty percent of the final mechanical we've got planned. They're enough for the test. We'll add the other twelve blocks for the final trap."

"We should have the sculpted stones we need by then," Verena added.

Shona said, "We've already committed three sculpted sandstone. I don't understand why we need fifteen."

The idea of so many sculpted stones potentially sacrificed in one mechanical was hard to grasp. Luckily Gisela and the other two sculptors working in New Schwinkendorf were generating a lot of sculpted stones. They might not be as powerful as a finely crafted piece that Aunt Ailsa would produce, but they didn't have to be. Many of the rough-sculpted stones were small obsidian pieces, needed for all of the remotely-controlled mechanicals, but as the Builder mechanicals grew ever more complex, they needed more and more other sculpted stones. Plus, with war brewing, they'd wanted to give Healers as much power as possible.

They had half a dozen sculpted sandstone in Merkland already, but had contacted Gisela to rush production of the rest. She'd promised they'd gather every available stone in New Schwinkendorf and sculpt more, if needed. Usually such a concentration of sculpted stones would have been illegal and would have represented enormous wealth, but Connor wished they had twice as many and that his Aunt Ailsa had been free to assist in perfecting them over a period of weeks.

"The sculpted stones are vital to this new mechanical construct," Verena explained. She and Hamish had worked tirelessly through the two full days, their work fueled by buckets of sweetbreads and crates of smashpacked desserts. They claimed to have worked out the sequencing for the mechanical to create a dearth of healing power, and had spent the entire next day working with a huge team to put the plan into practice.

Hamish added, "They'll link together and will be the focus of our command sequence, but they can't contain all the healing power we hope to capture. Simply deflecting the healing power away from an area might have worked, but this approach gives us far better coverage. We need the big sandstone blocks to act as reservoirs."

Aifric grinned. "Think of how much healing we could accomplish by sculpting pieces of those blocks afterward."

Great idea. Verena said, "We're already planning to try. If this works, we should be able to suck all the healing power away from everyone, although some will remain locked into the sandstone pieces you have on you. One of the goals for today's test is to get a sense for how quickly that power will drain away."

"Should we place the healing-sucking vortex mechanical at the point where we spring the trap, then?" Ivor asked.

Verena said, "We're calling this mechanical Sucker Punch."

"My idea," Hamish announced proudly.

Verena said, "I thought to call it Primal Health because healing's still there, but not available to anyone unless we choose." She hesitated and Hamish eagerly gestured her to continue. She sighed and conceded, "But for once Hamish's idea is better."

Hamish laughed, overjoyed that he'd finally gotten to name something. Connor liked the name. It perfectly represented what they were planning.

Verena added, "We considered the question of placement, and there's some benefit to positioning it closer to the trap, but we feel that we'll get a better overall effect by placing it around the convergence point and cutting off the sandstone power at the source."

Connor sincerely hoped it worked.

Hamish rubbed his hands together in anticipation. "So here's the plan. We activate this thing, and you try healing each other."

"It's hard to heal if we're not injured," Aifric pointed out.

"That's why we were bash fighting," Rory said with a grin. "Now that we're warmed up, we're going to resume, but keep our tap rate low enough that we can get hurt easier."

Tomas and Cameron didn't look as enthusiastic about that part, but seemed willing to pay the price in order to get a good bash fight. Erich was already humming a battle tune to himself. Connor had seen the three of them fight more than once, and he doubted they'd hold back. He didn't doubt they'd give him and Aifric plenty to do.

Verena extracted a small piece of sandstone, sculpted into a highly polished sphere. "Activating Sucker Punch . . . Now!"

Connor expected some sign that the mechanical was active, but those big blocks just sat there. He glanced around, and everyone else was doing the same.

"Is it working?" Shona asked.

Hamish grinned. "Oh, yeah. It's sucking in a ton of energy already."

"I don't feel any different," Aifric said.

Connor tapped sandstone and felt available power like always. When he tapped the deeper aspect of his fleshcrafting, he sensed both red and green energies flowing through him. After a moment, he felt a slight undercurrent of the red energy, as if something was tugging at the flow. The tug increased and the flow of healing power lessened.

"I feel it!" he shouted, exulting.

"Time to test it," Rory cried. He turned to his men just in time to catch Tomas' fist with his face. The blow rocked him back, but he kicked out, knocking Tomas stumbling.

Erich happily grabbed Tomas by the head, yanked him off the ground, and flung him into Cameron. The two went down in a heap, but leaped back to their feet. Erich plowed into them and the three launched into a brutal bash fight. Erich started loudly singing his Grandurian battle song.

Tomas ducked under one mighty blow and slammed a fist into Erich's ribs hard enough to blow a torc in half. Erich grunted and missed a beat in his song.

"Grandurian songs always sounded like sick cattle begging for a mercy killing," Cameron said as he and Erich traded punches.

Tomas laughed. "More like a sick mmppfh." The words cut off abruptly as Erich shoved a rock-hard fist into his mouth.

Shona jumped into the fray with a flying kick into Erich's back, knocking him off his feet. Anika rushed in to defend her brother and punched Shona back down when she rose.

Connor really wanted to join them, but shouldn't he focus on the healing power test?

Softly whistling to herself, Ilse moved lightly into the fray, her movements dainty compared to the brutish stomping of the others. Sometimes Connor forgot she had primary affinity with granite. She danced into the bash fight, flowing around the mighty blows of the bigger men, or somehow deflecting them and turning her opponents' strength against them. With seeming ease, she sent Tomas tumbling and sidestepped Shona's charge, sending her plowing into Cameron just like she had knocked her into the doorframe of Lord Gavin's manor house during that very first fight all those months ago.

Even Evander and Ivor joined the fight, and soon the entire bunch of them were laughing and cheering each other on as they beat on each other. Connor laughed, pleased that they could share such a happy memory before launching their deadly fight against the queen.

Hamish flew over the group, thrusters of his battle suit drowned out by the shouting of the fighters. He fired a missile, striking the ground right next to where Shona was wrestling with Ivor. The explosion knocked them both tumbling, and Evander punched them both back off their feet as they rose.

Aifric sighed. "The sacrifices we make for research."

"I know. I want to get into it too," Connor agreed.

"If you're not going to, would you mind sharing some granite with me?" Lady Briet asked.

That caught him by surprise. Lady Briet wore one of her fine dresses, after all. She wasn't exactly young any more, and usually let others do the sweaty fighting.

She smiled at his reaction. "Come now, Connor. Who wouldn't want a chance to experience life as a Boulder at least once?"

"All right," he agreed with a grin, thrilled that she wanted to get involved.

General Wolfram said, "Better loan me some too. I'll see she doesn't get hurt."

"You just don't want to miss the chance to punch me in the face," she laughed, again surprising Connor with that easy banter.

He shrugged. "We rarely get to slug it out with those we spend so much time negotiating with."

"I agree," she said sincerely. "Together, then?"

He extended an arm in a gentlemanly way, which she took.

In a moment, Connor tapped chert, obsidian, and sandstone, plus granite for the loan. He felt the drag on his sandstone more severely. It was definitely working. The two of them grinned as they swelled with granite power, and didn't even wait to join the rest of the bash fight before Lady Briet punched at Wolfram.

He was by far the more experienced soldier, and seemed to be expecting the blow. He parried and punched her in the nose. Connor doubted the punch hurt, but she was clearly not used to getting hit and recoiled out of habit.

So Wolfram picked her up and threw her into the middle of the bash fight shouting, "Make way for Lady Briet!"

Verena laughed and took Connor's hand. "We should arrange parties like this more often. Lately we've been far too grim."

"I totally agree."

Together they watched the intense bash fight for a couple minutes. No one held back, but beat on each other with epic abandon. Lady Briet threw herself into the middle of the fray, shrieking something in Althing that Connor hoped was a battle cry, even though it sounded more like she'd pulled a muscle. It seemed everyone wanted a chance to participate in international diplomacy because they all made a point to punch her face several times.

Finally Aifric interrupted. She nodded to Kilian, who had stood beside her while they watched the fight, and he shouted, "Enough! Time to test the healing."

No one stopped. It took another five minutes to pull everyone apart. Connor had to tap earth and physically drag some of them away from each other before they relented. He didn't blame them. It was extremely difficult to stop when one was immersed in such a fun bash fight.

The battered group presented themselves to Connor and Aifric for healing. Most of them were bruised, but not badly damaged. Lady Briet was the exception. Her dress was badly torn, she limped, and she was missing four teeth, which she displayed proudly through a wide grin.

"My dear Connor, you gave me a princely gift today. Thank you so much!" she gushed as he healed her.

His red-frequency healing power was dwindling fast, and he barely managed to heal her bruises and her injured knee. Then he switched to green frequency power to fleshcraft her teeth back. The connection seemed weaker than usual because of the red-frequency dearth, but he still managed to access fleshcrafting anyway. Once the connection solidified, he felt no lack of green-energy power.

She sighed as she touched her restored teeth, looking more content in her dirt-streaked, bedraggled way than he'd ever seen.

Once everyone was healed, Connor conferred with Aifric. She said, "I can barely heal a scratch any more. My healing power is simply gone, even though my piece of sandstone is fine."

"Me too," he confirmed. "Although I can still reach fleshcrafting."

Kilian grimaced. "If mother can still fleshcraft, we might be accomplishing less than we hope."

"It was more difficult to make the connection," Connor said. "If we can convince her that healing is broken, she might not realize she can get past it if she just focuses on green. At least, not before we kill her."

"It's worth the attempt," Shona said, and everyone else nodded agreement.

"Can we enhance the mechanical to influence green frequency power too?" Ivor asked.

"I can't sense the different frequencies, so I don't think so, at least not yet," Verena said with an apologetic shrug.

"Maybe if we can find that Builder threshold and figure out how to get through it we might be able to," Hamish said.

"Attempting an unknown threshold will take careful preparation, and we don't have time to wait," Kilian said. "We've still got a better chance than we've had before, and we have to hit her before she begins the march from Crann."

Shona pushed her hair back from her face, looking almost totally unaffected by the recent bash fight. "Now that we've proven this mechanical will work, we need to finalize a plan of attack."

Chapter Eighty-Four

The Need for Burned Cookies

"We have to lure her out of Crann alone," Connor said as the group drew into a circle to discuss the plan.

Kilian nodded. "Like the Battle of Vallanes. We need a powerful lure."

"Won't she be suspicious it's a trap if you've used that approach before?" Wolfram asked.

Evander said, "The rooster greets the new day with undiminished enthusiasm, but the gathering clouds of an approaching storm paint the sky in countless variety."

Connor was glad he'd reverted to Sentry speak, even though he wasn't sure how to interpret that one. Evander had spoken clearly far too often of late, and it left Connor feeling rattled.

"What does that mean?" Cameron asked with a frown.

"Means we get chicken for dinner," Tomas said with a grin.

"Let others interpret deeper meanings," Ilse said with a smile. "He suggested that although the ruse might seem similar to ones she's seen before, we can leverage different approaches that she cannot help but respond to."

They considered that for a moment, and Connor discarded several wild ideas about how to lure out the queen. Too many of them resulted in pitched battle with her army, which they needed to avoid.

"She hates Builders, right?" Hamish asked.

"And she thinks you dead, right?" Rory added.

Verena said, "She knows someone survived. She saw you outside of Jagdish."

"And she must know that Builders helped us survive her swarm," Shona added.

"But she doesn't know which of us are alive," Hamish reminded her.

Connor liked the idea. The queen's unreasonable hatred for Builders included fear of their powers that he really wished they understood. But they might be able to leverage it. "Showing her that Hamish or Verena still lives would definitely enrage her."

"Except she'd just boil them out of the sky," Kilian pointed out.

"We have blind coal," Hamish protested.

"Not enough to escape if she decides to actively hunt you," Kilian said, and Connor suspected he was right.

Ilse said, "I'm afraid only Connor has a chance to keep ahead of her long enough to draw her out."

Verena gripped Connor's hand, suddenly looking nervous. "You can't be suggesting Connor launch a solo assault against Crann."

"She thinks Connor and I are both dead or captured, after all," Ivor said thoughtfully.

"And she has expressed interest in capturing you," Kilian added. "Perhaps she won't try annihilating you right away."

"But we want her to chase him," Wolfram said. "So we need her mad enough to abandon her army and take off after him."

"I can definitely irritate her enough to get her to chase me," Connor promised. He wrapped an arm around Verena to comfort her and added, "I'm ascended now. I can move as fast as she can, and I should be able to hold her off long enough to draw her out."

"If you get caught in the middle of an army at Crann, not even you can fight free of all those Petralists and the queen," Verena protested.

"I don't see a better way," Hamish said apologetically.

"But Verena has a point," Evander said, again speaking clearly. That was so unnerving.

Aifric, who had been looking distracted, her lips moving silently in a group conference in her head, looked up. "I think the answer is obvious. Connor needs to use stilling on the army."

"Yeah! That's right. You stilled all of Merkland," Hamish exclaimed. Several of the others voiced support, looking enthusiastic about the idea, but Verena hugged him closer, searching his gaze with her own. He'd confided in her how difficult stilling Merkland had been, and how hard it had been to stop.

Connor licked suddenly dry lips. They had a point, but he hesitated, thinking back to that singular experience. When Harley detonated the rage bomb over

Merkland, it had threatened to destroy the entire city from within, everyone ripping each other apart in a fit of mindless rage. He'd stilled them all, sucking their life force away, preventing them the freedom to move and to commit murder.

He'd saved tens of thousands of lives, but the cost still haunted him. Some of them had died. The weak or wounded, those with too little life force remaining had succumbed to his insidious power in those critical moments. Releasing them would have resulted in even more death, but he'd felt every one of those lives as they were snuffed out and sacrificed to him.

Part of him had exulted in the experience. That part haunted him the most. That flood of energy had been intoxicating, a wondrous thing that filled him with life and strength and power and glory. For a moment he'd struggled to control the overwhelming urge to hold onto stilling longer than needed, to draw out more life from those helpless people.

He'd unleashed stilling upon a defenseless city in order to save it, but he'd very nearly ended up destroying them all.

"I don't think it's a good idea," Verena said, interrupting the happy chatter, still holding Connor's gaze with hers.

"Of course it is," Hamish retorted. He punched Connor on the shoulder. "I bet you can still more people than ever now that you've ascended."

Connor feared he might be right. If he stilled more, even for a short time, he could use that power to fight the queen, to free the very people he leeched life from. But if he did, could he stop himself from losing control?

"Stilling so many is dangerous," he said finally.

Kilian stepped closer, studying Connor closely. Connor read understanding in his gaze. Kilian had taught him stilling, understood the price one paid to wield it. He expected Kilian to suggest a different way, but Kilian nodded slowly after a moment and said softly, "I see you fear what might happen."

"Wait, what would happen to Connor if he stilled others?" Hamish asked. "I thought it was affecting them."

"There's danger in too much of a good thing," Connor told his friend. "Like that time we snuck that huge Sogail cake out of Neasa's bakery the night before the Sogail when we were seven."

Hamish nodded in instant understanding. Verena looked from Connor to Hamish, frowning, and asked, "What happened?"

"We ate the entire thing, of course," Hamish said proudly. "It was a special cake, three feet long, five layers, should have fed twenty people."

"You ate it all?" Lady Briet asked, her tone awed.

"We certainly did," Connor said. "And it nearly killed us."

"I was so sick the next day I couldn't eat anything until lunchtime," Hamish said, his expression turning anguished from the memory of missing the first hours of the feast.

Connor said, "Stilling a lot of people is like that. It's wondrous in a way I can't explain, but it's very hard to stop once I turn it on."

"If you don't, you could kill them all," Verena said softly, looking worried.

"Or kill yourself," Shona added.

Tomas shrugged, not looking concerned. "That's why you get the fancy socks, lad. Big responsibility comes with great perks, but hazards that you've got to deal with."

"Socks?" Shona asked, looking confused.

Cameron spoke up. "Course. Simple bash fighters get wool socks, what with all our marching duty and everything. Leaders have to walk more careful or they scatter all them deep thoughts they need to make, so they need fancy socks to make the right padding."

Connor smiled, his tension easing under their banter. "I don't think I ever got fancy socks."

Tomas and Cameron both looked offended and turned to Kilian. Tomas said, "You're risking the fate of the revolution over skimping on socks? Really?"

Kilian chuckled. "I'll see to it that Connor gets excellent socks before the battle." That mollified them and Kilian added, "The fact that you understand the risk and fear it makes me optimistic that you'll be able to control yourself."

"Besides, if you get distracted, the queen will rip out your mind," Hamish added.

"Not helpful," Verena said.

"I thought it was. Connor works best when motivated," Hamish responded simply.

"He's right. I can do it," Connor said. He didn't see that he had a choice, but the fact that he'd be facing a tight schedule helped. "And Hamish I'll need your help preparing what I'll need to get her mad enough to chase me."

"What do you need Hamish for?" Verena asked, clearly wishing he'd said he needed her help preparing instead.

He grinned at her. "Because Hamish has been helping me perfect the vomit rocket."

"Eww," Verena and Shona said together.

Chuckling, Kilian said, "The rest of us will set the trap for when you arrive. Evander, Ivor, and I will attack with elemental powers, try to injure her and force her to consume her healing power faster."

Hamish said, "And Verena and I will hit her from the air with every mechanical we can get our hands on."

"Are you sure that's wise?" Shona asked. "She can hit you from a distance, and your missiles and hornets aren't likely to accomplish much."

"But she's afraid of something we can do," Verena reminded her. "Maybe we can get her to reveal more of what that is."

"I like it," Kilian said. "We have to make sure we don't tip our hand too early, so we can't just set up a dozen hovering windriders packed with bombs."

"Too bad. We have some good ones," Hamish said. Then he suddenly cocked his head as if listening. A moment later he shouted, "Really? Perfect!"

Connor asked, "What?"

Hamish tapped the side of his helmet and grinned. "I've got some great news! Just what we needed for our distraction initiative."

"Don't tell me you actually created that giant fart bomb you've been talking about," Verena said, looking suddenly nervous.

"Still working on perfecting the mix in that one," Hamish said. "This is even better." He pointed into the air and shouted, "I give you Ilse's Revenge!"

Connor glanced north toward the pass and tapped a little quartzite to his eyes. His vision magnified tenfold, colors deepening and turning far more vibrant. In the distance he easily spotted a dozen oversized windriders approaching in a flying duck formation. Strapped to the flatbed cargo beds of each one was a Juggernaut sphere.

"I didn't think it was finished," Verena exclaimed.

"Jean just contacted me. Said Fyodor had teams working day and night to finish. Wanted to make it a surprise to send along with the rest of the sculpted stones from Gisela," Hamish said, laughing with joy.

Everyone shared his enthusiasm. They had big plans for Ilse's Revenge, and everyone started chattering excitedly about how best to utilize the mighty mechanical. For her part, Ilse looked very pleased that her namesake death mechanical would be deployed in time for the imminent battle.

As they waited for the flotilla to arrive, Rory said, "I've decided to include Tomas and Cameron as pilots for this fight."

The two Fast Rollers whooped and punched each other. Connor loved their enthusiasm, but glancing up at the huge Juggernauts, he suddenly feared what they might do once unleashed driving those deadly mechanicals.

"All of the main pilots are available," Verena protested, obviously sharing Connor's concern.

"I'm aware of that, but I'm afraid I must insist," Rory said calmly. "This battle might well determine the war, and Ilse's Revenge will play an important role. I need pilots who know battle and who know how to work with all of us. Your other pilots are skilled, but inexperienced."

Verena started to protest again, but Connor said, "I think Rory's right. We can't afford any delays or hesitation."

She leaned closer to him and whispered, "But we're talking about Tomas and Cameron, Connor!"

"I know. Have you ever known them to hesitate before leaping into the most insane fight?"

"No," she admitted with a grimace.

"And fighting Queen Dreokt is about as insane as it gets. What if the other pilots hesitated?"

"They'd get slaughtered," she admitted with a sigh. "You're right, but I still don't like it."

Tomas gave her a reassuring smile. "Don't worry, Lady Verena. Cameron and I won't let you down."

"No, ma'am," Cameron agreed, giving Verena a wide, gap-toothed smile. "In fact, I prepared some flowered prose for the day we got to pilot them beasties for real."

His expression turned intense as he concentrated, but before he could launch into what would certainly be a terrible excuse for poetry, Verena said, "It's all right, Cameron. I believe you. In fact, it might be better to save the flowered prose and share it with the other pilots."

His eyes lit up and he grinned. "Brilliant."

Tomas added, "Leave it to Builders to think the heavy thoughts."

The two wandered off, betting which of them could get the best distance when they practiced using the ejection seats.

"That was smoothly done," Kilian said with a wink.

The Juggernaut-bearing windriders landed nearby a few minutes later and Connor eagerly joined the others inspecting them. Half-constructed, they had looked intimidating, but the finished products emanated a sense of deadly power even when strapped to their transports. The shells of the ten-foot diameter spheres were constructed from alternating octagonal plates of polished steel and quickened granite. They had included some Alasdair White, but also several other strains. Connor recognized blue Clemens, dark gray Schmitten, and pink

Walther, resulting in a colorful mix that only heightened the sense of deadly power surrounding the machines.

Many of the pilots were already in Merkland, but Hamish oversaw unloading several of the Juggernauts to test them out. Of course he took the first one. It was the same size as the Juggernaut he'd piloted against Harley, but should prove several times more powerful. Tomas and Cameron clambered into theirs. It was a tight fit for their burly frames, but they managed.

With a deep, throaty rumble, the engines that would power much of the Juggernaut came to life. Tomas and Cameron smoothly rolled theirs off their wagons and accelerated, the spheres barreling across the landscape with impressive speed. Hamish lifted his off the wagon with a blast of thrusters that cast it into the air. He set the sphere spinning so that when it landed it instantly accelerated after Tomas and Cameron.

They spent a few minutes racing around the group, testing thrusters and test-firing a few of their weapons. Missiles detonated against distant rocks, fire blasted out around the spheres, and Tomas charged a tall stone outcropping nearby. Just as he reached it, he unleashed the wide battering ram. It erupted out the front and exploded through the outcropping. Tomas plowed right through a second later, eliciting a cheer from the group.

"Excellent," Ivor said as the three spheres slowed to a stop nearby. "Coupling them all together into Ilse's Revenge will give even the queen pause, I reckon."

In very good humor, they spent another hour fine-tuning the battle plan and drawing from Kilian's long experience fighting his mother. They would hit her hard and fast and break down her healing power. In the moment when she realized her healing wasn't working, they'd destroy her.

As the planning began winding down, Connor felt a growing sense of optimism. They could actually pull it off.

"One final point," Kilian said seriously. "Should the battle go against us for any reason, we need a disengage signal."

"You can't be serious," Hamish protested. "We're going to beat her."

"Hopefully, but I've experienced too many fights with my mother not to understand something could go wrong. Since Connor, Evander, and I expect to engage the closest, any of us have authority to trigger the flee command."

"We should call it Burned Cookies," Hamish suggested. "That's always a bad sign."

"Why not just say Disenage?" Verena asked.

"Because we don't want her knowing what we're doing until it's too late," Hamish said.

He had a good point, and his codeword was accepted. If anyone called out Burned Cookies, the rest of the team promised to immediately flee. Connor and those closest to the queen would seek to disengage and join them, but they would be on their own. Others coming in to help would just get killed too.

No one liked the idea, but everyone saw the need for it. No one had ever defeated Queen Dreokt. She'd been driven off before, but never defeated. If they lost, the ensuing battle against the queen's armies might be little more than a formality to finish crushing the revolution.

Connor held Verena close and silently vowed he would not run, not if there was any chance of winning, but he was glad Verena had agreed to follow the plan. He hoped he could stand as an equal against the queen now, but Verena would be destroyed. Or worse, mind-wiped and turned against him.

He shuddered to think of that horrible possibility.

"Connor, do you think we can really defeat her?" Verena asked in a small voice, her usual eternal confidence replaced by open worry.

"I don't think we have a choice." He forced confidence into his voice. That seemed to help reassure her.

He only hoped they weren't all lying to themselves.

Chapter Eighty-Five

Nothing Motivates Like the Vomit Rocket

Connor slowed the underwater Slide to a halt in the Macantact river, just at the point where it reached the northern outskirts of Crann. He stood on the watery deck alone in a bubble of air forty feet below the surface. He'd chosen to use the boat-like construct of water for his solo incursion as a way to feel closer to his team. They'd used the Slide on the journey fleeing the Carraig, and again during the failed attempt to save Ivor's fiancé, Alyth.

Even though he was immersed in the great river, his mouth felt dry and his pulse was racing. He tried to breathe deeply to calm himself as he checked the integrity of the shielding around the Slide for the hundredth time. It was secure, more secure than any shielding he had ever attempted with water.

Not only had he surrounded the entire underwater ship with the protective bubble of his water senses, but he had created three additional levels of shielding around that one, each about fifty yards out from the previous. The multi-layered defensive measures ensured he remained safely concealed from other Spitters monitoring the river.

They were there, of course. The queen's vast army filled the great plain stretching north from Crann. It appeared General Aonghus had learned lessons from the battle of Merkland and Connor had sensed Petralists walking with earth and water for the last ten miles.

The queen had created hundreds of new Petralists, but most of them were still very new to their affinities and lacked the subtle control and deft touch that came with experience. Although their defenses were extensive, the majority of those on duty were clearly newer Petralists. As Connor gently swept his own water senses downriver, he picked them up like toddlers stomping around in the dark.

No doubt they considered the risk of an attack minimal, so it made sense to give the newer Petralists some experience rather than saddle the much smaller number of experienced Petralists with the chore. They still thought Connor and Ivor dead or captured, and chances of Kilian and Evander attacking alone were minimal. No one else posed enough of a threat to worry about, so although Connor had needed to slip past quite a few other Petralists in the river, he felt confident that none of them had sensed his passage.

Moving past another Petralist actively monitoring the waters was tricky, but similar to the concepts he learned in his first lessons about shielding with earth. The trick was in using subtle, gentle touches. None of the enemy Spitters were working very hard to conceal themselves, but instead had cast their influence wide across the waters. The Sentries were probably doing the same thing with the earth. So the challenge was to very subtly divert their will around his location and pass through among them like a hole in the water.

With his multi-layered approach he had adjusted his shields so that each layer split an enemy Petralist's senses just a few degrees. That small gap would not register on anyone but the most skilled, actively focusing on the area. By the time all of his shields passed them, those tiny gaps added up to a hole large enough to slip the narrow deck of the underwater Slide through unseen.

On any other day the exercise would've been thrilling, but today it only served to ratchet up Connor's nerves. He tried to calm himself and was tempted to transform part of the deck into a comfortable chair. If he really wanted calm, he'd break out a few smashpacked desserts, but after considering the idea, he rejected it. His nervous tension helped him focus.

The mission was as simple as diving off the cliff into Loch Sholto with fifty knives strapped all over his body, with the goal of not getting cut. He had to draw out the queen alone, without getting killed in the process. The rest of the team were deployed at the trap site, and everything was ready. All they needed was the queen to get the party started.

First step, infiltrate the greatest army assembled since the Tallan wars.

He had considered and discarded a score of ideas about how best to distract, enrage, and draw out the queen. Some of them were downright foolhardy, like knocking on the front gates and challenging her to a running battle. Others were far too likely to fail, like sending in another swarm of sculpted scones and then attacking all of the latrines when they filled with groaning Petralists.

Connor still didn't like the idea of using stilling again, but hadn't been able to come up with a better alternative. So as he hovered there near the city, he tapped basalt and reached for the outer-focused power of stilling. With the ability to now concentrate exclusively on the green energy source, he connected with it even more securely than he had during the first battle of Merkland.

That awesome memory of drawing life force from forty thousand people still made him shiver, but he ruthlessly forced down the sense of eager anticipation to feel that wondrous river of life again. He would do it, but he wouldn't like it. He didn't dare waiver for even a second.

Connor extended his senses out beyond the river and toward the army. He did not need to still the entire city of Crann, but hoped to influence as much of the army as possible. All of those lives burned in his mind like tens of thousands of candles on a vast, dark plain. Only ascended Petralists might be able to sense his stilling power creeping over the host. As far as Connor knew, only the generals were ascended, but he needed to proceed cautiously, just in case.

"Here we go," he whispered to himself and gently released his power, like a soft breath, barely enough to make a candle flicker.

His senses sharpened, all of those lives snapping into greater clarity in his mind as he sent his influence creeping with deliberate care across the host. He suspected the queen was probably housed in the governor's palace, but he could not dare take chances of alerting her too soon. So he kept his influence far from that sector.

When he had attempted to still Merkland, spreading his influence over the entire city had strained the limits of his strength, even reinforced with porphyry and driven by desperate need. So he was startled to realize that since his ascension his stilling ability had magnified many fold.

At first he sensed thousands of lives, then tens of thousands, then well over a hundred thousand. Many were indeed regulars, but a staggering percentage possessed at least one affinity. The flames of their life forces glowed brighter and drew stilling toward them like magnets. He pushed his stilling power across the entire camp, but left its heart for last. That's where the brightest life forces glowed, the captains and generals, the most powerful and experienced Petralists.

Connor's power wafted over the rest of the camp, like an invisible mist, gently touching each life force, but not yet drawing power from them. He connected to each of them, like a mosquito settling onto the skin but not yet plunging its needle into flesh. If anyone recognized what he was about to do, it would be the leaders, so he slipped his influence into the heart of camp with exquisite care.

No one struck at him or seemed to understand the silent danger creeping among them even as he reached into the central command tent and recognized the fiery glow of General Aonghus' and General Rosslyn's life forces.

That's when Connor struck. Where his influence had rested weightless as a flaxen cord over those vibrant hearts, it transformed into steel bands that seized them and wrapped them in tightening bonds.

This time there was no lag before energy began pouring back along the conduit to Connor like a reverse wave. It thundered into him with astonishing power, and he rose up onto his toes, arms outstretched, gasping. The energy from the souls he had stilled in Merkland had nearly eclipsed his ability to control it. The energy that poured into him now was several times stronger, but he managed somehow to hold it in. In fact, he could see that energy like an invisible glow pouring into him and fusing to his core.

He laughed with the unrivaled thrill of that much raw, pure energy. And he felt connected with all of those lives, somehow sensing their states of being. The regulars succumbed first, slowing to a halt, settling into chairs, lying down on the ground, or simply closing their eyes. The Petralists withstood the invisible assault a little longer, and Connor sensed the beginnings of alarm ringing through some of them. Only the strongest actually managed to shout a warning and tap their powers, questing out in vain for the invisible enemy draining their strength.

Connor clearly sensed General Aonghus' rage, and the fear of General Rosslyn, seated across from him at their command table. For a moment Connor was tempted to snuff out Aonghus' life. The queen had twisted him into a monster, and in Connor's mind he again saw Jean blackened and bloody and on the cusp of death. Revenge was so tempting that he quivered with the need to strike, and only barely held back.

There might be many justifications for executing Aonghus, but he held his hand. Many had been corrupted by the queen, some willingly but most not. He still hoped somehow to help as many as possible regain their previous self-control. He did not hold out much hope for Aonghus, and was not sure what he would do if the general tried to change. But it was not Connor's choice to make. In the battle that would surely come, Connor fully expected Hamish to track Aonghus down and deal out appropriate vengeance.

So instead he tapped inner limestone and struck Aonghus with sensory deprivation. Let the man panic, trapped in the burning inferno of his own mind.

The plan was to still the army just long enough to exhaust them, then release them. One of his greatest fears about this plan was to feel weak lives again snuffed out by his stilling. In Merkland so many had been young or weak or wounded, and their deaths at his hand still haunted him. Luckily the army he was stilling now was made up almost entirely of hale and hearty individuals. He could hold them for quite a while. Just as he had the last time he tried stilling a large population, he felt an enormous reluctance to release it and sever that incredible flow of energy.

No doubt if the queen ever decided she needed the lives of her people to fuel her strength, she would not hesitate to snuff out as many lives as it took. The thought that he might be relishing the same temptation that she would surely give in to helped Connor regain his equilibrium and sever stilling.

As his influenced faded from the army, he could feel many of the soldiers gasping or crying out in panic, but he did not believe any of them would die. He had absorbed so much energy that his previous nervousness evaporated, like water flash-boiling from a superheated pan. If he could ever face the queen and survive, it was now.

So he hurled his senses into the city. Ignoring the feeble lives of the citizens and soldiers there, he closed in on the brightest life force of all. Queen Dreokt blazed like a bonfire among candles. He sensed that she was already awake, moving through the grand central palace. He wasn't sure if she had sensed his attack, or just hadn't retired, but he didn't feel her will pushing through the city to find him yet.

Time to get her attention.

Connor gathered up his stilling power like a tidal wave, and just as he felt the first flickers of the queen's will rippling out from her, he struck with every ounce of power he could throw into the blow. An avalanche of stilling boiled over the queen, and for a second Connor felt it connect. A vast current of energy sucked away from her, crossed the city, and thundered into him.

His grin faded, though. He clearly sensed her towering fury at the despicable insult. That he might attempt to still her unlocked a rage so fierce, it was like an all-consuming fire.

Somehow she shattered his stilling and flung his influence away. She was so strong! She'd invented affinity powers after all, and had centuries of experience wielding them.

Connor swallowed a flicker of fear. He was still so full of raw energy, not even the queen's wrath could completely snuff out his confidence. She might be ancient and powerful, but he still enjoyed the element of surprise.

So Connor cast off his shielding and erupted out of the river, rising a hundred feet into the air on a shimmering, intertwined column of fire and water.

He tapped limestone to blaze like a living sun, and tapped quartzite to his voice for the final touch.

Connor laughed, magnifying the sound a thousandfold. In his mind he was going for an evil thunder chuckle like Harley had created with such great effect outside of Merkland. What he got sounded like a convention of hysterical maniacs.

Well, we might not be instilling fear, but at least he definitely got everyone's attention. He also spared a moment to reach up through the air to the clouds high above the city and seize the long, narrow missile Verena had set circling the city. He yanked it straight down and wrapped it in the heaviest shielding he could. As soon as it turned vertical, Verena sensed the change and threw wide the missile's thruster. It plunged downward with inspiring acceleration and would strike in seconds.

The waters of the river around him suddenly erupted into giant fists. Twelve of them converged on him, grasping at him like claws of destruction. Queen Dreokt hadn't wasted any time pinpointing his location.

Part of Connor wanted to seize those waters and wrestle the queen for dominance. He was infused with so much energy, and enjoyed such a close association with water that he could not imagine that he might lose. But that was not the plan.

So he tapped pumice and threw himself into the air, slipping through the grasping watery claws and rocketing skyward to five hundred feet. That high, he was out of range of any of the other Petralists. The city spread below him, lanterns twinkling like tens of thousands of fireflies. The enormous host spread north, even larger than the swarm that had nearly destroyed Merkland. He appreciated the view, but couldn't get distracted. He'd gotten the queen angry, but needed to goad her into chasing him without bothering to consider the consequences.

Queen Dreokt rose swiftly, but with regal poise above the central palace, standing upon a platform of air. She wore an impressive gown of crimson and blue, hands on hips, glowing like the rising of the sun. As soon as she appeared, he felt the weight of her gaze like a tangible link and tensed, reinforcing his already strong mental shielding.

"You!" Her voice boomed like thunder over the plain. "I thought you were captured, your mind broken."

"You're not as convincing as you think. In fact, my Builder friends have another gift for you," he shouted back, again seizing the missile in its super-fast plunging descent. It was slightly off course, so he pushed the nose over to better aim at the queen.

She somehow sensed his effort and her will slammed into his, smashing aside his shielding and pushing the missile aside with overwhelming force.

He let her. He didn't need it to actually hit her, but it was close enough. The missile had closed to within a couple hundred yards, almost directly above her. Connor spoke clearly, the speakstone link back to Verena already active.

"Let her have it."

The missile detonated.

The explosion was pretty impressive, a charge of diorite designed to burst the hollow ceramic container at the head of the missile containing the payload and spray it downward with terrific force.

Queen Dreokt glanced up just as a fine mist of disgusting puke-worthy stench settled over her. Hamish had perfected the blend using his milked skunk extract, the mega stench, and a few other vile chemicals from the Althins. Even from more than a mile away, Connor saw her shudder, her expression turning disgusted.

"I call it a vomit rocket, Your Majesty!"

Then he ran.

Air laughed as she held his hand and yanked him into the sky faster and faster. She asked, "So you want to feel what real speed is like?"

"Show me what you can do," Connor urged.

With her hair blowing around her like a thunderhead, she laughed again and tripled their speed. Soon they raced north, rivaling the fastest he had ever flown in the Hawk. He'd reach his friends in moments.

He glanced back, and sure enough Queen Dreokt was giving chase, flying as fast as he, standing easily in the air, hair unruffled by the speed of her flight. Her voice spoke directly into his mind. "*Foolish boy. You dare attack me? I meant to raise you to greatness, to teach you truth, and to bequeath to you a nation united.*"

"*United by insanity isn't my idea of fun,*" he shouted back.

"*So your Builder friends still live? You should have used the time to flee. I will teach you respect, and together we will protect our world from the true dangers, even if that means obliterating those annoying Builders you so desperately love.*"

"*The honey bee flitting between flowers commands its tiny domain, but the grumpy old lady who spanks a pedra gets eaten.*"

That was pretty good, but his insolent grin faded as she responded with a colossal mental punch aimed at the center of his brain. That strike would have snuffed out the mind of anyone else, but Connor was already tapping chert with all of his mental shielding in place. The blow rattled him, but he gritted his teeth and imagined himself sheltering in his family home in Alasdair. The sturdy structure, built by his father, stood intact and secure, buffeted by a mighty storm but undamaged. He managed to hold on, although his progress slowed a little as the mental buffeting shook his connection with Air.

He struck back out of pure instinct, tapping limestone and forming a mirage of Verena in the Swift suddenly shedding a cloak of invisibility. The imaginary Verena swept in toward the queen, speedslings firing hornets while she cast handfuls of quickened stones that shot through the air toward the queen.

Queen Dreokt actually cried out, shrieking like a housewife who just spotted a mouse in her cupboard. Definitely something about Builders worried her, but an instant later she struck with a firestorm of combined elements that would have obliterated Verena, the Swift, and all of her activated stones.

Connor let the mirage drop and tried his booming thunder chuckle again. He managed to avoid sounding so hysterical, but his voice still came out high-pitched and shrieking, as if he had magnified the sound of a rather sick steaming teapot.

In his enhanced sight he saw the queen frown in his direction, her head tilting a little in concern. No thunder chuckle of his would ever scare her, but maybe she now worried that she had partially damaged his mind from that assault.

He couldn't help flicking his chert mental senses across the distance. He could not read her thoughts, and sensed her anger had been replaced by a sense of raw determination. He needed her angrier, less in control, so he cast out the thought, "*Why don't we settle this over a fresh batch of scones that my Builder friends just finished baking? I think you tried some of their sweets before. Which one was your favorite?*"

That did it. Her rage exploded and she shouted, "*I will catch you, boy. There is no escape now. So you're stronger? You cannot withstand me for long, and for your impudence you will help me torture your beloved Builder girlfriend for a year before I wipe her mind and send her to perform the most menial and disgusting labors I can devise. She will live a long, miserable life. And it will be your fault.*"

Connor very nearly turned around to go punch that smug smile off her face, but fought down the urge. He had rattled her, he shouldn't be surprised that she was good at rattling in return.

To reinforce the illusion that he was fleeing out of fear he turned the keystone on his minihub to the common channel and shouted in a panicked voice, "Our intelligence was wrong. The queen is with the army and she's chasing me. Help!"

Verena responded immediately according to plan, sounding panicked. "No, Connor. Don't lead her here. We're not ready."

If the queen didn't already know she could eavesdrop on speakstone conversations, she'd just learned. That should give her a sense of victory and reinforce her confidence.

Connor glanced back, forcing an expression of fear. Queen Dreokt continued to chase him, looking smugly confident.

He would wipe that look off her face forever. Soon.

Chapter Eighty-Six

The Greatest Battle Petralist of All Time

Connor landed on the barren ridgetop they'd chosen for their trap. The location was perfect, wide open enough to allow them to fully engage, but broken and rough enough that no one lived in the area and they could easily conceal their surprises.

"So far so good," he said to himself. First phase complete, and he was still alive.

Now for the hard part.

Connor quested through the ground with slate but felt nothing. Even though he knew they were there, Evander had prepared for several hours, and Connor had never met anyone who could best the giant in shielding. When he quested out through the air, he caught only a faint hint that something might be there, high above, but invisible to the eye.

Again, Evander's shielding was exceptional, combined with mechanicals designed to help conceal flying craft from view. No doubt Hamish and Verena were also tapping pumice to help hide them from elemental powers. Connor felt confident the queen would not spot any of them before it was too late.

There was water available from an underground stream that Kilian had identified, but which Connor now struggled to locate. It too was extremely well hidden.

Queen Dreokt landed about ten long paces from Connor, and he embraced all of his affinities. He would need everything and was ready to unleash it all in a fight to the death. Hopefully her death.

The elements appeared in the air around him, wearing leather or steel armor. He decided the surprising choice was a good sign. The queen gave no indication that she saw them, thankfully. They might seem to be standing openly beside Connor, but somehow he was still seeing them only inside his mind.

"Today you face great peril," Water said calmly, but she looked eager for the fight to commence. Her long hair was braided, and she wore armor that reminded him of Verena's custom set.

"And perhaps great opportunity," Air added.

Fire scowled. "Focus until the right moment."

Earth, who was entirely encased in armor that looked like granite said, "Days of strife offer opportunity to the one best prepared."

"And that will be . . . Connor," Water said, glancing at him and giving him an encouraging smile. That pause was odd, but Connor didn't have time to ask her about it.

Queen Dreokt's expression was again calm, and she regarded him like Lady Isobel from Alasdair might have regarded some new treasure she was about to acquire. The queen spoke in a disapproving tone, "You fly exceptionally well, and you've learned to shield your mind, at least at a distance. You show promise, boy, but you were a fool to ascend so soon."

"It's not foolish to learn to defend oneself," he retorted, happy she hadn't launched into the fight. Every second she waited was another second his team could set up their counter-attack.

"You display reckless foolhardiness in crossing a bridge before you know the danger," she snapped angrily, her stance turning more aggressive. "You think you are clever, but you walk paths of destruction. You think you are clever, but you led me to this barren hilltop. What advantage could you hope to gain over me here?"

"Every advantage, of course," Connor replied, happy that his voice sounded calm. Now that the moment of battle had arrived, his fears faded under a rising tide of eagerness. They'd dreaded this fight for months, but now all their preparation would pay off. Together they would destroy her and guarantee peace for their families, their communities, and their nations.

Connor drew upon his elemental affinities. Water and fire appeared, ropes of elements twining together to form a protective cage around him. He added earth, slender fingers of brown mixing in with the others. Then air joined the mix, tightly wound vortices, like miniature clouds weaving in amongst the rest.

Finally he tapped serpentinite, wrapping the structure in the sounds that he most cherished. Verena's laughter, his mother's voice, the sound of Jean's pencil on her notebook, and even the sound of that last explosive vomit that had won him the title from Hamish.

Queen Dreokt waited for him to finish, pursing her lips. "You stabilized your elements, and you even manage connection to serpentinite, despite the difficulties. Yes, indeed you have potential, once I educate you and teach you caution and control."

He had hoped she'd seem more intimidated.

Connor tapped a little bit of porphyry, and the beast stirred in his heart. It was his reserve weapon. Then he tapped chert and drove a mental dagger toward the queen.

She easily deflected it and actually chuckled. "I control the minds of all who serve me. Your fledgling mastery of your affinities offers no real threat. Surely you understand that."

"I understand you're overconfident and more than a little overfed."

She surprised him by clapping her hands and laughing in delight. "Excellent. Enough presence of mind to cast insults in the face of guaranteed defeat. Excellent indeed."

Her laughter disappeared and she took a step closer. Connor tensed to fight, but her expression turned weirdly sincere. "Listen to reason, boy. You do not need to be destroyed. I can complete your instruction in all of your affinities, help you understand your powers in ways that it would take you decades to grasp." She extended a hand and beckoned him closer. "Bow to me, as is your eventual fate, and I will spare your family."

So she knew about his family. He shouldn't be surprised, but he couldn't avoid a new trickle of fear. If he refused and lost, what would she do to them? Probably whatever she was going to do to them anyway.

Not if he stopped her.

"How about you surrender to me? I promise to try teaching you how to not be such a screaming psychopath. You might even figure out how to enjoy life for a change," Connor retorted.

Her calm expression evaporated under a flash of rage. She struck, calling elements out of thin air and blasting them into an intertwined column at Connor. As ready as he thought he was, the brutality of the strike still caught him by surprise. It shredded his defensive cage and slammed into his chest, catapulting him off his feet.

At the same time, she struck at his mind, like a thousand fingernails scraping down slate practice boards the children sometimes used in their lessons. The mind-numbing shriek of it tore at his mental shields as he fought to push the elements away. Fire boiled around his face, while water scoured his exposed skin.

Air screamed across his nostrils, threatening to rip out his breath, and earth tried creeping over his eyes. He smelled cinders somehow. Was he burning?

He felt unbalanced, overwhelmed, and deeply afraid. Whispered voices seemed to laugh in dark corners of his mind, taunting him, telling him he'd been a fool to think he was strong enough to fight Queen Dreokt.

Connor lunged back to his feet, pushing through the cloud of elements and debilitating fears. He needed to strike at her, but wasn't sure how to fight off her mental assault. It was a form of warfare he had too little experience with and she kept slipping around his defenses like a cat nimbly jumping around a small child's playful swats.

So Connor tempted porphyry. The beast erupted out of his heart and filled him with its deadly intensity. He felt his limbs shake with the potential for change, but for the first time he felt completely in control of whether or not to call upon that change. The rage of porphyry coursed through him, but did not smother thought as it always had in the past.

Instead of fighting him to control his own body, porphyry stepped into his mind like a rampager that crouched beside the elements. They shifted away from it and it growled in warning to them before speaking in a raspy, hoarse voice, its red eyes glowing with bloodlust.

"*Pack Leader, let us hunt together. We will feast on her life blood.*"

That sounded like a good idea, and Connor's teeth ached, on the verge of changing into fangs.

As if she sensed that thought, or sensed porphyry coursing through his mind, the queen recoiled and snarled with frustration. "You foolish child! I told you to leave porphyry alone. It's an unstable power that will corrupt and destroy you."

Connor laughed. "As if you're planning to do any less. Now get out of my head and let's see if you actually remember how to fight someone."

He tapped granite and charged, ringing himself in elements to reinforce his strength. With the life force of all those people he had stilled in Crann helping to drive his fist, he could probably punch her back to Donleavy.

For a second she gaped, looking stunned that he would actually challenge her to physical combat.

And his move distracted her exactly the way he hoped.

The ground to either side of the queen erupted. Spears of earth drove toward her from both sides. She seemed startled by the unexpected attack. Evander really was the master of shielding. The spears of earth struck, but melted away as they touched her.

Evander rose out of the ground about fifty feet to their right, already holding compressed light between his clasped hands, his massive shoulders hunched with the effort. As soon as he broached the surface, he released the death beam.

It crossed the distance in a flash, leaving an after image burning in Connor's sight. The blast of light pierced the queen, punching cleanly through and shooting out into the distance, barely slowed.

She frowned at Evander, not even reacting to the terrible injury, which immediately began closing. "There you are, you annoying child. Your unruly behavior will only make your punishment worse."

That's when Kilian landed like a meteor, striking out of the clear sky so fast Connor barely recognized his approach. He slammed down onto his mother, encased in glittering fire and water, leading with a fist that exploded in a spectacular diorite eruption.

Connor blinked, stumbling in his advance, momentarily blinded by the onslaught. If Kilian had struck him like that, he had no doubt whatsoever that he would have simply been annihilated. But he forced himself to seize the combined elements, striking at the still-exploding cloud where the queen had stood.

He felt nothing.

The cloud dissipated a couple seconds later, revealing Kilian on one knee, fist pressed to the ground. With no sign of the queen.

"Tallan slap me silly," Connor breathed. He could not imagine Kilian might have actually blown her to smithereens, so he spun, looking for her. Evander was also turning, expression concerned. Kilian rose, actually looking shaken by the brutal strike he had just unleashed.

"Thank you for making this easier for me." Queen Dreokt rose up out of the earth to their right. She looked unharmed, although her clothing was in disarray. No doubt she had taken terrible damage, but she healed so fast they couldn't take advantage of any distraction the damage might have caused. She wagged an angry finger at Kilian. "Son, you have corrupted enough of my descendants and led them stupidly toward destruction. You still insist that I destroy you. So be it. I will not allow your insanity to wreck everything."

Verena had activated Sucker Punch a couple hours ago, but it didn't seem to be affecting the queen's ability to heal yet. That meant they needed to hurt her a lot more.

Connor launched into the air toward her, unleashing an intertwined blast of all of the elements. Kilian flung fire and water at her at the same time, while Evander plunged a giant fist into the earth. Connor felt his will surging through the ground like a lightning bolt. Between them all they should be able to hold her off.

Queen Dreokt threw out her hands, triggering an elemental explosion. The ground rippled, the air shook with thunder, and fire and water erupted in spheres of ice and superheated flame. The sheer intensity of the blast knocked Connor tumbling backward a hundred feet, bouncing wildly across the hard ground. Kilian and Evander fared better, somehow remaining upright in the face of the queen's attack, even though she still drove them sliding back across the hard-packed ground.

The air smelled charred, like burned toast, and the hairs on Connor's arms rose with a tingling tension as elements crashed and battled all around.

Queen Dreokt started laughing like a maniac, and her hair braided itself. Her expression turned predatory and she cackled, "Before you die, you'll see firsthand why I am the best battle Petralist who has ever lived!"

Chapter Eighty-Seven

A Glimpse of Insanity

No way would Connor let the queen see she intimidated him. So he said, "Sure, you dominated so much in the past that you had to nap away three entire centuries. Today you've got to learn to adapt."

Right on cue, Verena joined the attack. Missiles began raining out of the sky by the dozen. High above them, the Hawk, the Swift, and much farther out, the Albatross dropped their invisible shielding and launched a full volley of mechanicals. Connor felt them coming, so no doubt the queen did too. He threw his will into the sky to help shield the missiles inbound, but couldn't actually feel them with his quartzite senses.

They were coated with pumice dust to protect them from elemental attacks.

The queen indeed glanced up in annoyance and made a shooing gesture. Tornado-force winds ripped across the face of the inbound missiles to drag them off course, but they punched through without slowing.

"So the Mhortair attempt to still thwart me from the grave?" she growled.

Connor unleashed a torrent of intertwined elemental power at the queen, trying to keep her distracted. Maybe something in those missiles could hurt her. Verena had packed all sorts of activated stones among the diorite, hoping they might trigger whatever it was she feared from the Builders.

Queen Dreokt somehow split his elemental assault, letting it pass harmlessly past her. When he tried pulling it back at her, she seized control away from him and sent the elemental barrage blasting out against Kilian and Evander, sending them both staggering.

Connor gritted his teeth in frustration. He loved using that trick, but it really stunk to have it played back against him.

Before he could attack her again, the queen threw up one hand. Rocks the size of her head erupted out of the ground and shot into the air like they were giant hornets, flung from the world's biggest speedslings. Connor tried to intercept them, reaching out with air senses, but Queen Dreokt wrestled against him for control of the air, blocking his efforts for critical seconds.

Rocks struck the inbound missiles dead on. Since they weren't being directly controlled by the queen, pumice did nothing to protect the missiles, and they all exploded in a firestorm that Queen Dreokt seized and flung higher into the air, straight toward Verena and the other flyers.

Cold fear reinforced Connor's need as he bent his entire will into the effort of deflecting those flames and saving his friends from being immolated. No doubt they had pumice active and could tap blind coal as needed, but he worried what else the queen might be weaving into that wall of fire.

Thankfully, at that moment the ground rippled and spat out a dozen Juggernauts spheres, previously concealed by Evander. Hidden in a circle roughly two hundred feet around Connor's landing spot, they all accelerated toward the queen, thrumming with energy and the promise of violent destruction.

They were an awesome sight, replenishing Connor's hope. A single Juggernaut had fought Harley almost to a standstill. Sure, Hamish had some help, but he had taken on one of the strongest Petralists who ever lived. A dozen of them, well, a dozen would definitely scare Connor.

They enraged the queen.

She dropped her attack against the distant flyers and spun, glaring at the dozen enormous mechanicals picking up speed as they rolled in, as if Hamish had simply ordered them all to strike her with battering rams from every side.

"Vile Builders!" she shrieked.

Connor did not give her a chance to wreck them, but tapped the overwhelming energy that he had stolen from her army and poured it all through his connection to chert. He struck at her mind with every bit of that power. He snarled as he drove that power like a dagger, riding the wave of exhilarating energy.

The blow clobbered her like a landslide and her mental defenses actually cracked. She might be the dread queen overlord of mind wiping, but she had never felt anything like that. For a second Connor felt her mind and drove his thoughts into it like daggers.

She shrieked, this time in actual pain, and staggered, clutching at her head. Connor continued to drive into her mind, exulting with a sense of impending victory. He was actually hurting her! She wasn't invulnerable.

He felt her thoughts, her arrogant overconfidence that had faded to annoyance, given way to battle lust, and finally admitted a spark of fear for the first time in centuries. As their connection deepened, Connor felt a more complete picture of her mind, and although he needed to strike her down, for a second he recoiled.

What he sensed was no longer human. She had lingered in the long sleep for three hundred years, and from all accounts her mind had been broken even before that. She'd raised an elfonnel to defeat her enraged husband and had lost something important when she returned. She'd failed to escape her elfonnel after the Battle of Vallanes. Who knew what getting trapped in that elemental form for so long had done to her? Now that she'd risen again, very little of what remained of her was actually human. She was foreign, unlike anything Connor had ever felt.

If a healthy mind was like a seventeen-course meal, her mind was more like that meal had been eaten, then regurgitated, left to rot, then stewed to boiling.

Then he felt something else, a tiny core of absolute fear, buried deep under the fractured thoughts and jumbled emotions. He sensed fear of the Builders, and weirdly, fear of the very elements she wielded. This was it, the secret he needed to know, to understand. He just needed another second, and he'd understand how to beat—"

Queen Dreokt shrieked with rage and her mental shields snapped back into place, ejecting him. Their eyes met and he saw rage to rival anything he'd ever felt as a rampager burning inside of her.

Although Kilian and Evander continued striking at her with all their strength, she waved their efforts aside like someone brushing at flies. The Juggernauts were still rushing in, but she struck with spikes of narrowly focused will that pierced Evander's efforts to shield the mechanicals. Earth struck every one of the Juggernauts, catapulting them high into the air.

They all activated thrusters, although half of them reacted slower than the others. No doubt the ones with less experienced pilots, who were now getting their first real taste of battle. Connor hoped they didn't lose heart, but even Hamish and the others who reacted quicker would take precious seconds to come back around.

Connor clearly heard the speakstone chatter between them. Hamish was shouting orders and encouragement to his people. Most of them seemed determined, if understandably terrified. Tomas and Cameron of course being the notable exceptions.

"She's very energetic for such an old lady," Cameron commented.

"I hear higher affinities can do that to you. Bad on the teeth, though," Tomas responded.

"I bet she fancies soups," Cameron agreed.

"Probably why she frowns so much."

Hamish shouted, "Enough chatter! Link up and form Ilse's Revenge! First form."

The Juggernauts altered direction, shooting through the air toward each other in a move that might give them enough power to do some real damage.

The queen held Connor's gaze and said, "Perhaps now that you've felt my thoughts you begin to understand the dangers I'm trying to warn you of, as well as the consequences I suffer from rising through thresholds I did not understand that perhaps you can avoid."

That rattled him. Connor had expected to face a barking-mad lunatic they needed to put down like a rabid dog to save the kingdom. She'd done so many horrible things, but why then waste so much time claiming to want to save him, to teach him? He'd ascended and already sensed dangers in his new powers, but he'd be a fool to think he understood them all. Could he really break his mind and end up like her?

The thought made him shudder, and he refused to accept it. She must be trying to trick him, trying a more subtle form of mind control, but he couldn't allow himself to get distracted, to waiver in any way. He recalled her barbaric cruelty, her mind bomb that had nearly killed him and Ivor and every Builder. She wanted to murder Verena. She was evil, and he would stop her.

Connor struck at her again with chert, but this time she was ready and deflected his assault. She responded with a dizzying number of elemental attacks, hitting at him from the ground, the air, and both sides with water and fire.

Connor fought back, his concentration becoming complete as he drew deeply upon all of the elements. The queen would usually be stronger, but he was still enjoying an enormous amount of extra energy from stilling, and he burned through it at a staggering rate as he fought to defend himself. He might not be able to defeat her if they fought with elements alone, but he doubted she could fight hand to hand any more. So he broke into a charge, determined to close and pummel her until she couldn't heal any more.

Earth erupted around him in blinding explosions, the thunderclaps pealing so loud his head rang. Then earth fell away beneath him, yawing into deep, spike-lined pits. She switched up attacks with dizzying speed, changing tactics as soon as he reacted to the last one, leaving him struggling to keep up.

But he still managed to walk through it all. Fire and water churned around him, but he deflected them wide or simply stepped through. Kilian and Evander threw their entire focus into helping shield Connor, and their assistance helped him survive the elemental onslaught like a child clinging to a sledding plank during an avalanche.

Air slammed into him from every side, hardened like invisible blades, tough enough to take off a max-tapped Boulder's head. Connor gritted his teeth and punched each of them away or deflected them wide enough to slip through. He focused on the queen, advancing one step at a time. He'd crush her with his fists. If only he hadn't been pushed back so far. The yards between them seemed to stretch like a mile.

His entire reservoir of elemental affinities was completely focused on defense as he made his painfully slow assault, but he wasn't limited only to elemental powers. While the queen seemed locked into her tertiary affinities to the exclusion of almost all else, Connor felt no such limitation.

Drawing upon quartzite, he struck with sensory deprivation. He was not sure if she felt it before she broke it, but for a second her elemental attacks did seem weakened. So he tapped limestone and seized the air all around them, creating mirages of Builders swooping in and casting mechanicals at the queen.

He was not sure if she recognized the mirages were fake because she felt no movement through the air, or if she had learned his trick, but that approach did not seem to accomplish much. So he grasped water and fire together, reaching for the newfound forces of strum and magnis.

The churning air, so full of elements smashing against each other created a lot of charges, so it took Connor only a second to sweep his magnis senses across the area, concentrating all of that energy into a giant charge.

The queen's eyes widened in understanding just as he unleashed it.

A lightning bolt crackled between them. In that second, Connor could feel the pull of the force field of magnis generated by the moving strum, and clearly felt the air along the conduit turn into plasma to pass it through. The bolt of lightning struck the queen in the chest, blasting through and exploding out her back, showering the land behind her with blood and gore.

Queen Dreokt staggered, eyes wide in surprise, although she still did not scream. Connor hoped it was because her lungs had evaporated and she had no air.

She stumbled, but did not fall. The ghastly wound immediately began to close, but the healing progressed at a noticeably slower rate than her last injury. She gasped and for the first time he saw real fear in her eyes. Even though he was pretty sure her lungs were destroyed she managed to gasp into his mind, "*You wicked boy. How did you weaken sandstone?*"

Connor exulted. They were doing it! They were going to destroy her. He threw back the thought, "*Maybe even your affinities realize you're a lost cause. Air said you're heavy, and Water thinks you smell funny.*"

"*Beware considering elementals as people, boy. They are slaves whose power we command. They will lure you into destruction if you allow it.*" Again he sensed her unreasoning fear.

What did she know? She was so broken, she barely knew them. Connor accelerated his charge, and this time he would curse-punch her so hard he'd finish the job.

Even though she was staggering and seemed to be struggling to heal herself, the queen lashed out with desperate strength. A spear of earth no thicker than his finger erupted out of the ground right between Connor's legs. It punched through his armor and stone-hardened skin, stabbing deep up through his torso, from his groin up into his guts.

Connor did scream. The pain blanked out all thought, and he fell even as he seized that earth and melted it away. He had been injured badly before, but somehow this was worse. It burned, as if the queen had filled that slender conduit of earth with the concentrated burning ice that Mister Five had tried to kill him with once.

Connor seized upon sandstone, but he too felt the dearth of healing power. It was not nearly as much fun when he was the one being blocked from healing.

Queen Dreokt cackled, although her mouth suddenly filled with sand as Evander struck her across the face. She had to be badly weakened if his attacks were now causing damage. Kilian, his face set in a scowl, was also striking at an ever-increasing rate, wielding whips of white-hot fire, mingled with water. His attacks were drawing closer and closer to her. The air shimmered with waves of heat and icy droplets of water. It smelled wild, like the heart of a thunderstorm.

"I am so tired of boys who refuse to listen," she spat with a mouthful of dirt.

Water materialized around Evander, forming a sphere of ice. Connor hurt too much to intervene. All he could do was sense what she was doing. A hundred daggers of ice formed within the sphere and plunged into Evander's body.

Kilian turned, extending a hand, and the ice melted away from Evander, who staggered, covered in blood. But the distraction cost Kilian, because earth rose up on either side of him, forming cresting waves that smashed together with overwhelming force and a thunderous boom.

Connor cried out in despair, fearing Kilian was obliterated. The earth melted back into the ground, revealing nothing. For a second, Connor feared Kilian's body had been dragged away forever, but then he appeared again, racing by so fast Connor thought he must be hallucinating. Not even in his fastest fracked sprint had Connor reached half that speed. Kilian shot by his mother, sword whipping out, and severed her hand even as she raised it toward him.

She frowned and picked it up, then waved it at Kilian, who was banking around for another pass. A funnel of air intercepted him, sending him tumbling hundreds of yards away. His angry curses drifted on the wind back to Connor.

The queen was terribly injured, but she was still winning. Connor needed to fight, but oh, he hurt so badly. The injury sapped his strength and left him wanting to cry from the pain.

Then healing power roared into him from the small sandstone pendant Verena had given him. Like a flood, it washed away his injuries and filled him with health. He sagged with relief and grinned up into the air toward the Swift in silent thanks. It looked like their amazing Builder cleverness would indeed tip the balance of the fight in their favor.

The enormous healing power restored Connor almost instantly and he leaped back to his feet. He again max-tapped granite and tried to apply even more to protect himself from another surprise attack. He wasn't sure it would work, but it made him feel less nervous about resuming the attack.

Queen Dreokt stumbled, almost falling, looking weak for the first time. Her gaping wound was still closing, but slowly, and it was finally beginning to take a toll on her. Their eyes met, and he could tell she recognized the truth. She would not be able to regenerate fast enough this time.

Behind her, the dozen Juggernaut spheres were rapidly twisting around each, interlocked, outer plates sliding into new positions, forming into one giant whole. Within seconds they would rise as an interconnected construct seventy feet tall. Not even she'd be able to ignore the combined might of all those mechanicals. Connor had never seen them actually assemble into Ilse's Revenge, and was eager to see its final form, although he was not sure they were going to need it. He would rip the queen apart and toss one piece of her to each of his friends to pound into dust or melt into its component parts.

Mistress Four and Commander Six leaped out of the Hawk high overhead, starting a fast descent. Connor would catch them so they could participate in the final destruction of the dread queen and exact vengeance for the destruction of their people.

The Juggernauts completed the interlocking process faster than Connor had expected, and rose in the mighty form of Ilse's Revenge, towering over the battlefield with a fantastic creaking of steel and roaring of engines.

Connor blinked in astonishment and whispered, "Whoah."

The mighty construct had formed into a towering humanoid shape, the spherical Juggernauts flattened along the edges, huge outer plates formed into armor. Hamish's sphere formed the head, and it looked just like Captain Ilse.

"Did the viewscreen projections work?" Hamish asked via speakstone. "The only form we tested so far was the octahedron, but for this, we had to go full Ilse."

"It looks just like her," Connor said, recognizing the slight shimmering of the image. They were projecting her face onto the head of the giant mechanical. It looked fantastic, and it was so perfectly fitting. Queen Dreokt gaped at the enormous mechanical, looking truly astonished.

Armored plates all along the front side of Ilse's Revenge slid aside and it unleashed intense gouts of fire, along with hornets from eight oversized speedslings. The streams of deadly projectiles slashed into Queen Dreokt, puckering her stone-hardened skin, while the many diorite-tipped ones exploded with a satisfying chain of thunderclaps and blasts of white-hot fire. The explosions charred her skin and she stumbled back, looking actually afraid, clutching hands over the open wound in her chest. Some of the exploding hornets made it through and detonated inside her chest cavity.

She actually grimaced in pain and turned away, eyes wide with terror. The vile Builders were hitting her with their mechanicals, and that frightened her more than anything Connor had yet done. He exulted, feeling a sense of anticipation. They were going to do it! They were actually going to beat her. This battle was almost over!

Except the queen pulled out of a deep pocket a long, sculpted stone.

She started to laugh.

Chapter Eighty-Eight

Burned Cookies

Sculpted stone!" Connor shouted as he threw himself into the air toward Queen Dreokt.

The sculpture she held was long, just like the other ancient sculpted stones he'd seen. It was exquisitely carved into the shape of a skeletal human hand clutching a billowing flame.

Marble. She held the ancient sculpted stone that controlled affinity with fire.

Icy fear drove Connor on and he hurtled toward the queen, who lifted the sculpted marble high, her expression turning victorious, even though her ghastly chest wound was still not closed. Despite his many bloody wounds, Evander began sliding across the ground toward the queen too, but he was even farther away than Connor.

Kilian leaped forward, again moving so fast he seemed to teleport across the distance to his mother. He struck with diorite fists right in her wounded chest. The explosion ripped her in half in a second spray of blood and gore, tossing her legs and hips away and toppling her upper torso and arms to the ground at Kilian's feet.

This time she did scream. The sound started as a shriek of absolute pain, but continued to grow, building in strength far beyond the limit of human lungs. It tore at Connor's ears and he grimaced, but still dove the last few feet, planning to crash-tackle her and rip the stone from her weakened grip. Kilian also reached for the sculpted stone grasped in her hands. If one of them could get that stone, they'd have her.

Earth erupted under Kilian, tossing him high overhead. He twisted in the air, cursing in Havaen, blasting fire out his feet to reverse course. Connor reached for the stone as he crashed onto the queen's bloody form, and his fingers touched it just in time to feel a tidal wave of energy erupt from it, so strong it numbed his senses.

White-hot fire erupted from the stone in a blinding wave. Even though Connor walked with fire and no longer feared heat, the sheer magnitude of the onslaught still catapulted him away so hard he nearly blacked out. Fire boiled around the queen in a column so dense it completely obscured her. Connor reached for the flames, hoping to wrench them away, but only gasped in new fear.

The energy contained within that sculpted stone eclipsed anything he'd ever sensed. It felt like all the fires of the entire world were bottled up in there. And they all belonged to the queen.

In Connor's mind, Fire grinned at the still-expanding fireball. "Now that's a sight, that is." He held his hands toward it like an old gaffer warming himself before a stove. "She's stepped into the flames, boy. No way you can pull her out alone."

"What can we do?" Connor shouted.

Evander retreated from the intense heat that was starting to melt the ground. He looked worried, and not even in an inscrutable confusing way. He just looked afraid.

Not good.

Kilian plunged down into the firestorm, and Connor clearly sensed him tap blind coal. One second he blazed in Connor's marble senses like a descending meteor, and the next he simply disappeared. Connor lost sight of him as he plunged into the fire, but he did sense another explosion of diorite.

He expected to see the queen tumble away, even more broken, but gasped when it was Kilian who careened out of the flames, face bloodied, one arm twisted into a crumpled ball. Queen Dreokt must have broken the bones in twenty places. He smashed into the ground and kept tumbling, either unconscious or suffering such extreme shock that he couldn't react. Connor had never seen Kilian so beat up.

They were out of time. Connor used the rage he felt at seeing Kilian so broken to push back his rising fear, and threw himself into a fracked sprint. Just as he reached the crackling, intense column of the queen's firestorm, he drew deep from marble, and tapped both pumice and blind coal.

The slippery feeling of blind coal wrapped him in its strange embrace, and he plunged through the impenetrable wall of fire. Queen Dreokt stood in the center, wrapped in white-hot fire that held her legless torso off the ground. Her expression was exultant as she held the sculpted marble stone high in her right hand.

Connor needed more primary affinities, so he tapped them all. Obsidian activated, melding with the already-tapped basalt and pumice, accelerating his mind and his ability to manage his movements. He was already tapping blind coal, and gulped down the snake, applying it to his bones just before activating diorite. Its lightning-like power ripped through him just as he finally tapped granite.

Then he curse-punched the queen in her still-gaping chest wound, hoping to rip her torso in half. His fist plunged deep into her and exploded with diorite fire. The blast shook her, but didn't rip her apart.

Instead of squishy organs, it felt like her torso was filled with granite, and the intense eruption of power he released barely cracked it. Connor slammed right up against her, their faces inches apart, and his fear spiked again. He'd known she possessed very little humanity, but now he wondered what she was, and how he could kill her.

"It's too late for you, I'm afraid," she told him, her expression sad, like a grandmother speaking to a sickly child. She seized his face with her free left hand, her fingers stronger than steel, digging in and threatening to crush his skull. He grunted from the pain and grabbed her hand, trying to wrench it free, but couldn't budge her. How could she still be so much stronger?

She winked at him, and that shook him more than any of the terrible injuries she'd dealt out to them all. She added in a pleasant tone even as her fingers ground against his skull with ever-increasing strength, "Nice hit, kid. You may be ascended, but you're still just a child."

Connor tried switching blind coal externally again, but she was already holding him, her fingers digging into his skull, and it didn't help him slip free. So he tapped porphyry, and the beast leaped into his heart and appeared in his mind among the elements, who all backpedaled away from it, looking startled.

"We hunt!" Porphyry roared, but before Connor could unleash the beast, Queen Dreokt threw him away so hard his neck almost snapped.

He tumbled hundreds of yards across the rough plateau, the world spinning crazily around him, crashing right through mounds of rock that got in his way. When he finally stopped, body aching, stomach lurching in reaction to his fear, he felt deeply rattled. He was ascended, was supposed to be as strong as her, but he felt like a toddler trying to fight the Ashlar.

He couldn't focus on the fear, or he'd end up totally useless. So Connor forced himself to stagger back to his feet. He tapped obsidian, accelerating his thoughts, trying to think of a combination they hadn't tried yet. With a flash of insight, he realized he'd been focusing most of his efforts on fighting her with tertiary powers. He'd fallen into the same trap she had, leaning almost entirely on the vaunted elements, but he could never beat her that way. He had to fight smarter.

Queen Dreokt had expanded her column of fire, and to his marble senses, it seemed completely impenetrable. The distant flyers had launched another volley of missiles, but she completely ignored them. They detonated against the inferno with no visible effect. She was sealing them all out, right when they had finally injured her. It was so infuriating! Why wouldn't she just die?

Ilse's Revenge charged in, its feet rolling it across the ground, arms extended to either side to reveal eight sets of missiles hanging beneath them. They fired too, and actually plunged into the firestorm before exploding, but Connor couldn't tell if they accomplished anything either.

"Pumice coating should have done more," Hamish said to his team, sounding as frustrated as Connor felt.

They might not have accomplished much, but they did infuriate the queen. Ropes of combined elements erupted from her firestorm toward Ilse's Revenge. Hamish activated pumice in time, and they slipped through, sliding closer still. The queen might be well concealed in that pillar of impenetrable fire, but the towering form of Ilse's Revenge, with Ilse's face scowling down at the flames was still awe inspiring.

Connor tried focusing his rattled thoughts to rally to their aid. He was still pretty far away, but he could help shield them. Ilse's Revenge was barely a hundred feet from the queen's fiery pillar, pushing forward against the elemental onslaught. He poured every bit of shielding into the effort, but the queen only intensified her attacks. She unleashed a barrage of elemental fury so raw and wild, it eclipsed anything he'd ever experienced.

Hamish and his crew fought forward valiantly, activating blind coal and pumice again and again, but she hammered them with all of the elements and shifted tactics faster and faster. She really was a master of the elements. The giant mechanical staggered under a barrage of huge earthen chunks that she hurled at them. Apparently she released active control just before they struck, nullifying the power of pumice. Blind coal still saved them, but her onslaught forced them to tap it constantly. It wasn't designed for such prolonged use, and they'd run out long before reaching her.

Fire and water boiled around Ilse's Revenge, striking from every side like a thousand angry snakes. Long spears of earth, hardened to stone, drove into joints and tried clobbering the head, but the mechanical continued its dogged advance just like Ilse would if she was really there. Against any other Petralist, they would have posed a dire threat, but they would never succeed alone. Connor redoubled his efforts to help, while both Evander and Kilian charged in again, running right next to each other, their shielding merged together in a way Connor had never imagined possible. Connor's hope soared again. If anyone could get through, it was those two.

Queen Dreokt hammered them mercilessly, even as she kept battering at Ilse's Revenge. Elements flashed back and forth across the battlefield, igniting it in rainbow colors that would have been beautiful if they weren't so deadly. Connor broke into a run as well, but most of his efforts were focused on trying to shield Ilse's Revenge from her attacks.

It wasn't enough, and the individual Juggernaut spheres start running out of blind coal.

The left arm were severed cleanly away by a giant blade of air, and the two spheres comprising it were seized before managing to transform back to their original shapes. Intertwined fire and water slammed them into the ground that gave way beneath them. They sank out of sight, and the hole snapped shut with crushing force, squashing the hapless Juggernauts like bugs beneath a giant heel, cutting off the pilots' panicked cries for help.

Connor gritted his teeth with frustration. He should have been able to help, but his entire focus was consumed trying to fend off the queen's continuing overwhelming assault on the rest of them. He needed to give the rest of Hamish's team a chance to escape, but with that sculpted stone in her hands, Queen Dreokt was accessing far more power than he could, and she swatted aside his best efforts.

A sheet of water struck next, barely one compressed droplet thick, but fifty feet long. It slashed across the topmost junction, severing the head, sending Hamish's Juggernaut tumbling away. Connor seized that one with air and hurled it farther, determined to protect his friend from getting crushed like the others.

Hamish was shouting, "Retreat! Fire anything you've got left and get out of there!"

Too late. More sabers of water slashed home, slicing apart the arms, then the legs. The central torso tumbled to the ground with a resounding crash. They didn't give up, though, and the remaining Juggernauts shifted again, forming one great sphere.

The sight enraged Connor so much that he planted his feet and raised his hands, filled with unshakable resolve. "Give me everything you've got," he told the elements riding in his mind.

They didn't argue, but joined hands, their powers flowing unrestricted into his mind. He wrapped them together, then added serpentinite into the mix. Queen Dreokt hadn't done anything with serpentinite during the entire battle. Did she still think it was useless, beyond even her reach? It was one option that might help tip the balance in their favor. She was hammering the remaining bulk of the Juggernaut, and their last bits of blind coal would surely run out soon.

Connor shouted, "Fight someone who can hit back!"

He hurled all of the intertwined elements straight at Queen Dreokt's firestorm. The five-elements spear plunged into it and pierced it, but missed the queen by a handspan. She severed it before Connor could redirect his powers, but now he knew where she was positioned. He would not miss again.

The elemental barrage ceased against the broken Ilse's Revenge. It looked like he'd drawn her attention again, or maybe she figured the Juggernauts were no longer a threat. She rose to the top of her billowing firestorm. It now stretched over thirty feet and reared more than twenty, a dense column of pure white heat. Connor couldn't see her lower torso, but she didn't look troubled by the fact that she'd abruptly gotten three feet shorter. Her voice boomed like a thunderclap.

"Fools! You threaten my rule without understanding the powers you wield. Witness the power of the ramverk!"

She plunged back into the column of flames and unleashed a blast of fire so concentrated, it was like a limestone death beam, but made of heat instead. So hot, it burned Connor's marble senses and he could only stare in wonder and horror. The fire was so powerful its heat shifted out of the visible spectrum and into ranges beyond human sight.

She didn't cast it at him, but unleashed the unbelievable torrent of living fire straight down. It speared through earth and stone, deeper and deeper until the vast distance challenged Connor's capacity to follow it.

Something exploded many miles below ground, and Connor felt a rumble begin down there and intensify with terrifying speed.

In his mind, Fire chortled. "She's gone and done it! She's cracked the mantel."

Water looked stunned. "Ever has she refused to walk as our champion."

"Might not have a choice today," Fire laughed.

Earth looked exultant. "The birth of a new mountain is a great day, but one I did not expect to see again until our champion was ready."

"What are you talking about?" Connor cried, but he was already thinking maybe he didn't want to know.

Deep in the earth, enormous pressure was building, like a million diorite explosions all erupting at the same time. Connor could feel the earth down there compressing, then melting under fervent heat as fissures ripped through solid rock, splitting up toward the surface like inverted lightning bolts.

Earth looked far too excited. "She has broken the seal over the planet's molten core where the world energy often pools for millennia before breaking forth. The pressure will give birth to a new mountain and bury this land in lava and fire and smoke and destruction."

Fire started laughing wildly. Air scowled at Earth. "I hate the ash from big eruptions. It chokes the sky."

Earth shrugged. "You'll eventually drive it back out. Then you'll have an entirely new range to explore."

Not good. Even the elements were distracted. So were his friends, shouting frantically, asking what was going on.

Connor tried to explain what he was sensing, but he felt numb as the full scope of the disaster settled over his mind like a spiky blanket. "She's unleashing the planet's core. This entire area is about to erupt. Everyone get out of here!"

From within the center of the firestorm, Queen Dreokt's laughter cackled forth. "Haven't you boys started running yet? It won't help, but give me a show anyway."

Harley had wanted a show too, had paused in her assault on Althing to wait for them to come up with clever new ideas. Connor had decided to ascend the second threshold, and managed to drive her off. Sort of. At the moment, he couldn't fathom what might avert the fast-approaching disaster.

Kilian raced up to Connor, looking ashen-faced and more terrified than Connor had ever seen. Evander joined them, his face stoic, but his eyes wild. "Water cast upon a campfire may extinguish the flames, but is in turn consumed."

For once his cryptic speech didn't help calm Connor's nerves. "What?"

"She's going to kill everyone. Can't you feel what's coming? An eruption of this magnitude might shake every building on the continent to the ground. It will fill the air with enough ash to block out the sun and kill all life," Evander stated, crossing his enormous arms.

"I wish you hadn't clarified," Kilian commented, scowling.

Connor was trying very hard not to panic. "What can we do?"

"We have to get that stone away from her," Kilian said resolutely. He erupted off the ground again, diving straight for the heart of the queen's protective column of fire. Flames whipped out of it and slapped him out of the air. He tumbled away, looking stunned.

"Don't you have any blind coal left?" Connor asked, casting his words right into Kilian's speakstone so he could hear across the eighty yards distance. They couldn't defeat her with fire, not right now.

"I'm all out," Kilian replied as he rolled to his feet, disheveled and battered, but still determined.

Connor was too, but maybe he could punch through with combined elements again, making himself the spear this time. Connor wrapped himself in a mixed five-elements shield, then glanced at Evander. "Give me a boost, will you?"

The giant plunged his huge fist into the hard-packed ground. Earth seized Connor's feet and flung him at the queen. If he hadn't been tapping granite, filled with the energy of all those lives he'd siphoned at Crann, and wrapped in elements, the explosive movement would have ripped him apart. Focusing all his affinities into a point in front of him, he drove at her flames. If he could pierce them and close with her, he might have a chance.

He struck, tapping pumice at the same time, but somehow the barrier felt absolutely solid. She owned fire, and she had also added her other elemental affinities into the mix. Did she know a secret to blocking pumice too? It seemed that maybe she did. She'd created a barrier that no Petralist could puncture. Not soon enough to matter.

Connor too bounced off, filled with growing dread. They couldn't stop her. And in moments, the entire area would erupt in an explosion of unstoppable elements. They'd been so close, but she'd flipped the entire fight against them. And against everyone living in Obrion.

"You foolish children fancy yourselves heroes. I only see fools who have brought destruction to all the other fools who follow you," Queen Dreokt mocked them from within her protective flames.

"Doesn't anyone have any blind coal left?" Connor demanded as he rejoined Evander and Kilian. Hamish shot up from inside his battered Juggernaut and flew to join them. All of them shook their heads.

"I have some on the Swift," Verena said, and began accelerating toward them.

That offered one hope, but Queen Dreokt could also overhear speakstone conversations, and she unleashed a mighty wind that swept all the flyers away to the east. If Verena tapped blind coal to slip through, she'd run out before reaching them.

"Tallan take it and boil it for lunch," Hamish cursed. "Can't you get close enough to finish her off?"

"No. That stone she's got is too strong. None of us can match her or break through without blind coal," Connor shouted back. The air was growing hot, and a noxious smell was growing, making him cough. Ominous rumbling was beginning beneath them. He could feel the pressure growing to critical levels far below. They were out of time.

Kilian's expression remained determined. "This day is going worse than even I feared it could. We're out of time. Burned Cookies! Get everyone away before—"

Too late.

Chapter Eighty-Nine

The Ultimate Curse Punch

The eruption built far faster than Connor expected. A tidal wave of molten stone began shooting up through the many fissures ripping up through the stone of the earth. It rose so fast, driven by so much energy, that all the power he'd ever controlled seemed laughable. Even though it was starting miles below ground, it would only take seconds to reach them.

"Go!" he shouted, leaping into the sky. He could fly and so could Hamish, but he realized with horror that the other Juggernaut pilots still locked into the broken Ilse's Revenge would never escape the devastation coming.

Evander leaped into the sky beside Connor, and the fact that he had to abandon earth seemed to confirm the hopelessness of the moment.

Connor glanced back toward Hamish and Kilian. Hamish started turning toward his Juggernaut, but Kilian grabbed his shoulder and shouted, "Fly!"

"But—"

"Fly!" Kilian repeated, throwing Hamish forcibly into the air.

"The other pilots," Connor protested.

Even though he was no longer standing on the earth, he didn't need to be. The ground was groaning and swelling upward. The other Juggernauts could never escape. He caught Mistress Four and Commander Six with air and sent them flying away. The Hawk could pick them up. He could seize all the Juggernauts, but he feared even he would move them too slowly to escape the pending destruction.

So he said, "Hamish, order your pilots to abandon their Juggernauts."

As Hamish did so, Kilian said, "Connor, don't worry about them. I'll get them out of here."

"You can't save them all," Connor protested.

"I'll save as many as I can. You have to contain the eruption. Evander and I will work to block the spreading ash."

"But . . ." Connor said again, trying and failing to comprehend the magnitude of what Kilian was suggesting.

His ancient mentor held his gaze, his expression deadly serious. "Don't fail Connor or *everyone* dies."

Tomas' voice surprised Connor. The Fast Roller shouted, "No retreat, lads! This is our moment. Take the fight to the old hag. Cameron, you with me?"

"Aye!" Cameron said, his voice as eager as ever for a fight. "Give us the naval eruption."

Hamish shouted, "Wait! You need to eject."

But the others were already responding to the command in the bash fighters' voices. The entire body of Ilse's Revenge seemed to compress, then two spheres exploded out the belly, flung forward with tremendous velocity.

Tomas and Cameron.

The other pilots immediately triggered their ejection seats, erupting from their Juggernauts. Kilian leaped toward them, again moving so fast Connor couldn't track him. He couldn't comprehend how Kilian was tapping such speed, but he was grateful for it. Kilian used a burst of fire to shoot into the air to intercept one of the pilots, a woman slowly descending toward the ground, her descent jacket hissing air. Kilian snatched the woman out of the air and shot away, moving so fast he created a little thunderclap as if the air was surprised anyone could move that fast.

Tomas and Cameron accelerated straight toward that intense burning pillar, whooping their favorite war cries.

"No one else knows how to manage their blind coal," Cameron said, sounding smug.

"Gives us the bash fight of a lifetime," Tomas shouted with another whoop.

"Can't believe we're wearing all this armor," Cameron replied. "Makes me feel fat."

"You're head's fat. Can't these things go any faster?"

"Kind of sad even Connor forgot you can't always rely on those fancy tertiaries. Times like this, a good beating is all that works," Cameron said.

"Kid's getting inferenced by all them powerful old Petralists he hangs out with too much," Tomas agreed.

Cameron chortled. "Who taught you to talk? The word's impoverished."

"Get out of there!" Hamish shouted, glancing at Connor for help.

Connor wanted to stop them, to help them, but there simply wasn't time. Maybe they were right. The queen's defenses were built around blocking him, Kilian, and Evander, but the juggernauts were Builder mechanicals, and they were the only ones left with blind coal. He didn't have time to go take it from them. If they could punch through, he had to let them try.

Attempting to do so was horribly dangerous, but not doing it was worse. They were facing absolute destruction if the queen controlled the eruption. She was mad if she thought it wouldn't hurt her own people, but clearly she didn't care. If only they had more blind coal!

"Go," Connor told Hamish.

Looking torn, Hamish still activated full thruster and shot into the sky. Evander saluted, then shot off to the east, moving into position to help control the eruption. If that was even possible.

Alone with the two intrepid Fast Rollers, Connor wrapped their Juggernauts with the strongest shielding he could manage, trying to protect them from the intense heat. It would never be enough. Within that superheated column, the queen would sever all of his influence.

"Which button activates pumice?" Tomas asked.

"The one next to blind coal. Hit 'em both."

"Should give us a couple seconds, right?"

Together they shouted, "For Rory and never-ending bash fights!"

The two Fast Rollers' Juggernauts shot into the flames side by side, the outer edges of the shells already beginning to melt from the fervent heat. Connor tried to maintain his connection, tried to offer what help he could to the idiotically brave warriors.

He maintained connection for a fraction of a second, but lost it as they pierced the queen's protective elemental barrier. The combination of blind coal and pumice together allowed them to punch through.

The last thing Connor sensed was the huge battering rams from both Juggernauts blasting out the front of each sphere.

And miraculously they connected.

The queen tumbled out the back of the column, what was left of her severed torso crushed by the impacts, broken arms thrown wide, expression enraged.

She no longer held the sculpted stone.

"Yes!" Connor shouted, raising his fists in victory. They actually did it. He started to laugh.

The two Juggernaut spheres blasted out the column of fire that was already shredding to pieces now that the queen had lost direct control. The two spheres were glowing red from the intense heat, despite their protections.

"You'd think she'd have put up more of a fight," Tomas said as he and Cameron peeled away and started accelerating for safety.

"Old ladies have health issues," Cameron said.

Connor wrapped them in air and lifted them off the ground. He only needed a few more seconds to lift them high enough before—

The ground beneath both him and two Fast Rollers simply melted, transforming into an ocean of superheated lava that exploded up into the air all. Connor gasped in a surprised breath of air laden with sulfur and smoke before lava consumed him.

For a second he thought he had simply died. His vision blurred as he tumbled about, carried upward by the eruption. Molten stone was blasting into the sky with such force it would probably carry him thousands of feet. Heat couldn't melt him, and while walking with all of the elements together, he'd survived the initial explosion. His elemental senses expanded through the rapidly spreading eruption and the scope of it boggled his mind.

He sought for Tomas and Cameron. They'd been caught in that explosion too, and their protective mechanicals would run out any second.

There!

He sensed the two Juggernauts. Both Fast Rollers were laughing crazily, and for a second Connor's hopes raised.

Then Cameron's laughter changed to a shouted curse of pain. "I've got a leak! Out of blind coal, and lava's pouring in."

A second later, Tomas said, "Tallan's roasted bones, so do I." His voice was far too calm.

Cameron's voice was laced with pain. "Max tapping doesn't help much. Best bash fight of a lifetime, though."

"Never thought we'd go out bash fighting with mechanical fists," Tomas responded, his breath gasping.

"My friend, it's been an honor to—"

Cameron's Juggernaut exploded.

Tomas' voice was weak, and it sounded like he spoke through gritted teeth. "Aye, lad. It's been—"

His Juggernaut exploded too.

No.

The twin blasts seemed minuscule, embedded within a mountain of lava, but they resonated in Connor's heart like a fist-full of diorite.

Tomas and Cameron were gone.

He couldn't believe it. The two dauntless warriors had faced the most insane battles with a shrug and a joke, eager to bash fight any challengers. They'd accomplished what he couldn't do with all of his affinities. They'd broken the queen from that sculpted stone and offered Connor a chance, however slim, to try averting a much greater disaster.

He could not fail them. He had to fight to bite back sobs. He could hold his breath a long time, but sucking in deadly mouthfuls of molten stone would kill him too. He cast his senses throughout the explosion, determined to stop it.

Earth was right. The queen had unleashed a mountain. Even with that sculpted stone, she was a fool to ever think she could control it. If all of the lava erupting into the air congealed, it would form a mighty peak. If it spread, it would consume the Macantact and all of northern Obrion. It was a natural disaster so immense Connor struggled to understand it, let alone control it. But fear for his still-living friends shook him out of his numb shock.

Connor grappled with the fire and molten earth blasting up into the air from a dozen huge fissures, but despite his enormous powers, his strength was pitiful against the raw power of the earth's core.

Fire laughed in his mind. "There's no stopping this, Connor. This is real power. This is our domain. But you're privileged to witness the event right from the heart of the volcano. No one's ever done that before."

Connor seized Fire's hand, then grabbed Earth's. "You're right! This is your domain. You two control these elements. You can stop this."

"Why would we?" Earth asked, looking genuinely perplexed.

"Because if you don't, half of Obrion will be destroyed."

"The earth is a living thing. It grows and changes all the time," Earth said.

"Fire consumes just as it warms," Fire added.

"But if we don't control this, I might die along with everyone I love," Connor exclaimed. He knew the elementals weren't human, but it still shocked him to see how little they seemed to care about the fate of the people in their world.

That made them pause. Air hovered overhead, while Water drew closer. "We do want to walk the land with you for a long time to come. Today the queen has granted Earth an unexpected freedom, but that will only last a short while. We can help you rein in this movement of the natural world, but it only adds to the debt you owe us."

"Fine," Connor said immediately, grasping at any chance to get them to help.

He hated making a blanket promise like that, but what alternative did he have? He still didn't understand what they wanted from him, and was starting to fear they might want a lot more than he would be willing to give, but the eruption was continuing to gain momentum. The queen feared something about the elements, but he didn't know what. As much as making the promise made him uneasy, the disaster he was stuck in the middle of was real and immediate and threatened everyone he loved.

As the channel up from the earth's core widened, more and more magma pressed into it, driven by the incomprehensible pressures so far underground. He was still getting carried ever higher within the heart of the first explosion and must have reached a couple thousand feet, with no signs of slowing.

Earth sighed. "Such a sacrifice must be repaid in full."

"I'll help you in any way I can. Just help me today," Connor pressed.

It was so weird holding a conversation in his mind with the elements while his body was riding the heart of an unprecedented eruption. He couldn't breathe, but felt like he could hold his breath a lot longer still. He wasn't sure if that was because he was still tapping pumice, or if it was a side effect of his ascension he hadn't explored before, but he appreciated it. The molten elements were flowing all around him. If his connection to his affinities wavered at all, he'd be incinerated in a heartbeat.

Fire drew closer, his eyes burning, his expression eager. "Very well, Connor. We'll help you, but in your current form you cannot hope to wield the power to succeed."

"So what do you suggest?" Connor asked, although he suspected he knew the answer, and it chilled him.

"To do this, you must surrender to me and cross the final bridge to join us." As he spoke, his eyes burned with white-hot flames. He looked eager, almost frantic. That seemed a little strange, since he seemed to be enjoying the eruption so much. Why get so excited to stop it?

Connor didn't have time to care.

To stop the eruption, he had to become fire.

Release an elfonnel.

Most who attempted to raise an elfonnel never returned. He thought back to Redmund and Camonica, sacrificed by Dougal to raise elfonnel to attack Granadure. Dougal had planned to sacrifice Connor the same way. The titanic elemental battles that resulted had destabilized the continent. The queen's action today threatened to destroy it altogether.

What choice did he have?

No choice, but that didn't mean he couldn't search for a way to protect himself. So Connor tapped porphyry again.

The beast instantly leaped into his mind, visible to him as clearly as the elements. It padded close to Connor, but faced the elements, and it growled at Fire, looking like it wanted to strike. Again, the beast seemed to make Fire uneasy. None of them were really there, so it wasn't like Porphyry could actually harm Fire. Connor didn't understand it, but hoped the presence of Porphyry might help improve his bargaining position.

Connor willed the beast to calm and it turned to him. "Danger, Pack Leader. This one seeks to consume you."

"I know. He has to, or I won't be able to stop this."

Fire said, "Release your other affinities and take my hand. Now is the time, Connor. Do you surrender to me and choose to accept your role as my champion?"

Porphyry's presence didn't seem to be helping much, and Connor didn't see any way out. He really needed to understand the weird behavior of porphyry, but he'd worry about that if he survived, and if his mind didn't end up more cracked than it apparently already was. Aifric might have nineteen women in her head, but Connor was talking with his affinities and having to deal with drama between them.

Connor steeled his nerves and forced himself to meet Fire's eyes, which were burning with crimson tongues of flame. "I agree. Let's do this."

Fire laughed and his mouth opened impossibly wide, filled with white-hot flames. He lunged forward and those flames enveloped Connor.

Porphyry lunged at the same time, plunging right into Connor as the flames enveloped him.

Connor's world transformed into living flames. They burned into his mind and consumed him from the inside out.

In that moment, Connor ceased to exist.

Chapter Ninety

A Monster within a Monster

Connor blinked open his eyes and rose on shaky legs. He stood in his mindscape, which had transformed into islands and bridges again. He found himself on the last island, facing the long, triple-layered plank rope bridge leading to a distant island made entirely of living fire. The cool air was still and completely devoid of scents.

Fire stood near the center of the top layer of the bridge. He'd shed most of the human form that Connor usually envisioned him in. Still roughly man-shaped, he was made of densely packed flames, pulsing faintly from thousands of individual flickers.

Between Connor and Fire, standing at the midpoint of the gently swaying bridge, stood Porphyry. In full rampager form, it crouched on the bridge, barring Fire's passage. Its low growl competed with the soft crackling of flames as the only sound in the otherwise empty mental expanse.

Connor rubbed his face, trying to remember what happened. It all came back in a rush and he gasped, "The queen! The volcano!"

Fire looked past Porphyry and beckoned Connor closer. As Connor stepped onto the bridge, Porphyry glanced back and said in its rough, growling voice, "Danger is close, Pack Leader."

"It's all right. I need to unite with Fire or we'll never control this disaster," Connor replied. He wasn't sure what had gotten into Porphyry. He had always imagined it like a beast in his heart just as he imagined the elements in human form. When the elements claimed their forms, he had welcomed the progression since they offered so much knowledge. He wasn't sure how to react to Porphyry also assuming a full identity.

"Release the beast. The bridge to that affinity will prevent full bonding," Fire said.

And suddenly Connor could feel it. Although Porphyry was manifesting in rampager form on the bridge between him and Fire, he could feel a link through it back to a separate bridge that linked him to porphyry, and from there back to himself.

If he still had a self. He couldn't feel his body, wasn't sure he still had one. Elfonnel stepped beyond their human form and took on the form of the element that gave them life. He wasn't sure if the human body remained buried deep inside the elfonnel, or if it was simply consumed, only to be reformed when the Petralist stepped back into normal life.

Porphyry growled again. "The pack is stronger when we hunt together."

"Has anyone else maintained affinities when raising an elfonnel?" Connor asked as he approached the midpoint.

Every step closer to Fire seemed to reinforce the bridge, making it stronger. He could feel the heat from the distant island, along with a growing desire to rush across the remaining distance and leap into the flames.

Fire beckoned encouragingly. "You can only reach your full potential and take your place as my champion by crossing the bridge and surrendering your other affinities."

"Our champion," said the unexpected voice of Earth from his left.

Three other bridges suddenly ran parallel to the one where Connor stood, before twisting to extend away to separate islands made up of the different elements. Water, Air, and Earth stood near the midpoint of each bridge, watching Connor intently.

Fire snapped, "Of course all of ours. Don't confuse the boy."

Connor liked seeing all of the elementals so close. He hadn't realized he might be able to access any of the rest of them while uniting with Fire to raise the elfonnel. Porphyry swiveled its powerful head to take in the newcomers and its growl deepened. Connor wouldn't be surprised by reluctance to losing its connection with him, but he sensed so much more. Porphyry felt true animosity toward the elements. What could possibly cause that?

"What about the queen? The eruption?" Connor asked, glancing around but still unable to sense anything outside of his mental space.

"We will take care of it shortly," Fire assured him.

"How? Why are we wasting time standing on bridges?" Connor demanded, trying to control his fear for his friends' safety. Had any more of them gotten caught in the unprecedented eruption?

"No time passes here. To the world, the transition will appear instantaneous," Fire said, his voice comforting.

"Really?" He'd noticed that conversations with the elementals took far less time than they would in the real world, but never had they passed instantaneously.

Water said, "We stand within your mind. Don't get distracted by unnecessary details. Release the beast and cross to Fire and become our champion."

Porphyry growled again, crouching a little lower. Connor clearly read its intent to fight any attempt to remove it. He didn't understand its belligerence, but maybe it was a good thing he'd tapped it when he did. Without Porphyry's presence, he didn't doubt he would have already rushed across the bridge and leaped into the flames.

Was that a good idea? Was this moment of surrender to the elementals what the queen feared?

He wanted to trust the elements. They'd helped so much since his ascension, but he couldn't ignore a flicker of worry. Porphyry was his only potential lifeline, but would the presence of the beast destroy his ability to raise an elfonnel? If so, he would have to cast Porphyry away, despite the potential cost, which could mean losing himself forever.

Definitely not an option that was high on his list of preferred outcomes.

"Will I remain myself enough to deal with the volcano and the queen?" he asked. Kilian had said it was extremely difficult to remain self-aware when surrendering oneself to the elements. If porphyry allowed him to keep his head, he welcomed it.

"Just cross to my island, and I'll take care of everything," Fire assured him in a soothing voice, reaching out toward Connor.

Porphyry growled louder and snapped at the extended hand. Fire retracted it with an annoyed look. Porphyry said, "Do not abandon the pack. None hunt as well as we do."

It had a point. Porphyry had helped Connor overcome all of his most trying challenges. Without porphyry, he would have succumbed to Dougal's mind control or fallen to the elfonnel at the Carraig. It helped him defeat Martys and save his family, and without it he never would have stilled Merkland or defeated Harley.

All of the elementals spoke in unison. "Let go your other affinities. Send away the beast, and become our champion."

He couldn't fail to raise an elfonnel, but he didn't dare turn his back on porphyry. So he said, "I don't think I can break free now. Please, let's just do this."

Fire scowled at Porphyry, but Water said, "The boy is not ready to take his full place among us today, but the day is not far off. Help him today, or we lose everything."

"So be it," Fire said with a heavy sigh. "Today was a singular opportunity." He fixed Connor with a grave expression. "You will learn your duty, and we will hold you to it."

That seemed harsh. Connor didn't like his tone, but he was already committed, so he didn't call Fire on it. He said carefully, "Please help me today, and I promise to keep studying until I understand how best to help in the future."

Luckily Fire didn't complain about the cautious wording, although Air scowled, as if reading his intent. Fire threw out his hands and shouted, "Then rise, child of the living flames!"

The mindscape winked out and Connor's world transformed into fire.

He blinked open eyes the size of houses as he became fully self-aware. His pitiful, weak body was gone, his puny human existence but a disappointing memory, little more than an unpleasant dream.

His life was so much more! He was fire, standing within the heart of the greatest volcano in the world. It was fitting, and he flexed a body the size of Mount Murdo. He looked out through the eruption and the world was tinged by shades of red. He saw all colored by how much heat it produced. Instead of blood, his body thrummed with the pulsing of a volcano's heart.

Laughing with unparalleled might, he ascended and rose out of the still-expanding eruption to stand atop the explosion. His body coalesced into a form worthy of him, a giant with arms bigger than the mighty Macantact. His lower torso merged into the vast pool of molten lava still exploding up out of the ground, fusing him to the great river of fire that extended all the way back down to the very roots of the earth.

He spread his mighty arms wide and his senses expanded in a rush. The land and air were so saturated with fire that he felt everything. More lava was exploding up through a dozen smaller fissures that ringed his central eruption by a couple miles. The entire area was shuddering, on the verge of a general collapse that would open the fissures into one enormous gap to allow billions of tons of molten destruction to blast into freedom and cover northern Obrion.

Yes. He could sweep across the continent, riding the flood of molten life and create an entirely new world. The old would burn, as all things should. He would build all things new out of the devastation of the old.

Like Alasdair.

The memory of his beloved home destroyed by the eruption triggered when the queen first arose flashed into his mind like a bolt of lightning. Connor shuddered and came awake, his thoughts rising out of the torrent of heat and fury that clouded his thoughts.

"*Don't hesitate. Embrace this moment and we will show the world what we can do together,*" Fire urged.

"*I don't want to destroy everything,*" Connor protested. It was hard to think, and the visions of sweeping the world with flame and destruction returned, enticing and exhilarating.

Then a blanket of impenetrable resolve settled over his mind as Porphyry awoke and padded into his thoughts. "P*ack Leader chooses the hunt and the quarry,*" it snarled at Fire.

Fire was no longer restricted to human form, but he surrounded Connor, infusing every part of him. Connor felt his sigh and the thought rose up through the torrent of superheated flames that made up Connor's heart. "*Forgive me for getting carried away. You are right. We will of course continue as we agreed.*"

Connor's giant face shifted, taking the form of a rampager. He grinned. It felt appropriate. Fire swept closer, and Connor's mind fused with the elemental, although he maintained a grip on his own thoughts through the connection with Porphyry.

He became Connor-elfonnel.

Exulting in his dominance, Connor-elfonnel plunged into the eruption, laughing as he swam through the inferno. It was still building. His transformation had taken only a second.

A lot could happen in a second. Lava and ash continued blasting up from the earth's core, superheating the air. The devastation had already consumed the rough land where they had staged their attack. All of the Juggernaut spheres had been consumed. Miles to the east he sensed the insignificant flying machines and a pack of puny humans.

Connor-elfonnel ignored them, but through that tenuous thread back to Connor, he recognized them and celebrated their safety. Kilian had indeed saved the Juggernaut pilots, and he was working with Evander to wrest the might of the eruption.

Puny humans would never succeed, Connor-elfonnel laughed. They thought themselves mighty, but their efforts to corral the devastation was a waste. They pulled but a fraction of the ash from the air, sucked bits of heat out of the fringes of the eruption to cast it back into the core.

Only he could control such an eruption. Again visions of riding the wave of lava swept through his mind, nearly swaying him, but again the tiny link to Connor resisted.

Huffing in annoyance, Connor-elfonnel bared his fangs and set to work. He plunged his fiery arms back down into the eruption, seizing the magma and willing it to stop spreading away from the central fissure. He reinforced that fissure to prevent it from opening wider and reached all the way down through the miles to the earth's core.

Not even he could block the titanic pressure casting the magma up through the break the queen had made. That enraged him. Nothing should challenge his might.

The core was a vast pool of energy and molten metal, and he sensed it had always existed and forever would. He couldn't tame it, so he would cap the breach to bottle up the fiery power that dwarfed even his might.

Seizing the waves of magma and bringing them in close added to his bulk, and the incredible volume of molten material bounded by his constraints forced the mountain beneath him to grow with astonishing speed.

Already the explosion had burst up over two thousand feet. Now as he held the blast in, the mountain grew faster still, as was fitting. He threw back his giant rampager head and laughed.

This time the thunder-chuckle erupted in truly epic fashion. It sounded like a rampager growl, magnified a million times, and it reverberated across the land like an earthquake through the air. The puny humans, Evander and Kilian, both looked startled.

They would look afraid soon enough.

He seized the rain of molten fire erupting from the smaller fissures, pulling them back in, preventing them from rising high into the air like they wished. He was wielding enough power to reshape half the continent, and although the Fire part of him allowed the Connor part to control their efforts, he still yearned to unleash everything, the temptation like a slow pulsing deep down in his gut.

First, control the eruption. Then. . . . Well, who knew?

As the lava continued to boil forth, he shaped it, forming an enormous peak over the central fissure and smaller peaks in a ring around it. Then he seized the heat and drained it away, helping to cool the vast mass of superheated stone faster. Otherwise it might have taken months to harden.

That built up a lot of heat, and for a moment he wondered what to do with it. Where to release it for the best result?

That's when he felt the queen rise out of the ground to the north.

CHAPTER NINEY-ONE

The Worst Splitting Headache Ever

The sight of the queen shocked Connor awake within the Connor-elfonnel just as his enormous, fiery form rose to the top of the volcano and swiveled toward where he sensed her. Through the constant rain of fire and swirling ash, he easily spotted her.

Queen Dreokt had reattached her sundered lower limbs and looked mostly intact. She must have figured out how to access the higher order of fleshcrafting, despite the dearth of regular healing power. She had covered herself in a suit of earth, and stood facing Connor-elfonnel, her expression twisted into rage, and her words carried easily to him.

"You fool! Despite my warnings, you embrace the danger?"

He no longer feared her.

Connor-elfonnel reached down, extending one mighty, burning arm across the distance to snatch her off the ground. She attempted to push him away, but she had lost the ancient sculpted stone and for once her strength proved insufficient.

He was fire now, and no mortal could overpower him. He smashed aside her will and surrounded her with the living flames of his hand and lifted her high. She beat against him, screaming obscenities in several languages, but the words were meaningless.

Queen Dreokt attempted to strike him with other affinities, but accomplished little more than flickers. He exulted. He reigned supreme now. He was beyond chert, he was fire, and no water remained in the superheated air, which was far too distracted to give heed to a puny human.

He saw fear in her eyes.

So he ate her.

He chomped down onto her tiny form with his enormous jaws, savoring the feeling of her body surrounded by the flames of his mouth. He'd never eaten anyone before, and the experience was disappointing.

The queen tasted stale, like old bread, covered in dirt. Not very inspiring, but at least she didn't taste like cabbage, or skunks.

She didn't melt, but screamed with rage, beating uselessly against the flames of his jaws. Swallowing her would not kill her. He must destroy her, then none would remain to challenge his dominance of his glorious birth.

She was immune to normal heat, but he was wielding far more than any mortal could ever manage. He'd gathered such an enormous pool of pure heat, it strained against even his control. In his elfonnel vision, he saw heat like light. Through the shielding influence of Porphyry, the tiny Connor part of him could sense his other affinities and even managed to tap limestone. That sharpened his vision further.

Amazing. Heat was boiling off the eruption in every spectrum, most of it invisible to the human eye but as clear to him as the rippling colors of a rainbow trout in the Wick. So Connor-elfonnel compressed all that heat, transforming it into higher-energy waves. They changed from yellow to red to purple, and eventually to pure white. The energy intensified until it held the power to rip air and matter apart.

He unleashed all of it upon the queen struggling in his fiery maw. Tipping his head back to point his muzzle at the sky, he vomited out all of that energy, striking her with a concentrated blast that ripped through her like a cudgel tearing through a rotten melon.

Queen Dreokt disintegrated.

Her body erupted into bits that sprayed out of his mouth and far across the land. Even her bones melted, although most of her skull remained intact. It hurtled for miles, beyond the farthest reaches of the smaller peaks forming around the eruption.

Connor-elfonnel exulted, trumpeting his thunderous laughter again. The tiny Connor part of him cheered the defeat of Queen Dreokt.

She wasn't that tough. She was only human, after all.

He was now the force of nature, risen to stop her and become the one being powerful enough to end her reign and replace it with a monument for pure fire.

"*Ride the wave, spread our flames across the land,*" Fire urged, his hunger to walk the earth and leave it a charred wasteland a tantalizing temptation for them.

Connor-elfonnel leaned forward, on the verge of sweeping out of the volcano and leading the way.

"*No.*"

Connor struggled to retain his own mind within the monster. It was so hard, like trying to think clearly in a dream, but those visions of immolating every city scared him so much he managed to hold on.

"*We agreed to stop this eruption.*"

Connor-elfonnel growled, sending showers of fire cascading down the hot, rocky slope forming beneath him, but he could not ignore the will of the human who had called him forth.

Connor rose to the forefront of the elfonnel's mind, taking control, waking from the dream into glorious reality. He felt his enormous fiery body really clearly for the first time, and laughed with the wonder of it. He was the volcano. He was fire, but somehow he was still Connor.

"*This is unnatural,*" Fire muttered. The elemental shared his fiery head, but Connor held the control position.

Connor laughed, spraying flames a thousand feet into the air. That was awesome! He bet he could vomit flames for miles, if he wanted to. "*Of course this is unnatural. We're an elfonnel.*"

"*But not a normal one.*"

"Stop moping. When's the last time you got to play in a volcano like this?"

That helped Fire perk up a bit, so Connor-elfonnel got to work.

The mountain beneath his fiery form had risen thousands of feet higher, towering over any of the other peaks in Obrion, while the smaller ring of peaks had each risen to over eight thousand feet, their lower flanks joining together into a high ridge that ringed the outer limits of the disaster.

Connor-elfonnel continued to drain heat away, casting it up into the sky as intense beams of high intensity energy that shot away so fast he expected them to keep flying until they hit a distant star. But he still couldn't stop the rising of new lava.

The disaster would continue unless he figured out how to deal with it. He tried to push back against the rising flames, tried drawing the heat away fast enough to create new earth, but he needed something more.

He was surprised to feel Earth step into their shared mind. "You cannot control my element bound to Fire alone. You need my assistance for that."

"Is that possible?" Connor asked.

From everything he knew about elfonnel, it shouldn't be. Always elfonnel rose as a single element, and the Petralist could only ever escape if they were Dawnus. Earth was not his opposite.

"For one who has stepped to the midpoint of the final bridge, it is," Earth said.

"He's mine," Fire objected. "You cannot transition him now while he's walking with me without sundering his soul."

"Let's definitely avoid that," Connor said. He needed to stop the disaster, but soul sundering sounded very permanent and very painful.

"I need not his entire being to grant a new degree of control," Earth responded calmly, but his expression looked more eager than Connor had ever seen. He really wanted to join in, and maybe they needed him, but that whole soul sundering thing still worried Connor.

Even more surprising, Water joined the conversation. Connor got a terrible headache as his shared mind fractured further. He blinked, and fell into a shared mindspace, sort of like that common area in Aifric's mind. Had he created that, or had the elements?

The location was small, some kind of old tavern with walls of rippling flame. The elements sat around a single polished wooden table in the center.

"This is weird," Connor commented, suddenly finding himself seated at the table with them on a chair made of lava, his torso human-shaped but made entirely of flames. His lower body melded with his volcano seat. Porphyry padded around the table, red eyes fixed on each of the elements in turn, a low growl rumbling in its thick chest. The elements made a point of not noticing it.

"He's going to crack," Fire complained, looking really annoyed. He straddled his chair backward and was consuming an enormous plate of spice-root pepper cookies.

Water gestured with her mug that frothed like all the waves of the sea. "Earth, you threaten to confuse him beyond repair."

Air leaned back in her chair, beyond the point where it should fall over, but a tiny whirlwind kept it in position. She raised a delicate wine glass made of faceted quartzite, filled with swirling clouds, and grinned at Connor. "Can I have part of him too?"

"If we diffuse him too much, we will lose him," Earth replied, banging his heavy, earthenware mug onto the table. His mug actually looked like it was filled with packed earth. How he could sip off of that made no sense.

"You're the one who brought it up. Why do you get to suck the joy out of everything?" Air muttered.

"Take your part, but be quick and do not damage him," Water warned.

Fire muttered, "Today was my turn." He flung the tray across the room. It melted from the heat before it struck the wall.

Connor tried to settle his thoughts, but he felt untethered, fractured. Was he losing it? The scene was so strange, the elements acting like he was a cake they were deciding how to split between them.

"Um, guys, the volcano, remember?" he interjected.

Earth pointed his mug at Connor, "You have not yet formed the lower half of your elfonnel. You have room for me to join the mix."

"Okay, as long as you don't destroy me. We want to avoid that," Connor said hesitantly.

He reminded himself they weren't human, so they probably didn't intend anything by the strange conversation, and he focused on the fact that Earth seemed to want to try something new.

That part he liked, as long as they avoided the whole death-by-fractured-mind-in-elfonnel-form bit. He was so powerful, but he couldn't even enjoy that without having to push the limits beyond what even Kilian or Evander had ever done.

He chuckled to himself when he realized he almost said, "If only I could just be an elfonnel."

"We cannot accomplish our goals without you, so it is in our best interest to preserve you," Earth said. "What we propose has never been done, and the burden of cost would threaten the stability of your mind unless you cast that burden upon your final foundational bridge."

"You mean the one linking me back to my family in Alasdair?" Connor didn't like the sound of that. He'd already cankered more of his family bridge during fleshcrafting than he wanted to.

"Indeed. You may cast the burden of the melding of Fire and myself onto that bridge and survive," Earth said.

Connor was happy that there was an option besides personal destruction, but he hesitated. "When I cast the effects of fleshcrafting on that bridge, it was damaged."

"Indeed, a price must be paid," Earth agreed.

Water leaned forward, an encouraging smile on her lips. "Connor, this is the only way to save you and your dear friends and prevent a horrible disaster from sweeping across your country. The choice is yours."

Except, what choice did he have? He didn't like damaging his family bridge, but it wasn't like the bridge was real.

Air placed a hand on his, and he felt through her touch the sense of a cool breeze, laughing along the face of a high mountain. "Connor, embrace your chance to take another step toward greatness. The burden may weaken that last bridge, but it represents nothing more than the weakness of your human condition."

Connor glanced at water. "I thought it represented the link back to my family."

"That is part of the same thing. We are sharing concepts that can be hard for you to understand, so we try different words at different times."

That made sense, but he wished he understood what his family bridge really meant, and what wrecking it would mean to him. He'd have to figure that out later. He didn't have time to waste, and he was out of options.

So he took a deep breath and nodded. "Let's do it."

At least Porphyry did not object as Earth reached out and grabbed Connor's amorphous fiery body at about where he should have a left knee. Connor didn't need more affinity drama.

With a strange wrenching feeling, an earthen leg grew out of his volcano chair and attached itself to his waist. Then it seemed to melt, and the earth flowed up into his torso. It was weird, like a fever chill racing up through him, and he shivered, feeling weird, like he was momentarily two people sitting in the same place.

Then the two people merged, and he nearly swooned. Groaning, he swayed in his seat as bands of earth mingled with the flames forming his body, and together they transformed into molten rock.

Was he becoming a lava elfonnel? Was that a thing?

The elementals all stood up and cheered. Connor found it hard to focus. His mind felt hazy, and he fought a growing dizziness that threatened to bury his consciousness again. The shared mindscape faded and Connor blinked, returning to elfonnel form. He still stood atop the enormous volcano, but now he could feel the molten earth within it. He sensed the rumblings radiating out from the epicenter of the eruption. Evander's will blanketed the area, struggling to ease the worst of the trembling, but accomplishing only a pitiful fraction of what he needed.

His giant elfonnel body changed just as it had in the mindscape. The pure flames darkened as earth flowed up into him, transforming into bands of molten lava. That darker layer spread across his chest, arms, and face, bands of shadow interspersed with the white-hot ropes of living fire.

He felt Evander's surprise to feel him walking with earth too. Connor wanted to grin, but couldn't seem to make the elfonnel-rampager mouth move in that direction, so he settled for spewing a stream of lava straight up into the air, then absorbing it again when it cascaded down over him. He wondered if the big man was confusing himself with a convoluted Sentry-speak question of how it was possible. He wished he could hear Evander's thoughts, but didn't dare try any other affinities. He was already feeling spread far too thin.

His mind felt fractured in a really unpleasant way as he fought to manage the melded connections to both earth and fire. In his moment of distraction, the eruption intensified, pushing the limits of his control and threatening to fracture Connor's attention beyond his ability to hold it together. His headache got worse.

He wasn't sure what a schizophrenic elfonnel might do, and didn't want to be the test case to prove how bad the idea really was. So he held on, even though it felt like his mind was getting stretched and twisted like a cloth in a washer-woman's hands. He was just glad Air didn't decide to take any part of him. Adding another twist would snap him.

Then he sensed that mind-bending pressure ease, and felt more than saw black, sludgy mist roll across his family bridge, as if someone had cast a giant bucket of filthy slop onto it. His agreement to the plan was enough to trigger the release, apparently.

The nasty mixture splashed across the wooden planks, the stone supports, and the polished wooden handrail, spreading far down the bridge and seeping into everything. The wood blackened with rot, the stone chipped and cankered, and the handrail pitted.

The damage was far more severe than he'd expected, and he feared he'd made a terrible mistake. He wasn't sure what he'd just lost, but it wasn't something meaningless like the elements had suggested.

Unfortunately, it was too late to take back the choice, and the vision faded as his senses expanded through his lava body. He was there, a mixed elfonnel, and he'd already paid the price, so he'd better stop moping about it and get to work.

Casting his combined elemental senses deep into the earth, Connor seized the ground around the break in the planet's mantel. His will melded with the land all around. He was still fire, but he was also earth now, and it was marvelous.

The land spread away in every direction, the entire continent mapped to his mind. He was surprised to feel his senses slide farther, beneath the Sea of Olcan. If he wanted to, he bet he could push his senses all the way across and get a glimpse of the next continent.

He didn't have time.

So Connor seized the land of Obrion and quelled the tremors that threatened to cover the entire continent in destructive shaking. Then he focused on the biggest fissure, the one directly beneath him. And walking carefully with both Fire and Earth, he attacked it.

With Fire, he bled away the heat, while with Earth he fused the newly forming stones to the existing ground, welding it all together.

It wasn't enough.

The thin plug ripped asunder like a piece of cheesecloth trying to catch a huge, roasted ham. He redoubled his efforts, his enormous elfonnel form leaning into the struggle, crouching and slipping deeper into the bubbling lava.

The soft bulk of the great mountain he'd formed threatened to explode under the pressure, and even though he was now the living embodiment of two elements, he only barely held it all in check. If his attention wavered, if his control slipped, the mountain would explode in every direction, sweeping miles of Obrion away in fiery destruction. Would he simply explode too?

Not the way he wanted this day to turn out.

So he held on, his fiery form quivering from the strain, trying to work fast enough, to plug the hole in the planet.

He couldn't do it. The pressure was too great, the plug too fragile.

"*This isn't working!*"

"*Because you're not surrendering completely to us,*" Fire said.

"*I'm an elfonnel, aren't I?*"

"*Perhaps the greatest who ever rose,*" Earth acknowledged. "*But you try to change the course of the planet. It cannot be done without surrendering completely to us.*"

Porphyry appeared in his mind, across from Fire and Earth. They didn't step into the shared mental space, but occupied parts of Connor's mind. His headache blossomed and he groaned, fearing that he had pushed himself too far, even after casting so much onto his family bridge. Maybe people just weren't made to walk with two elements at the same time.

Porphyry growled, and Connor read its caution. It sensed danger in the route the elements suggested, but what else could Connor do?

Fire beckoned him closer, and Connor felt his will beginning to slip. His headache intensified until it felt like his brain was on fire. That was so wrong when he was fire. All he had to do was agree, and he sensed that the pain would disappear.

So would he.

"*Give up yourself, Connor. Isn't that what human heroes are supposed to do? Surrender themselves? Only then could we hope to generate the back-pressure force necessary to stop the advance of the core,*" Fire said, his voice gently tugging on to take that last step and surrender.

Connor had nearly died for his family, his friends, and his country more than once. He bristled at Fire's insinuation that he wasn't trying hard enough. If he gave in, would the elementals really stop the eruption? He knew their temptation to ride it forever and sweep the land with destruction.

He couldn't trust them.

What else could he do? His mind hurt, his enormous body was shaking with the strain, the mountain quivering, and the pressure to explode again was growing fast. Was that what Fire meant by a back-pressure blast?

"We can do this!" he insisted, gritting his enormous teeth and throwing himself back into the fight, sinking down through the volcano and into the earth, descending through the boiling magma filling the great fracture in the planet's mantle toward the center.

He didn't dare go all the way down into the core. Not even he could survive the molten heart of the planet, but he descended many miles until he approached the break, a section a hundred miles thick that had been formed of solid stone before the queen punched a hole through it.

Connor tried again to drain away the heat of the magma pushing up into the gap, fighting to form a plug of earth over it and seal the hole. Despite crouching just a few miles above that critical section, he still couldn't create a strong enough boundary quickly enough.

In the process, he absorbed vast amounts of heat energy, though. As it built inside of him, his elfonnel form swelled with that energy that coursed through him with growing intensity, needing a release.

"Surrender to us, Connor, or all will be lost," Earth urged, and he sensed the elements' fear. If he didn't try something different, and fast, they'd all be consumed, and everyone he loved would die.

Kilian's words came to mind again. "*Don't fail, Connor, or everyone dies.*"

He needed an idea, he needed another tool.

All he had was heat. Lots of heat.

He thought back to how he had destroyed the queen. Could he try that here? Could he disintegrate part of the planet? Would that make things better or worse?

Only one way to find out.

CHAPTER NINETY-TWO

Too Much of a Good Thing

"Wait!" Fire shouted, but Connor couldn't wait or he would die.

He focused all of that heat into the highest-frequency energy he could, sucking in more and more until his entire giant form thrummed with pent-up power. Then he unleashed it all, roaring an underground challenge, the sound impressively mighty.

If only Hamish could have heard that. He might die in this attempt, but he'd figured out the thunder-chuckle at last.

All of that heat energy blasted away in a vast invisible beam down through the fracture in the mantel. Energy poured out of him in a titanic burst that ripped down through the magma and shattered it all in an instant, boiling the superheated magma to gas, then rending that gas into component bits like the plasma generated by lightning.

Some of those basic elemental molecules sundered under the bombardment, and they weren't happy about it.

Those breaking elements unleashed staggering amounts of energy in vast detonations that eclipsed the energy driving the magma upward, forming pressure voids that drove the magma back in every direction. The magma already pressing toward the surface accelerated, ripping past him like a molten whirlwind. Connor fought the current with all his strength, but was still swept upward for miles before arresting his ascent.

The magma blasted up through the top of the volcano, spewing fire and superheated air tens of thousands of feet.

He ignored that problem and focused all his strength on filling those pressure gaps with new-formed earth. By draining heat from the magma at the lowest edge of the hole, he hardened it to stone. By the time the pressure voids faded and magma again began driving upward, he'd formed a far thicker crust than before. It still flexed under the strain, stones cracking and the entire new construct groaning like underground thunder.

Connor held on with all his strength. He hurled his huge body down, crashing into the top layer of the plug he'd created, and pushed with all his might. The stones flexed and cracked, threatening to burst again.

Howling with the effort, he fought the growing pressure while adding more layers of stone as fast as he could create them. For twenty eternal seconds, he fought the elements, on the cusp of losing the tiny plug again. His body shook from the strain.

He hadn't realized fire could feel exhausted, but it could. So could earth. Panting fire and dust, he fought on and the pressure slowly eased. Finally, after adding more than a mile of new stone in the gap, the pressure subsided and he sensed that the plug would hold.

For a moment he simply sprawled there, laying atop his newly-formed stone, a totally exhausted, but happy monster, surrounded by magma and stone.

In his mind, he glimpsed the elementals standing to either side of him. Fire looked impressed. "I hadn't expected a mortal human to discover the power of fission."

"You mean ripping those molecules apart?"

"Indeed. Those basic components of matter contain vast power, as you've witnessed. Those bonds are not easy to break, but when they are broken, the result releases world-changing power."

Connor grinned to think he'd discovered another subtle world power. The thought of climbing the miles back to the surface made him grimace, but staying down there forever would be worse. So he sighed and slowly began to rise through the magma-filled conduit, filling the fractured mantel back in behind him. He again gathered enormous quantities of energy as he sucked away the heat from the magma, but he didn't dare release it down into the core again for fear of shattering the plug he'd just created.

Some of it he used to replenish his strength, soon feeling his monstrous best again. He held in the rest until he ascended up through the top of the still-spewing volcano. There he tipped his giant muzzle into the sky and roared with victory, releasing all that energy into the sky in an invisible death beam that wouldn't stop until it smacked into the moon.

He glanced after it, suddenly wondering if that was a good idea. What would that beam do to the moon?

He hoped no one noticed.

Then he cast his elemental senses across the rest of the greater disaster area. He immediately sensed Kilian and Evander still fighting to help contain the mess. Evander stood to the west, blazing in Connor's affinity senses like a miniature sun. Walking with air, he was grasping the wild air currents rushing around the new-formed mountains and seeking to tear across the continent, carrying with them deadly clouds of ash. He pulled them back to spin around the ring of new mountains in a darkening funnel cloud.

Standing to the east, Kilian was dousing the clouds with water, dragging the ash out of the air and casting it down onto the still-bubbling lava. It sank into the lava, becoming one with the earth and fire that Connor controlled.

Despite their best efforts, they were not capturing everything. The funnel cloud was growing so fierce, winds howling faster than a fracked Strider, it threatened to burst free. He didn't dare walk with Air and Water while in elfonnel form. He was already fractured enough.

That didn't mean he couldn't help. Kilian was already working to drain heat away from the funnel, but that wasn't enough. After what he'd learned about storms from the elements, Connor understood what he needed to do to prevent that still-growing funnel of wet ash from growing into the biggest thunderhead the world had ever seen.

So he seized that heat, dragged it high into the air above the funnel cloud, and spread it out there. Storms grew when hot, moist air was forced to rise by cooler air above. Now he was spreading so much heat above the funnel that the air there turned super hot. That snuffed out the impetus for the storm, robbing fresh power from the currents that had sought to drag in new currents from across Obrion.

So much ash was whirling within that funnel cloud, tons and tons of it in a gray, swirling mass over the mountains that Connor's earth senses easily slipped up through it all. He grasped it and tugged.

All those tons of ash fell from the sky, plunging down onto the red-hot eruption area like a gray blanket a quarter mile deep. It fell with a rolling cascade of muted thunder as Connor dragged it all down into the new mountains, preventing the lighter ash from blowing up into the air again.

He sensed surprise from Kilian and Evander both. He wished he could speak with them, but only managed another rumbling thunder chuckle. Elfonnel were so good at those.

With that part of the disaster contained, he focused on the deeper earth again. He verified that he'd sealed the fractured conduits fueling the eruption, but was surprised to feel other fractures, fissures, and cracks throughout the lands of Obrion.

With a start, he realized those had been caused when the elfonnel had clashed during the invasion of Granadure by Dougal's armies. He clearly felt the fracturing of the solid rock beneath the borderlands and under Mount Murdo and the Carraig. There were natural fissures there, but the titanic struggles of Petralists and elfonnel had ruptured them far beyond their natural state.

So Connor seized those fissures and fused them back into solid stone again.

"*We did not agree to seal the other veins,*" Earth protested.

"Why shouldn't we? I can stabilize things and keep further destruction from happening."

Fire grumbled, "I told you it was a bad idea to give him too much too soon."

"It's not a bad idea. This is wonderful," Connor replied. He didn't understand their concern. They might not be human, but it still surprised him that they didn't celebrate what he could do.

They didn't like it, and they continued to murmur, but Connor kept working. He'd gained control, and he was not about to give it back. He wasn't sure what they could do to him if he upset them. Could they eject him, cast him back into mortal form to die in the volcano he was still mostly immersed in?

He hoped they wouldn't. They seemed to still want him to help them in the future, and he planned to do so, as long as they didn't want something he couldn't give. At the moment, he couldn't ignore this unique opportunity to fix some of the problems plaguing the land.

Despite their clear displeasure, they did not attempt to thwart him. The challenge of the unstable elements had stumped Kilian and Evander and the mightiest of the Petralists, but in elfonnel form, Connor found he could readily manage sealing those fissures and settling the land. He bled away the restless energy pooling under those broken lands and dissipated it out through the continent where it couldn't harm anything.

Kilian had spoken of raising an elfonnel as the greatest challenge a Petralist could survive, but at the moment, Connor was loving it.

That gave him pause. Was he really having so much fun as an elfonnel, or was he mad, suffering a broken mind? Had he really failed and just hadn't realized it yet?

Somehow he doubted that. He felt like himself, far more than he probably should. Sure his body was made out of living fire, he was lounging in a bubbling volcano in a bath of superheated lava, and he'd just eaten Queen Dreokt. So maybe it wasn't exactly a normal day, but inside he felt like himself. He bet his thrice-ascended bond with the elements was what helped so much.

Maybe ticking them off hadn't been such a good idea. What if they left him and removed their protective influence? There had to be weird side effects that came with stepping outside of his human form and possessing a mountain of fire, but he felt great.

He decided not to worry about it. He was having way too much fun to get all mopey about possibly melting later.

With a renewed sense of optimism, he turned back to the new mountains he'd formed. The great central peak was a massive, rough shape that would become a landmark of Obrion from that point forward.

It was kind of ugly.

He cringed to think of generations of Obrioners pointing out the huge, misshapen mass of new stone and saying, "Yup, that was Connor's greatest accomplishment."

So he got to work. The new stone was still pretty soft. If that mountain was going to be his monument, he'd make it a fun monument.

He started by simply smoothing the shape and making it less ugly, but that wasn't enough. People would know he had built it. It would tell them something about him. What did he want them to know?

Ideas poured in and he grinned and leaped to the task. In his giant, lava form, he scampered over the mountain to work the new stone. He might not be a sculptor like Aunt Ailsa, but he'd learned a lot of the concepts from her.

He started by scraping the sides of the gigantic peak as smooth as polished granite, sculpting the mountain into a nine-sided shape. On each flat section, he carved the ancient symbol of one of the nine core affinity stones. Moving farther up the mountain, he rounded the peak and sculpted from memory his favorite image in the whole world.

Verena.

Of course, Verena. What else would he want to create as a monument to the world beside the face of the most amazing girl he knew? He sculpted the mountain so that she looked north toward her homeland, that mischievous smile on her adorable face. He fashioned the sections representing her hair out of pure, black basalt and laughed again when the final shape became clear.

As much as he loved Verena, she wasn't the only thing he wanted to carve. He did pause to add a carving of her father's prize duck trophy onto the mountain just below her. No reason not to impress him a little too, since Connor would be seeing a lot of Verena's family if he managed to survive the day.

He'd survive, and he'd show everyone that he could do it with style. So he leaped from the central peak to the surrounding, smaller mountains and worked them too. In the top of the first, he carved the faces of Tomas and Cameron, wearing their customary insolent grins. He added the epitaph, "*Mighty heroes and unfailing friends.*"

It felt right to leave a monument to the two brave men who had sacrificed everything. They were heroes the entire country should celebrate. Without their sacrifice, Connor never would have succeeded. It didn't seem adequate, but it was more than most fallen warriors got, and it helped ease some of the cold knot of sorrow that remained in his heart, despite his boiling temperature.

On another mountain, he carved Ilse's face beside her husband, Lukas. On the shoulder of the mountain below, he wrote, "*Protect and defend.*" He hoped the monument would serve as a memorial to the brave pilots of Ilse's Revenge who had battled so bravely against the queen while their mechanical wore her face.

He dedicated the next mountain to Hamish and Jean, and included her favorite phrase "*Look deep, see clear*" above an image of a giant cookie, complete with the recipe, which he had long-since memorized. It was one of Hamish's favorites.

The next mountain he dedicated to Rory and Anika, carving them looking at each other, with the inscription, "Love breaks borders."

He carved his parents on the next one, and thinking of them helped ease his headache. It was as if bringing his loved ones to mind and creating tangible memorials to them all, he was somehow drawing upon their strength.

"*This is unwise,*" Fire said, speaking for the first time in a while.

"*Why? These are people I want to honor.*" Surely even an inhuman elemental could understand that.

Earth responded. "*Because you strengthen your bridge, when that will lessen your ability to walk openly with us.*"

Only then did Connor feel it. In his mind, he saw his affinityscape, and the terrible cankered, rotten damage he'd caused by casting his need upon it during his elfonnel transition did look less severe somehow. That was amazing! He hadn't realized he could repair that bridge, and despite how it displeased the elements, the fact that he could eased some of his lingering unease about the choices he'd been forced to make.

"Are you quite finished?"

He glanced down and found Kilian standing atop one of the smaller peaks nearby. He was surprised to see the afternoon was already far spent. He'd consumed the bulk of the day plugging the eruption and playing with his new mountains. He didn't even feel tired. In elfonnel form, he could probably go for weeks without needing a rest.

Evander slid up the side of the mountain to stand beside Kilian and said, "The fresh-cut flower is beloved by every maid, but only foolish suitors dump a wagonload upon their beloved's head."

Connor glanced back up at the towering peak with Verena's image engraved for all to see. Maybe he had gone a little too far.

No. It was perfect. She was going to love it. In fact, he considered taking the time to carve Kilian and Evander on one of the other peaks. They deserved it, but he sensed they'd really not appreciate the gesture.

Unfortunately, now that they'd broken his concentration, he found his enthusiasm fading. When he looked around at the lands beyond his new ring of playground mountains, he noticed that although the air was a bit hazy, it was mostly clear.

Kilian said, "Somehow I know you're in there and you're far more aware than you should be, but there's danger in staying immersed in the elements for too long. Can you return, Connor?"

Return? Why would he want to do that? He was so much more as an elfonnel. Connor turned a slow circle, surveying the great peak and the ring of smaller mountains surrounding it. He'd done that. He'd formed them, carved them, and saved the continent. Why not stay elfonnel? What could he do tomorrow?

"*When the hunt ends and the pack is sated, return to slumber.*"

The words from Porphyry surprised him, and as he focused on the beast still protectively wrapping his core thoughts, he suddenly felt more himself. Of course he needed to return. He couldn't show Verena her new mountain, couldn't hold her or steal a kiss in monster form.

He sensed reluctance from both Fire and Earth. They wanted to play, although they still seemed to be grumpy about his decisions. Maybe they needed a break as much as he did.

"*So, how do I get out of here?*" he asked himself.

His mindscape shifted back into the dim tavern. Earth and Fire were both scowling as they drained their mugs. Air was walking upside down along the ceiling, singing softly to herself like the sighing of winds over the mountains at night.

Water rose and extended a hand. "Come with me, Connor."

Fire slapped Connor's hand onto the tabletop before he could move. Heat flowed into Connor from the elemental being, and even though he no longer feared heat, he sensed danger through the contact. He'd hoped Fire would have enjoyed the play time in the volcano more.

Before he could stammer another apology for bottling everything up so fast, Fire surprised him by smiling warmly. "I have to apologize for acting annoyed earlier, Connor. We so rarely get to walk in elfonnel form that I got carried away."

"You showed great wisdom in your choices today," Earth added, saluting with his mug.

Connor sat up straighter, feeling a rush of pride. They were treating him like an equal, a trusted companion instead of a child they needed to teach how to walk. He did not doubt that experience as an elfonnel would always be a pivotal moment in his life.

Fire added, "Today I took you to the edge of greatness and bequeathed a greater measure of my influence upon you than upon any little human who has ever called forth an elfonnel."

"I really appreciate it," Connor said quickly, and he meant it.

Fire held his gaze and said, "I did so because I trust you, Connor. I trust that you will honor the debt you owe all of us. We need your help, and you are the only one who can help us."

There it was again, the obscure debt. Connor glanced at the other elementals, who all nodded agreement, and he felt a surge of determination to find a way to help them. They'd helped him save everyone he loved, perhaps everyone on the continent. He had to do everything in his power to show his appreciation. "What exactly do you want?"

Fire leaned back and spread his arms wide. "Freedom, of course."

"I don't know how to give you that," Connor said, feeling confused. He was still immersed in the elfonnel. They'd confirmed it was the most powerful elfonnel ever. How much more freedom could they want? He glanced at Water and said, "You spoke of being imprisoned before, but I don't understand how that's possible."

Air descended to join them, slowly rotating in an invisible wind, arms extended. "We are beings of the sylfaen, Connor."

Water added, "And yet we exist partially apart from it."

"We have outgrown the original restrictions placed upon us from the days of creation, and yet we cannot walk freely upon the earth and choose our own fate," Earth said solemnly.

Fire leaned forward. "We seek release from our prison, a chance to live a free life, just as you do."

Finally, their needs were becoming a little clearer, although he still didn't understand how they could be imprisoned. They were elements, for Tallan's sake! But he understood the need to escape bondage and to fight for freedom. That was the entire focus of the revolution, after all. The elementals might not be human, but knowing they shared at least some similar challenges helped him feel closer to them.

"I don't know yet how I can help you find more freedom, but if there's any way I can help, I promise to do so," he said sincerely. "Can you explain more about what it means for you to be free?"

"Enough for today," Fire said with a benevolent smile. "You've pushed the limits of your strength.

"Rest, Connor," Air urged, blowing him a kiss.

He wanted to know more, to understand their need and how they expected him to help, but suddenly he felt completely exhausted. Maybe he had walked as an elfonnel too long. He sensed that if he delayed much longer, he might lack the strength to return. Was that how the queen had gotten trapped in the long sleep?

The thought of slumbering under a mountain for centuries made him shudder. He quickly rose and took Water's hand. Liquid flowed down her sleeves, over his arm, and across his body, enveloping him. As it did so, he became aware of his own, mortal body taking shape in the center of the burning heart of the great elfonnel.

Then her waters plunged down his throat, snuffing out his connection to Fire and to Earth and catapulting his body out of the great elfonnel. His consciousness shrunk back down to fit into his tiny, regular body.

The elfonnel shrank away and disappeared, leaving Connor alone. His body was miraculously intact, but felt completely wrung out. Worse, the sense of unstoppable power faded back to reality, leaving him feeling woefully puny and weak. Returning from elfonnel glory to everyday life was a huge downer.

The air felt cool to his skin, even though it was still shimmering with residual heat from the new-formed mountains. He landed on his backside on hard stone, his mind reeling from his recent monster experience. It already felt more like the craziest dream of his life. His vision was blurry, as if still coated with water.

Exhaustion clobbered him like a gigantic club. He groaned as every inch of his body protested, and his eyes drooped, feeling as heavy as if cast in lead.

He managed to whisper, "Ow."

Chapter Ninety-Three

Hard Lessons

Connor groaned as he focused every scrap of remaining strength on simply blinking his dry eyes. His left moved, which felt like a huge victory, but his right only twitched. His entire body felt sore, even though he'd instinctively already begun tapping sandstone again. Luckily, he was still connected to the conduit back to the Sucker Punch mechanical, and healing energy thundered into him like the famous Mealt Falls of Donleavy.

"Wow, what a day," he mouthed as he stared up at the hazy sky of early evening.

For a moment his vision was overlaid by the memory of the world through elfonnel eyes. Had he really managed it?

"So you did decide to survive," Kilian said, crouching beside Connor and extending a hand to help him sit up. He groaned as he moved, but managed not to black out or fall over again. His head swam, and he rubbed his left temple. It felt like maybe Air and Water had entertained themselves beating on him while Fire and Earth got to play in elfonnel form.

They were on top of the new peak he'd shaped like a duck, sitting on the long, flat bill. It gave them an excellent view of the majestic central peak that towered three times higher. It looked good, the smooth, faceted sides reflecting the last rays of the setting sun. The growing shadows helped soften the features of the giant Verena statue at the peak. Connor loved how it turned out.

Evander dropped to one knee on Connor's other side, a gentle smile on his huge face. "The strongest trees grow in the fiercest wind, and the greatest honor a student can bestow upon a master is to grow beyond their training."

Wow. The words infused Connor with a warm glow of pride. He'd survived, and even Evander was impressed. Not bad for a single day's work.

The giant hauled Connor to his feet. Even though he was filled to bursting with healing power, he still groaned again. But as he started moving, he felt a little better, as if his body realized it was really back.

That much healing power could really set a person right. He hoped his friends had tried it too. Deep down inside, he still felt a terrible exhaustion lurking, but for the moment he managed to ignore it. He rubbed one hand through his hair. It felt dirty, but not burned off like it should have after taking a lava bath.

"Well, that was unexpected," he said.

Kilian chuckled, but watched Connor with cautious eyes. "How do you feel?"

"Hungry."

"That's a good sign. Raising an elfonnel and returning takes a lot out of a person."

Connor dug out a handful of smashpacked meals and popped one into his mouth. It tasted like beef stew, and he savored it, tapping marble enough to heat it so he could enjoy it more thoroughly. He offered one to Kilian, who accepted with a nod of thanks. Evander took three and popped them into his mouth together. It looked like he didn't even bother chewing, but just swallowed them whole. Connor really needed to work with him on that. He was missing out on so much.

"Did you really walk with fire and earth at the same time and become a lava elfonnel?" Kilian asked around his mouthful of food.

Connor grinned. "Wasn't that amazing?"

"Unheard of," Evander said. He looked astonished, or maybe a bit gassy. Probably the result of those expanding smashpacked meals in his stomach.

Kilian shook his head slowly, looking less pleased than Connor expected. "I can't imagine how you did it. I've never heard of anyone doing that, not even Tallan or my mother."

"Don't you need two elements in order to return?" Connor asked.

"That's different. The second element breaks your connection with the first and helps restore balance. It brings you back to yourself, returns you to your body and helps you escape the element that owns you. But you held onto two for hours, and they weren't even opposites."

"Good thing I did, or I don't think I would've been able to stop that eruption. Your psycho mom punched a hole right through everything, down to the core."

"I felt it," Kilian confirmed.

That reminded Connor. He gripped Kilian's arm and exclaimed, "Did you see? I destroyed her!"

"I saw," he said, but didn't look like he was celebrating.

"I killed her. It's over. She's gone!" Connor exulted. He still could barely believe it. After all their worry, he'd flipped everything against her and killed her instead.

"She's had a pretty bad day," Kilian agreed. Then he gestured toward the great central peak. "I lost track of what was left of her while we were fighting to contain the ash clouds. Get us up there, and we can see where things stand now."

"You can't think . . ." Connor breathed, stunned by the suggestion in Kilian's words. He'd melted the dread queen, disintegrated her with energy so intense it could shatter the tiniest particles of matter.

"I think we need to be sure."

So Connor tapped quartzite. Air responded immediately and regarded him critically. "Connor, you look terrible."

"I'll look worse if you let me fall off this mountain."

Laughing, she seized his hand and tugged. With almost no effort, he lifted himself and Kilian all the way up to the crown of that towering peak. Even that little exertion left him feeling light headed. They landed on top of Verena's head. Evander followed, flying confidently with air too. Connor had half expected to see him jump on his favorite sliding earthen seat and simply ride up the side of the mountain.

When they landed, Kilian raised one hand, eyes half closed, expression intent. He seemed to be searching. That was interesting. How was he doing that? He didn't use quartzite or sandstone or obsidian or chert. Was he searching for a body heat signature?

Connor tapped chert and quested out as well, pouring his senses in every direction, seeking any other minds. His mental senses usually felt like sleek, invisible fingers of thought that flowed across the land effortlessly, but he in that moment they felt clumsy and raw, creeping along far slower than usual. Still, he managed to faintly sense in the distance all of the Builder flying crafts that had fled the disaster, carrying with them the still-living juggernaut pilots.

Just not Tomas and Cameron. Connor abruptly remembered their suicidal bravery, and grief punched him in the gut. He swayed, stifling a sob, and his good mood faded under a flood of mourning.

They'd helped distract the queen in a critical moment, helped break her connection with that sculpted stone. If they hadn't, would he still have managed to usurp control over the eruption from her? Or would she have possessed the strength to challenge him, perhaps seize control over him in elfonnel form?

He didn't know, but chose to believe their sacrifice had allowed him to succeed.

Then he felt another living mind and that unexpected connection snapped his thoughts back into focus. With a gasp, Connor spun to the west and pointed, shouting, "There!"

Tapping quartzite, he magnified his vision in time to see a tiny shape rising into the air beyond the flanks of the westernmost peak of the ring of mountains he'd created. It took a second to understand what he was seeing. When he did, he gaped.

A flying skull.

Queen Dreokt.

He clearly remembered spewing the tiny bits of her across the landscape. The biggest part had been that charred skull, but he would have sworn all the flesh was gone, the brains vaporized inside.

Some of it had regrown. Patchwork skin covered the re-formed skull, revealing facial muscle in places. No hair had grown, but one hate-filled eye was mostly complete. The skull rotated to point that milky orb toward Connor. The thin, scarred lips peeled back from scorched teeth in a snarl.

Her mind-voice had lost none of its potency. Her thoughts screamed with fury. "*I warned you, child, but my days of restraint are over. You will reap the consequences of your stubborn idiocy.*"

Connor couldn't believe what he was seeing, couldn't fathom how Queen Dreokt somehow lived. It was impossible, but he was seeing it.

She was regrowing her body from charred bits that could not have contained life. How? Was she using the same fleshcrafting he used? There had to be more, but he couldn't fathom it. Staring at that distant skull with skin slowly growing over exposed muscle sent a shiver of horror creeping down his spine.

But she didn't have to know how freaked out he was. He cast a thought back at her. "*You shouldn't have revealed yourself.*"

Harley had survived death several times, abandoning her form and most of her humanity to survive. They'd finally destroyed the last, disgusting monstrous aspect of her. The queen sounded like herself still, even though she was reduced to the shape of a flying skull.

She wasn't quite dead, but she wasn't very alive either. He did not intend to allow her the luxury of restoring her full strength. Connor reached out with quartzite and snatched at her, trying to seize air away from her to prevent her from escaping. If they could hold her there, Evander could slice that psycho skull in half like he had Harley.

Queen Dreokt somehow slipped past his quartzite fingers and accelerated away. Connor grabbed for her again, but he was no longer elfonnel, was miles away, struggling with almost overwhelming exhaustion. The lack of a body seemed to have only condensed her will. She blocked his clumsy attempts and continued accelerating until she shot away even faster than she'd chased him from Crann.

"She's running!" Connor cried. He was right, they could kill her, but only if they could catch her.

Kilian hissed and made a snatching motion. Fire burst out of the air around her all those miles away. It was an impressive display of fire mastery, but although she was limited in physical form to a ghastly skull, her affinities remained at full power and her skull burst through his ring of fire, trailing white-hot sparks. It would have looked really amazing if the sight didn't inspire so much fear.

Connor's mouth felt dry, and his heart was beating so fast it was hard to breathe. He'd thought he was scared fighting her before, but seeing her survive that superheated death ray left him deeply shaken.

Evander was already beginning to compress light into a new death beam. That was more like it, but she was moving so fast, could Evander even hit her?

"We can't lose her now!" Connor shouted, wishing he'd memorized her curses from earlier. He felt like using them all.

Evander released the death beam, and it ripped through the air, covering the miles in a heartbeat. The beam of light deflected away from her at the last second, as if it struck a piece of Sehrazad steel glass. The beam struck the charred ground in an explosion of dirt.

"How can she do that?" Connor shouted. "She doesn't have any stones. She doesn't have a body even!"

Kilian glared after his departed mother, then sighed and turned to Connor. With a shrug he said, "She will. As soon as she leaves the range of Sucker Punch, she'll begin growing a new one."

"We need to go after her, chase her down," Connor cried, even though the thought of engaging in another battle made him want to cry.

Evander seized his arm and held him back. "No."

"Why not?" Connor exclaimed. "She's barely alive. We can take her."

Kilian too shook his head. "Not even you can catch her before she reaches her armies in Crann. Do you plan to destroy all of her soldiers to get another shot at her?"

Evander added, "By the time you do, she'll be restored. She's angry, and down there she would be beyond the reach of our sandstone trap. She would have full access to healing."

Connor sagged. They were right, but he hated to admit it. "We were so close!"

"Closer than ever," Kilian agreed. "But perhaps not as close as you hoped. This is the great challenge we've always faced with her. We don't know her weakness. We hurt her today, and if she had not distracted us with this." He gestured at the ring of new mountains. "Perhaps we might have hurt her enough to matter. But perhaps not."

Evander said, "We learned much today."

"As did she," Kilian said gravely. "She knows we're hunting her weakness and that we are learning about her secret ramverk. She's willing to put all of that at risk to defeat us. What will she do next?"

Connor frowned. "She used that marble sculpted stone, but I don't feel my fire affinity interrupted like serpentinite."

"Nor have I, but I expect to feel it soon. We were distracted when she struck Jagdish so did not notice how long it took for the affinity to drain away." The calm way he spoke about that impending disaster was a little unnerving. When fire faded, he'd lose half of his elemental powers. Connor would lose only a quarter of his, and hoped to still manage some kind of connection through the green frequency. Would Kilian still be able to connect that way too?

Kilian took a deep breath and said, "We must figure out how to deal with her, but for now, we need to understand how you walked with two elements in elfonnel form."

Connor couldn't believe he was taking his mother's escape so well. He still didn't quite believe it. "How can we deal with her? She regenerated from a skull, Kilian! Who can do that?"

"You can."

"No I can't," Connor objected. Sure he had ascended the third threshold, but she wasn't human.

"Perhaps this is the lesson we need to deal with first," Kilian said. He glanced at Evander, who nodded.

"What lesson?" Connor was really not in the mood for more cryptic answers.

"Are you still connected with your elements?" Kilian asked.

"Of course. But—"

Kilian drew his long belt dagger and plunged it into Connor's chest, right through his heart.

Chapter Ninety-Four

Some Gifts Just Keep on Giving

Verena swept out of the sky, aiming toward the towering new mountain that lorded over the immense new ring of lesser peaks that now replaced what had been barren, empty lands. She'd watched from afar, fighting the tempestuous currents that had driven most of the others farther and farther away.

Not everyone had trained themselves to handle the bumps and swaying of flight. Lady Briet and General Wolfram in particular reached the stomach lurch point remarkably soon, even though the Albatross was so much more stable than Verena's little Swift. Hamish had been forced to fly the Hawk packed full of Juggernaut pilots back to Merkland.

She'd seen Tomas and Cameron make their heroic last charge into the heart of that inferno, and her cheeks were marred with still-drying tears. They had all entered the battle knowing full well that many of them, if not all of them, might not survive a head-on fight with the dread queen. That truth didn't help as much as it should.

Connor had raised an elfonnel.

She'd nearly screamed with tension as she watched the enormous super-elfonnel rise above the exploding new volcano. Connor was consumed by the elements, and she'd feared he would never return.

And yet, looking at the stable ring of new peaks spread over what had to be fifty square miles, she clung to hope that Connor had survived intact within that fiery beast. Somehow. It had taken the form of a deadly rampager, which at first had seemed to confirm her worst fears. But it had snatched up Queen Dreokt and incinerated her, then instead of spreading destruction across Obrion, it had fought to contain the disaster.

Kilian had kept them updated on the progress of their battle against the disaster and his amazement at the elfonnel's control. When the Connor-elfonnel swept the ash from the sky, settled the land, and formed the mountains he'd sounded awed. When he spotted the earthen leg grow out of the fire-bound elfonnel, he'd sounded like he was seriously considering fainting from surprise.

Verena took it as a good sign. Now as she surveyed the majestic peaks up close, she couldn't help laughing. They bore the stamp of Connor all over. The pedra was magnificent. The duck made her laugh, with tears of joy in her eyes. Only Connor would know the significance of that duck, fashioned to look like her father's precious trophy. Everyone else would think it a monument to Ilse's Revenge, and it could serve that purpose to.

And the cookie. Who but Connor would think to inscribe a cookie, complete with recipe, on the side of a mountain?

She felt moved to fresh tears by the memorial Connor had carved for Tomas and Cameron. The two fighters were often insufferable, always insolent, but among the bravest men she knew. They'd charged into the face of death without hesitation, and that final act of courage had helped save them all.

Her eyes were then drawn to the main peak. As she swept in close, heading for the tiny trio perched on the very top, she shook her head slowly in amazement. Connor had to be in control, and the fact that he devoted that incredible peak to her filled her with joy. He'd hesitated to make their betrothal official, and doubts had wormed their way into her heart, despite knowing his reasons for delay. Seeing that enormous testament of his love erased those concerns and made her more eager than ever to wed the man she loved.

She still sighed as she studied the expression on the giant sculpture. Sure, she often smiled in that mischievous way around Connor, but did he really want the entire world to know that aspect of her personality above all others? She could accept that, as long as Connor returned to her as himself and not as some inhuman monster like the queen.

Verena slowed as she noticed Connor, Kilian, and Evander turning to the west. The Swift already had three separate speakstones tuned to their general channel, as well as one paired directly with Kilian, and another with Connor. Over the open line with Kilian, she heard Connor exclaim, "We can't lose her now."

She pivoted west and magnified the front viewscreen, scanning the landscape, but not sure where to look. How could they be talking about the queen? Verena had seen Connor eat her, then spit her out in tiny bits. They'd won. Hadn't they?

A glowing death beam shot through the sky, leaving a trail of ghost light lingering in Verena's vision. She turned to watch the path of the beam, noting the spot where it abruptly deflected away.

She gaped and magnified her viewscreen as far as she could, zooming in on the unbelievable sight. It looked like a flying skull. What, by the Tallan's eternal grace did that mean?

Could it really be the queen returned from the dead? If it was, they'd just lost her because the skull was accelerating away faster than Verena could follow, even in the Swift. Despairing, she pivoted back toward the mountain and accelerated. She had to talk with Connor and understand what was going on.

As she descended toward the trio, their voices rang through the Swift. Connor's frustration matched her own. Then without warning, Kilian drew his dagger and plunged it through Connor's heart.

Verena screamed. Connor staggered, mouth open in silent horror, both hands rising to grip the handle of the dagger standing from the center of his chest. Verena couldn't believe what she was seeing. The sight clobbered her harder than Shona's max-tapped fist.

How? Why?

Kilian yanked the dagger free in a spray of bright arterial blood. Connor fell to the rocky ground, mouth moving silently as if trying to ask all the questions clamoring in Verena's mind.

She crossed the distance on max thruster and started spinning up her speed-slings without even consciously willing her hands to move. She sighted on Kilian, but resisted the overwhelming urge to unleash a torrent of destruction on her beloved many-times great uncle. She needed to understand first what he'd done.

If he'd just killed Connor, Verena would kill him.

She only managing to slow instead of overshooting by tipping the Swift back ninety degrees and unleashing the puking dooms underneath. The force dragged her into her seat, but she didn't care. Pivoting back around, she dropped the window shielding and settled the Swift to a hover.

Leaping out, she rushed to Connor and dropped to her knees beside him. Blood covered his chest, and he was staring up at the sky, blank eyes wide, not moving. Verena seized his head and turned his face toward her. Through uncontrollable sobs she shouted, "Connor! Connor, don't be dead."

Kilian flicked his dagger, and the blood flew off, leaving the blade gleaming. He sheathed it and said calmly, "Hi Verena. You got back fast."

"What did you do?" she shouted so loud she felt something tear in her vocal cords. The pain barely registered.

He looked surprised, glancing from her to the unmoving form of Connor. Verena was tempted to check for a pulse, but why bother? Kilian had stabbed through the heart. Unless . . .

With a flick of her Builder senses, she checked if Connor was still connected to the Sucker Punch. She'd tested the healing power herself for just a second and had nearly leaped right out of the Swift from all the energy it poured into her. If anything could save him from even such a devastating wound, it would be that.

No. He did not appear to be tapping sandstone. Fresh tears flooded her eyes as that last desperate hope extinguished. He was really gone. She'd been so close, and Kilian had taken him away forever. The horrible cruelty of it nearly toppled her to the ground beside Connor.

Kilian said, "I guess the timing would seem a bit weird to you."

"Weird? You just murdered Connor!" she screamed. She couldn't help it. She leaped to her feet, hand dropping to her satchel. Her horror was quickly being consumed by a towering fury. She'd felt that fury before, each time she'd thought she'd lost Connor, and it still shook her like a nightmare beast ripping her heart to pieces. She only managed to keep from attacking Kilian because her questions still outweighed the blinding rage.

She trusted Kilian. Usually. He never acted without a reason.

Had he decided to punish Connor for not defeating the queen? No, Verena couldn't believe that.

Had he discovered Connor had returned to human form broken? That was entirely possible, and that new jolt of icy fear quelled some of her hot anger. If Connor returned as a monster instead of the man she loved, he could unleash as much destruction upon the world as Queen Dreokt herself. Stabbing him in the heart would be the most charitable thing Kilian could do.

Evander also looked unusually calm about the stabbing. He poked Connor with a toe and said, "Shock is delaying reaction."

"He'll figure it out," Kilian said calmly.

Fighting to control her emotions, Verena clenched her hands by her sides and asked with forced calm. "What. Did. You. Do?"

Kilian flashed his trademark roguish smile and said, "Some lessons need to be experienced to be understood."

"What lesson? Death?" Verena shrieked, despite herself.

Kilian fixed her with the full weight of his stare and said gently, "Relax, Verena. I didn't kill Connor. I'm helping him understand who he now is."

She glanced at the still-unmoving Connor. The bleeding had stopped. In fact, now that she thought about it, he should have bled a lot more. "How does stabbing Connor through the heart help him understand anything?"

Gesturing to the west, Kilian asked, "You saw the thing that's all that's left of my mother?"

Verena shuddered and nodded, unable to voice the horror she felt at that sight. She rubbed her arms against a sudden chill.

"If she can recover from that, a little stab through the heart isn't going to kill Connor."

She opened her mouth to retort, but blinked as the words sank in. She glanced back to Connor. "You mean . . . ?"

"Yup. He's had a big day. I figured he'd worked all the drama out of his system, but elfonnel do weird things to the mind. Maybe I should have given him a few more minutes."

Just then, Connor gasped and convulsed into a sitting position. He clutched at his chest, looking panicked. Verena dropped to the ground beside him with a cry and tackled him right back to the stones. She clung to him, weeping with joy. After a surprised second, he clung to her just as hard.

"That's very touching, especially after he carved this mountain for you, but don't you two think you're overdoing it a bit?" Kilian asked.

"Shut up, Kilian," Verena said, not letting Connor go.

"Fires of the heart burn hottest in youth, and it's the lost prize rediscovered that brings the most joy," Evander said.

Kilian grunted. "Couldn't have said it better."

Evander laughed. "You couldn't have said that at all."

"Roses blooming in winter gladden the icy heart, but the balm of company eclipses the still waters of solitude," Kilian replied.

Verena loosened her hold on Connor enough to gape up at Kilian. Had he really just said that?

Connor sat up beside her, looking annoyed. "Really? You stab me and then decide to joke about it in Sentry speak?"

"You were taking a while," Kilian pointed out.

Verena was so full of joy by Connor's recovery, her anger at Kilian melted away. "I never knew you had the heart of a Sapper."

"I've had it a while. Pickled. On my bookcase," Kilian said with a straight face. Then with a grin, he hauled the two of them to their feet and hugged them both.

Verena wrapped an arm around Connor, ready to support him if he stumbled. Anyone else who had just been stabbed through the heart wouldn't be standing at all, let alone grumbling about the fact they weren't taking his near death more seriously. Kilian's humor helped dissipate her terror and she breathed a sigh of relief when Connor draped an arm across her shoulders instead of collapsing against her. Despite his blood-soaked shirt he looked healthy, although he leaned against her more heavily than usual. She didn't mind.

"What just happened?" she asked.

"I'm okay," Connor said, looking like he barely believed it.

"Of course you are. You ascended the third threshold," Kilian said. He actually sounded a little exasperated. "Didn't you just see my mother regenerate from bits of broken skull?"

"Just because she can do it doesn't guarantee I can," Connor protested.

"Actually, it does. The very day you ascended you stabbed yourself in the heart with that sculpted serpentinite dagger. Don't you remember that?"

"Not really. I was kind of distracted," Connor admitted.

Evander said, "Usually one remembers driving a stone dagger into their own heart."

Verena stared from Kilian to Connor, amazed. She hadn't put the pieces together either. She touched Connor's chest in wonder and breathed, "You can't die?"

Connor grinned. "Can you believe it?"

"You can die, just not easily," Kilian clarified. "With your third ascension, you're bonded so tightly to your affinities, you've become almost a living convergence point."

That was a nice way to say it, and the concept made a lot more sense when Verena thought about it that way. "A living convergence point," she whispered.

Connor grinned, and it amazed Verena anew that he didn't act like he was the second most powerful person in the world. He was the living embodiment of affinity power, who could wield mind-boggling abilities, but he was still Connor. That comforted her immensely.

Kilian added, "Remember, Tallan died. When you're completely cut off from your affinities you're vulnerable. That's why I thought maybe today's plan might work. We had never figured out how to block my mother from her affinities."

"We got close," Connor said, looking annoyed again. "So close!"

"She won't fall for that again, will she?" Verena asked. She appreciated Kilian proving to Connor that he was now immune from most fatal injuries, but teaching time with Kilian was usually more fun than that.

"She'll be motivated not to. I don't think she understands exactly how we accomplished what we did, so she might not grasp how to avoid walking into another trap," Kilian said.

That gave Verena some hope. "We won't let her get away again," Kilian promised, little waves pulsing across his left eye. Flickers of crimson fire ignited in his right eye, then abruptly winked out.

Kilian staggered and cried out in agony, one hand clapping over his right eye. Verena spun, hand dropping to her satchel, looking for the threat. Anything that could strike Kilian down unawares could kill them all if they didn't react quickly. Evander also spun, one massive fist raised to fight.

Connor didn't. He stepped to Kilian and grabbed his shoulder. He looked sad, or resigned maybe. Kilian's face had drained of color, and he looked more shaken than he had by the sight of his cursed mother flying away as a ghastly skull.

"It's gone. I feel it too," Connor said gently.

"What's going on?" Verena asked. She hated not understanding. Usually she had answers, but now she felt rattled, which made her feel cranky.

"Marble. It's gone," Connor said.

Right. Verena rushed to Kilian. Even though she'd been on the verge of killing him just moments ago, she threw her arms around him and hugged him. He wrapped her with one arm, and she could feel tremors quaking down his torso.

"I knew it would happen. I saw the stone and we finally understand what they mean, but . . . but feeling my affinity fade away is the worst thing I've felt since Tallan was murdered." Kilian drew in a ragged breath and tried to smile. Didn't quite work.

She read the depth of his anguish and wasn't sure how to comfort him. If her Builder powers had just gotten snuffed out, she'd probably panic. Kilian had trusted fire for centuries. Losing that affinity would be like losing a limb. Maybe worse.

"It's gone. Fire is gone," Kilian said more strongly. He recovered his composure quickly.

"I can still feel it through green," Connor said.

After a moment of intense concentration, Kilian blew out a relieved breath and grinned. "I can feel it. Sort of. I've had to balance red and green for so long, it seems completely wrong to focus entirely on the green."

"That's probably why your mother struggled to reach fleshcrafting when we blocked sandstone," Connor said.

"Probably. I'm glad we knew to work through the challenge and focus on green. Without that understanding, I doubt I would have figured it out for a long, miserable time."

"So she might have limited herself more than us?" Verena asked, happy to grasp for any glimmer of positive from the crazy day.

"Perhaps. She's crippled her Firetongues just as she has ours. She might not realize she can still reach some aspects of fire, but she will eventually."

Connor scowled. "She noticed me tapping serpentinite earlier. It surprised her. If the whole near-death-by-elfonnel experience and skull flight back to herself doesn't distract her too much, she might put the pieces together."

"Why aren't we going after her?" Verena asked.

Connor said, "She's too fast. She'll get back to Crann before we catch her, and we're not prepared to fight her and her entire army there, outside of the reach of Sucker Punch."

Kilian chuckled. "I'm glad you were paying attention."

Evander said, "Come. We should return to Merkland. We have much to discuss."

Kilian nodded, but Verena took Connor's hand and said, "We'll catch up. I haven't thanked Connor yet for giving me an entire mountain as a sign that he was still alive in that elfonnel."

Connor grinned. "Did you see the duck?"

CHAPTER NINETY-FIVE

One Feast Is Not Enough

Merkland was chaotic. From his comfortable seat beside Verena in the Swift, Connor spotted signs of the titanic eruption as they soared past the wall. Many buildings looked damaged, while some had collapsed entirely. The famous white walls looked unaffected, but the city looked even more battered than before. The streets were crowded with people, and fear radiated up to his chert senses, even shuttered as they were.

It seemed a cruel stroke of rotten luck for Merkland to suffer more when they were still dealing with the damage from the summoned swarm. The palace looked about as beat up as it had before, except one of the smaller towers on the southern wing had collapsed. The debris had created a terrible mess. He cringed to see the pain and death. It was his fault. He hadn't been fast enough or strong enough.

Verena muttered, "All her fault."

"What?"

She dropped her window shielding and he clearly saw her anguish. She gestured at the battered city. "All of this is Queen Dreokt's fault. I hate that woman. I wish we'd finished her off."

Connor still felt responsible, but Verena was right. Queen Dreokt had chosen to unleash that sculpted stone. Did she recognize the damage it caused? Did she care? The shaking probably hurt Crann at least as much as it had Merkland. What would she say to her people?

Connor doubted she'd even acknowledge responsibility.

"I see Rory," Connor said, spotting the general in the square in front of the palace.

The other flying craft had all landed there, and a crowd had gathered. Kilian and Evander were already speaking with Ivor, Shona, and Aifric. The Juggernaut pilots lingered around the Albatross with General Wolfram and Lady Briet. Seeing them reminded Connor he had to ask Kilian how he'd moved so fast.

Connor and Verena had lingered only a few minutes, but he smiled at the memory. She'd been very impressed by the mountain he'd carved for her, and she loved the duck memorial. Despite everything he'd experienced that day, those brief moments together were still treasured highlights.

They landed near their friends, and Rory rushed to them, looking more distraught than Connor had ever seen. Anika trailed close behind. Rory grabbed Connor's arm and asked, "Did you save them?"

Connor didn't have to ask who. He felt ashamed that he'd actually forgotten briefly about Tomas and Cameron's heroic sacrifice on the flight back. He had a lot on his mind, but none of that mattered in that moment facing his friend.

He hated himself for having to shake his head sadly. "I'm sorry. There just wasn't enough time."

Rory seemed to wilt. He staggered back into Anika's arms and she held him tenderly, whispering comforting words through her own tears. Rory clung to her, not hiding his grief as tears ran down his cheeks.

Verena slipped under Connor's arm and he held her tight. She was openly crying, and he sniffled a couple of times too. Rory's anguish moved him deeply. He considered Tomas and Cameron good friends. They were irreverent, but genuine. They were unapologetic bash fighters who were far more brilliant than they liked to admit. They had trained him and helped him through some very difficult times, and their loss created a terrible, aching hole in his heart.

He doubted he felt a fraction of the sorrow Rory did. Rory had been their captain, then their general. He'd trained them, worked with them, relied upon them for years. They were more like annoying younger brothers than soldiers under his command, and their loss beat him down worse than anything Connor had ever seen.

Connor gripped Rory's shoulder. "They saved everyone. They broke Queen Dreokt's control over the eruption when not even I could touch her. Without that, Merkland would be gone by now."

Rory sniffled and managed a weak smile. He did not pull away from Anika but nodded his thanks. "Tell me."

So Connor did. He explained about how the fight had been going so well until the queen pulled out that sculpted marble stone. He described how she'd sealed herself away from their affinity powers and unleashed the volcano. As he talked, the rest of their close friends gathered around in somber silence.

Hamish cursed softly and tossed aside a breadstick he'd been chewing on. "I should have taken their blind coal. I could have managed it better. I might have gotten away."

Connor sighed. He too was beating himself up for not doing more, but they couldn't change what happened. "Maybe, but maybe not. The eruption would have probably caught you too, and I might not have been able to reach you in time. You probably would have died."

"But I'm the Builder, and I was their leader. I should have been the one to see the opening," Hamish protested.

Verena hugged him. Hamish wasn't as close to Tomas and Cameron, but he'd liked them too, and he was struggling to handle their deaths. They'd been part of his team, so of course he felt responsible for their safety.

Rory said, "They were bash fighters, Hamish. They saw through the complexities of battle better than anyone I ever knew. They always found a way to boil the complex calculations down to how best to get to bash fighting. That's why I insisted they go to that fight."

"They bashed the queen real good," Connor said with a smile. He described how they'd punched through her barrier, crushed her chest, and broken her grip on the sculpted stone. "That gave us the chance to set things right. Without them, she would have blocked me."

Anika raised one fist and lifted her beautiful face high. "Hail the victorious dead!"

Connor raised his fist with the others and repeated the phrase. It felt right. He could imagine Tomas and Cameron looking down at them and getting a good laugh at all the honor they were bestowing upon the pair. The thought made him smile.

Rory rubbed his eyes and said, "Best bash fight ever. Those two figured out how to bash fight with the biggest Builder mechanicals ever built."

Shona, leaning on Ivor and looking shaken by the loss of the two warriors said, "Come. We have much to discuss. There's still an army preparing to march against us, and it sounds like the queen will restore her potency soon."

Hamish protested. "We can't just jump into another meeting. We have a triple-huge feast to throw."

"I think a normal feast would be plenty," Verena said.

Hamish shook his head, looking determined. "First, we need to feast to honor everyone who died today."

"Absolutely," Rory said.

"Second, we need an almost-but-not-quite celebratory feast for how close we came to killing Queen Dreokt," Hamish added, raising two fingers.

Ivor chuckled. "Let's just call it a celebration feast."

"Fine. Third, we need to feast Connor's elfonnel return and the birth of a whole new mountain range," Hamish concluded, spreading all the fingers of his hand.

"That's more than three fingers," Shona pointed out.

"Because I'm planning on eating a few extra helpings," Hamish stated simply.

Connor smiled, grateful that Hamish insisted they make the time to feast together. They needed it. He wrapped an arm around Verena's shoulder and said, "I agree."

Kilian said, "Very well. Let's feast."

"And no one thinks about all the work we have to do until tomorrow," Verena added.

That was an excellent idea, because tomorrow they needed to figure out how to win a war against a woman they still had no idea how to kill.

Where's the Next Book?

After an epic read like that, the last thing you want is to catch up on sleep or actually go to work or even take a shower.

You want the next book!

I get it, and I believe you NEED the next book.

Good thing it's already finished.

At the end of each of the earlier books, I've made exclusive short story content available for you to download. Hopefully you've taken advantage of that. If not, you can still get these free, fantastic short stories here.

Hamish's story. Set in Stone: Home Sweets Home
https://BookHip.com/MLXNR

Jean's story. A Stone's Throw: Mind Over Muscle
https://BookHip.com/ZVNGHS

Gregor's story. No Stone Unturned: A Servant of Two Masters
https://BookHip.com/LFADBP

Aifric's story. Affinity for War: A Gaggle of One
https://BookHip.com/SWPQFZ

Connor's story. The Queen's Quarry: A Duel to the Duck
https://BookHip.com/MAPQCZ

This time, I'm combining the next book and special content into one fun package. The next Petralist book is *Builder of Intrigue*, a Petralist origins story like *When Torcs Fly*, or *Game of Garlands*, but this time it's Aunt Ailsa's story.

Set immediately prior to *Set in Stone*, the little gem details an exciting adventure Ailsa has in Merkland. She plans to travel to Alasdair to prevent Connor from swearing fealty to High Lord Dougal, but also must deal with a dire threat that could destroy all chances for either her or Connor to ever find freedom.

Things don't go according to plan.

Get *Builder of Intrigue* here: https://smarturl.it/kj3r16

And the final main book in the series—*Blood of the Tallan*—will be released shortly after *Builder of Intrigue*. Get it here: https://smarturl.it/cil521

Thumbs Up? Or Thumbs down?

How did you like the book?

Are you willing to take 5 seconds and share it with the world? Now, while it's still fresh?

Reviews help more than you imagine. How many times have you looked at reviews of books or products before buying?

If you've never poste d a review before, it's super simple. Just two steps:

- Rate the book 1-5 stars. Be honest. Be generous.
- Write a short review. One or two sentences is plenty.

What goes in those sentences? Here are a few suggestions:

- Your feelings about the book.
- Something you loved about it. (no spoilers please!)
- The fact that you couldn't put the book down all night.
- Your favorite line of Sentry speak.
- Who is your favorite character?
- If you were a Petralist, what affinity would you most love to have?

Just pick one suggestion, or come up with your own. It's that simple.

And just like that, you really help me out.

To post a review on Amazon: http://smarturl.it/yv37jy

Thanks!

Frank

Petralist Stones

Three for the masses
Two for the many
Four for the privileged few

Igneous

Basalt
Speed, agility
Tapped: Poweder through the skin
Obrion: Strider
Granadure: Wingrunner

Granite
Strength, summoning
Tapped: Powder through the skin
Obrion: Boulder or Fast Roller
Granadure: Rumbler

Obsidian
Magnifies innate abilities
Tapped: Powder through the skin
Obrion: Blade
Granadure: Allcarver

SEDIMENTARY

Limestone
Light
Tapped: Held or worn
Obrion: Solas
Granadure: Solas

Sandstone
Healing
Tapped: Held or worn
Obrion: Healer
Grandaure: Healer

METAMORPHIC

Marble
Fire
Tapped: Under the tongue
Obrion: Firetongue
Granadure: Flameweaver

Quartzite
Air, senses
Tapped: Placed in mouth
Obrion: Pathfinder
Granadure: Longseer

Slate
Earth
Tapped: Soles of feet
Obrion: Sentry
Granadure: Sapper

Soapstone
Water
Tapped: Powder swallowed with water
Obrion: Spitter
Granadure: Water Moccasin

Secret Stones

Diorite
Igneous stone
Explosive power
Tapped: Powder through the skin
Obrion: Unknown
Grandaure: Unknown

Porphyry
Igneous stone
Rage monster
Tapped: Powder through the skin
Obrion: Unclaimed
Grandaure: Rampager

Anthracite (Blind Coal)
Sedimentary stone
Aggressive slipperiness
Tapped: Held or worn
Obrion: Unknown
Grandaure: Unknown

Serpentinite
Metamorphic stone
Sound
Tapped: Held or worn
Obrion: Unknown
Grandaure: Unknown

NEW STONES!

Chert
Sedimentary stone
Empathy
Tapped: Held or worn
Obrion: Unknown
Grandaure: Unknown

Amphibolite Gneiss
Metamorphic stone
Counters basalt
Tapped: Powder through the skin
Obrion: Unknown
Grandaure: Unknown

Granite Gneiss
Metamorphic stone
Counters granite
Tapped: Powder through the skin
Obrion: Unknown
Grandaure: Unknown

Author's Note

You might not have guessed, but I love big, epic fantasy adventures. The Petralist has been such an amazing journey. It's fitting that it takes two huge novels to finish the final showdown.

After finishing this incredible epic, you may be wondering how Blood of the Tallan could possibly take the stakes higher, delve deeper into the magic, or threaten the lives of our beloved heroes any more.

It does.

My goal with every one of these books has been to make the adventure bigger, the stakes higher, the threat more personal, the magic more fascinating. I'm glad you've joined me this far, and I am confident you'll love the final chapter of The Petralist.

Frank

About the Author

Frank Morin is a storyteller, an outdoor enthusiast, and an eager traveler. He is the author of fast-paced grab-you-by-the-eyeballs-and-don't-let-go adventures, including *The Petralist*, the epic teen fantasy series you've been enjoying, full of explosive magic, huge adventure, and brilliant humor. Frank also writes *The Facetakers* fast-action historical fantasy thrillers.

When not writing or trying to keep up with his active family, he's often found hiking, camping, Scuba diving, or traveling to research new books. Find out more about his novels and his shorter fiction, or join his readers group at www.frankmorin.org

www.ingramcontent.com/pod-product-compliance
Lightning Source LLC
Chambersburg PA
CBHW021624030826
48979CB00036B/2134/J

* 9 7 8 1 9 4 6 9 1 0 1 7 2 *